INTO THE FLAMES

Into the Flames
Copyright © 2024 by M.B. Thurman
All rights reserved.

First published in the New York, NY in the United States by Contrarian Publishing

This work is protected by copyright. Apart from any use as permitted under the Copyright Act 1968, no part of this work may be reproduced, copied, scanned, stored in a retrieval system, recorded or transmitted, in any form or by any means, without the prior written permission of the publisher.

This book is a work of fiction. Names, characters, and incidents are the product of the author's imagination and/or are used fictitiously. Any resemblance to actual persons, living or dead, is coincidental.

www.contrarianpublishing.com

Summary: When Hadley Weston reunites with her lover Fitz MacGregor, she discovers that he is a witch, and so is she. While training to master her powers and searching for a long-lost family artifact, the two discover that a rogue witch threatens the safety of human and witchkind. They must work together to reclaim the ring and stop the dangerous witch before he destroys the world as they know it.

Library of Congress Control Number: 2024917401
ISBN 978-1-965422-00-7

First Edition

Cover illustration and cover design by Jon Stubbington
Book design by Jamie Ryu

INTO THE FLAMES

BOOKS ONE AND TWO IN THE SUMMONED SERIES

An Omnibus

M.B. THURMAN

CONTRARIAN PUBLISHING

New York, NY | Est. 2024

This book is dedicated to my husband, Trent. Within these pages, readers will find the story of two imperfect beings who love one another unconditionally.

Thank you for discovering what that looks like with me.

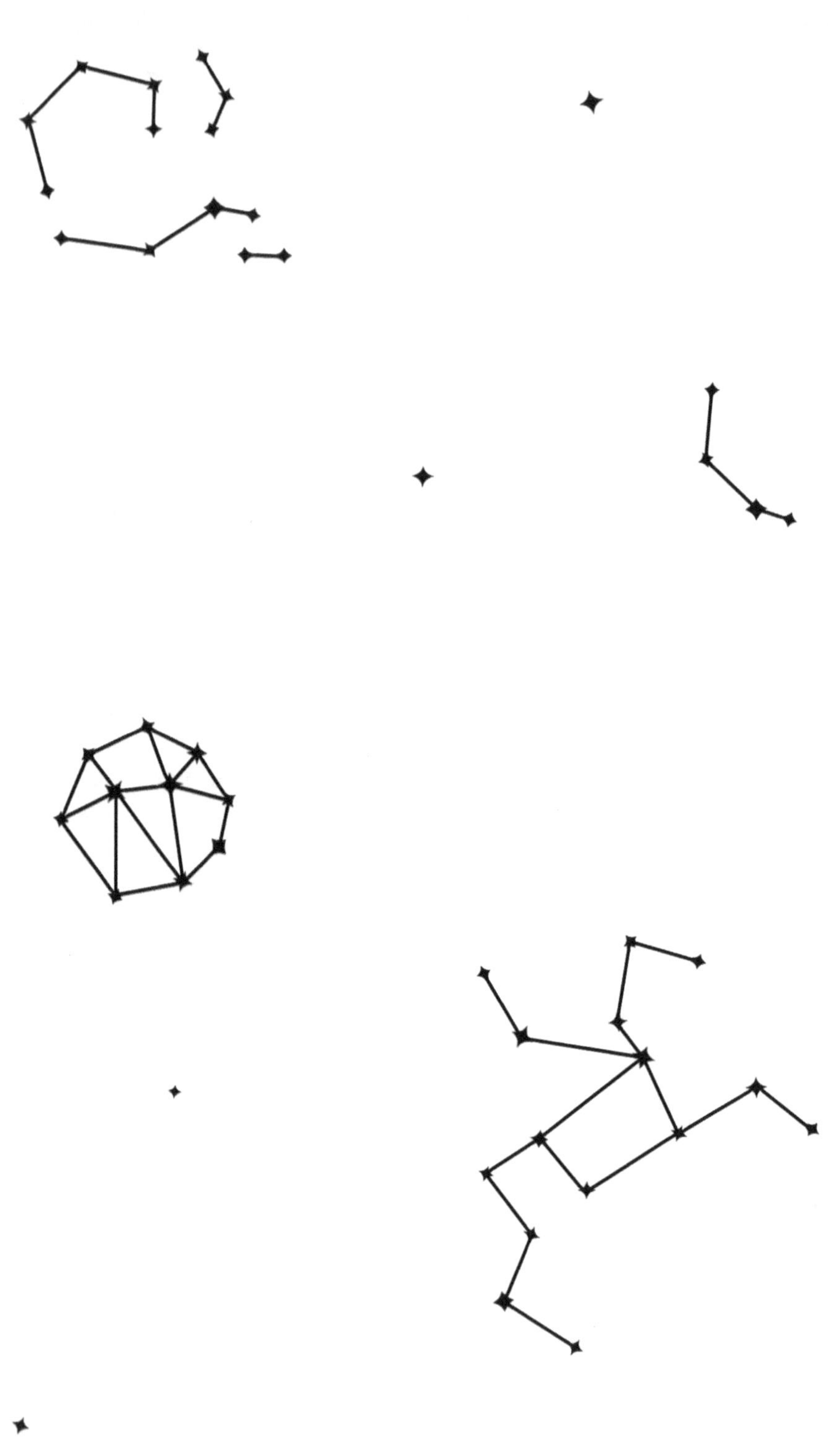

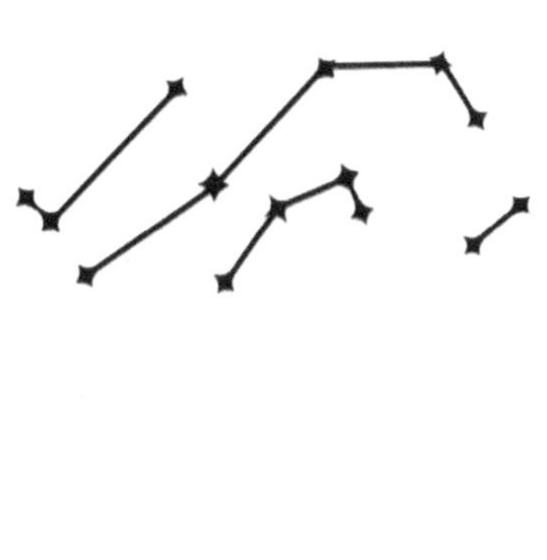

BOOK ONE

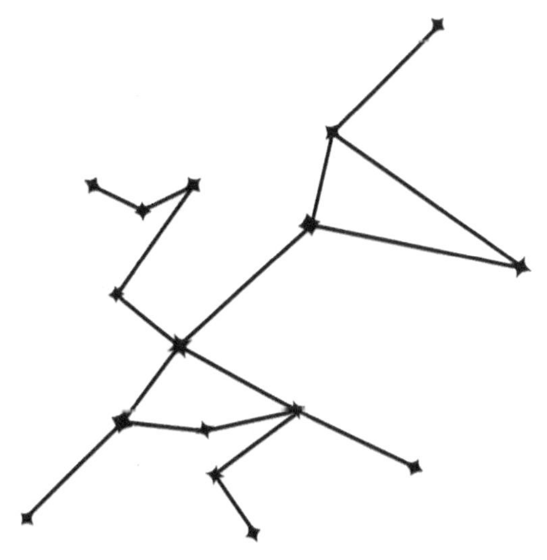

*Many a strange occurrence has come to pass,
but none so strange as the discovery that you are
not at all who you thought yourself to be.*

PART ONE

CHAPTER ONE

The note was tucked carefully under a stack of books on my old oak desk, and the paper's edges fluttered in the evening breeze filtering through the open window.

I froze as my eyes darted around the room.

I'd closed the window before popping down to the kitchen for a snack, and the unmade bed was littered with blankets from my rushed departure that morning. A cold cup of forgotten Earl Grey tea sat atop the desk, adjacent to the open laptop that lay nearby. Suitcases were scattered across the far side of the room.

Nothing else had been disturbed.

Only the open window and the mysterious note that lay just beneath it. I slowly crossed my bedroom to investigate.

I was accustomed to notes falling into my possession, but they were usually in unmarked envelopes that appeared in my mailbox or pushed just under my door. This was the first time I was certain someone had accessed my space. My fingers trembled as they tugged at the cream-colored paper.

> *Meet me Friday at 6 p.m.—the top of Notre Dame.*
> *Don't tell anyone.*
> *I'll adjust your travel arrangements.*

Friday . . . only five days away.

I had job interviews lined up in London for the following week, and this would move my travel up, shortening my visit with my mom.

I glanced at the note again. I didn't need to pull Fitz's letters from my purse to know the penmanship matched perfectly.

After eight months of us being inseparable, we had been forced apart. Fitz and I had kept in touch through burner phones that showed up at my apartment and letters I mailed to various locations around Europe after the addresses came inexplicably into my possession.

I'd considered walking away countless times, but I knew Fitz held the answers I needed to finally understand myself—to understand the things I was able to do.

The snap of a branch pierced the still night air.

I approached the open window timidly, peering into the endless dark of the moonless night. My eyes strained to make sense of the fathomless depths, but to no avail—I could see nothing. The noise had come from a woodland animal, I reasoned.

Still, I pulled my window closed and double checked the latch before tugging the curtains together. I poured a glass of whisky and settled onto my bed with the note.

I unfolded the paper again, studying the words scribbled across it.

Lake Crescent, Washington
June 2021

I stared through the large window at the sheets of rain blowing across the lake, mesmerized by what I saw.

Although the PNW held a tiresome reputation as the rainiest portion of the U.S., it didn't often rain like this. I pushed open the cedar-framed window and was met by the cool summer breeze. I relaxed at the scent of evergreens. The patter of rain echoed through my bedroom. Gram had told me it would let up soon. I wasn't so sure, but Gram was always right about those sorts of things—and well, most things, come to think of it.

I hoped the rain would stick around so I'd get out of berry picking. It wasn't that I was opposed to helping Gram, but I'd had the strange feeling that I was being watched. I knew it was ridiculous. I had no evidence. And yet, I couldn't shake the unsettling feeling that had crept into the back of my mind.

I sat in silence as the rain stopped, and then bounded downstairs to perform my berry-picking duties. Pretending not to notice Gram's smirk, I grabbed the bowl from the counter and headed out the door to find the best berries for her jam.

The air held a thick, humid atmosphere that was more intense than usual, and I had a distinct feeling we weren't done with the rain just yet. Storm clouds rolled into the distance, fittingly in the direction of Mt. Storm King, and sunlight began filtering through the lingering haze. The majestic peak took the brunt of the weather in the area, and being the misty mountain that it was, Storm King attracted much of its own legend.

I completed my outing in record time. The sun cast its golden rays through the nearby trees. The light kissed the fresh raindrops, which caused the ground to shimmer all around me. Mesmerized, I stooped to get a better look at the ethereal scene when a splash in the stream startled me. Berries scattered through the blades of grass. I turned toward the stream but didn't find the source of the noise.

I froze and listened for anything odd but only found the usual trickle of water, the chirping of birds, and the crash of distant breaking waves. I reached for the bowl but was disturbed by a branch snapping in the direction of the stream. I mustered my courage and walked slowly toward the source of the commotion.

There was an infamous story of a beautiful waitress who was murdered and cast to the bottom of Lake Crescent. Her body had been preserved by the waters of our curious lake. I'd picked up a book in my teen years about the unfortunate young woman, and the image of her body still haunted me. The incident had occurred in the 1930's, with little criminal activity around the area since, but the feeling of being watched had truly rattled my mind.

I was nearing the edge of the stream when a woman's voice floated on the summer breeze. It was so beautiful; I swore it was a siren's call. I strained my ears, trying to make out the words.

The wee birdies sing and the wildflowers spring,
And in sunshine the waters are sleeping.

Barely breathing, I lowered myself along the stones on the cliffside and stepped into the cool waters of the stream. It took mere seconds to find the source of the commotion, as one of the most beautiful women I'd ever seen stepped around the trunk of a massive spruce tree.

"Oh! Hello," she called excitedly.

She closed the short distance between us, her long, auburn hair hanging loosely down her back, complementing her tall figure. I would have been more in awe of her flawless, milky skin had her intense emerald eyes released me from their spell.

"I'm Izzy MacGregor," she said in a thick accent. Scottish, I thought. She extended her hand. "I'm sorry. Did I startle you?"

"A little." I laughed in response as I took her hand in mine. "I was just picking blueberries and heard some noise."

Her eyes dipped to my empty hands.

"I dropped the bowl. Berries *everywhere*."

Izzy giggled. "I'll help you pick them up. Lead the way."

"I didn't expect to see anyone else up here," I said as we climbed the bank.

"Oh, right. I'm visiting my parents. They just moved in next door, and I've been exploring the past couple of days. I was walking the stream out of curiosity."

"It's beautiful around here. Keep your eyes open though—a herd of elk have been congregating by the stream the past few days, and the moms can be aggressive with their new calves."

"Thank you. I'll be mindful of that," she said, grinning like there was some sort of inside joke I was missing.

"Have you seen them before? The elk."

She hesitated just long enough that I thought she wasn't going to answer my question. I turned the bowl right side up, and she finally met my gaze.

"They're fascinating creatures. I love wildlife." Izzy picked up a ripe blueberry and rolled it in between her finger and thumb, bringing it into the light. "Looks like the rain has been good to the crop. May I?"

I nodded, and she popped the berry onto her tongue, closing her eyes while she savored the taste. She was the kind of woman, I thought, who really *lived*. The kind of woman who stopped to feel the rain on her skin and whose laughter set a room alight, the kind of woman who lived intentionally. I couldn't place where the knowledge came from, but instantly, I *knew* her.

"They're sweeter this year than normal," I said, considering her. "You love nature, don't you?"

"Very much," she said. The sunlight touched her face, highlighting the freckles splayed across the bridge of her nose and cheeks.

Her gaze lingered on me, and she pursed her lips.

"What is it?" I questioned.

"My brother will be keen to meet you."

"Oh." I looked around like her brother might materialize at any moment. "He's visiting your parents too?"

"Aye. He's around here somewhere. Wanders the woods almost as much as me, that one."

"Why do you think he'll want to meet me?"

"It's just a feeling I have," Izzy said.

"Well, I look forward to meeting . . ."

"Fitz."

"Fitz," I echoed. A small jolt ran through my body at the feel of his name on my lips, and I took a deep breath, hoping to shake off the odd sensation.

I dropped another handful of berries into the bowl and dusted off my hands. I didn't know what else to say, but I didn't want our conversation to end. "Where is your accent from . . . if you don't mind me asking?"

"Scotland."

"I thought so. I'd love to visit Scotland."

"When you're ready, I'll tell you all the must-sees."

"Do you like Washington?" I asked.

"Very much. It's a bonnie place," she mused absentmindedly, dropping the last berry into the bowl.

"Iz—are you out here?" A man's voice broke the still afternoon air, and a thrill moved through me at the sound.

"Speaking of Fitz," she said conspiratorially to me. Then she called, "Aye, over here!"

Izzy eyed me pointedly before walking toward the nearby tree line. A man emerged from the verdant canopy. I studied his tall figure as he made his way to Izzy. He carried himself with ease and confidence. There was a prickle at the nape of my neck, though I couldn't understand the signal.

The two had a brief exchange before Izzy called across the clearing. "My dad needs me. It was lovely to meet you!"

She disappeared into the trees that separated our homes, and Fitz walked toward me.

As he came more clearly into focus, a small gasp disturbed the back of my throat. He was *beautiful*.

Fitz wore a thin crewneck sweater and jeans, and though there was something innately academic in his style, the way he carried himself was almost playful. As he neared me, I studied his structured jawline, which held the faint scruff of a few days without a razor, and I followed it to his strong cheekbones and his chestnut hair.

My heart beat wildly.

The world tilted beneath me as I met the emerald eyes of Fitz MacGregor. And there it was: the same feeling that coursed through me as with Izzy before. Fitz was complex, and I knew that instantly, the same way I knew he loved the sound of jazz and the taste of whisky on his tongue. Fitz was comforting, like the rain, a good cup of tea, the first few notes of my favorite album.

I *knew* this man.

His gaze was intense, somehow seeing straight through me, and my breath came short. His eyes lingered across my face, and at first, I thought I imagined it, but no—the rise and fall of his chest grew more exaggerated by the second.

We stared wordlessly long enough for my anxiety to flare. But he finally reached out his hand, and I placed mine into his expectant grasp.

An electric shock surged from my fingertips through my entire body, and I swallowed hard. My breathing grew more labored, and a jolt of panic coursed through me at my inability to understand the reaction.

"Glad to meet you." His attempt at civility couldn't mask the strain in his voice.

"I—I'm sorry, but I have no idea what's happening."

"You feel it too." It was more statement than question, but I nodded anyway.

"Should we . . ." I looked down at our linked hands.

"Oh, right. Sorry."

He released me, and it left me feeling utterly empty. Perspiration formed on my forehead, and my eyes flitted across Fitz's face searching for any signs of distress. He shoved his hands in his front pockets.

"The weather is mental. Maybe it was just static," he said.

"Static electricity? That's the best you've got?"

Fitz chuckled. It was a welcome sound. "Indeed, it is. Please, I'd love to hear a more plausible theory from you."

I raised my hands in mock surrender. "I don't have a theory yet."

"But you'll sort out a good one."

"I'll do my best." I smiled. Fitz's amusement was contagious.

The wind picked up, rustling his mess of chestnut hair, and a rumble of thunder pierced the quiet.

"Now, that's something you don't hear very often around here," he mused.

"We'd better get out of here before the bottom falls out, as my grandmother would say."

I wanted nothing more than to get to know Fitz. I wanted more time, and a wave of relief washed through me at his offer to walk me home.

We set off in the direction of my place and reached the porch just as the rain began to fall. I wasn't sure how to approach seeing him again without sounding overzealous.

"You're welcome to wait out the storm here, if you'd like," I finally said.

"Thank you. But I'm late for another commitment." I thought he seemed disappointed, but perhaps it was only my own hope. Still, he lingered, and his eyes studied me.

"I feel like I've met you before." The words tumbled out before I could stop them, and I groaned inwardly.

"I'd remember you if we had." Fitz smiled softly. "Perhaps in another life."

I wasn't so sure he was joking.

"I'd better be going," he continued. "But Izzy and I will drop by tomorrow if that's all right?"

"I'd like that."

"I'm glad to have met you, Hadley."

Fitz stepped into the rain. He paused, looking at me over his shoulder one last time as the rain streaked down his beautiful face. And with that, he disappeared into the trees that separated our homes.

I was so preoccupied I didn't realize until I walked into the house that I hadn't given Fitz my name.

CHAPTER TWO

Lake Crescent, Washington
Present Day

After Dad's untimely death eight months prior, my mother and I hadn't found the courage to organize his belongings. But I'd left my job as a public relations consultant in Boston two weeks ago and driven home to the glacial-fed waters of Lake Crescent in Washington State to spend time with my mother. I'd passed the better part of my trip home rifling through old chests in my father's study and sorting through his side of the closet with my mom.

When I'd first mentioned my upcoming trip to London to my mom, her face had fallen. Both of my parents had always encouraged me to see the world, and I knew my mom would never truly stand in the way of my growth. But life without Daddy was uncharted territory.

I settled into the oversized chair in the corner of my room and pulled my favorite blanket around me. The temperature had dropped earlier in the day, our first taste of fall, and it seemed a good time to conduct another search for job openings. I scanned one of the many career sites I'd been monitoring, and the hair on my neck bristled as my eyes swept over a newly posted opening: PR Manager, Edinburgh Castle. I followed the link to the "Careers" tab on the castle website and read the listing.

The position itself sounded like the right fit for my experience, and working somewhere like the castle would align with my love for history. And . . . Edinburgh was where I believed Fitz to be. I took a slow sip of tea as I debated my next move.

A knock at the door halted my decision making.

"Momma?"

My mom peeked her head around the door. "Ready to start dinner?" She'd lived in Washington State for over thirty years, but neither she nor my father had lost their Mississippi accents.

"I'll be right there."

She smiled brightly, and my stomach flipped. We'd cooked dinner together almost every night, but for the first time since my return, the experience wouldn't be pleasant.

My fingers flew over the keyboard. Within minutes, the application process was complete, and I was staring at a confirmation page.

There was no time like the present to inform my mom of my newly solidified plans.

"You're adding Paris *and* Edinburgh? Alone?"

"I've always wanted to see Paris. And I'm not positive about Edinburgh yet—I might not even receive an interview request."

My mom pursed her lips.

"This is something I need to do, Momma." I flipped the salmon I was cooking for dinner, trying to keep the conversation casual and hide the annoyance in my voice.

"I just don't understand why you left your job in Boston. Or why you're looking for a new one in Europe, for that matter."

I let my eyes linger on the pan while I rolled through my thoughts.

I understood my motivations for the change perfectly, but the thought of talking about it with Momma seemed overwhelming; being honest about my grief seemed impossible.

"You know I've always wanted to go abroad, at least for a while," I said.

"I think it'll do me some good."

My mom remained silent.

"And who knows. Maybe I won't even receive an offer from anyone. But this trip is about figuring all that out."

She narrowed her hazel eyes as she leaned against the counter. "Why can't Jordan go with you on the trip?"

Jordan had been my best friend since childhood, and we'd traveled to many a place together. But now she worked as an intelligence analyst for the FBI, and her team was always overtaxed.

"You know how difficult it is for Jordan to take time off," I said. "And after her promotion, she's swamped."

And if I was being honest, I needed to take this trip alone, even before Fitz's note had materialized in my room.

Silence.

"Can you pass me the salt?" I asked.

My mother sighed. She tucked the loose strands of her honey-colored hair behind her ear, taking her time.

"Do you really have to go right now? You could visit Gram for a couple weeks, and then maybe timing would work for Jordan to go with you. Or Tanner," she countered.

"Momma, if I do find a new job over there, I'll be living alone regardless. If I can't manage a solo trip, then I have no business moving halfway across the world."

"I don't know that you have any business doing that anyway."

I threw my arms up in protest. "You don't trust me?"

My mom paused, her eyes dropping to the floor for mere seconds. "Of course, I trust you, Hadley."

"Then what is it?"

"It's just your first time out of the country alone, and I can't help but worry."

"I'll be fine." I grabbed dishes from the cabinet to plate our dinner.

"I can't lose you too."

Her words stopped me in my tracks, and suddenly, I wasn't so concerned with dinner. I set the plates on the counter gently and met her gaze.

"Oh, Momma." My father's death had gutted her, but it was still unlike her to make such an honest confession.

She raised her hand. "I don't mean to sound dramatic. I just worry a little more these days. The world seems fragile lately."

"I'll be smart," I promised, my voice losing the last of its edge. "I'm not going anywhere for a very long time."

My words echoed through my thoughts—except in my dad's voice instead of my own. He materialized in my mind, his soft, gray eyes filled with pain. Even so, he wore a brave smile and reached for a hand I recognized well.

Is this Momma's memory?

My face was then reflected back at me: my concerned blue eyes, my favorite Mississippi State sweatshirt that I'd claimed from my father's closet the day prior, my hair which had inexplicably darkened to an auburn during the course of a couple weeks right after his death.

"She's so much like Matt."

My stomach lurched.

"Oh, no," her voice sounded again.

The world tilted off-kilter as the realization sunk in. This wasn't like before.

I was reading my mom's mind.

"Hadley, are you okay?"

I couldn't speak.

"Hadley!"

I nodded.

"Are the panic attacks back?"

They'd never left, though she didn't need to know that.

"You're scaring me, honey. Can you breathe?"

I nodded. My mom had me sit in a nearby chair, and I focused until I was able to steady my irregular breath and my racing heart.

"Better?"

"Yes. I'm sorry."

"Don't apologize. But . . . what brought it on?"

"I don't know," I lied. "I think it's just the life changes catching up with me, you know?"

"If this is still happening often, I don't think you should travel alone," she said.

"It isn't. I promise you I'll be fine. I need you to trust me."

My mom hesitated, but she nodded reluctantly. "I thought it would be nice for you to come back here. Cathartic, maybe. But now I'm afraid I did the wrong thing."

"What?" I asked. "No, not even close. I wouldn't want to be anywhere else right now."

My mom reached for my hand, and a pang of guilt filled my chest at the thought of leaving her alone again.

Lake Crescent, Washington
June 2021

I woke to an odd crackling noise. My eyes popped open and darted around nervously. I sat up and reached for the back of my head, feeling the damp strands in a state of utter confusion.

The night had settled in with the steady patter of rain, but at some point during the evening, the rain had moved out, and the moon's pale glow softly illuminated the forest. I was sitting on a fallen log, cocooned in a sea of deep green; verdant moss decorated many of the tree limbs, and lush ferns blanketed the earth. The leaves still dripped with the evening rain, and the earth was soft and quiet underfoot. I jumped from the downed log and navigated around several massive tree trunks attempting to orient myself.

Light glimmered from the opposite side of a towering spruce, and my eyes reeled to adjust to the sudden illumination. I crept to the tree and timidly peered around it. A tall figure draped with cascading auburn hair took shape in the glow.

Izzy.

She stood next to a large elk cow, and I almost yelled as Izzy reached toward its head. I had just warned her about this.

I'd seen countless elk over the years, but none that would allow you to even approach them. I was too late to warn her, and I froze as I awaited the animal's reaction. Surely, it would attack her.

The elk, however, seemed perfectly content as Izzy ran her hand down the side of its neck. The animal looked squarely into her eyes before tilting its head. A small calf limped toward its mother with an injured hind leg.

Izzy proceeded toward the calf and took a seat on the cold ground. She touched her hand to its leg and whispered so lowly I couldn't make out the words. After a few minutes, she stood, and the calf walked over to its mother without issue. It was healed.

"Impossible," I muttered. I clasped my hands over my mouth immediately. My words had been barely a whisper, but they didn't escape Izzy's notice. I stepped from behind the tree.

"Oh!" Izzy gasped. "Hadley . . . What are you doing out here?"

"I was just wondering the same thing. I don't know how I got here."

"Don't you?" Izzy asked.

"No."

"What's the last thing you remember?"

"Falling asleep in my bed. I don't know how I got here. Why am I here?" My voice was filled with panic.

Izzy moved closer, and she seemed to glide above the ground as the ivory train of her dress floated behind her. Izzy's eyes were wilder than I'd ever seen.

I gasped when I realized a soft glow of light was pouring from her pale skin. The sight was ethereal, and it left me speechless, completely in awe. Every hair on my body stood on end.

"Is this a dream?" I asked.

"How should I know? If it were, I'd only be a figment of your imagination."

"I think you know."

Izzy opened her mouth to speak but was cut off by a distant buzz that vibrated through the forest. The sound grew in intensity like the hum of an airplane as it fired up on the runway.

"What is that?" I asked, to myself as much as to Izzy.

"I—I don't know." Izzy cocked her head toward the commotion, and her eyes widened. And when she spoke again, it was with urgency. "You need to go. *Now.*"

"Why?"

"Someone's here. You aren't safe!"

"Izzy, what are you talking about? What's going on?"

"I don't know. I know it doesn't make sense. Please, Hadley. Please just get out of here."

"I don't see anyone. Are you sure someone's there?"

"This is dangerous. You must go."

A swirl of fog materialized in the distance. It was the softest shade of gray. It yielded a pair of eyes like pools of ink, and I could've lost myself in their depths. The sight was ominous—unnatural—and something in my gut told me that I should run, that I should be terrified, but I couldn't leave Izzy behind.

"Come on, Izzy! Let's go!"

Izzy shook her head, and in the face of danger, a calmness came over her. She placed her hand softly on my face.

"Go home," she whispered gravely.

A violent wind swirled through the treetops and formed a funnel cloud that plummeted to the earth.

Izzy stepped back. She pointed to the swirling cloud. "Run, Hadley!"

Taking a chance, I ran toward the cloud and was swept away. I screamed as the cloud engulfed me. I was robbed of my sight until I woke in my bed, gasping for air.

"A dream," I croaked out, still dragging in ragged breaths. "It was only a dream."

I fumbled my way to the bathroom sink and turned on the faucet, hoping a splash of cold water would do me some good. As I patted my face dry, something odd caught my eye in the soft illumination spilling in from my bedroom. I flipped on the overhead light and studied a patch of green caught in my strawberry blonde strands.

A jolt of panic shot through me as I pulled moss from my hair.

CHAPTER THREE

Lake Crescent, Washington
June 2021

The pebble bounced across the surface of the water before sinking to the lake's fathomless depths.

"You ever hear the native story about how this lake was formed?" Tanner asked, brushing his dusky strands away from his face.

Tanner and I had met during our undergraduate in a history class at the University of Washington and had bonded instantly. With his squared, chiseled jaw and athletic build, I'd seen him draw a lot of attention over the years, but it was his inward qualities that had endeared him to me. He'd been through the roughest chapter of my life with me, although he was there for many of the good moments, too. He'd grown up near Seattle after his parents relocated the family from Beijing when he was a baby. They'd bought a weekend home on Lake Crescent, only a few houses down the gravel road from my parents' cabin.

"Someone was talking about this at the lodge recently—warring tribes, right?"

"Yeah, the Quileute and Klallam tribes were fighting, and allegedly Mt. Storm King was tired of their battle and threw a chunk of itself into a river that was here at the time. They say it dammed the river and killed their warriors, but the lake was born. And so was peace."

"Seems like there's a lot of local legends about this lake."

"All that talk, but the lake still has her secrets," Tanner said.

A shiver ran through me. Tanner tossed another pebble toward the lake, and it skimmed the smooth surface before following its predecessor. It was one of the rare days where the lake looked like glass, and the temperature was cool for June. I'd thrown one of my dad's flannels over my favorite blue turtleneck, but I still found my layers weren't quite warm enough in the shade.

The sound of crunching gravel announced Jordan's return.

Her tall figure bounded down the hillside navigating the towering trees as she juggled three mason jars and a picnic basket. Tanner and I jogged up to meet her halfway, and a bright smile crossed her face.

"Compliments of Gram," she said.

"Oh, hell yeah!" Tanner reached for the basket, his eyes sparkling in anticipation. I swore they shifted with his mood. I'd seen them as dark as inky pools—onyx stones set against his golden skin. But other times, they appeared a softer shade of brown, bordering on russet.

Jordan passed off a mason jar to me, and I removed the silver, screw-top lid to enjoy some of Gram's famous sweet tea.

"Always makes me feel at home," Jordan said.

Jordan's family had relocated to Mississippi from D.C., and I'd spent all my childhood summers in the southern heat with my grandmother. Jordan and I met the summer her family moved to Starkville, and the two of us had become fast friends.

She had just graduated from Amherst in May, but her dream was to work as an intelligence analyst for the FBI. She was about to start the application process.

This summer, I had applied for an internship with the National Park Service to work at Olympic National Park, and luck was on my side. I was assigned to Lake Crescent Lodge, which allowed me to spend the season with my parents after my father's cancer diagnosis.

Gram wanted to spend time with Dad as well, and with Jordan's break before her application process, we'd pivoted our summer tradition to Washington.

It had been a little over a week, and the three musketeers were already deep into the outdoors—we'd spent the morning kayaking.

We scattered ourselves along the old, wooden dock, and Jordan pulled a book from her backpack. She was an avid reader, and I'd rarely seen her without a book nearby.

"What's this one about?" I asked.

"Oh, it's so good. It's about a band of magical pirates who get marooned on an island surrounded by mermaids."

Tanner chuckled. He was often amused by Jordan's literary tastes.

"Shut it, Tanner."

The sunlight filtered through the nearby trees, casting dancing shadows across Jordan's deep brown skin. I'd always been fascinated by the way the light pulled flecks of amber from Jordan's dark eyes. Her tight curls were the color of a starless night sky, and she wore two space buns pinned at the top of her head, the rest of her hair spiraling to her elbows. Tanner had gifted her a Pearl Jam t-shirt, which she had promptly cropped and tossed on under a jean jacket. With her black ripped jeans and oversized sunglasses, she looked every bit the badass she was.

After sunning ourselves, Jordan decided we should take a walk, and we meandered along the gravel road that hugged the side of the mountains. The lake houses were below us, their driveways jutting straight down from the roadway.

"That's where Izzy lives." I pointed through the trees to the cedar cabin with its gabled roofline peeking up at us.

"It's beautiful," Jordan marveled.

"I'm ready to meet this family," Tanner said. "They sound . . . interesting."

The day after I met the MacGregor siblings, Izzy and I had ridden our bikes around the lake, but the following day the family seemingly disappeared, and I hadn't seen nor heard from them for several days. Even now, the house looked deserted. Something felt off about the situation, but I guessed the lake and I weren't the only ones with secrets.

Tanner wandered ahead of us.

"What if the MacGregors are in the witness protection program?" Jordan's eyes filled with wonder. "Oh! Or maybe in some branch of government ops?"

I laughed. "Of course, that's where your mind went."

Jordan shrugged.

"I like that theory more than your others, though."

Jordan cut her eyes in my direction as a knowing grin pulled at the corners of her lips.

"Hadley Weston," she said reproachfully.

"What?"

"How exactly would you know about those theories?"

I groaned. "I'm sorry."

"It's okay. Lord knows you can't help it."

Even though Jordan had grown accustomed to my oddities, I still felt horrible when I knew things she hadn't told me. She'd always understood me on some level—she knew about my ability, but never once made me feel like I was different from her.

On our return to my house, two figures materialized at the top of my driveway. One's long, auburn hair gave her away instantly, and the other made my heart stop.

Izzy skipped into my arms. "These must be your friends?"

"Jordan and Tanner, meet Izzy," I offered by way of introduction.

As Izzy, Jordan, and Tanner exchanged pleasantries, Fitz walked toward me.

"Hadley, it's good to see you again," Fitz said.

The sound of my name on his lips sent a thrill sparking through my body. The world began falling out of focus again, and I fought against my mind for control.

"Glad to meet you," Fitz said to Jordan and Tanner.

My eyes followed his movements warily. He shook hands with both Tanner and Jordan seemingly without incident. My fingers tingled as I recalled the shock between the two of us when we had touched. I took a deep breath and exhaled slowly, hoping it would help with my nerves.

Fitz met my gaze curiously before offering a soft smile, and my nerves eased slightly.

"Mum was just about to put the kettle on when we left. Fancy a cup?" Izzy asked.

Jordan and Tanner looked to me for direction.

I nodded. "That sounds nice."

The MacGregor cabin was captivating. The high ceilings lent a roomy feel to the space, especially in conjunction with its open concept. The foyer opened into the kitchen and living room. Massive windows covered the wall facing south, allowing for a magnificent view of the lake and the short pier that jutted into the water. The tree line had been thinned in front of the house, but it ran wild on either side of the structure, maintaining the cocooned effect most of the homes around the lake boasted.

Izzy led Jordan and Tanner onto the back deck, but I meandered slowly through the space as I studied the details.

The interior of the home was mostly comprised of cedar boards, a real testament to the local logging community, and a stone fireplace promised a cozy winter spot. The furniture was a mix of creams and leather, and touches of tartan were spread across the space—the blanket on the couch, the dish towels in the kitchen, the runner in the foyer.

I turned to Fitz, who had stayed behind with me.

"The MacGregor tartan?" I asked, gesturing to the plaid pattern.

"You're a curious one, aren't you?"

"I apologize in advance."

Fitz chuckled. "I just completed my PhD, so curiosity isn't a crime as far as I'm concerned."

"Wow, congratulations. That's incredible. What was your area of study?"

"Scottish history with a focus in Divinity—medieval witchcraft and religion."

"Fascinating," I marveled. "Witchcraft has always been interesting to me."

"Oh aye?" he questioned, a gleam in his eye.

"I was *consumed* with the idea of witches as a child. My parents thought it was a phase, a passing fancy from Halloween. But then they realized my interest ran much deeper and that trying to sway me from the obsession was useless. It felt . . ."

"It felt what?"

I shook my head. "You'll think it's silly."

"Try me."

"It just felt so real. Like magic was all around me," I recalled sadly, remembering the child I had once been.

"No. That's not silly at all. I was fascinated by it myself."

"That's what led you to your focus in school?" I asked.

"Aye. I was so captivated by the subject, I traveled to the burghs in Scotland where accused witches were tried, and somewhere along the way I decided to study it seriously."

"What piqued your interest in that subject?"

"My family tree," Fitz said. "My father and I traced back to a grandmother who died in the witch trials in Forfar, Scotland in 1662."

"What was her name?"

"Esther MacGregor."

"I can't believe you were able to trace back to her. It must've been shocking to discover your ancestor was executed in a witch trial."

"I was horrified. It was a long time ago, but it felt personal. From there, I learned what I could about who she was and about the time period."

I nodded. "It changed your trajectory."

"I reckon you're right. I was debating on my degree program for university when we got our ancestry sorted, and this research settled my mind on Scottish history."

His eyes bore into mine. There was something unspoken in the air—I felt it—but whatever it might be, I couldn't quite grasp it.

He pushed his rolled sleeve a little further up his forearm, and a desire to touch him took hold. I wanted to know if he would shock me again. I balled my hands into fists, resisting the urge to reach out to him, when a noise startled me. I turned, losing my balance.

Fitz caught me just before I hit the ground and pulled me upright. A jarring shock pulsed through my arm from his touch, and we pulled away quickly.

"You good, Hads?" Tanner called, walking through the doorway.

"Yep, all good here," I assured. I turned to Fitz. "Sorry about that. I'm not usually clumsy."

"Nae bother," he said, his accent thickening.

"Have you ever had this happen before—the shock?" I whispered.

Fitz looked around, but the rest of our companions were lost in conversation on the far side of the room. He returned his focus to me. "Never."

"Me neither. I don't understand it."

"Neither do I."

A woman bounded down the staircase that hugged the east-facing wall. There was no question that she was Izzy's mother. Auburn hair hung just above her shoulders, framing an ivory face with a striking pair of eyes the same shade of green as her children's. A broad smile warmed her features as her eyes swept across us, and in that moment, I was certain that Ann MacGregor was every bit as charming, self-assured, and attractive as her young daughter.

"We're so pleased you're joining us for tea."

A round of thank-yous sounded before introductions were made, and I thought Ann's eyes lingered on me just a bit longer than with Jordan and Tanner. Ann moved toward the kitchen to boil water, and Jordan's pointed look toward me confirmed my suspicion. Fitz pulled out a barstool for me. Izzy set plates of shortbread cookies and a cake topped with almonds on the table while Ann steeped the tea.

"This one's a favorite," Izzy shared. "Dundee Cake."

"I've never heard of that, but it looks delicious," Jordan said.

"Mum's specialty," Fitz chimed in. "It has spices, oranges, and raisins."

Ann beamed at her children's praise. "Hopefully, you like it."

"Love it." Tanner covered his face with a napkin, his praise barely coherent with his mouth full of cake. The group laughed.

A door opened to reveal an office. The man that stepped through the doorway was as tall as Fitz and shared his chestnut hair. His face held striking blue eyes the color of storm clouds, but the trait that stood out most was the presence he brought to the room. Though his family was happy he was joining us, something felt off about him to me. Ann kissed him lightly on the cheek and placed a steaming mug in his hand.

"Ian, meet Izzy and Fitz's new friends."

Introductions were made, and yet another set of eyes lingered on me. And this time, I felt even Tanner's observation. The pattern was impossible to ignore.

As the afternoon wore on, we settled into a rhythm of conversation. Jordan and I had countless questions about Scotland while the Mac-Gregors had countless questions about us. And as the light grew golden, I realized we would be late for dinner with my parents. The rest of us were so consumed in our conversation that we'd lost Tanner and Ian.

Fitz and I rose in search of our missing companions.

The door to the study was cracked, and hushed voices floated from the other side. They were seated across from each other at an old wooden desk. The conversation looked serious.

"I've got it," Fitz whispered in my ear, sending a chill through my body.

He emerged with Tanner and Ian, and the latter two wore grim expressions. We exited the cozy home into the cool air of the June evening.

"What was that about?" I whispered to Tanner.

He shook his head in response. I was about to push him for more information when Fitz called my name. Jordan and Tanner walked to the top of the driveway, granting us privacy. Fitz leaned against the house, a smirk resting on his lips.

"May I see you tomorrow?" he asked.

"Gentleman." I smiled. "And the answer is yes."

"Late morning work for you?"

I nodded. "What'll we do?"

"You like plans, don't you?"

"I'm afraid so."

"Let's try skipping plans tomorrow. We'll let the day take us where it wills." He turned toward the door but paused, looking back over his shoulder. "Oh, but Hadley—wear something comfortable. We'll have ourselves a wee adventure."

CHAPTER FOUR

Lake Crescent, Washington
Present Day

As I followed the curves of Highway 101 around Lake Crescent bound for the airport, my mind was spinning. I'd promised my mom I'd be safe, and yet there I was, closing the distance between myself and a potentially dangerous situation. Truth be told, I had no idea what I was walking into, but I had to take that chance. I'd regret passing on the opportunity for the rest of my life.

I checked the time, debating whether I had enough of a travel buffer to stop at my favorite pullout along the lake.

Lake Crescent was a living, breathing entity—I knew it would sound odd to say it out loud, but it was. I'd never known another place so charged with magic. Even though I'd experienced so much hardship along its banks, I still found solace there. I didn't have time for a proper goodbye, but I decided I would stop for a few minutes and breathe its pure air once more before spending ten hours on a plane. I'd make it to Tanner's house in Seattle with a little less time to spare, but we had the airport haul down to a science.

I stepped from the car and walked toward the shoreline. The wind rustled the branches high above me, and the edges of my vision blurred with the deep green of lofty spruce, fir, and alder. The tree-topped mountains jutted straight into the smooth surface of the pristine lake from every side. I'd always felt shielded from the outside world here, like the lake was a world of its own. Its hues were dependent on the sun, and on that day, the light bathed the lake in aqua blue.

It was often said the lake didn't give up her secrets, and perhaps that was part of my kinship with her. The secrets I harbored were buried deep within me, just like the fathomless depths of the lake.

Lake Crescent, Washington
July 2021

I tugged at the rope as I took my final step onto the rocky surface of Mt. Storm King. Fitz and I had spent most of our days together over the past month, taking turns choosing our adventures. I'd decided to share one of my favorite hikes with him. There were countless trails with breathtaking mountainous views in Washington, but the perspective from high above my lake home was my favorite.

We walked cautiously along the center of the peak until reaching the best viewpoint on the mountain.

"Now, that's a braw view," Fitz marveled.

"That means good?"

"Oh aye. This is bonnie—you know that one by now?"

"Aye," I said, mimicking Fitz's tone.

He laughed, shaking his head.

I scanned the scene below us. Fitz was right: it was bonnie. The lake's sapphire surface was as smooth as glass below the plunging mountains surrounding it. The day had started out stormy, which wasn't common for July, but the clouds faded to soft gray, the wind died down, and the rain ceased its descent as we arrived at the trailhead, just as Gram had predicted. That woman was a marvel.

The storm had been enough to scare off the crowds that morning, which were usually thick in the summer months, and we shared the mountaintop with only a few others. We settled on to the edge of the rocky peak, and I stretched out appreciatively, happy to rest my feet for a bit.

"So, how's the job search going?" I asked.

"Slow. But that's by choice, so I can't complain."

"Same here," I said. "I'm stalling, but I can't stay here forever."

"I'm sure your parents are happy you're here."

"You're searching for a professorship?" I asked, steering the conversation away from my dad. He'd been feeling better the past couple of days, but the bad ones were still inevitable—and they were always in the back of my mind.

"What makes you think that?"

"Didn't you say you've always wanted to be a professor?"

Fitz's gaze jumped quickly to mine.

"What's wrong?" I asked.

"Nothing is wrong," Fitz said.

I narrowed my eyes.

"I never told you that—about wanting to be a professor." My heart dropped.

"This has happened a few times now—you've done this with Izzy too."

I remained silent.

"Don't be nervous. I just want to understand."

Silence.

"How do you know these things?"

"I don't know," I finally said.

"You're positive about that? That doesn't quite make sense."

I shook my head. My mind was racing.

Fitz grew pensive before swinging his legs around to face me. "Does this happen often?"

"No."

"Hadley . . ."

"What?" I asked.

"You're not being truthful."

"Excuse me?"

"I know that's a lie," Fitz said.

"And how would you know that?"

Fitz looked around, but none of our fellow hikers were in sight. "Because I know when people are lying to me. I feel it. I . . . see the lies."

My heart quickened. "See them?"

"Aye."

Why was he telling me this?

"What do you see when people lie?" I asked.

"The light around the person dims—it sort of wavers when they're not being truthful."

I paused before saying, "I—I know what you mean. Except that I see a transparent thread forming, and I feel it in the air. It makes the air feel heavy."

Fitz's eyes lit. "You have that ability too?"

I nodded, closing my eyes briefly.

"What happens with the thread?" Fitz asked.

"It depends. If it's a singular lie, it fades. I won't see the thread again unless we revisit the conversation. If they add on to the lie, another thread forms, and a knot ties them together."

Fitz smiled. "That's incredible."

"Is it?"

"I think so. It's certainly useful."

"I can't argue with that."

"Can you do anything else?" he asked.

I nodded my head.

"Like?"

I hesitated, not quite ready to share the rest.

"I'll go first?" he suggested.

"Please." My voice was shaky.

Fitz reached for my hand and gave it a quick squeeze. "I have a bit of a strange skill. It came on when I was a wee boy, and it's intensified as I've grown older. I'll show you, but it's a bit jarring."

"I'm ready."

He turned his head curiously, and suddenly, I could think of nothing but my conversation with Jordan and Tanner from the prior evening.

We were seated on the pier by Tanner's lake house, making plans for an upcoming hike. The memory was vivid. Waves licked the shoreline, and frogs croaked through the trees. I tried to push the scene from my mind, to focus on Fitz, but I couldn't escape it . . . until my mind went blank.

I looked at Fitz, but before I could speak, I spun into a June afternoon.

I was riding bikes with Izzy. We talked and laughed as we peddled our way around the lake.

The emotions that had plagued me that day came rushing back. I'd had the strange dream about Izzy wandering through the woods the night before, and I'd spent that afternoon in utter confusion, wondering whether it had truly been a dream. I gasped at the intensity, and my mind went blank.

"What the hell was that?" I asked, breathing hard.

"I'm sorry if that was intense. I wanted to find a couple recent memories that wouldn't be too taxing for you."

"You can read minds?" I asked.

"Not exactly. Not everyday thoughts as they run through people's minds, but I can latch on to memories. I can pull any of your memories to the surface."

"They felt so . . . vivid. It was like I was reliving them."

"Aye. It always happens like that."

"And I couldn't stop thinking about them. I couldn't get out of the memory."

Fitz nodded. "Not until I release you from it."

"Show me something else."

"Are you sure?"

"Yes," I responded, uncertain if I truly was.

Fitz searched my eyes, prying into the far reaches of my mind. Slowly, his expression changed. The memory that rose to the surface took my breath away.

A large field with deep green ryegrass stretched across the distance toward the horizon, and a quaint, two-story farmhouse came into focus, the home where I'd spent so many summers. I studied every last detail. The white paint, large windows framed in maroon shutters, and a wrap-around porch were forever burned into my mind.

"All I need is a glass of Gram's sweet tea," I said.

"I don't think I can help you with that one."

It was disconcerting to hear Fitz's voice while I was so completely lost in my own mind. Gram's front porch was still the only thing I could see.

"Oh, don't even try. I'm pretty sure Gram could reach across the lake and slap you for messing with her tea."

Fitz laughed heartily.

I closed my eyes briefly, savoring the feeling of Gram's kingdom, and opened them again to Lake Crescent.

My body could no longer contain my emotions, and I laughed, though tears ran down my face.

"I'm so sorry. Maybe I shouldn't have done that," Fitz said.

"No, you don't understand."

Fitz's eyes flickered worriedly across my face.

"I'm happy," I said.

"Happy?"

"I've felt so strange my entire life, Fitz. I've never known anyone who can do strange things too. I've never known anyone who could understand me."

Relief washed over his face. "Thank god. I thought I had upset you."

"Quite the opposite."

"Well, fair is fair. Tell me about your other gift. Can you read minds? Is that how you know things we haven't told you?"

"Not exactly. I don't know what's wrong with me to be honest."

"Well, first of all," Fitz said, "there's not a damn thing wrong with you."

I remained silent. I couldn't agree with him.

"So, your ability . . ." he prompted.

"I don't know how I can do what I can do. I don't hear thoughts. Information just shows up."

"What do you mean exactly?"

"I just know things. I have no idea how I know them. I just do."

Fitz nodded thoughtfully. "So, you aren't asking for the information? You're not trying to gather information from anyone?"

"No. Never."

"Ah, and that's why you think we've told you those things. Is this new?"

"No, the information has been coming to me since childhood. I've done a pretty decent job over the years of discerning where the information came from—whether someone actually shared something with me or not. But ever since I met you and Izzy . . ."

"What?"

"I'm having a lot more difficulty controlling it."

"I wonder if it has anything to do with me," Fitz said. "Maybe being around someone else like you has intensified your gift."

"How do you control yours?" I asked.

"Years of practice."

"Do you think you could help me?" I asked.

"I don't have your gift, but I think I can be useful. Let's give it a go, at least."

My heart swelled. "Thank you so much."

Fitz reached for my hand. After a moment, the shock faded to a dull roar that pulsed between us, but for the first time since I'd met Fitz, I counted that pain as a blessing.

CHAPTER FIVE

Seattle, Washington
Present Day

I pulled into Tanner's driveway, and his tall, muscular frame emerged from the front door before I could even put the car in park. He waved from the small porch before popping back into the house.

The cozy craftsman-style bungalow was painted a faded green and trimmed in white. Shrubs lined the porch, and a large spruce tree offered much-appreciated shade from the hot sun during the summer months.

Tanner reappeared and bounded down the front steps. I exited the car to greet him.

"Hads!" Tanner shouted lifting me from the ground. "God, it's good to finally see you!"

"It's good to see you too! Momma and I missed you last weekend."

"Some of us have to work for a living, Weston."

I scoffed, punching his shoulder lightly. "You know I'm heading to Mother England for interviews, right?"

"Nah, I'm glad you took some time off to help your mom. And I'm so proud of you for doing this. You excited?"

"Unbelievably excited. Momma? Less so."

He pulled a Mariners cap from his back pocket and pulled it over his dark hair. "Tell me all about it in the car."

Tanner was chattering in the driver's seat about a new training regimen he'd designed—he was one of the best personal trainers in Washington, and he'd built a successful business out of that.

"I was bummed to miss our annual Storm King hike, but it was the only day they could have me in for that interview. Even though my schedule is pretty stacked with clients, I think this gig could be a great decision, you know?"

"This is the one you mentioned the other night on the phone that you couldn't tell me about?"

"Yeah. I still can't tell you who it's with, but they're pretty major."

"Well, keep me posted—I mean, as much as you can."

My phone buzzed, pulling my attention to a new email.

Ms. Weston,

Thank you for your interest in our open PR Manager role here at Edinburgh Castle. The hiring manager for this position, Mr. Murray, would like to arrange an interview with you and has a strong preference for it to be in-person rather than via video conference. I see you've indicated you're traveling to the U.K. soon, and we would like to arrange the interview while you're in the area. If you'd like to move forward, please advise on your availability at your earliest convenience.

We look forward to hearing from you.

Sincerely,

Edna McLeod

Assistant to James Murray

"What is it?" Tanner asked.

"Nothing. It's just an interview request."

"That's awesome. Where?"

I hesitated.

"Spit it out, Weston."

I took a deep breath. "Edinburgh Castle."

"Scotland? I didn't know you were applying there."

"I wasn't . . . necessarily. This opening just came up while I was researching, and it looks like a great fit for me."

"I see." He paused. "Isn't that where Fitz lives?"

". . . I don't know for sure if he's still there."

Tanner cut his eyes to me. "You're playing with fire."

I gazed out of the passenger side window hoping Tanner would let the conversation drop. The skyscrapers of downtown Seattle flashed by. I'd always loved the drive down I-5 through the downtown corridor. An ache plucked at my heartstrings. I'd missed the PNW more than I wanted to admit, even to myself. Boston hadn't been easy, but Boston was over.

A new adventure was just what I needed.

Forks, Washington
September 2021

At first sight of the Cedar Creek Inn, a deep breath escaped my lungs, my mind momentarily devoid of trouble.

The three-story farmhouse oversaw a large field and the great trees covering the mountains to the south, white paint stark against deep green. Memories bubbled up—my dad walking me down the narrow lane along the inn as a child, in search of elk grazing the fields; my mother lounging on the front porch, a good book in hand.

I parked along the old wooden fence outlining the property, and Fitz emerged distractedly from the car. It had been his turn to pick our outing, and he'd chosen the inn without hesitation.

Tanner had given me a look of disapproval when I'd told him I was going to share my love for the inn with Fitz. I knew he was worried about my relationship with Fitz . . . whatever it may be. But as Fitz and I gazed at the inn, my happiness was palpable—it was one of the few places where I could always breathe easily.

"I see why you love this place," Fitz murmured under his breath.

A Scottish flag hung from the front porch, floating gently in the breeze alongside the American flag. Fitz turned to me, a question resting on his features.

"When guests visit from other countries, Ben and Sarah hang their flag alongside our stars and stripes," I explained. "They're welcoming you."

Fitz grinned broadly.

My eyes scanned the house and surrounding area, registering the subtle changes since my last visit—a fence repair, a fresh coat of paint on the porch, a new sign. But it was mostly just the same. The soft trickle of water from the creek was perceptible in the quiet afternoon. Cows dotted the field, their bodies basking in golden rays, strewn all around an old wooden barn. The structure was popular with tourists, likely one of the most photographed barns in the world. The wood had grayed, faded by the rain, and was contrasted with a blue roof, bright in the afternoon sun.

The front door swung open, revealing a familiar face. His eyes twinkled brightly in recognition behind silver-rimmed glasses, and a crimson Washington State University cap and gray Cedar Creek Inn polo proudly proclaimed his love of both.

"Hadley!" he exclaimed, his voice warm and inviting. "It sure is great to see you again."

"It's great to see you too, Ben."

A woman's voice floated on the afternoon breeze. "I thought I heard you, Hadley. Welcome home!"

Ben's wife, Sarah, stepped around the corner, her arms extended in my direction. She hadn't changed a bit. Her hair was the color of snow, framing blue eyes and a face defiantly untouched by time.

Ben and Sarah had been staples in my childhood. My parents and I had visited their inn for many years. They'd become like second parents to me, and occasionally, when college life became too noisy, I'd found my weekend escape in this very home. Introductions were made, which included a sly look from Sarah as Fitz shook Ben's hand.

I showed Fitz around the inn while Ben and Sarah pointed out their most recent updates to the rooms. Eventually, Fitz and I settled on to Adirondack chairs on the back porch. The promise of fall floated in the afternoon air, but the sun's warm rays kept us comfortable.

The back door swung open, and a young woman bounced across the threshold, her usual exuberance lighting up the space around her. Blonde curls tumbled to her shoulders, framing her storm-cloud eyes.

"Addy! I'm so glad to see you!" We embraced warmly. "I hated that I missed you last time."

"I was so bummed! But I'm glad I didn't miss this visit." Addy nodded toward Fitz.

"Oh, right. This is Fitz."

She grinned, eyeing me meaningfully before shaking his hand. "I did come out here on a mission. Sarah has fresh baked cookies. You want coffee or tea to go with them?"

We both requested tea, and Addy bounded back through the doorway.

"She's sweet," Fitz said, nodding toward the door.

"She's curious. The only guy I've ever brought here is Tanner." I rolled my eyes. "Why *did* you decide on coming here?"

"The way you've spoken of Ben and Sarah, the house, all of it . . . I wanted to see it."

I tilted my head. "But why?"

"Because it's important to you."

Addy flung the door open, a tray of cookies in hand. She was followed by Sarah, who held two steaming mugs and two plates.

"Cookies make any afternoon a good one," Sarah said as she handed off the mugs.

Fitz eyed the cookies appreciatively. "I couldn't agree more."

"Well, you know where we'll be if you need us."

Sarah and Addy headed for the door.

"You don't want to join us?" I asked.

"No," they answered in unison. They chuckled before closing the door behind them.

I groaned. "Sorry."

"For what?" Fitz asked innocently. He grabbed a cookie from the nearby tray and leaned back in his seat.

"You know for what."

He laughed. "Perhaps. Is their assumption incorrect?"

"That something is going on between us?"

"Aye."

"We spend a lot of time together. But we spend a lot of time with Jordan. Tanner. Izzy."

Fitz's gaze was unreadable. I babbled on. "Whatever they think is going on, I don't think that's your intention here."

"Oh aye?" Fitz cocked his head to the side and studied me long enough that my breath hitched. I hoped he didn't notice. "I don't think that's quite true."

"And what is?" I challenged.

Fitz's eyes flickered across my face, and humor faded from his features. "It's exactly what they think. I think you already knew that."

"I know . . . but you're confusing. You seem interested, but then you keep a distance from me." My eyes flickered to the space he'd left between us.

"I didn't want to make you uncomfortable. The shocking . . ."

I set my open hand on the arm of his chair. He hesitated before holding it in his own. Pain traveled through my body and goosebumps rippled across my skin, but I was determined not to let go. And after a moment, the pain eased.

"Not so bad," I said.

"All right then." Fitz said, amused.

We sat silently for a moment before Fitz's expression grew pensive.

"What is it?" I asked.

"This isn't just friendship, and we both know it. You and I gravitate to each other."

We sat, hands linked, while we enjoyed our afternoon tea, and after helping Addy with the dishes, we decided to take a walk. We meandered the old lane near the inn in companionable silence, taking in the scenery. We passed the barn, and the lane narrowed. The green fields stretched toward the low mountains, and a chorus of frogs was all that disturbed the quiet. The evening was still, peaceful, and the chill of dusk crept into the air.

"I have so many memories from this place," I said absentmindedly.

"Would you share one of them with me?" Fitz asked. I leaned against the nearby fence.

"You mean . . . ?"

"Aye. But only if you want."

I nodded.

"Think of one you'd like to share, and I'll take it from there."

I rolled through a few options before laughing. "I've got it."

The scene unfolded like I was living the moment all over again. I was walking the lane with my parents about ten years ago, and our dog, Max, was with us. Max was a border collie, and we were forever trying to help him run off his energy. My mom held his leash loosely in her hand while she talked distractedly with my dad about our upcoming family vacation. I studied my father. It was years before his diagnosis, and it was a real gift to catch another glimpse of his healthy years.

Suddenly, Max turned his head, and his ears perked up. He jumped the fence, ripping the leash out of my mom's hand, and tore across the field before we could even process what he had done. I was horrified when I realized the object of his focus. A herd of roughly forty elk were congregated in the back field.

"Dad!" I yelled. "The elk!"

"Oh, no. Here, Rach," he muttered, tossing his phone to Momma.

He jumped the fence and ran as quickly as his feet would carry him over Max's path.

"Matt! Be careful!" My mom yelled.

I jumped the fence and followed my father's path, my mother's protests fading with my progress.

Max was determined to do what collies did: herd. Max was running around the elk, and my dad was running behind Max. One of the elk chased Max while he chased the rest of the herd, and my dad stumbled backward, realizing the danger.

"We're going to have to tackle him," I said.

"Yeah, we just have to wait until the right moment," he said, eyeing the massive creatures.

After a series of unsuccessful attempts, we finally found our opportunity.

As Max zoomed past us, Dad risked it all and jumped with full force, landing unceremoniously on top of Max. Max yelped in surprise. My dad winced at his clumsy landing. I shrieked at the scene unfolding. But Max was caught.

By the time Dad and I returned to Momma, Ben and Sarah had joined her. They'd happened upon the scene during their evening walk. Luckily, no one was injured, and the whole episode ended in laughter.

As the memory faded, the group's laughter was replaced with mine and Fitz's. A few tears dropped down my cheek.

"Sorry," I stammered. "I forgot how funny my dad looked chasing that damn dog."

Fitz carefully wiped away my tears.

"It was nice to see Dad like that too—healthy. It felt real again."

"I'm glad," Fitz said softly.

As our laughter faded, we held each other's gaze, and though I felt the strangeness of the moment, I couldn't seem to look away.

"What's the matter?" Fitz asked.

"It's nothing really. Just sometimes when we lock eyes . . ." I trailed off.

"It's difficult to look away? It's the same for me," Fitz said.

But it was more than that. Sometimes the world felt like it was spinning out of control, but if I just kept my eyes on his, everything else faded out of focus. I think I would have found peace in it if I could just let the moment be.

Fitz reached timidly toward my cheek before letting his hand drop.

"Why, Fitz?" It was nearly a whisper, but I knew he'd heard me.

He shook his head and gripped my hand. The now familiar shock blew through me.

"I think we should give this a minute." He nodded to our linked hands, and I understood.

Once the pain eased, Fitz ran his fingers through my hair to the base of my neck. His eyes wandered from my eyes to my jaw, and his hand followed his gaze as his thumb skimmed the length of my face. It traveled slowly to my lips, and his eyes followed. His eyes darkened as he made his decision. He leaned forward and met me in a soft kiss. My entire body tingled with butterflies before a small tremor radiated through me. I gasped softly, and he pulled back.

"Are you good?"

"Yeah, I'm fine."

 He paused.

"I don't know where our paths lead from here, Hadley. There's so much uncertainty." His voice grew husky, and his accent thickened. "Would you still want to risk this if I told you it might *no* end well for us? If I told you I cannae guarantee your happiness?"

"No one can promise happiness. That's like promising sunshine in this rainy little town. Neither of us can guarantee anything . . . But I think we're worth the risk."

"We shouldnae be doing this." His brows creased, and a frown spread across his features. "You deserve better than what I can give you."

Fitz was right about the uncertainty of our futures . . . our careers, my dad, the oddities between us . . . There was so much we couldn't explain. But I wouldn't allow uncertainty to decide my future.

I shook my head and pulled his face to mine until our lips almost touched. "You don't get to decide that for me. I'll decide that for myself."

CHAPTER SIX

Seattle, Washington
Present Day

Tanner pulled into the departures lane and hopped from the car to grab my suitcase. He rolled the luggage to the sidewalk before pausing.

"Come on, Hads. Out with it."

"What do you mean?"

"You were distracted the whole ride over even before you got that email. Something is bothering you. Talk to me."

I sighed, debating telling the truth. It was Tanner . . . I'd never been any good at lying to him.

"A letter showed up in my room this week. Fitz asked me to meet him in Paris."

"*What?*"

I nodded.

"Oh, shit."

I laughed. "Yeah. My sentiments exactly."

"You're going to do it?"

"I have to. I've been waiting for this moment for over a year."

His dark eyes narrowed. "Are you sure? I mean, you're sure the note was from Fitz?"

"Positive," I said.

"And you're sure you want to do this?"

"Tanner," I warned.

"Nah, no hate. I'm just asking. You're ready for this? For whatever this is?"

"There's only one way to find out."

"You remember those self-defense moves I taught you and Jordan, right?"

"*Tanner!*"

"What? Just in case it's not Fitz waiting for you over there," Tanner said.

"He'll be there. I'm certain of it," I said, more confidently than I felt.

"If you say so."

"I say so. Now, I really have to go. I'll text you later."

"Knock 'em dead, Weston."

"Love you, big guy."

"Yeah, love you too. Stay safe. Call me if you need me, okay?"

I hugged him and sprinted for the door.

I paused at the entrance and turned back to find Tanner standing right where I'd left him, with his brows knit tightly and his lips straightened into a grim line. I'd seen a similar expression the first evening we'd visited the MacGregors when Tanner sat across the desk from Ian. My heart sank at the thought of leaving him with worry, and I thought about turning back. Instead, I simply waved before rushing through the doors.

Lake Crescent, Washington
March 2022

Fitz's parents were hosting a going-away party for me before I left for Boston, where my first job out of graduate school awaited. Everyone was there: my parents, Fitz, Izzy, Jordan, Tanner, Ben, and Sarah. The party was in full swing, but the emotions swirling through my body were too much to bear, so I sought out a quiet corner in the adjoining room. I stood near the window, my eyes transfixed on the rough surface of the lake.

Footsteps disturbed my reverie, and I turned to find Fitz. Over the last six months, Fitz and I had grown closer, spending most of our days together. His family had joined mine and Tanner's tradition of celebrating the holidays with our families at the lake. Fitz had been helping me navigate the ups and downs of my father's illness. We worked on recognizing patterns with our touch and came to understand that strong emotions heightened the intensity of the shocks.

Life hadn't been easy, but it was better with Fitz.

But over the last week, I'd sensed something was wrong. Fitz had been so proud of me when I shared news of my job offer with him. I knew how difficult this would be for our relationship, but I believed we could work through it. So why was it that I'd seen the distance grow in his eyes and had felt his increasing despondency washing through me?

Fitz reached for my hand, and a shock moved through my body. A soft smile spread across his lips, but his nerves radiated throughout the room. My chest tightened.

"A bit much in there?" he asked, his Gaelic dialect thick on his tongue.

"You know me. I'm loads of fun at parties."

"Part of your charm."

"Since when is anxiety charming?"

His eyes turned mischievous. "Since I met you."

I laughed, shaking my head lightly.

"I have something for you."

He placed a small box in my waiting palm. I ran my fingers across the silky, sage paper and the large, ivory bow.

I opened the gift slowly, my hands shaky on the paper, and a sort of reverence fell across the room. It was our last day together before everything changed, after all, and there was something sacred about these few peaceful moments I had alone with Fitz. I finally unboxed the gift, and I couldn't conceal my gasp.

A slim, golden band was lightly hammered and held a pearly white moonstone in a round bezel at its center. It glowed like its namesake in the soft rays of the pale sun. The light pulled hints of blue to the surface of the otherwise crystal-colored stone.

"Fitz! This is too much."

"How did I know you'd say that? Always underestimating what you deserve."

I shook my head softly.

"Tell me something. Do you like it?" Fitz's teasing tone fell to softness in an instant.

"Of course, I do," I whispered.

"Then promise me you'll wear it. Nothing would make me happier."

"I promise." My response was barely a whisper, but the smile on his face let me know he heard me.

I slipped the ring onto my finger and paused briefly before enveloping him in a warm embrace. He stiffened at the shock as our bodies met, but he quickly composed himself and wrapped his arms around me.

"Hadley," he said hesitantly. I released my grip and found his brows knitted tightly as his lips fell into a hard line. "After you leave tomorrow, you and I won't be in contact for a while."

My mind spun so quickly, I was sure the ground itself was slipping away.

"Why?"

"I'm not supposed to tell you why. I'm supposed to tell you something . . . anything but the truth, but I can't do that. I can't lie to you."

"I don't understand—are you breaking things off?"

"No, of course not . . . I know this doesn't make sense. I don't want it to be like this, but it isn't my choice."

I reached for his hand, holding it in both of my own. The pain returned before falling into a dull ache, and I wondered if my touch was adding to his discomfort.

"Isn't your choice? Then whose is it?" I asked.

"I know you don't understand it right now, but I promise that I'll be able to explain everything one day."

"When?"

"I don't know exactly. It won't happen for a while, but it will happen. I swear," Fitz said.

"You know what?" I released my grasp, feeling like I was letting go of more than his hand. "Screw this."

"Hadley."

"No. Maybe we haven't talked about it lately, but you and I both know damn well what we have." My voice rose, attracting the attention of our friends and family in the next room.

Fitz took my arm and led me onto the back deck, away from their questioning glances.

Though the sun was still present, the wind had shifted overnight and brought with it the cold air of the west, which tore through my loose hair and sent strands of strawberry blonde floating all around me. I pushed my hair away from my face, the act further incensing me, as Fitz turned on his heel, rage burning through his green eyes.

"I didn't say a bloody thing about not knowing what we have," he growled.

"So, what? You tell me something like this and then it's just supposed to be okay?"

"I know it's not okay! I never said it was. I'm doing my best here."

"Not good enough."

Fitz's glare tore through me.

"This is ridiculous," I said.

"Look," he began, pausing briefly. "You have no idea what this is doing to me. I have no choice. Please just try to trust me."

"How am I supposed to trust you?"

His eyes widened, the anger fading with my freshly delivered blow before he turned toward the lake.

"Don't you dare turn away from me," I said.

"I know you're pissed. I would be too." He paused, turning to face me once again. "I've already said too much, and that's because I care about you."

"I need more."

"You're different, Hads. And so am I . . ."

"Come on. Don't give me this crap, Fitz."

"No, you need to listen. The things we can do—that's why we'll be apart for a while. When I can come to you again, I promise I won't waste a second."

"Wait, this is because of our abilities or because of this weird connection we have?"

"Both."

"Are you in trouble?"

"Yes and no," Fitz said.

"Real helpful."

"Damn it, Hadley," he muttered under his breath.

"What? Give me something."

"Aye, it's about our abilities, but our connection has something to do with it as well. This isn't exactly normal—it's special to you and me. That's all I can say about it. You have no idea how much trouble you're getting me into."

"Except that no one else knows about this conversation, right?"

Fitz's lips curved into a humorless smile.

"I love your curiosity, your love for learning. But it's going to make you mental and get us both into trouble."

"Fitz, you have to give me a little more context, and I think you know that."

He paused as his eyes narrowed. "Give me a moment."

I nodded, and he disappeared inside the house. When he returned, a large blanket was draped over his arm, the red-and-black checkered pattern looking at home against the wooden cabin. Fitz draped the blanket around my shoulders and led me toward the trees bordering the house. Gravel crunched underfoot, and I already knew where we were going: a lofty evergreen that had fallen years ago. I'd had many a conversation, with both Fitz and Izzy, sitting atop that magnificently large old spruce.

My feet met the firm end of a broken branch with a certainty that came with familiarity, and I hoisted myself onto the spot we'd worn smooth. I settled in comfortably while allowing myself to adjust to the energy of the space. I couldn't explain it, but the air always felt different around the fallen tree.

Fitz eased himself down next to me, the tinny sound of his jacket disturbing the quiet. His eyes were distant, transfixed on the waves breaking on to the shore a few feet from us. Finally, he faced me.

"We've talked about our oddities, you and I."

I nodded.

"The truth is there are people who know about the things I can do. And those people . . . Hadley, they work for the government."

"*What?*"

"You're safe, but I'm going to leave the States for a while."

"Wait a second . . . like, the U.S. government?" I asked.

"It's more complicated than that. But I do need to leave."

"I . . ." I cleared my throat. "I don't understand. You're in danger?"

"I know they want to talk to me. I spoke with my family, and we feel it's best for me to leave the States, at least for a while."

"Won't they be able to trace you?"

"Don't worry about that," Fitz said.

"What would happen if we kept seeing each other? What would they do?"

"I'm not sure."

A transparent thread wavered between us. It wasn't an outright lie, but it wasn't the plain truth either. And that wouldn't work for me.

"What would they do, Fitz?" My voice was even, but the warning was clear.

"They haven't communicated consequences yet. But based on the information my dad and I have gathered . . . it would be bad. Unless you want me to *really* disappear from your life, we need to do as they ask, at least for a bit."

I was stunned. "No. That can't happen."

"We'll sort this out," Fitz said. "I'll find a way to communicate with you. And eventually, we'll find a way around all this."

"How do you know things will be okay?"

He turned his head ever so slightly, his eyes piercing mine.

"You're not going to tell me."

Silence.

"So, you're going to leave here, lay low, and then what?"

"I'll figure that part out eventually." He shrugged. "Right now, I'm focused on making my first move while keeping you safe."

"You need to worry about keeping *yourself* safe. Don't worry about me."

Fitz turned to me, placing his hands on either side of my face. "That's impossible . . . for me to not worry about you. Surely you know that."

I rested my forehead against his. I closed my eyes, attempting to quiet my raging mind, before pulling back, my eyes searching his.

"Is it crazy that there's a part of me that wants to come with you?"

He ran his thumb softly across my cheek. "The most selfish part of me wants that more than you know."

"But you're not going to let that happen."

"You know me well." He sighed. "I want to keep you safe. I need some time to sort this out, but I *will* sort this out. I promise I'll find a way."

"I could help you," I said.

He shook his head. "Go to Boston. Start this new chapter of your life. Stay safe, Hadley."

I opened my mouth to protest, but he was faster.

"Think of your father."

A lump rose in my throat. I understood Fitz perfectly. It was hard enough to leave for Boston while my dad was still battling cancer. If I went with him, there would be no regular phone calls, no video calls . . . and I couldn't do that.

"I choose you or I choose my family?"

"No," Fitz whispered. "You're going to choose a life for yourself. One where you'll still talk to your family and support your father."

There was a flurry of emotions inside of me: anger, sadness, fear— they were all racing for control. I wanted to object. It wasn't in my nature to accept defeat. But I couldn't do this. I couldn't disappear on my family. I couldn't put my dad through that. And I wouldn't risk Fitz's safety.

"Hadley . . ." he whispered.

I knew what he sought. "I'm okay."

"I'm so sorry."

A tear spilled down my cheek. "You say we'll find a way to overcome this, so why is it I feel like I've just lost you? I'm missing you so much even while you're still here. I already feel your absence, Fitz, and it is *everywhere*."

I found the courage to face him after my confession. Though his expression was impassible, tears fell from his eyelashes, staining his perfect face with grief. The ache in my chest intensified. I cradled his face in my hands, sweeping my thumbs gently across his cheeks.

"You said I had no idea what this was doing to you," I began, sniffling, "but you're wrong . . . because I can *feel* what you feel too."

His pain filled every fiber of my being. We'd likely never understand why we felt each other's emotions as though they were our own, but I was okay with the pain. It was the loss of that connection I feared most.

"I wish I loved you less," he said. "I don't want to put you through this. But there's no helping it." He pulled me closer to him, and I gasped at the charge of electricity that sparked through me at his touch. It was amplified. He loosened his grip, but I tightened my own, shaking my head.

"I don't want to hurt you," he said.

"I don't want you to let go."

He nodded.

"Is this hurting you?" I raised our linked hands.

"It's bearable. It . . ." He trailed off.

"It what?"

He shook his head.

"Say it, Fitz."

His eyes glistened with tears, and my body filled with the butterflies of uncertainty. His free hand slid to cradle the base of my neck, and I felt his resolve crumble just as strongly as if it were my own.

"It hurts worse to let go," he admitted.

"Then don't."

"I have to, Hadley."

CHAPTER SEVEN

Paris, France
Present Day

Though a rooftop in Paris seemed an unlikely place for our reunion, I stood atop Notre Dame, waiting expectantly. I pulled the note from my pocket and ran a thumb across my name written in ink, as if the note would disappear if I let it out of my sight. The paper's edges had already softened from my constant handling.

I turned to Notre Dame's sweeping view, the full grandeur of the city on display. Block after block of historic architecture lay on either side of the Seine down to the Eiffel Tower and beyond toward the high-rise skyline—surely a mesmerizing scene under different circumstances.

A faint chill crawled the length of my spine, rattling my already growing nerves.

Not for the first time, I considered that the note wasn't from Fitz.

I reached for my right hand, needing to feel the smooth surface of the moonstone ring I couldn't remove. I closed my eyes, anticipating the deepened state of awareness brought on by the stone, my thoughts churning, my senses heightened.

My nerves prickled from the back of my neck to the base of my spine, and I couldn't deny the gnawing sign of being watched. I'd felt the unsettling sensation countless times over the last couple of years—since just prior to meeting Fitz. The observations had grown more frequent since he and I had parted at the lake, and the feeling more intense.

I glanced over each shoulder, answering the compulsion that bordered on habit. Eyes landed sporadically on mine as I scanned the bustling, historic attraction, but I found nothing suspicious.

A cool breeze nipped at my neck, a subtle reminder that the day was fading. I checked my watch. It was an hour past our intended meeting time.

I meandered around tourists that lingered in the waning daylight, excited by the prospect of golden hour photos and sunset views. A couple wrapped their arms around each other as they gazed at the scene, tender smiles spreading across their lips. I tried to push my disappointment from my mind, but my chest tightened.

Finally, I had to consider that Fitz wasn't coming.

The setting sun and my fading optimism tempted me to trade the stone gargoyles of Notre Dame for a quiet space. Recalling a cozy little café near my hotel, I swept the Parisian skyline one last time before turning to leave.

I wound my way toward the door when the sensation of being watched prickled up my spine again. But something was different . . . and it stopped me in my tracks. A scene took hold of me, and I saw myself reflected from another point of view.

"Not again," I whispered, panic-stricken. I took in a deep, ragged breath before turning slowly.

A tall man stood near the stairwell, his head turning toward me. My eyes swept over him. From his brown oxfords and dark wash jeans to his gray sweater and the chestnut hair peeking from underneath the hood of his olive jacket, he was as perfectly put together as he'd always been.

He pulled the hood down, and the sun's golden rays illuminated a face forever etched into the fabric of my mind. As I neared, his expression grew easier to read. His eyes were hopeful, following my movements tenderly. His mouth was set tight, holding all his fear and doubt. I paused just before him, staring wordlessly into his emerald eyes. The breath caught in the back of my throat.

"Fitz."

He smiled.

And there he was. A perfectly familiar stranger. The ghost that had haunted me for over a year, the only person who held the power to break me over and over again. My heart ran wild, and I found some comfort in the fact that his must be doing the same. His fingers twitched, and I thought he might reach for me. Instead, he tightened his hands into soft fists. He closed his eyes briefly, an attempt to blink away the mist.

I took Fitz's hand in mine, and a burst of electricity coursed through me, taking my breath away. We broke away quickly, shaking our hands like it would help expel the pain.

"Oh, shite!" The intensity of his whisper made me smile. "We're off to a great start."

I shrugged. "It's pretty on-brand for us, to be honest."

He laughed softly, and between my nerves and the infectious sound of his laughter, I did the same.

"You've changed." He reached timidly for my hair, allowing my auburn locks to fall through his fingers.

"In some ways," I said softly.

His eyes were troubled as they swept across me, scanning for other changes, I guessed. A deep melancholy settled between us, and I was desperate to make it stop.

I extended my hand. "Let's try this again?"

"Aye, who needs their hands anyway?"

As our fingers met, a tremor radiated through my body, though softer than before, and I figured our calming nerves might have some thing to do with that.

"Now, that's better," Fitz said.

"Much better," I agreed.

A surge of emotion bubbled through me, and I had to be honest with myself about how badly I'd missed Fitz. My eyes welled with tears.

"Come here," Fitz said.

He tugged at my hand, pulling me into his embrace. A long-standing tightness eased from my chest, and I leaned into him, finally allowing myself to believe the whole scene was real. I hadn't dreamed it. He gave a tight squeeze and released me, the scent of whisky and spice dissipating with the warmth of his touch.

"I can't believe we're here," I said.

"Aye . . . surreal, isn't it?" he asked, his Gaelic dialect thick on his tongue. "I'm sorry I was late."

"Why *were* you late?"

"I was . . ." He trailed off, registering the people surrounding us, before dropping his voice. "I was followed."

"By?"

"No idea—not the usual folks."

My thoughts flooded with questions, but this was neither the time nor place for an inquisition, annoying as that was. The man had disappeared once before; I didn't want him to leave before we had a chance to talk— to really talk.

I nodded, crossing my arms as the wind picked up.

Fitz shrugged out of his jacket before I could even protest and placed it around my shoulders.

"Let's get out of the cold. Can I take you to dinner?"

I was caught off-guard by the realization that I hadn't eaten all day— I'd been too nervous—and he mistook my pause for disinterest.

"I mean, no pressure. We don't have to. It's just—"

I laughed, interrupting his panic. "Let's get dinner."

"What a great idea, Hadley."

We wound through the thick crowd just outside the cathedral. Fitz turned toward me, placing his hand on the small of my back. The gesture felt comfortable, like we were assuming our previous roles. A twinge of apprehension hit the pit of my stomach.

A couple of streets over, the sidewalks were free of crowds, and I let out a deep sigh. The wind blew gently across the Seine, which served as our guide toward the café. We walked in silence only a moment before

I broke the ice.

"I felt someone watching me before I saw you. It wasn't you, was it?" I asked, hoping maybe it *had* been Fitz watching me at Notre Dame.

"No. I had just climbed the steps when we met near the door," he said.

"So, it was someone else. I was really hoping I was wrong about that."

"Aye, but sometimes it isn't bad intent. Maybe the person was just curious about you."

"You think someone was watching both of us at the same time, and it was just a coincidence?"

"Did you just roll your eyes at me?"

I grinned. "Yes. But the question still stands."

"No. But it wasn't the government."

"And how do you know that?"

"I just do. I'm telling you this is different."

"You know we have to talk about all this, right?" I asked.

Fitz nodded. "I know. We have a great deal to discuss . . . and some decisions to make."

I waited patiently for him to continue.

"If it's all right with you, I'd like to talk about all that tomorrow, though."

"Tomorrow? Why?"

"I've looked forward to seeing you again for a very long time," he said. "I just want one night with you where we forget all the bullshite. Just one night, Hadley."

I couldn't pretend I didn't want the very same thing.

CHAPTER EIGHT

The café was charming. The host led us to a back corner, navigating mismatched, antique tables—products of a bygone era still serving as a catalyst for food and conversation. They looked at home amongst the sage walls, which were covered in mahogany shelves holding eclectic, vintage wine bottles. Although the restaurant was filled with patrons, the hum of conversation was soft, intimate.

Fitz pulled out my chair then proceeded to his seat. My eyes flickered across the table, wondering what it was about him that made every bit of my soul so incredibly aware of his presence.

His lips curved into a soft smile.

"What?" I asked, realizing my eyes had lingered far too long on my dinner partner.

"You. I forgot how observant you are. About everything."

"And you find it amusing?" I asked.

"I find it endearing."

I shook my head, butterflies dancing in my belly.

"Your mind is my favorite thing about you. There's always so much going on up there . . ." He trailed off, searching my eyes.

Silence fell. I would've felt embarrassed had it been anyone else.

The moment dissipated with the waiter's arrival at our table. We ordered a bottle of wine, and I suggested Fitz use his discretion to select food for the table. As I'd been in Paris only a day, it seemed wise to allow the veteran to take the wheel. Fitz was enthusiastic about sharing a couple of his favorite dishes with me.

He leaned forward. "Go ahead."

"What do you mean?"

"I can tell you have a burning question."

I pretended not to notice his amusement as I asked, "Why did you decide on Paris?"

"I didn't want to meet you in London, just in case Big Brother sorted out that you were going there next week. This is a close enough stop. And they think I'm in Budapest," he offered.

"You don't think they've figured out we're here?" I asked.

"I'd wager they've figured out I'm not in Budapest, but they have no trace to Paris."

"Nice."

"I needed to get away anyway, and Paris usually helps me sort out my head when I'm feeling stuck. You have impeccable timing."

"I remember that you love this city," I said. "I can already see why."

"Aye. It's a grand place for breaking monotony."

"What has you feeling stuck?"

Fitz's eyes grew distant, and an emotion stirred within me. Fear wasn't the right word for it, but something was troubling Fitz.

"My latest project," Fitz said. "Shall I bare my soul to you?"

I nodded in encouragement.

Though his words were lighthearted, he couldn't hide the tension that rose to the surface as he spoke. "I'm trying to solve a mystery surrounding my ancestor and an object they lost in 1662. I've hit a dead end."

"Is anyone helping you?"

"No," he admitted. "I haven't trusted anyone."

The look on my face must have betrayed my confusion.

"I don't want the government to know my family ever had possession of it, and I'm not sure who I can trust," Fitz said.

Why would it matter to anyone outside of his family if his ancestor had lost something hundreds of years ago? I'd spent far too much time on the mysteries of Fitz MacGregor and his family, and it seemed that pattern would continue.

"Is this about Esther?" I asked.

"You remember her?"

"Esther changed the course of your life. Do you think I'd forget something like that?"

He glanced down at his hands, his eyelashes fluttering as he smoothed out the tablecloth. When he looked up, his expression was unreadable. "I'm a slow learner."

I'd let his deflection go, at least for now. "Why are you telling me about it?"

"Because I trust you."

The waiter delivered our wine, and his request for Fitz to approve the Chateau de Ferrand broke our gaze. When we locked eyes, we could barely look away, as though we'd become aware of each other for the first time, a magical, invisible thread connecting us. It seemed to be some sort of communication we didn't yet understand—much like how we'd each developed the ability to feel the other's emotions and pain.

I felt his nerves across the dinner table, and I knew he felt mine.

The waiter poured the beautiful, deep burgundy liquid into my glass. After a brief swirl, I took a small, tentative sip, allowing it to trickle smoothly across my tongue.

"That's *delicious*," I said before taking another sip.

Fitz chuckled at my response and raised his glass in turn. "What do you taste?"

I closed my eyes, pulling another slow sip from the glass. "Dark fruit—black cherries. Spice. It'll open up nicely."

"Aye, it does want oxygen. It's a bit warm, which I fancy." He nodded appreciatively. "I'm glad you approve. Wine tasting has been a bit lackluster without you."

He deftly swirled the dark liquid, opening its full possibilities. There was something playful and unassuming in his manners. In his features, I'd found both a man that left me breathless and a boyish countenance that put me at ease.

I leaned forward. "You trusted me enough to talk about your secret project, so . . . let me help you."

"I'd be grateful for your help."

"How long have you been working on this?"

"Let's discuss more about the project later," Fitz said.

My eyes narrowed.

"Come on, Hadley. Let's save this conversation for another day. I don't really want to think about it right now."

"You know, there seems to be a lot of conversations being pushed to 'another day.'"

"You'll be here for a few days, so I think we'll have time to cover everything."

"Oh." My eyebrows raised playfully. "So, I can expect the pleasure of your company for several days?"

"If you'll have me."

I nodded. "Well, since we have several days in Paris, I have plenty of time to ask my questions."

"Here we go."

"Your good humor is appreciated. So, tell me more about what you're doing in Scotland now. You've been cryptic about your exact location—are you still in Edinburgh?"

"Aye. Conducting research and teaching a few Scottish history classes."

Edinburgh. Butterflies danced through me.

"Hold on. Are you teaching at the University of Edinburgh?" I asked in awe.

"Aye." Fitz smiled, clearly gratified by my response. The university was consistently ranked as one of the top in the world, and Fitz was only in his early thirties.

"I should have picked up on that. Your accent is stronger," I teased, pulling a laugh from him. "But that's incredible. This is how you landed back in Scotland?" I asked, reaching for . . . some sort of French cheese puff pastry at the center of the table.

"A couple of my mentors had asked me about my postdoctoral plans before I left for the States that summer, but I wasn't sure what I wanted. I doubted myself more than anything."

"So, what changed?"

"I came back to Edinburgh right after we left the lake that March, and I met with a few of those mentors. They thought I'd be a good fit for the history faculty. One thing led to another, and before I knew it, I was accepting a position as a lecturer."

He told the story nonchalantly, in his quintessential Fitz style, but I knew that accomplishment was no small feat, and I sensed the pride he took in his work.

"I teach in the School of Divinity, focusing on witchcraft and religion in Scotland during the 17th century."

"You seem happy with it," I said.

"Aye, and it's been nice to spend time in Scotland again. Seeing family is great too."

"I'm jealous. I have a long list of places in Scotland I want to explore, especially in the Highlands."

"I'd be honored to show you my country . . . if you'd like."

"I'd like that very much."

A broad grin spread across his face.

"Speaking of careers," I said, "I hinted at a change in my last letter, but I didn't want to put it in writing . . . I'm interviewing in London."

My heart skipped a beat as I omitted Edinburgh, but I wasn't ready to broach that conversation with Fitz just yet. If he noticed my nerves, he didn't show it.

"You'd be moving?" he asked.

"I need a change. Seems reasonable, right?"

"Perfectly reasonable I'd say, though I've never been the foremost scholar in reasonable."

I laughed knowing he was absolutely right, which I considered a mark in his favor.

"Are you staying in PR or looking into something different?" he asked.

"The same. I really enjoy working in PR. I just didn't want to be in Boston anymore." I shrugged.

"But why London?"

"The culture, the history, the architecture . . . it's always interested me. London has great career options—companies, museums, universities. I feel like it would be a good next step for my career."

"Aye, it's a good thought. I wonder—"

"What?" I asked, feeling a shift in his energy.

"I just wonder what's really drawn you to London. It's a proper Hadley story, but there's more to it."

"What makes you think there's more?"

"Because I know you, and I know when you aren't telling me something," Fitz said.

I thought about my father, my panic attacks, the emptiness that I thought might last forever. I thought of how I'd concealed all of this from my mom when she sought the same information only a few days ago. She and Fitz both knew me well enough to understand there was more to my decision . . .

I almost told him all of it, but the words stuck in my throat.

Not yet, I thought.

"Maybe you don't know me so well anymore," I said instead.

"I'll always know you," he responded, the soft smile fading from his face.

"You left, Fitz. I'm sure we've both changed. I know I have."

"I left? It's not quite so simple, is it?"

"Fine," I said. "We both moved, but I didn't end things."

"I didnae either. And you know this entire arrangement was for your protection."

"Do I?"

"Wow, Hadley. That's unfair."

I exhaled sharply.

"I dinnae want to argue right now. I just asked a simple question," Fitz said.

I closed my eyes in an effort to think clearly. "Truthfully, I thought about coming over here a couple days early, even before your note. I needed to . . . wrestle with my thoughts and process the past couple of years before jumping into interviews. With Dad . . ." I trailed off, willing the tears to stay in. "You know, I told you my dad died, and it changed nothing."

"My first priority was keeping you safe, and that's what I did."

"That's not what I needed most. I needed you there, Fitz."

"It would have caused a shite storm," he said. "It would have been far worse for you."

"You don't know that."

"I do know that. It would have been ugly, Hads. And what good would that have done you? You would've been dealing with the loss of your father, supporting your mother, and dodging the government? No." He shook his head. "You can be mad at me if you need to be. I'll take that. I *can* take that because you're here with me, and you're still safe."

I sighed. I was angry, but I couldn't decide if I was angrier at Fitz for what had passed or angrier at the fact that I couldn't stay mad at a man who was willing to sacrifice everything for my safety.

"How about we get out of here?" he asked.

"I could use a change of scenery. I think the jetlag is creeping in."

"We can go back to the hotel if you'd prefer."

"Absolutely not. I want to see Paris at night."

We wandered along the Seine, and the path was quieter than I expected. We strolled along in silence until I recalled a question I had about Fitz's research.

"How did you learn that the ring your ancestor lost was Esther's?"

"*Did I tell her about the ring?*" Fitz's voice echoed through my mind.

I froze.

What is happening to me?

Fitz laid a hand on my arm. "Are you all right?"

I was too confused to answer.

"Hads . . ."

"I'm sorry," I said.

"What's going on? Your energy feels panicked."

"I . . . You probably won't even believe this one."

"Hadley, have you met us? There's absolutely nothing normal about either one of us."

I hesitated still.

"There's no room for lies at this point—not between us. I'm not going anywhere, so you might as well be straight with me."

"I heard you thinking. I can hear people's thoughts now," I whispered shyly. "But it's not all the time. It just comes and goes. So, the random information I used to know about people?"

Fitz nodded.

My voice shook as I continued. "Now I can actually hear them thinking like they're talking in my head or see what they're seeing. I don't know what's wrong with me."

"There's nothing wrong with you. Please don't say that," he implored, his fingers sliding between my own, finding a firmer grip.

I nodded, not believing him, but unable to find the words I wanted to say. He rubbed the base of my thumb with his own, sending my feelings into battle with one another—pain, joy, anxiety, peace.

"When did it start?" Fitz asked.

"Right before I left for Paris."

"And no one knows about this?"

"No."

"Has anything else changed recently?"

I shook my head. "But things changed when Dad died. At first, I thought it was because I was grieving, but then . . ."

"What changed?"

"My hair thickened, and it changed color—from strawberry blonde to this auburn-ish shade that it is now. And it all happened so quickly, like in a week."

"That does seem odd."

I rambled further about the physical changes I encountered, the words tumbling out after seven months of secrecy. "My skin really smoothed out, and my complexion just . . . glows. And then I suddenly didn't need my contacts anymore. I know how this must sound, but it did happen all at once. I've been trying to find a connection, but it's difficult. I haven't talked to anyone about it."

"Don't you worry. We'll sort this out."

I nodded.

"Do you notice a pattern in what people are thinking?" Fitz asked. "Is there any sort of trigger for the mind reading?"

"No. It truly is all over the map. The first time it happened was with my mom."

"Give me some examples."

"There was the detail with Esther. And then, on the flight over, the person next to me was upset, and suddenly, I was hearing thoughts about their divorce." I shook my head. "And I . . . saw myself through your eyes at Notre Dame. I was in your mind, Fitz. I'm so sorry."

"Hey," he said softly. "It's all right. You didn't mean to do that."

I couldn't find my response.

"I think there's a connection between them," he said.

"What do you mean?"

"Every instance you recall is because you wanted insight. Who's watching me? Why is this person upset? And so on. Random information isn't coming to you—you're controlling the information you receive. We just need to figure out how you're calling them."

"I'm not asking for information, Fitz. That's what I'm saying. I'm not controlling this."

"You hear information you're curious about. Is it so hard to reason that your brain is asking for the information it receives? It seems logical to me."

"I just didn't think it would be that simple."

"You're close to the problem, so you're overthinking it."

I nodded, considering the new possibilities.

"That still leaves us with the biggest problem, though," I said. "I have no clue how I'm calling this information to myself. And I need to figure out how I even have this ability. I need to understand how it works if I'm going to control it."

Though Fitz's speech was casual enough, his nerves were wild. "I'm going to help you figure that part out relatively easily."

I paused momentarily taking a deep breath to dispel the nervous energy that rushed into my body.

"How are you going to do that?" I asked.

"Well, here goes our one night without the bullshite."

"What are you talking about?"

Fitz sighed deeply. "Hadley . . . I'm a witch. And so are you."

CHAPTER NINE

My stomach turned.

Fitz's words hung in the air, which suddenly seemed lifeless and stale.

Witches and witchcraft didn't exist. They were ideas created from the back of someone's mind many years ago. They were fabricated excuses used to persecute innocent women. They were Halloween stories and the subject of books and films, but they weren't real.

I looked at Fitz. The man who stood before me was no storyteller. He was a lucid, intelligent man who held an esteemed position at one of the foremost educational institutions in the world. I searched for the threads of a lie but found none. Fitz wasn't lying, but his statement couldn't be true. My mind wouldn't allow it.

"Fitz, do you realize what you just said to me?"

"Aye, I do. I think you're in shock. Here, drink some water," he countered. He pulled out a water bottle.

"Where the hell did that come from?"

"Don't worry about that." He twisted the cap and extended the bottle in my direction.

"I'm just fine, and I don't need water. You can't say something like that and then tell me how to respond. You can't just show up in Paris and casually throw out, 'Oh hey, I'm a witch, and so are you.'" I paused. "On second thought, do you want to take it back?"

"No, I don't. You *are* a witch."

"Yes, I heard you. Loud and clear."

He arched an eyebrow.

"Oh, Fitz," I whispered. "Listen, I just . . . my parents aren't witches. There's no way. I would know if they were. And I don't have some magical powers, okay? I can . . . read minds. I know it's strange, but not strange enough to call me a witch."

"You're right about your parents not being witches. Your mum can't know about this. Do you understand?"

I found myself nodding before I realized the harm in playing along.

"Good," Fitz said. "And there's nothing strange about mind reading. Or witches."

I looked around us, hoping to god no one was eavesdropping.

"Don't worry about them. No one can hear us." His eyes were wild, full of something bordering excitement.

"You say that so confidently."

"Oh aye."

I let out a slow, loud sigh, wondering how I was even supposed to approach a conversation like this. Fitz seemed to think we were discussing something completely normal.

"What have I gotten myself into?" I whispered under my breath.

Fitz stifled a laugh. I was borderline angry, and he was amused. It would've been just another day had he not uttered those unbelievable words only moments ago.

"I'll explain everything to you. I understand it's difficult to believe this after living twenty-nine years believing witches are just made-up stories, but this is no fabrication."

I thought about walking away. But some inexplicable force seemed to hold me in place as curiosity took over.

"For argument's sake, let's say that I believe witches exist. Which I don't," I clarified. "And that I believe I have my abilities because I am one. How could I be a witch?"

"Traditionally, witches are born into families of other witches. However, there's an occasional witch born into a family of humans. You've felt the difference your entire life, aye? It's one of the reasons you're so comfortable around me—why you were so comfortable around Izzy."

He gauged my expression before continuing. "We're not sure why it happens, but it appears to be some sort of genetic anomaly that shows itself after years of human ancestry. Somewhere down the line, there was a witch in your family tree."

I didn't see how Fitz could be right about all this, but if he was . . . then there was another person in my family who was like me. I wanted it to be true so badly it made my heart ache, but I knew that was ridiculous. I shook off the thought.

"It's not allowed, but that family member must've mated a human," Fitz said.

Mated . . . something about the term tugged at me.

"I see," I returned skeptically. "What happens with these newbie witches?"

"When they first show a sign of harboring powers, other witches are assigned to look after them until their powers are mature enough to access them. At that point, we're allowed to mentor the new witch as their power develops."

"So, you've what? Followed me?" I asked.

"Everyone in the family has an avid interest in keeping you safe. We monitor you through spells. We use spells that reveal where you are and how you're doing, but we're not physically present. If you were to run into trouble, we'd know immediately. Witches developing their powers tend to get themselves into interesting situations."

"So, your family was assigned to babysit me?"

"We were assigned to help you. My dad really is a university professor, but he also receives monitoring assignments from our council—our Scottish witchkind government—to monitor witches developing their powers. Izzy and I have trained with him, and we work with him from time to time."

Was I just some project to him? Was everything between us a lie? I wasn't so sure I wanted to know the answer to that.

"I don't need your protection," I said, turning to leave.

"Where are you going?" he asked.

"The hotel," I hissed and then froze.

The prickle working up my spine was undeniable. We were being watched.

"Oh, come *on*," Fitz spit out.

"Perfect timing."

"Well, you're not walking back alone."

We hurried down the sidewalk, not yet certain of our destination. Whoever was watching us, they didn't have good intentions. I could tell that much.

"If we walk around long enough, they'll lose interest. I think," Fitz said.

"And if they approach us?"

"I'm not sure. I don't think they will, though."

We turned down a less trafficked alleyway and picked up our pace, noticing the lack of witnesses.

We rounded the corner into a busier street near the Champs Elysées. The sidewalks were thick with crowds, and cars zipped down the streets. We tucked ourselves into an arched cove near an old, wooden door and pretended to be otherwise engaged. I focused on steadying my breathing, which was difficult with adrenaline coursing wildly through my veins. The seconds ticked by slowly, and after a while, I wondered if we'd lost our pursuers. But just as the question crossed my mind, two people passed our shelter. Their hooded jackets concealed much of their features, but I knew it was the people who'd been watching us.

Fitz's breath caught, signaling that he'd felt the same knowledge settle in. He gripped my hand, and we stepped from the doorway as prepared as we could be for whatever might follow. I met the gaze of our stalkers unabashedly, refusing to give any sign that I was afraid.

Their faces were impassible, but not their minds. They weren't anticipating a standoff. They held our gazes for mere seconds before sprinting off.

"That was . . . easy," I said.

"Too easy," Fitz said. "I don't suppose you heard anything useful?"

"Not really. They were surprised and didn't want a confrontation, but I have no idea why—my reception got a little fuzzy."

Fitz nodded thoughtfully.

"I'd feel better if I knew what they're after," I said.

"I agree. Something's not right about all this."

"Either way, let's get out of here?"

We walked the final stretch to the hotel in silence.

"Tell me everything," I demanded as we entered my room. "Clearly, there's a lot more you need to tell me than I thought."

Fitz entered the room calmly and took a seat on the bench. I stationed myself in front of him and crossed my arms.

"Okay, what do you want to know?" Fitz asked.

"Anything, Fitz. Everything. *What am I?*"

His response wasn't immediate, which allowed enough time for me to change my mind.

"Actually . . . wait," I said. "Show me magic first. I want to see it. I need to see it."

"You believe me, then?"

I struggled with the words, and I finally just nodded.

He looked toward the small, built-in desk across the room, and his eyes rested on a half-peeled orange. With his thumb and first two fingers slightly extended, he flicked his wrist, and the orange hovered in the air.

A brief intake of air was all that betrayed my surprise—I felt the blank expression still resting on my face. He looked at me from the corner of his eye and then returned his focus to the orange. With another flick, the peel unwound itself, as if it were the work of invisible hands, and floated into the trash can.

And with one final flick, the perfectly peeled fruit floated across the room, stopping in front of me.

"Hold out your hand," Fitz said softly.

I followed his direction, and the orange dropped into my open palm.

"Good god," I said. It was all I could manage. And when I looked up, I was met by an inscrutable expression. "Okay now, tell me everything."

He sighed. "I think we should get some rest and pick this up tomorrow."

"You think I can fall asleep after your little display?" I said as I stifled a yawn, and Fitz narrowed his eyes at me.

"I'm done in, Hads. You're exhausted—and don't try to deny it."

I looked at the clock beside my bed. 3 a.m.

"Fine," I said. "But we're discussing this as soon as we wake up."

I walked Fitz to the door.

His eyes flickered to my lips, and I wondered if he was fighting against his willpower the same way I was struggling with mine. There was so much I needed to know, so much I needed to understand.

But in that moment, the only thing I could think about was how badly I wanted to feel his body pressed against mine, how badly I wanted reassurance that we were more than just a project to him.

Tension swirled through the air.

The desire consumed me. Fitz's head tilted slightly, and my eyes lingered across his face.

Fitz wrapped me in his arms, and the ache in my chest eased ever so slightly.

Progress, I thought.

As he released me, his hands slid to either side of my face, and a dull pulse echoed across my skin. He looked deeply into my eyes before planting a slow kiss on my forehead.

"Goodnight, Hadley."

Fitz released me into a restless night, sleep eluding my troubled mind. I wrestled with myself for hours before finally deciding that despite the lack of a true scientific explanation, everything pointed to Fitz being truthful.

I'd wondered my entire life why I was different.

Had Fitz finally given me the answer?

CHAPTER TEN

Fitz smiled as he entered my room the following morning, but he couldn't hide the tension radiating through our connection. Dressed in dark jeans and an ivory sweater, he was as put together as ever, though his disheveled hair was a telltale sign he'd been stressed. Fitz sank into the oversized chair in the corner of the room.

"So, what's on the agenda for today?" I asked.

"You and your wee agendas."

"Tease all you want. But I want to know."

"I thought about going through your questions over lunch. But I'm not sure if it's safe for us to go out or not. I think we should stay in."

"Well, we can't just lock ourselves in our rooms," I said.

"Right, but we had people stalk us around the city last night."

"Yeah, I was there."

"Check the attitude, Hads. You really think we should go back out there and risk it?"

"These aren't the government people who normally follow you?"

"Aye, and that worries me."

"I get that. But these people knew how to find us at Notre Dame and again after dinner. If they don't know where we're staying, it's only a matter of time. I don't think being out in public puts us at more risk."

Fitz narrowed his eyes in thought.

"I'm not saying this doesn't worry me—it does," I clarified. "But we're probably just as safe out in the crowds as we are sitting in this room."

Fitz nodded slowly.

"Tell me what you know about these people," I said.

"All I know is they're different," Fitz said.

"You're *certain* this isn't the government?"

"This isn't how they operate. They wouldn't be chasing us around Paris. Their visit would be much more . . . official."

A chill ran down my spine.

Fitz continued. "And I lost them when I left Edinburgh. They haven't found us."

"You said 'witchkind' government' yesterday . . ." I trailed off.

"Aye, we have our own government in witchkind. They're the ones who mandated we stay apart."

"Why?"

"They weren't certain your full set of powers would materialize," he said. "They told me to stay away from you unless that changed."

"Because?"

"Because humans aren't allowed to know about us. Until we knew you'd come into your powers, they thought I was putting witchkind at risk."

"That's ridiculous."

"I'm fully aware, trust me."

His nerves resurfaced in my body. My mind was spinning as we both danced around the things we needed to say but didn't yet know how.

"Whatever it is that's holding you back . . . let go of it. Please, just talk to me," I said.

Fitz sat forward in the chair and rested his chin on his hand. I leaned against the wall granting him time to roll through his thoughts, and when he raised his gaze to mine, the resolve in his eyes was clear.

"I've thought through this a million times trying to decide the best way to explain it all. Turns out, there isn't one." I nodded in encouragement for him to continue. "The truth is you need to understand what we're facing. And you need to decide if you're willing to take this risk."

"Okay . . ."

"You're safe from the government right now. I'm confident they haven't found us. But that won't last." He paused. "Until you match with your powers, you're still considered a human by the councils' definition."

"What do you mean by match?" I asked.

"Your powers are trying to settle into you—that's why you have your abilities. But to become a true witch, your power needs to fully enmesh with your mind and body."

"You think I'll match," I said.

"I feel it, Hadley. You'll match."

I nodded.

"But if the councils catch us before you match, they'll erase your memories of me."

"*What?*"

Fitz shook his head. "I know how that sounds. But it's true. And if they were to do that to you . . . I'm afraid it would meddle with other memories I'm associated with."

"All of our time at the lake . . ." The first time Fitz had met Daddy; that night we stayed up to see the sunrise with Izzy; the base camp hike we did with Jordan and Tanner.

"And I don't know how far they'd take it . . . But they wouldn't take the risk of your family and friends bringing up my name, I don't think."

"So, they'd erase their memories of you too? We'd forget it all?"

"Aye. Or they might leave their memories intact and relocate you after erasing your memories. It's impossible to say which option they'd lean toward."

"They can't do that."

"They can," Fitz said. "If they catch us, they'll do whatever they deem necessary to protect witchkind."

Erasing my memories was bad enough, but I couldn't allow that to happen to my loved ones.

"And what about you?" I asked.

"It depends," Fitz said. "There have been many different penalties given in the past from imprisonment to mandatory government service, but . . . they've also spellbound witches. If they feel it fits the crime."

"Spellbind? They'd take your powers?"

Fitz's gaze dropped to the ground. "They'd ensure I couldn't access them."

I shook my head. "No. That can't happen. I need to match to my powers. That's the solution to all this."

"Hadley . . . there's no guarantee that they wouldn't spellbind both of us as punishment."

I paused. "I see."

"There's little that's worse for a witch than to be separated from our magic. I won't lie to you: It would be horrific. It would be losing a vital part of yourself." Fitz's nerves fluttered through me. "Think about all this and what you want."

I started to speak, but Fitz was faster. "No . . . don't answer right now. Really think about it. This is your future, Hadley."

I sighed. "Fine."

"I'll bet you have loads of questions. And rightfully so. You should learn everything possible, so you'll make an informed decision." He sighed, and his brows knitted together. "But I'm having trouble concentrating in here. Your energy is everywhere."

"Let's go somewhere else then."

"I know a place for lunch. Let's get a proper meal—and some caffeine, and I'll answer all your questions."

He chose an open-air café for our excursion, and it turned out to be the perfect spot to work our way through lunch. The bittersweet changing of the seasons was apparent in the crisp air, and I tilted my face toward the sky seeking the direction of the sun. I refilled my coffee cup, realizing it was my only hope to combat the jetlag that compounded my lack of sleep, as I watched the passersby stroll along the old stone street.

Though the conversation with Fitz had been sobering, I was eager to leave the hotel and see more of Paris. I wanted to commit the feel of Paris to memory, knowing I would miss the energy of the city when I left.

I reached for a croissant and leveled my gaze at Fitz. "I have questions."

"Let's hear them."

"I guess my biggest question right now is . . ." I studied the man across from me, searching his eyes, wondering again if the feelings between us were real. The question almost escaped my lips, but I asked about witchcraft instead. "What am I? I mean, what am I capable of? What can I do?"

"Well, truthfully, I can't answer that question. Every witch has different abilities. You're very close to matching with your magic—I feel your power so clearly—and once you do, we'll test your abilities and see where your strengths lie. But based on the feel of your energy, you're an elemental witch."

"What does that mean—elemental?"

"There are two types of witches: elemental witches and spell casters. Spell casters are exactly what they sound like. They're witches who use spells to work their magic. But you and I are elementals. We don't require spells to connect with the elements. We're in constant communion with them, and our powers link directly with the elements to work our magic."

"The elements . . . like air or water?" I asked.

"Air, water, fire, earth, the moon . . . witches gather power from all the elements, but elemental witches are especially influenced by one particular element. Mine is earth—once you match to your powers, we'll know yours."

"So, I'll connect to the elements, and I won't use spells?"

"In certain cases, you will. Elemental magic isn't the best choice for every need."

"Oh, right. You said you used spells to keep an eye on me," I recalled.

"Aye. It was easier and less invasive that way."

"Is one type of witch more powerful than the other?"

"Elementals are usually more powerful than casters," Fitz said. "A caster can't work elemental magic, but an elemental can work spells."

I nodded. "Do we need . . . wands?"

Fitz chuckled. "No, Hollywood. No wands required for either type of witch."

"Pointy black hats?"

"Myth. Do I look like a pointy hat-wearing witch to you?"

"I'm sure you'd look dashing in a pointy black hat."

Fitz shook his head playfully.

"Brooms?" I asked.

"Only for sweeping the floors."

"Are you a warlock? A wizard? Or is 'witch' the correct term?"

"Please never ask me that again." Fitz grimaced. "A wizard sounds like an eccentric old bloke with a celestial robe who reads spell books covered with cobwebs."

I laughed. "What about crystals, palm readers, tarot cards—all that stuff?"

A frown blanketed his features. "Crystals are accurately represented in human culture, but the rest . . . it's all tied to potential witches who never matched to their powers. Gifted humans, essentially."

"Basically, me if I don't match."

"You'll match."

His certainty gave me a little hope, but I couldn't ignore the doubts that nipped at the back of my mind.

What if he was wrong about me and I couldn't match to my power? What if he was forced to leave again? What if he left anyway?

I sighed. "Any of the witch legend true?"

"We're powerful," Fitz said. "We can manipulate the elements and bring fantasy to life. But we're as diverse as humans. We're not stereotypes."

I nodded. "What are some of the things elemental witches can do?"

"We control the elements to a certain degree—produce fire, work the air around us. Some are like you and hear thoughts, others are are time-walkers. Some speak with spirits of the departed or influence the weather—the list goes on."

"Time-walkers, like time travel? Speaking with spirits? Seriously?"

"Mm-hmm."

I was dumbfounded.

"This is loads of information, I know."

I nodded thoughtfully.

Fitz placed his hand on top of mine, and a surge from our unspoken connection flowed between us.

"Seriously, Fitz, why do we feel this energy? And don't you *dare* tell me you don't know."

"You won't like this," he began, his lip twitching. "But I don't know. I always feel when I'm coming into contact with another witch. I feel the difference in the air, and my chemistry reacts differently than when I interact with a human—and that's normal. But when I make contact with you, it's electric."

I nodded.

"I researched this while we were apart."

"Did you find anything?"

He shook his head. "I think it has to do with your powers stirring. I still don't understand why, but there must be a correlation."

I opened my mouth to respond, but I couldn't seem to find the words. A prickle worked its way up my spine like an assault of hundreds of tiny needles. Fitz's eyes widened before he regained his composure.

"This feels like more than one person watching us."

"Aye, and their energy is familiar.

"Oh," I said, as the realization settled in. "It's the same people from before."

Fitz nodded. "Let's go."

CHAPTER ELEVEN

We slid into the backseat of a gray taxicab waiting just outside of a nearby museum. The driver set down his newspaper and asked for our destination.

"We need to drive toward Sacré-Cœur but without taking a direct route."

Our driver glanced suspiciously at Fitz in the rearview mirror.

"We're being followed," Fitz said. "If that makes you uncomfortable, we'll call another car."

"It's been a while since I've had some fun."

And there it was again—the driver's thoughts entered my mind as if he'd spoken aloud. A slew of memories flashed through my mind of cars zipping through the streets of Paris.

"Oh, damn," I muttered under my breath.

Fitz shot a questioning glance my way.

The driver slammed on the gas, and we sped away from the museum.

A sign hung from the front passenger seat. The second row of text was in English. "Welcome. Your driver is Adebayo."

I hoped Adebayo was up for a challenge.

"What are they driving?" Adebayo questioned, a heavy accent rolling from his lips.

"The silver Peugeot," I answered, garnering a raised eyebrow from Fitz. "What? You think you're the only observant one in this car?"

"Can you make that turn?" Fitz asked.

Our driver laughed, shaking his head. "Can I make that turn? Of course, I can."

And indeed, he did—at a record speed, I was sure. I slid across the seat into Fitz. He shouted, laughing, and braced himself against the door, his head nearly slamming into the window.

As we rounded the block, a farmer's market came into view. Pedestrians were scattered through the street browsing the market. Shoppers' hands were full of everything from paper bags to ice cream cones as they dawdled along the stalls. I scanned the block searching for an exit but came up short.

Adebayo's eyes narrowed in concentration. "Brace yourselves!"

Fitz pulled me closer and prepared for whatever followed.

Several things happened at once.

Mass chaos ensued in the market. A young woman holding a tasting cup in front of a stall selling honey released a blood-curdling scream. Shoppers ran toward what they hoped was safety as Adebayo pumped the breaks and turned the wheel. The tires screeched as they slid against the pavement, but the car made a U-turn in the the middle of the street. Adebayo's execution was nearly flawless, but the backend of the car clipped the corner of a stall. The car made impact with a loud bang that echoed through the street.

Several small thuds sounded against the roof of the car before lemons, oranges, and berries rolled down the windshield and into the street.

"Did we just hit a fruit stand?" I asked incredulously.

Fitz chuckled. "Here we go!"

"Hold on tight!" Adebayo called.

Adebayo slammed on the gas once again, and the tires spun out. We took off in the direction from which we'd come.

The silver Peugeot was speeding down the street, but it slammed on brakes and angled itself in an attempt to halt our progress. Adebayo sped up and clipped the front corner of the Peugeot. The car spun, and we turned down the nearest street. Fitz and I turned to watch the corner, and sure enough: the dented silver car came into view.

Adebayo smirked. "Don't worry. I have the perfect spot to lose them."

I held tighter to Fitz's arm, which was wrapped around me, and he rested his hand on mine. The shock was uncomfortable at first, but I adjusted quicker than expected. Apprehension hit the pit of my stomach as I looked at our hands. What were we doing?

A tight alleyway came into focus, and I instantly knew the plan. Fitz and I braced ourselves as best we could, and Adebayo turned our car into the small space with precision. The Peugeot, however, was less fortunate. The driver couldn't make the turn and crashed unceremoniously into the building. Smoke rose from the car, and before I could even react, we were back on a main road.

"Brilliant," Fitz said. "I don't know how you pulled that off."

Adebayo smiled. "I grew up racing these streets with my cousins. I've outdriven many cars."

Our fearless driver turned down a narrow alleyway and positioned the car out of sight.

"We lost them. But you should walk through this building and call a different car to pick you up on that next street."

"Adebayo, my friend. A job well done," Fitz exclaimed.

He grinned. "It's been a while since I had excitement like that. Just like James Bond."

Fitz slid a card into Adebayo's hand. "Call this number, and we'll set things right with your motor."

They shook hands warmly before we followed his instructions. Since we'd lost our pursuers, we requested that the new driver take us straight back to our hotel in the 1st arrondissement.

We entered the hotel through a back entrance, making our way quietly to my room. Fitz secured the extra lock on the door, and I pulled the curtains closed.

"Maybe we should cancel our dinner plans," Fitz said.

I sighed as I slid into a nearby chair. "I hate this."

Fitz eyed me sympathetically. His energy stirred.

"What is it?" I asked.

"I've known what I wanted from the beginning, and everything I'm going through is worth it to protect you. But the stakes are high—you don't have to do this, Hadley. You can walk away from all this at any point."

"You might like that," I said.

"What are you talking about?"

"Would it make it easier on you if I did?" I asked. "Or would it just mess up your 'project?'"

"Do you really think you're a project to me?"

"Aren't I? I mean, you were assigned to monitor me."

"And what? I can't have fallen for you?" He laughed, but there was little humor in it. "Don't give me that much credit."

I shook my head. "I'm so confused."

Fitz's eyes softened. He knelt in front of the chair and took my hands in his. The shock was less intense than before. I was about to let go when a tremor worked its way from my fingertips throughout my body. I looked up from our linked hands to find Fitz's quizzical brow. Then energy blew through my veins like a gust of wind, momentarily stealing my breath. Fitz's emotions settled deep within me, and his pain was jarring.

I doubled over. "What the hell is going on?"

"I have no idea," Fitz said, his voice strained.

Fitz moved toward the gray linen bench and rested his elbows on his knees and breathed deeply. I followed his rhythm of breathing, and our heart rates slowed.

"I feel you so clearly," he said.

"It wasn't as strong as it used to be . . . until now."

"Aye. I noticed that too."

"I was worried. I guess I still am. I don't know what all this means."

Fitz nodded. "There's one source I haven't consulted. I could ask the government about it."

"No."

"I could phrase it as a lingering question from our previous time together. It might be worth the risk."

"We changed our lives for how long? For you to compromise yourself now? They'll know why you're asking. No, we won't go to the government. We'll find another way."

"There might not be another."

Silence fell.

"Does it bother you? Or scare you? That you can feel me so clearly?" he asked.

"Maybe it should, but . . ."

"What is it?"

"It's probably going to sound too weird," I said.

"Well, now you have to say it."

I groaned. "Okay. It's just that . . . whatever this connection is that we have, well, it feels normal to me. Natural, even. Feeling your emotions inside of me, carrying that knowledge of you . . . it just feels like it should be that way. When our connection was strained during our time apart, honestly, it freaked me out."

"It's the same for me. Don't you know that?"

I closed my eyes briefly, thinking.

"I know you're confused," Fitz went on. "I know this is unbelievable. But please don't question how I feel about you. My feelings for you have never faltered—not once."

There was no lie in his statement, not even the tiniest wisp of a thread. Fitz was being truthful, and finally, I decided I had to trust in his words.

I crossed the room and sat near Fitz. I timidly reached for his hand. The surge lessened, and I tightened my grip.

"This is our normal, I guess."

Fitz nodded. "Perhaps."

"We'll figure it out eventually."

"I want to find a way around the whole shocking bit. If we can navigate that, then I'm good," he said.

"Me too."

Fitz stood. "I'll be back. I'm going to have the hotel move our rooms next to each other."

"Speaking of which, the front desk wouldn't let me add a card to my room," I said.

"Aye, it's taken care of," Fitz said.

"Let me know the cost. I need to pay you back."

"Nae bother. We're good."

Fitz hadn't let me pay for anything . . . not since I'd met him. I wondered how money never seemed to be an issue for him.

"Oh, and I do think if we go out to dinner, it'll throw off whoever is watching us," Fitz said. "If we don't make sense to them, all the better for us. We'll be vigilant."

"Do you think they'll expect us to carry on like normal?"

He tapped his finger on the wooden desk. "I'd wager they're waiting for us to run."

"Eventually, though . . . that's what we'll have to do, isn't it?"

"Truthfully, I don't know. But you and I will decide what comes next—together."

CHAPTER TWELVE

Fitz would only share that we'd dine at a Parisian staple that evening—and that he planned to wear a suit. It took longer to dress than I cared to admit. I studied my reflection in the bathroom mirror, nervous about my newly acquired little black dress and how snugly it fit against my body.

I wondered if Fitz and I were making a mistake by going out for the evening. A deep breath escaped my lips as I tugged at the sleeves around my wrists and the hemline hugging my thighs, knowing my anxiety would flare higher the longer I sat idle. I slipped on the black heels I'd packed for job interviews and touched up my eyeliner and lipstick, keeping both my hands and mind occupied. A knock at the adjoining door startled me.

My heart rate quickened, and I opened the large, wooden door to find Fitz leaning against the doorframe. Dressed in a gray suit and a black cashmere sweater, he looked as handsome as ever. This man would be the death of me.

"You are . . . stunning," he said.

I was gratified by the dumbfounded look on his face. "Thank you. You look pretty good yourself."

"I had a witty line prepared, but I've lost it just now," he said.

"Well, hurry up and find it. I want to hear this."

"Oh aye?" He straightened up, cleared his throat, and offered me his hand. "Hi, I'm Fitz. I'll be your tour guide this evening."

I laughed, shaking his hand, and the afternoon's tension seemed to dissipate with our touch.

Soon we were again exploring the streets of Paris, the lights of Rue de Rivoli guiding us toward our destination. We walked in companionable silence, taking in the bustling streets saturated with happy tourists and well-dressed diners.

The night was intoxicating with the hum of activity, the sights around the Louvre, the cool breeze against our skin, and no signs of being under watch. Fitz carefully placed my hand in the crook of his arm and offered a timid smile in my direction.

"Gentleman," I said.

We turned down a heavily trafficked street which was illuminated by the warm light of streetlamps and the lanterns lining the buildings on either side.

And in a sea of beige, one section stood out amongst the rest: a dark wooden facade with a red banner. As we neared the entrance, I gasped. Maxim's de Paris. A Parisian staple indeed. The distractions of modern-day Paris fell away as we entered the world of Art Nouveau, a timeless dream.

I looked around distractedly. From writers to actors to musicians, this space had captivated the imagination of creatives for over a century. I'd dreamed about visiting the famed restaurant for years—and Fitz knew it.

Beautiful murals decorated the walls, intricately detailed columns and molding adorned the dining rooms, white tablecloths were spread across small tables . . . all cast in a dim haze of soft crimson. It was overwhelming.

"I'm not big on surprises, but this one . . . well done, Fitz," I said as we took our seats.

"I'm glad we could check this one off your list. I've not been here before either. This is grand."

Our waiter pointed out the table where President and First Lady Kennedy had dined during their visit, and he shared stories about everyone from Grace Kelly to Marion Cotillard, all of whom had dined in the magnificent establishment. A tuxedo-clad man crooned classic jazz tunes from a stage across the room, and soon enough, the music of Frank Sinatra and the Rat Pack morphed into the soundtrack of our evening.

"What's in this dish?" I asked, stabbing at one of the mysterious ingredients with my fork. I'd asked Fitz to choose an appetizer, but I was questioning whether that might have been a poor choice.

Fitz grinned at my reaction. "Go on. Take a wee bite."

"Absolutely not. I'm not putting that in my mouth until you tell me what it is."

"Stubborn as always."

"Part of my charm, right?" I asked.

"Oh, sure."

The waiter approached our table. "And how is everything tasting?"

"It's wonderful," Fitz said.

"And the appetizer? Is it to your satisfaction?" he asked, his gaze settling on me.

"Oh, absolutely." I smiled.

"Very well. Please, enjoy."

"*Escargots aux noix*" sounded through my mind.

"You sneak," I said. "I should've paid more attention when you were ordering."

"What?" Fitz asked.

"It has snails in it," I whispered.

"How did . . ." He paused. "Did you read the waiter's mind?"

"Don't look at me like that. It's not like I meant to."

Fitz laughed. "Aye, it has snails in it. But it also has walnuts, white wine, lemon juice . . . It's a fine dish."

I sighed and took another sip of wine. "When in Paris, I guess."

I took a tentative bite, and surprisingly, I couldn't argue with Fitz.

"Okay, it's pretty good," I conceded. "I think I mostly taste the lemon and spices. Parsley and . . . nutmeg, I think."

"Look at you being adventurous."

I narrowed my eyes, but he only smirked.

Food and wine kept our conversation light while we finished the appetizer, but once we ate our way into the main course, I decided to learn more about our situation.

"So, your dad doesn't know where we are?" The thought of Ian potentially knowing our location unnerved me. I didn't think he would betray his own son, but his work with the government bothered me.

"No, and it's to protect us both. It would place him in a compromising position if he knew more. Henry is the only one aware of our location."

"Your mysterious best friend." Fitz had mentioned Henry several times at the lake, and I longed to meet him.

"Aye, that's him. We've been running our own reconnaissance."

"What do you mean by that exactly?"

"Since we parted at the lake, I've built a network. Dad, Henry, and our friend Isaac partnered with me to research everything about witches acquiring their powers and about the witchkind government. Henry works in finance, so he also helped me with investments and properly allocating resources to fall off the government's radar. We knew the only way I could break the government's rules was to know them well and to be prepared for anything that followed."

"Wow . . ."

Fitz nodded. "We have loads of information."

"It still bothers me that you didn't tell me all this at the lake. I wish I had known."

Fitz sighed, setting his wine glass on the table. "I'm sorry. I was sorting things out as I went along. I didn't know what knowledge might put you in more danger, and I didn't want to risk the councils erasing your memories. And I didn't know what would make you more anxious, or even fearful. To lay that burden on you and then have to separate . . ." He paused, pursing his lips while deep in thought.

"Still," I said, "I think it would have been better for me to know the complete truth."

"Hadley, if I had crossed that line before I had the proper resources in place, we would have sunken quickly. So, what was the alternative? I tell you you're a witch who can't match to her powers yet and I'm leaving but don't worry because the witchkind government won't come after you to erase your memories as long as I'm gone, but they'll be watching us to ensure we stay apart?"

I squeezed my eyes shut.

"You forget how well I know you," Fitz said. "That would not have ended well. I know this was still a disruption to your life, but the alternative . . ."

I pushed my risotto around absentmindedly with my fork. "Fine. I see your point."

"I am truly sorry for what this did to you. I'm sorry that I didn't tell you. But I hope you know that every decision I've made has been for you. I would do anything to keep you safe, no matter the cost."

Fitz's honesty softened my anger.

He continued. "I can't say that I'd do everything the same way again—of course, I wouldn't—but what's done is done. In some instances, there were no better choices than the ones that I made. But for the others I could have handled better, all I ask now is that you forgive me."

"Forgiven. I know it was a big burden to carry. But don't keep things from me in the future."

"You have my word."

Dessert came and, in the midst of chocolate cake, I posed my next question. "Fitz, what happens next? My time here is almost over. I board the train tomorrow afternoon for London."

"Right. I'd like to travel with you and begin your training if you're comfortable with it? Help you get matched to your power."

"Yeah. I'd like that," I said.

"Good. I'll make my arrangements."

"How are you able to take time off like this during the semester?"

"I'm not teaching this semester," Fitz said. "I've been doing loads of field research in the Highlands, working from there or from Edinburgh. Or Paris, as it were. I'm building a new course exploring the policies of

King James I and how his prejudice polluted his kingdom for centuries."

"I'll bet there's a connection to witchcraft," I said.

"He had a lot of blood on his hands. We'll explore the effects he had on 16th and 17th century life in Scotland, along with his influence on religion."

"I'll be the first to sign up for your class, Dr. MacGregor."

"I'd be honored, Ms. Weston."

"But for now, I think it's time for a change in scenery. You still have an Eiffel Tower to show me."

"Let's go."

The cab deposited us below one of the most iconic structures in the world. The Eiffel Tower stretched high above us, and I craned my neck to take in the sight. Luckily, the line was short, and I soon found myself ascending the attraction with my adventurous escort. My breath was labored when we reached our destination, but not only from the exercise. I'd seen countless photos of the historic landmark, but nothing prepared me for the grandeur of the experience. We gazed at the countless lights of the city, the cool evening air granting us vitality as we soaked in the view.

We wandered around the top of the tower, navigating past the summit's champagne bar and the line of excited patrons awaiting their celebratory flutes. The wind was a bit cold, and I regretted leaving my warmer coat behind. No sooner had I expressed that sentiment to Fitz than he had us huddled in a corner.

"What are we doing?" I whispered.

"Just wait," he said.

He glanced around casually and once he was satisfied no one was watching, he moved his hand in a circular motion.

Then, he extended his arm, which turned transparent, and he pulled my coat out of thin air.

My jaw dropped. When I'd slightly recovered, I looked around. Fitz found my response thoroughly amusing.

"What if someone saw you?" I asked.

"No one saw. I used concealment. A human wouldn't have any idea unless they were standing right here with us."

I was speechless.

"Here," he said, holding out my coat.

I turned, and he helped me slide my arms into the sleeves. He then pulled me into his arms, and I rested my head on his chest.

My body was wired from the excitement of watching him use his magic, but as he held me in his arms, I was lulled into a state of perfect happiness, calm and sure. I smiled as we created a memory I would always remember, the type of moment people tell their grandchildren about, eyes closed, recalling how alive they felt.

Fitz and I grabbed drinks from the Bar à Champagne and found a less crowded corner to enjoy the views. We shared more about our time apart, both hungry for details of the other's lives, completely lost in the stories only we could tell. And eventually, our conversation meandered to the first moments of our reunion at Notre Dame.

"I dreamed about that moment for a long time," Fitz said.

"And did you also dream about us lighting each other up like a Christmas tree?" I asked, recalling the intensity of the shock.

"Well, I must say, things went a little smoother in my dreams."

"How boring then. I guess reality really is better than fantasy sometimes."

Fitz's laugh was genuine and unguarded, and a piece of my soul healed at the sound.

"I dreamed about that moment too. More than I should have," I admitted.

Silence fell, and Fitz reached for my hand, holding it in both of his own. A surge of energy followed our contact, but I found that it wasn't painful, as though we were readjusting to each other.

Fitz ran his fingers across the moonstone on my finger. "You kept the ring. It's one of the first things I noticed."

"I couldn't seem to take it off. I . . . feel better when I wear it."

He nodded. "It's charged with my energy."

"What do you mean?"

"The day I gifted it to you, Izzy suggested I channel some of my energy into the stone. She thought it might bring you comfort while we were apart."

"She was right . . . as usual." I paused. "You thought of everything, didn't you?"

"I did what I could. It wasn't enough, but it was all I could offer you."

His eyes were troubled—filled with memories—and I leaned into him, hoping my touch might quiet his pain. He wrapped his arms around me, and we fell silent as we gazed at the lights scattered on the horizon.

I wasn't sure how long we stood there, suspended above the city, reveling in the rediscovery of our long-lost companionship. At some late hour, we paused to appreciate the light show sparkling all around us before descending the tower in search of a sweet nighttime snack.

We were close to abandoning our search when we finally happened upon a small bakery. The owner was pleased to pause his closing tasks, supply us with end-of-day chocolate croissants, and bid us adieu as we wandered back into the dim evening streets. We ate in comfortable silence, happy to stay in that moment as long as it would allow, until the gold and maroon hallways of our hotel welcomed us home.

Fitz and I did a quick sweep of our rooms before deciding we were safe for the evening.

Anxiety bubbled as I thought about parting ways for the night.

"What's wrong, Hads?"

"Nothing's wrong. Are you tired, or do you want a nightcap?" I questioned.

"I have a bottle of Glenfiddich in my room. Care for a wee dram?"

"Yes, please."

Fitz retrieved the bottle while I rounded up a couple glasses, and we ended up on a blanket on the floor, leaned up against the bed, glasses in hand.

"I didn't want to bring this up at dinner the other night, but I want to clarify something," he said.

My heartbeat quickened—and so did Fitz's.

"When you mentioned your dad's passing . . . I didn't stay away. I came to the funeral home."

"You what?"

"I did. I needed to see you, to do what I could to help you. But I never made it inside." He laughed without humor. "I even saw you in there." He paused, clearing his throat. "I'm sorry I couldn't be there."

I scooted closer and placed my hand on his. He held on to it tightly, a flurry of anguish and regret floating through our connection.

"What happened?" I asked.

"A few of my father's colleagues showed up. They'd foreseen my decision and were waiting to see if I would go in or if I'd change my mind. As I was reaching for the handle, one of them called my name."

"They came to stop you."

"Aye. According to them, I let things go a little too far at the lake."

"How did they know that?" I asked.

"The councils are eager to understand how situations like yours occur, so our evaluations were detailed, and the councils agents checked in daily." Fitz sighed. "From one of Dad's reports, an agent realized members of the family were growing closer to you than normal."

"They figured out it was a relationship between us."

"And an agent was on our doorstep within a day of that report being submitted. Truthfully, we didn't realize it would be an issue. We believed you'd match—we never saw you as human. But the councils clearly didn't see it that way and they reminded me that a witch and a human being together is strictly forbidden."

"So, they tried to remove you from my case and separate us."

"Aye. They wanted me to leave and allow Dad and Izzy to finish the observation after I felt our connection. The councils expected I'd try to see you again if you went through a major trial before your powers developed, or even if they didn't."

"Well, they were right about one thing, then. They knew we'd eventually do what we've done."

"They knew I couldn't help it, the bastards."

"So, what happened at the funeral?" I asked.

"They reiterated the *reasons* to keep my distance and told me to be patient, to let things run their course. It was harder to walk away from the funeral home than it was to watch you leave for Boston. I thought that was going to kill me."

I paused, collecting my thoughts.

"Thank you," I finally said.

"For?"

"For trying to be there. For being honest with me."

Fitz nodded.

"I don't like that the councils try to dictate who we're involved with," I said. "Just look at our situation; it was pointless. Why do they do this?"

His expression darkened. "As long as it isn't a human, they don't care. They're terrified about our secret getting out."

"Do you think they're right about that?"

"I understand their worry, and at the same time, I don't," Fitz said. "Humans are unpredictable. I understand the councils' fear of them, but you can't control the lives of witches and humans like this. They were wrong about us—that's a fact."

"It feels like they paid special attention to us. I mean, showing up at my dad's funeral was disrespectful. I just don't understand why our relationship bothered them so much."

"They *really* want me to follow in my father's footsteps. I need to be the kind of witch who adheres to the rules for that to happen."

"Is that what you want?"

"Doesn't matter. They haven't forced anything yet, but I've had a feeling for a long time that it'll all come to a head one day. Now I'm sure of it."

I squeezed his hand. "Well, if it happens, I'll support you no matter what—as long as you want me in your life."

"The only way you'll get rid of me now is if you send me away," he said.

"I've been waiting for you to tell me this is temporary," I admitted, "that you're going to have to disappear again."

He paused. "Hadley, I'm not strong enough to go through that again."

Our emotions muddled together as they swirled through me.

"It still worries me," I said.

"I didn't have a choice back then, but I do now."

"And that's not going to change?"

"No, it won't," Fitz said. "I've been ready for a fight since the beginning. But we weren't prepared—we didn't have the resources, and I didn't fully understand what we were up against. But being here, together, this will change everything."

"I'm ready for whatever comes. I'm exhausted from the secrecy—from being apart."

"To be clear, I still don't know the full consequences of all this. They might go easy on us; they might not. But either way, you know the risk we're taking now."

"To hell with the consequences," I said. "We'll find a way to beat the councils."

"It's easy to say that now."

"Maybe. But this phase of our lives is over. It has to be."

Fitz nodded.

"You said something that's been on my mind," I said. "You keep using the word 'mates' . . . Fitz, is that what's happening between us?"

Fitz exhaled slowly, and as his eyes narrowed in concentration, his energy fluttered wildly through me. "Aye. I've thought that was the case since the moment I laid eyes on you."

"What does that mean exactly?"

"Witches often refer to their partners as mates, though it's really the same thing—only amplified."

"Amplified how?"

"When we find the person we're meant to be with, it's an incredibly strong connection."

"Is that why we feel each other's emotions?" I asked.

"Aye, I've observed it with other mates. The emotions seem normal."

"But not the shocking?"

"No," Fitz said.

I nodded.

He continued. "I think when you match to your power, our connection will intensify."

I placed my hand behind his neck and looked squarely into his eyes. "Good."

Fitz kissed my forehead tenderly, but when he pulled back, his features grew stormy. He tugged my body closer to him, one hand resting on my waist as the other cradled the base of my skull. My arms slid across his back, and instead of the jarring shock I anticipated, warmth pulsed through my veins like a vibrant life-source was channeling between the two of us. My heart raced as his eyes searched mine. He slipped a finger under my chin—holding my gaze until I was certain of his intentions—before dipping his head slowly and deliberately, as though he knew the prolonged moment would only make me want it more. To his credit, it was working.

As his lips found mine, electricity coursed through my body, chills rippling across my skin. My eyes popped open, and I found that his had done the same, both of us wired with the shock. My senses were heightened. Every touch, every feeling intensified until they outweighed the pain. Our grip tightened, and we continued to explore each other a few moments longer. He drew back as gently and deliberately as he had approached, eyes closed as he drank in the last intimacies of the moment.

"I'll remind you every single day just how much I want you in my life, even after you finally come to believe it," he whispered.

CHAPTER THIRTEEN

The following afternoon, I was seated next to Fitz somewhere high above Paris. The train had been my humble suggestion, but Henry had arranged a private flight for us. Though it felt extravagant, it had provided Fitz with the means to lose the witchkind spies in Edinburgh. Whoever was following us in Paris was about to receive the same treatment.

Sipping whisky on our brief path over the English Channel, my thoughts darted mercilessly around my exhausted mind. I was nervous to open my eyes and see the world for what it truly was and not for what I previously believed it to be.

But another feeling beat fiercely against the first for control. It bubbled up, refusing defeat: I was excited.

I recalled the little girl I once had been—the girl who was confident there was more to her than her human facade. A twinge of sadness accompanied the recollection.

By the time I'd reached adulthood, cynicism had crept into my bones and stolen my sense of wonder.

"What are you thinking about?" Fitz asked.

"My childhood."

Fitz swirled the whisky in his glass, his eyes distant. "You always knew who you were, Hads. You and your power have been trying to connect with each other for years. Your magic was already awakening you."

"Awakening me?"

"From an ordinary life. You were never meant to be normal."

Perhaps he was right. I needed to search inside myself to uncover that little girl and her unwavering belief.

Fitz leaned over, whispering. "Once you find that faith in yourself again, you'll be unstoppable."

"Stop doing that! It's so unnerving when you're in my head like that. You said you can't read minds."

"I can't. But I can sense your feelings and read your facial expressions. You smell doubtful, and you look like you're trying to solve a puzzle that's got the best of you."

"You can smell me thinking?" I asked, my face scrunched in full disbelief.

"Oh aye. It sort of smells like smoke."

I punched his shoulder playfully, though I was grateful for the comedic relief.

"Did I ever tell you about my favorite cat I had growing up?" I asked.

"Never."

"She was a large, fluffy black cat with these beautiful green eyes— almost the color of yours."

"What was her name?" he asked.

". . .Midnight."

"A witch-obsessed child naming her black cat after the witching hour . . . Oh, that's proper," he countered, amused.

"Can you see her?" I asked.

"Only if I bring that memory to the surface. We can do that if you'd like."

"Maybe later. I don't think I'm ready to revisit my childhood that vividly." I recalled how intense my memories were when Fitz recreated them.

Fitz's phone lit up, and his expression grew serious as he read whatever was on the screen.

"What now?" I asked.

"Dad said a council member called him this morning to ask for any information he might have on our whereabouts."

"They know we're together now."

"Aye. When we both slipped off the radar . . ." He trailed off.

"But they don't know we're headed to London."

"Which means we were successful in keeping things quiet when we booked your travel."

"How did my travel escape their notice?"

Fitz smirked. "There's a particular report that customs and border patrol send to witchkind government. Henry might have paid off a few people to prevent your information from being included."

My eyes widened. "How did he manage that?"

"That's a query for Henry, I'm afraid."

I shook off the thought and returned my focus to our current travel. "Okay. And you were right about the Parisian spies—they definitely weren't linked to the witchkind watchers."

Fitz nodded thoughtfully. "At least we're staying ahead of them."

"And our Parisian stalkers think we're headed to Istanbul—nice choice, by the way."

"See, there are a few perks to private air travel."

"There's something I don't understand, though. Can't the watchers find us using their powers?"

"That would typically be the case," he said.

"Why not in this instance?"

"Magic."

I groaned, which only humored him further. Then I asked, "When do I start trying to match to my magic?"

"Tomorrow."

"You've known for years about my powers. Why didn't I start this process sooner?"

"Your power materialized slowly due to human DNA obstructing its growth. When I first met you, you knew things about others because you were essentially pulling information from their minds, but you weren't yet hearing their thoughts like you do now. There are even humans, though rare, who have this ability. You simply weren't ready," Fitz said.

"How can humans have that ability?"

"It's like I mentioned the other day. They have magic somewhere in their lineage," he answered. "After a family mixes with humans, the power weakens with each generation until there's very little chance a descendant could match to their power. Every so often, that former magic shows back up in someone's DNA.

"Sometimes," he continued, "these people are like you and their mind and power can combine. For others, they'll possess some ability, but they'll always remain more human than witch."

"Do you know why my magic is matching with me? Like, my witch ancestor isn't too far back or . . . ?"

"My suspicion is you have recent magical ancestry on each side of your lineage. It would explain why none of your living relatives have abilities. It might just be the combination of your mum's and your dad's lineages."

"I've been wondering a lot about my family. I wish I knew who my magical ancestors were," I said. "I know Gram isn't a witch, but she's not too far removed from having some sort of power. There's just something about her. She has this . . . awareness about her, and her intuition is uncanny."

"We'll work on that mystery soon."

After years of countless questions, I was thrilled I would finally have my long-awaited answers. And the sooner I matched with my magic, the sooner I'd have them.

"Look," he said, pointing toward the window.

The city of London lay beneath us, a blend of generations of architecture stretching as far as the eye could see. I'd visited the city before, but there was something about it that always took me by surprise.

Fitz gently grazed my face with his fingertips. "When you're happy, excited . . . my god, do you take my breath away."

"How's my energy now?"

He lifted his arm, directing my attention to the goosebumps rippling across his skin.

A smirk pulled at his lips. "Electric."

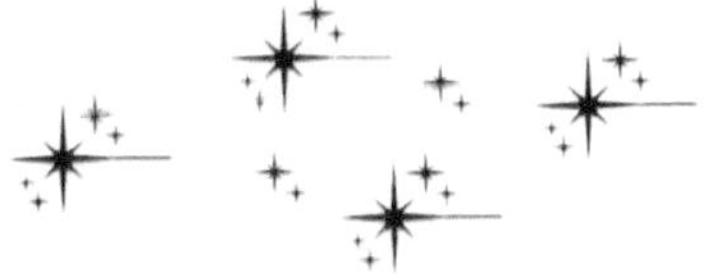

The next few days were spent in interviews. I'd always held an interest in European history, and options like The British Museum and The Institute of Historical Research were at the top of my list. Not only would they be a good career advancement for me, but I was genuinely interested in the work they did.

My career had developed at private firms, continuously pulled on to various projects, always consulting with multiple clients. Although the fast-moving environment had taught me a great deal, a steady partnership within an institution sounded like a fresh challenge and a desirable change of pace.

But after my recent interviews, I was unsure if that's what I still wanted.

After my interview with the sole private firm on my list, I traipsed my way out of the crowded ground floor of the modern high rise into the bustling streets of London. There was no city in the world quite like London, with its unique mix of palaces, tube stations, teahouses, and pubs. Fitz was waiting in a less trafficked area along the front steps of the building, and I settled next to him. We sat amongst office dwellers, most of whom sought to eat their lunches in the late September sunlight. As a native Seattleite, I understood their desire to soak up the last of the golden rays before the cold, rainy season set in.

"How did it go?" Fitz asked.

"It went well."

"You don't seem excited."

"The hiring manager talked about company culture and how great the benefits are, and the team seemed great . . ."

"This sounds positive," he said.

"Yeah, it is," I said. "I should be seriously considering this role."

"But you aren't, are you? Why is that?"

"I don't want to work in a firm anymore. I think I knew that before I even applied for the position, but now, I'm sure."

"You want to work somewhere like the museum instead," he guessed.

I had met with them the day prior. The museum seemed like a good fit, and they'd shared that the professional retiring from the position was more than willing to wrap up early—meaning I could start in less than a month.

"I thought I did, but now I'm not so sure," I confessed.

Fitz's questioning glance pulled more from me.

"I just . . . I'm different than I was a few weeks ago when I started this job search. My circumstances are different. I guess I'm really just questioning what I want for myself now that I know I'm a . . . you know," I said, glancing around to register how close our neighbors were.

"Aye, that's understandable."

I paused before pressing on. "There's another interview I haven't told you about yet."

"Let's hear it, then."

"When I was researching openings in London, another option came up."

"This last option isn't in London?" Fitz asked.

"No."

"Where then?"

"Edinburgh, at the castle."

I expected the words to elicit some sort of response from Fitz. Instead, he sat there quietly, eyes transfixed on the street below us.

Finally, I broke the silence. "I don't have to look into the castle if you prefer I don't come to Edinburgh."

"No, that's not it at all—I promise," he said, reaching his hand across to mine. "To have you in Edinburgh . . . don't you know how badly I want that?"

"Tell me what it is, then."

Picking at the square patch on his leather bag with his free hand,

Fitz led into his explanation. "I don't want to influence your decision. Of course, I want you in Edinburgh, but that isn't fair. I don't want you to feel pressure about coming to Edinburgh if it doesn't feel right."

"I—" The words stuck in my throat.

"Out with it," Fitz prompted.

"I can't do long distance at this point. Not after what we've already been through."

"Long distance never crossed my mind."

"And what's the alternative?" I asked. "You leave Edinburgh?"

His eyes flickered to mine. "Aye. I'd do that for you."

"Fitz." I laid my hand tenderly against his cheek. "You're finally home. You belong there. I wouldn't want you to leave."

"I want you happy."

"I'll go to the interview, and we'll sort it out from there," I said. "Let's take this one step at a time."

"It'll be tricky going back to Edinburgh with you."

"Because of the government?" I guessed.

"We'll sort it. I believe in us."

CHAPTER FOURTEEN

"No, come on, Hadley. You need to still your mind!"

Apparently, I was off to a rough start unlocking my magic. We sat near the floor-to-ceiling windows in our hotel room as I navigated the complexities of my mind. My current task was to meditate—but what for was unclear. When I squinted, Fitz knew I wasn't exactly following his guidelines.

"Your powers will never settle with all those bloody thoughts buzzing around in your mind. It's a wonder you get anything done. And I told you that when you do this, I can't concentrate either."

"Fine. Tell me how to do this."

"Quiet your mind. Stop thinking."

"I'm going to punch you again."

A slight tug at the corner of his mouth threatened to break his demeanor into a full smile.

"I can't stop thinking," I said. "How on earth am I supposed to just make it all stop?"

"You are actually overthinking the process of not thinking, aren't you?"

"Yes, hi. I'm Hadley. Have we met?" I quipped, extending my hand.

"You can control your mind, Hadley," Fitz said. "Our minds are one of the most powerful things in the universe, and you can control yours. You want magic? Power? This is the key to unlocking an entirely new world."

"I still don't understand how to do this."

"You'll have to sort it. Only you know the answer to this."

"Fantastic."

With my determination, Fitz's coaching, and the knowledge of everything at stake, I hadn't stirred from our two-bedroom suite for hours, and I wasn't going anywhere until some sort of breakthrough occurred. My focus shifted outside, searching for anything that would quiet my raging mind.

Shangri-La held an incredible view of London.

Gazing through the large windowpanes, I traced the path of the River Thames rolling ceaselessly through the city. Vessels floated brightly against the murky water, and countless buildings shot up on either bank. The blinking glow of the London Eye captured my attention. I focused on the wheel, studying its bright lights and steady, circular motion. As I followed the slow, rhythmic spinning, my mind stopped.

For a split second, I panicked at the loss of vision. Fitz had warned me not to fear its onset, and with the reminder that my condition was normal, I adjusted. The darkness took my mind, leaving a complete absence of everything else.

Then, slowly, a large eye materialized. An eyelid swept upward revealing an iris that swirled with fire—orange, red, and yellow flames roared to life. The eye's gaze darted about, as if it sought something in the abyss. Something stirred behind the eye, and I squinted, curious what might lie beyond the pupil, before everything evaporated like smoke winding its way into the night sky.

I gasped, and Fitz ran to my side.

"What's happened?"

"I found the darkness," was all I could manage as I scanned the room, my sight restored.

"That's good. What else?"

"There was an eye."

"Where was it?"

"I don't know, just in the darkness. It was huge—the only thing I could see."

His eyes lit up, though my own thoughts remained puzzled.

"What on earth was it?"

"You did good, Hadley," he began, reaching toward me before quickly pulling his hand back. "You saw your mind's eye."

"What exactly does that mean?"

"Your mind's eye is your witch's eye. It couples with your magic to show you the things you can't see with those baby blues of yours." He paused, his gaze suddenly curious. "What color was the eye?"

"It was several colors—it looked like fire dancing inside of the iris."

Fitz grinned. "Well, aren't you lucky?"

"What? Why?"

"You're a fire witch."

"Does that mean what I think it does?"

"Your power is fueled by fire. It'll be one of your most advanced skills, then."

My happiness was palpable—I couldn't contain it, and my cheerful energy zipped around the room.

"I saw something else too. It was past the pupil of the eye. I could only see movement. When I tried to see past the eye, the vision dissipated."

"You saw your magic."

My head snapped up, meeting his gaze. Butterflies danced in my belly, fluttering about violently. "Why did it disappear?"

"Why do you think it disappeared?"

I thought for only a moment before the disappointing answer surfaced. "Because I started thinking about what it was."

"You have to still your mind long enough for the interaction to occur between mind and power. You've only been meditating a few hours. Keep trying. It will happen."

I broke out into what must've been the goofiest grin of my life.

Fitz shot me a questioning glance.

"I saw my powers."

"Pretty damn cool, isn't it? I'm so proud of you."

"I'm a witch."

The outline of my witch's eye danced freshly in my mind, and my skin prickled at the proximity of my power. I swung my legs toward the window and closed my eyes, eager to answer my magic's beckoning call.

"Let's get a bit of scran before you start again."

"But I want to try again now," I whined.

"What you need is nourishment to help sustain you . . . especially before you get hangry." He eyed me dubiously. "Then, you can try again."

He was right, but the call of the witch's eye consumed me. Fitz reached for my hand and pulled me from the ground.

"So, just now," I said, "when I came back to this reality . . . ?"

"When you returned from the depths of your mind."

"Right. You reached for me, but then you pulled back. Why?"

"Oh, that. My instinct was to reach for you—to make sure you were all right. Then I decided you might need a minute. The mix of our energies after your encounter with your mind's eye might have hurt you more than it comforted you."

"Makes sense."

"You thought . . . what? I didn't want to touch you?"

"Well, of course, I went straight to the worst-case scenario!" I exclaimed, pulling a laugh from Fitz.

"It's going to take a long time for you to believe that I never wanted us to be apart. We'll never be forced away again."

"Promise?"

"Promise. And, Hadley? I'm always wanting to touch you."

Fitz pulled me closer and slid his hand behind my neck, illustrating his point, before kissing me longingly. He then extended his hand, and my jacket floated from a chair near the door to where I stood, hovering until I extended my arm.

"Ready?"

"Oh, I need to learn how to do that."

"Just think, magic could be at your disposal very soon."

I decided the break was worth it considering we wandered into Ye Olde Cheshire Cheese, taking in the history and good beer. A pub since 1538, and rumored to have been a 13th-century monastery prior to that, it had been rebuilt shortly after the Great Fire of 1666. It was relatively busy given that it was a Friday, and the chatter was nearly deafening as we navigated the upper floors. Luckily, we found a spot in the lowest level of the structure, which was far less chaotic.

Our meal was set to dim lighting, a roaring fire, and wooden tables set on cold, stone flooring. Literary legends like Charles Dickens and Sir Arthur Conan Doyle had enjoyed the food, drink, and company of this very establishment, and I was happy to do the same.

Fitz's phone lit up for about the millionth time since we'd sat down.

Henry was calling him again.

"Maybe you should answer that. It could be important," I said.

"We have a code for that sort of thing. Whatever he's calling about, it can wait until after dinner."

"Another text just came through," I observed, eyeing him pointedly.

Fitz sighed before reading Henry's text and turning the phone around for me to read.

Ignore me all you want, mate. You're the one who'll be pissed later.

Another text popped up: *I know the bartenders at the Cheese well.*

I gazed over Fitz's shoulder and found a handsome man dressed in a suit leaning against the bar, humor spreading across his lips.

"Uh . . . Fitz. You need to turn around."

Fitz's expression darkened before following my instructions.

The man crossed the room casually, never dropping that gloating smile.

"Henry Stuart," the man said by way of introduction. He extended his hand. "I'm glad to finally meet you."

"Likewise," I said.

When our skin made contact, a small tremor moved through my hand. Fitz was right—I certainly sensed contact with another witch.

But unlike the intensity I felt with Fitz, a dull energy pulsed just under the surface at Henry's touch and then quickly passed. A peaceful sensation rested briefly within me, and I couldn't make sense of it.

After shaking hands, Henry squeezed Fitz's shoulder and took a seat next to him.

"What the hell are you doing here?" Fitz asked.

"Good to see you too, Fitz."

I wondered if Henry could feel the annoyance pouring from my dinner partner. I took a sip of my beer and studied this dear old friend of Fitz's. His mischievous hazel eyes were set below a strong brow and hair the color of champagne. Combed into a deep side part, I found it reminiscent of old Hollywood, like Cary Grant. Henry appeared young, maybe younger than his actual age, and his thin figure was draped in an expensive and well-tailored suit. Though he appeared a bit aristocratic, his countenance was deeply warm and inviting, and I gave myself permission to like him straight away.

"Question still stands, Henry."

"I thought I could be useful." Henry shrugged, clearly unfazed.

"That wasn't part of the plan. What if someone followed you?"

"Come on, mate." He scoffed. "Give me some credit."

Fitz sat back in his seat though he held Henry's gaze firmly. "You are so bloody annoying."

"Aye, and you're a walk in the park," Henry countered.

Fitz pinched the bridge of his nose, and Henry caught my gaze and smiled. I couldn't help but laugh.

"And what exactly is so funny to you?" Fitz tried to keep his composure, but the edges of his lips were threatening a smile.

"I have no idea what you mean," I quipped.

"You might as well tell me why you're really here," Fitz said.

Henry considered his question for a moment before launching into an explanation. "A few reasons. Curiosity, a need to be helpful, but mainly: your update on the trackers in Paris worried me. I wanted to be nearby in case they come to London."

Fitz's expression softened.

"Isaac is keen to meet this one, as well." Henry nodded in my direction.

"And how much time do we have before Isaac arrives?" Fitz asked.

"He said you'd be pissed, so he was thinking he'd wait until you're ready. But considering I texted him to let him know I was about to meet Hadley . . . five minutes at best."

Fitz laughed, followed by Henry.

"Isaac . . ." I mused. "You've mentioned him before. He's a lawyer?"

"Indeed, he is," Henry answered. "He's also consulted for the English council for years. He's a talented reader."

"It's a magical skill. Isaac is damn good at reading the intentions of both humans and witches," Fitz explained.

"He's one of our closest friends," Henry said.

"Aye. He's helping us, same as Henry," Fitz said, refreshing my memory.

"That's right," I said, recalling our conversation about his network. "Thank you for that," I said meaningfully to Henry.

"Dinnae mention it, lass. I'd do more if I could."

"And there he is," Fitz said. He nodded toward a witch sporting a navy fedora, a long houndstooth overcoat, and navy slacks with thin pinstripes.

The overcoat was unbuttoned, perched atop his shoulders, and he shed the layer in one rolling motion, revealing the rest of his three-piece suit. He was tall like Fitz and Henry and had the lithe, muscular build of an athlete. Isaac and I shook hands, and the same odd sensation came over me. Suddenly, his connection to Fitz echoed through me, and I recognized a pattern—their bond of friendship sent a signal of peace quickly through my veins. Fitz had shared that as I neared matching with my magic that my instincts would grow stronger, and my intuition was growing stronger by the day. The feeling was odd, and *that* was going to take some getting used to.

Isaac removed his hat and embraced Fitz before sliding onto the old wooden bench next to me. His dark complexion suited his chocolate-colored hair that was combed into a pompadour. He smoothed back a few loose strands as a waiter set a plate in front of him.

"Thank you, Martin," Isaac said. His accent was identifiably Italian. "That was fast."

"You can thank Henry," Fitz said. "He let us know you were on your way."

"I didn't tell you I was coming."

Henry shrugged. "I knew you couldnae resist."

Isaac sighed before settling a striking pair of dark eyes on to mine. They were complex like the fallen leaves of November and filled with an endless depth, and Isaac carried himself with a certain wisdom. I was excited to get to know him better.

"*Carissima*, how is your power-matching going?" he asked.

While I described my experience, I was struck by the significance of that moment. Observing the three men gathered around the table, I realized their friendship knew none of the usual barriers that mine often held. I had concealed parts of myself for so long, and I was overwhelmed by the simple fact that, for the first time in my life, I wasn't hiding who I was. I had no reason to keep a secret. As far as that group was concerned, I was *normal*. When I shared the sentiment aloud, Fitz reached for my hand.

"That's over for you, lass. You're with us now," Henry said.

"That's true," Isaac agreed. "I already know you and I are going to be buddies —isn't that what you say in America?"

"Isaac is convinced your friendship was 'written in the stars.'" Henry rolled his eyes playfully.

"I'm assuming you already know a lot about me," I guessed.

Isaac grimaced. "A professional hazard I'm afraid."

"Well, if we're future besties, it's time to level the playing field," I said.

He grinned.

"So, you're Italian. Clearly."

He laughed. "Yes, darling. I was born in Iran, but my parents moved us to Italy when I was a baby. I grew up in Genova. It's a coastal city in the North of Italy. You might know it by its English name—Genoa."

"Oh, I'm going to have so many follow up questions to that."

"I'm bracing myself."

Henry chuckled and looked to Fitz, who shrugged, though he was equally amused. I ignored them both and continued my questions.

"And you're a lawyer . . . ?"

"Yes. I've just made partner at my firm, so I plan to stay here a while, much to Fitz and Henry's dismay."

"Dismay or not, staying here is to your own detriment, mate. I mean, London is nothing to Edinburgh," Fitz argued.

"Too true," Henry added before plucking a Scotch egg from Isaac's plate.

"Spoken like true Scots," Isaac said. "And I *was* going to eat that."

Henry shrugged, a sly grin on his face. He sliced through the egg before depositing half back onto Isaac's plate.

"Making partner is big. Congrats," I said. "You must like London then. Or does the job just hold you here?"

"It's not London so much as his mate," Henry interjected.

"Now I need details."

"Well, there isn't anyone yet," Isaac said. "A seer told me a few months ago that I'll meet my mate in London and gave me a description. I'm keeping my eyes open."

"Hopeless romantic, this one." Henry winked.

"I just worry, you know? What if I don't know he's 'the one?'"

"*You'll know*," Fitz and Henry responded in unison.

"Either way, that's not keeping me in London—Fate will take care of things one way or the other. I know her that well," Isaac added drily, eyeing Henry meaningfully.

"That was a joke, mate."

Isaac punched Henry's arm playfully.

"Come on, guys. We're in *civilized* company," Fitz interrupted, looking at me.

"Aye. Better make a braw first impression with your new best friend, Isaac," Henry said.

My phone vibrated the table, startling me. I flipped it over and sighed.

Jordan.

I know you're busy, but I'd really like to catch up and hear about your interviews. I miss you.

For the first time in seventeen years, Jordan and I had gone days without talking. I wanted to call her more than anything, but I didn't know how to talk to my best friend when I couldn't tell her everything. I knew she'd ask, "What's wrong?" the moment she picked up, and I couldn't be honest with her. I needed to protect her from the mess I was tangled in. I needed to . . .

"Shit."

"What's wrong?" Fitz asked.

I shook my head. I wasn't ready to talk to Fitz about the fact that I was willing to do whatever necessary to protect Jordan, the same way he had protected me.

As we worked our way through dinner, I found myself relaxing at the change of scenery, which allowed me to free my thoughts from the last few hours. I ran a finger around the rim of my glass, watching the dark beer swirl in tandem with it. The liquid ceased its movement only after my finger did the same. Stunned, I looked up to find a smirk on Fitz's face.

"When did that start?" Fitz asked.

"I guess right now?"

"You're close, Hads. Your power is so close."

I smiled, returning my attention to the glass. A small jolt of electricity pulsed through me, and as my finger resumed its previous path around the rim, the beer again answered the call of my magic.

CHAPTER FIFTEEN

We surrendered to the night, emerging from dim lighting and roaring fireplaces at Ye Old Cheshire Cheese into the cold air of the evening. The contrast between the warm pub and the night air jolted me from my relaxed state, and I felt invigorated as I scanned the scene just outside the door. Fitz instinctively reached for my hand as we wandered through the crowds in the courtyard, packed despite the weather.

Henry and Isaac returned to our suite with us to talk through the latest data they and Ian had collected regarding the Scottish and U.S. councils' search for us. Isaac proposed we create a barrier with the elements. Apparently, this would allow me to focus on matching to my magic undisturbed, and the guys could keep an eye on me while they worked through the updates. I couldn't quite wrap my mind around that one, but I sat and watched in awe as Fitz performed the honors.

He held my gaze and smiled, and I saw the tiniest ripple in the air around me—the kind of movement you'd never notice if you weren't paying close attention. He turned his head so his eyes could trace from one wall to the other, and then his gaze fell on me.

His lips moved, but I couldn't hear him. An awe-struck laugh escaped my lips, and I wondered if he could hear it. Fitz laughed in turn, waved, and joined Henry and Isaac's discussion.

I tried my best to push the scene from my mind so I could focus on acquiring my own power. I settled slowly into my former meditative state and began the process of quieting my mind. When I'd observed Fitz's daily meditation, it had seemed so natural for him—so necessary—and I was uncertain I could integrate it so effortlessly into my life. Fitz had been quick to remind me he'd been meditating since childhood, and once I matched with my powers, I would feel its draw and its promise to ease my mind's burden.

Even if I wasn't certain about that, I did feel more confident after seeing my mind's eye. And more determined. I knew what I was working toward, and my mind stilled with considerably less effort.

As I focused again on the large wheel and its bright circular motion, the rest of the world slowly faded to black. I reminded myself to remain neutral before I slipped into the abyss.

Darkness took hold, and I fought back against the rising hysteria, recalling that panic would pull me away from my magic. I breathed deeply, drawing in the positive and exhaling the negative. Peace wiggled inside, slipping from the pit of my stomach through the rest of my body, as though a healing power swept through my bloodstream.

On the coattails of the calmness came a heightened sense of awareness, and a dim shape wavered in the darkness. A large, translucent eye stared back at me, and I waited patiently as it regained its strength. It was a painting coming to fruition, each brushstroke breathing life into the unblinking object as the colors intensified.

Simply observe. Let the moment be.

The eyelid closed, slowly and deliberately, before lifting to reveal the flame-filled iris. A movement behind the eye shifted my gaze, and my power grew more distinct than before, drifting in an untamable cloud, all the while intensifying into the same mesmerizing colors as the eye.

It gathered itself together and slinked through the pupil of the eye, like smoke billows from a chimney. Rolling tentatively through the air, the cloud whirled closer, and its edges shimmered as they danced to some imperceptible tune. The hair on my body prickled, standing on end.

My curiosity almost got the better of me as a thought nearly slipped across my mind. My magic halted mid-air, threatening to disappear altogether, but I recovered quickly, dropping back into thoughtless observation. The cloud continued its forward movement. My mind and body both grew serene, increasingly at peace as the gap between us and my power—something I needed as much as the air filling my lungs—diminished. My arm instinctively greeted the cloud, closing the final space between us.

My fingers burned at the initial contact before a surge of electricity ripped through my fingers, consuming my hands, arms, chest, and eventually my entire body. My limbs contorted in pain, and my body fell to the ground, my legs unable to support my weight. Shrieks escaped my lips, a feeble attempt to relieve the pain building inside of me. The crippling ache lingered as power coursed through me, adjusting to its newfound home.

A throbbing sensation replaced the pain, like the dull beating pulse after stubbing your toe. Weightlessness followed, gradually radiating throughout my entire body from my fingertips, leaving behind no trace of the former discomfort. I perceived the air in a new way, freshly aware of its interconnectedness, understanding its relationship to the electricity snapping inside of me.

The air lifted me from the ground, suspending me.

My body lay limp for only a moment before my limbs began twitching, my entire body spinning and sputtering in the darkness. Once the twisting subsided, I floated back to the ground in utter exhaustion.

A heavy weight settled in my lungs, and I focused on inhaling and exhaling, finding comfort in the familiar rise and fall of my chest. I mustered the energy to sit up and looked in the direction of my mind's eye. The ever-present eye stared, expressionless, and I crawled timidly in its direction, proceeding slowly until I was mere inches away. I hadn't fully appreciated its breadth.

It stood at least fifteen feet tall, and the pupil was so large, I could step right through it.

As I studied the intricate detail of the iris, my proximity awakened its power, and the entire eye began to shimmer. I drew myself up and stood with my quivering legs before slowly raising my right foot and stepping through the center.

As my foot made contact with the ground, an explosion flung me across the empty space. I turned in the midst of the blast and inexplicably floated to the ground. Though my landing was graceful, the ringing in my ears proved the explosion was real. I turned to my witch's eye but found only darkness.

The final infusion had occurred, and both my magic and mind's eye rested comfortably inside my body, each in harmony with one another.

With my task completed, I woke from my reverie.

Fitz's usual carefree expression was replaced with creased brows and worried eyes. "Say something."

"Like what?" I asked grumpily.

"There you are. How do you feel?"

"Like a train toppled over me."

"Here, take these—they'll help with the headache." He handed me medicine and a glass of water. Even though I felt like I'd been run over, his preparedness demonstrated at least the discomfort was expected.

"Are Henry and Isaac still here?"

"We felt the shift when you matched to your power. They left to give you a bit of space, but they're just next door in Henry's room."

"Henry's room?" I asked.

"Aye, he booked a room next to ours in case we run into any trouble."

I looked around the room, hoping to orient myself, feeling the full weight of my dazed stupor. I was still sitting on the floor of our hotel room. The river and the gray skyline still lay beyond the windowpanes. And the London Eye still flashed brightly, though it wasn't quite as easy to gaze upon with the pounding in my head.

Fitz knelt before me and pressed a cold, damp washcloth against my forehead. I placed my hand at the base of his skull, twisting my fingers into his hair.

And for the first time since I'd met Fitz, we didn't shock each other.

I tugged until he moved his body closer to mine, our faces only a few inches apart. I closed my eyes, drinking in his deep scent, which was heightened after receiving my powers. His presence was tangible all around me, and I felt everything about him—his heartbeat, his energy, and his power. He was far more powerful than he'd ever let on.

I allowed the connection to navigate where it willed, and through my witch's eye, I saw a small stream of energy forming between the two of us. I couldn't fully comprehend it. It resembled the brilliant glow of vintage light bulb wires in a dark room. The connection I'd thought to be imaginary turned out to be real. Even though magic was fantastical to me, I had begun to understand it, innate as it truly was. I followed the length of the stream and found Fitz at the other end. It was only then that I noticed a second stream of light from Fitz back to myself. I opened my eyes to Fitz, who was still bent forward with his eyes closed.

"You let me in."

"What do you mean?" I asked.

"The streams. You saw them?"

I nodded.

"You found a stream that led to me—a path I created for you. I've waited a long time for you to find it. The other stream just formed between us . . . it came from you. You created a path for me to find you, as well."

"How did I do that? I don't understand what's happening."

Fitz crossed his legs and scooted closer until our knees touched. He took my hands in his. "I know this all must seem a bit scary, but this is normal for us. All right?"

I nodded. "What are these streams exactly?"

"Our energies formed a connection between the two of us. This type of connection—it only forms between mates," he said.

I paused. "You were right about us being mates, then."

"Are you good, Hads?" he asked. "I know this is quite a bit to sort through at once."

"I'm good."

He squeezed my hand.

"What causes the streams to form?" I asked. "You said yours has existed for a while, and mine just formed."

"They form as feelings and trust for someone develops. Once you trusted me, the connection formed. With the assistance of your magic, you created a path for me to find you."

His fingertips brushed the side of my face gently until my cheek rested in his palm.

"This connection is formidable, Hadley. These streams are life and vitality flowing between us. You have a direct line to my soul, and I to yours. You'll know immediately if I'm upset. I'll know if you're ever in danger."

"I've felt that already."

"Aye. I think that's partly due to mine forming so early on."

"Fitz, mine would have formed a lot sooner if I had my powers. I think part of it already existed from my side."

"I think that's why we've been shocking each other. That's gone now—for you too?"

I nodded.

"This connection was instantaneous," Fitz said. "I think your magic has been trying to match with you, and it's been trying to connect us."

The gravity of our connection hit me with full force, and the vulnerability that came with our interconnectedness left me feeling exposed.

"What's wrong?" Fitz questioned.

"It's nothing really. It's just that I feel naked—internally."

Fitz nodded.

"What if you don't like what you find in our connection?"

"Not even a possibility."

My heart raced.

Fitz's brows furrowed, and his eyes shut tightly. "Never worry again that I'll leave you."

"You feel that?"

"Aye, of course I do," Fitz said. "And god only knows why you feel that way."

"What if there's something about me that you can't deal with?"

"You're forgetting something: I know you, Hads. I know you better than anyone else, and I want you—all of you." He paused. "I have my flaws too. You know that. But you'll learn that it isn't our nature to run away from the tough bits."

Fitz's words were comforting, though his energy unnerved me—it was agitated.

"What's wrong?" I asked.

"I can't bear the feeling of your fear inside me. It's . . . painful."

I'd caused Fitz pain, and I didn't know how to remedy that. Closing my eyes, I succumbed to my instincts and allowed it to guide my actions. I closed the gap between us, pressing my lips firmly to his.

A slew of memories raced through my mind: the moment our eyes met at the lake, the electricity that drummed through me as we shook hands, the feel of his kiss the first time he pressed his lips to mine, the look in his eyes when we met atop Notre Dame. My emotions built with each memory, and warm desire pumped through my veins.

I anticipated the charge of the kiss, the final fusion of our connection. But the emotional intensity surprised me—it propelled me forward.

Unlike his slow, deliberate movements before, Fitz was consumed with need. One of his hands laced tightly to mine, and he cupped my face with the other. I responded by placing my free hand behind his back and tugged him closer to me.

He rocked back, pulling me onto his lap, and he stared into my eyes as his hands raked through my hair. He found his grip in the long, auburn strands and tugged my head back gently to expose my neck. His lips found the tender spot just under my jaw, and I sighed. He worked his way toward my chest before pulling at the left side of my V-neck sweater.

He paused.

"What is it?" I whispered.

"I feel you so deeply . . . much stronger than before."

"It's the same for me."

"My heartbeat—can you feel it inside of you?"

I nodded. I traced a path along his sweater and paused right where his heart lay. I pressed my palm to his chest, but it wasn't enough. I followed my instincts and pushed his sweater toward his head. He acknowledged my silent request and helped me with its removal. I unbuttoned his white dress shirt and tossed that barrier next to us on the floor before scanning the lean muscle of his sculpted torso. My breath caught when his eyes flickered back to mine. Fitz's gaze was intense.

I pressed my hand against his solid, bare chest, and his heartbeat intensified. The thump radiated through my body, and my own heartbeat raced to match his. Fitz slipped my sweater off my left shoulder and grazed his fingertips along the edge of the fabric until he found the soft skin over my heart. I closed my eyes as I tilted my head back, both reveling in the feel of his touch and willing my heart to not leap from my chest. Fitz leaned forward and pressed his lips to the spot his fingertips had just touched. I then tilted his head to meet my gaze, and whatever he found in my eyes—it lit a fire inside of him.

He slipped his hand behind my neck and pulled me forward, kissing me deeply before returning to my neck and lower. When he found my lips again, our motions grew in intensity, and I savored the feeling of our connection finally flowing freely. I'd never felt more connected to anyone or anything in my life. We lost ourselves to the intoxication of each other until I pulled back to search his face for any signs of its former distress.

Fitz grinned as he stretched out on the cool floor, dragging in the deep breaths his body sought. "I don't think I'll survive that again," he mumbled, pulling a hearty laugh from me.

"Well, I don't have to touch you."

"Oh, like hell you don't. You might kill me, but I suspect I'll enjoy every bit of it," he responded, leaning on to his elbows.

"I—" I paused, searching for the words. "I never could have imagined something like that. The feelings that channeled through that connection . . ."

"Aye, it's intense. Are you good?"

"More than good."

He laughed. "Well, that's grand."

"This is so different from the way humans approach relationships, though. I mean, it never felt right to me, and now I finally understand why."

"Aye," Fitz said. "We're programmed a bit differently. Once we find our missing half, we lose little time in starting our lives together."

"Desire is different for us?"

"Oh aye. Because we do have desire, but the impulse to find our mate is always just under the surface—always palpable—and we don't typically quell the loneliness by just hooking up randomly."

"But it happens sometimes?"

"There's an exception to every rule, but when there's such a strong urge to find your other half, anyone else just feels like a distraction—like someone who could throw you off course."

"You really feel this way about me?"

"You know exactly how I feel about you. You've known since the first day I met you—when I wandered into that clearing with you and Izzy. That was it for me."

My heart warmed at his confession.

He continued, "So, to answer your question: Aye, I really feel this way about you. I consider us bound together. Forever. Don't you?"

I ran my fingers along his jawline, and he rested his forehead against mine.

"Yes," I whispered.

Finally. A longstanding tightness released from my chest.

Fitz pulled back, a strange look blanketing his features.

"What is it?"

"There's nothing wrong." He paused momentarily. "It's just . . . I love you, Hadley."

"I love you too. I always have."

He couldn't keep the broad smile from his face, though I thought he was trying. His hand rested at the base of my skull, his thumb gently gliding back and forth, chills rising behind the warmth of his touch.

"Do couples separate in the witch world? Do they break this connection?" I asked.

"Not that I know of . . . it's just not in our nature to find our other half and then give up when things get tough. We mess up, we get angry, we have problems, but we fight for the love we've been given."

His words were comforting, and I released some of my previous anxiety.

"I could sit here forever with you, but perhaps we should have a little change of pace?" Fitz asked.

"What do you have in mind?"

"Power training?" he suggested.

I was on my feet before he could blink, my headache nearly forgotten. "What are you waiting for? Get up!"

Fitz rolled to his feet and slid his hands around my waist, pulling me back to him. "Yes, ma'am."

He kissed me quickly, a happy gleam in his eyes.

CHAPTER SIXTEEN

Fitz paced the room, his phone glued to his ear. Ian had finally called with more information, and my foot tapped nervously, awaiting the update. Ian's voice was bold and deep, and though I couldn't make out his words, the rise and fall of his cadence was distinct. His voice held as much presence as it would if he were standing in the room, and my reaction surprised me. Ian unnerved me, and even though I knew I owed it to our circumstances at the lake, the pit of my stomach still tightened.

Henry and Isaac didn't look any less anxious than I felt, and though the call was brief, it seemed to last an eternity. When Fitz punched the button to end his call, my stomach flipped.

"Dad says we need to meet with the Scottish Council, and if we give them what they want, he thinks things will be fine."

"Fine?" Isaac asked.

"He said he received a visit from the council this morning. They told him they've suspected Hadley and I were together ever since we both gave them the slip."

My breath hitched. Fitz sat next to me and took my hand in his.

"Dad told them that Hadley acquired her powers. After some back and forth, the council member left. They phoned this afternoon and said they want proof that she's a fully functioning witch now."

"Do you agree with that—that things will be okay?" I asked.

"No," Fitz, Henry, and Isaac responded in unison.

My eyebrows rose.

"Here's the thing . . . the councils work in strange ways. If they do let this go, there's a reason," Isaac said.

"Well, that sounds ominous," I said.

"I reckon it could be . . . they might want you for something in particular," Henry said.

"I don't understand."

"They might want to leverage a particular skill set for something. That's fairly common," said Fitz.

"I don't doubt that. This feels suspicious," Isaac said.

"I agree," Fitz said. "But I . . . I do think we should give them what they asked for, at least for now."

"How so?" I asked.

"We should provide proof that you have your powers."

"What if they decide to punish us? What if they spellbind us, Fitz?" My voice shook. I'd finally found myself, and the thought of losing my magic so quickly tore violently through me.

"I don't think they'll do that. And neither does Dad."

"I think it's more likely they'll ask something of you," Isaac said.

"We already know they want Fitz to work with them," Henry added. "I doubt that's changed."

"The only way to find out is to meet with them—and I think we should. If that's all right with you?" Fitz asked me.

"I don't think we have much choice unless we decide to run," I said. "But what are the odds they wouldn't eventually find us anyway?"

"Slim. We'd have to change our entire lives—give up our connection to everyone and everything," Fitz said.

"I don't want to live that way—not unless it's a last resort," I said. "Let's go and face this."

"Dad said this meeting is to discuss what's happened, and the council will collect whatever information they're seeking. If they decide there should be consequences, the courts will convene before a sentence is reached."

The room fell quiet. It was Isaac who first broke the silence.

"It's real now. We've prepared for this moment for a long time, and now we will see if we're ready."

"Aye, and if I'm being transparent, I'm nervous," Henry admitted.

Fitz nodded. "Same, mate."

"If anything goes wrong, we have contingency plans," Henry said.

"Which consists of Fitz and I disappearing?"

"Aye," said Henry sadly. "But if they move to spellbind you, your choices are to live a painful existence without magic or to run from the councils and disappear forever. I know it doesn't sound appealing, but you'd have each other—and your magic."

"Whatever happens . . . We'll be ready for anything." Isaac nodded once in our direction.

"You're good friends," I said. "I'm sure you know how much Fitz appreciates that, but I haven't thanked you properly. I want you to both know how much this means to me."

Henry smiled shyly. "You're a part of our wee family. We protect one another—no questions."

"We'll always have your back," Isaac added. The room fell quiet once again as we felt the weight of what was to come. I squeezed Fitz's hand reassuringly.

"Well, not to break up this tender moment, but it's getting late, and I promised Hadley one last evening stroll in London."

We were leaving for Edinburgh the following morning, as Monday's interview at the castle was only two days away.

"I won't see you in the morning before you leave, but I'll be in Edinburgh in a couple weeks. Sooner if the councils give you trouble." Isaac embraced me warmly. "Take care of yourself, Hadley."

"You too, Isaac. Miss you already."

He planted a quick kiss on the top of my head before embracing Fitz and then Henry. And as we dispersed for the evening, my heart tugged at me slightly. The spell was broken.

I was happy to learn Henry would meet us in Edinburgh, but it wouldn't be quite the same without Isaac. This small group of brothers had seen me through one of the most important and vulnerable moments of my life. And in our short time together, I'd learned just how much they'd contributed—and were still contributing—to help Fitz and me through this situation with the government. Though I was only just getting to know them, it felt as though they'd known me as long as Fitz had.

I waved goodbye to Isaac as we parted outside the hotel lobby. I didn't know much with any certainty, but of one thing I was sure: the next time I saw him, everything would be different.

PART TWO

CHAPTER SEVENTEEN

Forfar, Scotland
January 1662
Esther

I peered through the hazy windowpane, observing the snow drifting to blanket the earth in white. It was an exceptionally cold day, even for January, but I loved the way snow transformed the world into something new. As a wee bairn, the excitement had been almost unbearable when I woke to the brightly covered hills, and as an adult, the sense of nostalgia was strong. My husband Hamish wasnae fond of snow, which reminded me the fire needed tending before his return. Hamish had left for the village in the wee morning hours and hadna yet returned; my thoughts were further at war with one another the longer his absence stretched.

The fire roared with the crackle of fresh wood. Two figures materialized in the flames. My visions had troubled Hamish, but it had taken little time to discover who they were. I stared into the eyes of my many times great-grandson, as confused by his appearance as ever. Though I had grown accustomed to frequent visions, this one vexed me.

My foresight manifested as images in the elements—water, fire, earth, air, moonlight—as my power mixed with the spirit of the land. Often-times, I recognized those I saw—my kin, neighbors, and acquaintances—as I observed their futures, transfixed by their stories. Occasionally, my witch's eye watched the future for me. I'd foreseen the melancholy battle of Culloden Moor, the colonization of the New World as it headed west, and the invention of a horseless buggy—an automobile, I believed. With my mind preoccupied in times that had yet to pass, I had to be mindful of my speech—Hamish often said I spoke in strange ways. Perhaps I'd no been mindful of that as of late.

The flames grew restless, and I lost Fitz MacGregor and Hadley Weston in the all-consuming blaze. Their appearances set my nerves on end. Frequent manifestations meant I had a connection with their futures, and I felt Fitz and Hadley were in trouble. Their bodies floated through the in-between, an indication that they were on a lengthy journey through time or space. Long passages were tricky, and even with Fitz's power, I prayed they wouldnae attempt a dangerous expedition without a pressing reason. Perhaps I was wrong. Or perhaps they had caught my witch's eye for this very reason. Perhaps I was meant to assist them on their journey.

The light in the room brightened, and Hamish's figure filled the doorway.

"Did ye succeed?" I asked.

He eyed me dubiously as he shook the fresh powder from his overcoat.

"The truth, Hamish," I said.

"I pleaded with every witch in the area."

"None will help us, then."

Hamish cut his eyes sharply—he was searching for the right words, but he wouldnae find any. I reached out my hand, beckoning Hamish to my side.

"Damn them all to hell," Hamish said.

"Aye, and what would that do for ye?"

"I cannae understand, Esther. The council would do the same for their families if it came to it, and yet, none will stand now and fight."

"Come to me, *mo ghaol.*"

Hamish obeyed, my rising nerves undoubtedly registering in his body.

"Ye've done well, Hamish," I said. "There's nothing left to be done. Now, we must wait."

Tears welled in his eyes as he held me close. I rested my head on his chest, watching the flurry of activity on the other side of the panes. Icy flakes floated upon an invisible force, making their slow, winding descent to the ground, where they burst into flames. A chill ran down my spine.

Fate beckoned, and ere long, I would be forced to answer.

Edinburgh, Scotland
Present Day
Hadley

Scotland took my breath away. I surveyed what lay beyond the train window, already in love with the hauntingly beautiful land. The hills stretched as far as I could see, greeting the rolling fog like old friends. The land's beauty mixed with the nation's historical tragedies to create the perfect backdrop for fairy tales, legends, and the accounts of heroes. I wondered what my story might become in such a place. Perhaps it wasn't quite the substance of legend, but I was lost in my own fairy tale. How many people discovered one day that their childhood fantasy had been fulfilled? Even though Fitz and I would soon face the Scottish Council, I had to believe everything would turn out all right.

I felt the warmth of Fitz's hand on mine and turned to him, a man formed of this land. His strong figure seemed crafted to survive the harsh environment, and the magic about him was palpable. That magic transformed him into someone who'd stepped straight from the stories that his characteristically superstitious culture passed from generation to generation. Though the more I learned, the less superstitious I found those who heeded the warnings and tales of the past.

"We coexist much more easily with the humans now that they're, as a culture, more enthralled with their limited version of science," Fitz explained. "Most humans don't believe magic to be real, so they've turned to what they consider a more reasonable explanation of the mysterious. They certainly live less magical and informed lives than their ancestors. But to be honest, I think it's nice no one is trying to burn us at the stake. Let them have their science."

"It's unfortunate it has to be this way. It seems like witches could help humans quite a bit."

"Aye, but we can't tip the balance, anyway."

"And we keep this balance because . . ."

"Anything that significantly alters humanity must be left to Fate. There are consequences for pissing off Fate. She's a tricky mistress," he answered.

"You talk about Fate like it's an animate being."

"She is. Trust me, you'll see that. She can't really be explained or even fully comprehended, but she's there."

"What about God? Do most witches believe in a higher being?"

"In some form," Fitz said. "Our religious beliefs are as varied as humans', but with the power to see the world so clearly, it's hard to reason a higher being doesn't exist."

"So many people act like witches are all evil," I said. "Like we're devil worshippers."

"Aye. I'm not trying to commune with the devil myself."

"Really? I hear hell is nice this time of year," I said, pulling laughter from Fitz.

"I can't lay all the blame on the humans. We've had witches contribute to that narrative. But humans have posed as witches over the years, causing harm to our reputation."

"I'll bet some of the humans aggravated their captors with wild confessions."

"Devil's advocate, though. Some of them were just doing what they could to end things," Fitz countered.

"Because of the torture?" I asked.

"Days of sleep deprivation, the absence of food and light, and being held in freezing conditions would cause most anyone to confess, just to put an end to the torture. And that's only the beginning of what some of those poor men and women endured. Death seemed better than living."

"That honestly makes me sick to my stomach," I said. "I know there are still people today who want to cast a negative portrayal of the craft, and they're basing their judgments on false information. The overzealous witch-hunters might be dead, but the stigma lives on."

"It's frustrating that humans have turned us into caricatures. But the general belief in magical beings has faded. We've hidden ourselves, so we have to accept this version humans have created for their own amusement."

"How superstitious are people around here?"

"It's a modern city with modern people, but you'll be in contact with historians, English professors, archaeologists, and the like. Those humans are close to the past. They're researchers, observers of humanity. Superstitious, no. Perceptive, aye."

Fitz checked his phone, which quickened my pulse. I was wary of bad news.

"It's Henry," he said, undoubtedly feeling my nerves. "He's reminding me to use his estate outside Edinburgh for your magic training that's best suited for the outdoors."

"Estate?" I asked.

Fitz's lips tugged into a half smile. "Aye. His parents left him the family estate. His dad has some health concerns, and moving to a villa overlooking the ocean in Greece is his method of coping."

That was some coping mechanism.

"Are our health risks the same as humans'?"

"Serious risks like heart attack or stroke are exceedingly rare until we're quite old, as are the minor aches and pains. And cancer is almost non-existent in our world."

"How old is Henry's dad?"

Fitz hesitated before answering. "One hundred twenty-three."

"How is that possible? He would've been eighty-five when Henry was born? What am I missing?"

"Most witches choose to have children earlier than Henry's parents to stay on a more human timeline, but there are loads of witches who don't choose a traditional lifestyle. If you saw Henry's dad, you'd think he was in his late sixties now."

My curiosity got the better of me before I could halt my mind, and my eyes must've been the size of saucers.

"Hadley?"

"Oh my god. I'm so sorry."

"You're inside my head, aren't you?"

"I promise I didn't mean to. I just . . . lost control."

He exhaled slowly, requiring a moment to check his feelings.

"It's okay. You're new at this, and honestly, you won't develop proper control until I track down someone to help you with that power."

"Thank you for understanding."

He nodded.

"Do we really live to two hundred?"

"Aye, somewhere between two hundred and two-twenty-five typically. Our magical energy slows aging. It prevents major diseases from taking root. As our bodies finally age out, they become more susceptible to illness, but it takes longer."

"Wait, so how old are you?"

"Thirty-three. Don't worry, you're not with an old bloke."

"Thank god."

Fitz laughed, amused with my concern.

"Okay, so Henry's dad is ill much earlier than he should be?"

"Oh aye, and when Henry's ready, he'll relay his dad's tale to you. He was active in the First World War. Because of the damage, his body invited illness early. Luckily, what ails him now isn't life-threatening."

The train pulled to a stop, and Fitz smiled, the buzz of my energy swirling all around us. As we exited the bustling Waverly Station, the fresh air felt unusual—animated somehow—as its tiny movements danced wildly across my skin. My feet greeted the earth of Scotland and were immediately met by a burst of energy, which climbed rapidly, humming throughout my body. My energy, my blood, everything within me responded to an invisible force in the elements. I hesitated, glancing at Fitz.

"Magic grows stronger in certain areas of the world. Our spirits return to the places we called home, regardless of where we die. We feel that concentration of their power, and our own powers strengthen because of it." He grinned, bursts of his euphoria hitting me in waves. "Edinburgh has a rich, magical history. Your body is feeding on the collection of energy and spirit. Paris and London have strong footholds as well—you're becoming more in tune with yourself since you perceive the magic here."

The feeling of power pulsing through my body was sensation enough, but this knowledge was exhilarating. Standing in the midst of the historic city, my magical brothers and sisters across countless generations were granting me vitality.

People passed by us, consumed with their daily lives, completely unaware of the life transforming before their eyes. For the first time, I felt like I belonged to something on a grand scale. After years of searching in vain for others like myself, feeling ill at ease in my own body . . . I was no longer alone.

CHAPTER EIGHTEEN

Edinburgh exceeded my expectations, idyllic and dramatic as the city was. Throughout Old Town—fittingly the oldest part of the city—remarkable architecture, cobblestone streets, small pubs, and charming tourist shops filled with tartans and Scottish trinkets all culminated into a uniquely Scottish experience. And if that was somehow insufficient, the expansive and ever-present Edinburgh Castle sat atop Old Town, granting a glimpse into the ingenuity and realities of medieval times. Researchers believed it had been besieged twenty-six times in the castle's 1,100-year history. The massive structure had previously housed everyone from royalty to prisoners, but its seemingly final role was preserving history, educating and entertaining tourists, and adding jobs to the Edinburgh economy.

I strolled down the esplanade near the castle entrance. The gray stonework rose high above my head, and the thick, impenetrable walls held two large wooden doors in place, which opened to a courtyard filled with tourists. My chest swelled as I considered joining the ranks of the castle employees, preserving history and architecture for generations to come.

An hour later, I had lost myself to the castle, which was grander than I'd expected. The sights were breathtaking from the outer walls, granting an unparalleled view of Arthur's Seat, the ancient volcano credited as the main peak in Edinburgh's group of hills. St Giles' Cathedral stood out along the Royal Mile, the main street of Edinburgh's Old Town, which was filled with centuries-old buildings and throngs of tourists. My eyes scanned from Old Town to New Town over to the Firth of Forth, the estuary where several Scottish rivers rolled toward the North Sea. I wondered if this magical city might be the place I would soon call home. I wandered through the Great Hall, learning about Oliver Cromwell's army laying siege to the castle in 1650, and I couldn't help but think of generations past—and of witches like Esther. Her story had come to life for me, and that only brought the history of the castle further to life as well.

Engrossed in the history as I was, a small jolt of panic hit me when I realized only a few minutes separated me from my impending interview with Mr. Murray. I rushed through the doors of the Great Hall and navigated around the crowds of tourists scattered about the sunny courtyard. I thought I might have received some assistance from the supernatural in reaching his office on time.

Mr. Murray was a distinguished gentleman in his early sixties, if my appraisal was correct. A white button-up, a charcoal waistcoat with matching slacks, and expensive leather shoes accompanied his tartan-inspired jacket. As he drew closer, I took stock of his handsome features and the twinkle in the blue eyes shining brightly above a fluffy, gray beard. I found it odd when he didn't shake my hand, lightly nudging my elbow instead, guiding me toward his office. There was something protective in the gesture—almost fatherly. I settled into the leather chair opposite the desk from him and looked around the office.

"Not too shabby, aye?" he smirked, a thick Highlander accent rolling off his tongue.

Although not large, the space was comfortable. Two leather chairs nestled into a corner, and a nearby wooden table held two glasses with a bottle of Scotch cozied between them.

"My assistant wants to throttle me half the time." His hand swept over the stacks of books, magazines, and loose papers covering most of the mahogany desk.

I rather doubted that. Mr. Murray had a lot going on, but he was equally organized if the appearance of his desk bore any true reflection of his character—and in my years in the workforce, I found it usually did. Each stack appeared orderly, an organized system in play. The window near his desk opened to the center courtyard, his office perfectly positioned to observe the happenings of the castle. Not too shabby, indeed.

Mr. Murray asked various questions about my career path and what I sought from my next position. I, in turn, asked about the company culture and Mr. Murray's experience working for the castle.

"I was a bit surprised this job posting was open to international applicants," I said once Mr. Murray had finished sharing about his tenure with the castle.

"Oh? Well, I'm keen to find the proper fit, Ms. Weston. Your areas of focus in your previous positions are a good match for the needs in this one. And you mentioned your love for history. That's something I always look for in a candidate."

"Areas of focus, like my event work," I guessed.

"Aye. We dinnae have the budget for a fundraising manager, so that role is spread across several positions. The PR manager is head of the annual donor event. I was glad to see your experience in that area."

Running an annual event . . . though I'd worked on event teams in the past, this would be my first opportunity to head an event. And that sounded like the type of challenge I was looking for in my next move.

"Speaking of international applicants," Mr. Murray said, "perhaps I should have led in with this, but what has you interested in leaving the

States to pursue a career in Edinburgh?"

And at that precise moment, a tingle worked its way up my spine. It was fleeting, but the signal was clear—this man was no human.

Out of all the job opportunities I'd explored, I was banking on the one where I'd report to another witch. My mind raced wondering if he realized I was a witch, but of course, odds favored that he did. Surely, he knew. I suddenly understood why he hadn't shaken my hand at the beginning of the interview.

The thought unnerved me, but I responded as calmly as I could. "I'm ready for a new challenge and am very interested in expanding my horizons in another country. Scotland has such a rich culture and wonderful outdoor community. I think it's the perfect place for me."

"Oh, you're keen on the outdoors then?" he asked, stroking his neatly trimmed beard.

"Hiking and kayaking are both avid interests of mine."

"You're sure to have endless adventures here, especially through the Highlands."

I smiled, hoping to hide my growing apprehension.

"Well, if you dinnae have additional questions, I'll let you get on with your day, Ms. Weston. I plan to call your references this afternoon."

"That sounds great. I really appreciate your time."

I extended my hand, my eyes intently awaiting his reaction. He followed my lead, and a small tremor moved through my hand. Mr. Murray was certainly a witch, and a powerful one at that.

Walking down the corridor, I wondered if others of our kind worked within the castle. Could they determine I was a witch from afar, just as Mr. Murray had? I stepped into the courtyard and found Fitz.

"You know," I said, "If it weren't for your modern clothing, you'd fit right into this medieval place, you bloody Scot."

"You're a real charmer, you know that?" Fitz leaned over, planting a kiss on the top of my head. "Finally. I thought you were going to stay in there forever," he murmured, tugging me closer to him.

His warmth was inviting against the lingering nip of fall. I slipped my hand in his and told him about my experience with Mr. Murray.

"I'll ask Isaac to do a background check on him—he has access to those witchkind resources," Fitz said. "What's Murray's first name?"

"James."

"James Murray . . . that sounds familiar." Fitz's eyes widened, though he recovered quickly.

"What's that about?" I asked.

"Well," Fitz said, "there's a James Murray on the Scottish National Coven Council, but I don't know if they're one and the same."

"He works for the *government*?" I didn't like that at all.

"We don't know that yet," Fitz said. "Let me do a bit of research, and I'll let you know what I find out."

"I don't know how I feel about working for another witch, and if he's a part of the council . . ."

"Why are you unsure about working for a witch?" Fitz asked.

"I don't know. I'm not comfortable with my magic yet, and I guess I'm just nervous."

"That will change, though. Faster if you allow yourself to spend more time with other witches."

"Point taken," I said. "You know, I sensed the energy of the stalkers in Paris, but I didn't feel anything from Mr. Murray until we were nearly finished with the interview."

"You sensed them because they were tracking us—they were actively using magic," Fitz said.

"Murray definitely knew I was a witch though. How did he do that?"

"As your skills develop, you'll be able to determine if another witch is close, even if they aren't expending magic. Every witch has varying levels of power. You'll learn to pick up on their energy. It'll be even stronger between the two of us, though—I know you're not far by simply feeling your energy or catching your scent on the breeze."

"What do I feel like? How far away can you feel me?"

"A respectable distance, I suppose. When I walked through the castle gates, I knew you were still inside," Fitz said. "Your energy feels like sunlight dancing on my skin when you're at a distance. Similar to standing beneath the canopy of a tree on a day like today. The wind moves through the leaves, and I catch glimpses of your light and warmth. And as the gap between us closes, it grows warmer, more pleasant."

My grip instinctively tightened on his hand. "And my scent?"

He rested his face against the top of my head and inhaled slowly.

"Your scent is caramel." He paused. "Your scent is sweet, your warmth is palpable, and you're miraculously standing in front of me with your hand linked through mine. Who forgot to tell you that you deserve the whole world?"

I shook my head lightly, though his praise sent butterflies through me. "It's come on gradually, but I know your scent and feel as well."

"Like you're downwind from a farm?"

"Way to ruin the moment!" I laughed, pausing briefly to collect my thoughts. "You smell of oak . . . of a whisky with hints of fruit and spice. I noticed it when you hugged me that first moment in Paris. I assumed it was the scent of drink and cologne, but now I know it's you. It's comforting . . . You make me feel at ease."

That elicited a shy smile from Fitz.

"And the feeling your energy gives me," I said, "well, I'd liken it to your description. That feels just right."

"It's amazing, isn't it? That this sort of thing is real."

"It honestly feels unbreakable."

Fitz nodded. "Damn near it, I think."

The hair on our necks suddenly bristled. Though Fitz's expression remained blank, the shift in his energy buzzed in tandem with mine. We were being watched.

"*I don't know who this is,*" his voice whispered in my mind. "*We should go.*"

It seemed our exploration of the castle would have to wait for another day.

CHAPTER NINETEEN

The following afternoon, I sat cross-legged on the floor of my hotel room after meditating. Elemental witches may have been more powerful than casters, but we also carried a heavier burden. Because of this, Fitz placed a real emphasis on meditation becoming a part of my daily routine. I'd already recognized its necessity to ease my mind and release my excess energy.

I stretched lazily across the floor and reveled in the few moments when I felt perfectly centered.

I gazed up at the castle, smiling despite my recent protests with Fitz. The fact that he had upgraded my room to a castle view suite was something we were still fighting over. He wouldn't allow me to spend a dime—or, well, pence—as long as he was around.

The hotel was beautifully appointed, and the bathroom bigger than mine at home.

I jumped at the sound of my ringing phone. The number was local, and I answered quickly.

"Good afternoon, Ms. Weston. This is James Murray calling from Edinburgh Castle. I'm calling to let you know you'll hear from our head of HR later today with an official offer for our PR manager position. I hope you'll consider joining our team."

"Wow, that's great news," I said, hoping my voice was enthusiastic.

"I'm glad to hear it. I just have to say, you'll be a fine match for the role."

"Thank you so much. I look forward to hearing from the team."

After I hung up, I stared blankly at the castle, allowing my mind to roll through my thoughts. I wanted this job. Honestly, I wanted this life: living in this city with Fitz and working for an Edinburgh landmark.

But apprehension still channeled through me. Mr. Murray had done nothing wrong. In fact, he had done everything right. But Fitz and I hadn't yet met with the council, and I wasn't as honed into my new-found skills as I'd like to be prior to working closely with another witch.

And besides all that, Fitz had confirmed that James Murray did, in fact, sit on the National Coven Council for Scotland.

Fitz attempted to assuage my fears by telling me that James wasn't like the council members who had kept us apart and that Ian held him in high regard.

I was distracted as I readied myself for the evening. I was having dinner with Fitz at his flat, and though I was thrilled to see his place, the weight of this upcoming decision pulled at my good humor.

I had just poured a cup of tea when my phone rang for the second time that afternoon. It was the same number Mr. Murray had called from. I took a deep breath and answered.

Despite it being my idea, I was nervous as I walked over to Fitz's home. Fitz had offered to pick me up, but I argued against his need to protect me.

"At least call a car. Don't walk over alone," he'd said, after reminding me about the witch who'd watched us at the castle.

I shook my head and checked the directions on my phone again. Fitz would be angry if he knew I was indeed walking alone, but my desire to stretch my legs and admire the city at night was acute.

A shiver ran the length of my spine. I almost paused before instinct smothered my curiosity. Realizing I was about halfway to my destination, I picked up the pace. Although the night air was crisp with the chill of autumn, it wasn't the culprit of the sudden cold in my bones or the pinpricks of a glare assaulting my skin. I was being watched, and not by someone with mild curiosity either.

I glanced around confidently, remembering the advice I'd been given over the years: when alone at night, appear confident and alert. I hoped that advice was applicable to witches as I pressed onward. My heart beat wildly against my chest, and my sense of time was distorted. The minutes seemed to tick away slowly. Thoughts danced through my mind. Had our Parisian stalkers returned? Was it the council? *Was I in danger?*

My balance wavered as a silhouette took shape in my mind.

From the beige wool coat to the auburn hair, it was clear I was watching myself through my stalker's eyes. It took intense focus to keep moving forward as the scene grew more vivid, and even though my pace slowed, I threw my shoulders back and walked more confidently than I felt, all the while praying I wouldn't stumble and fall. From the stalker's point of view, I determined they weren't close, and perhaps they thought they were far enough away that I wouldn't notice their observation.

I shook my curiosity from my mind and focused on the path ahead of me. There was no discernible energy near me. Still, I feared the watcher would overtake me before I reached the street's next intersection, even though the Royal Mile was already in view. I reminded myself to breathe, releasing a deep sigh of relief upon rounding the corner on to Old Town's bustling main drag. The witch's stare faded along with the darkness of the street I left behind, and I focused on propelling myself closer to Fitz. Deciding I was safer amongst the crowd of people, my pulse slowed, and I checked the map a final time.

If I was reading the map correctly, Fitz's flat lay within one of the most impressive addresses in Old Town. Ramsay Garden towered over the city and only drew shadows from its western neighbor, Edinburgh Castle. I'd walked right past his home as I strolled down the esplanade to my interview. The majestic Scots Baronial-style building was beautifully adorned with white and beige stonework and trimmed in a contrasting red.

"What's wrong?" Fitz asked as he threw open the door.

"Nothing."

"I was about to call you. I felt your nerves."

"Well, there's no need for that now," I said.

"Hadley."

"Fitz."

He eyed me warily, and I reached for him instinctively, knowing his touch would quiet my agitated energy. "Don't worry about it. I'm just happy to be with you."

He ushered me through the doorway and kissed me quickly.

"So, what's on the menu?" I asked.

"We're making Scotch pies."

His answer made me smile.

"I know you're not keen on mutton, so I bought chicken instead."

My sigh of relief made him laugh.

Fitz gave me a brief tour of his flat, which was stunning. The wood floors were walnut, complementing the stormy gray walls of the living room. Large bay windows adorned the west-facing wall, allowing for ample light during the day, but were just then flaunting their view of the castle, all lit up for the evening. His furniture held deep, rich colors in the woods and warm brown leathers, rustic like a beautifully worn saddle. Books, new and old alike, were randomly stacked on most surfaces, and a half-empty decanter held a golden liquid, sure to be single malt Scotch.

The distant sound of jazz grew in volume as Fitz led me into the kitchen. My eyes flickered around the space, surprised by the comfortable size of it. Since his flat was housed in an older European building, I had expected a smaller kitchen.

"I decided on this flat solely for the kitchen. It was the largest I saw—the former owner was a chef and expanded it. You should've seen the rest of the place, though. It was tragic but completely worth the work for this setup."

"This place suits you."

The kitchen cabinets were mahogany and the counters a gray concrete. Copper and stainless steel hardware completed the look. His flat was warm and comfortable, just like him. I grinned as he set the ingredients on the counter, the thought of passing many an evening in this manner flitting across my mind.

Soon, my hands were buried in dough, and I relaxed into the rhythm of the evening. Fitz was preparing the filling. He set an onion on the cutting board and turned to me.

"Help me dice the onion?"

"Um, sure," I said. "Let me just wash my hands."

"No need. Just come over here for a second."

I followed his instructions, and he stood behind me wrapping his arms around my waist.

"Try to levitate the knife."

I craned my neck to face him. "Seriously?"

"Aye. Mind how you connect to the elements. Ask them for what you want."

"You're pretty distracting right now. You know that, right?" I asked.

He smirked. "I can move."

"No," I protested, holding firmly to his hands.

He chuckled and reached for a dish towel to wipe away the traces of dough.

"Go on," he prompted.

I scanned the materials the knife laid against—the gray counter, the worn, oak cutting board—before studying the knife. Its handle was made of dark wood, and the steel blade gleamed in the light that shone from beneath the upper cabinets.

My mind willed the knife to move.

Nothing.

"Feel the air with your energy," Fitz said. "Feel the elements that surround the knife."

I navigated the molecules surrounding me and felt my way slowly toward the knife. I jumped when my energy met the impermeable object.

"Now connect to the air around it."

The experience was more visual than I anticipated, but the air rippled as my magic infused with it. I timidly tugged my energy upward, and though it was wobbly, the knife rose from the counter.

When the knife fell with a clatter a few seconds later, I couldn't even be disappointed. I turned to Fitz.

"Did you see that?" I exclaimed.

"Aye. You're a proper witch."

Fitz kissed me, and goosebumps spread across my skin. I ran my hands along his neck, finding my grip along his shoulders. He cupped my face gently before resting his forehead against mine.

"I'm sorry," I said.

"For?"

"Pretty sure your shoulders are covered in dough now."

"Oh. Nae bother."

I ran water over a dish towel and Fitz lifted me onto the counter. He leaned into me as I wiped his shoulders clean, and my pulse quickened. He kissed me quickly before depositing me back on to solid ground.

I finished the dough distractedly as I watched Fitz command the knife to magically cut the onion for him.

"Do you do that often?" I asked.

"Cook with magic? No, but I hate chopping onions . . . the burning, watery eyes and all that. If I were ever captured, there's no need for waterboarding, just give me a hundred onions to dice."

"Oh, I really need to learn how to prep food with magic."

"You'll get there," Fitz said. "Patience."

"One of my strong suits."

The navy, ceramic plates looked beautiful as I set them onto the wooden dinner table. Fitz refilled our glasses with cabernet and took a seat, his face softly illuminated by the dim lighting.

"This is incredible," I said, savoring the first bite. The double-crusted pie was filled with chicken and just the right amount of gravy. "The combination of herbs and gravy creates such a great flavor."

"Aye. And the onions too. It's a controversial choice in some households, but I prefer mine with it."

I was about to comment on the onion controversy. Then I remembered. "Oh, I have news."

"I feel your nerves. Put me out of my misery, Hads."

"I accepted a job offer this afternoon."

Fitz set his fork down and paused briefly before his eyes flitted to mine. I couldn't place what I found in them . . . apprehension, maybe.

"Oh aye? What did you settle on?" he asked.

"Well, I'm moving to Edinburgh."

Fitz's gaze dropped momentarily, and a flood of relief washed through me—his relief. When he looked up again, a heartfelt smile graced his lips.

"Do you know how happy that makes me?"

I nodded. "I think I do."

Fitz laughed softly, a kind of laugh that captured perfect happiness, before rising from the table. He slid my chair back and pulled me into an embrace. I wrapped my arms around him and held him close, content to stay in that moment forever. I pulled his face to mine, kissing him deeply.

After dinner, we moved to the couch by the fireplace. Curled up under a blanket, I was relaxed and happy.

"How's Izzy?" I asked, taking another appreciative sip of wine.

"You like this one, don't you?"

"You have good taste in women and wine," I countered, pulling a deep laugh from Fitz.

"Aye, that I do."

His fingers skimmed the length of my thigh, taking their time in meandering back to my knee. "Izzy's good. She was in her last year at the University of Washington when you moved?"

"Yep," I said.

"She accepted a job in grant writing with Seattle Children's Hospital."

"That sounds like a good fit for her."

"She's always wanted to help others, and this is a good opportunity for her. I don't know how long it'll last, though," Fitz said. "It's hard on her to be indoors at a desk for so long. She told me just yesterday she'd like to open a shop to sell plants and herbs, teas, that sort of thing."

"Okay, now *that* sounds perfect for her."

"Aye, her heart's always been in nature."

I recalled the teas, salves, and whatnot she'd brought to Daddy while he was sick and how much that had meant to us.

"I'd like to see her," I said.

"She's anxious to see you again. We should arrange that."

"Really? That would be amazing!"

"I'll call her tomorrow and ask about her holiday time. She'll hop a plane in a heartbeat."

"I can't believe how long it's been since I last saw her," I said.

"That's partially my fault. She would have come sooner, but I didn't want to pull her further into this mess while you and I were breaking the rules."

"You were right to do that."

"There's no harm in it now," Fitz said. "You have her number. Call her any time you'd like."

Fitz insisted on walking with me back to the hotel, although I didn't need any convincing. Anxiety rolled through my body as we crossed the hotel lobby. I hadn't yet mentioned my earlier encounter. Fitz would overreact, but the thought of being alone haunted me. Fitz's internal battle raged, and his warring energy washed over me. We were feeding into the other's negative energy and leading each other down a rocky path. He'd known something was wrong before I even arrived at his home, and he clearly felt the emotions that now raced through me. As the elevator propelled us toward my floor, my internal struggle came to a halt. It was time to end our game.

"Someone was watching me again tonight."

"Excuse me?" he returned, his eyes immediately wild.

"Don't overreact."

"I'm not overreacting."

"Really?" I asked.

"First of all, *really*. You know I can't help it. And this sort of thing just isn't done. You don't watch other witches."

"Okay, fine."

"Where were you when this happened?"

"When I walked over to your place."

"I told you not to walk over," he growled.

"I told you not to boss me around."

"You still don't grasp how dangerous this is, do you?"

"I do."

"Then why did you put yourself at risk?"

"I thought it would be fine—it was a short distance, and I thought it would be more crowded than it was."

He met my eyes sternly.

"Look, they didn't get close enough for me to know for sure, but I think it was the same witch from the courtyard at the castle. They never made contact or anything and trailed off right before your place."

Fitz pulled me through the door, throwing a glance at the lock. It secured itself. He then nodded toward the far side of the room, and the curtains moved to obstruct our view of the outside world.

"I'd like to stay here tonight," Fitz said.

"Sounds good to me. You could probably call the front desk for a toothbrush. Unless . . ."

"Unless what?"

"Can you just produce that sort of thing with a snap of your fingers or something?"

"I'll call the front desk," he said, reaching into the air. Without warning, the phone flew across the room and into his impatient grasp.

"Oh god. Please teach me how to do that," I said.

"All in good time. You performed levitation tonight. You'll be calling up objects in no time."

Getting ready for bed was infinitely more fun as I considered the objects I could call into my reach, wondering if I could brush my teeth without using my hands. Upon entering the bedroom, I initially reached for my leggings, but after some debate, I settled on my pajamas. They outranked my leggings on the cute scale, and much of the top was a transparent lace. It wasn't an attempt to seduce Fitz necessarily, but I thought he might shoot down the request I was about to make, and I needed all of the ammunition I could muster. I marched into the living room to find Fitz lying on the couch.

"Well, don't you look adorable?"

"Are you coming in here or what?" I asked.

"*Hadley.*"

"What? Please, don't be a prude tonight. Besides, you're able to offer more reliable protection at a closer range."

"You are something else."

"Come to bed, Fitz."

I expected resistance, but he crossed the room, stopping just in front of me. My eyes searched his, hoping for an opening into his thoughts, but to no avail; he remained carefully impassable. He turned me around and led me into the bedroom. We held each other's gaze as we climbed onto the bed.

"What are you afraid of, Fitz?"

"I'm afraid of handling this wrong."

"What do you mean?"

"Our past is complicated, and I don't want that for our future. I'm being mindful of the changes you're working through," he said.

"Which I appreciate, but . . ." I trailed off.

"You asked me to not be a prude . . . have I really not made my desires clear to you? If you read my mind right now, my thoughts would make you blush."

My heart quickened, and Fitz let out an irritated groan, rolling on to his back.

"What now?"

"The last thing I need is your body responding to my confession."

I laughed lightly, taking hold of Fitz's arm and tugging him to face me again. "Okay. I'm calm."

His eyebrows rose at my response.

"Just . . . continue. Please."

"It's important that you and I do what we can to cultivate our relationship," Fitz said. "I don't want to rush things and then realize we should have taken time to let other aspects of our relationship develop first."

"I get that. There's so much going on between us, but also just with me. With my powers, my mind, my body. I agree."

"I don't want you flying into everything headfirst, and then regretting it later."

"I don't think that would happen," I said, "but I also appreciate that we're trying to take things at a reasonable pace. There's a balance, though, and we're currently tipping the scale."

"Are you comfortable with this? With me staying over?"

"This feels better already—more comfortable than being without you. If you still need some space, that's fine, but don't stay away on my account," I said.

"Have you gone mad, then? I had to talk myself down last night, so I wouldn't come over here and sleep outside your door."

"That worried?"

"You have no idea," Fitz said.

"No more of that."

"Deal."

I slid my body closer to his and rested my head against his chest. We shimmied ourselves until we fit snugly together, clinging tightly to our rediscovered territory. Peace radiated through me, and I closed my eyes, allowing foggy calmness to take hold.

CHAPTER TWENTY

On Wednesday, Fitz and I walked up the steps of the Scottish National Coven Council's main campus. The beautiful beige building towered high above us, its stonework contrasting little against the gray sky. As we neared the entrance and people became visible on the other side of the glass doors, I froze. My muscles tensed, my heart raced, and the overwhelming urge to run took hold.

"Oh no," I muttered.

Fitz turned quickly. "It's okay, Hads. Let's take a deep breath, aye?"

I nodded.

He led me through a few breathing exercises until my body eased. Then, he wrapped his arms around me and held me until I was calm.

"Sorry about that," I said.

"A bit overwhelmed?"

"My anxiety has been better over here, even with everything happening. But . . ."

"I understand," Fitz said. "But we'll face this together . . . we'll be all right."

Fitz's energy fluttered through me. I knew he was worried too, but I accepted his encouragement gratefully.

"I'm sorry to say this, but we're tight on time," Fitz said. "Ready, you reckon?"

I swallowed hard and nodded. Fitz reached for the door handle.

Perhaps it was my prior experiences with government buildings, but I'd painted the witchkind government offices as old, dilapidated buildings with buzzing, flickering fluorescent bulbs. A carefully curated space both preserving the building's history and boasting modern comforts awaited me instead. An attractive brunette's heels clicked down the hardwood hallway as she led us past large, black pane windows. I was struck by both the grandeur and the tastefulness of the offices. Everyone smiled or nodded as we passed them in the hallway, and they seemed genuinely pleasant. Several witches spoke to our guide, who was full of banter and laughter. She knew everyone by name.

Our guide left us seated by a desk in a small room surrounded by beige stone walls and a large picture window, massive trees full of red and yellow leaves swaying gently on the other side of the glass. The table was sturdy, good quality, and topped with a large Apple monitor. I tapped my fingers nervously on the wooden desk, and Fitz slid his hand over mine.

A petite woman with gray hair and framed Prada glasses entered the room, gliding effortlessly toward the desk.

"Hadley. Fitz. Such a pleasure to meet you both." She shook our hands, and her eyes widened. "Oh my. Such power you *both* have!"

I shifted in my seat, and Fitz once again reached for my hand. His nervous current of energy coursed through me, reminding me of our earlier conversation—how the Scottish Council had been trying to recruit him for years. He'd avoided a meeting like this for a long time. This must have been a worst-case scenario for him in more ways than one.

"Mrs. Cameron," Fitz said. "It's nice to meet you."

"Please, you can both call me Olivia." She smiled broadly.

I was surprised by her friendly nature, though it felt forced. Something was off.

I caught Fitz's glance through the corner of my eye.

"Oh, good," Olivia said. Olivia's eyes were fixed behind us. I turned to find a small witch in the doorway. "Thank you for joining us, Mia."

Strong waves of energy fired off her snowy skin and crackled through the still air like lightning warning of an approaching storm. Her eyes were as soft a blue as Lake Crescent's glacial-fed waters, and they were starkly contrasted by her raven hair. She felt equal parts ethereal and threatening.

"This is a rare treat," Olivia explained. "We don't often have Cardinal Court members join these types of meetings. But I'm pleased to introduce you to Mia Davies."

"A court member?" Fitz questioned.

"That's of little consequence," Mia said. "I'm only here to observe your meeting today."

Her soprano voice was melodic, though it held a tone of authority. She was used to giving orders, I thought.

Fitz's energy grew tight, and it was clear we both felt how strange the situation was.

"First things first. We need to verify Hadley's power," Olivia said, rising from her seat.

A flurry of nerves shot through me. "What does that mean? What do I have to do?"

"Oh, this will go quite quickly," Olivia said. "Hadley, I'll just place my palm on your forehead, and then I'll feel the palm of your right hand. Will that be all right?"

"I don't have much choice, do I?" I suddenly felt trapped, and my tone was harsher than I'd intended.

Olivia smiled, and my skin crawled.

"She's happy to oblige," Fitz intervened.

"This is a dangerous situation. Try to remain calm," Fitz whispered into my mind.

My eyes flickered with uncertainty. I wished I knew how to respond telepathically.

"No need to be nervous, Fitz," Olivia said. "I imagine I'd have the same response if I were in Hadley's position."

Olivia was, indeed, quick. She stood next to me and closed her eyes, muttering unintelligibly under her breath. Her palm rested gently on my forehead before she took my hand, palm up, in hers. She grazed and circled my open palm.

After a few minutes, she opened her eyes and smiled before turning to Mia, who was leaning against the brick wall near the window with both her arms and legs crossed. Olivia nodded, and Mia stepped forward, still studying me.

Olivia returned to the opposite side of the table, typing rapidly before hitting the enter key with force and meeting my gaze. "You certainly have matched with your power. There's no doubt about that. The power you each possess is extraordinary."

Fitz nodded once. My stomach flipped. The council knowing the extent of our power felt more dangerous than defying their orders had.

"Fitz, you were right about Hadley, but you both understand our concern?"

I felt like a child in the principal's office. Olivia's tone was coercive, like we should see her point of view, and it didn't sit well with me.

After all they'd put us through, they weren't allowed to tell us how to feel about it.

"I'm afraid I don't," I returned, meeting her eyes unabashedly.

"Hadley."

"No, Fitz. I don't understand, and I won't sit here and pretend I do." I returned my focus to Olivia. "I am a witch. I always have been. Fitz was able to see that. If the councils are so wise and use such discernment ruling over us, how could you miss that?"

Fitz shifted uncomfortably in his seat.

"We didn't miss anything," Mia countered.

"Are you kidding me? You kept us apart because you didn't realize I was a witch. That sounds like missing something to me."

"We kept you apart because it was uncertain you'd match," Mia said. "And in the end, you defied orders anyway. You should answer for what you've done."

"That was on me," Fitz interjected. "If anyone is to answer for these actions, that should be me, and me alone. I made these choices, and Hadley had no part in that."

"Fitz, no," I said.

He kept his gaze fixed on Mia.

"Fitz kept our secret until it was time for me to match to my power. He didn't do anything wrong," I continued. I wouldn't let him take the fall alone.

"There is an order to things. He stepped out of line doing this without the council's involvement," Mia shot back.

Fitz's energy stirred through me. I was making him nervous, but I was so angry I couldn't seem to stop.

"But it was time for me to match—clearly. Your order didn't make sense."

"It's worked perfectly for years. Our rules are in place to protect everyone—even yourselves."

"You protected us from nothing. You served your own self-interests, sure. But can you honestly tell me you did anything in my best interest?"

"This line of thinking demonstrates how much you don't know—which is a lot, by the way," Mia answered.

"Is that so? Please, enlighten me."

Mia shook her head. "That time hasn't come."

"What does that even mean? I'm tired of this, of hiding information. I think you're just trying to cover your tracks because you realized you were wrong."

"It's not that simple, I'm afraid," Olivia interjected.

"Oh, but it is," I said. "Things either are, or they aren't. I am a witch. The councils forcing us apart was wrong. You made the wrong call."

"We made the best decision we could, and we did it to keep everyone safe," Olivia said. "I know this must have been a difficult season for you."

"Do you? Tell me something: can you really understand what I've been through?"

Olivia quietly held my gaze, and if I wasn't so angry, perhaps her intensity would have made me uncomfortable. Mia's features were cross, but she held her tongue.

"No. I guess I don't," Olivia finally acknowledged, sighing.

"You have no idea what you did to us." I hated the strain I heard in my voice, but I kept my eyes firmly on Olivia before shifting my gaze to Mia. "You sit in here and make rules for the witches you govern, but do you truly understand the consequences of those choices?"

"Of course, we do," Mia said.

"Sometimes we're forced to make decisions that are best for witch-kind as a whole," Olivia said. "There may be negative side effects, but we can't always control every factor. It's impossible."

"Is that what I was? A factor?" I shook my head.

"You're quiet, Fitz. What do you think of all this?" Olivia asked. Perhaps she thought Fitz would see the sense in their faulty logic, but she was mistaken.

"Of course, I don't agree with the councils' choices regarding our relationship. I think we're all clear on that. But this moment isn't about me." He cleared his throat, and I didn't miss the way he pushed back his shoulders and sat straighter. "It's about what's been done to Hadley and about how you forced us apart unnecessarily. Hadley doesn't need me to speak for her."

"This truly was meant to protect everyone," Olivia said. "Humans are too dangerous. They can't know about us."

I met Fitz's eyes meaningfully. I wouldn't be coerced into believing the councils had intended to protect me.

"But here we all are. Hadley has come into her powers. There are no rules being broken now. You are free to move forward with your relationship without any further involvement from us."

"We're glad to hear that," Fitz said. "One more question, though."

Olivia nodded for him to continue.

"Someone watched us while we were in Paris, and now someone has been watching us from the shadows here in Edinburgh. Is it the councils?"

"No, we haven't had anyone watching since you've been back—and we didn't even know of your whereabouts when you were in Paris. We trusted you to come forward and meet with us, as you and your father said you would, so we stopped trying to find you, truthfully."

"You're certain?"

"Quite. Do you have reason to believe they're related?"

"It would be quite the coincidence if they aren't, but we have no hard evidence either way except that they have different energies."

"We'll find out who it is and ensure your safety." Olivia turned to Mia, who nodded.

"Thank you," Fitz said.

"We can assign an agent to you if you feel threatened," Olivia said.

"I don't think that's necessary," Fitz said.

He looked to me, and I shook my head. "We'll pass on that for now. But we appreciate the offer."

"We do need to assign a council trainer to meet with Hadley and assess her powers, though," Mia said.

"Why?" Fitz asked.

"It's standard procedure when a witch of . . . uncertain ancestry matches with their power, especially if it happens in adulthood," Mia said.

"What do you mean by 'uncertain ancestry?'" I asked.

"We don't know where your magical lineage comes from," Mia said. "But we'll find out."

"I'd like to know the answer to that myself," I said.

"Then you should cooperate with us."

"This assessment process isn't invasive," Olivia said. "They'll run Hadley through different spells, observe her using her magic, that sort of thing. We're continually improving our research so we may better assist witches in this situation in the future."

Fitz sat back in his chair, though he didn't immediately respond. His energy tightened.

Olivia broke the silence. "It'll be helpful to Hadley as well. The trainer will prepare a report with information regarding her best abilities and those you'll want to hone during training to improve on."

Fitz looked to me, and I shrugged.

Truthfully, I didn't love the idea, even if they were able to provide answers, but I wasn't sure if refusing the trainer would land us in trouble.

"On one condition," Fitz said.

"That being?"

"The assessment doesn't happen here. I think Hadley would be more comfortable elsewhere."

Mia stiffened, and Olivia turned her head slightly and nodded to Mia. Whatever occurred in their silent exchange prompted Mia to sigh . . . and then agree.

"Pick a location that suits both parties. We look forward to working with you both," Olivia said.

"So, that's it, then? We're free to go?" I asked.

"I think we can all agree on leaving the past behind us and moving forward." Olivia smiled warmly.

A chill ran down my spine. The guys were right: they wanted something from us.

"Aren't you a feisty one today?" Fitz quipped as we exited the council building.

"One minute I was panicked, and the next I was angry."

"Oh, that much I sorted out."

"You won't have to just 'sort it out' once you teach me how to communicate telepathically."

"Patience, Hads."

I groaned and then my mind turned back to the meeting. "I don't like Mia's involvement. I think she had something to do with our separation," I said.

"Because she was a part of this meeting or is it something else pulling at you?"

"Yeah. I mean, the Cardinal Court sounds like a big deal. And one of their members was present for our meeting? It seems odd."

"Aye, it does seem a bit much."

"So, do you think we're done now?" I asked, hoping he'd disagree with my instincts.

"No."

"Oh, great," I said.

"We'll hear from them again. Did you see her reaction to our power? Her surprise wasn't genuine. I think she already knew what she'd find."

"Fitz, why do they want you to join them so badly?"

"It's my abilities. They want me to utilize them for the council's purposes."

"I know you're powerful. I know you can bring my memories to life and all that . . . but what else can you do?"

Fitz hesitated. "Do you want me to tell you about them, or show you?"

"Show me. Definitely."

CHAPTER TWENTY-ONE

Henry's estate was straight out of a fairytale. A lengthy driveway wound across the rolling hills of the countryside, crossing property so extensive that no neighbors were visible, even with the lack of foliage. The Palladian-style home was grand, sitting atop a hill in the center of his acreage. The home had been constructed in the late 17th century by Henry's wealthy ancestors and had remained in his family for hundreds of years. It had recently been left to Henry after his parents moved to Greece.

We stepped through the French doors from the patio into a large sitting room. Two of the walls were covered in bookshelves that held countless volumes of literature. Paintings covered another wall with what I assumed were the likenesses of Henry's ancestors.

Though the suit jackets betrayed the time period of each portrait, the red Stuart tartan clearly spanned across generations. The far side of the room held antique maps and a stone fireplace that appeared to be just getting started for the afternoon. Tufted chairs and a large leather couch were near the fireside, and end tables were decorated with stacks of books and lamps emitting a warm glow.

"Happy birthday, Hadley!" Henry exclaimed happily as he entered the room. He enveloped me in a warm hug.

"It's so good to see you again, Henry," I said.

"It's lovely to see you, as well."

Henry had returned to Edinburgh the day prior.

"How's your special day been?" Henry asked.

"Well, let's see. Fitz woke me up with breakfast. And then I opened presents from him—look at my new watch," I said, showing off one of the gifts.

"Oh, that's bonnie," Henry said.

"Then we hiked Arthur's Seat and grabbed lunch."

"Gonnae train on your birthday?"

"She insisted," Fitz said.

"What better present is there than learning more about my magic? I mean, seriously."

"You have a point, lass," Henry said.

"Speaking of which, we should get started," Fitz said, laying a hand on Henry's shoulder. "She has loads of training ahead of her."

Henry nodded. "I'll be just here if you need me."

Fitz led me outside to my designated training location, and the afternoon passed as I learned to command my fire magic.

I dug the heels of my baby blue rainboots against the Scottish soil and pulled my body into the proper form . . . or so I thought. The wind nipped at my bare fingers, but it was of little consequence. My fingers burst with flames, and I shot a fireball toward the target.

"Are you joking?" Fitz shouted from behind a small fir tree.

"Obviously not."

"I ought to send one back, so you know how it feels."

"I can take it."

"Seriously, please don't set me on fire. It would ruin the afternoon."

I snickered, pulling a smile from him as well.

Mastering the skill of fire creation was a huge step in my training.

Once I'd understood how to commune with the elements, asking them for what I sought was easier and more intuitive than I'd anticipated, for which I was grateful. It made me feel like a real, certified witch, and that was a true confidence booster this early in training.

The next step was creating fire with my body and then using that fire to protect myself. I never could have imagined there were so many ways to command fire. I could throw it like a baseball, wield it through a bow and arrow, shoot it from my fingertips, and radiate it from my entire body. I was basically a dragon, I observed to Fitz, who rolled his eyes.

Throwing had taken little practice. Fitz had noted it was one of my most natural skills, with an appreciative nod. The bow and arrow had worked out quite nicely as well. My father had taught me to wield a bow and arrow long ago. Apparently, that was skill enough. Radiating fire from my entire body? Evidently, I wasn't half bad at that either. I had gasped as the air ignited all around me, absolutely in awe at the way the flames responded to my request.

However, using my fingers like a gun to shoot fire was an issue. I'd almost set Fitz ablaze with a misfire. Twice. Though he was trying to maintain his humor, I was sure nearly being lit on fire was a harrowing experience. He walked over to demonstrate again how my form should appear.

"One more time. Legs here. Back straight. Arms tight and slightly bent."

"Do I really need both arms out?"

"Your ability is still materializing, and you'll have twice the strength with both hands. It should fully develop in the next week," Fitz said.

"Best news I've heard all day."

"Arms just a little lower. It's a slightly different form from shooting a firearm. Aye, perfect."

I adjusted per his instructions and shot. My flames landed at the edge of the target.

"Now, that's better," Fitz said.

"I was a lot closer on that one."

"Try it again. Focus on what you want."

I took a deep breath, mindful of my form, and reveled in my desire to set the target ablaze, envisioning how flames would lick the air. I closed my eyes briefly and asked my magic to guide my efforts.

"Fire," I breathed, and took my shot. Flames leapt from my fingertips, brilliant against the waning daylight. "Oh my god," I whispered, mesmerized by the target, ablaze in magical desire made real.

"That was braw!" Fitz was beaming as he lifted me from the ground. My lips found his, both of us alight with excitement. "Let's see that again."

Firing off shots one by one, I hit my mark, my energy bursting at the seams. Finally, I paused, a sudden urge for Fitz taking hold.

"Damn," he breathed. "Your eyes."

My head tilted in curiosity.

"They're on fire, Hads," he explained, his hand resting at the base of my skull.

"I don't understand."

"They're red, orange, yellow . . . the same as your fire magic."

Like my mind's eye, I realized.

"Is that . . . normal?" I asked.

"Aye, I think it is for you." His heart rate doubled as he met me in a kiss, fiery in its own right.

"I wish I had a mirror," I said.

"Call one up."

I grimaced. I wasn't excelling in calling objects as quickly as I was with my fire magic. One of the main rules with calling forth an object was that we could never risk a human catching us in the act, so we had to work a concealment around us to hide the fact that we were pulling something from thin air.

"The concealment part of the spell is still giving me trouble," I said.

"There's no one around—I'm certain—so don't worry with the concealment. Just call it up."

I thought of the compact mirror in my makeup bag: the antique brass one that Gram had given to me years ago. I visualized the etched floral pattern on the lid. I could almost feel it under my fingertips. I reached my hand into the air and when I pulled my hand back, the mirror rested in my palm.

"That's brilliant. Nice work," Fitz praised.

I flipped open the lid, and sure enough, just above my bright smile, my irises danced with flames. I gasped.

"You good, Hads?"

It was an unnerving sight, but it was fresh proof of the power I held inside of me. "More than good."

"Why don't we head inside? You need to rest."

I groaned.

"Fine. I won't show you my powers then."

My eyes lit up. I'd forgotten. "You should have led in with that. Come on. Time to show me what you can do, Dr. MacGregor."

"Shall I pour drinks?" Henry asked as we entered the sitting room. Henry had a "no shoes" rule in his home, so I swapped my boots for a pair of cozy slippers—which Henry had bought me—before making a beeline for the warm hearth.

"That does sound grand. But something else vies for my attention this evening," Fitz said.

Henry's gaze turned curious.

"Hadley's asked to see the rest of my powers."

A grin spread across Henry's lips. "Oh aye? Well, prepare yourself, lass."

Henry padded to the kitchen, and I settled onto the couch next to Fitz.

"You remember at the lake when I pulled your memories to the surface?"

I nodded.

"There's more to that power."

"Show me."

Fitz turned his head, and I followed his gaze to find a familiar face staring back at me.

"Momma?" I asked, thoroughly confused. She couldn't be here, could she?

My mother walked toward me. "Hello, honey."

I tentatively moved closer, not realizing until that moment just how much I missed her. After everything that had happened—that was still happening—I wanted nothing more than to see her, to tell her everything about the witch I was becoming.

I touched my mom's arm, and she dissipated right before my eyes.

I stared blankly at where my mother had been.

"I apologize if that was too much—with your mum. When you asked me to show you, I just pulled out the first person I could find in your memories."

"She was an apparition?" I asked.

"Aye. My power mixes with your memories and recreates them like they're real . . . and they play out in front of your eyes."

"That wasn't like the mind trick before. That was . . . real."

"It's jarring, I know."

"Damn, that was incredible. You're *really* talented, Fitz. That took a lot of power—I can feel it."

"Oh aye. There's nothing much to it," Fitz said.

"Wait, are you blushing?"

"Don't look at me," he countered playfully, walking off to the kitchen. Though his remarks were lighthearted, I knew it was difficult for Fitz to be praised. I thought he would be used to it considering the vast amount of power he possessed, but Fitz was humble, and for that, I was inordinately grateful.

When he returned, he was flanked by Henry and holding two glasses of water. Henry settled into the armchair in the corner and began rummaging through papers and magazines on the side table.

"I have something else to show you," Fitz announced as he passed a glass of water to me.

"Bring it on," I said.

"Pick a place."

"What?"

"Just pick a place. Name somewhere that fascinates you. Anywhere."

"Why? Oh my god." My eyes must have been huge. "Can you . . ."

"I'm a time-walker, Hadley."

"Are you kidding me?"

A snicker from the corner of the room was the only sign Henry was listening to our conversation. His face was hidden behind the latest edition of *The Times*, one of the only London-based newspapers still offering print copies, but I didn't need to see past the paper to envision the grin on his face.

"Careful, lass. You'll catch flies with your mouth open like that," Henry said.

"How do you know what my expression looks like?"

Another snicker from Henry was all I could expect in answer. I redirected my attention to Fitz.

"We're about to transport?" I asked.

Fitz chuckled. "Go on, then. Tell me where we're going."

"The Virgin Islands."

"*Nice*, Hadley." He smirked. "Okay, chug that water."

I followed his instruction quickly.

"Now come here."

With one arm secured around my waist, he urged me to remove my slippers and pulled me snugly against his body.

"Hold on tightly," he whispered, his breath warm on my ear. "And whatever you do, do not let go of me while we're in the in-between."

I was about to ask what he meant when the world spun, sliding away from the light, and weightlessness consumed our bodies. Ever so slowly, stars came into focus, their illumination momentarily jarring after the absolute darkness. Mesmerized, I extended an arm before Fitz reminded me to hold on to him. The stars faded away, replaced by many indiscernible objects, each swimming around us. Color returned, bringing shades of blue and green into my vision, along with the oppressive weight of gravity.

The spinning ceased, revealing ocean, sun, and land. I gasped when my toes met smooth, warm sand.

Unlike the beaches I'd visited in my short lifetime, the lush tree line mingled with the sand, the palm trees providing a welcome refuge from the bright rays of the sun.

"Welcome to St. John."

Stunned, I grasped his hand tighter and walked toward the crystal-clear water, mesmerized as it sparkled like hundreds of diamonds in the afternoon sun.

"How long can we stay?" I asked.

"We don't have to be back in Edinburgh until tomorrow morning."

"Will Henry be worried?"

"Not in the slightest."

"This is the best birthday gift I've ever received."

We journeyed over to Cruz Bay, securing essentials for an afternoon by the sea. We traded our warm clothes for swimsuits and staked our claim on a deserted stretch of sand. As I sank into a beach chair, Fitz floated a Corona in my direction, and I fired off my first question.

"Does it always happen like that?" I asked.

"Like what exactly?"

"The darkness, the stars, the spinning."

"Oh aye. It's always been like that. We're navigating through elements and time in order to find another place."

"How difficult is that for you?"

"Very," Fitz said. "It takes loads of practice and concentration. It's my most difficult power to control."

"Can you go anywhere?"

"Anywhere on Earth. Any further and you begin to deal with gravity in a different way. The distance alone is pretty troubling."

"You say you're navigating through time," I said. "Can you visit the future or the past?"

"I can visit the past, not the future. Though witches can see the future, it isn't a certain track. We're not omniscient, so we only see the future in a limited way."

"What do you mean?"

"There are unknowns," Fitz said. "Everyone changes their mind. When we make a decision, we alter the future. If we change our mind, we alter the future again. Then there's Fate . . . and God."

"So, with varying levels of power mixing with God and Fate, witches have limited future vision," I said.

"Right. You might set out to travel to one particular part of the future, but with the threads of time and humanity changing, you could land in some type of non-reality, basically trapped in time."

"That sounds like my worst nightmare."

"It would be anyone's worst nightmare," Fitz said.

"So, the future is an ever-changing beast, best left alone."

"It isn't stable enough for someone to physically transport themselves, especially with how quickly it changes."

"This is so fascinating!" I said. "Do you transport often?"

"No. It's tiring, especially when I bring someone along. Of course, that depends on the distance or how far into the past I'm traveling. But sometimes I take off on a whim."

"What about the past? Have you visited it much?"

"Some. I only stay for a short period of time. I don't want to accidentally alter the past. It's tricky and tiring, but the experience is truly incredible," Fitz said. "We'll pick a year and go when we have more time."

The sun descended, announcing the approaching evening, and I envied its calm path, sinking into the arms of the night. It was a stark contrast to the thoughts pinging around my mind. The past swirled all around me. My mate could transport us to anywhere in the world, and to any time in the past. We were witches. I'd fallen for him at twenty-seven, nearly lost him, and found him once more.

I climbed out of my chair and waded knee-deep into the gentle water of the Caribbean. I questioned who was nearby, awakening my mind's eye. A boat lay far off the coast, loaded with wealthy college students on school break. Around the corner—separated from us by large, slippery rocks—were two newlyweds, caught up in each other. Outside these few people, Fitz and I were alone on this tiny portion of the island, for which I was grateful.

I felt Fitz's presence behind me. His hands found my waist as his face nestled into the crook of my shoulder, planting a kiss on the sensitive skin. A low sigh escaped my lips, encouraging him as he slid his hand across my abdomen, leaving a trail of goosebumps in the wake of his fingers. Magic brought his desire to life as it twirled my body around slowly to face him. He searched my eyes, his fingers tracing the length of my cheek before planting a slow, long-awaited kiss on my parted lips.

Even though forming our connection had solidified our relationship and crafted a profound intimacy between us, everything felt more precious after facing the council together. But regardless of the cause, desire coursed through me even stronger than before. Fitz paused, his eyes searching mine.

"Do you know how much I love you?" I asked, running my fingers along the stubble on his jaw.

Fitz leaned into my palm, kissing it. "I can't even think straight. Our desire is clouding my mind, and I . . . Hadley, I know we've tried to pace ourselves, but my god, do I want you."

"Then don't hold back," I whispered.

A shift sounded through our connection, and for a few seconds, I struggled to identify what it was. Then, exhilaration pulsed through me, and I identified the former feeling—happiness had replaced a restrained tension that had existed from the very moment we'd met. It was so familiar that I had thought the sensation normal, and the newfound freedom in Fitz's energy was intoxicating.

He lifted me into his embrace. I wrapped my legs tightly around his waist as he walked us toward the dense tree line. He flicked his wrist, and a large blanket appeared under the canopy of the palm trees. Fitz dropped to his knees, lowering us onto the blanket.

Fitz scanned the area around us, and the air shifted. He was creating a privacy shield.

I took stock of my mate, and he watched as my eyes swept his body. I traced the muscular outlines along his chest with my fingertips and further down to his sculpted abdomen. His head tilted back, eyes closed, before a smirk formed on his lips. A burst of euphoria hit me as our connection intensified.

I slipped my hands through his hair as he leaned forward and kissed me. I tried to tug him closer to me, but he pulled away. He shook his head playfully before reaching behind my back to untie the strings of my swimsuit and tossed it aside. His eyes lingered, and his attention quickened my pulse.

Fitz ran his fingers across my collarbone to my shoulder, then lightly down my spine before tracing lower to my hips where he found his grip. His lips took their time studying the curves of my body, like he meant to learn every inch of it through touch. Goosebumps spread across my skin, and my mind grew thick. I was operating on instinct as the final threads of our connection began to take shape.

When Fitz's eyes returned to mine, a small intake of air rushed through his lips.

"What is it?" I whispered.

"Your eyes," he returned softly. "They're in flames again."

"Fitting."

"Aye. Fiery you are." He ran his thumb across my bottom lip. "My wee firecracker."

I looked deeply into his eyes, and my breath hitched. "I would have waited forever for you. Lifetimes, even. This—what we have—it was worth the risk," I said.

Fitz's gaze softened, and as I leaned in to kiss him, he wrapped his strong arms around me. His touch was filled with desire, but it was his energy I noticed most. For the first time since I'd known Fitz, all of our troubles melted away, and our bodies released the last of our tension, our anxieties. We were perfectly at peace with each other, and I finally knew Fitz in his purest form.

As our desire propelled us forward, a fire raged within me, and the warmth pumping through my veins grew until I thought it might consume me from the inside out. I moved against Fitz, and he rolled us to the ground. We were beyond words now, and the air was quiet except for our quickening breath. I was no longer in command of my body, my mind lost in the haze, and instincts took full control.

I arched my back as we embarked into the last of our unknown territory. Sparks floated lazily in the space surrounding us like fireflies lighting a horizon at dusk. I was certain I had lost myself in a dream as we cradled each other in magic, untamed and infinite. Time seemed to stand still as we held tightly to pink sunsets, warm breezes, and the most devoted hearts.

CHAPTER TWENTY-TWO

The following afternoon found us back at Henry's. Fitz and I continued our work on my fire skills, and eventually, we decided to retire to Henry's sitting room to relax.

Henry grinned broadly before passing wine glasses to Fitz and me.

"Hadley, I hear this is a favorite of yours, so I ordered a few bottles for the bar," Henry announced, his large, hazel eyes twinkling mischievously. My mouth gaped as I sniffed the dark liquid.

"This is the Chateau de Ferrand we had in Paris."

I looked to Fitz, who nodded in affirmation.

"Henry!" I said. "I can't tell you how appreciative I am of all this, and not only the wine. Thank you for letting me practice here."

"Oh, dinnae mention it, lass. You know you're welcome anytime."

Henry raised his glass, and we followed suit. "*Slàinte mhath!*"

We sank into large, leather chairs near the unlit fireplace.

"Hadley, perhaps you could do the honors," Henry said.

I inhaled deeply and envisioned the neatly stacked wood alight in flames . . . and it was.

"Nicely done," Fitz said, a proud gleam in his eyes.

"Brilliant," Henry concurred.

I settled deeper into the couch, allowing the sounds of the crackling fire and the taste of good drink to relax me as my toes warmed from the nearby heat.

"Well," Henry began. "The council called. They're sending out that trainer."

"Today?" I asked.

"Aye. They phoned about ten minutes ago and said he would be here soon."

"Ready or not," I muttered.

"If you're no ready, I'll request he come back another time," Henry said. "You've had a busy few days, and this is last minute."

"I'm fine to meet him today. I don't think we'll be doing any training this afternoon."

Fitz nodded.

A noise in the hallway disturbed the quiet of the sitting room. I turned toward the door, noting the extra wine glass sitting on the table. I had missed that earlier. Soon enough, Henry's housekeeper, Olga, shuffled into the room to announce a visitor. Henry requested she bring our guest in, and she smiled softly before nodding and disappearing through the entryway.

I wasn't sure what I had expected, but it surely wasn't what followed. A tall, muscular frame filled the doorway, and though I recognized his face instantly, I wasn't prepared for the charge of energy that accompanied him.

"Holy shit. You're a witch."

Tanner. He was one of the few people I thought I knew like the back of my hand, but I had clearly missed one very important detail.

Tanner ran a hand through his dark hair and crossed the room, lifting my rigid body off the ground and into a warm embrace. "Nice to see you too, Hads."

"You've got to be kidding."

"Now, is it the witch part or the council part that's throwing you off here?"

"Uh, both. Obviously," I said.

"Right, *obviously*." Tanner grinned. "The witch part does make sense when you think about it, right? I mean, didn't you ever wonder about us? Everyone else did. How we could be so close, spend all that time together, but with nothing happening in the romance department?"

He was right—we were magnets, but there was never any sort of romantic chemistry between us. Everything was starting to make sense.

"Everyone found our relationship odd, except for us," I said.

"We were kindred spirits—the same species surrounded by a lot of humans."

"Jordan . . ."

"Jordan was used to your oddities years before I ever entered the picture," Tanner said. "I probably make about as much sense to her as you do, but it works somehow."

"Well, I declare."

"You sound just like Gram!"

"You do know how to compliment a girl," I said, beaming ear to ear.

Staring at my companion of many years, the urge to give him a nice smack to the back of the head overwhelmed me, and I acted on that desire.

"What was that for?" Tanner asked, rubbing the back of his head.

"For keeping a secret from me," I said.

"Because I had a choice?"

I gave him an amused look.

Fitz interjected into the conversation, and he and Tanner shook hands. I couldn't help but think of all that had passed since I'd witnessed their first meeting over that very gesture. Tanner's expression dulled. I didn't expect him to have the same reaction to Fitz as he did to me, but something seemed off between them.

An introduction to Henry followed. Henry offered Tanner a drink, and we settled back by the fire.

"Is our friendship organic?" I asked.

"What do you mean?" Tanner asked.

"She's wondering if the council prompted you to make friends with her," Fitz clarified.

"This might be difficult to believe, but no. Our friendship was totally organic. I had no idea I'd be asked to assess you one day."

"But you knew I was a witch coming into my powers, right?" I asked.

"Yeah, absolutely. I figured that out pretty fast. I wanted to be careful around you, but we just bonded, you know? I didn't think our friendship would be a problem, but I got the MacGregors' blessing once they entered the picture."

"Really?" I turned toward Fitz.

"Dad told him to be careful around you, but he didn't see any harm in it."

"Okay, wait . . ." I said, trailing off.

"Yes, detective?"

"You started training hard right before I left the lake for Boston."

"Yeah," Tanner said. "The council hired a buddy of mine—you remember Slingshot?"

"How could I forget?" I returned drily. He'd never been a good influence on Tanner.

"Yeah, so they hired him as a trainer around that time, and he knew another position was going to open up in about a year or so. These positions are the kind you work your ass off to get a shot at because they don't come up very often, so I decided to go for it."

"When did the council hire you?"

"You remember that interview I was telling you about on the way to the airport?"

"No way," I said.

"Yep," Tanner said. "Apparently, they canceled the rest of the candidate interviews after meeting with me and offered me the job. Pretty strange actually."

"Are you moving to Edinburgh then?" Fitz asked.

"I don't know. I started working with the Washington council, and they asked me to consult on a 'special project,' so I got on a flight two days ago, and now I'm here . . . to assess your powers."

Silence fell, and truthfully, we were all a bit shellshocked.

"Well," Henry finally began. "I dinnae know about you, but none of this sounds like happenstance to me."

Fitz shook his head. "It can't be. The councils know about their connection. That's why they transferred Tanner over here."

Tanner nodded slowly. "Are you comfortable with this, Hads?"

"I wouldn't trust anyone else. You know that."

We decided Tanner would begin his assessment the following day, and with that, we allowed the conversation to meander toward everyone growing better acquainted. Touching on the subject of acquiring our powers, Henry shared his own story of coming into the craft.

"You caused an *earthquake?*" I marveled.

"Aye."

"What on earth were you doing to cause an earthquake?"

"Oh, that's the best part, isn't it, mate? He was planting a garden for his mother," Fitz answered, howling with laughter.

"And, of course, earth witches think this story is quite funny," Henry said eyeing Fitz. "It was a minor occurrence, but an earthquake nonetheless. It takes air witches a bit longer to command the earth elements, but eventually, I sorted it out."

"I heard that," Tanner said.

"You're an air witch too?" I asked.

"Yeah," Tanner confirmed. "It's the most common for elemental witches."

Henry took notice of Fitz's lingering amusement, and his eyes narrowed. A book then flew from a nearby table, its trajectory set for the back of Fitz's head. Just as I thought it would make contact, Fitz caught the book mid-flight, and with minimal effort.

"Fitz is annoyingly proficient in his magic—almost impossible to catch off guard," Henry offered, rolling his eyes.

"He's quick too," I said. "You should've seen him *move* when I almost lit him up with my fire pistols."

It was Henry's turn to laugh. "Maybe I should join your training after all."

"I'll inevitably entertain you with my witchy antics."

"Of that, you may be certain," Fitz added, a boyish grin spreading across his lips.

I took Fitz's hand in mine, and our energies relaxed. After tying our threads together in every possible way, I found our connection was stronger—and more palpable—than ever.

"Oh, shit," Tanner said.

"What is it?" I asked.

"You two are mated."

I laughed softly and nodded.

"When did that go down?"

"A week ago."

"It's pretty intense," Tanner observed.

"Aye," Henry agreed. "They have a strong bond. It's impossible to find where one energy ends and the other begins. It's all tangled up, and I cannae sort it."

"That's quick."

"I think she's known subconsciously since we met," Fitz said. "A part of our connection formed long ago."

Tanner whistled.

"Aye, muddles your brain, doesn't it?" Henry said.

Tanner nodded. "Well, I'm happy for you, Hads."

Tanner's energy didn't match his words, but I decided to let it slide until I had a chance to speak with him alone. His eyes flickered to mine, and I nodded, reassuring him that I was fine. Tanner's eyes were noticeably lighter than normal, seemingly russet and rimmed in gold. They brought a long-standing observation to mind.

"Tanner, why do your eyes change color?" I asked.

"You noticed that?" he asked. "Damn, I thought I was so careful with you."

"Not much gets past her," Fitz said, shaking his head lightly.

"Electrokinesis is one of my powers. When I use it, my eyes get lighter—something to do with the electricity. Anyway, it takes a while for them to fade back to a darker brown."

"So, you can . . . manipulate electricity?" I clarified.

"Yeah. I mean, it's nothing crazy. The same way you have fire, I have electricity." He shrugged.

The look on my face made him smile, and I was glad to see him release some of the tension from our previous conversation.

"How does that work if you're an air witch?" I asked.

"Electricity is energy. The way that the air fuels my magical energy generates electricity."

My mind reeled in complete wonderment.

We spent a few more hours beside the fire, and eventually our energies all settled into one another. Tension faded from the air, allowing me to breathe easily again. At some late hour, we began trading stories of our magical experiences and laughing like old friends. And for those few hours, I was content to let myself believe everything would turn out all right.

As we drove back to town, I asked Fitz about a couple of observations I made about Tanner.

"Is my energy off, or was it Tanner's?"

"What are you asking exactly?"

"I felt a tension between the two of you," I said.

Fitz sighed. "Aye."

"Care to expand on that?"

Fitz shot a look from the corner of his eyes.

"Please," I said.

"It's complicated. It all started at the lake."

I nodded.

"Dad was following orders, and Tanner disagreed with the way your case was being handled. He didn't like having to hide who he was from you. And we agreed with that—none of us wanted to conceal our true selves from you."

"Did he know your plan?" I asked.

"Not for a long while. But the day you left for Boston, Tanner paid me a visit." He paused. "It wasn't pleasant."

"What happened?"

"We argued, but eventually, I shared my plans with him. And he offered to help."

"*Really?*"

Fitz nodded. "I didn't think you would be keen on it since you care for Tanner like a brother, so I was hesitant. But he was persistent. If you want to know the god-honest truth, he applied to that position for you. It was his way to break into the councils' ranks."

"And no one thought to tell me this?" My voice rose.

"His tale isn't mine to tell. He asked me not to say anything so he could share everything with you himself. I think that's a conversation he'd like to have with you one on one, and I've already said too much."

I sighed, perhaps a bit dramatically, but Fitz kept his focus on the road. "Is there anything else you know that's going to blindside me? Because if you do, tell me right now. I'm tired of this."

"Hadley . . ."

"Are you keeping something from me? Anything at all?"

"Hadley, I've told you that you're a witch, what the councils knew, how I was feeling, all that. This is different though. I'm not even keeping my promise to Tanner by telling you this much. Damned if I do, damned if I don't."

"This is so messed up," I said. "I hate what the government has done to us."

Silence fell. I watched the rain streak down the passenger side window as I allowed my thoughts to roll through the new information about Tanner.

"Just tell me this . . ."

"Hadley."

"Did he already know I was meeting you in Paris before I told him?" I asked.

"No. Henry was the only one who knew ahead of time. I wanted someone to know where we were, but I was worried about the councils finding out, so I kept those details from everyone else. Of course, Tanner called me as soon as his best mate shared the secret with him . . ."

"Yeah, that one was my bad. But I only told Tanner because—"

Fitz waved his hand. "I'm not angry with you, Hads. You don't have to explain it to me."

I sank further into my seat, focusing on the patter of rain falling outside the car, and wished for the millionth time that these circumstances had never found us.

CHAPTER TWENTY-THREE

We'd just finished breakfast the following morning at Fitz's flat when I pushed for more information on Esther's ring.

Fitz topped off his coffee and settled onto the couch beside me. His finger circled the smooth surface of the moonstone in my ring. I leaned forward.

"I told you Esther was murdered in the witch trials. She wore the ring until the end of her life. Her husband Hamish was meant to retrieve the ring immediately after her death, but he was consumed with grief . . . Our family thought after strangulation, the captors would burn her remains at the stake. When collecting the ashes, he would also collect the ring . . ."

He trailed off momentarily.

"But they didn't?"

"They decided to burn the bodies in barrels of hot tar."

"Holy hell," I said. "I mean, I know it's all horrible, but that feels even more barbaric? I mean, it honestly just feels weirder somehow."

"Aye, it was."

"So, he didn't have any remains to collect," I gathered.

"Right. Then he wasn't sure about the ring, whether or not it was still in the tar or if it was taken before that. So, he and another witch combined forces and discovered someone removed it right after she was strangled."

My stomach turned as I considered how horrible an end those poor souls had endured, and my heart sank thinking of Esther.

"I feel so badly for Hamish. I can't imagine."

"Right. Hamish had already been through hell before he even lost Esther."

"Like what?" I asked.

"Oh, I'll give you a history lesson later," Fitz offered with a wink. "The MacGregors were outlawed by the king. Esther and Hamish assumed the last name Lockie for a time."

"So, you come from a distinguished line of outlaws?"

"Aye, just like me." He smiled. "We found his journal in the attic at my great-grandparents' house when we were organizing a few years back. Hamish never forgave himself for not solving the mystery of the ring. He felt like he dishonored Esther by not carrying out her final wish."

"Fitz, there were a lot of innocent souls lost to the trials, and most of them weren't even witches. But Esther was. Why didn't she resist or flee?"

"She had a good reason," Fitz said. "The most powerful witch in Scotland sat on the witch-hunting committee."

I gasped.

"He infiltrated them to prevent as many deaths as he could, but he had to remain inconspicuous. He couldn't be overzealous."

"This witch couldn't save Esther?"

"No, and he wouldn't allow Esther to resist by utilizing magic. She was quite powerful, but not powerful enough to stand against him. She also had three children to consider."

"He would've leveraged the children against her," I said.

"In a heartbeat. She had no choice but to bow to Fate. So, she didn't resist arrest, endured torture, and was brutally murdered."

"How was she compromised?" I asked.

"There was a woman named Helen Guthrie at the heart of the Forfar witch trials," Fitz explained. "She was arrested along with her thirteen-year-old daughter. Helen realized that as long as she remained useful to her captors, she would stay alive and have the chance to protect her daughter."

"It would be easy to hate her if it weren't for the fact that she was a mother protecting her daughter—no matter the cost."

"Harsh times, harsh measures I suppose. Helen told all she knew and all she could imagine. She implicated several women: some witches, some humans. Helen exaggerated Esther's ability of foresight and claimed she used it to alter the future in evil ways, doing the bidding of the devil. Esther didn't stand a chance."

"How did she know about Esther being a witch?" I asked.

"I can't say for sure, but I imagine it was the result of Esther slipping up in front of the wrong person. Or another witch sharing information on Esther to protect themselves."

"Makes sense."

"Hamish searched tirelessly for the ring," Fitz continued. "He scoured the village, used locator spells, but the ring was gone. Another witch must've taken it; a human couldn't have concealed it from Hamish. I'd like to honor Esther and Hamish by finding that ring."

Esther and Hamish MacGregor. Though I couldn't alter the past, I could at least ensure they weren't forgotten.

"What has you worried?" I asked.

"You feel that, huh?"

"Of course, I do."

"Esther saw her fate as a young woman, and it haunted her family until their last days. Her parents, aunts, and uncles all channeled their powers into the ring right before their deaths. Before Esther's capture, her only living aunt brought the ring to her. There was nothing Esther could do, and her aunt Annabel was left with a big responsibility."

"This was their attempt to save her life?"

"Aye, the ring held immense power—power that was forbidden. One of our laws states that you aren't allowed to host or harbor a witch's power in an object."

"Why?"

"Two reasons: taking power from another witch is a heinous act," Fitz said. "But it would also make anyone too powerful if they controlled the power of multiple witches. You see how your strength grows in certain areas, and that's only from our energies reacting with each other's. Can you imagine controlling the power of five witches?"

You'd be unstoppable, I realized.

"The ring could fall into the wrong hands. Maybe it already has . . . I think of the evil our kind has battled over the years and wonder if my family's power is being used by the wrong team."

"I know you have meetings to prep for, but show me your research later? After all, you did agree to let me help you, remember?"

"Aye. Thanks, Hads."

— CHAPTER TWENTY-FOUR —

With Fitz's afternoon schedule full of meetings at the university, I used the time to pack the last of my neglected belongings in my hotel room. We hadn't spent a night apart since the evening the witch followed me, and it seemed like staying at his place was a natural progression in our relationship.

I walked halfway through the room before realizing my suitcase was propped open near the window—not where I'd left it. Housekeeping might have moved it, I reasoned, though I'd declined service for days. I tiptoed the final distance, holding my breath as I peeked into the bathroom. Unused towels were strewn about the floor and vanity.

Not housekeeping.

I assessed the remainder of the room, prepared to shriek and run for the door should I find someone lurking under the bed or in the closet—I'd watched one too many horror movies when I was younger. I came up empty-handed and fell onto the bed in relief, allowing my heart rate to steady.

Realizing I'd forgotten my phone on Fitz's coffee table, I scanned each of the misplaced items, committing them to memory. I closed my eyes and searched the energy of the room, seeking any sign that it had been the work of the Parisian stalkers. The energy slowly registered, and though it felt familiar, I was certain it wasn't them.

I tossed my belongings into the suitcase, tugged at the zipper, and made a mad dash for the lobby, strong waves of anxiety rolling through my body. I rushed through checkout as the prickle of another witch hung heavily in the air, a warning that I was under watch. Unlike the previous occasions, no witch's glance chilled my back, but though the witch attempted to mask their stare, my witch's eye perceived their presence.

I paused at the front door, allowing the bellman to load my belongings into the cab. Standing in the cool afternoon light, I sensed an energy shift, and slowly but surely, an icy chill ran up my spine.

The bellman opened the cab door, and I slid into the backseat of the taxi, taking the opportunity to follow the trail of energy.

A man stood in the hotel doorway, unmistakably witch, and the chill grew stronger as I met his eyes. His pale, icy blue eyes glowed against his light brown skin and dark hair. His triangular face was chiseled and covered in dark stubble, and his light V-neck tee showed off a strong body. He would have been attractive if not for the uneasy feeling his gaze sent through me.

The slamming of the car door did little to dispel my growing anxiety. I held the witch's gaze firmly, refusing to release him as the cab drove away.

Fitz was waiting at home when I arrived. He must have felt my nerves; he was wearing holes in the hardwood as I entered the living room. When I shared that a witch was watching me at the hotel, his eyes darkened.

"Again?" Fitz yelled.

"You don't have to yell," I said. "You're such a brute when you're pissed."

"That's what this witch is about to learn."

"Oh god."

The look he sent in my direction could have killed someone, but he took a deep breath and exhaled slowly as I stared unfazed in his direction.

"I don't know what the hell they want, and it worries me," Fitz said.

"He."

"What?"

"You don't know what the hell *he* wants."

"You saw him?"

"Yeah, or I saw someone," I said. "I can't say for sure it was the same witch all three times, but I think so."

"What did he look like?"

"Tall, built, maybe mid-thirties? Light brown skin. And blue eyes."

I shuddered. "They were this icy, transparent blue. When our eyes met, I felt cold."

"I don't know anyone who fits that description. If this isn't the council, then I have no idea who it is. I'll call my dad and see if he might know him."

"That's a good start. We need to figure this out."

"We'll sort it, but for now, maybe you shouldn't be alone unless necessary."

"You think he'd approach me?" I asked.

"Maybe. He probably wouldn't cause a scene in public. If he caught you off guard with no one around, though . . ." He trailed off, his knuckles white from clenching.

"He was pretty brazen, like he wanted me to see him, but if he had any intention of approaching me, he had his chance."

"Hadley. What are you not telling me?"

I paused, taken aback by the venom in his voice.

"Please," he whispered, squeezing his eyes shut. "Just tell me."

"Someone ransacked my hotel room."

Fitz's eyes flew open, though he remained silent.

"I thought maybe it was housekeeping at first. But it wasn't. Someone moved my stuff, threw towels around—I guess to see if I'd hidden anything? And there was a . . . strange energy in the room."

"So, this bastard went into your room."

"It seems that way," I said.

"Seems that way?"

"Well, I don't have hard evidence it was him. It just seems highly likely considering he was watching me."

"I'll kill him," Fitz said.

"You'll do no such thing!"

"You'll no sit here and defend this bastard," he returned, teeth gritted.

"I'm not defending him."

"If you dinnae want him harmed, you'll be disappointed if I see him, if I *ever* feel his presence again."

"Fitz . . . You'll *have* to show some restraint."

"I cannae help myself. My instincts will be too strong."

"You'll control yourself. I know you can be smart about this."

Fitz shook his head, his gaze fixed on the open window.

"Look at me," I said.

He made no effort to do so. I closed the gap between us and reached for his jaw. He caught my hand in his, and his eyes were stormy as they met mine.

"Do you no want my protection?" he asked, though his voice was losing its edge. "You may no want it, but you need it. You're still learning. You're still growing in your magic."

I sighed.

"I told you my stream formed long ago, and with it, I gave you my love, my loyalty, my protection. I've focused on shielding you from harm for so long . . ." He trailed off. A breathy laugh escaped his lips humorlessly. "I'm content to be your sword and your shield for as long as you have need of it. Truthfully, I dinnae know how to be anything other than this."

His confession filled my veins with tender warmth. I'd been so caught up in what he'd hidden from me that I hadn't truly understood the toll our situation had taken on him or the role it had forced him into.

With my free hand, I ran my thumb along his lips. He raised my hand that he still held in his and leaned forward to kiss my wrist.

Goosebumps rippled across the tender skin.

"I want all of you, Fitz. Every little bit that makes you who you are. But I'm growing into my power. I'm not the lost girl you fell in love with at the lake."

Fitz nodded. "I know."

"There's a freedom in that," I said. "A freedom for us to find our balance. We'll both want to protect each other, but that's not your identity. That's not your sole purpose."

"My purpose is to love you. I protected you because that's what you needed most."

"Now, I need a partner in life. And I know that's what we'll be to each other."

"Aye." He pressed his forehead to mine. "But when it comes to this witch who's watching you . . . I don't think you should be alone. It's not wise."

"I'll text Mia," I said, inwardly groaning at the thought of our partnership with her.

"Good."

"We'll figure this out. This witch won't win."

"You might be right, but if it's all right with you, I think I'll act as your shadow for a wee bit longer—until you're further along in your training." He slid his arm around me absentmindedly, pulling me tightly against his chest.

"Fitz," I whispered, warm adrenaline pulsing just under the surface even though the thought of my supernatural stalker was far away.

Fitz rested his hands on either side of my shoulders and placed his forehead against mine. We stood motionless, suspended in time, closing our eyes to savor the moment.

Then he tilted my face upward to meet his gaze before kissing underneath my jawline. He worked his way to my lips, kissing me thoroughly. My sigh encouraged him further. He pinned my hands above my head, and I stood on my tiptoes to kiss him again. Our energy flowed freely between us—witch to witch—until we found what we sought and ended up tangled on the floor, watching the rise and fall of our chests moving in time with each other.

I wrapped my leg around his and pushed myself against him, my head tucking tenderly under his chin.

"The way I feel for you, Hadley . . . words aren't sufficient."

"I hope you know I feel the same. Never doubt my love for you."

CHAPTER TWENTY-FIVE

The next day, I sat on the back porch of Henry's estate, waiting for Tanner to wrap his mind around how to explain everything to me. He'd listened to my long-winded argument about how unfair I found the situation without interruption.

Finally, he broke the silence.

"I understand how you're feeling. I'd feel the same way. It feels like we've bamboozled you, right? But I want you to know something. We only did this to protect you, and I know we would do it all over again if it means you're safe."

I leaned back in my seat. I knew that, and I appreciated it, though I wasn't ready to let him know that.

"I don't like that I'm just finding all this out," I said.

"I know. But you needed to know you were a witch before you could understand the reason behind any of this."

"I get that. But learning that so many witches were keeping me safe while I didn't understand a damn thing about it is not a fun feeling."

"Yeah, I bet," Tanner said. "No one ever wanted to hide anything. I promise you that. We just wanted to figure this all out so you could move on and be who you were meant to be."

I nodded, parsing slowly through the information.

"We tried to make the right decisions," Tanner said. "I mean, I was against it at first, but once I understood everything, it was an easy decision to help."

"What changed your mind?" I asked.

"When we were at the lake, I fought a lot with Ian. I felt like it was unfair that you were being observed without your knowledge. I didn't get how complicated your status was. I'd never spent time around someone in your situation. If the councils didn't do this, you might have gotten yourself into a lot of trouble or hurt yourself. But it still felt wrong."

He paused. "I fought with Fitz too. I'm sure he told you that. But he was the one who helped me understand how dangerous your situation was. I didn't understand the stakes. And once I understood, I stopped fighting and started helping. All we wanted was to find a way for you to match to your power and live a good life."

"And you thought it was best that I didn't know too," I said.

"Yeah. You can't sit there and tell me that if you knew the truth, it wouldn't have wrecked everything. I know you better than that, Hads. Fitz does too. You would have obsessed over it. Plus, we knew the government might wipe your memories. So, I decided to help him figure out how to beat the councils."

I thought about the time I'd spent apart from Fitz: the panic attacks, the heartbreak, wondering who I was—*what* I was. Not knowing the facts had caused a fair amount of worry. I wondered if it would have been better—easier—if I had known the complete truth. I thought so, though if I was being fair, I couldn't know that for sure. It was irrelevant now, anyway.

"I know you'll be angry at all of us for a while," Tanner said. "That's okay. I'm just happy you're safe and that we can be open about everything now."

"You're right. I'll have to work through it. But even if I'm angry, just know that I understand the weight you carried—all of you."

Tanner nodded. "Fitz most of all. Go easy on him. I didn't at first, and I still regret that."

"You do?" I asked.

"I don't regret pushing him to a point where he let me in. But when he did, I realized how much of a toll it was taking on him . . . and that it would continue for however long it took us to sort all this shit out."

"Thank you for telling me that."

"It's something you should know."

"I'm sure I'll have more questions later. But for now, I guess we shouldn't keep Henry waiting much longer."

"Let's go get you assessed, woman," Tanner said.

Tanner, Henry, and I were sprawled out in front of a fire in Henry's sitting room in the midst of a training session while Fitz worked on his family research in Henry's office. As Tanner and I progressed through my assessment, we learned that I was gifted with mental transport. Though it felt like being a spirit-traveler was far less exciting than Fitz's abilities as a time-walker, mental transport did have one benefit over time-walking. I could travel through time and space, much like Fitz, but I couldn't be observed by the naked eye.

"Do you think spirit-travelers are to blame when humans think a ghost is around?" I asked.

Tanner and Henry looked to each other, their expressions quizzical.

"I've never thought about that before," Tanner said.

"Aye, me neither. That's a good question, lass." Henry paused, lost in thought.

"Some of their energy would be in the room. I learned that my first day on the job in Seattle," Tanner said. "We were assessing another spirit-traveler, and I felt the shift of energy when her spirit came in the room."

"Do you think a human would notice it?" I asked.

"That's the million-dollar question," Tanner said.

"We should test the theory sometime," I said.

"Aye, but you'll need to learn about the skill first," Henry said.

Henry wasn't gifted with mental transport but knew a great deal about it. After a fair amount of discussion on the subject, he agreed he'd provide training to the best of his ability while Tanner worked alongside him to assess the power. I'd need a couple of trainers to help me through my new skill set, and Tanner agreed Henry was a good fit.

"We'll start by identifying what you want," Henry said.

"Food."

He laughed.

"That is the most Hadley line I've heard in a long time." Tanner shook his head but smiled.

"A girl after my own heart, but I dinnae think that's going to help us here," Henry said.

"Right." I thought hard. "I want to see Gram."

"See her right now or in years past?"

"That's an option?" I asked.

"Aye. You can see her now, or you can see her at any point in her past. You have the power for it."

You have the power for it. I liked the sound of that.

"Do you have anything of hers on you?" Henry asked.

"These earrings." I tugged at the back and slipped an earring from my ear. "My grandddad gave them to her when they first married."

"Just one is sufficient. Hold it in your hand where you can see it."

"Like this?" I asked. The gold button earring sat upright in my palm, a delicate chain holding a diamond in place at the center.

"Perfect," Henry said. "You won't always need an object, but it's helpful when you have it, especially until you're proficient in the craft. Take a few deep breaths and relax."

I followed his instruction and fell into the steady rhythm of breathing.

"I can feel that you're trying to relax," Tanner said, "but your mind is too excited. Forget everything. Just breathe and listen to Henry's voice."

I closed my eyes and focused intently on my breath, pushing everything else from my mind. This was no different than my regular meditation, I reminded myself. My magic was instinctive, fueled by both need and strong desire. It had no use for frivolous thoughts.

"Connect with the earring and tell me what you feel," Henry instructed.

"I feel its strength . . . the ridges from how it's cut. The gold that keeps the diamond in place."

"Ask your witch's eye about the person who created it."

Nothing.

"Let everything else go," Henry prompted, sensing my difficulty.

The darkness faded as I focused, my curiosity taking root and revealing a dim, windowless room where a jeweler peered through a microscope. A cut jewel lay on the table in front of him, ready to be set.

My eyes popped open, pulling a smirk from Henry. "I saw the jeweler. He was looking at the diamond."

"Well done, you!"

"Nice job, Weston," Tanner said, typing notes on to the tablet resting on his lap.

Henry requested I navigate to the same vision once more before we moved to my next task. I did so dutifully, my sights set on mastery of another skill.

"Now you'll repeat the process, but I want you to find the day they were sold to your grandfather. Once you're in that vision, ask it to navigate to the time the earrings were given as a gift to your grandmother."

"Got it."

"Dinnae lose focus. Ask your vision for what you want to know—breathe. You have full control over where time takes you. It answers to *you.*"

Time revealed a salesman standing behind a jewelry counter filled with rows of gold, silver, and precious stones on a maroon bed of velvet. The salesman placed cash into the register while speaking with a handsome man in a navy suit. I recognized my young grandfather instantly, having seen his likeness in a frame by Gram's desk for as long as I could recall. The salesman handed a box topped with a big white bow over to Granddad, who ran his hand nervously through his short, blond hair before accepting it.

As he disappeared through the doorway, I asked time for a glimpse of Granddad gifting the earrings to Gram. The edges of my vision blurred, and the darkness grew until it was once again all I could see. I waited quietly, attempting to maintain focus, hoping I hadn't failed. I tore my interest away from the thought, returning to peaceful nothingness.

Light dawned, and Granddad walked into a room where a woman sat in a satin dress the color of pearls. Her long, auburn hair was curled about her face, which was carefully painted for the festive occasion, her blue eyes bright against her porcelain skin. Gram was beautiful, and I was grateful to catch a glimpse of an event I couldn't imagine if I tried. Their wedding photos had been destroyed in a fire years ago.

Granddad handed the box to Gram, who opened it slowly, as though she already knew what precious treasure lay inside. Once opened, a single tear ran the length of her cheek, and she embraced Granddad tightly. When Gram had gifted the set to me, she'd shared that Granddad was living on a small wage at the time and had gone without quite a few comforts in order to afford the gift.

I slowly navigated to the present and opened my eyes to Henry's studious face.

"How was it?"

"I don't have words . . . amazing."

"Think you're up for one more tonight?" Henry said.

"Yes, of course!"

"I dinnae want to overtax you."

"Henry, you two made me rest all day," I accused, pointing in Fitz's general direction in the adjoining room. "An entire day without magic! I'm going to explode magical energy everywhere if you don't let me do this."

Henry turned. "Tanner?"

"She's doing good, and her energy levels seem good too. I think it's fine to keep going."

I looked to Henry, a gloating smile on my lips.

"You were telling us earlier about the first time you accidentally read Izzy's mind. What if you traveled to that day? You can pick a scene from your own past," Henry said.

"That's going to be strange," I said.

"To say the least. But you need a recent destination after the last journey. Fitz has the watch Izzy gave him that summer."

Henry held the item in his open palm, a mischievous grin on his face.

"You sneak."

He passed the watch to me, and I sat motionless for a moment, preparing for another venture in time.

"Focus on what you want. Ask time to take you there."

I clutched the watch tightly and listened for the ripples of time, more aware of the experience than before.

I opened my eyes to a summer day in June. Everything was spectacularly clear through the kitchen window—giant spruce trees, swaying ferns, the sparkling lake.

I took a deep breath, trying not to lose my nerve.

Gram was working in the kitchen. She narrowed her big, blue eyes in concentration and reached for another mason jar. For as long as I could remember, she'd worn her hair cropped above her shoulders, warm auburn with sun-kissed strands, a testament to the amount of time she spent in her garden. Someone bounded down the stairs, pulling her focus away from her task, and my former self strolled into the kitchen.

The scene was vivid, and I could've sworn I was living the moment all over again.

"Where are you headed off to, Priss?" Gram asked, her southern accent thick. My heart swelled at the sound of her familiar, gravelly voice, which sparked countless treasured memories.

"I'm riding bikes with Izzy this afternoon."

"Nice girl."

"She *is* nice. There's something about her, though, that just doesn't . . ."

"Doesn't what, honey?" Gram questioned, a coy look on her face.

"This is going to sound stupid, but there's something about her that just doesn't seem quite human. She's too ethereal, too graceful."

Gram chuckled at my response, but an odd note rested in her laughter.

"What is it, Gram?"

"Oh, nothing. It's a silly thought, but I do know what you mean about her. The whole family is that way."

"You met the rest of her family?" I asked.

"Sure did."

"Did her family seem—I don't know—like her?" I recalled how desperate I was for information on the family. I had hoped to make sense of what I thought had happened the night before in my dream—or dreamlike state.

"I'd say so. Both kids were handsome, and how did you put it? Ethereal and plenty smart, too." With Gram that usually meant they had a quick sense of humor, one of the traits she admired most in a person.

Fitz and Izzy had stopped by that morning, just as Fitz promised, and I was thrilled when Izzy had asked me to hang out that afternoon. I wanted another chance to observe her—to make sense of her. I recalled the way Fitz had filled my mind with possibilities from the moment our eyes met. He was the first person to see me for who I really was. The girl before me had no idea about the love and magic that awaited her.

"What did you think about her parents?"

"Smart, funny, both seem pretty successful."

"I wonder what's up with them," I said, my mind spinning with possibilities.

"Maybe nothing, maybe something," she remarked, a twinkle in her eye.

Gram was more superstitious than anyone I'd ever met. There was rarely an old wives' tale or nontraditional remedy she didn't heed and pass along for future reference. As a child, I'd found it fascinating about her. As an adult, I'd found it quirky and endearing. And as a witch, I suspected that part of my power must have been passed down through her.

A rap on the door disturbed our conversation.

"I've got it," I said.

I was met by Izzy's bright smile when I swung open the door.

"I come bearing gifts." She passed through the door holding up a brown paper bag in one hand and a vase full of greenery in the other.

"What's all this?" I asked, eyeing the bag suspiciously.

"Your grandmother mentioned your dad's illness earlier and how she's been trying natural remedies to help him feel better in between treatments." She set the bag on the old, wooden buffet and pulled a large glass jar from it. "This is a blend of herbs that makes a nice tea. It'll help with the fatigue and with the nausea, too."

"Is that Izzy I hear?" Gram's voice floated in from the kitchen.

"Hi, Mrs. Weston!" she called. "I brought those herbs we talked about this morning."

Gram's eyes lit up as she entered the room. "Oh, that was fast. Thank you! And call me Gram—everyone does."

"Very well, Gram." She grinned.

"Izzy said she grows these herself, so I'll bet they have twice the healing power of what I've been getting at the store," Gram said.

"You grow this where you live in Seattle?" I asked.

"Aye. My roommate and I live in a townhome near the university, and we have a bit of yard. It's not nearly as much as I'd like, but it's a grand little space."

"What about this?" I asked, pointing toward the vase. Ferns were arranged beautifully around small branches of lush evergreen trees and expertly draped bunches of moss. A piece of burlap was topped with a sage ribbon and tied around the vase.

"Oh! These are for your dad's room. I harvested responsibly, but I wanted to bring a wee bit of nature to him. I know some days it's tough on him to be outside."

My eyes misted, and I caught Gram's gaze. She nodded. While my mind had been tied up in suspicion about my odd dream, Izzy had gone out of her way to be kind to my dad.

"That was really thoughtful. Izzy, thank you," I said.

"Don't mention it. Oh! And one last thing." She reached into the paper bag and pulled out a large mason jar filled with tiny crystal-like rocks. "These bath salts are the best I've found. All the way from Scotland." She winked. "But they smell lovely and soothe aches and pains. If they help, I have loads more at the house."

"Oh yeah, these'll do fine," Gram said, unscrewing the lid and taking an appreciative sniff. "Thank you, Izzy. This is mighty kind of you."

"Nae bother at all."

And in that moment, I didn't care about what had happened the night before.

I couldn't help but to hug her. She wrapped me in a tight embrace—the kind where you know the other person understands, the kind that stitches you back together when you're falling apart. She granted me comfort and validation in the way that only another woman could.

"Okay, let's get going?" I asked. "I could use some fresh air."

June was a tricky month on the Olympic Peninsula. One day might be hot and dry, while the next was cool and rainy. Izzy and I peddled along the gravel path until the tree line gave way to a clear view of the lake. We hopped down and walked to the end of a nearby pier. We sat in silence for a few moments, watching the cars zip along the 101 across the lake from us. Izzy laid back, stretching her arms and legs as far apart as possible.

"Do you think you'll take that job?" I asked.

"Which job?"

"The one your dad wants you to take after graduating?"

After a brief silence, Izzy pulled herself forward, leaning back on to her elbows. Her expression was indecipherable, but I already knew what I'd done.

"Or at least I thought you mentioned that yesterday. I must've made that up."

"You didn't make it up," she said.

"We don't have to talk about it. I'm sorry I brought it up."

"No, it's fine. I don't mind talking about it. I just don't remember telling you."

"You must have," I said. "I mean, how else would I know that?"

"How indeed," she pondered. I recalled how her gaze had lingered on me long enough to make me uncomfortable, but the end of her internal battle was clear in her eyes. "Well, if you know about it, I must have said something."

I had allowed my mind to grow too preoccupied with an event that must have been a dream . . . and I'd slipped with my very real oddity because of that.

I followed our path back to the cabin where Gram had fresh

lemonade waiting for us. A man's voice filtered through the front door, and I froze in recognition. Daddy. My thoughts raced around haphazardly. I knew I wasn't ready to see him—not like this. Tears welled as I asked time to release me back to my rightful place.

Tanner's eyes met mine, and he gave me a soft smile.

"I think I'll join Fitz and type up my report. Let's call it a wrap for the day." Tanner grabbed his tablet and left the room.

"Henry?"

"Aye, lass?" he asked.

"You said you don't have this power. How do you know so much about it?"

He sighed and reached for the nearest bottle of Scotch. "Fancy a glass?"

"I'm fine, thank you."

He poured a healthy serving, taking a sip of the amber liquid, and I waited patiently for him to begin. I came to the idea that perhaps I shouldn't pry, but then he began.

"I haven't talked about this much, but it'll be good to tell you. My mate, Emily, possessed your ability. I was with her during her training— that's why I know so much about it."

"I haven't heard you mention Emily before," I observed, leaning forward curiously. Neither Henry nor Fitz had ever talked about Henry's mate.

"It's no a story with a happy ending. I'll tell you nonetheless if you'd like."

I nodded sheepishly.

"I was thirteen when I met Emily. It's pretty rare, you know, for witches to find their mate so young, but we were lucky. Emily was beautiful and smart, with a quick, dry wit." He laughed, though without humor. "I was hopelessly in love with her. Our parents let us wed at sixteen. Our family and witch friends celebrated with us, but the humans wouldn't understand, not with our age."

He paused, pulling slowly from the glass.

"We did everything together. Studying, school, traveling. She loved to travel, and after we completed secondary school, we took a few years off, traveling and working around the world. We decided to come back to Scotland for uni. Dinnae get me wrong; things weren't perfect, but we were happy.

"Then a business trip to Inverness changed everything. We made a short holiday of her work trip. We drove up the Friday before and enjoyed the weekend. We were driving home—just outside the city. We were so close."

He hung his head quietly, breathing deeply. I placed my hand on his free one, and he held it for some time before pressing on.

"A drunk driver hit us. Nasty pig. Our bodies can withstand a great deal, Hadley. We can push past loads of human limits, but Emily couldnae do it. He was flying eighty miles an hour down the old lane. He slammed into us, pinning our car between his and a nearby building. Emily and I were both crushed. She died instantly."

"Henry . . . I am *so* sorry," I whispered. "I am so sorry this happened to you."

"I was a real mess after," Henry said. "Almost died myself. Broke most of the bones in my body, went into cardiac arrest, was in a coma for two days. I had a long road to recovery, and that was only physically. I didnae give a shite about anyone for a long time."

"You clearly do now."

"Aye. I was twenty-eight when Emily died. After about a year, I met Fitz. Best thing that could've happened to me. He helped me turn things around, go on to pursue my graduate degree, and honestly helped me become the man I wanted to be for Emily."

I smiled. That sounded like Fitz all right.

"I've been over it time and time again, punishing myself. Convinced there was something I could've done differently. I wish every day I had died instead of her. I'll never understand why it had to be her."

A tear rolled slowly toward his jaw.

I could have told him he lived for a reason. How grateful Fitz and I were to have him in our lives, or how Fate gave him a second chance, but none of it would change the fact that Emily was gone.

Instead, I wrapped my arms around him, locking us quietly in an embrace.

"I'm sorry," Henry said.

"What on earth are you apologizing for?" I asked, releasing him.

"You didnae ask me for all that."

"I'm sorry if bringing it up was too much," I said.

"No, I need to think about it sometimes. It ultimately helps, I think. I need to remember all of it—even the worst part of our story."

"Thank you for telling me about Emily. I'm glad you felt like you could."

"I had fifteen years with her," Henry said. "It was far too brief . . . but I know what it is to love someone with everything in me, and I'll carry that with me always."

"That's a gift for sure. And to have experienced so much life with her. A lot of people never have that."

"But you do—and you'll continue to grow. There are so many good things to come, Hadley."

"I'm a lucky girl," I said.

"Aye, and Fitz is one lucky bastard. He knows it too."

It was good to hear Henry laugh.

I couldn't begin to imagine what a loss like Henry's felt like, but my admiration for him grew. Those like him were special—the ones who loved, lost, and found the will to live again after tremendous tragedy.

Right on cue, Fitz entered the room, embracing Henry in an overly dramatic hug, pulling laughter from us all. Tanner followed shortly after, and we all stayed at Henry's late into the evening talking and laughing in a way that's only possible once you've opened yourself up to one another. When we left for the evening, I held Fitz tighter and dearer to me than before.

CHAPTER TWENTY-SIX

I sat on the edge of the bed the following morning while Fitz showered, reflecting on the many changes that had occurred over the past couple of years. I tried not to think of the past too often, following my therapist's advice that it was healthy to allow myself to feel and process grief, but it wasn't healthy to dwell. With all that had occurred since Paris, it had become difficult not to think about the summer I met Fitz. And in doing so, countless memories with my dad also bubbled up.

As my head sank into the soft pillow, I allowed my mind to return to a day I'd tried to forget for a long time. I closed my eyes, allowing the onrush of pain . . . but also the happiness of seeing Daddy's face again.

November 22, 2021 was a date I'd never forget. While my friends' families prepared for the upcoming holiday season, mine was focused on keeping my dad comfortable and in good spirits. He'd decided that morning that he wanted to go outside, and we had helped him walk to the back deck. He'd turned his face to the mist that drifted from the gray rainclouds and asked to sit in the doorway wrapped in a blanket.

But on his way back to bed, my dad had fallen in the hallway, unable to stand, and we had helped him to the bedroom. I'd never forget the pained look on Gram's face or my mother's strained response.

"Oh—Matt!"

It was her voice that had pierced me the most. It was almost a whisper . . . the whisper of a woman who felt completely defeated.

The chemo dragged on for months, the promise of it extricating the cancer turning to ash in our mouths. After each treatment, Dad felt increasingly weak for the following few days. My own mental strength withered with him, but I couldn't give up—my hope wasn't yet gone. After all, my dad was a tough guy, and growing up with him had been a splendid adventure. We'd spent countless days on the trails, chasing the mystique of the mountains. He'd always split his own firewood and fixed anything that broke around the house. As a child, I was convinced he could do anything.

But his illness finally forced me to acknowledge how completely helpless I felt.

I noticed the change of expression on his face, how his features seemed less bright and his skin less vibrant. I could no longer ignore the hollowness of his face, the loss of his beautiful dirty blond hair, and how his thick, athletic figure was wasting away. His structured jawline and gray eyes were the only familiar features I recognized in this foreign face.

Once we settled him into bed that afternoon, he was too weak to get up on his own again. His joints ached, he struggled to keep food down, and my entire world was crashing all around me. Mom, Gram, and I rotated sitting with him, helping him out of bed as needed and procuring anything that might make him more comfortable.

We discovered that if I made dinner, he wouldn't refuse to eat. So I handed Dad a bowl of pasta and sat at the foot of the bed to have dinner with him. He smiled before focusing on his food, and my heart warmed.

"I need you to make a promise to me," he said.

"Anything."

"You need to find a way to stop worrying so much about me."

"Dad . . ."

"I'm serious, Hadley." He leaned over in pain, even the act of conversing taking its toll on his energy, but I knew better than to tell him to rest. The man had always done just as he damn well pleased.

"Dad, you always put yourself last, but now isn't the time for that."

"I know you can't understand this now, but everything your mom and I have done from the moment we knew we were expecting you has been for you. Every decision with our home, our careers, our lifestyle . . . it's all been for you," he said. "You are my life's work. Having you put your life on hold for me would be the opposite of what I've wanted for you for the past twenty-eight years."

I had been debating my career decisions for post-grad school, and my dad encouraged me to look outside of Washington. I'd always dreamed of moving around but had decided against it when I learned of my father's diagnosis.

With this talk, he finally convinced me to follow my instincts and find the right fit for me, no matter the location.

When the job offer in Boston came up three months later, I discussed the offer with him. My dad told me I needed to take it. I'd never seen him prouder of me.

"I'm going to get better, and I'm going to come see you in Boston, Pumpkin," he said. "We'll have a blast."

I knew if I stayed in Washington rather than accept it, I'd not only let my father down, but I'd take away from any happiness he had while battling that monster.

It was with renewed purpose that I faced the soft glow of my laptop one late February evening, replying to the offer that had changed the course of my life.

In the couple of months after my move, he rallied, and we all felt real hope again. He somehow convinced my mother to drive him across the country in their camper. The doctors advised against it. My mom fretted the entire trip. I nearly had a stroke over it.

It took them two weeks because my mom worried about him being on the road. We meticulously planned the road trip so they could stop for his treatments. We didn't want to risk his health with the trip, but Dad was insistent. And he was extraordinarily happy sitting in my living room, a wide grin highlighting his features.

His miraculous turn continued for a couple of months, but he'd declined quickly last December. And that was that.

He never healed. I never had the chance to show him the harbor, the Freedom Trail, or my favorite parks—the particularly verdant ones that reminded me of home. We'd mourned beside his casket in January. But he had made it to Boston because he was my dad, and he was a man of his word.

CHAPTER TWENTY-SEVEN

"I think I found something," Fitz yelled across the room.

We'd practically, or perhaps not so practically, torn apart Henry's attic over the span of the past three days.

I was starting my new job on Monday, and we wanted to make some real progress on Fitz's family project over the next week before my attention was divided.

With Fitz delving further into his research, his dad sent over all the family records: journals, grimoires, enchanted objects, and the like. And by sent over, I meant that I stood in Henry's attic one afternoon with Fitz and Henry while the items suddenly materialized in the space.

The three of them felt the collection would be more difficult to locate in Henry's home should someone come snooping for information on the ring. All information regarding how to access the vast power held inside the ring needed to be carefully concealed. I had expressed concern over such a treasure lying in someone's attic, but Fitz was quick to point out how heavily protected it was.

"There's no need to worry. This protection spell Dad and I worked up is intricate. It would take someone a considerable amount of time and effort—enough that we'd feel it. And with the alarm spell, if they ever did sort it out, we'd know immediately."

"Sounds like you've thought of everything," I said.

"Almost."

As we turned most of our attention to the MacGregor family mystery, Fitz's dad partnered with the Scottish Council to investigate our problematic witch's identity. Divide and conquer, as they said. Between spending most of my time with Henry and Tanner, and with Fitz indeed acting as my shadow, I hadn't seen nor felt the snooping witch over the last week.

The three of us worked our way into the middle of a large, wooden chest and discovered a grimoire and a corresponding 1662 journal wrapped neatly in linen. The fabric alone betrayed their age, its color resembling that of the leather-bound books that surrounded it. Both had belonged to Esther's aunt, Annabel. Since she was the last living relative in the family pact and had gifted the ring directly to Esther, if there were any details surrounding spells for the ring, we'd find them in either of the two books.

Though Henry had assisted us in tearing through the attic earlier in the day, he drove to town for the evening and gave his housekeeper the night off—meaning Fitz and I would be able to examine the materials undisturbed by Olga, who was sweet but intrusive.

The oversized leather couch in the sitting room was to be our stage for further investigation of the books, and I bounded down the stairs, happy to leave the drafty attic behind.

The sitting room was a bit cool itself, and I extended my arm, tossing flames toward the neatly stacked logs in the fireplace.

They burst into a roaring fire, and I sank into the couch next to Fitz feeling quite satisfied. I'd never tire of fire bursting to life at my fingertips.

As an afterthought, Fitz nodded his head and a bottle of Glenfiddich and two glasses landed on the table in front of us.

"Henry keeps a few bottles around for me," Fitz said. "He prefers Bunnahabhain 25 Year, but I find I'm just not that extravagant."

I smiled at Henry's innate taste for the finer things and floated Annabel's journal to Fitz's side. In return, a crystal glass landed in my open palm, a thistle pattern distinct against the generous amber pour, and we settled down to the task of solving the mystery.

We found ourselves engrossed in Annabel's writings.

She'd left very specific incantations for her magic in the grimoire, and her journal held a fascinating account of life in 17th-century Scotland. Although the objective might have been searching for specific spells, we couldn't help but relay various spells and passages back and forth to each other.

The fire crackled through the evening, a soft soundtrack to the slow sipping of Scotch and the happy conversation between two history buffs combing through 17th-century artifacts.

Fitz was reading aloud from the journal, enjoying a particularly humorous account of Annabel's conversation with the local butcher, when the next passage caught his attention.

Took the wee item to E today while H and the bairns were away. Exceedingly surprised and angry at first, claiming we broke our word and wronged our brothers and sisters. She refused. I advysed hir of the great sacrifices we experienced to pass this to hir. Said she would be unable to use this item to hir benefit at any account. Eventually relented. Showed her S and P.

"'S' and 'P' . . . do you think she's referring to the spells?" I asked.

"Let's find out." Fitz lifted the grimoire on to the table and flipped back to the first page.

Each witch had a unique method for casting their own incantations, which ranged in complexity and strength. Though magic wasn't always worked through spells, Annabel had certainly cast a spell on this occasion. She would have taught Esther her spells in the hopes that only she would be able to access, use, and summon the ring—Esther, and her bloodline.

We carefully made our way through the incantations, and as we identified spells that were potential fits, I recorded them on my laptop. Then, Fitz recited the spell, and we waited. The spells worked, but the ring remained to be seen.

After four attempts and hours of study, we were losing steam.

"We'll find it," I said.

"Aye. Of course, we will." He placed his hand at the base of my neck and kissed me. "I'm glad to be doing this with you."

I smiled and squeezed his hand. "Here's the next spell." I turned the laptop to face him.

He sighed.

"We need a bell and fire. Luckily, we have fire right here." I called my magic forward and my forefinger blazed hot with flames.

Fitz chuckled.

"Where are we going to find a bell?" I asked, my eyes darting across the room.

"That's an easy one."

Fitz disappeared, and when he returned, he held an antique gold bell roughly the size of my hand.

"What is that?"

"A bell with the Stuart Clan Crest on top. Excuse me, the *Stuart of Bute* Clan Crest. Henry keeps it in his office—he rings it when something good happens."

"Why?"

"Don't ask me. Have you met Henry?" Fitz retorted, shrugging his shoulders.

He handed the object to me, and I turned it over for further inspection. The handle had been crafted into a lion, its upper limbs positioned in attack. The bell itself was simple, except for the inscription at the bottom: "Nobilis Est Ira Leonis."

"What does this say?" I asked.

"The lion's anger is noble."

"Sounds about right." I passed the bell back to Fitz. "Let's do this."

Fitz performed each spell twice. Once with an ordinary object in mind to test the spell. The second time was to summon the ring.

"*Light the fire and hearken the bell . . .*" Fitz began.

I called forward my flames as Fitz rang the bell.

"Bring forth the object I remember well."

The pen I had set in the adjoining room materialized. We repeated the spell, and this time . . . Nothing.

"Onward, it seems," he said.

Hours passed, and we finally reached the end of the grimoire.

"Ready to give this last one a try?" I asked.

He scanned the instructions once more.

"We need two candles, a topaz stone, cinnamon, and sage." He scoffed. "This one is *no* gonnae work."

"Not with that attitude it isn't," I quipped. "You're cute when you get worked up. Your accent gets so thick."

"Cute, am I? Well, I'll be keeping that in mind."

"Okay, now focus!"

"To the kitchen we go," he said, laughing.

Olga kept a well-stocked kitchen, and we found cinnamon immediately.

"Candles and sage," I repeated, tapping my fingers on the counter.

"In that pantry there."

I opened the nearby door to a room as large as my childhood bedroom. The shelves were stocked with countless dried herbs and spices, and rows of drying plants hung from the ceiling. At the far end of the pantry were candles of all colors, shapes, and sizes.

"Whoa," I muttered.

"Aye, he has an impressive collection."

I meandered to the end of the pantry, scanning the labels. Bay leaves, mandrake root, yarrow, belladonna, and the list went on. An impressive collection, indeed.

"Which colors?" I asked.

"White for protection and blue for communication."

I grabbed each color in the smallest size and turned to find Fitz leaned against the doorway, his arms crossed and his eyes mischievous.

"What?" I asked, walking toward him.

He wrapped his arms around my waist, slipping one hand in my back pocket. "You make me very happy," he said.

I tilted my head to face him, and he met me in a deep kiss. His hands wandered, and I broke away. "No, do not distract me right now. You're going to make me drop the candles."

"Who cares about the candles?" He reached for me, but I eluded his grasp.

"This is not focusing!"

He caught me and pulled my body to his. His kiss left me breathless, and for a second, I forgot about the spell.

"After you." He signaled toward the doorway.

When we returned to the sitting room, I felt hopeful again.

"Her spells are so many different forms," I said. "Some are just words and thoughts, others require objects, and then there are others that are sentences long."

"Usually, witches create spells in whatever form works best with their magic," Fitz said. "They also vary depending on what they're asking of the elements. But you're right—Annabel's are all over the map. This is the grimoire of a witch who was trying to throw others off."

"She suspected someone would come snooping."

"Aye. And she didn't make it easy on us."

Fitz scattered cinnamon across the coffee table, and I lit the sage and handed it to him. He waved the bundle through the air, and the fragrant smoke wafted through the room. He placed the sage at the center of the cinnamon base and placed the two candles at the top. I tossed fire at the wicks, which promptly burst to life.

"We forgot the topaz," I realized.

"Nae bother." Fitz closed his eyes and opened his hand. A topaz stone materialized in his palm. "What's the spell again?"

"You tell me," I said, pointing to the words.

"*Ghairm mi.* It means 'I summon.'"

I nodded. "And you'll need to think about the object you want to send for while you say it."

"I hate spell work," he said, his face cross. I stifled a laugh.

"I'll start with another crystal from Henry's collection to test the spell, and then I'll try the ring." He paused. "*Ghairm mi.*"

A moonstone materialized in his open palm.

"How clever," I said.

He smiled. He then repeated the spell.

Nothing.

"I'll just cross that one off the list then," I said.

He narrowed his eyes at me and reached toward the grimoire. It flew into his expectant grasp. He ran his fingers slowly over the book before feeling the air around it.

"Come feel this," he said.

I crossed the room quickly, feeling the return of his excitement. I ran my fingers across the book but felt nothing.

"I think Annabel left me a clue. We were so focused on the spells, I didn't investigate the energy as I should have."

"What do you mean?"

He flipped the book open and turned the pages until a smile spread across his features. "She hid a page of the book. Feel again."

A small twinge of energy nipped at my fingertips. I gasped.

"She enchanted the grimoire." He pointed to a small brown smudge on one of the corners. "This is her blood. She enchanted the book, so only her blood kin would recognize it."

"And I can feel it weakly because of our connection," I concluded.

"Exactly."

"Let's see what she hid from prying eyes."

Fitz laid his finger on the blood mark and closed his eyes. The other pages fluttered, and a soft illumination grew from where Fitz's finger met the page. He reached between the pages and tugged—and a new page pulled from the center of the book.

"You did it," I said, breathless.

"Annabel, you crafty witch."

Fitz read the summoning spell aloud:

That which was lost
Soon shall be found
Desire in your heart
Bring the ring
Here and now.

Flames leapt in the fireplace, and the hair on my neck stood on end. "The elements," I said.

Although no ring appeared in our midst, it was clear the elements understood Fitz's request.

"Aye, it seems the spell recognizes my blood, but I think something was omitted."

"You think Annabel left something out on purpose?" I asked.

"If she was this meticulous in crafting her spells, and in hiding the correct spell in the grimoire, she'd have made the spell itself difficult, too."

"May I?"

Fitz placed the grimoire in my open palms, a curious expression on his face. This was intricate and required focus and strength, but my lessons with Henry were going well, and I felt confident. This was the purpose of my magic, after all.

I sat and placed the book on the worn, wooden planks in front of my crossed legs, as Fitz retreated quietly to the couch, sensing my need for space. I simply stared at the pages, which were illuminated by the fire. I felt life within the grimoire, and I drew closer, taking an experimental sniff. The scent of aged paper and long-dried ink rose from the book as I searched for details of the woman who'd put ink to paper. The scent grew stronger still, and I rode the waves until I found the path I sought. My fingers traced the text, seeking the subtle changes of the page.

The air grew musty and damp and heavy with smoke, along with the nostalgia of a distant memory. Everything was fuzzy, like I was peering through foggy glass, and I closed my eyes briefly as my sight cleared.

I found myself in a rustic cottage. The walls and flooring were simple wood planks and stone with visibly rough craftsmanship, though the walls were in good shape. The counters were heavily marked, the result of the wear of sharp knives over the span of many years. No fridge, no dishwasher, no electricity . . . I was searching for any sign of modern convenience when a woman emerged from an open doorway. I jumped at her sudden appearance, but my presence didn't register with her.

"I'll be with ye soon enough, Alannah," the woman barked out over her shoulder. "The mistress will be none the happier for it either!"

Alannah's counterpart was a plain, middle-aged woman draped in a simple period dress. Her chestnut hair held streaks of gray, and a severe expression hardened her worn face. As she cleared dishes from the counter into a large wooden bucket, I thought how pleasant her features might be should she allow even a hint of softness. But times must have been difficult for many people, especially those in her line of work.

"Murdina!" a voice rang through the doorway.

My newfound companion turned quickly on her heel, clamoring out that she would be a moment more. Murdina's eyes then landed in my direction, and as her quick footsteps brought her closer, I held my breath. To my great delight, she walked right through me.

"I did it," I exclaimed under my breath. Recalling the events Annabel recorded in her journal, I gazed through the open window at the early morning light. Annabel would prepare for the day in a less trafficked area of the house.

Though simple, the house was larger than I expected, and I wound through several rooms and one lengthy hallway before perceiving hushed voices on the other side of an upstairs door.

I proceeded timidly, calculating the odds that I could transport myself through the door. I touched the door softly and asked my magic to deposit me on the other side.

A small but tidy bedroom was brightly lit, the morning sun pouring through the east-facing windows. A large, four-poster bed stood boldly in the middle of the room, covered in thick, wool blankets.

My eyes scanned over the few items crammed beside the bed and landed on an oak desk in the far corner of the room. Annabel sat at the desk, deep in discussion with a man I discovered was her husband.

What, is he human? I marveled. My heart softened as I thought of Fitz's and my challenges before I'd matched to my power. I could only imagine what this couple had faced.

My mind wandered to my human-witch ancestry. What challenges might my own family have encountered?

The man jumped from his seat, and his brows furrowed angrily as he stalked out of the room, slamming the door behind him. Annabel's left hand extended toward the ceiling, her journal materializing into her open palm. She set the book gently on the old, wooden surface, and the pages flew open to a blank sheet. Her hair fell loosely past her shoulders, the gray strands not yet smoothed back for the day. I moved closer to peer over her shoulder when my vision dissipated like smoke on the wind, and I was left staring at Fitz.

"No! I was so close."

"You lost concentration, that's all."

"How long was I gone?" I asked.

"Maybe ten minutes."

"Ugh."

"Just focus. You've got this," Fitz said.

Miraculously, I returned to where I left off, peering over Annabel's left shoulder. The passage was a few days prior to her encounter of passing the ring to Esther. I was close, but not quite close enough. I closed my eyes, asking my witch's eye to work with time to guide me forward.

The world went dark, and I was sucked into a wind tunnel, billowing around with total loss of control.

I'd once endured a tornado with Gram. We weren't far from her home when a large, swirling funnel appeared on the horizon. We had little time to react, jumping from Gram's car and running frantically toward a ditch behind other carloads of people, clinging to the hope that they knew what was best. I'd never forget those few horrifying moments when the elements betrayed us, and objects flew impossibly through the air. That experience was the closest to which I could liken this moment, but even that didn't feel quite sufficient.

When the wind died down, my sight was restored, and I watched Annabel gather her belongings. Excitement coursed through my veins as I followed her into the streets of Forfar, Scotland circa 1662.

CHAPTER TWENTY-EIGHT

Annabel made her way down a dirty path, which was lined with horse dung and the contents of chamber pots, one of the less appealing attributes of the time.

Annabel's narrow lane was soon behind us, and we strolled down the main thoroughfare of town, greeted by the sounds of a marketplace in full swing.

Though she spoke to very few, Annabel was watched by all she encountered. Merchants, housewives, and children regarded her path through the busy street, and a few made eye contact. It seemed that Fitz's family was well known by the small town's human population. She even seemed to be watched by other witches, who undoubtedly knew the witchhunt was coming for Esther.

The sight provoked a fresh wave of gratitude for the lack of human observation in modern times.

Annabel, though simply dressed, was vibrant against the crowd and held a stately appearance—the woman demanded respect. Her gray hair was twisted away from her face and mostly covered by a linen cap. She held her head high, meeting the gazes of others unabashedly. Annabel turned down a wide lane lined with trees, and eventually made her final steps toward what I hoped was Esther's home.

A row of two-story homes lay ahead. It could've been a string of townhomes found in modern times, albeit a little rustic for our era. But they appeared sturdier and cleaner than the area around Annabel's home, everything indicating this row was more affluent than the main street of town.

A thick, arched wooden door swung open to reveal a large foyer. A young servant girl stood aside, allowing Annabel to pass into the grand, open space. The girl didn't speak, though her doe eyes flitted timidly back and forth. She then signaled for Annabel to follow her, allowing me the opportunity to view Esther's home.

The house spanned two floors, and a balcony emerged from the stairwell, stretching the length of all four corners of the room and revealing several doorways—almost as many as the ground floor. The room was mainly comprised of wood and stone, and though each had the rustic appearance of centuries past, the masonry and carpentry work were of good quality, the materials in the space all working together seamlessly and in harmony.

A sizable tapestry was suspended from the second floor's vaulted ceiling, lying flat against the far wall, the soft, faded tartan colors forming a backdrop to the clan crest. It must have served as a symbol of family loyalty for many generations. A crowned lion's head was at the center, and the Gaelic words "'S Rioghal Mo Dhream" formed a half circle around it. I wondered if the tapestry had recently been added to the decor, or if it had been hung openly in defiance of the king's orders against the MacGregors. I thought of all the tartan-clad items I'd seen at Fitz's flat and at Ian and Ann's cabin at the lake. Esther and Hamish would have been proud to know the MacGregor pride lived on.

Stag antlers further decorated the solid wood half-wall of the balcony, and tables and chests alike were strewn against the backdrop of the stone walls, made from the same deep wood that constructed the stairwell and balcony. Esther's home was well-kept, and I wondered how many generations of Fitz's family had called these walls home before Hamish and Esther had come to know them.

A lady's maid walked Annabel into the sitting room without hesitation, where she received a warm greeting from Esther. Esther was beautiful, and I discerned both expressions and features I recognized from Izzy's fair skin, emerald eyes, and auburn hair. She was too ethereal to be human, and I was sure many humans in the small community were resentful.

"Aunt, I thought ye would never return," Esther said.

"Och aye. Same as I, truth be told."

"Well, I'm pleased to have ye home," Esther said. "Do take a seat."

Annabel looked down at her hands, an uneasy expression washing over her face. "Ye ken, my business that took me away, it was of a delicate nature."

"Oh aye?" Esther asked as she poured a dram of whisky, handing it over to Annabel.

"Aye, and I must speak to ye about it."

Esther narrowed her eyes in curiosity.

"Through the years, the family has endured torturous thoughts and visions, finding no rest even in sleep, even in death—"

"Aunt," Esther interrupted.

"Hear what I have to say."

"We struck an accord, or have ye forgotten?" Esther asked. "We are never to speak of these things."

"I remember well, child. Do not think because my body ages that my memory ages in turn."

"Why do ye trouble me then?"

"I have good reason, and ye must hear it," Annabel said.

"Make it brief. Hamish will return soon. I'll not trouble his mind today."

"Your parents believed they would pass before your vision came to fruition, and as such, they entrusted a grave task to me," Annabel fumbled along, her nerves clearly rising.

Esther shifted in her seat, taking a deep breath, but allowed Annabel to continue uninterrupted.

"Child, I do not speak of the past to harm ye, but to tell of our burden and our cause."

Esther nodded wordlessly.

"Before their deaths, your parents called each of the living family forth and held counsel on what could be done to prevent your early death. Each side of your family was heavily represented, as ye must ken that we each wanted to protect ye."

"I had no knowledge of this," Esther said.

"Oh, certainly not. It was arranged with great secrecy and maintained in such."

"When did this pass?"

"Some fifty years ago. We convened for days upon days. We considered every course of action. Somewhere in the deep of night, an idea emerged."

Annabel fidgeted slightly. This was it.

"This idea . . . this is why ye've come."

"Aye."

"I willnae like it."

"Nae, but there's no helping it. What's done is done." Annabel leaned forward, looking Esther in the eye, before proceeding. "Your own excellent parents wrestled with the idea, but in the end, there was nothing else to be done, and each of us would risk more than this to save ye."

"Aunt, what have ye done?" Esther asked, her voice barely audible.

Annabel reached into her pocket and removed an object neither of us could yet see. "Open your hand."

Esther obeyed, though slowly, just as a small, shiny object caught the sunlight and fell into her waiting grasp.

I gasped and instinctively ran my fingers over the moonstone on my own hand. They were practically identical. My mind raced. How had Fitz procured my ring? With their similarities, it couldn't be a coincidence.

Tearing my focus from my own finger, I gazed upon the horrified face of Esther.

She looked from the ring that lay in her grasp to her aunt before dropping the item to the floor. "Ye have brought great shame to this family!" Esther yelled, making no attempt to conceal her anger.

"Esther, my child."

"No, do not attempt to justify these perverse actions!" Esther said.

"Ye are too harsh. Hear what I have to say."

"This is a crime! I won't let my husband and bairns take part in the blame for this. They have endured enough."

"They dinnae have to endure any more suffering."

"What are ye saying, Aunt?" Esther questioned as she paced the room, walking off her violent energy.

"Hear what I have to say," Annabel responded softly, pointing toward Esther's seat.

After a moment's hesitation, Esther followed her instruction.

"Ye say this is a crime, and though that may be true, the law does no always dictate what is right. Humans have done a great evil to our kind. They fear the unfamiliar, but fear does no justify killing the innocent. Ye have done nae wrong, nae evil to them. Ye, who are blameless, do no deserve to be put to death. As such, we have placed our powers into this object."

"Surely no yours as well?"

"I have no yet done so. My death before your capture wasn't foretold, but I'll forfeit my power to this ring before ye are taken."

"Ye will do no such thing," Esther said. "Who still living knows of this?"

"Only I and your Uncle John." Annabel stooped to pick the ring up from the floor. "What is foretold is wrong, but we have provided a path to fight this evil. We will alter the future; we will make it right."

"We could suffer dire consequences changing the future in such a way," Esther said. "Fate would be none too pleased."

"Perhaps. What would ye have us do? We're your family. Would ye no do the same for your own bairns?"

Their arguments continued, but finally, Annabel made some headway.

"This was the dying wish of your parents, Esther." Annabel's eyes filled with tears. "Do ye no understand, child? Ye were their last thought.

Think of your parents. Think of your bairns."

Esther hung her head.

"Ye dinnae need to make me any promises today, but accept this ring, Esther. It holds your parent's power. Hold them close."

Esther nodded. It was weak, but it was progress. Although Esther would ultimately refuse to utilize the enchanted object, I wondered if her family's power had given some measure of comfort to Esther in her final weeks.

As the initial shock passed, Annabel continued her mission, giving instruction to Esther on utilizing the ring. I wasn't sure I heard correctly at first, but Esther repeated the words back to Annabel:

> *That which was lost*
> *Soon shall be found*
> *Desire in your heart*
> *Ignite with the moon*
> *Bring the ring*
> *Here and now.*

"I only need to alter the word 'moon?'"

"Aye. My powers draw strength from the moon. Yours, from the earth. Alter only this word, and the right to summon is yours. Let's have a try, shall we?"

Annabel tapped the ring, muttering unintelligible words under her breath, resulting in its sudden disappearance. "Proceed."

Esther held up her hand and recited Annabel's incantation.

The ring materialized in Esther's open palm.

I could've easily lost myself for hours with these women, but it was time to return to the future . . . or the present, as it were. With my research complete, I envisioned Henry's sitting room. I thought of Fitz's anxious face and my desire to be with him once again.

The heat of a nearby fire warmed my face, and the familiar scent of Scotch welcomed me back to the present.

"I know what we need to do," I whispered.

CHAPTER TWENTY-NINE

We sat by Annabel's grimoire, and Fitz's hunger for knowledge was palpable. I squeezed his hand and focused on relaying my recently acquired information. Fitz's powers were fueled by the earth, just like Esther's. He repeated the modified incantation, and when the last word escaped his lips, the fire again roared. This time, the ground rumbled, and the lights flickered as well. But yet again, no ring appeared.

Fitz worked the spell several times, the fire flaring higher, the ground shaking harder, and the lights flickering longer with every attempt. Although the elements yielded a greater response, the ring remained to be seen. Fitz sighed, turning to me.

"Are you sure you saw this correctly?" Fitz asked. His tone was accusatory.

"Of course, I'm sure."

"Don't be snippy. It was only a question."

"Your tone speaks volumes."

"What tone?" he quipped, the tone in question still lingering in his voice.

I arched my eyebrow but remained silent.

Fitz sighed. "I don't mean to sound frustrated with you. I'm just disappointed this isn't working."

I slid my arm around his waist. "We're going to figure this out. It's not you. Your words are exactly as Annabel taught Esther."

Fitz nodded, and his face grew pensive.

"Would I be able to use the spell even though I'm a different bloodline?" I asked.

"It might work; it's less likely outside our bloodline, but possible. The spell might recognize you since we're mates."

"How about I try? It'll at least help us narrow down what's going on."

"A fine idea," Fitz said.

I ran my fingers along the enchanted page of the grimoire and closed my eyes thinking of the missing phrase that held the key to this spell. I'd commanded fire and used my mind to see past events, but this was my first spell. Excitement coursed through my veins, and I used the excess energy to fuel my efforts.

When I opened my eyes, I was ready to pull the ring to me.

"That which was lost
Soon shall be found"

An energy rumbled through me, and my heart raced.

"Desire in your heart
Ignite with the fire"

My fingertips glowed red.

"Bring the ring
Here and now"

As the last word escaped my lips, an unfamiliar room materialized around me. Dark gray walls spanned the space, and several large paintings popped brightly against the deep color. A large wooden door was closed at the far end of the room. I crossed the worn hardwood floors, curious about the maps hanging from the opposite wall, hoping they would lend some clue about my location. The largest map was a rendering of Europe dated 1648, along with a smaller map of 1600 Scotland and a 1650 version of Forfar and its surrounding area. Wondering if I had left Scotland, I rummaged around the room.

Two oversized mahogany chairs and a matching table were positioned in a corner of the room. Letters were strewn on the surface of the table, all addressed to a Dr. Belmonte. I sifted through the items, not even certain what I was seeking, but when I lifted the final letter, I gasped. Esther MacGregor's magical ring lay at the center of the table, glimmering like it hoped to be discovered. Upon seeing it up close, I was struck by the exact detail my replica held to the original. I reached for it hungrily, but I was met by an invisible force, sending a small shock through my fingertips.

The ring was enchanted by an unfamiliar energy. Though I tried, nothing would grant me access to the magical item, and there was precious little I could do about that. There was nothing I could do with the ring without my physical presence anyway. If I wasn't able to secure the ring, I could at least continue my search around the room.

I was unable to open the door, nor was I able to transport myself to the other side, and I was confident that whoever Dr. Belmonte was, they understood the treasure in their possession. The thought stopped me in my tracks. Would a witch so powerful be able to detect that I had been in the room? If only I could see outside or into the hallway, maybe I could learn a little more about where I was. I scanned the room yet again, hoping I missed something in my initial search. Another door lay at the opposite side of the room. There hadn't been a door along that wall before—I was certain. I tried the handle, but it was also locked.

I wondered why the room had no windows, but no sooner had the thought crossed my mind than a window appeared. I hesitated briefly, trying to wrap my mind around this odd room, before tossing the curtains open to find a mountain range just beyond a small, snow-covered valley. The range was impressive, answering my earlier question. I might have been gazing upon the Alps, but surely not Scotland.

Turning from the spectacular view, another map caught my eye. Rather than my having overlooked it the first time, my instincts whispered that the enchanted room chose what to reveal and when. To my great surprise, a map of the Olympic National Park in Washington State hung from the wall, covered in red ink. A large "X" marked the High Divide Trail, which wasn't far from my mom's home. There was no indication of what might be along the trail, and having spent a considerable amount of time there, I was at a loss. I committed the details to memory and combed over the room one last time before asking my powers to deposit me back in Henry's home.

I was surprised to see Henry waiting alongside Fitz for my spirit to return to my body. I practically choked on my words while relaying the details of my adventure, describing the room and the great power holding the ring in place.

"You actually saw the ring?" Fitz asked. The light in his eyes was enough to draw a wide smile across my lips. He'd committed so much time to finding the item, knowing that he might never discover what he sought. Here was his answer after years of research—and bursts of his excitement flowed through me. "I can't believe we finally have a lead on its whereabouts."

"I just hope this name leads us somewhere," I said. "I could find my way back to the room, but if I can't open the desk drawers or exit the room, I think we're at a standstill."

"Most of the maps were of Scotland, you said?" Henry asked.

"One of Europe, one of Scotland, and one of Forfar. All were dated from the 17th century and at least looked like original drawings. The good doctor is clearly interested in the time period when the ring was created."

"And Forfar," Fitz added. "That's where the ring was certainly forged, but I just can't make sense of all this."

"I think we need to keep in mind that there was an Olympic National Park map too," I said. "The others were a bigger focus, but something about it is tugging at me."

"You know the area well, aye?" Henry asked.

"I can't even count the number of long weekends and summer

camping trips I took with my parents in the area when I was growing up. My . . . mom lives by a lake in the park."

I'd almost said "my parents." Would it ever get any easier?

Fitz slipped a hand onto my shoulder. "Henry, it's close to where Hadley and I first met."

"Have either of you been to the trail?"

"Yes, of course, but I don't remember anything out of the ordinary," I began, trying to recall any useful details. "The trail is pretty long. I think eighteen miles or something like that—diverse terrain."

"I think it's worth our notice," added Fitz. "Hads, think on it further and see if anything comes to mind."

"Fitz, show me the spell you've been using," Henry said.

Fitz performed the summoning spell, the elements answering in the same frustrated manner as before.

"Well, it's apparent the elements are irritated. Hadley's right: someone definitely has the wee thing under a potent protection spell."

"That means they've been waiting on someone to call the ring. Do you think this person knows who we are?" Fitz wondered.

"Not necessarily," Henry said. "But they realize this power can be called forth and are either using the ring for their own purposes or buying time until they figure out how to tap into its power. The incantations Annabel used are strong; not just any old bloke could hack into that power."

"Okay, so let's start researching Dr. Belmonte, cross-reference Scotland, Forfar, and Washington State, and see what we can come up with," I added.

"Aye," Henry agreed. "Great work, Hadley. You'll make one powerful witch yet."

CHAPTER THIRTY

Fitz arrived back at his flat from a day spent in the archives of the National Library of Scotland to find me prepping dinner. He kissed me quickly before throwing on an old sweater and helping me dice carrots for a stew.

"Your energy's off," Fitz observed.

"I'm nervous about my meeting tomorrow with the council."

"Did they confirm who you're meeting with?" he asked.

"Mia for a touch base about the Paris stalkers." I slid chopped onion into the pan. "Then I meet my new trainer."

"Do you want me to go with you?" Fitz asked.

"I don't want to pull you away from your research. I'll be fine."

"It's just computer work tomorrow. I'll work from the lobby so I'm around . . . if it helps."

"Of course, it helps."

"It's settled then," he said.

Fitz reached for the bundle of celery on the counter and placed it on the cutting board.

"So, I hope you're ready for a little family bonding." Fitz raised an eyebrow.

"What do you mean?"

"Izzy is coming over on holiday. And so are my parents."

"Wait, really? The whole family?"

"Izzy is excited to see you. They all are. And Dad is interested in our progress with the ring."

"That's great, Fitz. I can't wait." I focused on choosing the right spices from the cabinet, hoping my forced smile only read as distraction.

I knew he must've felt my conflicting emotions, but he didn't pry. I was thrilled to see Izzy and Ann, but I was nervous to see Ian again, if I was being honest. Ian had always been polite but distant. For the longest time at the lake, I had been convinced he didn't like me . . . and then there was the observation. I still had a lot of complicated feelings to unpack when it came to Ian.

"When do they arrive?" I asked.

"Izzy arrives two weeks from today. Mum and Dad arrive the following Monday. They're staying for a couple weeks."

"How did they get that amount of time off work so last minute?"

Fitz eyed me meaningfully. "The councils."

"So, the councils have basically infiltrated everywhere."

"You have no idea," Fitz said.

"I'm starting to get an idea."

"Mum and Dad offered to bring items from your mum's place if that's helpful."

I was lucky on the move front. My mom had volunteered to oversee the process in the States, and I only needed to collect my belongings on the east side of the pond. My mom had always loved a project, but after Daddy died, they'd become somewhat of a saving grace for her—something she could pour all her attention into.

With that business settled, my next task was finding a place to live in Edinburgh. Though it seemed Fitz and I were headed in the direction of living together, this flat was his space. He hadn't yet asked me to officially move in, and I hadn't addressed it with him, but time was running out.

"I need to figure out where I'm going to live," I said.

Fitz set the knife on the counter and faced me.

"John is moving out." John lived right next door to Fitz. "He just accepted a new job in Glasgow. The two flats would make a grand space if they were opened up."

I eyed him.

"You might not want to move in with me," Fitz said, "but I've . . . gotten used to you being here. I don't want you going anywhere."

"It's not that I don't want to be here. Fitz, I'm not sure I can afford a place in your building."

"We could purchase it together," Fitz suggested.

I hesitated.

"There's also the council," Fitz said, "though I'm not sure you'll want to have any ties to them."

"What do you mean?" I asked.

"If you want the help, the government will send you monthly payments, plus they'll help you sort out wherever you want to live."

I turned the stovetop off before turning. "Excuse me?"

"Humans, as a whole, might not know about us, but the leaders of their countries do," Fitz said. "They understand secrecy is imperative, meaning there's a specific branch of their administrations that carries out business with witchkind. Only their highest levels of leadership are aware of our existence."

"What ensures their secrecy?"

"The knowledge that almost every country in the world has an agreement with us, so they don't need to make enemies. We could take down an entire nation if we so choose. If they blow our secret, our Cardinal Court could have it ordered to take them out. It's a pretty compelling reason to be discreet."

"My god. But how does that affect my bank account?" I asked.

"Each country funnels money into secret accounts that fund the supernatural within its borders. So, you'd be funded by lovely Great Britain." He paused briefly. "I told you Henry's father was involved in the First World War. And I mentioned how I think the council wants something from us. We're occasionally asked to support our government with our talents. It's rare in times of peace for regular citizens to be called into any major action, but every once in a while, it's warranted."

I was astonished.

"Countries vary in the amount they funnel, depending on their economic state and how many witches live within their borders. You'd be amazed at what else your tax dollars fund, but we won't get into that."

My head was already bursting with information.

"So," Fitz concluded, "the money would basically keep you on retainer. But if you were ever needed, they wouldn't hesitate to ask."

"That seems kind of . . . scary?"

"Aye. It's one of the reasons I'm worried about Olivia's reaction to us. I've thought a lot about it since our meeting. I think she already knew about my power. Yours took her by surprise a bit. But that gleam in her eye . . ."

"I don't know if I want that tie to them."

"I've declined their help ever since we left the lake."

"I understand why."

Fitz nodded distractedly.

"What is it?" I asked, his nerves present in the pit of my stomach.

"I told you about Henry helping me invest my money."

"Yes . . ."

"I have a decent amount stocked up."

I tapped my fingers against the concrete countertops.

"So, how do you feel about the flat next door?" Fitz asked. "I know you won't let me buy it for you, but we could buy it together. And I do think if we have this place and the one next door, we could open the spaces into one large flat. If you'd want to do that, that is . . ."

"I think it's a brilliant idea. I feel a little funny about you splitting the cost of the flat with me, but if you want the larger space anyway . . ." I paused.

"I want to build a home with you," Fitz said.

And I longed for the same thing. It was decided, then.

"Let's do it."

Fitz smiled, shaking his head softly.

"Are you ever going to stop being surprised I want to be near you?" I asked.

"Absolutely not. I'm beginning to think someone enchanted you. How else can I explain it?"

"Explain what?"

"You're intelligent, powerful, stunning, and funny," he rattled off, a mischievous twinkle in his eyes. "What are you doing with me unless it's enchantment? Oh god . . . or pity. I'd like to think it's enchantment myself. At least it makes for a more romantic story."

I pulled him closer to me. "Hmmm, what am I doing with you? Besides the fact that you have the body of a Norse legend, intellect, and humor, let's also not forget that the power you possess is far beyond reasonable."

I asked the air to close the final gap between us, and it silently responded, pressing Fitz's body against mine.

"*Very* nice, Hadley."

"Shhh . . ." I placed my finger across his lips. He proceeded to kiss my finger slowly before brushing his lips along my arm. As he reached the tender skin between my neck and shoulder, I released a satisfied sigh. In the past several weeks, I'd discovered a completely new world full of wonderment, but at that moment, the only marvel on my mind was calling Fitz undisputedly mine.

CHAPTER THIRTY-ONE

The following morning found me in the one place in Edinburgh I did not want to be: Mia's temp office at the Scottish Council's headquarters. Seated across the marble-topped desk from her, I was far from comfortable. My nerves were almost as high as the first time the stalkers had tracked us. I'd hoped she would be more pleasant at this meeting, but she remained as cold as her cryokinesis powers.

"You and Fitz haven't given us any useful information on your stalkers from Paris," said Mia, her tone bordering on accusatory.

"Trust me, we want to know who they are as much as you do," I said.

"Trust you? How am I supposed to know that you want this as much as we do?"

"Why wouldn't I want them caught? Being stalked is not one of my favorite pastimes."

"You'd be surprised," she responded tartly.

I was coming to the idea that I couldn't do anything right in Mia's eyes—she'd combat me at every turn.

"You know, for someone who's meant to help us, your annoyance with Fitz and me has been painfully clear from the beginning. You've turned our meetings into accusations rather than collaborations."

"That's fresh coming from you."

"Oh, please do expand upon your position, Mia."

"You clearly distrust witchkind government. You act like I'm your enemy when I have done nothing but help."

My blood boiled. "Help? Are you kidding me?"

"If you'd like to calm down now, that'd be great."

"I'm fine."

"Really? Cause deflecting your fire is not on my agenda today," Mia quipped, though her eyes shifted warily from my eyes to my fingers.

Crap. My fire magic. I closed my eyes, exhaling my anger with each breath.

"Okay, sorry. I didn't mean to get angry."

"Let's just focus on why I called you in today. The reality is we can't generate a lead in any form. We have no idea who these witches are," Mia continued.

"Where does that leave us?"

"You haven't felt them watching you again since you've come to Edinburgh? Not even the slightest hint of something odd?"

"Nothing. This new watcher—he's different."

"Have you felt him watching recently?"

"Not since I last messaged you, but we've been spending a lot of time at Henry's and at our flat." A thrill ran through me at my first mention of Fitz's place as "ours." "We've been careful."

"And you still want to decline an agent being assigned to you."

"Yes, that feels more like imprisonment than help."

Mia's eyes flickered to mine, but she let my comment go.

"This is pretty rare, you know," she said.

"Being watched?"

"Not only that, but being watched by three witches the councils can't identify."

I nodded.

"We'll keep running searches, but if you think of anything else in the meantime, let us know. Something isn't right. And regardless of what you might think, your safety is important to us," said Mia.

"Thank you . . . seriously. The experience was nothing short of violating, and it's always in the back of my mind. Being watched gets under your skin. So, you can trust me when I say if I think of anything new, I'll let you know immediately."

"We'll do our very best with this."

"If that's all on that topic, I have another question."

Mia nodded for me to proceed.

"Did you have anything to do with my separation from Fitz?"

Mia's energy stirred, but her face was impassible. "Do you think I did?"

"You were involved in my first meeting with the council, so it seemed like you had an interest in it."

"That doesn't equate to my involvement."

"Correct. But you've made your opinion decidedly clear about it."

"Yes, because you broke the rules."

"I don't understand you."

"What is that supposed to mean?"

I ignored her question. "Did you have any involvement—any at all—in mine and Fitz's separation?"

She held my gaze, neither of us willing to look away first.

"I didn't give the order if that's what you're asking," Mia said.

"Then why do I feel like you were involved?"

"Spare me your questioning."

My blood boiled. "Did you give orders related to it? Consult on it?"

Mia sighed. "I was consulted, yes. The issue was raised to the U.S. National Coven Council—Ian fought hard for you and Fitz."

I nodded.

"No one wanted to vote against Ian, but they were conflicted because you were breaking our laws. One of the members called to consult with me."

"And what did you tell them?"

"That we govern based on the law."

I scoffed.

"Perhaps the laws need revisiting," Mia admitted, "but that is a different conversation. My duty is to uphold the law."

"That's shortsighted," I said.

"And you're judging the situation emotionally," Mia said. "Take emotion out of the equation and revisit it with fresh eyes. Everyone thinks they deserve to be the exception."

"Take my emotions out of it?" I repeated incredulously. "This is my life, Mia, not some textbook math equation!"

Mia's eyebrows rose.

"And Fitz wasn't a crush. We are mates. The council forced apart two witches who are mates. I think you have other laws that should have been considered."

"You made your position perfectly clear at our first meeting," Mia said. "We don't need to revisit it."

I shook my head and stood. "Do you need anything else for my statement?"

"No, we're done."

I stalked across the room but turned back before leaving.

"You know, I'm sure you're a talented witch, Mia. But you're as cold as the ice that spills from your fingertips. And that is your biggest detriment."

I raced from Mia's office and tumbled right into a young woman with dusky hair in the hallway.

"I am so sorry," I said, reaching for the woman as we balanced ourselves.

"Don't worry about it," she said, a hint of a smile crinkling the corners of her wide, umber eyes.

"I was just heading back to the training department's reception area, but I think I'm a bit turned around."

"Straight down that hallway on your right."

"Thanks," I said.

She nodded and dragged her black combat boots down the hall. I waited until she was out of sight and leaned against the wall, breathing deeply. My meeting with Mia had unsettled me. How could I accept help from this group of witches if I couldn't trust them? I took another deep breath and turned in the direction of the training department.

Tanner was waiting for me in the training reception area.

"You good, Weston?" he asked eyeing me suspiciously.

"Yeah. Just met with Mia," I offered in explanation.

That satisfied Tanner, and he escorted me into a training room.

Two new faces greeted us. One was short and slender, with bronzed skin and raven hair. Her dark eyes seemed to perceive everything, and I was struck by their intensity. Her physical being was almost otherworldly, and the lighthearted energy of a free spirit wafted casually around her.

The other had wavy, blonde hair that hung to her lower back, bleached by the sun, much in the same way her tanned skin had been kissed by it. She looked young, but her cunning blue eyes held wisdom and experience.

Tanner introduced the latter as Chloe—a Cardinal Court member, just like Mia. I groaned internally.

"Chloe is from Australia," he said. Tanner's energy was off, and there was something in his voice . . . strain, I thought.

I observed Chloe. There were few places in the world that made as much sense as Australia did for this woman. Her build was that of an athlete, and I wondered if perhaps she owed years of surfing for her sculpted, lean muscle.

Chloe had been assigned as my lead coach, meaning she was responsible for appointing and overseeing my training.

"Right on. I'm so happy to meet you, Hadley. I'm sorry I didn't make it over here to meet you sooner. I had some urgent business back home, but all is well now."

"Australian witchkind was on the brink of civil war about a year ago. But Chloe's been working to bring the two parties together," Tanner explained. "Really amazing work."

I didn't miss the admiration in his voice or the twinkle in his eye.

"It hasn't been easy, but we're finally in a good place—settling down and moving forward. Of course, that doesn't mean we don't have the occasional hiccup," Chloe said, winking.

An entire world existed within the one that I thought I had known so well . . . and everything I'd thought to be true was being challenged.

Chloe smiled. "Well, let's get started, shall we? This is Maka."

Chloe had chosen Maka from the Cheyenne River Sioux Tribe of the American Dakotas to improve my understanding of my abilities and to assist me in controlling them.

"I'm so happy to meet you," Maka said, extending her hand.

A warm energy traveled up my arm, and I returned her greeting.

"Maka will be working with you a few times a week until you master your mind reading and your mental transport," Chloe said.

"It sounds like your mind reading is your biggest challenge right now, so we'll start there," Maka said. "I'm excited to get started."

"Maka will send reports to me, and Tanner will continue to monitor your progress. We'll make sure you have the support you need until you're proficient in all of your abilities."

"Does that mean I won't be working with Mia any longer?"

Tanner had mentioned a rumor floating around headquarters that Mia was going to be assigned as my lead. Since she had been involved in my first meeting and on the stalker investigation, we gave some merit to the rumor, but I was thrilled to have this report disproven.

"She'll continue her work on the investigation, but the court decided I'd be a better fit for your training. I hope you're not too disappointed."

"No disappointment at all," I assured. "I look forward to working with you."

"Rad. Maka will meet you here tomorrow at nine. I know you start work on Monday, so we'll adjust your training sessions to fit your schedule."

They offered a chorus of niceties as I left the training room, and though I wanted to believe they had my best interest at heart, I left the room with a heavy amount of skepticism lingering in my mind.

Fitz was waiting for me in the main lobby. From the leather briefcase to the book in his hand to his wool waistcoat, he looked every bit of the scholar he was. Fitz kissed me quickly and gathered his belongings.

We were halfway to the apartment, and I was recounting the morning's chain of events to Fitz, when my breathing came short. I froze and cast a nervous glance to Fitz. Fitz's breathing grew labored for just a few seconds before he breathed deeply and reached for me.

"What's wrong?" he asked.

"I—I think I'm on the verge of a panic attack." I glanced around anxiously at the people who passed us along the sidewalk.

"Hey, look right here," Fitz said, his voice soft. "Keep your eyes on mine."

I followed his directions.

"Good. Don't worry about them. It's just you and me here, aye?"

I nodded.

"Breathe. Keep your eyes here and breathe."

I followed his directions. My heart still pounded in my chest, but I began to feel like I might catch my breath.

Fitz's eyes grew distant but before I could question it, a bit of peace flowed through my heart and into my bloodstream. A sense of calm seemed to glide through my veins, easing my nerves as it washed through me. My heart rate continued to slow and my breathing came easy.

Fitz extended his hand. "May I?" he asked.

"Of course," I said weakly.

He slid his arms around me, enveloping me in a safe, warm space. I leaned into him and closed my eyes. Edinburgh fell away—the people, the sights, the sounds. For a moment, only the two of us existed, and I had nothing to fear.

The wind whipped furiously as we worked our way to the top of Arthur's Seat. The ancient volcano boasted one of the best views in Edinburgh, being the highest peak in the hills surrounding the city. It was little wonder Robert Louis Stevenson had described it as "a hill for magnitude." Fitz and I were quiet on our ascent, content in each other's company and the sweeping views.

We found a seat near the edge facing the Royal Mile and pulled trail mix from his backpack.

"We should discuss your panic attack."

I dropped my gaze. Fitz had suggested a hike, knowing it often worked well to dispel my excess energy—and anxiety. But I knew the conversation wouldn't wait.

"You're not too keen on sharing this kind of information with me, but you expect that I tell you everything. That's hardly fair."

I wanted to tell him he was wrong, but I couldn't find an argument to support it.

"What do you want to know?" I asked.

"When did they start?"

"The moment I left the lake for Boston." I paused. "I felt like something was missing, like my gut was telling me something was wrong. I had a panic attack in the airport, but that was only the beginning. By the time I reached Boston, I felt a bit of hysteria. I can vividly remember sitting on the plane on the tarmac, waiting to exit, and feeling like my stomach was flipping."

"Do you have a theory on what triggered it?"

"I wondered if I was just nervous to move so far from home and leave my parents on the other side of the country, especially when Daddy was so ill, and I know there was some level of that. But . . ."

I gritted my teeth, hesitant to share more.

"What?"

"But I couldn't get you out of my head. I kept seeing your face, and I felt like I was missing something only you could give me."

Fitz's heartbeat raced through our streams.

"The first night in my new apartment, I was brushing my teeth when I was seized with hysterics. I basically fell to the bathroom floor and couldn't catch my breath. It was absolute panic and fear, which was only multiplied when I couldn't figure out why it was happening. Everything felt wrong. I was so worried about you."

"I'm so sorry." Fitz's face was downcast, but it wasn't my intention to make him feel bad about the past. I knew he had struggled too. "Sometimes, this anxious feeling would take hold of me. Since I didn't want to overstep in our relationship, I asked Izzy to work a spell to check on you when it felt like she'd be a better choice. She always said you were fine—that you were stressed about something—but she never told me the extent. She knew I'd take the next flight out. I didn't even know they were panic attacks until your last letter."

"Izzy did the right thing. You didn't need to worry about me with everything going on."

"There is nothing more important to me than you. You were all I was worried about."

I leaned over and kissed his shoulder. I couldn't have asked for a more thoughtful mate.

"Can we calm others from a distance?" I asked.

"Any witch can craft a calming spell, but it takes a powerful and exceptionally intuitive witch to craft the spell and then send it across the country."

"I thought as much."

"Izzy cares for you like a sister."

"Sometimes, I'd be in the middle of an attack and then inexplicably feel fine. It was something I couldn't explain—until now. What you did earlier today . . . I'd felt that before."

"It was Izzy. I'm sure of it."

"Thank god for her," I said.

"And what about now? Have you had more that I don't know about since we've been together?"

"No. This is the first one since I matched to my powers—well, aside from the one I almost had the day we met the council. But today . . ."

"Today was intense. Arguing with Mia after you were already nervous to meet with her, being introduced to a new court member and your new trainer."

I nodded.

"We'll run through an extra meditation tonight and work on a few calming techniques for tomorrow. You've got this, Hads."

CHAPTER THIRTY-TWO

I stood across from Maka in her training room at the council head-quarters, readying myself for my first training session with her. I wanted to get to know her better. There was just something in Maka's energy inviting me to trust her.

"Maka, your name is beautiful. I've never heard it before."

"Oh, that's because it's a nickname. It essentially means earth. In Lakota mythology, it's related to our earth spirit. When my mom was pregnant with me, she knew my abilities would be strong. Since she could feel my power so clearly, she named me Hope. But because they didn't know definitively what we were, many members of my tribe only sensed my strong connection with our earth. The nickname just stuck," she said with a smile and a shrug.

"Well, it's lovely, and I think you might just be an earth goddess after all."

Maka began by learning more about my struggles with mind reading.

"I have so little control of that power," I said. "I've started before I even know I've begun. And sometimes the thoughts are a little fuzzy or in and out. I really need to get a handle on it."

"I hate to tell you this, but controlling your mind is a matter of practice," Maka said. "You'll make progress as you continue to focus on controlling it."

"I've tried to be cognizant around others, but it's difficult to maintain that focus in a crowd of people."

"When you first learned to ride a bike," Maka said, "you had to focus on your balance, peddling, and where you wanted to go, but at some point, balance and peddling became innate. This talent will be the same. Keep focusing on what you want, and together, we'll get there."

"It's been tough. I'm so happy to have help with this now," I lamented with a smile.

"Oh, I know exactly how you feel. I've been there too."

"It's encouraging to talk to someone who's been through this."

"It must seem overwhelming right now, but you haven't had the benefit of training since you were young. You're just now discovering the world the rest of us experienced since childhood. I know without a doubt that you'll master everything in the time we have together—you harbor such strong and unique magic inside you."

"Thank you, Maka."

"Okay, we're going to work on some basics today: meditation and setting your intentions with mind reading. Mastering these are the first steps toward controlling your mind, and we'll start each session this way."

I nodded.

"Have you been meditating?" Maka asked.

"Yes," I answered truthfully. Fitz meditated daily, and we'd fallen into a routine together.

"And yoga?"

I grimaced.

"It's all right; you aren't in trouble," Maka returned, laughing. "But I want you to make room for it. You carry a massive amount of anxiety in you. Other witches' and humans' negative thoughts and energy will linger in you. Regular yoga practice is just as important as meditation in your case. They'll work together to remove all the negativity from your body, your thoughts, and your spirit."

"I know," I said. "That's horrible, isn't it? I know it'll help me, and I still haven't made room for it . . . I'm just having trouble balancing everything. I want to do better."

"Oh, Hadley," Maka began. "You have so much going on right now. You discovered you're a witch only a couple of weeks ago, and you're mentally wading through those changes and what they mean. You're moving to a new country. You're in a relationship that, yes, began a couple years ago but is different now in many ways. And you're starting a new job."

I laughed softly, nodding my head.

"No one would find their balance quickly, and you shouldn't blame yourself for not getting there with the snap of your fingers."

"Thank you."

"You're tired," she stated. It wasn't a question, but I answered anyway. "Yes."

Maka took my hand gently. "For someone with your talents, it's imperative you get into a routine. And once you do, you'll feel the anxiety peeling off, layer by layer. You'll feel yourself moving closer to your balance. Don't deprive yourself of inner peace."

I dutifully promised to adjust my routine. I wanted better for myself.

"Okay, look around the room and find where you're most comfortable," Maka instructed. "Settle into your meditation in whichever position feels best."

I looked around the carefully curated space. This training room was small, about the size of my living room, and it was cozily furnished. The stone walls held two windows at the north end, allowing pale light to filter on to the stone flooring. A large, cream-colored rug took up a sizable portion of the floor, bearing gold vines and burgundy flowers. There were egg-shaped lounge chairs tucked into a corner near the windows. Made of bamboo with plush cushions and draped with cozy blankets, they added to the relaxing atmosphere of the room. Natural sounds of rainfall drifted through the open windows, and the burning incense in the room was cinnamon—the scent was said to increase concentration and decrease muscle tension.

All the elements worked together to create a peaceful environment where I felt like I could achieve true connection between my mind, body, and magic.

I sank into one of the lounge chairs and tucked my feet underneath me. There would be much to learn, but meditation wasn't one of them. I already had the tools to be successful with this first step, and I was immensely grateful to Fitz for that. I closed my eyes, focused on my heartbeat, and allowed the outside world to fall away.

When I emerged from my reverie, Maka opened her eyes and rose from her chair across the room.

"How did you know I was done with my meditation?"

"I'm an energy reader," Maka said. "I felt your energy shift. Studying your energy while you meditate will help me make the most effective training program for you too."

"Being so attuned to people's energies, I bet you're proficient in feeling intentions."

"There are witches more specialized in that area, but yeah, I can usually figure out if someone has good intentions or not." Maka tilted her head curiously. "What is it, Hadley?"

"I was just wondering how Mia's energy feels to you."

Maka's eyes shifted warily, her face lost in thought. She pursed her lips. "I haven't really spent time with her. Anyway, let's get back to it. Let's move into setting your intentions."

I accepted her deflection—for the time being—and refocused my mind.

We deliberated the truest purpose of my skill and ultimately settled on this: the purpose of my mind reading was to only gather information that was necessary to me. I'd work daily to ingrain into my mind that I need only call upon this ability when appropriate.

"What constitutes it being necessary?"

"We usually say you shouldn't use it unless you're working with the council in some sort of official capacity. The mind is a sacred place. Outside of training, you shouldn't access someone else's mind unless it's truly necessary. But if you're ever in danger, you can use it to gain the upper hand."

"If the stalkers get brave."

"Exactly—if you're ever in danger, don't hesitate, Hadley. Use it to your advantage," Maka said.

"Understood."

"And if you ever find yourself in that situation, you might run into shielding, meaning you wouldn't be able to read your opponent's mind anyhow."

"Shielding?"

"It's when a witch protects their mind. It isn't something that's done and forgotten about. It takes constant energy to keep a shield in place, so most witches don't bother with it unless they really have something to hide or they're in a situation where they feel like someone is watching them."

"Is there a way around it?"

"Absolutely. It's difficult to break through a shield, and the witch will definitely know someone is doing it. So, proceed with caution."

CHAPTER THIRTY-THREE

On Monday morning, I stood in front of the bathroom mirror studying my reflection. I'd been meticulous in selecting my outfit for my first day at work, wanting to feel my most confident for the occasion. I pinned my hair away from my face and then smoothed out my new houndstooth blazer. I took a deep breath. I was ready for this.

My Oxford heels clicked against our hardwood floors, pulling Fitz's attention from the *The Student,* an independent newspaper produced by students at the University of Edinburgh. A broad grin spread across his lips.

"Oh, *there's* Edinburgh Castle's new PR manager."

I giggled. "And the outfit—first day at work approved?"

"Give me a proper spin."

I followed his instructions.

"Aye, very bonnie." He walked over and kissed me. "Now, come take a seat."

I checked my watch.

"You have plenty of time. I have a wee treat for you."

"Well, in that case." I took a seat, and Fitz wandered into the kitchen. When he returned, he set a steaming cup of tea and a chocolate croissant in front of me.

I gasped delightedly. "A croissant!"

"Your favorite. I found a local bakery owned by a French pastry chef."

"Oh," I said. "I'm going to be spending a lot of time there."

Fitz chuckled. He reached into his leather bag and pulled out a small box wrapped with a green bow.

"What's this?" I asked.

"Just a wee something for your desk."

I tugged at the bow and opened the box to find a small marble bowl with crystals inside of it. I pulled the crystals out to examine them— opal, citrine, moonstone, and rose quartz. I held up another. It was bright blue and speckled with gold.

"What's this one?" I asked, examining the stone.

"Lapis lazuli—it supports truth and helps with decisiveness. It seemed a good choice for your office."

Each of his selections was tied to something that would be beneficial to me, from my October birthstone to my truth-supporting crystal.

"This was thoughtful, Fitz. Thank you."

Fitz nodded. "I thought you might want to add your blue lace agate and black tourmaline."

"Great idea."

Post-breakfast, I attempted to call my coat forward from the closet, but I was still struggling with the concealment piece. When I reached through the air, I felt nothing. I sighed and reached for the coat again, foregoing the concealment. No one was around anyway—practice would have to wait.

Fitz walked with me to the castle gate, where we parted for the day.

"I'd wish you luck," Fitz began, "but you don't need it."

"Thank you—for all of it," I said.

He leaned forward and kissed my forehead. My heart fluttered.

"I'm proud of you. Go get 'em, firecracker."

The esplanade was already packed with tourists, and I navigated my way to the staff line and scanned my digital pass that HR had sent the night before. I turned as I reached the castle doorway and found Fitz right where I'd left him. He didn't need to tell me he was proud of me—it was written on his face. He smiled and waved, and as I passed through the entrance, I carried the peace of the morning with me.

The HR office was compact, only a couple of small rooms that had been modestly decorated with modern desks and antique photos. The young woman at the reception desk was friendly, and the morning passed with new hire training and filling out paperwork. Soon enough, it was time to meet Fitz for lunch in the castle's tea rooms. I walked through the castle courtyard and into the restaurant, finding Fitz and Henry already seated.

"This is a nice surprise," I said as I took a seat next to Fitz.

"I had a last-minute meeting arise in town this morning and thought I'd have tea with Fitz if he had time. This is better," Henry said.

"I can't disagree with that," Fitz said. "So, how's the first day going?"

"Nothing exciting to report. Just routine stuff. I'm glad they left my lunch open. This is a nice break before the afternoon."

"First days are usually slow, I'd reckon," Henry said.

"And I'm good with that. I've had plenty of excitement in my life lately. I'm content with a slow start to my new job."

We chattered on aimlessly, talking about work and plans for the week. It was nice to decompress from visits to Dr. Belmonte's office and power training by passing the lunch hour in casual conversation. As we wrapped our lunch, a text from Isaac in our group chat turned our conversation in a different direction.

Conference call Friday at 7 p.m.? I should have all reports back on Dr. Belmonte by then, and we can discuss the findings.

"That'll work fine for me. You two?" Henry asked.

Fitz nodded as he placed his teacup back on the table.

"Me too. I'll text him back," I said.

I sent the message and grabbed my purse. "I'd better be going. Glad you could join us, Henry."

"Aye, I'm happy for you, lass. Enjoy the rest of your first day."

I was halfway across the courtyard when a prickle worked its way up my spine. The watcher. He had returned. I glanced back, but Fitz and Henry had already disappeared.

I pulled out my phone and sent a text to Mia.

The watcher is back. I'm in one of the castle courtyards. I'm heading back into new hire meetings, but maybe this can generate a lead?

I hit "send" and hastened my steps.

I knew I'd recognize the watcher if I saw him again. I scanned the crowds thoroughly but couldn't locate him. I searched for his mind, but I found nothing promising—there were far too many thoughts swirling through the area, and I found it completely overstimulating. The witch's gaze faded as I entered the building, and I ran up the steps, determined not to be late.

I took a deep breath and reached for the door.

The next item on my agenda was a tour of the castle offices, and I was thrilled at the prospect of moving around rather than sitting in an office for the rest of the day.

And I might catch sight of the snooping witch again, I thought.

A familiar face stepped into the office. Mr. Murray's assistant had offered to be my tour guide.

"Edna, it's great to see you again."

"It's lovely to see you too," she said.

Edna led me through all of the buildings, and it was strange to see the modern office life existing in such a historic structure. Once we worked our way into the building that housed PR, marketing, and the rest of the business team, I paid special attention to the layout where each team was located. We peered into the breakroom as a young man was vacating a small table on the far side of the room. He made eye contact, and I smiled. He met my gaze and then looked at Edna, who was sharing more about the space, before his expression turned sour. He picked up his bag and headed for the exit.

"Oh, this is Mark Cunningham," Edna said. "He's on the marketing team. Mark, this is Hadley Weston, our new PR manager."

"Nice to meet you, Mark," I said.

He looked at my extended hand for a few seconds too long before shaking it quickly and nodding curtly.

"I'm looking forward to working with you," I said.

Mark nodded again. "If you'll excuse me, I'm late for a meeting."

I was curious about his cool reception and my mind wandered into his. I caught myself before I'd heard much of anything, but I got just far enough to understand that he wasn't pleased about Mr. Murray's decision to hire me.

"Did I do something to offend him?" I asked.

Edna hesitated.

"I don't mean to pry. If you don't want to answer the question, that's fine, but I just wanted to be sure I haven't done anything wrong."

"Oh no. You haven't," Edna said softly. She paused. "Mark recommended a good friend of his for your position."

"I see."

"Aye. A good friend who's native to Edinburgh. He felt a Scot would be best in the role. So, don't take it personally. He'll get over it." She smiled warmly. "You were the most qualified candidate, and you are the best fit."

"Thank you," I said.

"Let's keep going?" she asked.

I tried to forget about the interaction, but it stewed in the back of my mind. Mark was the first of my colleagues I'd met who I'd partner with in my responsibilities. And that wasn't a pleasant start.

As we neared my office, we bumped into Mr. Murray, and his face lit up.

"Ms. Weston! I am so pleased to see you."

"It's wonderful to see you again," I said.

"I was relieved when I heard you accepted our offer. You'll do great things here."

"I'm looking forward to it."

That Wednesday after work, I settled in front of our flat's roaring fireplace and set my laptop before me, taking a deep breath.

It was time to call Jordan.

When I'd texted her earlier in the day to schedule a time to talk, she'd proposed a call this evening. I thought about pushing it for a few more days, but I'd put off the call long enough. I needed to face this new reality with my best friend, whatever it was. Fitz kissed me on top of my head and padded down the hallway to the bedroom to grant me some privacy. The bedroom door closed with a soft click. I initiated the call and checked my expression, determined to wear a bright smile when she answered.

The call connected, and Jordan popped onto the screen.

She squealed in delight. "Hads! I'm so happy to see your pretty face."

I laughed. "I've missed you so much."

Jordan's midnight hair sat in a large bun atop her head, and she wore blue silk pajamas.

"But you know you really should be asleep right now. I know you have an early morning," I said. It was 11 p.m. on the East Coast.

"What? And miss this? Not a chance, sis."

"I'm glad we found some time to catch up," I said.

"I'm glad you decided to stop avoiding me."

"Jordan!"

She smiled mischievously. "Don't deny it."

"There's just been a lot going on."

"Yeah, yeah. So, how's the job?"

I filled her in on my first couple days, from Mr. Murray to Edna to Mark.

"Pretty sure Mark hates me."

"Who would dare hate you?" Jordan said. "That's messed up."

"Exactly what I thought."

We both laughed.

Jordan asked about my mom, and I, in turn, asked about her parents, and then her job.

"I've been pretty swamped myself. We lost the analyst I've been partnering with—her last day was yesterday—and they haven't replaced the position yet. I think they're hoping I'll absorb both caseloads, but I don't see how that's possible."

"Your hours are intense already. I can't imagine adding more to your plate," I said.

Jordan sighed. "Yeah, well. If you can convince the FBI that work life balance is a thing, let me know."

I shook my head lightly.

"My parents arrive on Friday for a visit, but I don't know how much I'll see of them. I asked for time off weeks ago, which was approved, but now that this analyst is gone . . ." She shrugged.

"It's tough finding a balance when you're in a different city than your family."

"Speaking of which, how is your mom handling the distance?" she asked.

"She's less than thrilled, but I think she'll be okay. Gram is spending some time with her."

"That's great," Jordan said. "How are you both holding up?"

I paused.

"We don't have to talk about it if you don't want to," Jordan said.

"I honestly don't know. I've been thinking of Daddy lately, and it's hard, you know? One minute I'm fine and the next . . ."

"I think that's normal, Hads."

"I think so too."

"So, it sounds like things are on again with you and Fitz?"

I nodded. "He met up with me in Paris, and . . ." I trailed off, smiling.

"Oh, damn. It's *really* on, isn't it?"

"It is. It's . . . serious."

Jordan's eyebrows raised. "I mean, that's good, I guess. But are y'all working through all this stuff from the past year?"

"It's complicated, but yes. We're sorting it all out."

"Does he have a good excuse for why he left?"

I hesitated. It was about to get tricky. "He does."

Jordan's expression was clear. She wanted an explanation.

"It's complicated and a bit . . . personal."

"I see," she said.

"I know that's not a great answer, but it's something that I can't really share with you."

Her lips twisted as her eyes dimmed in thought. "This is why you've been distant."

"Well, not exactly."

"Then what is it, Hads? What's going on?"

"I can't talk about it."

Jordan shook her head. "Nah."

"Jordan . . ."

"We're sisters, you and I. That's what we've always said, right? We tell each other everything. We always have each other's backs. But now, you're closing your life off from me. I don't understand it."

"That's not true."

"Is it because of Fitz? Are you doing this because of a guy? After everything we've been through . . ."

"That is absolutely not it."

"Seventeen years, Hadley Weston. That's how long it's been. And we've barely missed a day talking to each other. But you left for Paris and just dipped."

I sighed.

"Don't you start sighing on me, either. What you need to do is start talking."

Silence fell, and we held each other's gaze. Finally, I made my decision.

"You know I'm different," I said. "I've always been a bit . . . odd."

"Like knowing my thoughts," she said.

I nodded. "Well, turns out, there's something to that."

Her eyes narrowed. "What are you telling me?"

"There are other people who are like me. People that can do the same type of thing."

"Like the MacGregors," she said.

My surprise registered on my face.

"Oh, come on, Hads. I'd have to be pretty oblivious to miss the fact that they're an odd family."

Despite the serious nature of our conversation, I couldn't hold back my amusement. A smile nipped at Jordan's lips.

"So, what does that have to do with you and me?" she asked.

"I can't talk about the things I can do, or the things they can do. We can't tell anyone."

She eyed me suspiciously.

"It would put you at risk," I continued. "Major risk."

Jordan mulled over my words. "And who is the threat?"

"People like your employer." I eyed her pointedly.

She sat back in her chair and closed her eyes, releasing a deep sigh. "That is not what I wanted to hear."

"I know you understand my meaning. We can have a relationship—we're still sisters no matter what. But we can't ever talk about this stuff."

Jordan nodded her head slowly, her eyes shifting in consideration. Finally, she met my gaze. "I understand what you're saying."

"Jordan, you are one of the most important people in my life. You are family. I can't lose you, and I won't put you at risk. We *have* to be very careful. Do you understand?"

"Are you in danger?" she asked. "Because I have the resources to help you."

I smiled softly. "I appreciate that so much. But no, I'm not in danger—as long as we abide by this rule."

"You're sure I can't help you?"

I nodded.

"I need you to make me a promise," she said.

"Anything."

"I need you to promise me that if anything changes—if you find yourself in danger—you'll let me know immediately. Let me help you, Hadley, if I can."

I hesitated but then nodded.

"Tell me. I need to hear you say it."

"I promise, Jordan."

"I love you, Hadley. And I'll do anything to protect you."

I wondered if she truly understood that I was concealing information from her to keep her from harm.

"I know. I love you too, Jordan."

I returned from the office late on Friday evening. An all-staff meeting had run long, and I rubbed my aching neck as I passed through the doorway. I found Fitz in deep discussion with Henry. Isaac's voice sounded from the phone sitting on the coffee table.

Fitz rose from his seat and kissed me quickly.

"Sorry I'm late," I said.

"Tough day?" Henry asked.

"Just a long one. It's been a long week, actually."

"Did you have training tonight?" Henry asked.

"No, we're doing a Tuesday, Thursday, and Sunday schedule," I said, taking a seat next to Fitz.

"*Carissima*, is that you I hear?" Isaac asked warmly.

"It sure is. How are you?"

"I'd be better if I could figure out this Dr. Belmonte for you."

"Nothing?" I questioned.

"We've narrowed down our list, but it's still extensive. And we haven't found anything that matches all of our search criteria yet," Isaac said.

"Isaac mentioned one guy captured their attention, but his trail has gone cold," Fitz explained.

"I've consulted my best resources in the business. Ran background—nothing. Traced accounts—nothing. Looked into any and all documentation we could find—nothing. We found some old records, but they don't tell us much. Then he disappeared completely two years ago."

"If your team cannae find a lead on this guy, we have a problem," Henry groaned.

"If we search all of his connections, something is bound to turn up," Fitz said.

"Is it worth speaking with the councils about?" Isaac asked.

The group paused.

"Perhaps, but we shouldnae rush it," Henry said. "I think we should wait a bit. Fitz, Hadley?"

"I agree," Fitz said. "I'm not keen on bringing them into this yet."

"I'd prefer the councils not be involved if we can avoid it," I said.

"We'll hold off then," Isaac said.

"How many of his connections have you identified?" I asked.

"We have twelve decent leads to research," Isaac answered.

"And if none of the people on this list turn up anything useful? Where do we go from there?" I asked.

Isaac hesitated. "I think we'd need to ask you to pay Dr. Belmonte's office another visit if you were comfortable with it."

"Why don't I do that anyway?"

"Do you know if there's any risk associated with that, Henry?" Fitz asked.

Henry mulled over the question. "I dinnae think so."

Fitz turned to me.

I nodded. "I'll go back to Dr. Belmonte's office tomorrow."

CHAPTER THIRTY-FOUR

The following morning, I set Annabel's grimoire on the table in front of me and traced my fingertips lightly across the surface. Hundreds of years had passed, but this magical book still teemed with Annabel's magic. I felt its presence more clearly than I had when I'd first held the book. I wasn't sure if I owed that to my progress in training or if it was tied to me using her spell. Either way, I found a solace in her energy. There was something comforting in the fact that we existed so vibrantly even long after our deaths.

Fitz emerged shirtless from the bedroom, rubbing a towel over his damp hair, and effectively halted my process.

"What?" he asked.

"Nothing. Just admiring the view."

"Is that so?"

He crossed the room, and my pulse quickened. He knelt in front of me and pulled me forward. I wrapped my legs snugly around him, and he kissed me. When we pulled back, he flipped my wrist over and kissed it. The blood hummed under the surface, and I closed my eyes.

He ran a thumb over my ring, which reminded me: "Esther's ring looks just like the one I wear."

"It's a replica."

"How did you know what the ring looks like?"

"I don't know firsthand, but had it made based on a vision of my aunt's. Her mind's eye saw the ring, and she sketched it for us. That sketch is somewhere in Henry's attic actually."

"Why did you give this to me?" I asked.

"Because I believed you were my mate."

"And what does that have to do with Esther's ring?"

"Hads . . ." he whispered. "I risked everything to keep you safe, just like Esther's family did for her. It seemed a proper gift."

I ran my fingers along his jaw before pressing my lips to his.

"Okay, now get out of here," I teased. "I can't focus."

He chuckled. "I'm going for coffee. Earl Grey latte?"

"Yes, please."

With Fitz out of the room, I returned my focus to the grimoire.

The problem with being summoned by the ring was that I had no idea where I had traveled. Had I traveled through time to reach Dr. Belmonte's office, or had I remained in the present? To return, I'd have to rely solely on instinct, trusting the ring and my magic to guide me back.

We'd moved Annabel's grimoire and journal to Fitz's flat as it had become increasingly difficult for me to be apart from them. Henry said he'd seen it before with Emily—items used as a catalyst by spirit-travelers became a part of them.

I recited Annabel's summoning spell. A large map of Europe materialized . . . and then a room with dark gray walls. I crossed the room quickly, anxious to check if the ring still lay on the table. My sigh of relief disturbed the deafening quiet, though I still couldn't obtain the enchanted object.

Fitz and I had worked on my opening skills—or break-in skills, as I called them—after work over the previous couple of days, and I was ready to unlock Dr. Belmonte's sealed desk drawers. I sank into the rolling chair and placed my hands on the desk. Mental transport was such a strange experience. Though my body wasn't physically in the room, my hands felt as though they truly touched the desk, and my feet perceived the imperfections of the wooden planks on the floor. I ran my fingers across the cold surface of the desk, lingering along the coarse grain of the wood, allowing my mind to connect deeper with the elements.

Its life had begun in a lush, green forest with innumerable trees, alive with untouched vitality, and I watched as men cut the trees and hauled them to a mill. The tree became lumber, and the lumber was then worked into furniture before a young woman stained and sealed the desk, crafting it into a finished product. And finally, a staggeringly handsome man with dark eyes and a lithe but chiseled physique bought the desk and brought it home. This would be Dr. Belmonte, I reasoned.

Though Dr. Belmonte was attractive, something ominous rested in his features, and the longer I watched him, the more uncomfortable I became. Adrenaline coursed wildly through my system, and anxiety rested in the pit of my stomach. I momentarily rested my mind, contemplating my next move, before closing my eyes once more. I waited patiently, borrowing knowledge from the elements, asking them for intelligence on what had passed in this room.

Dr. Belmonte spent countless hours writing in code, making indecipherable calculations and hiding his work within this desk. His voice sounded in my ear, imparting the words that would open the drawers. I took a mental record of the spell, allowing the vision of Dr. Belmonte to dissipate, and promptly recited my new prize.

To my delight and amazement, four soft clicks fractured the silence as each of the locks unbolted themselves. I tugged at the top drawer.

But before I could look through the drawer, the click of another lock disturbed my progress. I froze.

I returned the desk to its former state and jumped from the chair just as the door swung open to reveal the man I'd begun investigating. He locked the door and tried the handle, ensuring no one else could access the room before leaning against the door for a moment, his eyes closing. His clothing was . . . odd. He shrugged out of a black velvet coat, which boasted a high collar and silver buttons. The ivory undershirt tucked into high-waisted trousers hid little of his toned figure. He looked as though he'd stepped off the set of a medieval film.

Dr. Belmonte crossed the space decidedly, though looking distractedly around him, before taking a seat in the chair I'd vacated only seconds before. He called for the locks to open and pulled at the bottom drawer. I was blanketed in security. I'd escaped his notice.

But suddenly, Belmonte paused. He slowly cocked his head in my direction, and a slight smile rolled across his parted lips.

"I can feel you, spirit-traveler. I know you're here," he stated plainly, as if he were offering to pick up the check for coffee.

Belmonte leaned back in his chair and placed his arms behind his head, clearly waiting for my next move. He wore a taunting smile, and my stomach turned as I realized he wanted a game. My mind ticked quickly through what I knew about spirit-travel, and I realized I didn't have an answer for my most pressing question: I didn't know if he could hurt me.

Think, Hadley.

I had crouched on the floor in my panicked dash from the chair, and I rose timidly, certain I'd hear the creak of floorboards even though I knew better. His eyes flickered in my direction and flitted around restlessly like he was trying to make sense of exactly where I stood.

I slinked around the room, catlike in my movements, and moved past the window, slowly circling the space to put distance between the two of us. He closed his eyes and brought his fingertips together in front of his chest. When he opened them, his gaze had found me again.

I gasped.

He chuckled. "Are you enjoying yourself? You may keep trying all you want, but you won't shake me, spirit-traveler."

An icy chill crawled through me. Something about the way he drew out his words was playful, and his speech unsettled me even more than his ability to follow my spirit. I didn't have a way to communicate with him, and I was too new in my powers to know any tricks.

We were at a stalemate.

"I may not know why you're here or who you are, but I will find out. No one enters my home without my permission, not even someone who smells as lovely as you. Make no mistake; I'll know you when we cross paths again."

"Hadley!"

"What is it?" I mumbled, struggling to regain consciousness.

"Thank god. Are you all right?"

"Of course. What's your problem?"

"My problem is I came home to find your limp body uninhabited, white as a ghost, and perspiration on your forehead. You scared the hell out of me."

"Crap, I'm sorry. I didn't mean to do that. It's just that I found the room again and I was finally on to something . . ."

He sighed. "It's all right, take your time."

"I figured out how to open the desk drawers, but then I was interrupted by Dr. Belmonte. Fitz, he couldn't see me, but he knew I was in the room. I mean, he didn't know it was me, but he knew someone was there."

Fitz held me, listening quietly until I related the chain of events.

"Dr. Belmonte knew where I was. His eyes followed me."

"That's odd," Fitz said. "I don't know how that's possible since it was only your spirit there."

"He said he could *smell* me."

"Now, that one I don't believe. Maybe he tried to unnerve you by saying something creepy like that."

"Well, it worked," I said.

"Hey, you don't have any reason to fear him. You know why?"

I shook my head.

"Because I'll never let anyone hurt you. And more importantly, you're a fiery, strong, mesmerizing witch. No one can mess with you unless you let them."

Fitz believed in me, and that counted for something.

CHAPTER THIRTY-FIVE

I hung up the phone and stared from my office window. Though the castle relied heavily on government funding, donations from members of the U.K.'s elite were equally vital. And I'd learned that because many of those donors were witches, only a witch could be chosen for the role I now filled.

Between phone calls with donors, meetings with the event planners, getting to know my new coworkers, Fitz's family mystery, and my magical training schedule, time was slipping away quickly.

Mark had emailed me last year's donor pamphlet that afternoon. Though the rest of my colleagues had been helpful and welcoming, Mark was still as distant as he was on my first day. I hoped time would benefit that relationship.

The phone rang again, and I checked the time: 6:15 p.m. I sighed and reached for the phone.

"Good evening, this is Hadley."

"Oh, hello there. Is this Edinburgh Castle's fancy new PR manager?"

I giggled. "What do you want, MacGregor?"

"When do you get off work? I miss you."

"Did I even give you this number?" I asked drily, though a smile nipped at my lips.

"No. But I'm a researcher. It wasn't much of a challenge, Ms. Weston."

"I see. Well, as it happens, I miss you too. But I'm very busy and important."

Fitz chuckled. "Oh aye. That much I know."

"I can head out soon—but I'll have to bring some work home."

"I'll be going quite late on this course material, as well. It's due for the Dean's review this week. I'll order in tonight?"

"See you soon."

I placed the phone back on the receiver and gathered my belongings from the wood-topped standing desk. According to Edna, Mr. Murray had insisted on a new desk when the castle hired me. He wanted me to feel well taken care of, Edna had shared. My space was small but comfortable. My window was smaller than Mr. Murray's expansive courtyard view, but it did boast a nice view of the Firth of Forth seascape, so I had no complaints.

I'd already added a few touches of my own to the space, and pops of green now contrasted against the stone walls and wooden doors—plants, courtesy of Izzy. A baby blue mini fridge was tucked in the corner, which Fitz had bought and stocked for me—lunch often appeared inside of it midday. I'd told him he didn't need to worry with it, but he consistently made lunch or had it delivered for me. With my magic training adding to an already busy schedule, he wanted to help where he could.

I waved goodnight to Edna, who never left before I did, and dashed home. Fitz was seated near the fire, and stacks of papers, a few books, a notepad, and his laptop were spread haphazardly around him. As I crossed the threshold, he rose to meet me. He hugged me tightly to him, and I pulled his face to mine.

We opted to eat near the fire and between the warmth of the flames and the taste of fish and chips, I relaxed into the evening.

"How's the event coming along?" Fitz asked before popping a fry in his mouth.

"Good. I think it'll be pretty swanky."

"Aye, I've always heard it's quite posh."

"Better get your tux ready," I said.

"Only if I'll have a hot date."

"You'll probably have a tired one, but I do hear she cleans up nice."

"She's *always* bonnie," he said, his features turning sweet.

"And how's your course coming along?" I asked. "Your students going to hate King James or what?"

"That man was a blight on humanity."

I nodded. Fitz had shared his research with me, and I couldn't disagree with his assessment.

"I need to get my hands on a particular book tonight at one of the libraries."

"How late are they open?" I asked.

"They're closed. But the director owes me a favor, so he's arranged access."

"Well, aren't you important."

"Aye, right. Didn't you know that already?"

All jokes aside, Fitz had an uncanny knack for being granted special access to academic institutions that didn't make exceptions for just anyone. I suspected, in Fitz's case, that had more to do with the distinction of his work than his network.

"Come with me?"

"Sounds like a perfect way to end the day."

Mahogany shelves stretched down a lengthy room with an arched ceiling, and the book covers were faded, dulled by the ravages of time. I walked slowly along the dimly lit center aisle and ran my fingers along the shelves. There was something innately romantic and timeless about libraries. While humans and witches would come and go, these volumes spanned the centuries. Long after I'd returned to dust, the stories in this very room would live on.

Fitz was seated at a small wooden desk, and he typed furiously at his laptop with an aged volume of literature open on a book stand. I peered over his shoulder and found an account of an accused witch during the North Berwick trials in Scotland in 1590. Fitz carefully turned the page of the book. He resumed typing, and a soft sort of heartache traveled through my chest. It wasn't only the thought of Esther's death that troubled us. Learning about the persecution of our kind was difficult, and a certain sorrow lingered within us as we dug deeper into the past.

I had wandered further into the archives by the time Fitz was done. He found me flipping through a book I'd found on Queen Victoria.

"This was so much more interesting than the work I brought with me," I said.

"And what do you have here? Ah, Victoria. One of the better monarchs this country has seen."

"Her story is fascinating—the reform she brought, the legacy she left."

"She was a powerful woman. Just like you, aye?"

"I can only hope."

I slid the book back into the empty slot.

"I love how she and Albert worked together. I always wanted a love like theirs," I mused.

"And did you find it, my love?" Fitz brushed his fingers along the side of my face.

"Even better," I whispered.

Fitz cradled my head in his hands before dipping his head to kiss me gently. Our lips worked slowly, passionately, as we sorted through our feelings together. Gradually, we grew in intensity, and Fitz lifted me from the ground. I wrapped my legs around his waist, and he pinned me against the wall. My hands ran through his hair, across his neck, down his back. He gripped me securely with one arm while his free hand slid up my shirt. The library was quiet, disturbed only by the distant ticking of a clock and the rise and fall of our labored breaths.

I dipped my head backward as his lips found my neck, and suddenly, another sound fractured the silence: the click of a door. We froze, our eyes wide. But we didn't sit in suspense for long.

"Dr. MacGregor, you in here?"

"It's Lawrence. He's with maintenance," Fitz whispered.

I tried to stifle a giggle unsuccessfully, and Fitz slid his hand over my mouth.

"Aye! What can I do for you, Lawrence?" he called in response.

"We're done for the day. Just checking on your progress."

"I'm returning the books now. I'll be just another minute."

"Very good. I'll be in my office if you'll let me know when you're heading out."

The door shut, and Fitz and I broke into laughter.

Fitz kissed me once more. "All right, firecracker. Let's not keep Lawrence waiting."

CHAPTER THIRTY-SIX

"Izzy!" I exclaimed, running for the door. I had still been at work when Fitz picked Izzy up at the airport, and I was pacing the living room impatiently by the time they arrived at our flat.

"Oh, Hadley! I've missed you!"

We embraced warmly—a hug that was years in the making—as two women who could finally be transparent about who they were. The last time we'd seen each other, too much couldn't be said aloud. It was exciting to be able to finally talk openly with her. I showed her around our new apartment, explaining our future plans regarding the space.

"The sale is still pending, but the seller is motivated to close quickly, and so are we. It's all happening so fast, my head is spinning," I said.

"This will be incredible. You'll have loads of space, and Fitz's flat could use a woman's touch," she said, winking.

"Not to interrupt, but are you two ready for a bit of scran? I'm starved."

"Oh aye," Izzy answered. "I'm famished."

We chatted about Izzy's trip as we made our way down the rain-soaked streets of Old Town. As we wandered into Whiski, our restaurant of choice for the evening, the warmth of the space was nearly jarring against the bite of late autumn that blustered through the city.

The pub was cozy and quaint, and something about it just felt like home. Tables were randomly strewn about the front room; a lovely bar was decorated with countless bottles and a busy bartender. The front door bordered a wall of windows, and I could see the charm of sitting amongst the window tables, watching tourists explore the Royal Mile. A traditional Scottish band sat in the front corner, their melodic stories tumbling out in Scots Gaelic alongside the captivating sounds pouring from the instruments in hand.

We settled into a corner booth, and I noticed Mr. Murray talking with the bartender. He waved and walked over.

"I trust you're enjoying your evening, Ms. Weston."

"Very much. Mr. Murray, this is my partner, Fitz, and his sister, Izzy."

"It's wonderful to meet you," Izzy said.

James shook her hand and then introduced himself to Fitz.

"I'm glad to meet you," Fitz said. "Hadley has spoken highly of you—and so has our father."

"Your father is Ian MacGregor?" Mr. Murray asked.

"Aye."

"Second to none, that one. Your father has been a huge asset to the Scottish Council. An honorable witch."

Fitz beamed at Mr. Murray's praise of his father.

We passed a few moments in idle chatter before Mr. Murray excused himself and moved closer to the band.

"He does seem like a nice fellow," Fitz said once he was out of earshot.

"He just looks like someone who'd sit on the national council, doesn't he?" Izzy said.

"Aye, he's distinguished all right."

"And he's also your manager at work?" Izzy asked.

"Right. I was nervous about that, but he's honestly been great."

Izzy inquired about how my new job was going.

"I was a little worried about the volume of work that came with this position, but I love it," I said. "I finally feel like I'm back in my element, you know?"

"I see that in your eyes."

Izzy went on to ask about Fitz's curriculum and, in turn, she told us about her career and the life she'd built in Seattle.

"Your work sounds incredible," I said, "but Fitz tells me you're missing nature."

"I'm a green witch through and through." She smiled. "I know the work I do at the hospital is important, but I miss growing things. I need more time to cultivate my garden properly. It pains me, Hadley."

"I understand just what you mean," I said. "That's what you were meant to do. It doesn't mean your other work is less important. It just means nature was meant for you, and the other job is meant for someone else."

"It sounds simple when you put it like that," Izzy said.

"Isn't it, though? We worry so much about letting others down or what's expected of us. But ultimately, this is your life and your gift. It's time to use it again, Izzy."

"A fine argument. Now I just have to save up for a shop."

"Do you think you'll stay in Seattle?" I asked.

"I don't know. I love Seattle, but I've thought of returning to Scotland, too."

"Oh, Iz. I didn't know that," Fitz said softly.

"Well, I didn't want to get your hopes up in case I couldn't sort it. But I'm quite serious about it."

"Well, I don't want to pressure you, but . . ." I trailed off, my eyebrows raised.

She giggled. "I understand your position on the subject perfectly. I'll take it into consideration, Ms. Weston."

"What will you sell?" I asked.

"A few plants, to be sure. Tea, herbs, salves, and the like. Oh, I was just thinking of your dad the other day. I perfected a salve that he would have loved."

Her eyes misted, and I took her hands in mine.

"I'll never forget your kindness to him," I said.

"He was a wonderful man, Hadley. I know you must miss him greatly, but just know that you aren't alone in that, aye?"

"Thank you," I managed.

The night wore on in conversation and good food, and sometime after dinner, I finally asked Izzy about a long-ago occurrence I always questioned: the night I thought I'd dreamed about wandering into the forest with her.

"You're right. That night wasn't a dream," she said.

"Even the night it happened, I knew deep down it wasn't a dream, but I couldn't make sense of it. I thought it couldn't have happened."

"I'm an earth witch, and my power is tied so closely to nature. I spend time healing the natural world and its wildlife when I can. When you stumbled into the forest with me, I had no idea what to do."

"You must have panicked a little."

"You have no idea."

I laughed. "Okay, but I have to know . . . was I hallucinating or was your skin glowing?"

Izzy grinned, and Fitz laughed heartily.

"Sorry," he said. "I can only imagine what went through your head when you saw Iz *glowing*."

"Oh aye. It took me quite a bit of practice to sort that one out, but essentially, I pull the elements to me in such a way that my energy reacts to the air by creating light. The light is far better than headlamps and that sort of thing."

"That really freaked me out," I said. "But now that I understand everything, that's an impressive feat, Iz."

Izzy smiled shyly.

"The other thing that's been bothering me is why were we in danger," I said. "Who was it that showed up?"

"I can't say for sure. At the time, I just knew whoever it was, they didn't have good intentions, and I couldn't risk anything with you. Now that I know everything happening with yous, I wonder if it was one of the folks who've been watching you recently."

"What a terrifying thought."

"Iz and I did our best to find out who it was, but our research didn't yield any leads. We had so little to go on," Fitz said.

"It's strange they turned up in the woods with us like that," I said.

Izzy's face was distant, lost in reflection. "I wouldn't let it worry you considering that's the only time something like that has happened. That *is* the only time, right?"

"Yeah, you're right." I said, though the pit of my stomach twisted.

Rain misted through the city streets, lending a hazy dreamlike quality with the soft illumination against the stone buildings. Though the wind had quieted, the air was still cold with the promise of winter. The weather didn't dampen the mood of the countless groups of people bustling across the streets, and the mix of voices and distant bagpipes echoed down the Mile.

We wandered back toward our flat and as we reached St Giles' Cathedral, I tugged at my scarf, hoping to find the source of the draft at my neck. Fitz paused, helping me to adjust it.

Church bells rang through the square, announcing the eleventh hour. Izzy closed her eyes and turned toward the sound.

A prickle worked through me.

"Do you feel that?" I asked.

"Aye," Izzy said.

"And it's not a friendly gaze," Fitz observed.

"It feels . . . familiar." I glanced around us, attempting to appear nonchalant. I scanned across the Mile—tourists taking photos, groups of friends laughing as they meandered down the road, couples walking hand in hand—until I found the source.

His icy blue stare was just as unsettling as it had been the day he'd watched me outside my hotel.

"To your right," I said. "Green cable knit sweater. He's leaning against the building."

"He's the one you saw outside your hotel?" Fitz asked.

I nodded.

"You two stay here," Fitz said, walking toward him.

"Not likely," Izzy retorted, and we fell into step beside him.

My stalker noticed us and walked briskly down a nearby alleyway, the entrance reading "Roxburgh's Close." He was at the end of the close, and we chased behind him as quickly as possible. My adrenaline was high, and I felt Fitz's energy running through me. It was oddly invigorating.

Our suspect turned the corner, and we followed suit. The close opened to a small courtyard. I scanned the buildings, their varying shades of beige and gray stonework jutting up around us, hoping I'd find something useful.

A hotel was just in front of us, and Fitz walked over to peer through the large windowpanes. "Nothing over here."

"I'll look on the far side by the restaurant," Izzy suggested.

Our mystery witch darted from a hidden corner near the restaurant as Izzy grew near, and we scrambled to follow him. I couldn't stand the thought of him getting away, and that propelled me across the courtyard faster than I thought possible.

I grabbed on to a lamppost, using it to launch myself into a right turn, and I was soon on Izzy's heels.

Another close was positioned at the far side of the courtyard, and our guy neared the end of it. I bounded down the dark stairwell and tripped about halfway through. My body stabilized, though I couldn't take credit for the action.

"*Keep moving!*" Izzy said into my mind.

Fitz was already out of sight, and when I emerged into the bustling street, I ran right into an unsuspecting tourist.

"Hey, watch where—" The man cut himself off as his eyes scanned across my features. "Are you okay?"

"I'm fine. I'm so sorry," I called over my shoulder, already running in the direction where my connection knew Fitz would be.

I found Fitz and Izzy breathing hard as they looked around.

"Hadley," Fitz called. He wrapped his arm around me and kissed the top of my forehead.

"We lost him," I guessed.

"Aye," the MacGregor siblings answered in unison.

"On the bright side, we've all seen him now," Izzy said.

Fitz pulled out his phone. "I'll update Dad and the guys."

I nodded.

"Thanks for the hand back there," I said to Izzy, still panting.

She nodded.

"Let's get out of here?" I asked. "I think we should head home."

CHAPTER THIRTY-SEVEN

The distant sound of bagpipes and the chatter of friends and families filled the streets of Edinburgh. The culmination was distinct, and I knew the moment was a core memory that I would carry with me always. We spent the day popping in and out of shops, restaurants, coffee houses, and bars. Izzy was excited to return to all her favorite haunts, and she had Fitz and me try everything she ordered.

"Fitz! You *have* to try this," Izzy said.

"How are you still going? I don't think I can eat another bite, Iz."

"Well, you'll have to find room. Hadley, make him try this."

"You two are something else." I laughed, reaching for my buzzing phone.

"What's the matter?" Izzy asked, noting my expression.

"Oh, it's nothing. I was just responding to a text from Jordan."

"You don't seem too pleased."

I hesitated before nodding.

"Mind if I ask why?" Izzy asked.

"To be honest, I was ignoring her calls for a while."

"You have to conceal too much from her now," Izzy guessed.

I nodded.

"That's always a tricky balance with human friends. But Jordan is your best friend. It takes a bit of work, but you'll be happier with her still involved in your life."

"I let her know in a roundabout way that we can't talk about certain things. She understood."

"Aye, that I can imagine. Jordan has always known something was different with you. She's been understanding in the past."

Fitz eyed me.

"He was telling me the same thing. I finally listened." I nodded in Fitz's direction.

"He was right. This time."

Fitz wore an offended expression, and we laughed. He snatched the cranberry scone from Izzy's hand and took a bite.

"Now, was that so hard?" Izzy asked.

"I still like the blueberry better."

"Aye right. That's because you're wrong."

"Okay, you two. Behave."

They grinned.

"We need to get moving—it's time to meet Maka."

When we saw her, Maka's face was tilted expectantly toward the sun enjoying the cool sunlight that had broken from the clouds earlier that morning after several days of clouds and rain.

I made introductions before we headed inside the coffee shop. Fitz and Izzy secured a table while Maka and I ordered at the bar. The shop was darling, all stone walls and cream-colored paint with pops of pale blues and verdant plants.

While awaiting our Earl Grey tea, Maka issued a challenge telepathically. We'd been working on telepathic communication, and I felt like I was finally growing proficient.

"Okay, Hadley. I know it's crazy in here, so this will be a good test for you. Do you hear people just talking right now or do you hear their thoughts too?"

"No thoughts. I have them shut out."

The small shop was crammed with young professionals and tourists, and the noise was almost deafening, even without the extra clamor of their thoughts buzzing through the air.

"Open the flood gates. Let it all in."

Over our past few sessions, Maka had taught me how to open my mind to hear other thoughts, the same way my ears heard their voices in a crowd. It was miraculously simple. I only had to find that particular wave in my mind and open it. Though the action was easy, the result was terrifyingly overstimulating, and I only attempted it when instructed during training.

Suppressing the flow of information was the toughest part. I focused my mind and opened the wave. Suddenly, my brain filled with thoughts. From breakups to vacation plans to storylines as people read nearby, my head swirled with information.

"Whoa," I said aloud.

"It's okay, Hadley. Breathe through this. You hold the information, not the other way around."

I nodded.

"Find one train of thought and focus in on it."

Scanning the crowd, I picked through the voices and slowly shut out anything that didn't suit my objective, obeying Maka's orders dutifully. Someone was reading a familiar story, and I found their voice soothing. It was fascinating to me how some people had a voice inside of them that read aloud in their mind as their eyes scanned the pages. It was my favorite revelation to come from training my mind reading ability.

Pip.

It clicked.

They were reading one of my favorite classics—*Great Expectations*. I'd first read the book in college, and though it held its fair share of tragedy between its covers, Pip's dry humor had me laughing through the story.

"Now, shut out their thoughts again."

I tuned out every thought in the room, and as focused as I was, I barely registered the change as they all fell away.

"You are a true proficient," Maka said aloud.

"I have a wonderful tutor. I'll give you her number."

As it turned out, Maka was a blessing in more ways than one. Magnetic energy channeled between the two of us, strengthening what would have certainly been an already natural friendship, and that made training far more enjoyable than it would've been otherwise.

Finally, the council had done something right.

CHAPTER THIRTY-EIGHT

When Monday arrived, it was the first day I felt disappointed by going to the castle. I rolled my eyes when Fitz insisted on walking with me to work, even after I argued that it was only a two-minute trek. I couldn't withhold my good humor when he promised he and Izzy would meet me at the castle restaurant for lunch. The day turned out to be quite busy—lunch was delightful—and before I knew it, the workday was gone.

I tapped my foot nervously as I leaned forward on our sofa and swirled my whisky glass a bit aggressively. Fitz's hand landed on mine, attempting to steady my movements. Izzy eyed me sympathetically.

"There's no need to be nervous, Hadley," Izzy said.

"I've been trying to tell her that," Fitz said.

"Easy for you two to say," I quipped.

Fitz pulled me closer and wrapped his arms around me. "Dad likes you, you know."

I scoffed.

"He does," Izzy echoed. "He always says he maintains a professional distance when it comes to our cases."

Her tone was clearly meant to mimic Ian's, and Fitz and I chuckled.

"He's nervous to see you again too," she offered seriously.

The knock on the door startled us all, and as I rose from the sofa, a montage of memories flashed before my eyes: the curtains moving in the upstairs window when I was outside with Izzy, his cool reception when I entered their home, his distant side glances when he noticed me walking through the yard, his expression the afternoon I saw him talking with Tanner in his office.

Fitz swung open the door, and my heart stopped. Then Tanner strolled in.

"Oh, you've got to be kidding me."

"A warm welcome, as always," Tanner said.

"Sorry," I muttered.

"She thought you were Dad," Izzy explained.

"Ah, she's nervous."

"Yeah, and we don't need to unpack that right now, just so we're all clear," I said.

Tanner raised his hands. "Wasn't gonna."

A rap on the door sounded through the flat once again, and this time, the party didn't wait before entering. Henry walked through the door, a huge grin on his face. I was just about to complain when two figures filed in behind him.

"Look who I found," Henry said.

A slew of exclamations followed his statement, but my eyes darted straight for Ian MacGregor. We made eye contact instantly . . . and then he smiled. And just like that, I could breathe again.

Ann hugged Izzy before pulling her over to Fitz and embracing him too.

"Both of my wee bairns under one roof again! Oh, I think I might greet."

"Mum, come on," Fitz teased, though he planted a quick kiss on the top of her head. Izzy beamed before making a beeline for her dad.

I took the opportunity to greet Ann while Ian reunited with his children. It made me happy to see the admiration in Fitz's eyes when he looked at his dad.

"Hadley, we are so glad to see you!" Ann began. "You have no idea how happy I am to be here with all you kids again."

Ann was right—the tears spilled out, and I hugged her tightly, grateful to meet her again under far better circumstances than when I'd last seen her.

Ian made his way over to us, and I turned to face him. I thought, somehow, he and Fitz looked even more similar than before. He dropped his blue eyes to the ground momentarily.

"Hadley, I want you to ken how happy we are for you and Fitz. And I hope we can spend some time together while I'm here, so I can have the opportunity to ken you better . . . firsthand." His lips dropped into a lopsided smile.

"I'd like that."

We shook hands warmly. There were conversations to come and feelings to sort through, but I knew in that moment that we'd be all right in the end.

Henry set a couple bottles of whisky on the table as we settled in. While Ann wanted a full report on my time in Scotland, Ian had questions about my experience working at the castle and Tanner's work with the council. Conversation was smoother and less tense than I had anticipated, and I grew more comfortable as the evening progressed.

"I worked a few projects with James Murray over at the castle," Ian said.

"I didn't realize you worked together directly," I said, "but he did speak highly of you."

"It doesn't surprise me that James didn't mention it. He's humble when it comes to his work, but his position on the Scottish National Coven Council is well-deserved."

"What type of work does he do in a position like that?" I asked.

"We haven't fully covered government structure yet," Fitz clarified to his father.

Ian nodded. "The Scottish Council seats are elected positions. He put in countless years at local levels before even being considered for nomination. One representative from each national council is sent to the European Coven Council—that's held monthly in Vienna. Then two representatives from each continental coven council are sent to the United Covens Affairs quarterly on the Island of Little Cumbrae."

"Where is that?"

"Here in Scotland," Henry answered.

"Aye, a wee island west of Glasgow," Ian said. "The owners are a part of the Scottish National Coven and offer the estate for their meetings."

"We're an organized bunch, huh?" I asked.

"You have no idea," Izzy said.

"I've been a bit nervous about working with James because of his seat on the council," I said.

"Dinnae let it trouble you, kiddo," Ian said. "Murray is a good guy. He's one of the few members of the councils that I respect completely."

"He's still a part of the council," I argued.

"Aye, but he had nothing to do with our separation. We need to give him a fair chance," Fitz said.

I still resented the councils for their actions against us, but my time with Maka had shown me that there was good to be found as well. And my experience working with Mr. Murray had been positive so far.

"I'll give it my best shot."

"That's all we could ask," Henry said.

"Tanner, Fitz mentioned that you're helping Hadley?" Ian asked.

"The council has me assessing Hadley's powers."

"I thought you were hired as a fitness coach," Ian said.

"Yeah, I was. They're teaching me to assess powers because they want me to create training regimens that best supplement agents' powers to make them as strong as possible across the board."

Ian shook his head. "Usually, they have someone specialized in that area onsite with you, and you build the plan together."

"That's how they explained things in Seattle," Tanner said. "But when I got here . . . they sent me out solo."

"Doesn't make sense, does it?" Henry questioned.

"Not at all," Ian said. "I'll do some digging into this. I'm not sure what they're playing at."

"Thanks, Dad," Fitz said.

"Of course."

"I should be going—I have an early morning," Henry began. "But, Hadley, I wanted to hear everyone's thoughts on your encounter with Belmonte."

"Oh, right."

I recounted the series of events.

"My experience is that spirit-travelers can't be harmed while they're outside of their bodies. Have you ever heard any different, Ian?" Tanner asked.

"No," Ian said. "Their spirit is separated from their physical body, so you cannae harm them."

"But how can I move things around if he can't harm me?" I asked. "How can I feel the desk and the floor but walk through a door?"

"You're focusing your energy into moving objects. You aren't moving them with physical force. You're asking the elements to move them for you."

"I swear I can feel them on my fingertips."

"Have you ever heard of phantom limb syndrome?" Ian asked.

I nodded.

"This is similar biologically," he said. "Your spirit has stepped outside of your body, but there's still a connection. Your mind is walking through the process of your movements, and your brain and your nerves are still speaking to each other."

"How did he figure out I was there?" I asked.

"Your energy. If you've attuned yourself to energy shifts, you can identify them."

"What about him saying he smelled me?"

Izzy visibly shuddered.

"Rubbish," Ian said. "He was trying to get under your skin."

"There would be minimal risk in Hadley returning to his office then?" Henry asked.

Ian considered Henry's question for a moment. "I'd say so. The risk is low, but keep in mind that we dinnae ken how powerful Belmonte is.

There are no guarantees when it comes to magic."

"I want to go back—I want to try again."

"Let's give it a go tomorrow," Ian said. We can walk you through some exercises that might be helpful. If you play your cards right, you can sort through his protection spells. You have that in you, Hadley."

"Tomorrow then." I smiled even though my blood ran cold.

CHAPTER THIRTY-NINE

The next evening, our small crew gathered around the living room coffee table ready to learn more about Dr. Belmonte. Ian had located a few council records with matching names, and only one set had been sealed. We had a hunch that he was our guy. Ian submitted a request for the records, but in the meantime, Isaac began a new background search based on Ian's findings while I focused on a successful third trip to Dr. Belmonte's home.

"When you finish your initial assessment of the type of magic he used for his protection spell, feel your way around the energy. If he's good, there will only be the tiniest wisp indicating where the spell was sealed," Ian explained.

"You'll need to really focus, Hads. Push everything else out of your brain," Tanner added. "True focus is the only way you'll recognize the edge of the spell."

"Then what?"

"Let your mind and your energy connect to the edge," Ian said. "You can either ask the air to disperse the energy, or you can use your own energy to tug it loose. Either way, the spell should unravel."

"How would a caster do this, Dad?" Izzy asked.

"They probably wouldnae, Iz. They might be able to work a spell to have the air pull at the edges, but unless they're lucky, I doubt they'd find a way to be in tune with the elements enough to tug open the seams."

"Are you ready, Hads?" Fitz questioned.

I nodded. "Yeah, I think I'm ready."

"Let's give her a little space, then," he instructed.

Everyone dispersed to the edges of the room aside from Fitz and Ian, who remained close by to monitor me. Ian wasn't positive they could pull my spirit back into my body if I ran into trouble, but he was confident Fitz could follow my path physically to help sort things out.

I closed my eyes, a bit distracted by my audience. But recalling that I was attempting a tricky passage, I cleansed the day from my mind and fell into my own abyss. Sensing I was in the right state to travel, I whispered the summoning spell to myself, and when I opened my eyes, the gray walls of Dr. Belmonte's office welcomed me back.

My first order of business was to check for the ring. I searched the table where I'd found it just over a week prior, but the ring was gone. I rummaged around the room and in the desk drawers, but again, came up short. The desk drawers were empty, and I realized Dr. Belmonte wasn't taking any chances with me. I walked toward the door and tried the handle, as if I expected anything to be different from last time, but my hand tingled as it met the invisible force protecting the exit. I took a step back and closed my eyes, feeling out the energy in the room.

The room was deafeningly quiet. Nothing stirred, and I couldn't even detect the sounds of electricity. I finally detected a hum of energy overhead and looked in its direction. For the first time, I realized the room's light came from torches mounted on the walls. I couldn't imagine having missed them on my first two visits, and I suspected the magical room was playing tricks on me once again.

I stared at the light, contemplating what I was seeing. The light didn't seem to be fire exactly, but instead some sort of glow that closely resembled it. I shook my head and moved on. The secondary hum radiated from the doorway. I paused in front of it and focused my mind on the energy circling it.

I sat cross-legged on the worn wooden floor and allowed my energy to saturate the space. I found that it was easier to focus on the energy's makeup by closing my eyes and allowing all of my senses to focus on the feel of it. I pushed my way around, poking and prodding until I found a tiny wisp floating at a far edge.

It was flitting about elusively, and it took several attempts before I was able to grab on to it. I didn't expect the charge of electricity that seared through my fingertips. My eyes flew open at the pain, and I released it quickly.

I breathed deeply, willing the sensation to pass. I reminded myself that my fingers didn't actually hurt, and my nerves calmed. I closed my eyes again and refocused on my task. The wisp was easier to locate the second time around, and I braced myself for impact as I again gripped it between my fingers. My chest tightened with the contact, but I pushed through the pain and tugged until the opening widened.

The further I pulled the spell, the less it hurt, and I jumped to my feet and ran for the opposite wall, pulling as hard as I possibly could. The spell unwound, the energy dispersing through the space like tiny fireflies all around me, and I walked timidly to the doorway.

I held my breath as I reached for the old, wooden door, but there was no need for hesitation. I walked right through.

The hallway was dimmer than the magical room, and my eyes adjusted slowly to the lack of light. Torches lined the space, and their flickering revealed gray stone walls and flooring. An ornate floor runner provided the only color to the space. The cream-colored base was decorated with swirling patterns of indigo, forest green, and flowers of rusty red. Nothing indicated which direction I should investigate first, so I decided to head to my right. After a few steps, I noted a door to my left and pressed my ear to it in silent request.

Nothing.

The next doorway yielded something more interesting. Though I couldn't make out the words, the rise and fall of voices filtered through the large, arched door. Half of my body leaned through the door, and I found two women sitting by a fireplace. I debated if I should risk them perceiving my presence or not, but they appeared deep in conversation, so I decided to cross into the space. The stone fireplace took up most of the wall to my left while rows of windows took up most of the space on the far wall. A large painting hung from the wall to my right, and I moved closer to investigate.

The painting reminded me of the Italian Renaissance works I'd studied in my college art history class. The scene was unfamiliar.

Countless figures were draped in Renaissance-style cloaks, and they were gathered around roaring firepits and mounted torches. A figure stood in a red cloak near the center of the painting, and he was pointing toward a woman whose back was turned. She had cascading auburn hair and a navy cloak with whimsical swirling patterns stitched in silver. Something about the painting felt ominous, and I studied it thoroughly, unable to look away. Finally, I tore my eyes from the painting and moved on.

Encouraged by their lack of observation, I moved closer to the women warming themselves near the fire. They were both ethereal, and their energy radiated through the space; they were powerful. But that was where their similarities ended. One of them had her honey-colored hair pulled into a neat chignon, and her eyes were the palest blue I'd ever seen. She was poised and held a teacup between her delicate fingers. Her energy was reserved, and I realized it would take time to read her.

The second woman sat across the fire from the other, and it was her energy I noticed most. It zipped around the space wildly, and her nerves pricked at the edges of my own anxiety. I breathed deeply before proceeding. Dark hair spilled down her back, cloaking it with strands the color of a midnight sky. There was something in her hazel eyes I couldn't quite discern, a wisdom. And a sadness. She leaned against the stone wall, and she rested her arm across her knees, a teacup hanging lazily from her fingertips. One of her legs was exposed through the slit of her floral dress, and a jagged scar ran the length of her calf.

The scene felt off . . . something was wrong. From the strange flaming torches to the women's medieval inspired clothing, it was an odd scene. Was I at some sort of Renaissance Faire?

I miss freedom, Camille," the black-haired woman said. "I long to return to Thalassa."

"Give it time."

"It's unnatural for me to be away from the sea this long. My heart is frozen like the wasteland outside those windows." She shivered, though I didn't suspect it was from the cold. "Don't you miss France?"

Camille swirled the black tea in her cup, considering the question. "I'm not like you. I don't miss anything I've left behind."

The black-haired woman sighed and leaned her head against the stones. "I should like to see France. I'd give anything to see Earth."

The world seemed to tilt on its axis as my stomach flipped.

"I'm fonder of Opimae myself," Camille said.

"Anything would be better than this frozen hell."

"Mind your tongue, Gabriella."

The room fell quiet. Camille finished her tea in silence while Gabriella stared wordlessly toward the windows. A blizzard raged outside, causing total whiteout conditions. I turned back to my newfound companions to find Gabriella's gaze settling on me. I thought perhaps she was watching the storm, but as I moved around the space, her hazel eyes traced my progress. I froze.

Camille snapped her fingers, and her teacup disappeared.

"He's back."

She rose from her seat and headed for the door. It closed softly behind her, and I returned my focus to Gabriella. Her dress billowed in her wake, and my breath came short as she stopped just in front of me.

"You'd better go. You wouldn't want him to catch you lurking again." She closed her eyes briefly. "Are you well-intentioned? I feel that you are. I hope I'm right about that."

She made her way to the door and her fingers rested lightly on the handle for a few long seconds before she turned back to me.

Her brows knitted in concentration. "I should be more careful than this, but . . . if you're the one from the prophecy . . . his name is Lorenzo Belmonte. Come quickly, before he learns how to use that ring."

And with that, she was gone.

I awoke in my living room feeling confused and unnerved. My heart raced and perspiration peppered my body. I looked around and registered the worried expressions of six faces I knew well.

"Hadley, my love. Are you all right?"

I focused on Fitz and wrapped my arms around his neck. He held me tightly until I was more composed, and I pulled back nodding.

"I'm okay."

Fitz lifted me from the ground and placed me carefully in a comfy chair near the fire. Henry slid a dram of whisky toward me. I nodded in gratitude and took a sip, allowing the fiery single malt to warm my belly before launching into my explanation.

"Sorry about that. The return was incredibly disorienting this time."

"Your body was stressed almost the whole time you were gone," Tanner said.

"Whatever it is that happened to you in Belmonte's realm, it agitated your body and spirit to a point that the reinfusion was jarring for you," Ian explained.

"That makes sense," I said.

"Take your time, but Hadley . . . what happened?" Izzy asked as she knelt to the ground in front of me. She touched her hands to my feet, and calm energy pushed through my veins, quieting my agitation.

I started from the beginning and ran the group through the chain of events. The story was littered with gasps and questions, but we finally made our way to the end, and the room went silent for a moment before Ann broke the quiet.

"I was a historian before I retired, you ken? I spent years in the archives researching a legend that most witches discredited. But for whatever reason, I couldnae seem to let it go."

Ian's head snapped to Ann, his eyes wide.

"Oh god," he whispered.

Ann nodded before continuing. "You see, there are a few records that turned up from the late 18th century that reference another world—a world where witches were allowed to travel to and from."

Her gaze shifted to me. "That world was called Opimae."

A gasp escaped Izzy's lips. Tanner rose from his seat and began pacing the room. Fitz and I locked eyes.

Ann continued. "I dinnae ken what I believe. Even after years of research, I've found the evidence is conflicting. But . . . I wouldnae discredit what Hadley heard in that room."

"I'd like to see your research, Ann," Henry said.

"Me too." Tanner turned to face us again.

"I think I need to talk to James Murray," I said.

"Are you sure about that, Hads?" Fitz asked.

"No. But he's on the council. If I tell him I heard about a world called Opimae, I'll at least know if his response is truthful or not."

"I dinnae think there's a risk with James. He might not reveal anything, but I foresee no danger," Ian added.

"I'll talk to him soon, then."

"I'll come to the castle in case you run into any trouble," Fitz said. "And Isaac arrives Friday, so if you meet with Murray then, I'll bring Isaac with me."

With Fitz's family in town and the chaos of my spirit-travel, I'd forgotten Isaac was coming for a long weekend. That was a bit of good news, at least.

"We could meet before then to review Ann's research?" Henry suggested.

A round of affirmatives filled the air.

"This started as research into a family mystery, and now we're discussing prophecies and foreign planets," Izzy marveled. "I can hardly believe it."

She was right. Life was about to get a lot more interesting—and fast.

CHAPTER FORTY

I asked for a meeting with James Murray on Friday. Apparently, his day was packed, but Edna had sent him a note to check in with me if he found some time in between meetings. I decided to go about my day as usual while Fitz and Isaac spent the afternoon at the castle exploring in hopes that I'd have a chance to connect about Opimae.

I crossed the castle's Great Hall to photograph a recently repaired wall near a suit of armor when footsteps echoed behind me. For a moment I froze, worried my supernatural stalker had returned, but almost as quickly, I recognized the energy.

"Mr. Murray, it's nice to see you."

"Good afternoon, Ms. Weston. Might I ask what you're working on this fine afternoon?"

"I'm gathering material for a pamphlet Marketing and I are pulling together. It's for donors attending next year's function. The new year will be here before we know it."

"Brilliant. I cannae wait to see what you pull together."

"I'm hoping Mark and I will make some strides together on this project. I don't think he's pleased that I'm here."

A soft smile tugged at the corner of Mr. Murray's lips. "He'll warm to you. Give it time, Ms. Weston."

I nodded.

"Well, I'm guessing the reason for your visit is due to my request for some of your time?" I asked.

"Indeed, it is. I have about thirty minutes open."

"Great. Could we head to your office? It's not something I'd like to discuss out here."

Mr. Murray signaled for me to lead the way. We stepped from the warmth of the Great Hall into a blustery scene. The wind gusts were excessively cold and strong, and I slipped my camera strap over my shoulder before pulling my hair back and braiding it as we crossed the courtyard toward our offices. Tourists were laughing as their hair blew straight up, and one gentleman was running after his ballcap, which was tumbling toward a castle wall.

I was relieved when I took my seat across the desk from Mr. Murray, warming my hands on a steaming mug filled with tea. But my relief was short-lived. Mr. Murray's energy was off, and something about it prickled at my witch's eye.

I cleared my throat and began.

"There are a few things I wanted to ask you about. They aren't related to castle business."

Mr. Murray arched his eyebrow but nodded for me to proceed.

"What do you know about Lorenzo Belmonte?"

He hesitated before answering. "A fair amount I suppose. I sit on the Scottish National Coven Council—I assume you've grown familiar with the witchkind government structure?"

I nodded. "So, is Dr. Belmonte involved in the council with you?"

His voice rose. "He no longer deserves the title doctor. He violated his oath to do no harm many years ago."

"So, that's a no, then."

Mr. Murray sighed. "Why are you asking me about Lorenzo? You shouldnae be looking into him."

"It's too late for that."

"Ms. Weston, please. There's so much you cannae possibly understand."

I paused, considering my next move. I decided to take a gamble.

"That's actually what I wanted to talk to you about. I . . . well, I gathered some information that doesn't quite make sense."

"What do you mean?"

"Have you heard of a place called Opimae, by chance?"

Mr. Murray sat back in his seat and rested his chin on his linked hands. "Do you ken what you're asking?"

"I do. Or at least, I think I do."

He eyed me suspiciously. "What are you getting at, Ms. Weston?"

"I believe that's where Lorenzo is—in Opimae."

"How did you arrive at that conclusion?"

"All signs pointed in that direction," I said.

"And what signs were those?"

I gave no answer.

"You shouldnae be researching this. And whatever you do, do *no* return to Lorenzo's home."

My blood ran cold. "Excuse me?"

Confusion flashed across Mr. Murray's features for only a second before recognition sank in. He knew what he'd done.

"How did you know I was in Lorenzo's home?" I asked. "Have you been watching me?"

Mr. Murray gave no answer, but his eyes were distant. I waited until he found his explanation.

"I'm a seer," he stated with some resignation. "I admit I was looking into you more than necessary. I apologize, but your position is important to the success of the castle and our restoration project. I care about this place immensely."

"What did you see?"

"I saw you in an office. Hadley, Lorenzo Belmonte is dangerous. He *will* find out who you are, just as he told you. I ken you haven't calculated your next move, but I'm concerned."

"I can't believe you were watching me."

"I apologize—truly. Hear me out?"

I nodded.

"You are still adjusting to your magic, and I worried about an issue arising around the castle. Our secrecy is imperative. And truthfully, I didnae have time to await information from the lower councils—not if we were going to make an offer quickly.

"With your . . . history, I've checked in occasionally. I wanted to warn you, but I need approval to discuss it. The councils are effective, but we're not always the most expedient."

"Approval?"

"From the upper council and the Cardinal Court."

"If Lorenzo is dangerous, I have to wonder why you waited to warn me regardless of their approval."

"That wasn't my call. There would be consequences if I stepped out of line."

"Then you and Fitz's father are more similar than I'd like," I said.

His eyebrow arched, though he remained silent.

"This isn't just about me being a newly matched witch, is it? You know about me and Fitz."

"Aye," he returned through pursed lips.

"Did you know our story when you hired me?"

"I thought you two were quite brave."

As much as I appreciated his sentiments, I didn't have much time with him, and I needed to return our focus to the reason I had requested this meeting.

"I need more information on Lorenzo."

Mr. Murray sighed. "I cannae talk any further—not yet."

"I think we could reach some sort of mutual disclosure. I think we could help each other."

"I'm as interested in Lorenzo as you are. But I'll need approval from the Cardinal Court to discuss this any further."

"If I may offer a suggestion?"

He nodded for me to continue.

"Chloe Wilson is overseeing my training. Raise this question to her."

Mr. Murray hesitated and then said, "Aye . . . I'll do it."

I had one last effort to give. "I know you're limited in what you can share, but Mr. Murray . . . I transported to a strange place. Please, can you just confirm this for me? Did I travel to Opimae?"

He held my gaze, and I thought for a brief moment that I had won him over.

He finally responded. "I'll speak with Chloe immediately, and hopefully, I can reveal more information soon."

I thanked Mr. Murray for his time and headed for the door.

"Ms. Weston?" he called as I reached for the handle.

"Yes?"

"It would not be wise to return to Lorenzo's home. He is a danger to you."

I checked my phone as I exited the building—a text from Jordan.

Still on for our FaceTime date tomorrow? she asked.

Wouldn't miss it, I replied.

And I wouldn't.

We'd talk about our jobs, how much we missed each other, my relationship with Fitz, her parents' recent visit; and I would continue to carefully avoid talking with her about the changes that I most wanted to share, the secret that burned inside of me like a searing hot knife in the pit of my stomach.

But I was learning the balance of my new life, and I was grateful Jordan could still be a part of it, even if our relationship had to look a little different than it had in the past.

I slid my phone back into my bag and headed for the castle exit.

Fitz and Isaac were waiting just outside the castle to walk home with me. Isaac lifted me from the ground and spun me around.

"I am so happy to see you, *Carissima.*"

When we entered our flat, the whole gang was there, and I was glad we were closing on the adjoining apartment. I had the distinct feeling we were going to need the space.

I recapped the meeting for them. "I'm trying to be open-minded here, but this is still strange to me. I can't believe he was watching me."

"I understand why he did it, but typically, we need clearance from the councils to engage in any sort of surveillance," Ian said.

"From what I understand, James Murray is a rule follower, so this was a huge risk on his part and—honestly—out of character."

"The councils have been riding that line for years though," Isaac added. "This does not surprise me."

"Let's not forget that because Murray has a seat on the council, he knows a great deal more than he's letting on," Fitz said. "As soon as a witch of human lineage who, along with her mate, defied council orders and then crossed this border, you can bet the Scottish Council did everything in their power to find details on us."

"That's true. I wonder what he's been plotting," Henry wondered.

"That's an eerie thought. Just when I thought things were settling down," I said.

"Being a witch is different from being a human in a lot of ways. This is just another example. We're all so connected, it's harder to keep secrets. It's just our nature," Tanner said.

"Speaking of secrets, do you think he believes in the existence of Opimae?" Ann said absentmindedly.

"He chose his words carefully, but I'm certain that's why he's seeking Chloe's approval. I think he wants to talk to me about it."

Izzy reached for her mom's hand. "You will keep us updated, won't you?"

"Of course, Iz," Fitz answered.

"And I dinnae ken what type of partnership he might try to build, but keep us updated on that as well," Ian said. "You ken as well as I do that the council doesn't offer information like this unless they intend on recruiting you."

"I know, Dad."

My chest grew tight.

My mind began ticking through all the little signs: the council offering us an olive branch, their long-time desire for Fitz to join them, their decision to bring Tanner to evaluate me, James Murray hiring me for my position at the castle . . . and I knew Ian was right.

James wouldn't share this information unless he wanted something from us.

This was it. This must have been the reason the council had gone easy on us.

"In the meantime, I think we should do a bit of our own information gathering," Henry said.

"What do you have in mind?" Ian asked.

"I propose Hadley return to Lorenzo's home. Each time she's gone, she's gathered new intelligence."

"It's a good idea," Fitz agreed as he turned to me. "But it's solely your decision, Hadley."

I looked around the room at the faces anxiously awaiting my decision. "I'll do it. Tomorrow."

CHAPTER FORTY-ONE

The following evening, I sat in our apartment, flanked by our friends and family. James had spoken with Chloe and was awaiting an answer from the court, but we decided to push forward with my return to Lorenzo's home instead of waiting for a final decision.

I closed my eyes and asked time to take me to Lorenzo's kingdom.

I expected to open my eyes to the office, but instead, the room appeared distantly before me, like I was peering through a snow globe. At first, I saw nothing but darkness around me, the scene floating in an abyss, but as my sight adjusted, weak light took shape in the depths of the void. I'd seen the swirling constellations of the in-between with Fitz while transporting, but I'd never encountered it during my spirit-travels, nor had I ever seen the stars so dim. I returned my focus to Lorenzo's office as I pushed back against the anxiety nipping at the edges of my consciousness. I willed myself closer to the scene and ran headfirst into an invisible barrier.

I instinctively reached for my aching head before realizing it would do me no good and reminded myself that my spirit and my body were less connected than normal: *mind over matter.* I reached timidly toward the room, and my fingers sent waves of energy rippling through the air.

Lorenzo had increased his protection spells.

But my training was going well, and it would take more than that to stop me. I closed my eyes and ran my fingers across the edges of his spell, picking at anything that felt suspicious. Eventually, I found the wisp that tied the energy strands together and tugged.

The energy unraveled, though it lingered through the air like it was searching for something. I paused, suddenly understanding the energy was meant to cling to the witch who unraveled it—it was meant to tie them to Lorenzo. A shiver ran through the core of my spirit, and I held my breath until the curious energy drifted through me. It continued onward in its search for the physical manifestation of me that it wouldn't find.

The air shifted, and an opening into Lorenzo's office appeared before me. I stepped through and fell to my hands and knees. A sigh of relief escaped my lungs.

I worked my way around the room, searching for anything that might be helpful. The ring was nowhere in sight, but since the summoning spell had brought me to Lorenzo's office, I knew it must be nearby. I scanned the stone walls. The maps were missing, and the windows were gone.

Windows, I thought, and they appeared.

At least I was getting something right. Though the skies were gray, visibility was decent, and I scanned snow-covered peaks that stretched as far as I could see.

I turned back to the room and decided to try Lorenzo's desk drawers again. I was standing in an enchanted room, after all. Perhaps the answer had been right in front of me this entire time.

I sat in his chair and shuddered. He'd been there recently—the chair was still charged with his energy. I shook off the thought and searched for the edges of a protection spell. And sure enough, it was there. It took only a few seconds to find the opening, and I tugged. I repeated the process of unwinding his spell. With the final tug, the drawers opened.

Finally.

"Files," I whispered.

Countless files materialized, and I set to work. About halfway through, a page caught my attention.

Though the paper was dulled by time, the ink hadn't faded. I swept my fingers across the pages, searching for anything useful. I was met by the magic that had been intertwined into the ink by the letter's author. The text was foreign to me—Latin, maybe—but I recalled a spell Maka taught me that would translate languages and recited it quickly.

The letters faded, and my heart dropped, but then, the words materialized in English. I read the page twice trying to commit the information to memory.

Lorenzo,

Take your mother to Opimae. Unexpected issues hold me in London, but I'll join you as soon as I'm able. The plans for the fortress are enclosed. The modifications needed are slight, but they're necessary. With the ring, the councils won't be able to stand against us, and we can finally overturn their faulty thinking.

May Fate grant us favor as you carry forward our plans. Remember what I told you about the in-between—vary your threads. I'll be with you soon.

- Father

I thumbed through the attached floor plans for the layout of the fortress before stumbling across a map of Opimae. A mountain range rose from Opimae City toward the northwest and near the top of the range someone had drawn a red "X". I checked the elevation charts: 22,438 feet. The nearest mountain town was Terra Firma, and per the scale, it looked like the fortress was located roughly ten miles north.

I felt my heartbeat quicken somewhere . . . *on Earth.*

If these papers were correct, then I'd confirmed Lorenzo's location was in Opimae—and I'd found his *exact* location. I sat flabbergasted for a moment before returning the paperwork to the desk. I rushed to the window under a compulsion to look once more at the landscape.

I threw open the arched pane window and was met by jagged, snow-covered mountains.

I closed the window and turned.

Lorenzo stood near the doorway with his eyes fixed indisputably on me. I studied him quickly, noting that he was again dressed in black, though his attire seemed to echo a medieval warrior. His overcoat held four large buckles that secured dark leather straps into place, and my eyes traced a dark leather strap to a quiver resting on his back. He moved slowly to the desk where he pulled the quiver over his head and rested it gently on the wooden surface.

I scanned the closed door, wondering how he had entered the space, before returning my gaze to the face of my opponent. His dark eyes remained fixed on me, and though I couldn't wonder why his eyes held so much anger within them, their intensity sent a chill through the pit of my stomach.

He moved toward me slowly, and I froze, remembering that he couldn't harm my spirit. I thought he might walk straight through me, but when he was merely inches from my face, he paused and closed his eyes.

"Ah." He fractured the silence and opened his eyes. "It's you again. I thought as much."

The slightest hint of a smile tugged at his lips, and he linked his hands behind his back before he paced the room seemingly lost in thought.

"Why don't you tell me a few things? You could begin with your name, for instance." He looked again in my direction, and my heart rate grew perceptible in my chest. He'd be handsome if it weren't for the ominous energy lingering around him like a cloud. Something about him felt . . . unnerving.

A noise escaped my lips—more breath than laugh—and unbelievably, it didn't seem to escape his notice.

"Impossible," I muttered.

Lorenzo's grin widened. "No. I'm afraid nothing is impossible. Didn't the councils tell you that?"

"How can you hear me?"

"You aren't the only gifted witch in this room. You might have penetrated my spells, but don't believe even for a second that you're more powerful than I am."

"How would you know?" I asked.

Lorenzo paused as he cocked his head in my direction. "Oh," he whispered. "It *is* you, isn't it, Hadley?"

My blood ran cold. How could he possibly know my name?

"I thought so. Who else would it be?" He nodded thoughtfully. "Why have you come here?"

I hesitated, choosing my words carefully. "I wanted to know if Opimae was real. Is that where I am?"

"Surely, you already know the answer to that."

"I want to hear you say it."

He laughed. "Then you'll remain in want."

I stayed silent.

"See, you've broken into my home before. Why should I tell you anything when you're sneaking around looking for things that don't belong to you?"

"Fine. I want to understand why you took Esther MacGregor's ring. What do you want with it?"

Lorenzo tilted his head considering my question. "I want to fix what the councils have broken. The ring will help me set things right."

"Like what?"

"The councils force witches to live in secrecy. We hide from the humans like we are ashamed of ourselves." Lorenzo shook his head. "And for what? Because we fear their persecution? It does not make good sense," he said.

I hesitated.

"We need a revolution. Reform won't come to us unless we demand it," he said. "The councils have overstepped, and they must answer for the injustices they've inflicted on to the very group of magical beings they've vowed to protect."

I thought of their threat to wipe my memories. I thought of Fitz's fear that they'd spellbind us, our speculation that they'd force us to partner with them . . . on something related to Lorenzo.

"The councils are trying to help me. They said they'd protect me," I said weakly.

"Is that so? But you know better than that, don't you?" he asked. "They only protect themselves."

Hadn't I expressed the same sentiment to Mia the first day I'd met her?

"They don't care about witchkind. I wish to change that," he continued.

"The councils say this arrangement protects us, that it would be detrimental to us if humans knew we existed." The words tasted bitter on my tongue. They echoed the very sentiment Mia and Olivia had expressed to me. But I needed to push Lorenzo—keep him talking until I could figure a way out.

"And have they protected you?"

I didn't answer.

"They're all liars, Hadley. Have you not learned that by now?"

"No."

"But that's not quite true, is it?" He came closer. "What does it feel like when someone lies to you, Hadley? To me, the truth feels like cool water trickling across my tongue. But lies? They run me dry. And right now . . . I thirst."

His eyes were like inky pools that longed to pull me under.

In the buzz of the moment, I'd forgotten to shield myself against my enemy, and Lorenzo stood so close that my head grew thick at the intensity of his energy. His scent permeated my senses with frankincense and amber. There was something else—vanilla, I thought. The ancient scent was too strong, overwhelming in some way, but I still needed a deep breath to push back against the ambush of his energy.

I steadied myself before drawing in the deep breath I sought, and upon my exhale, I asked the air to disperse the sweet, musky scent, and the effect was immediate. My head cleared, and I prepared myself for what would follow.

"You want some truth? You got it. I don't believe a thing you say. For you to have that ring . . . you've stolen power from another family. You disgust me."

Lorenzo tilted his head back ever so slightly, and as he mulled over his response, I took the opportunity to pick at the edges of his mind. Like his home, his mind was protected, but I was growing proficient in recognizing the patterns in his magic.

"What are you doing with the ring, anyway?"

Lorenzo's mind ticked through a myriad of thoughts, and so quickly that they didn't quite make sense. But soon enough, I heard something useful.

"Oh," I whispered. "You haven't found a way to access the power of the ring."

The anger burning through Lorenzo's eyes was palpable. He grabbed my wrist and pulled me mere inches from his face. "No one can read my mind."

My mind was frantic. How was he touching me?

"How did you do that?" Lorenzo asked.

I tried to pull myself free.

Lorenzo shook his head. "Answer me!"

"Let go of me!"

"Hadley," he growled.

"Don't you dare speak to me that way."

"I don't take orders from anyone," he spat. "You better remember that, fire witch."

I attempted again to pull myself loose from his grasp, but he grabbed my other arm and held them together. I wasn't thinking clearly. I'd let the shock of the moment get the best of me and that needed to change if I was going to make it out of that room. I looked around, orienting myself, grounding myself back to the scene around me.

"Stop looking around and talk to me," Lorenzo said sternly.

"How do you know I'm looking around?" I asked.

"The outline of your energy shimmers. I can see you; I can feel you. Now, how can you read my mind?"

I shook my head. "I don't know. I just can."

"Don't toy with me. It won't end well for you."

My mind finally caught up. I needed to return to my body. I just needed to call myself home. I closed my eyes and thought of the room where my body lay.

I thought of Fitz and the feel of his touch rather than the uncomfortable grip of Lorenzo's. The air shifted, and I opened my eyes to a hazy scene. The details of the room mingled with those of Lorenzo's office, and I knew it—I was suspended somewhere between the two places. I thought of my home, of the roaring fireplace, the smile on Fitz's face, but suddenly, the scene disappeared, and I was back in Lorenzo's office.

"We're not done here." It was a demand. "And if you'll stop being stubborn, I'll tell you why you should come to Opimae."

"What are you talking about?"

"Join me, Hadley."

"*What?*"

"We shouldn't be fighting against each other. You belong on the right side of things—not the councils' side."

His eyes were wild as they searched mine.

"What are you talking about?"

"You're working with the councils, yes?"

"They're helping me."

Lorenzo chuckled. "That is so naïve, it's almost endearing."

"Well, they aren't holding me against my will, so that's a start."

"And you think they wouldn't have wiped your memories clean to protect themselves? They say they're protecting us." Lorenzo scoffed. "Are you working with them? Are you here to spy for them?"

"What? No. I just want the ring back. And I want to understand what's happening."

Lorenzo's eyes narrowed in thought.

"Join my side, Hadley. I have forces greater than you can imagine. Together, we will ensure the councils will never punish another witch for who they love."

I hesitated, and Lorenzo smiled.

"You know I'm right. Work with me, and we'll set things right in the witch world."

I paused, unsure of my next move, before pulling back from him. He tightened his grasp and shook his head. "Stop doing that."

I gathered all my courage and settled my gaze squarely on Lorenzo before pulling my energy into a whirlwind all around me. The energy pushed violently against Lorenzo, and despite his best efforts, I pulled myself free. He knelt and struck his hand to the floor. The ground beneath me rippled. As the disturbance met my feet, a burst of energy slammed me against the wall. Before I could recover, Lorenzo was in front of me.

He pressed me against the stone that crept from behind the crumbling plaster wall.

His hand rested on my collarbone, and his fingertips pressed uncomfortably into my neck. His eyes flickered across me, and he moved closer until his breath was warm on my ear.

"You will not win this fight, Hadley." His voice was filled with venom. "You have no idea what you're up against."

"Neither do you," I whispered. I gathered every bit of energy that channeled within me. I called to the air and asked for her favor. I pulled at every stray energy in the room, and I worked them into a growing funnel within me. When the force of the motion threatened to overtake me from the inside out, I whispered to the threads of time, and I asked to return to safety. The energy spilled out, and Lorenzo released me in utter confusion. Wind whipped through the room, and when he reached for me again, the shock between us was so intense, I screamed.

A spark lit the space between us. Lorenzo cradled his hand protectively against his chest, but I could make out the fresh burn marks. His brows knitted in pain, and his wide eyes were the last thing I saw before darkness overtook me.

"Hadley, please." It was barely a whisper, but Fitz's voice echoed through the stillness.

Why is he worried? I wondered before my mind caught up. *Lorenzo.*

I needed to wake up. I needed to tell everyone what he was trying to do, and what he could do. I needed to tuck myself safely against Fitz's chest until I'd steadied myself again. I focused on pulling my spirit back into my body and found the constellations of the in-between.

I searched for anything of substance, anything that gave me a sense of direction, but it was fruitless. Panic would make everything worse, I realized.

I closed my eyes and focused on my breathing until my heart returned to a normal pace. Then, I set my intention. I would find my way home. It was that simple. The stars began to swirl, and I navigated through them until I ran into a soft glow. I could go no further, but suddenly, a familiar energy washed over me.

Fitz.

I focused on Fitz: his energy, his soft smile, his voice. The illumination grew brighter until I could see nothing else, and my mind grew heavy. Just when I thought my mind was slipping under, Fitz appeared.

"Fitz! What are you doing here?" I asked.

He looked around curiously. His face lit when he found my energy.

"I can hear you in my mind. That's a good sign," he said. "Are you okay?"

"I think so. How did you get here?"

"I felt your panic, so we decided I should follow your path," Fitz said. "The threads were fragile, but our connection wasn't. I was able to follow it through the in-between and straight to you. It was quite the journey."

"What do you mean?"

"Hadley, this was a ridiculously far journey for a time-walker. I think it's true. This is a whole different universe."

A whole different universe.

"Then I'm surprised either of us made it here."

"You still don't understand how powerful we are."

I nodded before remembering he couldn't see me. "I've landed in the in-between twice. We need to get out of here."

"Aye, but can you leave? Your power feels weak, and I can't carry your spirit like I can with your body. I think you need a bit of help."

"I'm not taking a boost from you, Fitz. You need all of your strength to return to Earth."

"I'll return home and channel my power toward your physical form."

I considered that. "Okay, then."

"I'll see you soon," he said.

Fitz closed his eyes and his brows knit, and soon . . . he was gone. After a few seconds, bursts of energy channeled through the connection and into my system. The feel of his power inside of me created a sense of euphoria, and I thought I'd be delirious by the time he was finished. When the transfer was complete, I knew what to do.

I closed my eyes and envisioned my home. The faces of our friends. The cool air that leaked from the old windowpane near my favorite leather chair. The scent of whisky welcomed me to safety.

My eyes flew open, and I immediately turned to Fitz. His worried eyes were already studying me. I flew into his arms, crashing into him with a thud. He chuckled and held me tightly in his strong arms.

"Oof," I muttered.

"Aye," Fitz said. "You took a beating in Lorenzo's office."

"I'll help," Izzy said as she moved closer.

Izzy squeezed me gently before resting her hand on the side of my face. She whispered words that were lost on me, but a warm, fuzzy state of serenity took hold.

A calming spell.

"Thank you."

"We can't keep the questions at bay for long, but hopefully this will help you get through it all."

I nodded and looked at Fitz. "Your power is unbelievable," I muttered. "It was good for me to experience it like that."

"Like what?" Ian asked, bringing me back to the world around us.

"Oh," I said, pulling back.

I found Tanner at the opposite side of the room. His eyes were flooded with concern, but when I met his gaze, his features relaxed.

I tore my focus back to Ian's question. Fitz had already shared some information, but we explained the rest of the encounter.

Ann shook her head. "You two make a great team."

"Fitz's power has always been a marvel. I never thought anyone would come along who could be seen as his equal . . . not until you," Ian said.

"You're pretty powerful yourself, Ian," I countered.

"The MacGregors are legendary," Isaac said. "Their magical lineage is distinguished."

"The earth has granted us favor. But none are as distinguished as Fitz, though," his dad said. "He's the most powerful living MacGregor."

"All right, enough of all that," Fitz muttered.

"Allergic to compliments." Izzy rolled her eyes.

"We need to discuss our next move," I said, pulling our focus back to our situation.

"We need more information on Lorenzo, plain and simple," Isaac said. "There's more information for me to go on, so I can continue my searches. But Opimae complicates things."

"Surely, we'll have an answer from the court soon," Henry said.

Fitz nodded. "They have the information we need—they're our most viable information source."

"Aye, I think it's time to put pressure on James," Ian said, his gaze resting on me. "You spoke directly to Lorenzo. James—and the rest of the councils—will want to hear about that. You just found your leverage."

CHAPTER FORTY-TWO

Ian was right about the leverage. Monday after work, Fitz and I found ourselves at Whiski ready to meet with James Murray. When I had demanded to see him that morning and shared that I had encountered Lorenzo again, James asked to meet with Fitz and me at 7 p.m.

The warmth of the pub was a relief as we filtered through the doorway. It took little effort to follow Mr. Murray's energy trail to the back of the bar where he sat nursing a dark beer and scanning the crowd through its narrow opening.

"Can you feel that?" Fitz asked.

An invisible barrier hung around Murray's table, and the air was heavy with the sign of protection. I was becoming quite proficient at identifying privacy spells.

Though the front of the restaurant was cramped, empty tables surrounded Mr. Murray's booth. We took a seat across from him.

"Hadley. Fitz. I'm so glad you both made it."

It was the first time he'd ever called me by my given name.

"Of course. It's a pleasure to see you again, Mr. Murray," Fitz said.

"The pleasure is all mine. Please take a seat, and you both can call me James."

We ordered drinks and dove right into the conversation.

"I paid Lorenzo another visit."

"I told you to stay away from him."

"Yes, I know. You were right about him being dangerous."

"Are you all right?" His eyes swept over me.

I nodded.

"As it happens, I received approval from the court last night to speak with you two." James sipped his drink and sat forward in his chair. His eyebrows knit tightly. "The word '*opimae*' is Latin, you ken? It means luxurious or lush, and the terrain is certainly that."

I nodded, though it didn't make sense. The landscape I'd seen from the windows hadn't exactly matched that description. And what did this have to do with anything?

"You noticed the maps on the walls in Lorenzo's office, I'm sure?"

"I did."

"We've been trying to make sense of them, James, but we haven't found a correlation in all of the locations," Fitz said.

"You wouldnae—not without access to council records. You see, Lorenzo acquired those maps while on the run, and he plotted the perfect escape from the councils. The area he sought refuge in is located in the Olympic National Park—right in the midst of your homeland, Hadley."

"Why there?" I asked.

"There was a particular area he needed to find."

"I saw markings along the High Divide Trail. Why would he go there? Easier to lose the councils?"

"There's a portal located off the trail."

"A portal? Where does it lead?"

Mr. Murray leveled his gaze. His eyes met Fitz's, and then mine. "To another world. The portal leads to another universe."

Silence fell momentarily.

"So, Opimae truly is another world?" I asked.

"Aye."

"How is that possible?" Fitz asked.

"It's magic," he quipped.

"I've heard rumors of another universe inhabited by magical beings, but until now, I discredited those accounts," Fitz said.

"The UCA—United Covens Affairs—gained knowledge of a portal around two hundred B.C. The portal was adjusted to what is now Washington, and it was a secret shared with no one outside witchkind, not even the human leaders of the day." He smiled. "As you can imagine, it seemed a safe location at the time, and it has remained one of the most discreet locations in the world. Shortly after its creation, we began to patrol the portal to ensure no one entered or exited who shouldnae."

"What do you know about this world?" I asked.

"Magic is practiced freely and openly, without fear or repercussion. Their convention is similar to our structure, and much of our knowledge and communication is through them. We've maintained a peaceful relationship over the centuries. Unlike Earth, their world is made up of many magical beings—witches, elves, dragons, and even water witches, or mermaids, as we call them here."

Fitz and I caught each other's gaze, marveling at the new intelligence.

"How is it possible?" I asked. "That so many mythical beings exist . . ."

"Well, for one, there aren't humans in Opimae. The beings all once existed here but were run close to extinction. Those left on this side were sent through the portal for protection. Another reason the portal has fallen to myth, even in witchkind."

"Fear anything that's different: the human motto," Fitz stated plainly.

"Unfortunate, but true. We saved those we could. It's imperative we maintain control of entrances and departures. Any magical beings, apart from witches, are not allowed to cross the portal into Earth. It's simply too dangerous at this time."

They'd never stand a chance here, I realized. They'd be captured, poked, and prodded until humans pulled every bit of information possible from them. Our way of life would end.

"But witches may cross openly? Most of us don't even know the world exists," Fitz said.

"The portal has been closed for about two hundred years to anyone outside of government business," James said. "It was a request from the Opimae government. But that recently changed. We haven't yet decided how to share this information at large. It could cause chaos."

"How did Lorenzo ever make it through?" I wondered.

"The answer to that question has evaded us for years—it's a mystery. There are no records of his passage through the portal that we can find. But the Opimae government has confirmation that he is on their planet."

"What I'd like to understand is why the council has decided to trust us with this information and what you hope to gain from it," Fitz said.

"We dinnae ken what Lorenzo is capable of, and that must change. Hadley wandered her way into Lorenzo's *home*—do you understand that no one with the UCA has been able to do that? The councils have searched for years for a witch who could do what Hadley has done. You clearly seek him for a reason of your own, something of immense value to you. We would like to partner with you to combine our efforts to pinpoint his exact location. Then, we'd like to bring him to justice for crimes he has committed."

Fitz nodded to me, confirming he felt truth in what James said.

I thought of my conversation with Lorenzo. I thought of his belief that the witchkind governments were the ones in the wrong.

"What are his crimes?" I asked.

Mr. Murray sighed. "Lorenzo went rogue years ago. He claimed our government prevents witches from reaching our full potential. He believes we should rule over the humans rather than coexist. He caused quite a stir and almost exposed us to humankind. It's all rubbish, of course, and we were able to stomp out his wee movement before it escalated beyond repair."

"And then?"

"We called him to trial, then he disappeared. We have reason to believe he is planning another uprising, and that would end in tragedy—he cares little for the carnage he creates."

I mulled over the information.

"And he has no regard for human life." James shook his head.

I found James's statement odd considering he was high-ranking in a government that would have erased my memories when I was considered a human.

"So, if we were to join you . . . is this working behind the scenes, or are we talking fieldwork?" Fitz asked.

I had suspected the conversation would lean in this direction, but I wasn't sure I was prepared for what may follow.

"It would be both, and I'm afraid the fieldwork has a real level of danger. It's one of the reasons we've spent years searching for the proper individuals to fill these positions."

"What exactly do you mean by fieldwork?" I asked.

"You'd both play major roles in the mission against Lorenzo," he began, clearing his throat. "With that being said, you'd be essential in the planning phase, and during this time you'd also undergo some training. This would happen in Opimae with their council, though members of our government would also accompany you—you wouldnae be alone in this. But you would be key players in enacting our strategy to stop Lorenzo. You could be preventing war."

"You believe we can do that?" I asked.

"Look at what the two of you were able to do on your own. The councils tried but couldnae prove you two were even in contact, even with the most skilled seers available. When you decided to slip off the radar, you did. And you weren't located until you allowed yourselves to be found. You believed in something, and you accomplished it. Then you broke through Lorenzo's spells and entered his home—something we've been unsuccessful in doing for years. If you can do that alone, imagine what you'll accomplish with the councils' resources."

"Well, when you put it that way."

James chuckled. "And that's in addition to your power, your intuition, and your innate sense of good—of right and wrong. You're the type of witches others will follow, which is immensely important."

Fitz nodded absentmindedly.

"Maka's reports have been undisputedly favorable," James added.

"Chloe recommends you for this role. And Fitz, it's no secret the Scottish Council has desired a partnership with you for years. We'd be thrilled to have you finally join us."

I took a deep breath. "Can you see the future of this mission?"

"No," James said, "but I've done extensive research on what is needed to defeat Lorenzo. There's a . . . prophecy about this mission."

"A prophecy?" I asked, though Gabriella's words echoed through my mind.

"*If you're the one from the prophecy . . .*" she'd said.

"The Opimaeans have a prophecy of old. It tells of a great conflict that is brought to their peaceful planet. The Opimaean folk partner with Earth and a team of crusaders. Two of these crusaders have a strong connection to one another, and Fate ultimately leads them to the conflict. They possess great power and hold the key to bringing peace once again to the nations of Opimae."

"And you believe we're those crusaders," Fitz said.

"Aye, I do. And I believe that together, we can accomplish what the prophecy has foretold."

Fitz and I looked to one another.

"You have exactly what we're looking for in our crusade leaders. Even though Hadley is new to this world, she's demonstrating great mastery of her skills, and clearly, we have need of her abilities. And when I discovered you two were mates, I thought perhaps this was the connection referenced in the prophecy."

I nodded, still at a loss for words.

"And beyond that, you two are more powerful than most witches I've known. Your powers exceed normal standards alone, but together . . . well, it's extraordinary." He paused and looked between the two of us. "I believe Fate led you to the council for this reason—she has prepared you for what lies ahead."

"*Came to dinner with my boss. Might join a crusade to fight evil on a foreign planet,*" I said to Fitz's mind.

"*Aye just another day.*"

"Lorenzo must be stopped," James continued. "And I believe we need both of you to do so. Will you join forces?"

Lorenzo had posed the same question to me only two days prior, and now I was tasked with deciding which side was right and which was wrong.

Fitz and I exchanged a glance.

"*I think we need to take a moment to really sort this,*" Fitz said to my mind.

"James, would you mind if we take just a few minutes to talk?" I asked.

"Absolutely not. This is a lot to process. I need to make a call anyway."

James exited the room, his phone in hand, granting us privacy to discuss our future.

Fitz swirled his drink, the Scotch trickling back down the length of the glass. It was a sign I knew well—he was about to share something he found no pleasure in. "You know we don't have a choice?"

"About joining?"

"Aye."

"This is one of those moments where we're called and have to answer."

He nodded. "Right."

"And what happens if we refuse?"

"I think we'll face the consequences of our previous actions."

"Spellbinding," I said.

"Aye. This is why the council played nice when we returned to Scotland. Think about it: Olivia Cameron's reaction, Mia—a Cardinal Court member—attending the meeting and working on our case. Chloe being assigned as lead over your training."

"They were already curious about me because of the way I came into my powers, and they've wanted to work with you for years," I said.

"Then we defied their orders and effectively dropped off their radar. They realized we weren't their average case," Fitz said.

"And when we showed up in that office and Olivia felt our power . . ."

"Exactly," Fitz said.

"Shit."

"Aye . . . shite."

"So, James probably had his eyes on us from the beginning, and then I paid a visit to Lorenzo's home . . ."

"Right. Your break-in sealed the deal."

"And here I thought I wowed him with my PR skills."

"Of course, you did. But that wasn't the only thing about you that wowed him."

"I don't trust the council," I said.

"How could you?" he agreed, shrugging. "We take it a day at a time. James wasn't responsible for what happened to us. He's a good guy. That's as far as I can see right now."

"That's a good way to look at it. We take things a step at a time and assess as we go."

"And some of the members have helped you—Maka, Chloe."

I couldn't disagree.

I thought of our only alternative: run. I thought of Jordan's offer to help. I thought of Henry and Isaac's backup plan they'd put in to place when we first met with the council. But our alternative plan wouldn't bring us closer to the ring . . .

"Regardless of any of the rest of this crap, you need your family's ring back. Lorenzo can't have it. We have to fight this."

"I want that ring back more than I resent helping the councils."

"And there's larger implications to consider . . . the unrest Lorenzo could cause."

"Aye. This rebellion could affect countless lives in both worlds."

"We can't allow that to happen," I said.

Fitz agreed.

"Why are you looking at me like that?" I questioned.

"Oh . . ." His smile widened. "Honestly, I'm just in awe of you sometimes."

"What? Why?"

"You're so sure. Courageous."

"No. I'm scared, Fitz."

"Me too. But we're facing this head-on, my brave lass." Fitz took a sip of whisky, his face turning pensive. "I'm debating how much we should share of what you learned from Lorenzo."

"We both believe Lorenzo is wrong, correct?"

"Aye."

"Then I think we tell James the location of the fortress. Maybe it helps shorten this whole partnership if I'm just forthcoming from the beginning. Speed this thing along."

Fitz paused momentarily, and then nodded.

We knew what we had to do. I gripped Fitz's hand tightly. Fitz waved to James, who was waiting patiently near the front door pretending to be otherwise engaged.

"Well then? You've reached a decision?"

"Aye, we'll join you."

"Oh brilliant! I cannae tell you how pleased I am to hear that," James returned, clasping his hands together happily. "Come to the the Scottish National Coven Council meeting at the castle on Saturday. We'll discuss the particulars of your travel."

I'd come to dinner with my manager and had somehow agreed to travel to a magical land in another universe to fight a warmongering witch. Was I making a mistake?

No, I knew I wasn't. I wasn't human; I was a witch. With my power and intuition, I knew we were right to trust James, and we needed to honor Fitz's family.

"There's only one condition," Fitz said.

"Anything," James replied sincerely.

"He—Lorenzo—has something that belongs to my family. I want it back."

"And what is that?"

"He has a ring that belongs to my family," Fitz said.

James's face lit in recognition, which was quickly followed by his eyes growing wide. "You mean . . . your ancestor's ring?"

"You know about that?"

"We've known about the ring for a long time. You see, we were the ones who first took the ring after your grandmother's death. The local coven knew what she possessed but believed she wouldnae fight her way free. The leaders decided there was no danger in leaving it in her possession until her death unless her decision changed. They hoped it would grant her some comfort as she suffered in her last days.

"The council leaders sent representatives to collect the ring with the intention of locking it away until your grandfather was composed enough to release the powers. They thought it would give him closure. But the ring mysteriously vanished one night under careful watch. The guards were incapacitated, and all the spells meant to protect the ring were disarmed."

"Oh my god," I whispered.

James nodded. "It requires vast aptitude and force to undo the work of so many other powerful witches. When the guards awoke, the ring was gone."

"And you have no idea who took it?" I asked.

"It appears our investigation has yielded nothing of significance. When I looked into council records earlier this week, I found the file on the MacGregor ring. It seems the search for it was abandoned. The case was marked as suspended."

"And now Lorenzo has the ring. God only knows what his plans for it are," I said.

"And you're certain it's the proper ring?" James asked.

Fitz and I shared the details of our investigation and my experience with the ring.

"We've been unable to penetrate the perimeter of his home—that is until Hadley broke in," James said. "That's the only reason I was able to see inside. You casually discovered something we've been unable to for years, my dear."

"I didn't do anything special," I said. "I talked to the elements the way I always do."

"It seems Hadley disarms others' spell," Fitz said. "When I couldn't utilize Annabel's summoning spell but Hadley immediately transported to the ring, I realized her powers find the loopholes in others' spells and latch on. She couldn't call the ring to her either, but the ring somehow summoned her. It's incredible actually."

"Extraordinary!"

I took a deep breath before I shared the last of my major news with James.

"There's something else," I began. "James, I think I know where Lorenzo is located. It's a fortress in the northern mountains on Opimae's portal continent. If you provide me with a map, I think I can find it again—or at least I can get close."

James exhaled deeply, his expression blank. He looked down for a few seconds, and when his gaze met mine, the determination in them was clear.

"Incredible," he mumbled. He pulled out his phone and typed furiously before sliding it back into his jacket pocket. "You'll have maps sent your way immediately."

I nodded.

"Is there any further intelligence you gathered?" James asked.

"Nothing of importance. Lorenzo was cagey with me, but I think you're right to suspect a rebellion from him."

"If you think of anything else, you ken how to reach me. We'll have you give an official statement on Saturday at the council meeting."

I nodded.

"Hadley, take the rest of the week off from the castle. If my suspicions are correct, you'll be in Opimae before the end of the year."

My breath came short. The new year was only six weeks away— only six weeks and then my life would look completely different.

"Is everything all right?" James asked, his brows creasing.

"It's nothing. Just . . . I feel like I finally found my place here in Edinburgh, and it's all about to change. And honestly, my work at the castle has a lot to do with that."

James's face relaxed, and he nodded. "Your position will be waiting for you when you return."

"Who will fill my role in my absence?" I asked. "Who will head the event?"

James hesitated, which told me exactly what I needed to know.

"You're thinking of asking Mark's friend—the one who applied for this position," I guessed.

"He was the most qualified candidate, after you."

I had to wonder if James was being truthful about me being the most qualified. Or had he only hired me to recruit me for this mission?

"It's only temporary, Hadley. The position is yours."

Mark will hate me more than ever when I return, I thought.

"And the ring?" I asked. "Will it be returned to Fitz?"

"Aye. The ring will be released to Fitz once we free the power from it. Consider it as a part of your reward for helping us."

"Is that something Fitz will be able to help with? Releasing the power?"

"Of course."

James insisted on picking up the check, citing council business. He took his leave, turning on his heel before pausing.

"Oh, and one last thing . . ." James called back, over his shoulder. "Welcome to the crusade."

CHAPTER FORTY-THREE

The following morning, our group gathered at Henry's to discuss the new information we'd received from James. The room fell into chaos.

"You *agreed* to that?" Ann asked. Her soft features were scrunched in horror.

"And what if they had refused?" Ian returned. "Would it have done any good?"

"You think the council would have really called them on it?" Tanner asked.

"This is huge. Of course, they would have," Isaac answered. He sank into a nearby chair. "This is bad. This is very bad."

"So, we're past the point of questioning this as reality?" Henry asked. "We truly believe Fitz and Hadley are traveling to another universe?"

The room fell silent.

"Murray is highly regarded amongst the ranks of witchkind government. He's a sensible fellow. If he says Opimae exists, then it does," Ian said.

"How can this be?" Izzy asked almost to herself. She met my gaze frowning. "You're sure about doing this?"

I considered her question, my mind rolling through the past twenty-four hours. "Even if I'm not . . . it doesn't matter, Iz."

"It matters to me."

"Thank you." I squeezed her hand lightly. Her gaze fell on her brother. He nodded softly.

"Okay, so . . . we're doing this, right? I mean, we're all going to fight for a spot on this mission in some form or another?" Tanner asked.

"Aye," Henry answered.

"No," Fitz said taking on an authoritative tone.

"And why not?"

"You've been able to elude the councils. Don't mix yourself up now."

"That's no your call to make."

"*Think*, Henry."

"Fitz . . ." I began.

"Hadley, this is dangerous. I'm already up to my eyeballs in anxiety over you. I won't have your back like I normally would, Henry. I'll be focused on protecting Hadley."

"I can handle myself, mate. Besides, you'll need me in Opimae to help protect Hadley, keep her power hidden from Lorenzo."

His gaze shifted to me. "We'll all be in some level of danger. But Hadley . . . none of us are able to locate the loopholes like she can, and Lorenzo is already sorting that out. I'll do my part to protect her."

"You truly want a part in this?"

"I hail from a long line of warriors, and though I have seen little battle, their valor rests in my veins. I'll do what I was born to do."

Fitz exhaled slowly.

Henry continued. "Hadley needs me too. She's family now, and even you willnae prevent me from protecting our family."

Fitz placed his right hand on Henry's shoulder.

Though his energy was tight, he knew Henry well enough to know he'd made up his mind. "Then I'm proud to have you fight with me, brother."

Ian cleared his throat. "I'll join, as well."

"Ian," Ann whispered.

His face grew tender as he gazed toward his wife. "I'll not let Fitz and Hadley run headfirst into danger on their own. Besides, what's the likelihood the council willnae ask this of me anyway?"

Ann's face fell. "Slim," she answered.

"I can feel it coming. But I'll make this decision for myself. For our family."

Ann dropped her gaze. The room was suspended in silence.

When Ann raised her head, the resolution in her eyes was clear. "I'll volunteer my services on the intelligence teams," Ann responded. "I'm not meant for battle, but I'll do my part."

"A fine offer," Ian returned as he slipped his arm around her.

"This group will need a reader. Reading others' intentions has never been more imperative," Isaac chimed in. "Count me in."

"I'll join mum and offer my hand at research," Izzy said. "My plants can wait."

I had to laugh. It was such a classically Izzy line.

"And I'll ask for a transfer to this project," Tanner said. "Either as a trainer or a team member—as long as I get to help somehow."

I smiled. "Wouldn't want anyone else kicking my ass."

And there we were: a family willing to risk it all for one another and for the greater good.

Later that night, Fitz and I lay in bed as we talked though the implications of our decision.

"I don't know what to tell my mom," I admitted to Fitz.

"Stick as closely to the truth as possible. The closer to the truth, the better you'll feel, and it'll be easier to remember your story."

"I don't think she'll understand that I'm tangled up in some mission that won't allow me to communicate for a while. She's just getting used to me being over here, and now I have to tell her this."

"Look, Hads. I don't know how much your mother already knows . . ."

"What?" I sat up, my elbow sinking into my pillow.

"I saw your dad before he died. He asked for a good portion of our conversation to stay between us, so I'm not going to share much with you—I'm sorry."

"Fitz. Shit . . . you say something like that, and then you can't tell me much?"

"Aye, this is why I haven't said anything. I know you'll be pissed at me, but it's a promise I intend to keep, and you'll have to get over it, unfortunately."

"You have a way with words sometimes, you know that?"

"Here's why I brought it up—I told your dad what I am . . . that I'm a witch."

"How did *that* go?"

"The man looked me dead in the eyes and asked if you were a witch too—if that's what was going on between us."

I laughed, caught off-guard.

"I told him what you were and how you didn't know yet. I showed him magic. Hadley, I broke every damn rule in the book. I told the man everything."

"Why?" I drawled out.

"Because I knew he wouldn't make it much longer," Fitz said. "You were heartbroken—he knew that. I wanted him to know his little girl would be all right. That one way or the other, you would be fine and happy. I wanted him to know the councils wouldn't keep us apart in the end."

"Oh my god . . ." I whispered.

"Hads, he died knowing who you are, and with a couple of promises from me . . . which will stay between him and me."

I nodded, not trusting my voice.

"I'm telling you this because he said he wasn't sure if he'd share anything with your mum—a fair amount he promised he wouldn't. But some of it, he might have found a way to share with her cryptically. She might not be all that surprised by what you tell her."

"So . . . there are things she might know, others she definitely doesn't?"

"Your dad wouldn't have told her you're a witch . . . but maybe that you're different, and I'm the same kind of different."

"But you wouldn't have known about any of this . . ."

"No, *but* my dad sensed something strange for years before I met you. He said I'd find someone to equal my power. And my mate and I would embark on something grand . . . something unbelievable. I told your dad I knew we had a big calling in life.

"So, back to your mum. I'd say you have until the day we cross through the portal to talk to her, but the longer you allow this to sit in the back of your mind, the worse you'll feel."

"I guess I should call her tomorrow."

"I think that's wise," he said, brushing his thumb across my cheek.

"I can't believe I'm going to leave her completely alone." A tear spilled down my cheek.

"Hads," Fitz whispered.

"My dad leaves her. I leave her." I shook my head. "I feel awful about this."

"I'd tell you not to worry, but I know you better than that."

I laughed despite my tears.

"Try not to carry that weight. You can't help the circumstances."

I nodded.

"And don't worry. You'll come back to her."

"We'll both come back," I countered, more confidently than I felt.

The following afternoon, I stared at my phone calculating the time difference. *9 a.m. Pacific Time.* There was no time like the present.

I sighed and reached for my phone. I stared at my mother's contact card and hesitated for only a moment before punching the FaceTime button.

My mom beamed as she answered the phone. "Hi, honey. How's everything going?"

"Good. How are things in the Pacific Northwest?"

"Nice. It's a weirdly dry week for November. You just missed Gram—she went for a walk."

I'd forgotten Gram was visiting her. It was her second trip since I'd left for Paris, and I instantly felt better knowing Gram was with her.

"Why don't you tell me what's wrong, Hadley?" my mom said, her brow creasing.

"Momma," I started. I paused, resting my head in my hands, wondering how to begin. "I'll be gone for a little while, and I won't be able to reach you."

My mother's expression changed slightly, confusion flashing across her features. "What do you mean?"

"Fitz and I have been asked to take care of some business that will have us away for quite some time."

"Just you and Fitz?" she asked warily, her hazel eyes narrowing.

"A few other people are joining us."

"I don't understand. Wherever you're going . . . we can still talk?"

"I don't think so," I said.

"How long will you be gone?"

"I'm not sure. It depends on how quickly we finish."

"Hadley, you've got to give me something here. This sounds ridiculous."

"I know."

"This can't deal with your work," my mom said.

"It deals with another type of work," I said, "but I can't talk about it, Momma."

"Why on earth can you not tell me about this?"

"Because I'm not supposed to tell anyone about this."

"But I'm your mother," she said.

"This is a mission of sorts, one I can't talk about. There would be consequences for both of us."

She stared, searching my face, and a fire rested in her eyes that I well recalled from my teenage years. She was angry, and I knew why. This couldn't make any sense to her, and I wasn't even doing a decent job of explaining the information I was able to share.

"Okay, here's the deal: we've been recruited for an assignment by a branch of government and are under strict orders to keep it confidential. I don't know how long this mission will take, but I'll contact you as soon as we're back. I can't tell you any more than that."

"Is this with the military?"

"You could say that."

"This is still not good enough," she returned, her voice terse.

"You know I've always been different," I said. "I know you realize Fitz and his family are too. We're the same type of different, okay? People like us are called to duty sometimes because of our skill sets."

My mom remained quiet, but I saw the conflict raging through her features. My departure would hurt her, and the thought broke my heart.

"I can't accept that."

"You have to accept it because you don't have another choice. And if you can't accept it, then you won't be able to see much of me in the future. Please understand what a difficult position I'm in."

"I'm sure we can get you out of this. I wish your father—" she broke off, trying to suppress tears.

"If Daddy were here," I said softly, "things wouldn't be any different. He told you a couple of things about a conversation he had with Fitz, didn't he? Right before we lost him."

My mom's eyes widened.

"Look, I don't know what he told you, but . . . Daddy knew everything there is to know about me, and about Fitz. And if he were here, knowing what he did, he'd tell you that I have no choice. I'm doing what I need to do."

"Oh god, Hadley."

"I know, Momma. It's a lot. And Fitz would be in a ton of trouble for sharing what he did. The same would happen to me if I told you everything now."

"Meaning I just have to trust what you're saying and never expect any more explanation," she finished, her expression flat.

"Pretty much. But what we're about to do—it's a good thing, I promise you that. I'm on the right side of things."

"Do you really have to do this?" she asked, echoing the same question she'd posed to me before I left for Paris.

I nodded. "Yeah . . . I do. I wish I could explain this better, but I need you to trust me. Please . . . have faith in me."

"I've always had faith in you, Hadley."

"I love you so much, Momma. And I'm so sorry."

CHAPTER FORTY-FOUR

Fitz had surprised me earlier that morning, sharing we'd dine somewhere nice that evening. My mind was weary from the call with my mother and all that lay ahead of us. A night out would do some good—one night out in our city before our worlds changed forever.

I felt bold as I dressed for the evening. I donned a burgundy, floor-length dress for the occasion. Though the sleeves sat off the shoulder, my arms were covered in soft fabric, which guarded against the cold, Scottish air. With a plunging neckline and a silhouette that hugged tightly to my torso, I intended to capture Fitz's full attention.

I carefully applied makeup and coiled my hair at the nape of my neck. By the time I shimmied into the living room, I felt better than I had in days.

Fitz stood by the fire, draped in a tux, complete with a white button-up and black bowtie, a glass of Scotch in hand.

"Holy hell," he mumbled as I walked through the door.

"Okay?"

"You're bonnie," he whispered, his hand sliding around my waist, pulling my body toward his. He kissed my neck, carefully avoiding my freshly painted lips.

After assisting with my coat, Fitz held out his arm and led me into the cold, damp evening streets of Edinburgh. He was tight-lipped about where we'd dine, but as we turned deeper into Old Town, I narrowed down the options. We avoided the steady trickle of water rolling down the street, and I turned my eyes toward the sky, finding that the clouds had cleared, a welcome break from the heavy rain of the day.

Reaching the Royal Mile, Fitz turned toward the esplanade of the castle rather than the many restaurants of Old Town. As we approached the gates, I looked at him curiously. There was a teahouse inside, but the castle was closed for the evening. He smiled, and a rap from his free hand resulted in the large wooden door swinging open.

"James?"

"Good evening, my lady. Sir." He nodded at Fitz, who was struggling to keep his composure.

"Right this way."

We followed James to an upper courtyard set with a table draped in white linen. A beautiful array of plants and flowers surrounded the table, and strands of lights spanned the distance of the ancient stone walls. The courtyard was open, exposing us to the cool night air, though roaring chimeneas were placed strategically around the space, all alight in their promise of warmth. The soft illumination of the castle's medieval architecture was a magical backdrop.

James took my coat, replacing it with a soft, fuzzy wrap, and seated us properly before disappearing under a dark archway.

"Why is my boss here?" I whispered.

"He made this evening at the castle possible. And then he asked to help with dinner." Fitz shrugged.

"What in the hell is going on?"

"Patience, Hads. Just enjoy the night," Fitz answered, smiling coyly.

Soft music floated in the breeze as a waiter arrived with Chateau de Ferrand to begin our meal.

"This always reminds me of Paris," I said

The waiter took pride in our dinner, explaining that the chef had selected and prepared the meal as a direct complement to Fitz's wine selection. The meal was, indeed, flawless, but I was distracted by Fitz's mounting nerves all through the main course.

As dinner was cleared from the table, I leaned forward. "Oh, is this all?" I teased.

Fitz reached for my hand, and his brow creased. "Actually, there's something I'd like to talk to you about."

"You know you can tell me anything."

"We've faced some tough moments in the last few months. But the way you stood against Lorenzo . . . you fight so bravely, my wee firecracker."

I laughed softly at his nickname for me.

"I couldn't be prouder of you."

I laid my hand tenderly against his jaw.

"But facing that danger and making the decision to join the fight against Lorenzo has reminded me that life isn't promised to us. Nothing is certain . . . except for us. You're my anchor, Hadley."

He knelt before me, and I inhaled sharply, anticipating what came next.

"I've loved you since the day I met you. You're my best friend . . . the only one I need by my side. I'll love you long after time itself has fallen away."

I raggedly exhaled, my heart pounding in my chest.

"I don't want to travel into the next world without this ring on your finger. Hadley . . . will you marry me?"

He opened the box, revealing a ring. Platinum metal bands held the infinity diamonds into place and were molded together to form an "X" at the front and again at the back of the ring.

I dropped from my chair and into his arms. With my lungs unable to grant me the air to respond, I pressed my lips against his, and his fingers wound through my hair. I pulled away, laughing nervously and took a napkin from the table to wipe my lipstick from his face.

"I think I was dreaming. Say it again," I said softly.

Fitz grinned. "Marry me, Hadley."

"Nothing would make me happier. Of course, I'll marry you."

His hand stroked my cheek gently before presenting the ring. I extended my left hand, inviting him to slip the beautiful ring onto my finger.

We clung to each other as we rose from the stones. So engrossed in the moment as I was, I didn't notice the figures emerging from the shadows until they were standing beside the table.

"Aye, Fitz!" Henry shouted before pulling me into a warm hug. "Congratulations, Hadley."

Alight with excitement, he then embraced Fitz as the others surrounded us with smiles and laughter. Izzy, Ian, Ann, Henry, Isaac, Tanner, and even James and Maka. Fitz had invited the crew to join us for drinks and dessert, and it couldn't have been more perfect; they were all present and ready with congratulations.

"Hads! Get into these loving arms," Isaac exclaimed, beaming.

"Isaac! Oh my god!" I laughed, holding him tightly.

"I know, baby girl. Now, let me see those diamonds."

"I have a sister!" Izzy exclaimed.

She wiggled her way into a group hug with Isaac and me, only to be followed by Tanner.

"Hads, I have a wee present for you," Fitz said. "Henry and Isaac have been helping me work on your family lineage."

"Wait, really?"

Fitz nodded. "You're Scots Irish."

I laughed. "How fitting."

"Gram was a Galloway before marrying your grandfather, the bloodline pure on both her mother and father's sides. Your grandfather—now he bore the name Weston, as do you, but upon tracing back, your people are *no* Westons."

"What do you mean?"

"Remember the story of Esther and Hamish's last name?"

"They changed it because your last name was outlawed by the king."

"Aye. Your grandfather was a Munro. Your ancestor changed his surname from Munro after escaping English troops. He was almost captured after surviving the Battle of Culloden. The Jacobite survivors were branded traitors and hunted by the English."

"My god," I gasped.

"Your mother's side is Irish—but it seems they fled to Ireland from a neighboring country. We're working to verify where they fled from, but my money is on Scotland."

"And what about my magical lineage—any leads yet?"

"Not yet," Isaac answered. "But now that we've traced back pretty far, we'll start referencing additional council records to find the witches hiding in your family tree."

My eyes misted.

"You good, Hads?"

"Yeah, I'm good. I just—thank you all so much for looking into this. You have no idea what this means to me."

A few tables were brought in so our friends and family could join us for celebratory champagne, and we fell into the rhythm of laughter and happy conversation.

Ian tapped a spoon against his champagne flute, and he and Ann rose from their seats.

"If we could have everyone's attention for a moment. I promise I willnae bore you for long."

The group laughed.

"But Ann and I want to offer our congratulations to Fitz and Hadley."

He turned to Ann, who began to speak. "I didnae have to meet Hadley to ken she'd one day join our family. Fitz left the lake house one summer afternoon in search of Izzy, and when he returned, he had changed. His entire world shifted in a moment."

I turned to Fitz, and he shrugged shyly, a smile spreading across his lips.

"It's been a long road to get to this night, but I think we all ken it was worth the fight. The world tried to write them off as star-crossed lovers, but even the world couldnae keep them apart."

Ann looked to Ian.

"Ann understood in an instant," Ian said. "But I had seen the consequences of defying council orders firsthand. I worried that these two didnae understand the challenges that lay before them. But they had more love and more courage than I thought possible."

Ian cleared his throat, and Ann slipped her hand into his.

He continued. "You two inspire me. Ultimately, your courage is what led us all here. When we face whatever the coming months bring, it is courage and love that will carry us through it. Thank you for reminding me of that. I'm so proud of you both. Congratulations."

Ian and Ann raised their glasses, and we all followed suit.

After the toast, tears were dried, and second glasses were poured. Sitting atop Edinburgh, one fiancé and eight friends made me feel as though I was sitting on top of the whole world.

After a night of celebration, Fitz and I wanted time to ourselves. The following morning would bring our first meeting with the Scottish National Coven Council, but for tonight—there was only us and our city. I held Fitz closely, and the world spun away.

The swirl of stars from the in-between faded, revealing the softer glow of our own galaxy far above and the expanse of Edinburgh below. Fitz wandered toward the cliff's edge.

He'd brought us to Arthur's Seat.

"I can't believe it's only been a few weeks since I first brought you here," he said.

"A lot has happened . . . And now this could be our last trip up here before we leave for a foreign planet."

I crossed the distance, taking my place next to Fitz. The city lights sparkled endlessly across the horizon.

"I can't even begin to grasp what our future holds."

"Neither can I," he returned. "We found a place to call home together, and now everything is changing." He slipped his hand in mine. "But I know our future is together. As long as that is true, I can face any trial this new world brings."

I rested my head against his.

"We'll come back, Hads. We have to."

"We'll be different."

"Aye."

A fleeting sadness crossed his features before he pulled me close. "You're cold."

"The wind is freezing."

"We can go."

I shook my head, pulling myself free from his grasp. I reached my hand into the empty air, and as I pulled it back, my favorite gray coat materialized, draped across my arm.

Finally, I had mastered concealment.

"You're proficient," Fitz said.

"Once I understood the elements . . ." I shrugged at his compliment, but I was truly proud of my accomplishment.

"How are you feeling after your encounter with Lorenzo?" Fitz asked.

"I'm mostly okay. I handled it better than I thought."

"Aye, you've done well, Hadley. I'm proud of the force you've become."

My heart swelled at his compliment. He'd never know how much that meant to me.

Silence fell as we gazed at the city lights.

"Perhaps this is our last time here for a bit. Perhaps not. But either way, let's have some fun."

"What did you have in mind?"

Fitz broke into a wide grin and walked to the edge of the cliff. He turned to face me and took a step backward. Instead of tumbling off the cliffside, his body floated high above the ground.

I closed my eyes momentarily, though I already knew what I'd find—there was no one nearby. I asked the elements to support me as I stepped off the ground and into the cool night air alongside Fitz. I laughed, albeit a bit nervously, and worked up the courage to look down. The sheer drop was sobering, but I'd come to know the elements well. I reminded myself I had nothing to fear.

"That first night we came here—could you have ever envisioned this?"

"Not in my wildest dreams."

Fitz tugged on my arm, pulling me into his embrace. I ran my fingers the length of his face, before planting my lips firmly against his. He met me in a slow, deliberate kiss as the air cradled us high above our city. When we floated back to the earth, we descended the landmark hand in hand, still hopeful, regardless of the days to come.

EPILOGUE

Lorenzo's Fortress, Opimae
Present Day
Gabriella

Gabriella's heels echoed loudly through the stone hallway. The door hinges of her master's dinner chamber groaned in protest as she turned the large iron ring and pushed the towering wooden door open.

"Gabriella, my darling girl," Lorenzo's thick Italian accent floated on the wintry air. "What news do you have for me?"

She crossed the room quickly, having been the subject of both his impatience and his disapproval of delivering information from across the room. The chill against her bare arms was insufferable. Gabriella couldn't understand why Lorenzo preferred to dine in the cold, damp air of the windowless room.

"*Signore*, they're preparing to cross over." Gabriella winced as her master's burning gaze rested upon her.

"What have I told you about information?"

"That it should always be clear and concise."

"Would you care to try that once more, *darling*?" he questioned, a mocking tone resting on his favorite term of endearment.

Gabriella cleared her throat. "Three members of Earth's witchkind councils will cross the portal into Opimae. They will bring a team with them."

"That includes Fitz MacGregor, yes?"

"Yes, *Signore*."

Lorenzo turned to his dinner partner, who remained silent. "Alexander, what do you make of this?"

"Things are progressing in accordance with the plan the informant provided."

"We need Fitz to perform his duty."

"And he will."

A soft laugh escaped Lorenzo's lips as he swirled the wine in his glass. Gabriella wasn't supposed to stare at her master, but she couldn't help herself. How could someone be so beautiful . . . and so cruel, she wondered. She'd promised herself she would escape, but something about Lorenzo was magnetic. Once you joined his ranks, it was impossible to leave—and she hated herself for it.

"You Russians are too straightforward. It's always gotten you into trouble. This is tricky, Alexander, and you'd better remember that. These witches are dangerous."

"Of course, sir."

"Gabriella, is the woman with him?"

"Yes, Signore. Had—"

"For God's sake," Lorenzo interrupted, delivering his strike in a a calm, icy tone. "You do not say her name . . . none of you say her name. Not yet."

His eyes blazed as his fist met the table with a startling blow.

Camille glided through the doorway, holding a tray of Lorenzo's favorite cigars. Gabriella wasn't sure how Camille did it, but somehow she always appeared at just the right moment and calmed their master. She lit Lorenzo's cigar of choice, and his eyes cooled as he exhaled more than the smoke. His lips curled around the cigar, and Gabriella followed his every movement, wondering what they—no.

She wouldn't allow her thoughts to travel there, not again. Once the crusaders arrived, she'd be free of Lorenzo's grip—and free of the thoughts in her mind that were no longer her own.

Lorenzo motioned for Gabriella to move closer. He tucked her raven hair behind her ears, his gaze intense. "You know I prefer your hair pulled back." He looked over her appraisingly. "But that dress does make your eyes greener. I like it."

"Thank you, sir. I'm sorry to displease you."

Lorenzo nodded, and she followed his eyes to Camille. Her honey hair was swept on top of her head, a few delicate tendrils escaping along her neck. Camille never displeased the master. Gabriella knew she must learn from Camille if her time in the fortress was to pass without incident. She would fly under the radar as much as possible—it couldn't be much longer.

Gabriella took solace in one belief that she considered absolute truth. Hadley and Fitz would bring one hell of a fight to their army, and she hoped to god that she was standing in the fortress of the losing side.

Forfar, Scotland
1662
Esther

I sprang up in bed, my heart pounding, my breath ragged, and my energy scaring the hell out of Hamish.

"Esther! Is something the matter?"

"Aye," I returned breathlessly. "It's Gabriella. I've connected to her once more."

Hamish's sleep ravaged mind finally understood. "What did ye see?"

"I saw him. The witch who's been watching Fitz and Hadley."

"Breathe," he returned, rubbing my back gently. "What more?"

"The crusaders are preparing to cross over. Oh, Hamish . . . he knows. He's been waiting for them."

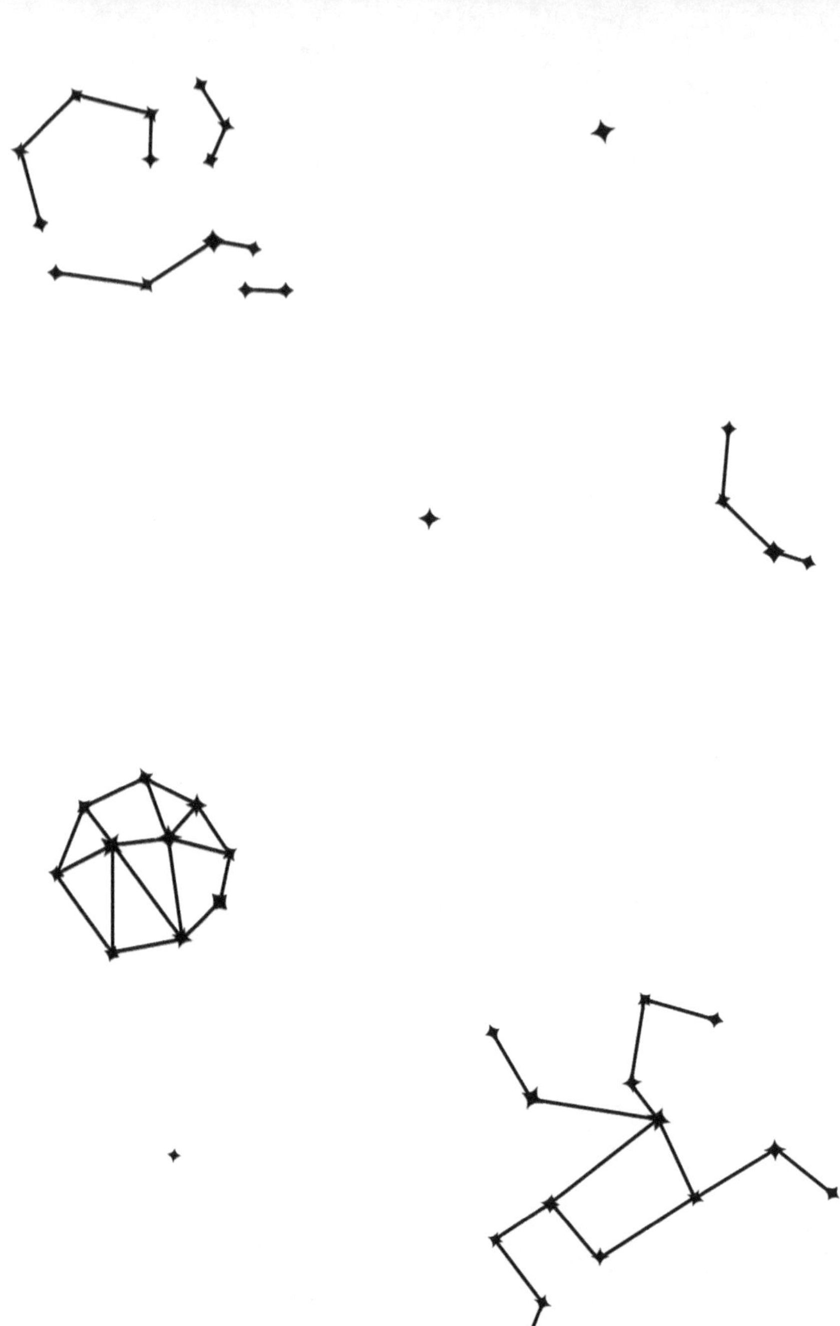

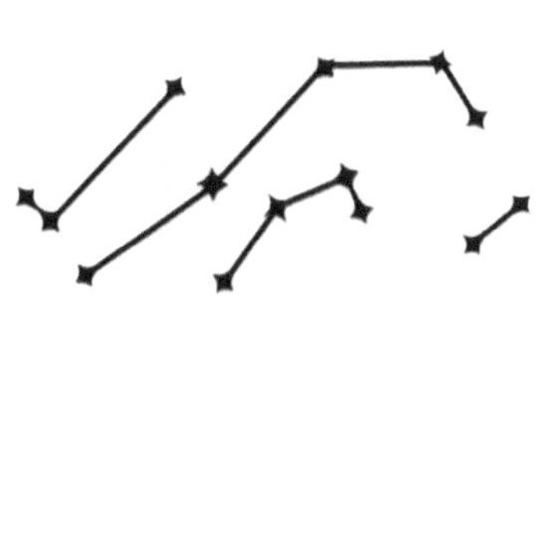

BOOK TWO

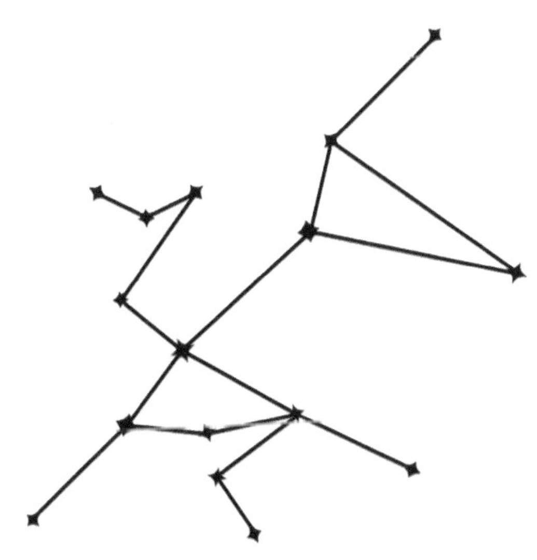

PART ONE

CHAPTER ONE

The Cedar Creek Inn had always been a place of refuge for me. From childhood visits with my parents to weekend escapes during college to the first time my fiancé kissed me, the inn held countless memories and offered a tranquility I'd rarely found in other places. A feeling of peace enveloped me as it came into view.

As my fiancé, Fitz, and I pulled into the driveway, the house buzzed with countless witches lost in preparation to cross over to the foreign planet of Opimae. After agreeing to a mission to stop Lorenzo Belmonte, a powerful witch preparing an uprising, we were meeting with our team and the top governing officials in our witchkind government—the Cardinal Court—to discuss details.

I put the car in park and turned to Fitz. His chestnut hair was tousled, his telltale sign of being stressed, but an encouraging smile graced his lips as his emerald eyes flickered to mine.

"Ready to do this thing?" I asked.

He rested his hand on my collarbone and ran a thumb down the length of my jaw.

"Oh, aye," he said, his Gaelic accent thicker than usual. "I feel your nerves. It'll be all right, Hadley."

"There's no going back now, anyway," I said, turning off the car.

His nerves fluttered through our connection, spilling into me like butterflies in a jar. I leaned forward and kissed him quickly. When I'd discovered only three months ago that I was a witch, Fitz had helped me match to my magic. As it turned out, we were also mates, and after I'd come into my power, our magical connection to each other had formed.

I exited the car and walked to the nearby fence, eager to stretch my legs after the long journey from Edinburgh and distract myself from my guilt. I'd seen my mother's cabin from the highway. It was more difficult than I'd imagined, seeing the cabin and knowing I was so close to her. But I was under strict orders—I couldn't stop and visit her. Part of me wondered if I'd survive the mission that lay ahead of us. Would I ever see my mom again?

The Pacific Northwest's signature mist clung to our hair and dampened our bare hands as we unloaded the car. As we crossed the parking lot, I couldn't help but pause momentarily. Even with the complications, there was a certain peace that came with returning home. The last time I'd been here, I hadn't yet matched to my power, and my heart swelled at the thought of how far I'd come, how much I'd learned about myself, how I'd found myself as a witch.

I scanned the white three-story farmhouse. Holiday lights were strung across the roofline, along the fence, and through the trees, and a Christmas tree twinkled from the sizable picture window at the front of the house. Across the old wooden fence was a large field thick with the mist's haze and low-hanging clouds. A faded, grayed barn with a bright blue roof sat in the field, and beyond it were towering trees blanketing the low mountains to the south. Fog rolled lazily through the treetops, adding to the magic in the air.

The skies were shifting from mist to rain, and we picked up our pace and stepped inside the house. The silver, green, and gold holiday decor was beautiful against the soft white walls. Several unfamiliar witches were congregated in the front room, spread across two wooden tables and lost in maps and calculations. In the second room, a roaring fireplace lent a cozy feel to the space. Another group of witches was discussing the Opimaean government, but still, we found no one we recognized. As we neared the kitchen, Fitz's best friend, Henry, emerged holding a steaming cup of tea.

With his champagne-colored hair, he was as handsome as he was aristocratic, hailing from a wealthy Scottish family. He was every bit Scottish nobility right down to the Stuart tartan pocket square.

"Finally," I whispered.

Henry had left Edinburgh before us to see his parents in Greece, and our other good friend, Isaac, had accompanied him. Henry's father was a decorated war hero, and he'd sought his father's council on military strategy before we headed to Opimae.

Henry hugged us both. He wore a warm smile as he ran a hand through his hair, smoothing it into place, but his hazel eyes betrayed him. The usual mischievous twinkle was dormant. He, too, was nervous.

"Glad you arrived safely. I'm due for a meeting on the portal crossing, but Ben and Sarah are in the kitchen—they're keen to see you."

Ben and Sarah were the owners of the inn, and they had become like second parents to me over the years. Though I hated to trouble them with our Cardinal Court meetings, their inn was the perfect solution to our needs. The house wasn't far from the trailhead that led to the portal—which would transport us to Opimae—and it had plenty of space for the core team.

The kitchen was bustling with food preparations, but when Sarah turned around, her blue eyes lit with joy. She wiped her hands on her sage apron and walked over to me. Her snow-colored hair was pulled into a barrette at the nape of her neck.

"Welcome home!"

It was something she'd said each time I returned to the inn, ever since I was a young girl, and there was a great comfort in that—especially now. She embraced me warmly. As we drew back, Sarah reached for my hand, pulling my engagement ring into sight. She beamed as she studied the two platinum bands that formed an "X" on my finger. The diamonds sparkled even in the soft light.

"Congratulations to you both. I'm so happy for you."

She hugged Fitz as Ben rounded the corner, flashing a bright grin at the sight of me.

"Boy, are we glad to see you," Ben said, his voice full of genuine warmth. Like Sarah's, his apron was stitched with the Cedar Creek Inn logo, though his was gray, and a crimson Washington State University cap covered his head.

We embraced before he moved to shake Fitz's hand and then rested his hands on his hips.

"I've never seen the inn quite like this." I pointed in the general direction of the groups scattered through the common areas. Ben and Sarah were human, and they had no idea they were hosting a house full of magical beings. I had to wonder if they felt the oddity of our situation.

"We were a little uncomfortable with it right at first. We weren't sure we could accommodate what you needed," Ben admitted.

"I know this must seem strange, but we appreciate you making room for us," I said.

"Anything for our girl," Sarah said.

"Well, let's get you two settled. James mentioned your meetings start this afternoon," Ben said. "We've got you in Country Clover. You know the way."

Ben and Sarah had, of course, reserved my favorite room for me. Sarah had brightened the room with a fresh coat of paint, but the large, king-sized bed remained the same, with its signature white picket fence headboard and comfortable bedding. The far window held a lovely view of the field and mountains while the side windows gazed over the yard and into town. Fitz's eyes rested on the large, jetted tub in the corner of the room, his eyebrow arched.

"Of course, that's where your mind immediately wanders," I said.

"You can't fault me when my roommate is so bonnie," he replied, sliding his hands down my back. A rap at the door halted the moment, and Fitz raised his voice, inviting our intruders inside.

"I'm in love with this place," Isaac declared. Though his features reflected his Iranian roots, Isaac's accent was classically Italian. His deep brown eyes were set in a handsome face of dark olive complexion, and his chiseled body spoke to the time he spent training.

Henry leaned against the doorframe. "What a braw room," he said, surveying our space. "I see why it's your favorite, lass."

Henry and Isaac had quickly become family to me. When Fitz and I had defied government orders, his two best friends had dedicated themselves to keeping us safe, gathering information on the council, and helping us formulate plans. We were lucky to have them by our side on this crusade.

A text from James pulled my attention from the guys.

"I hate to break up our little party, but James is ready for us."

James was waiting at the bottom of the stairwell, and his big blue eyes were alight with excitement. James was my boss at Edinburgh Castle, where I worked as the PR manager. But James also sat on Scotland's National Coven Council and was the very witch who had recruited Fitz and me for this mission.

Though I wasn't sure of James's age, he must have been at least a hundred years old based on his lengthy service with Earth's witchkind councils. Due to the slow-aging and prolonged life of witches, he appeared roughly mid-sixties with eyes that sparkled like Lake Crescent's waters on a sunny day and a fluffy gray beard.

James's greeting was warm, though brief, as he excitedly ushered us toward the front room. He explained that Fitz and I would meet with the Cardinal Court while the others met with a few members from the Washington Coven Council. They would join us later in the afternoon. The doorway sent energy tingling through my body as we passed through it: the work of a privacy shield. As I stepped into the front room, my skin felt the full assault of careful observation as the eyes of the court danced wildly upon us. I hastily took stock, my eyes darting across two witches—along with many new faces on a large screen.

"I ken you've met Chloe and Mia, but I'm so pleased to introduce you to the other members of the Cardinal Court," James exclaimed, slightly overzealous. "Comprised of the top twelve governing officials from all over the world, this court has been elected by witchkind and sworn in after approval by the United Covens Affairs. They're called to intervene for the most pressing matters—issues where the lower levels of government are unable to reach a decision or in situations that are crucial to our worldwide community. Allow me to make introductions."

From the Americas to Africa to Asia, each populated continent had elected officials to represent their interests in the highest court in the witch world.

One of the U.S. representatives needed no introduction. Mia Davies.

Mia carried herself with her usual authoritative air, and from her plaid blazer to her cropped raven hair, she was the definition of chic. Her familiar icy glare fell upon me.

"Mia," I acknowledged.

"Hadley." She nodded.

"I'm surprised we're here if you had any say in it."

"Majority rules. Now you have the chance to prove to me that you actually deserve to be here," she said as she strutted past us.

I looked at Fitz. "Did that just happen?"

"Well, this should be fun," Fitz whispered under his breath.

The afternoon passed quickly. Spending time with Mia wasn't an exciting prospect, but I was keen to learn more about our new colleagues and the government hierarchy. Mia walked us through the finer points of government structure. Even though Fitz seemed knowledgeable about government details, he was able to garner some new information, and I was glad the meeting wasn't a total waste for him. When another court member, Solomon, began speaking about the portal, Fitz's energy shifted, buzzing hungrily for details.

"You've crossed the portal?" Fitz asked.

"Earlier this year to meet with the leaders in Opimae."

Solomon was dressed in a traditional Ethiopian gabi, which was a simple off-white, but bright green, orange, and pink decorated the end of the sleeves and the bottom of the garment. The stark contrast between the white robe and his dark umber skin was stunning, and his smile immediately put me at ease. His eyes were ever-changing, alive like the Northern Lights.

"What was the journey like?" I asked Solomon.

"Are you nervous about the crossing?" Solomon leaned forward in his seat and rested his elbows on his knees, clasping his hands together.

"A little," I admitted. "I just don't know what to expect."

Solomon nodded. "The portal is filled with magical energy. It beckons you—pulls at you. But the journey through it was brief. It was over before I knew it."

The front door swung open, bringing with it a gust of wind and a figure I recognized instantly. Fitz's dad, Ian.

Unlike his children's bright green eyes, Ian's were storm cloud blue, but his chestnut hair was indisputably the same as his son's, as was his structured jawline.

"Hey, kiddos."

A large group filtered in behind Ian. My eyes scanned across them. Henry and Isaac. Fitz's mom, Ann, and sister, Izzy. My old friend Tanner Chen, a witch I didn't recognize, and one very special human.

"Jordan." I gasped.

I wasted no time in embracing my best friend since childhood.

"What on earth are you doing here?" I asked skeptically.

Her coy smile confused me.

Though I'd found a way to maintain our friendship without her knowing I was a witch, it had been a delicate balance to strike. Jordan and I had been texting only yesterday, and she hadn't said a word about this. Clearly, I wasn't the only one in our friendship holding on to secrets.

My life had been turned upside down when the council had thought I might remain human and not match to my magic. So, how could it be that Jordan was standing before me?

"I'm here to help you and Fitz."

"Jordan, do you . . . I mean, are you aware we're . . ."

"That you're a witch?"

"Oh."

"At least I understand now why you were dodging my calls for a while."

"Jordan, I am so sorry."

She waved off my apology. "Don't worry about it. As long as you never do that again."

She eyed me pointedly. I realized her dusk eyes had changed ever so slightly; the flecks of amber had intensified, almost the color of Henry's favorite whisky, and the irises were framed in black.

I laughed. "I don't think I have any more giant secrets."

"Ian brought me up to speed. Honestly, when he first told me about all this, it was one of the weirdest conversations I'd ever had, and I work for the FBI!"

Ian grinned.

"But then I thought about it, and we've always known you're gifted, right? And we knew something was up with the MacGregors when we met them." Jordan looked at the family in question as she referenced the summer that we'd first met them. "No offense."

They laughed.

"None taken," Fitz said, amusement clear in his tone.

Jordan took my hands in hers. "Then I thought about that conversation you and I had, and it clicked. This makes a lot of sense. And Hads . . . I'm so happy you've found yourself."

"I think I'm in shock, but . . .thank you."

Now that Jordan knew, I would no longer have to hide this side of me from her. I could finally breathe again.

Jordan had always understood me on some level—she knew I was odd by human standards but had never once made me feel different from her. Jordan's skin was deep brown, and her hair was dark like a starless midnight, pulled away from her face in knotless braids. She'd paired an olive bandeau top with dark high-waisted jeans and a black leather jacket. She might have been human, but there was nothing ordinary about Jordan. From her height to her ability to command a room, she was a force to be reckoned with.

"And this guy, too!" she exclaimed and pointed to Tanner. "I mean, what the hell?"

"Sorry, J." Tanner shrugged. Tanner was tall and chiseled, which was owed to his love for physical fitness. He'd worked as a personal trainer prior to joining the crusade. His eyes always changed colors, and today, they were an inky black, almost the same shade as his cropped hair. He wore a dark plaid hoodie and jeans. I'd rarely seen him in anything other than workout attire or clothing that was quintessentially Pacific Northwest.

The three of us referred to ourselves as the three musketeers, and I had been just as surprised as Jordan when I had discovered Tanner was a witch.

"And these two." She pointed toward the MacGregor siblings. "I was literally the only human that summer. I guess I should feel honored you even let me in your club."

Izzy grinned and walked over to Jordan.

"We're the ones who are honored, ma'am," Izzy countered. Her green eyes were the same emerald as her brother's, but instead of chestnut hair like Fitz and Ian, she'd inherited her mother's shade of auburn and the freckles that splayed across the bridge of her nose. She was easily the most ethereal witch I'd ever known.

As conversation continued, Fitz leaned into me. "You know what this means, right? Why Jordan's here."

Oh, no.

I had been too caught up in the excitement of seeing her to think it through.

"This isn't happening," I barked louder than I intended.

The room fell quiet.

"Everyone close to me has joined our fight," Fitz said.

"Yeah, and they're all witches. I don't understand how she's here, but the court can't force anything on Jordan."

"You and I know too well that the councils don't expose our kind to humans. If she's here, there's a reason," Fitz said.

"Don't be reckless, Fitz." Not awaiting his response, I turned to Jordan.

"Tell me this isn't true," I said. "You're not coming with us, right?"

"I am. I've been recruited, same as you."

"No, this doesn't make sense."

"Ian said you'd need my intelligence skill set. I've already agreed, Hads. From what it sounds like, there's no turning back."

I shook my head. "I need you to consider what a human body is capable of withstanding. There's more magic in this world than you can even begin to comprehend, and you'll have no defense."

"That's not exactly true," Mia interjected. "When you arrive in Opimae, she'll develop some kind of power."

I looked for James in the crowd surrounding us. "Is this true?"

James seemed to know more about Opimae than anyone, and he'd be the least biased.

"Aye, it's true. There's no telling what type of power she'll develop, but a few humans have passed into Opimae on council business, and each has developed powers."

"Why have humans crossed into Opimae?" I asked. "Why do they know about us?"

The room fell quiet before Solomon answered. "It's a delicate matter . . . it's rare, and it has only ever happened for very specific reasons."

Fitz and I exchanged a glance. We'd discuss this later. But for now, I returned my focus to Jordan.

"What type of skills might Jordan develop?" I asked.

"Well, I wouldnae expect her to develop a witch's gamut of powers, but she might, for instance, develop superhuman strength and speed," James said.

"How is that possible?" I asked.

"We believe it's due to human body chemistry interacting with the elements of a foreign planet. Their bodies are adapted to Earth, but if you remove them from their home planet and place them on to a world charged with magic, their bodies will acclimate to that new environment. It's rapid adaptation, so to speak. Your powers will intensify as well. Something to look forward to," he said dreamily.

"Jordan has a sense of otherworldliness already," Ian said. "It's one of the reasons I asked the court to consider her for the role."

"I appreciate what you're saying about Jordan, but she's still human," I said, eyeing my best friend. Jordan leaned against the wall, arms crossed.

"Yeah, but she's smart, intuitive . . . I mean, she's always fit in well with the two of us. She gets it," Tanner said as he ran his hand through his dark hair.

"And with her background in the FBI, I dinnae think there's a better fit for this role than Jordan," Ian said. "She's one of the rare council exceptions."

"How can you even get away from your job?" I asked. Jordan had been with the FBI for a couple of years and had advanced quickly in her career. Taking time off had been difficult from the very beginning.

Jordan turned to Ian, who turned to Mia.

"We've handled her leave from work just as we did for you." Mia's tone betrayed her annoyance.

I turned to Jordan. "You don't need to do this."

"I would do this if it gave you a better chance of success alone, but it's more than that. This is about my future, too. It's about all our futures. Witches aren't the only ones who will be affected if this disagreement ends in war. I won't sit on the sidelines."

"You're on the sidelines right now because you're human! Don't you understand that? You have no self-defense against a witch."

"I'm not a liability, Hadley. I'll develop a skill that will help, and that's in addition to what I already bring to the table. I have a role to play on this mission. I need to do this."

"Hadley, we don't know what the court will do if Jordan refuses this mission. Our secret has already been shared with her," Fitz sounded in my mind. *"I know you don't want them meddling with her memories."*

I simply nodded in response. The thought was sobering, but perhaps we could still sort things out later on.

"Lorenzo possesses great power, and he might learn to access the power of the ring at any moment," Solomon said. "Identifying a group of powerful witches was first and foremost, but we needed specific abilities that complemented each other. This group holds those powers.

"Ian made a great case for Jordan. She's always known about your abilities and accepted you without question. Jordan exercises an understanding and discretion that is almost beyond human. She is analytical and calculated but can accept information that can't be technically understood, at least not by humans. She will assist in calculating and assessing plans. And Opimae intelligence hopes to utilize her skill set. Jordan brings a fresh perspective."

"Hadley, Fitz . . ." Solomon continued. "We believe you are the warriors from the Opimaean prophecy who will lead a strong team from Earth to defeat Lorenzo."

Mia shifted in her seat, but her face remained carefully impassible.

I reached instinctively for Fitz's hand. James had told us of the prophecy the day we'd agreed to the crusade, but the thought of being part of a prophecy still boggled my mind.

I looked across the team. From energy readers to warriors to time-walkers and many skills in between, we made a powerful unit. Ian would bring invaluable experience from his years working with the councils, and Fitz and I had already looked to him many times for guidance.

There was only one witch among us that I couldn't identify, though familiarity tugged at the back of my mind. Mia followed my gaze to the doorway.

"I'm sure you're wondering about Molly," said Mia, her hand raised in the general direction of the new witch. The final addition to our party was propped lazily against the doorframe. "Molly, come meet everyone."

Molly's tall figure was dressed in black jeans and a graphic tee that read "Hex the Patriarchy," and colorful tattoos decorated her arms. Molly dragged her black combat boots across the space. She sported shoulder-length hair, dusky in color, except for the few blonde streaks jolting through it. With milky skin and wide, umber eyes, she was striking.

"Hi, everyone," she muttered. Rude wasn't the proper descriptor for Molly, but a casual, almost disinterested atmosphere hung about her, which piqued my interest. It seemed odd that she could stand next to Cardinal Court members, who were introducing her to a host of new witches with whom she would soon travel to a new universe and remain so relaxed. She almost seemed bored.

And then it clicked. I'd bumped into her the day I'd left my rocky meeting with Mia at the Scottish National Coven's council headquarters in Edinburgh. She caught my gaze, and recognition flitted through her eyes. She nodded.

"Molly comes from a long line of prestigious witches in North America," Mia said. "Her ancestors have been nomadic since they escaped the Salem Witch Trials. Molly harbors the power of transport, among many other skills. She's a chameleon and a quick thinker, and she'll work alongside Jordan to help with planning. We've selected her as your final travel companion. Well, aside from the council members: Solomon, Chloe, and James."

Chloe represented Australia on the Cardinal Court, and she had been the court member selected to oversee my training in Edinburgh after I'd matched to my magic.

A mix of welcoming voices followed Mia's explanation. Molly nodded once, the slightest smile spreading briefly to her lips.

"Welcome, Molly. We're excited to have you with us," I said. And then Mia's last words sank in. My head snapped over to James. "You're coming?"

"Aye! The court told me just today. I'm thrilled."

"So are we," Fitz said. "You're a great addition to the group."

"Thank you, Fitz. I'm honored to be a part of this." Henry shook his hand as James added, "And Molly is going to be fantastic."

"James has headed research and data collection from the inception of this mission. With his knowledge of the situation, his gifts, and his commitment to this project, we feel he is the best lower council representative to accompany you. He will also be a good fit for group morale," Mia explained.

I agreed with her assessment of James, though I wasn't quite sure what Mia knew about group morale.

"There, of course, will be others to help you in Opimae, but we are pleased to have such a strong team coming from this side," Solomon said.

"We've waited a long time for this group," James said.

"You were each born for this. It seems Fate found a way to bring you all together." Solomon nodded.

"*Fate,*" I echoed.

CHAPTER TWO

The next day, we used our time to sort out any last-minute details and have a final meeting before crossing over. The court wanted us fresh for our journey, as the travel through space and time would be draining. We were congregated in the front room of the inn, reviewing new records that had been sent over by Opimae's intelligence teams.

"This is the exact point where we'll exit Earth into Opimae City at the other side of the portal. It was confirmed today—Charles is our liaison on the other side." James paused, savoring a mouthful of spring roll from the takeout we'd ordered before our meeting convened in the common area. Our maps and documents had cluttered the floor even before we'd littered it with plates, boxes, several witches, and one human.

"Is that a positive development?" I asked, my curiosity piqued.

"Charles is one of the most powerful witches I've ever met from either side of the portal. He might even give you and Fitz a run for your money. He's the director of the Opimaean response to the Lorenzo crisis. He came to Earth to meet with the councils about a year ago to discuss this initiative to prevent war—he seemed honest. I think we're fortunate he was the one voted into this role."

Footsteps sounded from the dining room, occasioning a brief pause from the team as Ben emerged through the doorway, water pitcher in hand.

"Anybody need a refill?" he asked cheerfully. Ben made his way around the room, refilling as he progressed, before the maps attracted his attention. "Those are pretty neat. Is that an old map of Scotland?"

As he and Ian fell deep into conversation about antique maps and a college trip to Edinburgh, Isaac tucked himself into a corner with his government-issued laptop. He'd been scouring the council records for as much information about Opimae as he could possibly find, and he was perhaps the most anxious of all of us to see the world we were studying so closely. I shifted my gaze to Fitz, who was seemingly lost in reverie, a stern look obscuring his face.

I looped my arm through his. "What are you thinking about?" I whispered.

He planted a kiss on my cheek. "Take a walk with me?"

Walking with Fitz in the last few moments of daylight was more than enough to tempt me outside. Though the short December day was already fading, the rain had paused, allowing us a window to enjoy our time alone.

We meandered the old lane near the inn in companionable silence. The evening was still, peaceful, and the chill of dusk crept into the air. A sense of calm wanted to wiggle in, but Fitz's agitated mood radiated through my body. Excitement and anxiety both swirled around us, our impending trip through the portal never far from our minds, but I hoped to forget about the mission for a few delicious minutes.

Fitz and I had overcome a great deal in the past few months. Fate had woven our paths together, but that hadn't come without difficulty. Our beginning had been confusing for me, especially after the witch-kind government had forced us apart. Everything shifted when we'd finally challenged the councils. Fitz and I had fought for our love, and we'd found our way through the tough seasons together.

"It's been over two years since I first brought you here," I mused. I had still been human at that time, and I had struggled to understand what was happening between the two of us.

Fitz halted, scanning the field. Finally, his chiseled jaw relaxed, and his gaze turned tender as his eyes swept to me.

"Aye. I was nervous about what our future held."

"I didn't understand that at the time. But now I can understand the weight you carried," I said. When we'd defied the order to remain apart, we'd taken a dangerous risk. And ultimately, our actions had set our involvement in this crusade against Lorenzo into motion. I didn't realize the burden our situation had placed on Fitz until we were through the worst of it.

We continued down the lane, just as we had on our first visit to the inn together. Fitz suddenly pulled me to him and kissed me deeply. My breath came short, and I wrapped my arms around him. When he pulled back, he rested his forehead against mine.

"Do you remember when we stopped here last time . . ." He trailed off and shifted to meet my gaze, his eyes questioning.

I grinned. "You kissed me for the first time. I'll never forget that day."

I recalled the uncertainty of that time. I'd instinctively understood Fitz in many ways from the moment I'd met him, though I couldn't make sense of our connection. Our first kiss had been charged with an intimacy, a vulnerability I had never known before. But that human version of myself couldn't have grasped the love that awaited her— how much deeper our connection would grow.

I studied the man I loved so dearly. I'd come to know his thoughts, his intentions, and his energy as intimately as I knew the precise shade of green that colored his eyes—how they grew brighter when he was happy, how they dulled when he was displeased.

"Fate favored me the day she crossed our paths," Fitz said.

I smiled, but with all our recent discussions around Fate and the path she'd laid for us, I couldn't help but wonder if Fitz and I had been fated to fall in love, or if we had chosen this path for ourselves.

Did we even have a choice in the matter?

"She favored us both," I said, hoping Fitz didn't hear the distance in my voice.

"Fate has been kind to us, but I find myself wondering if she'll favor us on this crusade," Fitz admitted.

"It would be hard not to. I hope she wants peace."

"Aye. I can't imagine how Lorenzo could be right in what he's done."

"I know our mission is to stop Lorenzo, but you and I need to take every opportunity to get closer to the ring," I said.

I looked down at the gold band on my finger. It was lightly hammered and held a moonstone in a round bezel, an exact replica of the magical MacGregor ring.

Fitz's ancestors had channeled their power into a ring in the hopes that it would save Esther, his many-times great grandmother, from the witch trials in Forfar, Scotland. The ring had vanished after her death. Before I'd accidentally spirit-travelled into Lorenzo's fortress one evening, no one had seen the ring for hundreds of years.

"I hope we'll gain more information around the ring. I don't know how much we'll learn in Opimae until we find ourselves near Lorenzo," Fitz said.

James had told us the intelligence teams pulled all information on Lorenzo after we'd shared that he had the ring. I didn't expect they'd find anything useful in the council archives, but I would be glad to be wrong.

"I'd feel better if I knew Lorenzo hasn't found a way to access its power," Fitz continued.

"He hadn't figured it out the last time I transported to his fortress." Besides, Esther's aunt Annabel—who had been the one to protect the ring and pass it to Esther—had made it incredibly difficult to access the ring for anyone outside of the MacGregor bloodline.

Fitz nodded absentmindedly.

"Have you heard back about your position at the university?" I asked. Fitz was a lecturer at the University of Edinburgh, and he was the last of our team awaiting confirmation that his position was being held for him upon his return from Opimae.

"Aye, while we were in the last meeting," he confirmed. "Looks like the council came through."

I could only hope we all returned safely from Opimae to fill the roles that we'd secured before our lives turned upside down. After finally finding myself as a witch, I had just started to build a home in Edinburgh with Fitz, and we both loved our careers. I'd found my place only to be uprooted again.

"We should probably turn back," I said, checking my watch. "We have our last briefing at 5 p.m. about the portal crossing details."

Fitz turned. "Just think, by this time tomorrow, we'll be on an entirely different planet."

A jolt ran through me at the very thought.

CHAPTER THREE

The journey from the inn to the trailhead for the High Divide was familiar, and memories from my childhood flooded my mind. My dad and I had hiked the High Divide countless times over the years. It had been almost a year since we'd lost him, and I couldn't help but to think of him as we neared the turnoff, allowing myself to feel just how much I missed him. Lost in reverie, I was disoriented when the car came to a stop. I buzzed with excitement, though my nerves tingled through me in equal measure. Fitz and I had both tossed and turned most of the night, and my acute desire for sleep only muddled my feelings further.

I looked around the vehicle, realizing I wasn't the only one in somewhat of a trance. Everyone was a bit dazed. I closed my eyes momentarily, taking in the pops of electricity radiating through the car, nervous energy clashing through the air. Fitz squeezed my hand, for his own reassurance as much as mine, and we jumped from the van, our feet crunching against the gravel road. The gate that allowed access to the parking lot was closed, meaning snow had accumulated on the road and hadn't been cleared.

Two large vans parked behind us, carrying the additional time-walkers. Like Fitz and Molly, they harbored the power of transport and would help us reach the portal since we couldn't hike the trail this time of year. The December weather wouldn't go easy on us either. The road was pooled with water, and the rain thumped heavily through the thick tree canopy on either side of us. I pulled my rain jacket tighter, shivering against the frigid air as Fitz opened an umbrella and held it above my head.

Chloe jumped from one of the vans, and her smile brightened as she met our gaze.

"Great to see you again, Hadley," she said in her identifiably Australian accent. Blonde curls tumbled loosely down her back, and her cunning blue eyes were bright, even in the dreary morning.

"We're happy to finally have you with us," I said.

"I had a bit more business to tidy up before I crossed over, but we've got some great council members stepping in to help Solomon and me while we're away," she said while zipping her navy puffer coat all the way to her chin.

Right on cue, Solomon stepped from the van, ending a phone call and reaching for a long overcoat.

"You ready for this?" Chloe asked, nodding toward the forest.

Solomon shrugged. "Who could ever be ready for a journey like this? But I am ready to see more of this world."

Fitz and Molly grouped with the rest of the time-walkers as they reviewed a few final details. I wandered to the edge of the road until I felt the buzz of the privacy shield and turned around. Countless witches were scattered down the roadway chatting through our plans and making last minute phone calls. Molly was at the far end of the shield, standing with her eyes closed while being briefed. She had been distant ever since her arrival, and I wondered if she felt left out, having no prior connection to anyone on the team. I made a pact with myself that I'd try to help her integrate into the group as quickly as possible.

Isaac's voice pierced through the chatter. He was talking excitedly with one of the lower council members about elves. I smiled. The information he'd been so captivated by was about to come alive for him.

Mia caught my attention standing across the roadway from me. I'd learned that Mia had spent most of her formative years in Seattle. Had it been anyone else, I would've thought we could connect over growing up in the Pacific Northwest, but Mia and I still hadn't found our footing with each other.

Mia was focusing her energy on the falling rain. Every few seconds, she pointed her finger and froze random droplets. They hovered in the air until she flicked her finger, tossing the ice aside. I struggled against a wry smile, thinking of how fitting her cryokinesis power truly was, when Fitz called my name.

It was time to say our goodbyes.

Ann embraced Fitz and then me. "Take care of each other," she whispered as tears rolled down her face.

"We will—and Ian, too."

Fitz hugged his sister for the last time for only God knew how long. Izzy smiled, tears welling in her eyes, before she turned to me.

"Thank you," I paused. "Thank you for everything the past couple years. I wouldn't be where I am without you."

"It's been the greatest honor of my life watching you grow into the witch you are."

"I'll miss you, Iz."

"No more than I'll miss you." She hugged me tightly. "Now, go do what you were born to do. Show him a real fight, love."

James called everyone to order, and we paired off for transport. Fitz wrapped his arms around me. I did the same to him.

"Remember: don't let go of me, and don't lose focus," Fitz reminded me.

I nodded, recalling that if I did either of those things, it could result in me being trapped in the in-between, a possible death sentence.

I looked around one last time at the towering trees, damp ferns, and thick moss. There was something poetic, I thought, about crossing into a new world with Fitz in the very place where our journey had begun—where my magical awakening had started. Chloe caught my gaze as she passed Tanner. The two smiled at each other, and something prickled at my witch's eye. Tanner's gaze flickered to mine, but he looked away quickly.

Everyone stepped into position, and Solomon sounded the countdown. The world around me spun away, and it was replaced by a midnight sky and the swirling stars of the in-between. The seemingly endless void held the threads of space and time, allowing time-walkers to navigate through the past and present—to anywhere in our world, and sometimes beyond.

I hadn't traveled through its depths since my last mental transport to Lorenzo's fortress. This journey was much calmer—and brief. In less than a minute, we stepped from the in-between into a startling scene. Snow swirled viciously, assaulting my face with large flakes. I looked around, but I could discern nothing. The snowfall was so thick it obscured my vision.

"Fitz!" I yelled. "Can you see anything?"

The wind tore at our exposed faces, and we huddled together for warmth.

"Nae!" he shouted back, his accent thickening. "I cannae see a thing!"

"Where should the portal be located from here?"

Fitz closed his eyes, and his face scrunched as he tried to focus on the answer.

"I cannae tell with the weather like this, but I feel an odd energy in that direction." He pointed behind me.

I turned around and focused on locating the energy he'd found through the chaos. Something nudged softly against my face, and I had a feeling Fitz was right.

"Support me for a second?" I asked.

He nodded, understanding.

I focused on the faint energy until my spirit separated from my body, and I followed the path carefully. When I met a privacy shield, I knew I'd met my mark. We were close—maybe twenty yards away. I quickly returned to my body and was greeted by several familiar faces when I opened my eyes.

Jordan's eyes were inky pools in the dim light, but it was clear that they were troubled. I reached for her, pulling her close, realizing she hadn't yet seen me in this state.

"You okay, Hads?" she asked.

"More than okay. I know the way to the portal."

Fitz pulled me back to my feet as more of our companions materialized through the whiteout conditions.

We began pressing forward along what seemed to be a ridge line, and Tanner warned everyone to be mindful of where they stepped. My heart fluttered with anxiety. The team was quiet—focused—and their mix of nerves permeated the air. Our progress was slow and timid, but we made some headway as we labored through the blizzard.

Then Isaac's foot pushed through a large snowbank, and he began to slide toward the cliff's edge. Without thinking, I turned and asked the elements to cradle his body, but Fitz was one second ahead of me, so connected to the elements as he was, and he floated Isaac next to us.

"Are you okay?" I shouted above the wind.

Isaac nodded, his breath short. I embraced him and pushed a bit of calming energy into his system. His heart rate eased, and we prepared to move forward.

"We should walk single file," Tanner said.

"Aye, and we need to lead carefully," Fitz added.

"I'll lead," I said. I had spent countless time on the trails, but beyond that, I had a decided advantage over the others.

"Hads, no." Fitz shook his head.

I held his gaze as I called forward my fire magic, and within seconds, my fingertips were covered in flames.

A soft smile rose to Fitz's lips, and he motioned for me to walk ahead of him. I focused on the ground before me and cast bursts of flames into the snow until the rocky terrain was visible. The fresh, falling snow sizzled against the baking rocks, but that wouldn't last. I moved as quickly as possible, clearing a path until I met the privacy shield.

"Do we just walk through this?" I shouted back to James.

"Aye!"

I kept my fire burning, unsure of what I'd find on the other side of the shield, and stepped through.

Chills crawled the length of my spine, my second sight awakening to the presence of the portal's power, even as I was met by the warmth of flames that I could not claim as my own. I gazed at the snowless scene before me. Three witches sat around a campfire. The scent of coffee, smoke, and damp earth permeated the air, along with the sound of laughter, though it abruptly ceased as they settled their gaze on me. The light within the shield was dim, almost like we had stepped from day into night. Tents were scattered near what appeared to be a rocky cave, and countless books, maps, board games, and laptops were strewn around the fireside.

"Looks like it's time for the big group," a woman at the far side of the fire said.

"Come on in, guys. I know it's bad out there," the man next to her said.

I imagined being a portal guard wasn't all that exciting, especially during the winter months, but it looked like they'd made the best of it.

"How is this happening?" Jordan asked, her eyes wide.

Henry chuckled. "It's magic, lass."

"But . . . how?"

"Looks like the government set up a permanent shield," I observed.

"Aye," Fitz agreed. "The privacy shield would be permanent, but this protection shield is certainly set up for inclement weather."

Jordan nodded slowly. "Okay. Whatever y'all say."

I couldn't help but laugh.

James, Chloe, and Solomon met with the crossing guard and secured the last details of our journey. They lined us up to cross—groups of two would step into the portal at a time.

"We're all rooting for you guys," one of the guards said warmly.

Nervous smiles and nods echoed through our warm cocoon.

"If you're ready, so are we. Let's get started," the woman said.

We slowly made our final steps to the entrance of the next world. The naked eye would perceive nothing of importance, only boulders fallen from the mountainside, but the reverberations of energy hummed through the air. The energy grew louder and stronger as we progressed until it was almost unbearable. One more step would send us into the oblivion of the unknown. My mind's eye scoured the area, granting me as much intelligence as it could possibly gather, and I found where our world opened to the next.

I turned to Fitz. "See you in the next world," I whispered.

"I love you."

I gripped his hand tightly, and together we stepped through the unknown, and into the curious world of Opimae.

CHAPTER FOUR

The air was too thin.

My lungs craved more oxygen than they could garner from the atmosphere of the in-between. I breathed deeply, pushing back against the rising panic at the edges of my mind. The portal crossover was supposed to be brief—mere seconds, in fact—but time was ticking slowly. The path was so dim I couldn't distinguish Fitz or any of our companions, but I gripped his hand tightly, finding reassurance in the fact that he was still with me.

As more time passed, I grew concerned.

"God," I whispered. "Fate . . . if you can hear me, please . . . favor us."

A light flashed weakly ahead, and everything within me agreed it was the exit into Opimae. I pulled at Fitz, my arms and legs flailing about in the weightlessness of the portal. But my efforts amounted to nothing—I was no closer to the exit than I was to understanding what was happening to us. I squeezed my eyes shut and gasped for air, oxygen seemingly growing even more scarce.

Think, Hadley.

Anchoring deeply to my magic, I summoned my witch's eye to connect to the in-between and discover the truths hidden within it.

An entire universe existed within the portal. Brilliant stars shone vibrantly across a night sky until it grew pale against the glowing rays of a distant sun. The energy of my companions radiated from their bodies, buzzing wildly, filling the void with nerves, tension, and uncertainty.

A glowing cloud beneath us held the threads that connected planet to planet, but as I scanned the mass, the pit of my stomach twisted. As the cloud reached Opimae its glow waned, almost as though it was plagued by a sickness. A heavy energy buzzed ominously from the exit.

For the second time, I made a feeble attempt to move toward the exit of the portal. And again—nothing happened.

Not like that.

A distant memory echoed through my mind, and with it came a sudden realization. The portal wasn't pulling us toward the exit as it should. We would each have to propel ourselves forward. Whether it was my magic or Fate, I didn't know, but I trusted in this new enlightenment and focused my mind and my power on one common goal.

All at once, everything blurred.

I squinted at the sudden illumination as my feet found something solid, and between the lack of oxygen and the tricks of gravity, I fell unceremoniously to the cold, damp ground, my hands meeting something loosely resembling grass. After the warmth of the guards' campfire, I was unprepared for the chill of the afternoon air.

A hand materialized in front of me.

"Fitz?" I asked weakly.

"Hadley?" an unfamiliar voice questioned. "I'm Keoni. I'm here to help you."

"Where's Fitz?" I couldn't hide the panic in my voice. When had I let go of his hand?

"I'm right here, Hads." His Scottish accent was thicker than normal, a tell that he was tired, frustrated—or both.

His cool fingers grazed my own as he took a seat next to me and wrapped his arms around me. I could breathe again.

"Are you having trouble with your sight?" I asked.

"Aye, but it's improving. Are you all right?"

"Yeah, I'm acclimating."

Though shapes were still fuzzy, I discerned Fitz's chestnut hair and his striking green eyes. I looked behind us to further test my eyesight. I made out several figures seemingly helping our teammates before Tanner came into focus. He was sitting with Chloe, and though they both looked a bit shellshocked, they were talking. Jordan was next to them, and my heart dropped until she offered a thumbs up to let me know she was okay.

I glanced back to Keoni, realizing I hadn't yet responded to him.

"Keoni, you said?"

"Yes, ma'am. How are you?"

"I'm okay. I'm sorry; I've been rude. I'm just a bit groggy."

"Passage isn't usually this difficult," he returned, his voice soft. "You're the second group to cross today, and the first was in the same state."

"What does this mean?" James asked. He moved slowly to take a seat on the ground next to Fitz.

"Lorenzo seems to have further affected the portal. Crossing has been odd in recent months. However, this . . . this is new."

"We must get word back to Earth, as well."

"Of course, James. We've already dispatched a messenger across the portal."

"Fitz! Hadley! Are you all right?"

"Isaac!" I reached my hand toward him. "We're okay. How are you feeling?"

"*Carissima*, you're freezing."

Isaac pulled a blanket from Keoni's grasp and placed it over my shoulders. I pulled him into an embrace, unable to fully voice both my relief and my gratitude, and his strong arms cradled me reassuringly.

"It looks like everyone is recovering. Let's get you into the warm vehicle waiting for you," Keoni said.

I cast my gaze upward, and Keoni extended a hand to help me stand.

With my eyesight nearly restored, I came face to face with the first witch to greet us in Opimae. His dark eyes were set against golden brown skin under a strong brow. His jaw was chiseled, and a wide smile spread across his lips. Jet-black hair fell loosely on to his shoulders, which were draped in an overshirt of thick, dark wool. The sleeves revealed gray chainmail, and as my eyes scanned his clothing, I found him reminiscent of a medieval warrior.

Soft laughter escaped Keoni's lips. "We stick closely to the dress of our ancestors around here. You'll grow accustomed to it."

"Shoot, I'm sorry. I just—"

Keoni waved his hand, dismissing my apology. "Please don't apologize. This is the first of many differences you'll see on our planet. You wouldn't be very observant if you didn't notice."

"Speaking of which," Jordan began as we all meandered toward the vehicle, "is it winter here—or fall, maybe?"

My best friend ran her hands rapidly across her arms, and I quickly draped my blanket around her. Jordan's hair had always fallen to her waist in tight curls or braids, but she'd shortened it just before our departure. It was quite the adjustment for me after seventeen years, but her natural hair was pulled into space buns, and I was certain no one had ever looked more casually cool in the style.

"It is indeed fall here in Opimae. Although, you'll never find it to be very warm here. Our suns are too distant."

Jordan and I exchanged glances. "Suns?" she whispered. That bit of information had been omitted in the intelligence reports. Jordan tilted her head toward the sky, the pale light illuminating the flecks of amber in her eyes.

Conversation was cut short as Keoni ushered us into a sleek SUV. A hand slipped on to my shoulder.

"You kiddos all good? Breathing all right?"

"We're good, Ian." I managed a smile.

"Are you all right, Dad?" Fitz questioned, his brows knitting tightly.

"Oh, I'm fine, son."

A stern look from Fitz pulled more of an explanation from him.

"I might ask for a bit of oxygen. I'm all right, but that journey did take it out of me."

Ian had entered the portal just behind us, and as my foggy mind ticked through recent memory, I realized Ian had sat nearest the portal when we exited into Opimae.

"How long were you in there, Ian? Did something happen?" I questioned, concern for my future father-in-law flooding through me.

"Ian entered just after you," James said. "But he exited last—ensuring no one was left behind, I suspect."

My gaze shifted back to Ian.

"Dad," Fitz whispered.

"No need to discuss it. We're all here now. I'll get a bit of oxygen, and we'll be all good."

"We'll have a few healers awaiting our arrival at headquarters to assess everyone. They'll take good care of you all." Keoni looked pointedly to the young witch in the passenger seat, who nodded and sent word of our needs, along with our ETA.

The driver accelerated, and a tall stone wall blurred in my periphery until we reached a thick, wooden gate attended by several guards. Like Keoni, they wore vaguely medieval attire, though they boasted charcoal armor atop their woolen clothes.

A guard approached our vehicle before confirming our passenger list and then waving his hand near our driver's face. A bright glow materialized in the air. The guard nodded, and with the wave of another guard's hands, the gate opened, allowing our departure. Several blacked-out SUVs were parked near the gate, and they fell into line, flanking our car as we sped down the blacktop street.

Tanner whistled, settling more comfortably into his seat. His eyes had turned russet after our portal crossing, a sign that his electrokinesis had awakened.

"Now, that was state of the art security," he said.

"Life in the age of Lorenzo, I'm afraid," Keoni responded. "We utilize both magic and technology in an effort to be as ironclad in our security measures as possible."

"Much has changed, I'm guessing?" James prompted.

"Much more than I wish." A humorless smile spread to his lips, and I didn't miss the glance he exchanged with the driver in the rear-view mirror.

On our journey through the city, Keoni shared he was assigned to our team as an Opimae intelligence resource. He was second in command to Charles, the highest ranking Opimae official actively working on the Lorenzo case. Keoni was to be our liaison, and perhaps more importantly, he was in charge of delivering us safely to headquarters to meet with Charles.

"I thought Charles was meant to be our liaison?" I asked.

"Think of me as an extension of Charles," he said. "We'll both be working closely with you, but I'm more accessible than Charles currently. He and I work as a team, so no need to worry."

"*An interesting start,*" Fitz voiced to my mind.

As we progressed through the city, Keoni shared more information.

"You're in Opimae City now. This is the largest city in Opimae and where your beginning efforts will focus. Headquarters is located here, and you'll soon have the pleasure of meeting governing officials from each of our continent's nations."

They must have been meeting over the Lorenzo situation. Something in Keoni's tone didn't invite discussion over it.

"We understand your planet has been a peaceful one, historically speaking?" James asked.

"Very much so. We're not accustomed to unrest."

"If only we could say the same of Earth," Isaac lamented.

As we meandered deeper into the center of Opimae City, the streets turned to cobblestone, and Keoni pointed out the more interesting sights of our trek: statues, landmarks, and the river that wound through the heart of the city.

It was beautiful—I found the architecture reminiscent of Bruges, Europe's most well-preserved medieval city. Ancient buildings lined the river, primarily comprised of stone, brick, and a variety of rich woods, which culminated into a scene that beckoned me back in time. The structures nearest the river seemed to jut directly from the water, and the subsequent rows of buildings swelled upward toward the foothills of the nearby mountains.

But unlike many of the medieval cities of Europe, Opimae City held a considerable amount of space for the natural world, even at its core. Trees, shrubs, and grass were visible between buildings, on rooftops and balconies, and spread throughout the neighborhoods that were scattered through the foothills. I was struck by how naturally the sprawling city intertwined within the deep foliage of the mountainsides.

If the city was reminiscent of Bruges, then the nature was vaguely Portland, and the two intermingled in the most ethereal way.

And yet, there was something even greater fighting for the attention of my senses: magic. A rush of energy radiated through me, and it was clear that the inhabitants of this city were purely magical beings. This, I realized, would take time for my body to settle into.

As we approached a particularly ornate bridge, I studied figures carved into the stone: dragons, pegasus, sea-like creatures, and figures of prominent witches. I found myself wondering how many magical creatures might exist on this foreign planet.

"We're here," Keoni announced.

My eyes scanned an impressive stone structure sprawling the length of the block and rising several stories in height.

"I know this is going to be difficult, but try not to stare."

"Stare?" Fitz questioned.

"Yeah, at the species who aren't witches." Keoni smiled before leaving the car to greet a tall, graceful woman approaching us. Her cascading, honey-colored hair and intense green eyes complemented a pale triangular face. She clearly wasn't human, but it wasn't until she stood near the vehicle that we noticed her ears.

"Ah, an elf, then," James said.

"Let's get out of the car and get a better look," Isaac said impatiently.

"Remember, no gawking," Henry returned, flashing a warning look at Isaac.

"You are so bloody annoying sometimes." It seemed British vernacular had seeped into Isaac's vocabulary, and that subtle reminder of my new home made me smile.

As we exited the car, I realized distance hadn't done the elf justice. Everything from her lean muscle to her lightness of foot suggested a lithe warrior, a soldier who could quickly answer her purpose. Her nimble fingers were perfect for wielding the bow slung across her back, and I imagined thousands of years of evolution had likely crafted hands stronger and steadier than my own. Human legends hadn't gotten much wrong in this department.

"Everyone, please meet Lana. She is head of your team's security. I'd ask you to introduce yourselves," Keoni began with a smile, "but there is no need. She is already well-acquainted with each of you."

"What do you mean by that?" Ian asked.

"Your profiles were sent ahead of you. Photos. Strengths, weaknesses. We've been studying the team to prepare for your arrival," Keoni answered.

This explained why Keoni had recognized each of us at the portal.

"We're pleased to have you with us," Lana said. "I look forward to spending time with each of you. But for now, if you'll follow me, I'll escort you to Charles."

She turned quickly, and as we followed her lead, I took the opportunity to further observe her. Her attire was much like Keoni's. A dark woolen tunic was cinched at the waist by a burgundy leather belt that dipped crookedly from the weight of a holster at her hip, and her bow and arrow sat neatly in a back quiver of matching leather.

Lana led us down a coved walkway, lined with large lanterns, and upon further inspection, the flames seemed to float, suspended at the center of each lantern. I'd seen this type of lighting once before— in Lorenzo's fortress. Keoni noticed our divided attention.

"The flames are a manipulation of the elements—they are simply light," he explained. He opened the glass door of the nearest lantern. "Feel," he invited.

I timidly reached for the lantern, and when my fingers met the flame, they passed through the light without any discomfort.

"Brilliant," Fitz mumbled behind me before testing the theory himself. Our eyes met in wonder.

"Once the elements are pulled into place, the light holds steady for about a week before requiring a tune up."

"Is this to save energy?" I asked.

"We did experiment with artificial light, but many of the staff didn't take well to the change, so we kept magical lighting through many areas of the building."

We paused again at the end of the walkway, where a group of guards flanked two large wooden doors with iron hinges. The guards were dressed the same as the first group at the portal exit: wool to keep them warm, armor to protect their weakest points.

"You were briefed about being added into our government database?" Lana confirmed.

"Aye, we've all agreed to the terms," James answered.

Lana moved us into place in front of several guards, who set to work. They waved their hands in front of our faces before asking our names, inputting data into small handheld devices, and signaling us forward.

"How does this work?" Ian asked.

"The guards pulled a miniscule amount of your energy so the device could read the frequency and makeup of your magic. The device then recognizes the energy of those who have access," Lana said. "You're now in the system."

"My god," Molly whispered under her breath. She met my gaze, and her mouth twisted into an unsure expression. I nodded in agreement, and she quickly returned her focus to Lana.

Lana led us down a lengthy hallway with cream-colored walls and intricate ceiling murals, depicting witches and elves, all cast in the glow of magically lit torches that were mounted to the walls.

My pace slowed as I studied the murals, though I wasn't well enough acquainted with Opimae's history and legends to make sense of them. When a hand within the mural moved, I stopped, mouth agape.

"Hadley?" Fitz nudged.

"I'm sorry. It's just—is that . . ."

"Oh," Jordan said. "The murals are moving."

"*Bellissimo*," Isaac whispered. "How is this possible?"

"Magic," Lana said. "For some witches, weaving magic into their work is a part of their artistry."

"It certainly brings them to life," James added, gazing distractedly toward the ceiling.

We eventually turned the corner into a large room with rows of wooden tables and thickly trimmed windows, which allowed the soft afternoon glow to grace the worn wooden floors. The space felt scholarly, resembling a library with its rows of books along the walls and the lamps spread across tabletops. And though the table lamps were fueled by magical fire, the overhead lighting was bright—and I thought perhaps they weren't magically constructed.

Keoni ushered us in and signaled for healers to attend us, ensuring we were each recovering from our journey. I was only half cognizant of the healers, my mind swirling with information, when a tall figure walked purposefully through the doorway.

He was unmistakably witch. A palpable energy pulsed through the air all around him, one of the strongest auras I'd ever sensed. His eyes were dark, and his skin a deep brown. He carried himself with the intention and self-assuredness of someone who'd known leadership long enough to no longer be frightened of it. Though his tunic was of a similar medieval style to that of Keoni and Lana's dress, the dark fabric was inlaid with intricate designs and trimmed in silver.

He extended his hand, introducing himself to each of us.

"What an immense pleasure to finally have you with us," he said. "I'm Charles."

"We're delighted to be here," James replied.

"I know you must be tired from your journey and longing to settle into your new space, so I'll keep this brief." He smiled. "Keoni and Lana will escort you to your accommodations. I know it's not home, but we trust you'll find it comfortable for the duration of your stay with us."

"Thank you, Charles. We appreciate the hospitality," I said.

"You're most welcome, Hadley. We are appreciative of our alliance with Earth."

Nods and faint smiles went around the room—though the group's energy still felt skeptical at best.

"The next few days will be busy, but for now—please rest and prepare yourselves for the grueling weeks to come."

CHAPTER FIVE

Fitz and I joined our companions upstairs in the great room of our new home for breakfast. As we entered the lofty space with its high columns and cliffside views, I shook my head, wondering how long it would take to grow accustomed to our beautiful new home. The arched, black pane windows allowed for ample natural light and held a lovely view of the valley below us. The walls were a mix of soft cream plaster and beige stonework, and they were adorned with oil paintings and thick, decorative curtains. The wooden floors were full of character, and area rugs were scattered about.

Jordan was tucked in the nearest corner at a small table. She extended her hand absentmindedly in front of her as she searched for her drink, and her eyes were transfixed on a book that lay open on the table.

"You always find time for a book," I said.

"There's a library in here. *A library*," she said, her eyebrows raised. "I think I'll just stay here today and learn about Opimae's literary scene."

"Dinnae you want to go explore Opimae? Isn't that all you could focus on yesterday afternoon?" Henry quipped.

"Henry, respectfully . . . shut your mouth."

Henry chuckled before returning his focus to the headlines spread across his computer screen.

"Keeping up with business, I see," Fitz said, peering over Henry's shoulder.

"Aye. Best I can," Henry said. "I'll have to send communications through a messenger across the portal, but at least there's a news stream here dedicated to information coming from Earth. It is semi-helpful."

Fitz met my gaze with a smile. *"Henry will be Henry."*

"This place has everything we could want except for peace," Ian said, gazing through the floor to ceiling windows. He glanced toward Tanner, before giving me a pointed look.

Tanner had been quiet since crossing the portal, and I was worried he regretted his decision to join the crusade.

Jordan suddenly floated out of her seat and I gasped.

"She's perfectly safe, lass," Henry muttered, his focus remaining on Jordan.

"Good morning, team!" Keoni said warmly as he entered the great room. When he caught sight of Jordan, he laughed. "I see you're having a bit of fun this morning."

"So much fun!" Jordan said enthusiastically, her eyes wide with delight. Henry floated her gently to the ground, and she padded over to the refrigerator.

Keoni turned to face most of the group. He looked the part of a warrior, draped in a dark waist-length tunic held tightly into place by a leather belt atop matching black trousers and tall leather boots. A black armored vest trimmed in bronze completed his ensemble.

"I hope you are well rested, because we have a lot of Opimae to see today."

"Oh, how marvelous!" James exclaimed, rubbing his palms together excitedly.

"When is our first briefing with the Opimae intelligence teams?" I asked.

"Your first meeting hasn't been set, but we'll work that out soon enough."

"I don't understand. We've come all this way to work with you on the Lorenzo crisis, and we're spending our time sightseeing?"

"Will we mostly be sightseeing these first few days?" Isaac asked.

"Charles—and all of us really—thought it important to teach you about Opimae before diving into meetings so you may understand us better. The idea is to acclimate you to Opimae—give you a real feel for this new environment. There is much to see in Opimae and the surrounding area. It is one thing to read facts about this land and its cultures. It is quite another to experience it, to see it firsthand."

"Of course," I replied.

Fitz and I met each other's gaze pointedly.

"We're meant to be preventing war, not playing tourist," Fitz said telepathically.

"I don't care what their reasoning is—this doesn't make sense."

"Aye. Let's play along today, but if this continues, we should speak to Charles."

I sighed softly before asking the air to deposit my jacket into my waiting grasp and headed for the door.

"Where are we?" Isaac asked.

We stood in a large courtyard at what seemed to be the heart of the city. Large statues rose above our heads, carved from something akin to gray marbled stone, depicting figures dressed in robes and bearing pointed ears. The elves were grouped together as though they were in conversation, and their feet met rectangular stones of the same material. A moat of crystal-clear water encircled the monument, which was then bordered by a patch of grass. The grass met the cobblestones that were common through the inner corridor of the city. Benches were scattered about the courtyard where witches and elves basked in the pale rays of the suns.

"Iter. It is a popular courtyard that pays homage to the elves," Lana explained.

"Many places in Opimae are named in Latin," Isaac shared with the rest of us.

"Yes, very good," Lana returned. "*Iter* essentially means 'the journey.' The statues were built by my folk to honor the leaders who brought our ancestors across the portal during The Great Passage."

"I'm anxious to learn more about The Great Passage," Isaac said. Without legal cases to consume his mind, it seemed Isaac's zest for research would be satiated by continuing to learn as much as possible about Opimae.

"And so you will—soon."

"This is a famous spot in the city," Keoni added, returning our focus to the courtyard. "Street performances are common here—especially traditional elven music. And on sunny days you'll always find witches painting. It's quite enjoyable to watch them work," he said, pointing toward a witch who was seated on a bench doing just that.

Through a mix of sweeping motions, the woman commanded paint on to the canvas. A buzz of energy radiated aggressively from her body, perceptible even at our distance. I thought of the motion-filled paintings at headquarters, though this painting seemed to be headed in a different direction. The scene unfolding was a countryside, and though the grass swayed to the rhythm of the wind, the sun caught my attention most, as a soft glow radiated from the canvas.

I leaned my head against Fitz's shoulder and scanned the waterway below us. I wondered at Fate and this path she'd led us down as my eyes followed the small boats that skimmed the river. As the vessels transported a mix of magical beings to their destinations, I considered the passengers' lives and where they were headed. I couldn't help but wonder if any of them believed in Lorenzo's mission—were any of these beings his followers?

"Are those water taxis?" Jordan asked.

"Yes," Lana returned. "And speaking of river boats, we have one awaiting you once everyone is ready."

"What's next on the agenda?" I asked.

"A tour of the city."

"What are we waiting on then?" Isaac exclaimed, his eyes wide.

"Let's get moving!"

An elf stood on a wooden box turned makeshift stage, deftly pulling a bow against his fiddle. A small accompaniment of elves sat below him, playing their instruments in harmony with his. The magnetic energy called to us, and many of the beings across the courtyard broke into dance. Though they seemed happy, a palpable uneasiness rested in the air. I wondered if that was due to Lorenzo—did the citizens of Opimae City know the danger they might be in?

As I scanned the scene, one woman caught my attention as her skin began to glow.

"What's happening there?" Jordan asked.

"Faeries glow when they're happy," Keoni answered.

"Stop it," Jordan said. "She's a *faerie?*"

I laughed thinking about the number of faeries Jordan must have read about in her books.

Lana and Keoni exchanged a smile before Lana answered. "Faerie sightings in Opimae City are uncommon. This is quite special."

"Why is this uncommon?" I asked.

"The faerie folk don't often wander from their kingdom." Our gazes were fixed upon Lana, awaiting more information. After a moment's pause, she acquiesced. "You've heard the human tales of faeries, I'm sure. They claimed faeries were troublemakers, and the faeries were blamed for many tales of woe on Earth. When they crossed into Opimae, they moved far into the east country. They keep mostly to themselves even now. They've only grown more reclusive since Lorenzo's arrival in Opimae."

Keoni met Lana's gaze, his eyebrows raised. Her jaw tightened before breaking their silent exchange to look toward the growing crowd. Even with their efforts, Keoni and Lana couldn't hide that something was wrong.

Once the song ended, applause echoed loudly through the courtyard, and we walked toward a set of stairs that led to a boat launch. The river was quiet; the only discernible sound was that of the water splashing against the side of the boat. The wind rustled the leaves of the many trees that lined the river.

Isaac was talking with Henry and Molly as they found their seats, and I hoped Molly was feeling more comfortable with us. Fitz extended his hand, helping me on to the boat, and I laced my fingers through his, pulling him along with me in my search for a good seat. I passed Tanner, who was deep in discussion with Chloe, their expressions serious. My mind wanted to know more, but I quieted my ability. I wouldn't be reading anyone's mind today. I found my seat next to Jordan, and Fitz slid on to the bench beside me. Jordan dipped her hand into the water, though she quickly pulled back as a gasp left her lips.

"Jordan. What is it?"

"I—I'm not sure."

The group exchanged glances warily before I looked to Keoni. "Is there something odd about the water here?"

"No." His brows knitted tightly before he dropped his hand into the water. He shook his head as he met my gaze. "There's nothing amiss."

"Jordan?" Lana prodded. "Can you tell me what you felt when you touched the water?"

"It felt . . . alive. My fingers tingled. That isn't normal?"

"I'm afraid not. Although I have no idea whether a human's body chemistry would react strangely to the river."

"Maybe she's tuning in to magical energy here?" Keoni guessed.

"I can't say," Lana returned, pensive. "Jordan, will you touch the water again and see if you have the same reaction?"

Jordan timidly returned her fingertips to the river. "Yeah, it feels the same."

"How odd. We'll ask around at headquarters if this might be normal for humans. Very few have passed over, but we do have records regarding their journey and how they responded to our elements," Keoni offered.

As we meandered through the city, we pointed toward architecture that we found especially beautiful. The buildings truly took me back in time. I could easily have persuaded myself that I was swept up in an Earth-side adventure from centuries past had it not been for the vast amount of magic floating through the air. Though the air was saturated with magic, it wasn't heavy. On the contrary, it felt vibrant.

"And as you can see, there are many cafes and coffee shops all throughout the city," Keoni said.

"The coffee shops suprised me," Jordan said, her face scrunched.

"We enjoy caffeine just as much as humans do," Keoni said.

"Our coffee shops *are* different from yours, though," Lana said. "We have minerals and properties that differ from those on Earth, of course, and that alters the flavor of our coffee, tea, and so forth. But I think you'll enjoy these nuances."

"And we offer natural additives to help your body in targeted ways," Keoni added. "Our kitchen witches craft delicious potions, whether you need a shot of energy or wellness."

Fitz explained quietly that kitchen witches were casters who had specialized powers in cooking, growing herbs, and concocting potions.

I marveled at the new knowledge as a courtyard came into view, and countless figures sprinkled the scene. Some dawdled about with their companions. Others sat quietly, typing on laptops and writing in notebooks. Some walked quickly with shopping bags tucked under their arms or swinging from their fingertips. Suddenly, a prickle worked its way up my spine, and to my horror, I recognized the energy. I gripped Fitz's hand.

"What's wrong?" he whispered.

"The watcher from Edinburgh. I feel his energy."

"*What?*" Fitz asked, though he looked around hurriedly.

My mind spun. Could he really have crossed the portal?

I closed my eyes briefly, focusing on the familiar energy. I followed the prickle toward the courtyard, and finally found who I was looking for. My eyes popped open, and sure enough, I met the icy blue stare of the witch who'd watched me in Edinburgh.

"There!" I whispered intensely to Fitz.

The watcher's eyes flickered to Fitz's. He disappeared so quickly, I questioned if he'd ever been there at all.

"Is everything all right?" Henry asked.

"It was the watcher—from Edinburgh," Fitz said, his tone disappointed. "He disappeared as soon as we located him. He must be a time-walker."

"What's this about?" Keoni asked, his eyes narrowing suspiciously.

I explained the situation to Keoni and Lana.

"And you're sure it was him?"

Something felt off about Keoni's response, and I hesitated in answering.

"It's not that I doubt you," he explained, noting my pause. "I only wanted to double check before we file a report about this."

"I'm sure."

Lana and Keoni wanted a full report to put on file, and Lana sent the witch's description to local government agents to be on the lookout for him. It was unnerving to know he'd found me on a foreign planet, and though I tried to put him out of my mind, it took a while for my heart to steady. Fitz offered a push of calm energy, but I declined. I didn't want to grow reliant on that every time my anxiety rose.

Luckily, the next couple of hours passed uneventfully on the water as we learned more about this magical new world. Isaac was full of questions about everything from the faerie kingdom to water witches, and the subject matter made it easier to relax—until the conversation turned toward government.

"There are twenty-four separate nations in Opimae," Lana said. "Each is comprised of its own government structure. Some have a monarchy, while others don't. They all have elected officials for various positions within the government, but ultimately, their highest-ranking officials all have seats on our international council."

"Are the monarchs figureheads, or do they rule?" Henry asked.

"They actively rule, though most of these kingdoms also have an elected official who essentially represents the interests of the folk in the kingdom. They work together with the monarchy to ensure the kingdom's inhabitants have their voices heard," Lana answered.

"How many of these kingdoms have a monarchy?" I asked.

"Seven out of the eight on this continent," Keoni said.

"Thalassa, the kingdom of water witches; Athdara, the Northern kingdom of elves; Constantina, the Southern kingdom of elves; Arregaithel, the kingdom of the dragon keepers; and Bain, the kingdom of druids, all have dual government representatives—a monarch and an elected official. Kevardhu, the faerie kingdom, and Hurlee, a southern witch kingdom, both have monarchs who rule alone, though I can't imagine why," Lana offered.

Tanner released a low whistle. "There's a whole lot to unpack in what you just said."

Lana laughed. "I suppose there is."

"So, it's true then. There *are* dragons here?" Fitz questioned.

"Yes. They live in Arregaithel under the capable watch of the fire witches." Lana's gaze settled on me. "The keepers of the dragons are a nation of witches that formed at The Great Passage. They have a way with the creatures and have made it their mission to train and protect them."

I marveled at the thought of a nation comprised of fire-fueled witches like myself. *Could I manage a dragon?* I wondered. Fitz caught my gaze, undoubtedly wondering the same.

"You mentioned druids," Ian said. "Are they similar to the druids of Earth?"

So, those legends were true. Druids really did exist on Earth.

"Your druids are essentially descendants of the ones who did not seek refuge in Opimae. I believe humans have heavily infiltrated those familial lines," Keoni answered.

"What exactly makes a being a druid?" I asked.

"Druids aren't human, but they're not witches either. They're a separate species who draw energy and knowledge from the earth. They don't have a witch's gamut of powers, but they're tied to nature and to the spiritual world—to the unseen."

Information flowed much like our path down the winding river. By the end of our boat tour, we'd seen much of the downtown corridor and learned of our magical brothers and sisters.

Perhaps there was something to Opimae's method of introducing us to its culture after all.

CHAPTER SIX

The following morning, I woke early despite going to bed later than planned. I wanted nothing more than to fall back to sleep. But there was no drifting back to my dreams when I remembered where I was. Instead, I left the bed quietly, trying to not disturb Fitz. I tiptoed down the hallway to the communal kitchen and made a cup of tea. The house was quiet, and I tucked into a breakfast nook to enjoy a hot drink that bore a striking resemblance to chai.

I pushed open a nearby window. The air held a strange quality on this foreign planet, calmer somehow, and its suns softer and steadier than the fleeting light of Earth. Even though there were two suns that hung in the skyline, they were distant, accounting for the pale light that basked this planet. We were in the height of Opimae's fall, and the light would allegedly grow weaker with each passing day until the winter solstice. Unbelievably, Keoni had shared that during the summer season, a third sun made an appearance in the northern sky which boosted the summer daylight to a brightness similar to Earth's.

Once I'd drained the mug, I padded softly down the hallway to wake Fitz before our breakfast meeting with Lana. I opened the curtains and delicate sunlight cast itself across the room. Fitz rolled over into the soft rays and slowly opened his eyes.

"There you are," I said, taking a seat next to him on the large, four-poster bed.

His fingers lightly traced my cheek. "Hmph. Not a dream after all."

"Can you believe this?" I asked.

"I didn't expect it to be so . . . bonnie?"

"Neither did I," I agreed. "Admittedly, I didn't even think about things like what the architecture would be like here, but medieval Europe wouldn't have been my guess."

"Aye, nor mine."

I stifled a yawn. "I should've gone to bed earlier. I'm still tired from the crossing."

"I don't want to get up either, but it's not sleep I crave."

"*Fitz MacGregor*," I teased.

"Aye?" he questioned. Fitz pulled me closer.

"We need to be ready soon," I murmured as his lips found my neck.

"Come here."

Fitz flipped to his back, pulling me on top of him. He gazed intently into my eyes, and my heart quickened. I'd never tire of that.

"You're looking at me like that, and I'm meant to get up now? That's hardly fair," Fitz said. He sat up and ran his fingers along my jaw before tucking my hair behind my ear.

I moved my head to the side, leaning into his touch. He tucked his face into the crook of my neck, lingering there as his lips brushed lightly against my skin. Goosebumps rippled across my body.

"You're making it really tough to be responsible right now," I mumbled.

"Aye, I see. I'll just stop then," he said, a mischievous smirk resting on his lips.

I slid my hands on to his firm chest.

"You'll stop when I tell you to stop," I whispered. I pushed against his body, and he sank back into the bed. One arm bent behind his head in support while the other traveled to my hip.

I dipped my head, and once my lips met his, my resolve wavered. He kissed me deeply before we pulled away.

"All right, then. Time to prepare for the day." He raised an eyebrow and continued. "But we'll be picking this up later tonight."

He rose to kiss me again, and it was enough to make my breath come short.

"I'll be thinking about that all day," I said.

Fitz threw on a shirt and wandered down the hallway in search of caffeine. I sat on the bed for a few minutes longer, studying our bedroom.

Our space was beautifully appointed, the walls the same mix of soft white plaster and stonework that were in the great room. They were sprinkled with landscape paintings, and one had caught my attention last night. There wasn't much to the painting, except that it was different than the rest—this was a garden scene rather than an untamed land-scape. Two women sat on a bench with their backs to the viewer. One sported auburn hair, which was pulled into a low, flipped ponytail that cascaded down the center of her navy tunic. The other had hair the color of a moonless night sky, which fell in loose curls down her back, and she wore a simple, burgundy-colored smock dress.

I felt the energy around the painting, but there was nothing perceptible that I could find. I removed it from the wall and examined the backing. Again—there was nothing odd. I felt the elements that comprised the painting, searching for information on the artist or the origin of the components used to create the artwork. I'd once discovered information about Lorenzo in the same manner, but this time . . . I was stumped. Something tugged at my mind, though I couldn't seem to grasp it. I placed the painting back on the wall and returned to readying myself for the day.

A cup of tea materialized on the dresser. I smiled as my fingers met the mug, feeling Fitz's lingering energy. I closed my eyes, enjoying the peace that accompanied the feeling of his magic streaming across my fingertips. Our power was already increasing in these first few days in Opimae due to the vast amount of magical energy that coursed through the planet, and as our power grew, so did our magical footprint.

Opimae felt both strange *and* familiar, and I guessed we owed the familiarity to the concentration of magic constantly surrounding us. Truthfully, we were most comfortable around our own species in a world where we were allowed to be ourselves.

I glanced in the mirror, smoothing down the gray tunic draping my figure. After yesterday, the team had decided collectively that we needed to blend during our time in Opimae, so our last outing had been a shopping trip. The beings of Opimae clearly observed the customs of their ancestors, attire included, and we would be no exception. I asked the air to pull my long, auburn hair into a braid as I drained my second cup of tea and rushed off to the great room to meet the team for breakfast.

"And that's when I learned women are easily twice as smart as men."

Laughter erupted as I walked into the great room. "I rarely walk into a room with you in it, and not walk into roaring laughter."

Tanner shrugged and pulled a sip from his usual breakfast smoothie. "What can I say? I just tell it like it is, and I guess people think it's funny."

"Tell it like it is? *Oh my.*"

He winked at Jordan and Chloe, who laughed in turn.

"You shouldn't encourage him like this." I smiled and rolled my eyes playfully at Jordan, who simply shrugged. Truthfully, I was glad to see Tanner acting like himself again. After considering his distance the last couple of days, I realized he'd truly not been himself in months. But I couldn't wonder why—he'd joined the council to help keep me safe, and the crusade had soon followed.

I sat next to Jordan on a large, linen couch, which felt like sinking into a puffy cloud.

"Is Molly here?" I asked, scanning the room.

Jordan shook her head. "She came and got coffee, but she said she had some things to take care of and went back to her room."

"I think she had some fun yesterday, though. We'll keep reaching out," I said.

Chloe pulled my focus as she rose from an armchair near the stone fireplace and took a seat beside me. Her somber expression warned of a serious conversation, and I took a deep breath.

"You know, Hadley, I wanted to talk to you about something."

I nodded.

"I can feel in your energy that you're still a bit skeptical of me and Solomon."

"Chloe—"

"No, it's okay. I just want you to know I understand. I would feel the same way after what you and Fitz went through."

Not the conversation I had expected. "I appreciate you acknowledging that. It hasn't been easy."

"I've launched an investigation into the lower councils, and I hope that will help."

"An investigation?"

"Based on what I've heard, I don't believe things were handled well, so there will be an investigation. I'm sorry for what happened to you and Fitz, and I'm here to help you every step of the way through this crusade."

The councils had put us through hell over our relationship, and none of their members had seemed to care about how it affected us. It surprised me how much Chloe's genuine acknowledgement of our feelings meant to me.

"I have a question about all this," I said.

"Go for it."

"This connection we have to our mates . . . it's unique."

Chloe hesitated, her eyes narrowing ever so slightly. She nodded. "I know—not firsthand, but I know."

"Do the councils believe that Fate leads us to our mates? Do they believe our bond is sacred in witchkind?"

"Yes, that's commonly believed by most of witchkind."

"Then it's difficult for me to understand why mates are forced apart, human or not. If that's the case—if our bonds really are that strong— then why do the councils take action against witches who've fallen in love with humans?"

I was looking for Chloe's opinion on mates just as much as I sought her answer for the councils' involvement, I realized.

My own energy wavered as I thought about the concept of Fate. The same question echoed again through my mind.

Did I have a choice?

"It's widely believed the bond isn't as strong between a human and a witch as it is between two witches," Chloe explained.

"Has anyone making these rules experienced that?"

Chloe pursed her lips.

"Because I've experienced those feelings as both a witch and a human."

"And what is your opinion on the matter?" she asked.

That stopped me in my tracks. "You actually care about my answer, don't you?"

"Of course, I do," she said. And I realized she meant it.

"I can't argue that the connection isn't stronger between two witches. My connection intensified quite a bit when I came into my powers. But I have to say, it was incredibly strong before I matched. I know it isn't cut and dry, and it likely varies by situation, but . . . Chloe, it wasn't normal for a human. That much I can tell you."

She nodded.

"Maybe these matches only happen with humans who have magical DNA." I paused, considering. "But I think it's worth the councils' time and resources to *really* investigate this, and not just in relation to Fitz and me. I'd like to see this investigation grow to all witch-human relationships. Being pulled apart from your mate is traumatizing. It pains me to know there are witches *and* people out there experiencing something like what Fitz and I went through."

"I agree."

"I thought you might, considering your current call for an investigation."

Chloe held my gaze and then leaned forward, resting her hand lightly on my arm.

"I think what you and Fitz have is incredibly special, and you're lucky to have what you do." She nodded once, letting that sink in. "And I don't believe you should have been forced apart."

Intuition nipped at me as I considered Chloe's stance. I had a feeling she wasn't as anti-human as many on the councils seemed to be.

"You fought for Jordan to be here even though she's human, didn't you?" I asked.

"Allowing a human to know about us *and* bringing them to Opimae is a big deal. I had to fight for a majority vote from the court to bring her on the mission," she said, her voice dropping even lower. "It was a split vote, but Fate favored Jordan."

I wasn't sure that Jordan's presence on Opimae was Fate favoring her, but I understood the sentiment.

"Why make the exception for Jordan?" I asked. "After the hell Fitz and I went through . . ."

"I see a change in some of the court's opinions. We do have to be incredibly careful about humans finding out about us, but not all situations are the same." She hesitated. "I can't really say much more than that right now, but just know that some of us are fighting hard for change."

I nodded, silence falling as I thought through her position on the subject.

A strange prickle nipped at the corner of my mind, and I turned to find Tanner studying Chloe. I knew him well enough to feel concerned over the change in his energy. But as quickly as I took notice, it was over, and Tanner changed the topic of conversation.

"Can you believe this? The three musketeers here in Opimae to help save all that's good in the world."

"It does seem pretty unbelievable, doesn't it?" I asked, rising from my seat to walk toward him. "Although if we have to camp while we're here, we're pros."

"Or have to eat nasty ass dried food."

"Or use whisky to disinfect wounds," Jordan offered.

"And disinfect our bellies while we're at it," Tanner added seriously before we broke into laughter.

"You know what I can't believe? That you were training for this council job for over a year. And here Hads and I were thinking you were a personal trainer for regular ole humans like me," Jordan said.

"Come on, J. I couldn't exactly share that with you two before all this shit went down."

"I guess I see your point," Jordan conceded.

Fitz's voice sounded through my mind, capturing my attention. He was seated at a table with Henry and Keoni. I excused myself and scanned the breakfast spread before them.

"Hads, Lana and her mate Saoirse made a traditional elven breakfast for us," Fitz explained.

"Wow, this looks incredible. It's wonderful to meet you!" I offered warmly, reaching to shake Saoirse's hand.

Saoirse was easily as ethereal as Lana and dressed in a similar style of clothing, though her outfit included an armored breastplate. Her storm cloud eyes contrasted against her deep brown skin, attributing to the otherworldliness of her elven nature. Her build was similar to Lana's, and as she turned back to the kitchen, I noticed the leather quiver across her back holding her bow and arrow.

"Saoirse is a military scout. She has an assignment today." Lana's lips curved into a humorless smile, a sign I knew well.

"That worries you," I said.

"You know how much, I'm sure," she returned, eyeing Fitz.

I laid a hand briefly on her shoulder before shifting conversation back toward a lighter tone. "This was kind of you two."

Saoirse beamed as she stepped back into the great room. "We wanted to share a bit of our culture with the team."

My eyes scanned over the large spread. Various fresh fruits, nuts, and breads lay on the table. I picked up a piece of bread. There was certainly a time when I couldn't have even dreamed of a moment such as this—enjoying a breakfast made by elves—and I vowed to savor the experience.

"Caora bread. It's one of my favorites," Saoirse offered. "And Lana's specialty."

I turned the caora bread over, scanning the components that brought it together. It looked similar to a scone and had been baked with various berries and nuts.

I took a bite. The interior was still warm, and I closed my eyes, savoring that first moment. Not too heavy for breakfast, the fruit lent a bit of sweetness to the treat, its flavors reminiscent of dates and cranberries.

"The berries grow wild by the riverside in Athdara," Saoirse said. "We're famous for them."

Saoirse set a plate of what looked to be smoked fish on the table before pulling her long box braids into a ponytail at the crown of her head. Both Saoirse's and Lana's movements were graceful as they flitted about the space, and it struck me how their divinely ethereal nature intertwined effortlessly with their warrior energies. The balance was truly otherworldly.

The team pushed a grouping of tables together to form one large table that would accommodate us all. Everyone—including Molly—gathered round and filled their plates. There had always been something extraordinary in this simple act for me: bringing loved ones around the table together to share a meal, filling ourselves with nourishment, strength, and happiness. I glanced at the familiar faces softly illuminated by the morning light. Despite the hardships that awaited us, I was inordinately grateful to Fate for this moment. And in the soft light of a strange new land, sharing the table with those beautiful souls, I began to feel strangely at home.

Fitz flicked his wrist, and an orange flew across the table and into his waiting grasp.

I smiled. "Always reminds me of Paris," I whispered.

Fitz held my gaze as the orange peeled itself, a nod to a Parisian evening that seemed so long ago, and I kissed him quickly.

"While we have everyone gathered here, we wanted to mention the upcoming autumnal festivities," Lana said, depositing another plate on the table. "It's a celebration between all of the magical beings here in Opimae, and we hope you will join us—it's this Saturday evening."

"That sounds grand, Lana. Thank you for the invitation," Henry said.

"This is your largest festival, right?" Isaac asked.

"Yes," Saoirse answered. "Our fall celebration is the largest of all the elven gatherings, but it's also the largest celebration across all cultures here."

"The closest thing we have is the true celebration of All Hallows' Eve," Isaac said.

"That's right," Saoirse said. "And the elven celebrations are most similar to Samhain in Celtic cultures."

"I bet it's incredible," I said.

"It is! And everyone dresses up for the occasion," Saoirse said.

"The food and drink are plentiful. And the rituals are fascinating ancient practices. You'll have a great time," Lana said.

"What are the rituals like?" Jordan asked.

"Chanting. Dancing. Praying. And there are recreations of important historical events. The elves each give something up in sacrifice for the week leading up to the festival, so we feast today, then we name our sacrifice. And we feast once again at the festival. Elves love a good excuse for a feast."

We decided to sacrifice something in solidarity with our elven sisters. Jordan and I sacrificed sweets.

"I suppose I'll give up my pipe," James said.

"A noble sacrifice," Henry said. "If you can go a week without tobacco, I can match a week without whisky."

Isaac whistled. "Stay out of his way this week, mates."

"Aye, and what'll you give up, then?"

Isaac wrinkled his nose.

"You're actually considering it?" Fitz asked.

"If Henry can do without his whisky . . ."

"No espresso?" I guessed.

Isaac nodded. "No espresso."

"I'll join Henry—it'll be a dry week," Fitz offered.

Solomon and Ian joined Isaac in giving up their precious coffee, and Molly and Chloe sacrificed tea.

"Use this week to honor your sacrifice and find the gratitude you'll maintain even through the difficulties of this season," Saoirse instructed.

"And remember, my friends. The end of this sacrifice brings feasting," Solomon said, a twinkle in his eye.

"Lana, you mentioned something yesterday about the elves' preservation initiatives. Could you explain that a bit?" Jordan inquired, shifting the focus of the conversation.

"Of course. The folk of Athdara have partnered with Bain to ensure nature conservation efforts are in place. Our concern for this land and its inhabitants has grown in tandem with Lorenzo's forces."

I noticed Keoni's brows knitted tightly, though his focus remained intent on the caora bread on his plate.

"We worry that war will bring irreparable damage to the land, and we've worked tirelessly to maintain the purity of Opimae as best we can," Saoirse added.

"And the druids have been instrumental in this process with us. Their own abilities wane if the land suffers, so tied to it as they are," Lana said.

"I'm sure there are countless animals who would suffer alongside them," James said.

"Of course. Many animals were brought over from Earth. Strangely, the only life on this planet prior to our passage were plants and sea creatures. The creatures are similar in nature to Earth's, but there are differences. There are shark-like creatures, for instance, but they favor something you'd consider as Prehistoric Earth."

"We've often thought the origin for all sea creatures is similar, but their adaptation results in the differences we see in the creatures of the two planets," Saoirse added. "Much like the difference between Earth's horses and our pegasus."

"I've been curious about pegasus," James said. "They weren't included in any of the reports we reviewed before crossing over."

"Earth's witchkind councils keep decent records on the witches of Opimae. Other magical beings, not so much," Keoni interjected.

"Do the pegasus live in a certain area of this world, the same as the dragons?" Isaac questioned. I could see his mental Rolodex turning.

"They're mainly in Athdara, but there are some pegasus in Constantina as well—the southern elven kingdom. The elves and the pegasus seem to be intertwined in some way. Our legends claim we were bound to them as their keepers. Sometimes I rather think it's the other way around," Saoirse answered.

"How so?" I prodded.

"They're incredibly intuitive beings. We tend to their needs, but they are magical, after all. And when a bond is formed between a pegasus and an elf, they become attuned to the thoughts and feelings of each other. Soliana knows my mood instantly. And when I'm feeling sad, she always senses it. She'll push this peaceful bit of magic my way."

"Saoirse does little field work without her partner in crime, Soliana. She's beautiful," Lana said.

"On Earth, the depictions of pegasus are usually white in color," James said. "Is that accurate?"

"No, pegasus are many different colors."

Lana smiled. "Soliana is a creamy white color at her core, but her beautiful mane is like dark chocolate, and her legs are the same. You'll have to see her sometime."

"*Oh my god*," Isaac began. "Yes, please."

The group snickered, but Isaac's gusto for Opimae's cultures was more than simply amusing. The yearning to learn respectfully about and understand the cultures of others was touching. This was how we were meant to be.

My mind spun, thinking of the magical species like pegasus and dragons, and I longed for the opportunity to meet these incredible beings.

"Speaking of Soliana, I'd better be going. Have a great time today, everyone." Saoirse gathered her belongings.

"Be careful out there," Lana whispered.

"Always," she replied.

This was Saoirse's job, but I imagined there was a level of danger to her days. My chest tightened, and I reached for Fitz's hand.

Saoirse hugged Lana tightly, planting a kiss on the top of her head, and flashed us a warm smile before heading for the door. A chorus of goodbyes floated through the air, and Lana's lips curved into a forced smile as the door clicked behind Saoirse.

"Okay, team," Keoni said. "Let's get moving. We have a fun day ahead of us."

CHAPTER SEVEN

The van zipped over the first mountain pass as we headed to a training center in the northern mountains where a fun surprise allegedly awaited us. The team chattered excitedly, speculation running wild. Lana and Keoni had been tight-lipped about the day's main event, both wearing smug smiles. It was the most I'd struggled to stay out of my companions' minds in quite some time, but I'd made a promise not to pry into the minds of those around me unless necessary, and that was a promise I intended to keep.

I gazed out the window, surveying the subtle changes in scenery as we climbed the mountainside. Massive evergreen trees stretched toward the sky, their sprawling branches decorating the faintly blue expanse above us. Deep forests, pristine glacial lakes, and rushing waterfalls accounted for most of the landscape. The sunlight intensified as we climbed toward the northern sun, and though it offered no extra warmth, it was pleasant.

"Is this sun bothering you?" Jordan asked me, squinting. She was rummaging through her leather bag.

"Not really. Are you okay?" I asked.

"I think so? This light just feels so intense." Her hands emerged with a large pair of sunglasses.

My gaze met Keoni's. He shook his head before looking to Lana. She shrugged, though her gaze lingered on Jordan. My chest tightened, though I pushed back on the feeling, not allowing myself to worry. She was a human on a magical planet, after all. We'd known she'd adapt differently from the rest of us.

"Do the glasses help?" Lana asked.

"Yeah, they make a big difference. Much better."

Keoni and Lana exchanged another look.

Our journey ended as we pulled into a parking lot positioned in front of a large stone building. Another massive stone structure stood behind it, and with its pitched gray roof and rectangular layout, I reasoned it must be some sort of barn. We stepped from the car into the soft crunch of snow. The snowpack had increased with our elevation, and no one had thought to clear the lot.

Instead of entering the nearest building, we navigated around it, sinking a couple feet into the snowpack with each step as we slowly progressed toward the barn.

"Could everyone pause for a moment?" Henry asked. "This willnae work."

He raised his arms forward and closed his eyes. When he opened them, a flurry of snow rose from the ground and stacked itself to either side of a newly cleared path, like the work of an invisible snowplow.

"You'll tire yourself quickly working magic like that," Ian said, smirking.

"Aye, but no more than trudging through this mess, I'd reckon," Henry returned.

"Laisrén will be thrilled," Keoni said to Lana before extending his arm for her to proceed.

We stopped just short of the barn, and Keoni proceeded solo toward the large iron doors. He pushed forcefully, opening one just wide enough to allow his entrance. It was strange that the doors were made of such a heavy material. Why not something more practical, like wood? When Keoni reemerged from the barn, a hearty witch followed his path, and together, they opened the doors fully.

With a full head of fiery red hair and a beard to match, the man stood in great contrast to the fallen snow. He wore coveralls of a strange material, and he dropped a large helmet by the doorway before crossing the distance to greet us.

"Good afternoon, Crusaders! My name is Laisrén," he offered in greeting.

"A fitting name!" James returned.

"*Laisrén* means fire or flame in Gaelic," Ian explained for those of us who didn't speak the language.

"Welcome to Arregaithel, the fire witch nation. We're mighty pleased to have you with us."

My heart skipped a beat.

We exchanged greetings before Laisrén finally revealed our afternoon's purpose. He whistled to another witch by the door, a petite blonde woman in a wool dress with a cloak made of the same material that Laisrén wore, and she disappeared quickly into the barn. When she reemerged, she wasn't alone.

"*Oh. My. God.*" Jordan whispered.

Gasps and murmurs went all around. My eyes met Lana's as I tightened my grip on Fitz's hand.

"Unbelievable," I muttered.

Not twenty feet from us stood one of the most legendary beings to have ever existed in either of our worlds. It stood at least seven feet tall, dwarfing the young woman who held its reins in her tiny hands. The creature stood on four legs, boasting two large wings atop its back. Steam rose from its elongated snout, which was proportionate to its long, lean neck. The beautiful creature was covered in scales that ranged from burnt umber to the darkest shades of ruby. But as the dragon came nearer, the sun kissed its scales, beckoning shades of crimson and poppy into a shimmering glow. Its large evergreen eyes swept across us, and when those eyes met mine, something ancient stirred in my soul, responding to a call I didn't quite understand.

"This is the fire witch?" Laisrén confirmed, nodding in my direction.

"Yes," Keoni responded.

"She'll gravitate toward you, ma'am. She senses your fire magic already," Laisrén explained.

I nodded, words failing me, my eyes never leaving the incredible creature. As she took her final steps toward us, a distinct hum of magical energy exuded from her.

"Róisín is well trained for battle. She's not wild. You have nothing to fear," Laisrén continued. "She'll want to sniff the lot of you—dragons are curious creatures. But she won't harm you. Remain still until she's familiarized herself. Once she's comfortable, we can move around, and you can get to know her better."

The young woman walked Róisín down our newly formed line-up, and she inspected the team until she made her way to me. Róisín's forest-colored pupils were distinct against the shimmering red of her scales, and they seemed to soften as she settled her gaze on me. She sighed, releasing a rush of steam, and a small laugh escaped my lips. She shook her head like a wet dog, but with the movement, a rush of energy flurried all around me.

Embers floated between us, and I instinctively reached my finger toward a glowing spark.

My hand tingled. The energy that rushed through me pulled an almost giddy feeling to the surface. Róisín was full of magic, and I suddenly understood that her magic was a communication tool—one that, to my great surprise, I understood. A curious feeling prodded at my energy, feeling around, and I let my guard down instinctively.

Róisín stood motionless for only a moment before nudging my shoulder. I slowly moved my hand toward her before pausing.

"May I?" I asked. Róisín closed her eyes, nodding. I looked toward Laisrén.

"She understands you," he confirmed. "Go ahead."

Fitz's energy tightened, and I turned, flashing a broad smile in his direction. I expanded the flow of our connection, allowing him to absorb my experience, helping him to understand what I knew to be true: Róisín wouldn't harm me. He nodded, and I reached forward timidly before sliding my hand down Róisín's neck. Her scales were clearly protective, nearly impenetrable I imagined, though they were also smoother than I expected. Her eyes closed, and she leaned into my hand. Tears misted over my eyes.

"Pretty special, isn't it?" Laisrén said, his eyes full of pride.

"I feel like she knows me."

"She recognizes that the same fiery magic resting inside her also resides within you. We're different, of course, but our magic . . . well, it's similar. She sees you as family."

Róisín pulled back, and I swore a smile formed at her lips.

"Show her your magic," Laisrén encouraged.

I looked to Fitz, who was now wearing a smile to rival mine. He nodded, understanding my silent request, and stepped back. I anchored deeply into my magic, and when my hands rose, flames burst to life from my palms. Once I'd channeled a hearty flame, I twirled my fingers in distinct motions, shaping the fire like a painter before a canvas. Movement by movement, the fire transformed until the figure of a small, fiery dragon took shape. My magical dragon breathed fire before dissipating into the cool afternoon air.

The team clapped and cheered, but it was Róisín's reaction I noticed most. She bobbed her head enthusiastically, and her joyous energy filled the air all around me. I'd thought a dragon would move slowly, but Róisín turned quickly and breathed fire above us. She expertly directed her fire into rings that grew larger and larger and then dissipated into smoke.

Laisrén had arranged an afternoon tea for us, and we settled on to an outdoor patio near a large chimney hot with fire, courtesy of Róisín's fire magic. She curled up at my feet, keeping them nice and warm as I snacked on a croissant.

"She likes you," Laisrén said.

"The feeling is mutual." I smiled. "How long have you worked with dragons?"

"Oh, for many years. My parents said they always knew this was my calling. I was constantly sneaking out of the house to a field nearby.

Dragons often grazed there, and I loved to watch them be. Fascinating creatures."

"And we're in Arregaithel now?" I asked, confirming his earlier greeting.

"You're just over the border. But aye, you're in a kingdom of witches just like you."

I nodded. "Do you like it here?"

"Oh, very much. We're only a few hours from Opimae City, but it feels like a different world up here. It's tranquil."

I looked around at the snow-covered mountains, listening for the perceptible rush of a nearby waterfall, and nodded. I understood perfectly. Something about Arregaithel felt like home to me. Perhaps it was my fellow fire witches' energy, or perhaps it was how much this beautiful landscape reminded me of the Pacific Northwest. But no matter the reason, I leaned into it, enjoying the distinct comfort.

Afternoon tea passed with companionable chatter while we learned more about Arregaithel and my fire commanding brothers and sisters. We were just finishing up the tea service when Jordan's predicament caught my attention.

"Henry," I began. "Jordan is having trouble getting back on to the ground."

When Henry had floated Jordan around the great room our first morning in Opimae, he'd started something that Jordan wouldn't tire of. He usually floated her toward her seat and then asked the air to release her slowly, but today her legs were flailing around as she attempted to descend to the ground.

Henry looked up from his conversation with Keoni and glanced at Jordan only a second before the two of them smiled widely at each other.

"What's going on?" Molly asked, her curiosity overcoming her reserved demeanor.

"Henry isn't floating her today." Fitz grinned, grabbing another sandwich and slipping his free hand on to my thigh.

"Henry?" I prompted, ever so slightly distracted by Fitz's touch.

"He's right. I released her like normal. I didnae realize she wasn't seated." He shrugged.

"Oh my god."

"Dinnae worry," Henry directed. "I've got her. She willnae fall to the ground, at least."

"You're a real one. Thanks, Henry!" Jordan exclaimed.

"So . . . Jordan's picked up her power then," Isaac said. "This should be fun."

We knew this was coming, but it was really something to see. Her face was aglow with pure happiness.

"Hell yeah, Jordan!" Tanner exclaimed.

"You can feel her energy already, huh?" I asked.

"Oh yeah," he answered enthusiastically.

Henry walked Jordan through the process of returning gracefully to the earth, and I embraced my best friend. I wasn't sure if she'd acquire any other powers during her time on Opimae, but this alone was special.

After a few hours spent in the realm of the fire witches, we bid adieu to Róisín and Laisrén. I lingered for as long as I could next to Róisín, surprisingly dreading my separation from her. I suddenly understood Saoirse's connection to Soliana. Róisín rested her head on my shoulder, and I wrapped my arms around her.

"Will I be able to see her again?" I asked.

"We'll keep in touch with Laisrén. Perhaps we can find another opportunity," Keoni offered.

I nodded, returning my focus to Róisín.

"I have to go now, but I'll find a way to see you again."

Róisín nodded. She leaned her head against mine before releasing me. I paused as we meandered back to the car, and I turned back to Róisín, who was sitting near the barn, intently observing my departure.

I didn't know how, but I'd see Róisín again. Our paths hadn't crossed by accident. I was certain our destinies were intertwined—that Fate had written it in the stars.

CHAPTER EIGHT

We found ourselves at Opimae's government headquarters the following morning, awaiting our introduction to our combat trainers. The weather had turned stormy, and I shook the rain from my jacket as Tanner and I were called into a large training room, where mats were spread across most of the stone floors. Draped along the far wall was the same fire-resistant material I'd seen in Arregaithel. Chloe, Solomon, and Keoni turned to greet us. They were working together to ensure everyone on the team was trained properly—Chloe and Solomon included—and Chloe wanted to continue assessing my powers to ensure I was still advancing as I should.

Two witches sat cross legged on a table across the room. The woman stood and was followed by the other witch, who rose slowly from his seat, unfurling like a cat stalking his prey. His icy gaze pierced straight through me.

"Hadley, is everything all right?" Solomon asked, his brow creasing in worry.

I realized my face must have revealed my horror, but I couldn't seem to speak. My gaze held my stalker's, neither of us rushing to make the first move.

"Hadley," Chloe said, her voice betraying her confusion.

"Why is he here?" I asked, my eyes still fixed on the witch. His curly dark hair had been cropped, drawing more focus to his chiseled features and pale blue eyes set against light brown skin. I had almost forgotten just how attractive and how alarming he was. My skin crawled.

"This is Jess Evans," Keoni said cautiously. "He's one of your trainers."

"*Him*? Are you serious?"

"You've met?" Chloe asked.

"Oh, not officially," I said, still unwilling to release his unsettling stare. Chloe's gaze shifted warily from me to Jess. "But he's been following me."

"Following you?" she said. "You don't mean . . ."

"That's exactly what I mean. He's the Edinburgh stalker."

"Oh, hell no," Tanner said, shaking his head.

Keoni's eyes widened. "Excuse me?"

"Hadley, are you positive?" Solomon asked.

I finally looked away from the mysterious witch and met Solomon's gaze. His eyes were soft, though his features looked wary.

I nodded. "Absolutely positive."

"This can't be true," Keoni said, exasperated. The room went silent as Keoni shifted his gaze to Jess. "Is Hadley right about this?"

Jess held my gaze a few seconds longer before looking to Keoni. "Yeah, she's right."

I had expected him to deny my claims, and it caught me off guard when he confessed.

"Why?" Keoni asked.

"I didn't mean to alarm you," Jess said, turning to me. "The chamber shared their interest in you, and I knew I'd assist in your training, should you agree to this mission. I wanted to observe the new prospect in her natural hab—"

"Bullshit," Tanner said, cutting him off.

"Clearly, Jess was a bit overzealous," Keoni said. He watched Jess warily as he spoke. "However, he is the best coach in our ranks. He's trained most of our special forces."

The unfamiliar witch exchanged a look with Keoni before resting her eyes on Jess.

"I'm sure he is. This just doesn't sit well with me," I said.

"I apologize," Jess said.

"That's it? That's the apology?" Tanner asked.

"That doesn't seem awfully sincere," I said.

Everything within me was burning. Jess's entrance ignited my fire magic, and his continued presence only stoked the flames higher. I closed my eyes momentarily, willing my body to cool down.

"I truly am sorry," Jess returned, a grim expression settling on to his features as his gaze dropped to my fingertips.

"Jess, why don't you explain to Hadley how you're going to help her?" Keoni prompted.

His frosty gaze sent prickles across my skin. As my powers developed, I was learning that the sting of a witch's gaze usually faded with time. The longer you knew someone, the lesser the reaction, and the longer you were in contact with another being, the more the sting dulled into comfortable familiarity. Yet the pricks of Jess's gaze offered no signs of abatement.

"We're going to have a lot of fun," Jess said. "You'll learn task execution with me. We'll focus on hand-to-hand combat, martial arts, and the like. This training will be vital in the field."

I nodded once, though I considered walking out of the meeting. I looked to Tanner, whose energy felt angrier by the second. The government couldn't force us to work with Jess.

"This is Sadie," Jess continued, gesturing to the woman next to him. "We'll work together in this training, and she'll act as one of Hadley's sparring partners."

Everything about Sadie seemed as pale as Opimae's suns, from her milky complexion to her green-ish hazel eyes to her ashy blonde hair. But her energy was stormy, and the scowl on her face suggested she wasn't thrilled to be working with me.

"It's nice to meet you, Sadie," I said anyway.

Sadie looked at me wordlessly and nodded.

"Sadie is a member of our special forces. She'll prove to be a great partner for you," Keoni said.

I had my doubts, but I held my tongue.

"Chloe has volunteered to continue monitoring your progress. She'll work with you on power enhancement training," Jess said.

"I'm thrilled because it's the special part," Chloe said. "Maka taught you control. Jess will devise your self-defense and strategy, and Sadie will push you to outlast your opponent. Power enhancement is the added boost that will take each of those abilities to the next level. We'll cover magical combat like crafting spells and generally leveraging magic for added strength. Then, we'll heighten your instincts."

Finally, something I could look forward to.

"Now that we've covered that bit of business, we'll have Hadley run through a training session with Jess," Keoni said. "Tanner, you can break for a while, and we'll call you in after Hadley."

"Yeah, I'm not going anywhere," he said, eyeing Jess.

"I'd like to speak with Chloe and Solomon first," I said.

Keoni looked troubled, but he forced a smile and nodded in agreement.

We stepped aside, and I motioned for Tanner to join us. I asked the elements to withhold our conversation from the others in the room. Once I felt the privacy shield settle around us, I began.

"I can't train with Jess."

Solomon nodded. "His behavior was outrageous. No disagreement there. But I think we'll have to be careful in how we approach this situation."

"Here's what we know," Chloe said. "Jess is well-respected in Opimae as one of their best trainers. The Opimaean government made it clear that we all have to train with Jess for consistency in combat."

I released a long, frustrated sigh. "So, what are you really saying? That I can't object to this?"

"No, I'm not saying that at all," she said. "I object too."

"As do I," Solomon said. "All we want to say here is that we must find the right way to object without causing offense in the Opimaean ranks.

We must be strategic, hm?"

I understood his meaning. "This could read as Earth being un-cooperative."

"Exactly."

"Additionally, Solomon and I received letters from several Cardinal Court members stating they've worked with Jess in the past and were enthusiastic about him being appointed to our training," Chloe said.

"That's not good," Tanner said.

Solomon nodded. "Jess is respected among many in the European governments—apparently, he worked closely with them before he accepted this role. And that sentiment of support trickled through South America, India . . . this will be a divisive issue on the Earth side as well."

Keoni approached our group and pointed to the air between us. I reluctantly dropped my shield.

"Is everything all right? We really should move into your training session," Keoni said, eyeing me.

I called the shield back into place and pushed it over to include Keoni.

"You clearly skimmed over the issue back there, but Jess stalked me. *Stalked me,* Keoni. I was fearful for months. And now you tell me I have to train with him?"

Keoni's face turned pensive. "I understand your position. And I understand how you're feeling. The issue is this: the chamber won't support a change. They've decided he's the best fit, and I can guarantee they won't change their minds."

"Respectfully, I disagree with their assessment. He didn't watch them. They don't know how this feels."

Chloe nodded slowly, her face unreadable.

"You're right—they don't," Keoni said. "But the chamber chose the most qualified candidate for each of these training positions. These are your lives on the line."

"Come on, man. That's weak," Tanner said.

Keoni's eyes flickered to Jess, and his conflicting emotion washed over me.

"I'm going to raise this issue to Charles no matter your arguments," I said.

"And I support her," Chloe said.

"As do I," Solomon added.

"Then here's what we should do." Keoni paused. "I think you should find a way to get through this training session. Make this a proper gesture and see how it goes."

"Why?" Tanner asked.

"It'll demonstrate to Charles and the rest of the chamber that Hadley tried—that she gave it an effort before requesting a change. I know that seems like a lot to ask, but I can assure you it'll go a long way with Charles."

Keoni's gaze bore into mine, but I wasn't quite ready to give an answer.

"I'll stay through all of today's training. Chloe and Solomon will be here for the full session, as will Sadie. Tanner is welcome to stay too. You won't be alone with Jess."

"Fine." I sighed. "I'll try to get through this—just for today."

Chloe and Solomon exchanged a long look before nodding in agreement. I dropped the privacy shield and stalked over to Jess.

This would get me one step closer to Lorenzo, I reminded myself. This would get me one step closer to the ring. I just needed to get through one day.

"Ready to get started?" he asked.

I nodded, though I shivered at his cool tone. There was more behind his words than he said aloud.

"We'll start with light rings today."

As much as I didn't want to learn from Jess, the subject matter piqued my interest. "I haven't heard of those before."

"They're difficult to create but highly effective in combat." Jess stepped back and flipped his arm right side up. A ring of light materialized, roughly the size of the palm of his hand. "This is a defensive move. I don't suggest it as a regular practice in combat, but it's a good skill to cultivate in case you ever find yourself in a tough spot. And even more importantly, I'll teach you how to deflect them."

"Do they hurt?" I asked, eyeing the magical ring.

"No, they don't hurt the creator or the recipient. But they will stunt the recipient's power, which gives the creator the upper hand. Think of it like temporary spellbinding."

I nodded.

"So, how does it work?"

"Tanner?"

"Come on, man," he said tersely.

"She needs to see it in action. I know you've worked as a trainer, so I thought you'd be fine with helping out. But if you're worried about taking fire, Sadie can step in."

"Worried?" Tanner scoffed. "Nah, I'm not worried about your light ring."

Tanner strode across the room. I felt a slight energy shift in the corner and turned to find Chloe struggling to conceal an amused grin spreading across her lips.

"Okay, Evans. Give me your best shot."

Jess grinned, and I adjusted my stance warily. It would take everything in me to stand aside and watch him hurl the ring at Tanner. I wiggled my fingertips, hoping the burning energy that threatened to spill out would dissipate.

"Hadley, watch the ring as it gets closer to Tanner," Jess instructed. "I'll release it as slowly as I can."

Jess tossed the ring through the air, and it expanded as it neared Tanner. By the time it reached him, the ring had grown to the size of his body, and I held my breath as it engulfed him and disappeared.

Tanner looked unscathed except for the scowl on his face. He crossed the room and stood in front of me.

"Do you feel Tanner's energy?" Jess asked.

"Yes," I said, then hesitated. It was strange—stifled. "It still feels like Tanner, but something's wrong."

"His magic is stunted. It's agitated because it wants out, but he can't release it in his current state. Tanner, do you mind if she touches your arm to feel the difference when you make contact?"

Tanner turned his head slowly toward Jess, clearly annoyed, but nodded. I reached my hand timidly toward his forearm and paused.

"He won't feel any discomfort, will he?"

"I'm good, Hads. Come on."

I held Tanner's gaze. He nodded, which propelled me forward. When my fingers met his skin, a soft energy radiated through them. It wasn't the usual burst that accompanied another witch's touch.

"How long does this last?" I asked.

"About ten minutes. Enough time."

I shivered.

"So, this is a defense technique that we'll work towards, but you'll learn a lot of useful skills along the way. You'll start by learning to channel your magic in defense. Once you've mastered that, you'll move on to pushing that power outside of your body and manifesting it into various forms—like light rings. And finally, you'll work on your form to effectively execute the maneuvers."

I closed my eyes briefly, feeling my magic's call within me.

It was ready.

Next we focused on proper posture to support my back safely through combat. Jess adjusted my stance, his hands lingering on my hips. His touch caused a flurry of emotions in me—and none of them good. My entire body went rigid as my anxiety roared. Tanner's eyes narrowed, his gaze firm on Jess's hands and his jaw set tightly.

I had promised my former trainer, Maka, that I'd stay out of the minds of those around me, but that was a resolution I decided to break. I breathed deeply, willing my focus to shift to the elements. I found the air and followed its path to Jess. I awaited the typical onslaught of thoughts, feelings, emotions, and heard . . . nothing.

Absolutely nothing.

Unfortunately for Jess, Maka had taught me about mind shielding, and the lesson lay freshly in my mind. Why would Jess protect his mind around us? What exactly was he worried about?

I tried again. Nothing. I had found the loophole in Lorenzo's mind, but I couldn't seem to break through Jess's mental protection. I was missing something . . . and I didn't know anyone who could help me with this issue that I trusted.

I had little time to consider the situation. Fitz's violent energy washed through me seconds before he burst through the doorway into the room. I moved quickly away from Jess and toward Fitz.

"You cannae be serious!" Fitz shouted at Keoni. He pointed to Jess. "He stalked my mate in Edinburgh, and then he turned up here watching her. And you put him in a position of authority? What are you thinking?"

"Fitz," Solomon said. "This wasn't Keoni's doing. We're going to sort this out."

"Sort this out? Is that what's happening here? Because from my perspective, it looks like he is training Hadley."

"I'm sorry if I caused any trouble. That was not my intention," Jess said.

The look on Fitz's face was one I hadn't seen before. His eyes darkened as his nostrils flared. He closed the distance between himself and Jess until he was mere inches away.

"*If* you caused any trouble? You know damn well what you did. If you're gonnae act like that, at least own your shite."

Jess looked blankly at Fitz, neither anger nor fear in his features. I moved closer to them.

"Since you seem to be unclear, let me make things clear to you." Fitz's voice was low and calm, and there was something in his tone that made my heart beat faster—danger, I decided. "You've harassed and stalked my mate, you bastard, and if you ever do it again, I swear I will take care of you myself. And when I do, you willnae be capable of repeating your indiscretions."

Jess held Fitz's gaze unwaveringly, though he also held his tongue. Keoni moved toward them, but Solomon reached out his hand to stop him.

"I wouldn't," Solomon said simply.

Tanner stood nearby, his arms crossed, his body pulled tight, and his head tilted up. He was ready to jump in if needed—ready to assist Fitz in taking Jess down. I took another step closer.

"Hadley," Fitz growled.

I continued forward, though slower. "Let's go, Fitz."

Nothing.

I took another step. Fitz's eyes darted to me before returning to Jess.

"Training is over. Let's go home." I closed the distance and placed my hand on Fitz's arm, so he could feel my energy. He glanced to my hand and then to my eyes. Just when I thought I'd lost, he nodded. He looked again at Jess.

"You'd do well to mind what I've said here today," Fitz said, an air of condescension swirling around him.

Fitz took my hand in his, and we left.

Fitz and I stepped into the nearest uninhabited room. Rows of books lined old wooden shelves, and three tables sat in the middle of the space. A small library of sorts, I guessed. Fitz shut the door behind us, and when he turned to face me, I realized none of his anger had faded.

"Fitz . . . take some deep breaths. Try to calm down."

He sighed deeply but nodded. "This is unacceptable."

"I agree."

"Was he training you?"

I filled in the blanks for Fitz, explaining everything from the earlier conversations.

"Keoni shouldnae have asked that of you. He should have raised the concern to Charles himself—the moment you told him what Jess had done."

"That would've been the best outcome. I do think Keoni is trying to help, though."

Fitz shook his head. "Maybe. But that doesn't matter much when this outcome was the same."

I couldn't argue.

"Something has to be done."

"We're taking this to Charles. And we can say that I tried in today's session, but that I'm still uncomfortable with Jess."

"Did he touch you?" Fitz asked.

I wavered.

"The truth, Hadley," he said, his eyes clouding.

My heart beat faster as I thought through my answer. "He readjusted my stance during training."

Fitz squeezed his eyes shut.

"We'll talk to Charles and go from there. We'll figure this out," I said.

"He cannae train you. This cannae happen."

"They might force our hand. We have to be prepared for that."

"If we cannae convince Charles to remove him, then we'll rearrange the schedule, and I'll attend your sessions with Jess."

"I don't know if that's such a great idea." Fitz might lose his patience again, which would only perpetuate the issue.

"His actions toward you have been nothing but inappropriate. I feel how uncomfortable he's made you. I should've done more in that room back there," he said angrily. "It's no too late."

"No, Fitz. You are not going back in that room right now."

His eyes pierced mine, and his lip quivered with rage.

"Why are you mad at me?" I asked.

"I'm no mad at you. But I'll no have that wee bastard near you again, Hadley. Dinnae you understand? Does this no bother you?"

"It does bother me." I threw my hands up. "Of course, it does. Exactly *what* is it you're implying right now?"

"I've implied nothing. Why do you no want me in your sessions?"

"Fitz, we haven't even talked to Charles yet. Don't overreact."

"Overreact?" he asked.

"I can handle this situation myself."

"Can you now? It dinnae seem handled ten minutes ago when I walked into that room, and he was standing right next to you with his eyes lingering on your body! But if you're no bothered by that, then fine."

"Are you worried about something?" I growled. One of the few light bulbs in Opimae City shattered above my head.

"I just find you to be a bit naïve about the whole thing," Fitz spat, observing the glass shards distractedly. "Jess is no harmless, Hadley. You'd do well to be mindful of that. I'd hate for him to catch you off guard one day—dinnae forget he rifled through your hotel room in Edinburgh."

His demeanor grew wilder by the second.

"This is ridiculous. Look, he creeps me out, and you're not helping. Why would you talk about him catching me off guard? God almighty, Fitz."

Fitz sighed, though he didn't argue.

"I thought witches didn't have stray feelings for someone other than their mate," I said, wondering if that's what had Fitz so worked up.

"Aye, and I told you there are exceptions. He doesn't have a mate. Maybe he's obsessed with this sort of thing. He's clearly demented."

"I doubt he's daydreaming of stealing my affections. I think you're just pissed about him following me."

"Of course I'm pissed."

"And I get it. It pisses me off, too. I think he's a weirdo," I continued. "I don't like him. I don't want to be around him. He makes me uncomfortable. I'm going to try to remedy this situation."

"Aye right. Nothing for me to worry about."

"You don't have to be a jerk about it."

"Neither do you. You're acting like I'm being completely unreasonable."

"Well yeah, I definitely wouldn't call you reasonable right now. I haven't done anything wrong, and you've thoroughly lost your temper," I said.

"Aye, right."

His sarcasm ripped apart the last of my patience.

"What do you want, Fitz?" I yelled.

"What do I want?" he said, his voice rising. "What I want is to corner Jess in a dark alley and cause him enough pain that I feel he's atoned for every thought of you that has ever crossed his mind." Fitz moved closer to me until we nearly touched. "What I want is for him to never lay eyes on you again, for him to never experience what it feels like to be this close to you."

My breath grew ragged. I'd never seen Fitz so angry. His eyes were wild—primal—and his energy buzzed through the room, making it difficult for me to focus. My hair stood on end at the proximity of his electricity.

"What do I want, Hadley? I want every single part of you. I want to pull every thought of you from Jess's mind. And I want you to hear me because I dinnae want to explain this again."

Fitz paused, registering my energy—feeling my nerves, my flurry of emotions. He stood motionless for a few seconds before reaching toward my face, a bit timidly. I didn't move, and he placed his hand tenderly against my cheek. As he pulled away, a flurry of broken glass lifted from my hair and the fabric of my tunic. The shards traveled toward a nearby trash can.

I shook my head. "*Why are we like this?* One minute we're rational creatures, and the next . . ."

"This is our nature. I know this magical world is still new to you, but as displeased as you might be with me right now, I need you to consider the situation more carefully—and from my perspective."

I didn't answer.

"Hadley . . . do you no understand that no one could replace what you are to me? You might think I'm reckless, but I'll always protect you, especially from the things you might no see the danger in. I dinnae much care about the consequences as long as you're safe."

He looked away for a moment.

"What, Fitz?" I whispered.

"Perhaps I *am* a bit reckless when it comes to you. But I think you are worth fighting for. And I think we are worth fighting for. And I will do what I must to protect you and what we have."

I nodded, considering his words.

"The thought of watching helplessly as you walk into that training room with him . . . for you to be subjected to working with a trainer who stalked you. Watching your mate go through something like . . ." He shook his head. "I want better for you. I dinnae mean to make things more difficult. I—I just want to fix it, Hadley."

I rested my hands against his firm chest and stared into his emerald eyes. Traces of his anger still lingered, but his eyes cooled as his hand slid along the base of my neck.

Fate might have meddled in our emotions, but I couldn't deny that our feelings for each other were real and strongly woven through us. I couldn't deny that I would set the world on fire for this man.

Fitz had stood by my side and encouraged me as I'd found myself. He had been willing to risk everything to keep me safe and grant me agency in deciding my future. He'd reminded me to believe in myself again.

"Look, I understand. If the situation were reversed, I'd probably have set Jess on fire when I walked into that room."

Fitz chuckled lightly. The sound was welcome—we were turning a corner.

"Set him on fire? Now, there's an idea," Fitz said.

I ran my fingertip along his jawline. "I love you, you know."

He rested his forehead against mine. "You have all of me," he whispered.

His lips found mine as we clung to each other. Fitz gripped my thighs and picked me up, and I wrapped my legs around him as he walked us haphazardly toward the nearest table. He whispered to the elements against my lips, effectively locking the door. He set me on the table, and I fumbled along the leather belt that held his tunic in place until my fingers met the cold metal of the buckle. The belt dropped to the floor with a thud as I pulled Fitz's tunic over his head, revealing his sculpted torso. My lips traced along his collarbone, and his head tilted back, eyes closed. I worked my way along his neck, and he met me in a deep kiss.

Fitz pulled back and hastily removed my tunic, his fingertips tracing the curves of my body. My back arched, his touch driving me toward the edge of my self-control. Fitz scanned my body and released a low, ragged breath. The heated gleam in his eyes quickened my pulse.

Our bodies were caught between lingering anger and tender confessions, and the mix of emotions only heightened the feeling of his skin against mine. I reached behind his neck and pulled his face to mine.

His lips were slower than before as they traveled across my skin, searching for the sensitive spots that made me gasp as we shed the last of our clothes.

And amid the stormy afternoon, we slowly, and intentionally, sorted out our differences.

CHAPTER NINE

Flames leapt high into the night sky, breaking the dark of the evening and casting shadows across the open field. At the end of our first week in Opimae we were gathered at the autumnal festival, where Samhain and All Hallows' Eve were celebrated by both the elven and witch folk alike, culminating into one massive autumnal celebration.

The garb of the evening only added to the magical feel of the festivities. The crowds were dressed in hooded Renaissance-style cloaks, which ranged in color, textile, and pattern, creating a sea of masked magical beings masquerading in the moonlight. Though all the masks were domino style, their designs and decor were just as varied as the cloaks. The idea was not to conceal the face, but rather, to frame it.

Our attire was formal, though we'd incorporated touches of armor that proudly proclaimed our status as warriors. Fitz and I both wore cloaks of deep navy comprised of thick wool to ward off the chill of the fall evening. Silver embroidery crafted a distinct pattern of stars along the proximity of his collarbone, meant to complement the same pattern of my own. In contrast, my shoulder armor was made to mimic dragon scales. Fitz's mask was night—navy to match his cloak, while my own was silver satin and trimmed in pearly white moonstones. Light and dark. This evening was about balance.

The world glowed dimly tonight, differently, magically—somehow equal parts comforting and unsettling. A conflict of emotions I couldn't reconcile swirled restlessly within me as the world seemed to move in slow motion. From the flames to the movements of my magical companions, the world was off kilter, strange.

I gripped Fitz's hand as we made our way around one of the fire-sides, seeking our companions after being separated in the previous ritual. I'd considered Fitz's words after our conversation about Jess. I didn't question my feelings for Fitz, but the idea of Fate nipped at the back of my mind. I'd chosen Fitz and I'd chosen my life . . . hadn't I? I shook my head and pushed the thoughts into the back of my mind, focusing instead on the night of festivities.

It was a time to celebrate the harvest, to ask for protection, to thank God and Fate for the bounty that had been received, but also to pray for, ask for, plead for safe passage through the winter months. I pondered how we celebrated Halloween back home in the States. Many cultures referred to the celebration as All Hallows' Eve, the same as Opimae, and I wondered if those Earthen cultures had remained truer to the traditions observed in Opimae than where I had grown up. I couldn't help but think of the little girl I had once been, unknowingly seeking my magic. But as lost in the commercialization of Halloween as we had been in my household growing up, I had never grasped the true origins of the holiday. The juxtaposition of All Saints and All Souls in the days that followed had been lost on me.

But in Opimae, I learned of its importance, its necessity.

We soaked in the elven traditions and learned how the ancient Celtic practices and traditions of Earth all stemmed from the elves. It was amazing how most of human culture was influenced by those who were not human. Magical entities like the elves.

Magical beings like us.

This festival was much like Samhain—or rather, Samhain was much like the elven rituals we were taking part in. It was far grander than I could have anticipated. The elven celebration of Samhain maintained that private home rituals took precedence, similar to the human Samhain practice, but the elves also believed a large celebration was in order, and its main purpose was for magical beings to come together to honor the harvest and to honor the dead.

Though the druids and the faeries weren't as involved, they did hold a presence at the celebration, and a mix of magical beings gathered in the firelight, awaiting the start of the evening's rituals. Witches joined in the elven celebration, and as I opened my mind's eye to the magical beings around me, I came to better understand the power of the elves. The magic that swirled within them didn't manifest the same way as it did with witches, but it did fuel them in similarly superhuman ways.

I gazed across the fire, and even in the shadows I picked out our companions. I spotted Lana and Saoirse and waved. Lana's olive cloak was a beautiful contrast to her long, blonde hair, which spilled in waves down her back. Saoirse's cloak was royal blue. Her hair was pulled into two braids, and even in the firelight, her pale eyes glowed blue. Lana and Saoirse were a truly striking pair.

Jordan, Keoni, and Isaac were standing near them and walked over as they caught sight of us. Jordan and I embraced warmly. Isaac followed suit.

"We lost you in all the bustle!" Jordan exclaimed.

"We couldn't find you anywhere." I smiled. "Have you seen the others?"

"Henry left to find Molly and Tanner, though he did wander off in the direction of the mead. I think he's glad the sacrifices are over." She laughed.

Fitz rolled his eyes. "Aye, that sounds like Henry."

"Are the celebrations to your liking?" Keoni asked, his cheeks likely flushed from the nearby fire and the warmth of the mead.

"This is absolutely incredible," I said.

"I agree," Isaac chimed in. "There's something inherently magical about these rituals—about the firelight. About the transition from summer to winter and the season of bounty that falls between them."

"This feels like stepping back in time," Jordan said. "I look around and see absolutely nothing modern, from our drink to our cloaks, even these masks. We could be in any era right now."

Fitz smiled. "There's something timeless about this world."

Keoni turned to Fitz. "Is Earth not the same?" he asked.

"Timeless? It can be. But there's something about this place, and even amid all this trouble, the energy of Opimae is different. It's not as weighed down as the energy on Earth. It hasn't experienced the same violent history."

Keoni nodded. "We *are* a planet of refugees. I suppose it makes sense we haven't come here to war monger."

"It's unfortunate," Isaac began, "that war might find its way to such a peaceful planet. The beings here left Earth to escape the violence of humanity, but now, Lorenzo is threatening to bring that violence here."

Keoni dropped his gaze thoughtfully before responding. "Many things have crossed that portal over the years—energy, magical beings, strange tales. And not all of it has been good—which is why Opimae has a military presence at all." He paused. "But most of it has been good, I'd say. And when it hasn't been, our folk try to handle it quickly because we know the cost of evil."

We sat in silence, feeling the conflict of his emotion.

"Some of Opimae's inhabitants have argued over the years that we should simply keep the portal doors closed indefinitely. I'm not of that opinion. Far more wonderful things have crossed that portal than evil."

Silence hovered over our group as we stared at the fire. Fitz slid his arm around my waist, pulling me closer. There was something in the fire and the masks, the cloaks and the call of celebration, that made me feel alive in a different way. Some ancient, ethereal part of me awakened, and I guessed I had the elves to thank for that.

The spell broke as our other companions entered the circle, passing around cups of mead and cider. I looked across the fire and spotted two familiar witches.

"Fitz," I whispered. "Look at the two witches in the black capes."

He looked around and his eyes settled on them. Even with their masks, we knew them instantly—we knew their energy. These witches were seared into our minds.

"The Parisian stalkers," he said.

Two witches had stalked us in Paris when we had first met up after our time apart. Their identity was a mystery yet to be solved.

Our group followed our gaze.

Isaac dropped his head quickly. "Guys, stop. We shouldn't all be looking at them."

I dared to look out of the corner of my eye to ensure we hadn't attracted the attention of the witches who had captured ours.

Luck was on our side. The witches continued chatting. One of them pointed in the opposite direction, and they walked away in search of whatever had pulled their focus.

"Stay here," Fitz commanded to the group. "Hadley, Isaac, let's follow them."

We wandered from the fire. Fitz paused, halting the three of us as he looked back to Tanner in silent request. Tanner nodded and joined us.

We slowly made our way around the fire, taking turns keeping the subjects in our line of sight, trying not to tip them off. They stopped in front of a tall witch draped in a green cloak.

Isaac and Tanner angled themselves in front of Fitz and me, so we could gaze casually past their shoulders, pretending to be in conversation with each other. Just when I thought about moving closer, the three of them disappeared. I met Fitz's gaze, disappointed.

Tanner and Isaac started back toward our group, and Fitz and I trailed behind them. I hesitated once our group was in sight, countless emotions fighting through me for control. Then I grabbed Fitz's face and pulled his lips to mine. His flurry of emotion was apparent, but his lips met mine hungrily just the same.

We pulled away, staring into each other's eyes, feeling out the other's energy. The kiss had done what I thought it would—it had taken the edge off both my nerves and his.

"Fitz . . ." I trailed off.

"I know, Hads. I don't want to ruin a night of celebration. This just . . ."

"Scares you. It scares both of us."

He nodded.

"The first time we lost them, we didn't know what we were up against. This time? We'll find out what they're after."

"Aye, that we will."

Fitz met me in another fiery kiss before the sound of drums and the lonely, ancient reverberations of Celtic song rose loudly on the air. The next ritual was beginning.

As we returned to the fireside, Tanner walked over to Chloe, and they fell into easy conversation. There was truly something odd about their interactions, though I couldn't quite place my finger on what was wrong. Either way, it was enough to arouse suspicion, and I vowed to keep a closer eye on them.

We quickly filled in the rest of the team on how the stalkers' trail had gone cold.

"We should send for Mia," Chloe said.

All eyes flickered to me. I sighed, weighing the options. But truthfully, whether I liked Mia or not, she was good at her job, and the Parisian stalker investigation had been given to her to oversee. Finally, I nodded.

"Great. I'll send word now," Solomon said.

"I'm going to get a refill," I said quietly to Fitz.

He extended his hand. "I've got it."

"I could use a minute."

He hesitated. I held my ground, my expression not inviting argument. "Aye. But please be careful, Hads."

I nodded and meandered toward the nearest drink table. I felt Fitz's eyes trailing me, his concern never far away. The line was moving quickly, but between the sea of attendees, the roar of countless conversations, and running into the stalkers, my nerves were rattled. I navigated to the edge of the crowd and found I was near the cliff. I moved closer, seeking the sounds of the ocean that would drown out the noise.

Fitz would be unhappy with my choice to wander around alone, but in this moment, I didn't much care. Both his concern and the intensity of our connection only added to my overwhelmed state of mind.

The breeze carried a fine mist of sea spray, which dampened my face, and I closed my eyes, soaking in the moment. My nerves quieted, and I slowly opened my eyes to a large moon on the horizon. Its pale glow cast a reflection on the waves, highlighting their rise and fall as they crashed against the cliffside. I looked back to the moon, basking in the elements that granted strength to many of my magical brothers and sisters, wondering at all the moon and the sea had seen of witchkind.

Realizing I'd been gone too long, I turned back toward the celebration, but found a figure draped in a black cloak advancing toward me.

"Jess."

"Good evening, Hadley." His mask sparkled with onyx stones.

I smiled weakly.

"I'm sorry to interrupt your solitude."

"That's okay. I was just leaving to meet Fitz."

The thought of Jess pushing me from the cliffside suddenly flitted across my mind, and I took a step forward. Jess caught my arm, and my body stiffened in response.

"I don't mean to startle you," he said, releasing me. "I only wanted to say I'm sorry."

I paused. "For what, exactly?"

"For my behavior in Edinburgh. I never intended to alarm you."

"I don't see how you could possibly think it wouldn't worry me."

"I made a mistake."

I remained silent.

"I did have your best interest at heart. And I still do. I hope we can focus on the future, so we can prepare you for what's ahead."

There were a great many things I wanted to say to Jess, from how he'd frightened me in Edinburgh to how he still made me uncomfortable to how angry I was at him for behaving as he did. But all I could think about in that moment was how to get away from him—to return to the safety of the crowds.

"We'll see," I finally said. I held his icy gaze, hoping he couldn't sense my nerves. "I need to go."

I shoved past him, not looking back, and almost ran into Henry as I neared the crowd. His brow was creased in concern.

"Are you good?"

"Jess found me near the cliffside." I nodded behind me.

Henry's expression darkened. Based on the feel of his agitated energy, he'd spotted Jess.

"Where's Fitz?" I asked.

"Looking for you—mad with worry. He felt your nerves, but there's loads of energy here, and it's jumbling his perception of your threads."

I closed my eyes, calling to Fitz, and in a matter of seconds, he materialized before me.

"Hads, what's going on? Are you all right?" Fitz laid his hands on my shoulders, examining me.

"Jess approached me. He . . ." I trailed off, noting Fitz's change in mood. I shrugged. "He just wanted to apologize, I think. But I didn't want to talk to him. That's all."

Henry's eyes pleaded what his mouth would not—*don't do something stupid, Fitz.*

I knew the precise moment Fitz found Jess in the distance. It was the same moment Fitz's eyes grew stormy. By the feel of his energy alone, I knew he was indeed going to do something stupid.

Fitz released me and disappeared. By the time I turned around, he was already standing in front of Jess. The roar of nearby waves mixed with the buzz of the crowd, and as I ran across the open field, I couldn't make out what they were saying to each other. I nearly slid into Fitz but caught myself at the last second, teetering on my tiptoes like Fitz's wavering self-control.

"What did I tell you? Hm?" Fitz growled. "Did I no tell you there'd be consequences if you did this again?"

"Do what? Apologize?" Jess retorted.

"Well now, considering I felt Hadley's nerves crackling through our connection, I dinnae think that's quite right."

"Should we do something?" I asked Henry.

Henry tilted his head, assessing the situation.

"Nae," he said. "Let Fitz sort this one out."

"*Henry.*"

"Aye?"

"There will be consequences for this," I said.

And this isn't his fight.

Henry sighed. "Aye, I suppose you're right."

"You should take a deep breath. Calm down," Jess said.

I grimaced. That wouldn't go over well.

"Dinnae tell me what to do." Fitz's voice was entirely too calm, and the hairs on my neck bristled.

Henry released a low whistle.

"Hadley," Jess said to me. "I was just apologizing to you. Can you tell Fitz that?" His tone betrayed his annoyance, and I realized Fitz's anger wasn't the only threat to the situation.

"Take. Your eyes. Off. My fiancée."

"You know what?" Jess asked, never removing his eyes from me. "No."

Fitz's cheeks flushed, and there it was—he was fresh out of patience.

Fitz's fist met Jess's jaw before my mind could catch up. Jess staggered backward and spit, staining the sage-colored grass red. He snapped his head to the side and rubbed his jaw briefly before charging at Fitz. He ducked and connected with Fitz's core, and they went tumbling on to the ground.

My heart raced at the thought of them rolling over the cliffside.

"Aye, right," Henry said. He neatly drained his cup and tossed it aside before calculating his next move and launching himself at Jess.

"You've got to be kidding me," I muttered. It appeared Henry was trying to pull Jess away from Fitz, so I focused my efforts on tearing Fitz away from Jess.

When they realized I had entered the tussle, Fitz and Jess both grew distracted, and I used those few seconds to tug Fitz away before calling up my fire magic faster than I ever had before. My fingers blazed hot.

"Let me be clear about something," I said. "One wrong move, and I will make a scene none of you will soon forget."

Silence.

"Jess, enjoy the rest of your evening," I said.

He understood my meaning and rose from the cold ground. He stared at Fitz longer than necessary but stalked off wordlessly into the dark.

"Thank you for your assistance, Henry. We'll see you back at the ritual."

Henry nodded and walked back to the crowd. As he left, the energy shifted. He'd placed a privacy shield around us. I'd been so distracted by the fight that I hadn't noticed until now. Good. At least no one else would have seen the scuffle.

"Hadley," Fitz said.

I shook my head, my hands still covered in flames.

"Come on, Hads. We can talk about this, but there's no need for that." He pointed to my hands.

I sighed but extinguished the flames.

"That was absolutely reckless," I said.

"Aye."

"And you have no remorse, do you?"

Fitz rose to face me, and his eyes pierced mine.

"If you hadn't been here, he would be in far worse shape. Why did you stop me?" he asked. "Why defend him?"

"I didn't defend him, Fitz!" I yelled, stepping closer to him. "I defended *you*."

"That was unnecessary."

"Think of the consequences," I argued. "You can't do things like this."

"Aye, I can. And I will—he'll learn his lesson yet."

I took a deep breath, willing myself to calm down. I understood why he was angry, but this was exactly what we had discussed only a couple days ago. He was going to have to do better.

Fitz closed the distance between us until he was mere inches from my face. "I told you I'd protect you no matter the cost. I willnae stand by and watch while he makes you uncomfortable. I'll no have it, Hadley."

I held his gaze. I thought of our conversation back in Edinburgh, how he'd offered himself as my sword and my shield. I sat with my anger just long enough to recognize it as fear. I worried about the consequences of his actions. I worried about what this could lead toward in our relationship.

But mostly, I couldn't stand the thought of Fitz being hurt on my account. When I shared that sentiment with him, he softened.

"Is that your concern, my love?" He traced his fingertips along my jawline. "I'd suffer any consequence to guarantee your safety."

I leaned into him, and he wrapped his arms around me, holding me securely. I rested my head on his chest. My mind was confused, but my heart was sure.

"Back in Edinburgh, I told you I needed a partner, not a sword and shield."

Fitz was quiet.

"That's still true, Fitz."

"Aye, and I told you I'd always protect you when you needed it. Jess isn't harmless, and I think you know that."

I sighed.

"Are we always meant to be fighting about this?" he asked.

"You're infuriating, you know that?"

"Aye. And I'm grateful you love me despite that wee fact."

There was nothing small about that fact, but I indisputably loved him despite it. Frustration still echoed through me.

"We'd better get back to the team," I finally said.

"Aye. Lead the way."

Fitz and I meandered through the crowds until we reached the first large fire pit. We were navigating around it when a tall witch in a red cloak caught my attention.

Had I seen him before?

The lighting was dim, and my eyes strained to study his strong jaw-line. Even covered in dark stubble, there was no hiding the chiseled structure of his face. His dark eyes were like endless orbs in the soft glow. Though his head was cloaked, his raven hair shone in the firelight, and I recognized his energy instantly.

Oh god.

Fitz grabbed my hand. "Your energy is troubled. What's going on?" he whispered.

"The witch in the red cloak. I know him."

Fitz's eyes rested firmly on my face—glaring, waiting. I met his gaze, his green eyes bright in the ominous scene.

"It's Lorenzo," I breathed.

The rest of it happened so quickly I could barely process it. I dropped Fitz's hand and pushed through the crowds.

Lorenzo's eyes locked on to mine, and his lips turned upward in a smirk. He mouthed my name—it was clear.

"Hadley."

A figure standing next to him in a blue cloak placed their hand on Lorenzo's arm. Before I could reach them, they disappeared.

I gasped. He was just . . . gone.

Fitz reached for me. "Hadley," he said firmly.

"He got away," I lamented.

"What were you thinking?"

"He knew I was here. He meant for us to see him."

"Aye, and you almost walked right into his grasp." His energy buzzed between us.

"That's not true," I said firmly, meeting his gaze. "He wasn't going to take me anywhere."

"How do I know that?" His teeth ground together.

"Because neither of us would have let that happen," I said. "But that's not what's important right now. What matters is that he did this on purpose."

Fitz took a deep breath, checking his temper. "Aye, it seemed intentional. Let's get back to the rest of the team."

Fitz extended his hand, and I hesitated for a moment before accepting it and rushing back to our group.

The team's relief was short-lived at our return. We told them of our Lorenzo sighting.

"I can't believe he was here," Lana said.

"This is concerning. Lana, we'd better give orders quickly," Keoni prompted. His eyes flickered around the fire cautiously.

They stepped away, radioing to headquarters and asking for additional security to be stationed around the celebration for the remainder of the evening.

"Should we get out of here?" Tanner asked.

"No," I said firmly. "We continue the festival. We see this thing through. This is important to the Opimaeans, and I know it's important to all of us. And we definitely don't want to let Lorenzo know he got under anyone's skin tonight."

I met Fitz's gaze. He nodded.

"This feels violating," Jordan said.

"It was brazen," Henry said. "Why risk something like this just to make eye contact and leave?"

"I honestly don't know," I replied. "He's made his statement. I just wish we knew exactly what it was."

Our speculation continued as we took our seat near a roaring fire pit. Fitz settled into a nearby chair and pulled me onto his lap. Jordan's eyes flickered across us, and her eyes narrowed in silent questioning. I knew what she wanted to know. Were we okay?

I nodded and mouthed "later" to her. She returned to her conversation with Isaac. Henry took a seat next to us and set drinks in our hands. Soon after, conversation ceased as the final elven ritual began. Though I was looking forward to the performance, I couldn't help but cast glances around the fireside. Additional security was already filing into place.

I pushed as much worry from my mind as it would allow, focusing instead on the lead dancers taking the stage. Lana had taught us the dance so we'd be able to participate at the appropriate moments, and it was exhilarating to move in step with thousands of others as we meandered around the fires, cloaked and masked, dancing to the strums of harps and drums. Saoirse and Lana helped us along with the more repetitive songs.

We were lucky enough to be standing near a set of performers. Isaac leaned forward, seeking the best view of the scene.

I smiled at Lana. "He's been studying all week for this," I whispered.

They were reenacting the tale of the Great Passage, explaining the departure of their elven ancestors from Earth, and as the tale went on, witches joined them on stage. The performance was so captivating, I started to relax.

"This is my favorite part," Saoirse murmured, almost to herself.

"I'm having a little trouble keeping up," I admitted.

"You understand that they're leaving Earth?"

"Yes."

"Okay, so they are gathering at the portal. The Great Passage occurred during the autumn season."

"What? Really?"

"Yes, just as the harvest had come in. Much was left behind, just so our folk could carry the essentials with them to this new world."

"It must have been terrifying."

"I'd imagine. But see, this part is my favorite because this is when my folk realize they are not alone. Your folk have come too. We realize we have each other."

I glanced at Saoirse, her cream-colored mask contrasting her deep brown skin and framing eyes the color of a winter's sky. Her excited energy was palpable, and I smiled.

"I love that."

"The rest of the story belongs to us both."

My folk joined the elves, and they bowed to one another. They crossed the portal together, offering supplies and aid. And when they arrived in Opimae, they were surprised by the warm greeting they received by the few who had come before them. Their journey ended as they settled on the nearby land. A tall elven man with braided blond hair stepped forward and told of the magical beings who spread across the land, forming nations, and of their commitment to those who had welcomed them home and to the land that received them—and of the bounty that followed.

Claps and murmurs of enthusiasm followed.

The crowd parted, and I strained to see what was happening. A tall elf in a dark cloak walked gracefully toward a wooden table with ornate decor. His long blond hair hung loosely under his crown of golden vines, and the elves bowed as he passed. He nodded at the crowds. His arm was extended, and an equally ethereal elf rested her hand on his arm as they moved in tandem. Her raven hair cascaded across her green velvet cloak, and a gold crown of leaves encircled her head.

Lana and Saoirse bowed as they passed our group.

"King Copandir and Queen Emlyn of Athdara," Lana whispered reverently after they'd passed.

The crowd grew loud as everyone migrated to long wooden tables spread with cuisine from both of our cultures. Elven breads and the freshest fruit straight from Athdara lined the table alongside smoked and fried fishes, countless vegetables, large cauldrons of soup, and goblets of ale.

Elves performed music throughout the dinner service, and a group of them danced near us. Their ancient movements were captivating. So engrossed as I was, I didn't notice Fitz and Henry had sneaked off until they returned with chalices for Jordan and me. I took an experimental sniff.

"Honey-wine?" I asked, turning up my nose.

"This one is only mildly sweet." Distance lingered in Fitz's tone.

The mead met my lips, and I took a small sip, still not convinced. Hints of cinnamon and clove washed over my tongue, with a touch of sweetness—honey and perhaps currants? I was amazed.

"Okay, you're right. This is pretty good," I said, striving for normalcy.

Lana chuckled at my response.

"How is this so good?" I asked.

"Thousands of years of practice—mixed with a bit of love and magic."

"I'm surprised by the spices."

"It's a popular drink around here. There's always some on hand."

We returned our attention to the dancers, and between their rhythmic motions and the taste of honey-wine, I was lost in the experience. The beat of the drum stirred something ancient in my soul, and my magic answered its call. Before I could quite finish studying the motions of the dancers, Fitz flicked his wrist, sending our drinks to rest on the table as he pulled me up and into his arms.

He stared straight into my soul, and my breath hitched. Strange energy crackled through our connection, charged with our heightened emotions. Anger and fear still swirled through us, along with the questions that lingered in my mind, and I wanted nothing more in that moment than reassurance.

"Kiss me," I whispered.

As our lips met, the magical energy that channeled between us was wild and untamed. Fitz pulled back and stroked the length of my cheek before reaching for my waist, spinning me around. Noticing the many bare feet, I knelt to remove my shoes. The cool grass felt divine against the soles of my feet. Fitz and I fell into the rhythm of the drums that now beat around us, finding our steps in unison, following the example of our elven brothers and sisters.

For a few delicious minutes, it all fell away. We weren't even in Opimae—

we simply existed somewhere in the realm of the elves. There was no Lorenzo, no battles to come, no heartache. There was no Jess, no Fate, no questions troubling my thoughts. There was only the soothing sound of elven music, the sight of thousands of years of tradition, the taste of aged drink, and the comfort of excellent company.

The All Hallows' Eve traditions of the witches followed dinner. Just like the elven Samhain practices, certain rituals were left to the privacy of our own homes, but there were two practices the group would participate in together—a prayer of thanksgiving for the harvest and a blessing and offering for the dead.

As we walked back toward the fire from our dinner table, I took the opportunity to talk again with Saoirse. She was telling me more of the passage when her eyes emitted a soft glow. With her hood draped over her head, the pale light radiating from the shadows of her cloak was truly ethereal.

"My eyes are glowing, aren't they?" she asked.

I nodded. "It's mesmerizing. Is this common with elves?"

"It isn't. You might catch our skin glowing softly at times." She winked. "My eyes are glowing because my great-grandmother was a witch."

"I'm not following."

"My lineage is purely elven except for my mom's grandmother—she was a water witch."

"And that's common with water witches? I'm sorry, I'm trying to learn as quickly as possible, but there's a lot to learn."

"Oh, don't mention it, Hadley. I'm happy to help with your continued education."

I grinned. "Thank you."

"Water witches' eyes glow. Mostly when underwater, but as their power shifts around in them, they can have surges which cause their eyes to glow even above water."

"That's fascinating."

"Yes, I suppose you're right. Sometimes we forget how incredible our magic is until we see the sense of wonder from someone new to our planet."

"Do you feel like you have other witchy traits too?"

"The witch magic is so little with me—my eyes do glow sometimes, but they don't shine like a witch's would under water. But occasionally, I have the knowing."

"Wait. You have foresight?"

"It comes and goes. Mostly goes these days, it seems."

"Is that not an elven trait?"

"It can be, but not in my familial line. Of course, my great-grandmother was well-renowned for her foresight."

"Are interspecies relationships common here?" I asked.

"I wouldn't say common. But it isn't taboo—sometimes Fate throws us outside of our own species. I often wonder how and why that happens, but it does." She shrugged.

"You credit Fate with that?" I asked.

Saoirse bobbed her head from side to side, considering my question.

"I think she brings the right beings into our lives at the right time."

I couldn't argue with that. "But you think we choose to accept those beings into our lives?" I asked.

"I think there's always a choice, Hadley," she said.

I hoped that her words were true—that we always had a choice.

"I like how accepting your culture is here."

"I've heard stories about Earth's prejudices. I know that Lana and I would not be welcome everywhere, even if we concealed our ears."

"That's true."

"Maybe I'll just stay here in Opimae." She smiled, and I laughed lightly in turn.

"Earth has its problems, but maybe one day when all of this is over, you and Lana can come visit Scotland, so we can show you the good parts too."

"We are honored by your invitation." She bowed her head slightly. "I hope we do have the opportunity to discuss it one day."

I hoped that very much myself—I hoped Lorenzo's carnage would be far less than we feared. I wasn't naïve enough to think we could change Lorenzo's mind and come out of this peacefully, but I could at least hope for the best possible outcome for us all.

A stunning witch took the stage as the ceremony of thanksgiving began. Her champagne hair tumbled in curls to her lower back, and bright blue eyes shone behind her cream-colored mask. She raised a prayer and thanked Fate for her favor. Other witches joined her, and they asked for safe passage through winter, reciting what sounded like poems and spells.

After a short intermission, we resumed with a blessing for the dead. The veil was thin tonight, and we all felt that strongly in the air, in the life energy around us. Apparently, on such a night, with the thin veil and the gathering, praying, and communion of so many magical beings, even those like me, who didn't possess the gift of communing with spirits, would be able to see them.

Silence fell over the crowd, and the air was still as the communion began. I held Fitz's hand tightly as we focused our energy, set on a common goal. Powerful communers called to the dead. And suddenly, shapes materialized through the crowd. The spirits showed themselves to confirm they had received our blessing and to offer a sign of peace and solidarity with us.

Our ancestors were a life force for us, Fitz had told me when I'd first arrived in Edinburgh. Their power lingered in the air after their passing, and we drew extra strength from the presence of their magic. They forged a path for us that we each walked, and we owed much gratitude to them. It was an honor to be visited by those gone before us.

As the spirits appeared, Molly grew pale enough to match their lifeless pallor. I couldn't understand why. Strangely enough, this process felt natural. Our connection to our ancestors was always strong, even if we couldn't see them, and I'd known they were around us. But as tears streamed down her beautiful face, I realized quickly that Molly was upset.

The wispy figure of a tall, handsome witch stood before her. He looked at Molly longingly as they raised their fingers toward each other. I wondered if she could feel his touch. *But who could he be?* I wondered. Molly was from Earth, and none of Earth's spirits would be here . . .

I scanned the crowd and found Henry looking toward Molly. A curious expression blanketed his features too as he studied her movements. Henry must have felt my own gaze, and he turned his attention to me. I looked to Molly and back to him. He shrugged, though his look turned pointed.

The air filled with soft murmurs and sniffles, and I could only imagine my reaction if I were to see my own father. I closed my eyes tightly, blinking back tears as the crowd's attention turned to the stage. The figure of a young woman hovered in front of the living representatives. Her dark hair tumbled down her back, and instead of the lifeless pallor the other spirits held, her bronzed skin was glowing with a golden light.

"She was selected to receive the blessing on their behalf," Isaac whispered to me and Fitz. "Lana was telling me about this earlier today. The blessings are already flowing into her spirit. Soon she'll be able to speak to us, and then she'll carry our blessings back with her to the others."

"Take heart, my children," the apparition said. "We know of your burden. We know of the great evil that has settled into this land. We are peaceful, but we are strong. Goodness will prevail." She glanced around the crowd, and her eyes settled on our group. "There are beings here with such goodness in their hearts. We stand with you." She nodded her head, and we bowed ours in return. Her lips pulled into a slight smile. "Thank you for this gift. We remember you as you remember us. Go in peace."

In an unbelievable moment of communion between the living and dead, I was again struck by the balance of opposites. The entire night was about our species working together for a common purpose. I glanced around the fire, processing the sight that would soon be a memory. Countless spirits hovered through the crowd, some peaceful, some clearly emotional at the sight of their loved ones. It was overwhelming. Standing in the dimming glow of the fire, I felt a peace resting within me unlike anything I'd felt before.

It was then that I realized—we weren't the only side offering a blessing tonight.

PART TWO

CHAPTER TEN

The house was abuzz with excitement when we returned after the festival despite the late hour, and the team gathered in the great room to have a nightcap before bed. Molly tried to excuse herself, but I took the opportunity to pull her aside.

"Molly, could Henry and I speak with you for just a second?" I asked quietly.

She hesitated briefly, her mouth twisting in uncertainty. But after a few seconds of debate, she nodded. Her energy tightened as we stepped on to the balcony.

The air was still. The world was quiet except for the click of our shoes on the stone flooring. We settled into lounge chairs near the fireplace. Henry set down three glasses and a bottle of whisky before waving his hands, and firewood floated from the nearby stack and into the pit. I called forth my fire magic and threw flames toward the neatly stacked wood.

Henry poured the amber liquid and floated the glasses toward us. He sat back and swirled his dram of Scotch, his gaze wistfully set somewhere beyond the glass. Henry and I hadn't spoken about his mate since the night he'd shared the details of her death with me, but I knew his mind must have been dancing with Emily after tonight's final ritual. It seemed impossible that such a magical being could have died in a car accident, that Henry could lose his mate in the blink of an eye. I knew it was difficult for him to talk about her openly, even after all these years.

I feared we were about to have a similarly heavy conversation with Molly.

I took a deep breath and began.

"We don't want to pry, Molly."

"But you're going to."

"Yeah, we are," I said. "I know you're upset. If you want to talk about this later, it can wait. But . . ."

"But you're wondering how a witch from Earth could experience what I did with a spirit on Opimae."

Henry and I nodded.

"I knew it wouldn't escape your notice." She shook her head.

"We're observant," I said.

Molly laughed softly before sighing. "Let's get it over with."

"Who is he, Molly?"

"His name was Finn." She paused momentarily, looking from me to Henry and back. "He's . . . my mate."

I nodded encouragingly, hoping my face hadn't contorted into some sad expression—I had a feeling Molly would hate that.

"Oh, Molly. I'm so sorry."

"Thanks," she returned simply. "Here's the thing . . . no one here knows that I've been to Opimae before. I asked Prisha and Ella not to say anything—it was my one condition for joining the crusade, and they agreed."

Prisha was India's Cardinal Court representative, and Ella was one of the European members.

"So, Chloe, Solomon. . . no one else knows?" I asked.

Molly shook her head.

"Why?"

"I was in Opimae for three years with Finn. When he died . . . well, it was horrible. I know you can imagine the pain of a lost mate, and honestly, it's fifty times worse than that."

My eyes flickered to Henry. His eyes hadn't wandered from his drink.

"And you didn't want us to know about it," I said.

Molly shook her head, a tear rolling down her cheek. "I. . ."

"Take your time, lass." Henry's face was soft, understanding.

After a moment, she said, "I didn't want to relive it with you. I didn't want to explain it. And I didn't want to be the poor girl who lost her mate that everyone was going to worry about. I mean, knowing I was coming back to the place where I lost him. . . Tell me you wouldn't have worried."

"You're right, of course," I said.

"I couldn't take any of it. I just couldn't. So, I asked them to conceal it."

"And you saw him again for the first time tonight."

"Yes," she whispered.

"Dear god."

Molly sniffled but chuckled softly. "Yeah, exactly."

"How was it? Seeing him again," Henry asked.

Molly hesitated, but when she met Henry's gaze, her expression softened.

Henry glanced down. "You know about Emily, then."

"Prisha mentioned it. I'm so sorry, Henry."

He smiled sadly, his eyes distant.

"It was just how you think it would be," Molly finally said. She hesitated, clearing her throat. "It was the best moment because I saw him again. And it was the worst because I—" She hesitated. "Because I had to let him go all over again."

"I think you might be stronger than I am. I'd give anything to see her once more," he said. "But to say goodbye a second time . . ." He trailed off.

She shook her head. Tears welled again in her eyes, but her face was resolute. She didn't want to break in front of us.

To see your fallen mate for only a few minutes before they disappeared from your life again seemed like Fate's cruelest trick.

Henry set his glass on the end table and leaned forward, resting his elbows on his knees.

"Will support from an acquaintance make it better or worse?" he asked.

Molly held his gaze and then shrugged. Tears spilled out and rolled down her face. Henry moved to the armrest of her chair, and Molly leaned into him as he held her tightly.

I stood and moved toward the fireplace, suddenly feeling like an intruder in the intimacy of the moment. I debated what to do—should I go?

Molly and Henry's feelings ran deep like fathomless wells. Henry had always claimed Emily's love had been worth the pain of her loss, but his emptiness gutted me, and so did Molly's. Their circumstances were wholly unfair. It wasn't right, and more than that—it was cruel.

The idea of losing Fitz was devastating, and my body trembled at the thought. How could Fate chart our courses to each other and then allow mates to be so tragically ripped apart? Why go through all this trouble to bring them together only to devastate them in the end? If our love wasn't our own, why did mates hold on to their lost loves? That didn't seem like a symptom of Fate.

Though I could make a case for Fate wanting us to feel the pain of our fallen mates for a purpose, that theory didn't feel right. No, it couldn't be that simple. There had to be more to it.

Henry's voice registered through my mind. "*Dinnae go.*"

I nodded and sat back down. Henry and Molly's pain was palpable in the air, and my heart ached.

After a few minutes, Molly sat back and Henry returned to his seat.

"Sorry about that," Molly said through sniffles.

I reached for her hand. "Don't you dare apologize."

"I've been doing okay lately. But seeing him tonight . . ." She trailed off.

"I can't imagine," I said.

We sat in silence, and I tried to suppress the question I wanted to ask more than anything.

"Oh, Hadley," Molly said.

"What?" I eyed her skeptically.

"Just ask." She looked at me pointedly.

Henry chuckled softly.

I hesitated a few seconds. "What happened, Molly?"

She took a deep breath, closing her eyes, seeking composure. I waited patiently.

"It happened when Lorenzo overtook Terra Firma to create a base camp below his fortress," she said. I looked to Henry, but he shook his head.

"We didn't know about this," I said.

"About Terra Firma?" she asked.

"No, lass. They've no shared that with us," Henry said.

Molly met my gaze, uncertainty filling her eyes.

I had discovered the location of Lorenzo's fortress in my spirit travels to his office. Or at least, we had thought it was a discovery. Had Opimae's intelligence teams known his location this entire time?

"*I should probably ask Charles about that,*" I said to Henry telepathically.

"*Aye, and you should ask the Cardinal Court if they know about it.*"

Molly was in a vulnerable state, and I didn't want to push her too hard, but this revelation was troubling.

"When was this?" I asked.

"A year ago," she said.

"*A year ago? I thought we were brought to Opimae to prevent Lorenzo from making his first move.*"

"*Aye, and if Lorenzo has already taken over this town, why has he no made another move in a year?*"

I looked to Henry.

"*You wouldnae be remiss in asking for some of Charles's time tomorrow,*" he suggested.

I fired off a quick message to Charles asking him to meet with me and Fitz the following morning. I returned my focus to Molly. "I'll deal with this tomorrow, but for tonight . . . Terra Firma?"

"Right. So it's a small mountain village, and it was Finn's home. He . . . died defending the village during the invasion." She paused, her leg shaking nervously. "I'd come to Opimae City that day to pick up some things we needed back in the village. By the time I heard what was happening—"

I gasped softly.

"Yeah."

"So, that's why you're here," I said.

"No one hates Lorenzo more than I do," she whispered. "And I swear to god, Hadley, when I come face to face with him one day—I'll gut him."

I reached for Molly's hand, squeezing it gently. "I'll hold him down," I offered before asking, "How are you feeling about the ritual now?"

"I haven't processed it yet. It felt so real, but it didn't at the same time. It's hard to explain."

I nodded, and silence fell. Finally, Henry broke the quiet.

"Do you think we can do that sort of thing on Earth?" he asked.

Molly mulled over the question.

"I'm not sure. Magic is so different here," she said. "Obviously, there are mediums, but this . . . this was something else."

Henry nodded.

"Did you ever consider speaking with someone on Earth? Someone that could connect you two?" Molly asked.

"Of course. But I've never gone through with it." We waited, allowing him to roll his thoughts around in his mind. "I couldnae stand the thought of trying to speak with her through someone else . . . that they would stand in between us. That they'd become a part of what should only be between the two of us."

"God." I exhaled deeply, feeling his pain. Our connections to our mates were powerful. Anyone stepping in between us felt like sacrilege. "I'd never thought of it that way before."

"You dinnae have to. Your mate is still here."

"Henry . . . I'm sorry."

"Dinnae apologize, lass. I didnae mean it that way." He rested his hand briefly on mine.

"I know," I returned, squeezing his hand gently. "There are a lot of emotions swirling around the group tonight."

"You must be thinking of your father tonight. I know how close you were."

"He was one of my very best friends."

"Have you considered speaking with him?"

"Of course. But I knew I was losing him—I had months to talk with him, to remind him how much I loved him. He was taken from me, but he wasn't taken unexpectedly."

"Is that better or worse, you reckon?"

"I couldn't tell you. I think it's a wonderful thing to have that time with your loved one, but you also wake up every day knowing the end is growing nearer. Loss is loss, whether you know it's coming or not."

"Aye. That's true enough. In the end, we're all just grieving our losses, licking our wounds. It doesn't matter if you know the end is coming. There's never enough time."

"Exactly. And I think trying to commune with my father would be the same way—it would never be enough. It would just pull me into the past and make me focus on what I lost. It would be easy to convince myself that I just need to talk to him one more time, but . . ."

"But you know that isn't true."

I nodded. "But that's my situation. Henry, I don't know what's right for another being, especially when we're talking about losing a mate. But I do know that having had the opportunity to say goodbye to my father gives me some measure of peace. When someone is ripped from your life unexpectedly—maybe one last conversation would be helpful for closure."

I looked to Molly. Her expression was pensive.

"I don't think you'd regret telling Emily one last time that you love her, especially knowing with certainty that she can hear you," I said.

"There is a peace in that," Molly said, her gaze rising to meet Henry's. "I know Finn heard the words I said to him tonight. I didn't realize how much of a burden I was carrying until that moment."

Henry smiled sadly. "Perhaps you're right. My heart belongs to Emily, and it always will." He paused momentarily. "I'll make you a promise, then. If we survive this mess and make it back to Earth, I'll try to reach her. And I'll remind her once more that I'll never stop loving her."

"I'd like to hear about Emily—if you want to talk about her. It's okay if not," Molly said.

"Aye, lass. I'll tell you about her. But only if you'll tell us about Finn too."

Molly smiled. "I'd like that very much."

Henry took one slow sip of Scotch and set the glass gently on the table. His eyes grew distant, and a soft smile rose to his lips. Molly leaned forward in her seat, while I settled in for the sad tale I'd never forget.

CHAPTER ELEVEN

Charles had agreed overnight to meet with Fitz and me, so the following morning found the three of us in a small conference room at headquarters. The stone walls were bare, but it was a corner room, and streams of pale light filtered in through the windows. We settled on to the uncomfortable wooden chairs, and I turned to Fitz.

Our energy was still unsettled after the events of the previous evening. Though our distance tugged at me, I knew Fitz and I could push that aside while we talked with Charles. He made eye contact briefly and nodded that he was ready. I called the meeting to order.

"Charles, last night I heard some information about Terra Firma."

His expression didn't waver, but his energy wasn't quite as controlled. He hadn't expected this.

"One of our crusaders was living there when it fell. What's interesting to me is that we had no idea Lorenzo had made any advancements like this."

Uncertainty flickered across Charles's features.

"That information wasn't included in the briefings we sent to Earth?" he asked.

Fitz and I exchanged a quick glance.

"No," Fitz answered. "Your reports were minimal, to speak plainly."

"Charles, we thought we were brought over here to prevent war. We didn't know an attack had already occurred. We weren't even aware the Opimaean government knew the location of Lorenzo's fortress."

Charles nodded. "An oversight."

I wasn't buying it.

"Perhaps we can start attending meetings and reviewing new intelligence now? And I'd love to get Jordan started in intel."

Charles set his pen down, his gaze following the movement distractedly. "We've had a vested interest in helping you and your team acclimate to Opimae."

"Which we've appreciated," Fitz said quickly. "But we'd like to get to work now."

"We've caught up pretty quickly—we've seen much of your beautiful nation, the city, Arregaithel . . ." I trailed off. "But we're ready to make progress with Lorenzo. Let us do what you brought us over to do."

Charles sighed. "Terra Firma is a small, quiet mountain village in Arregaithel. Lorenzo took over the village about a year ago. We have full reports on the incident. I'll share them with you."

"That's a great start," I said.

The arched wooden door opened, its hinges creaking in protest, and a young elf stepped through. He didn't look much older than a teenager, and his golden hair and pale blue robe added to his otherworldly presence.

"I've been sent for you, sir," he said, looking to Charles. "The intelligence teams have urgent reports for you to review. It's Lorenzo—his numbers are far greater than we anticipated."

Charles's energy shifted. It wasn't only surprise that charged the air around us. There was a bit of anger, too. He eyed the elf disapprovingly, and I imagined a silent message was being transmitted to the boy, considering the look of surprise on his face. Clearly, Charles was unhappy he'd shared the information in front of us.

"I'll be right there. Thank you," Charles said simply.

The boy nodded and closed the door behind him.

"Pardon the interruption," Charles said. "Now, the business about intelligence updates for your team."

"We want to be updated in real time," I said. "Starting with whatever information Intelligence has gathered about Lorenzo's numbers."

Charles held my gaze wordlessly.

"I'd like to call in the team so we can be briefed on this news," I continued.

"And Charles," Fitz said. "Hadley and I want in that chamber. We want to start sitting in on meetings with the nations' leaders. Starting this afternoon."

"I agree. Earth deserves a seat at the table. We deserve to have our voice heard, too," I said.

Charles hesitated, leaning back in his chair. Finally, he nodded.

"Gather your team and meet me in the conference room beside my office."

The meeting room was less fussy than most areas of the council's building, consisting of simple stone walls and small windows. Tables and chairs were lined neatly across the wooden floors. Pendant lights hung overhead, compensating for the smaller windows. Keoni shared that the room had once been used for storage but was recently converted into a meeting room as space at headquarters grew scarce with the influx of resources—us included.

It could've been a meeting on Earth: thermoses and coffee cups scattered the tables along with notepads and laptops. Magical beings occupied the rolling chairs around the tables, some catching up, some whispering in pairs or small groups.

Keoni crossed the room distractedly and sank into his seat quietly. When he met my gaze, he offered a smile, but his efforts weren't enough to fool me. His expression seemed forced.

Fitz and I found seats between Molly and James. The former gave me a half smile as I settled in next to her. Though I was pleased with the progress we'd made integrating Molly into the group, she still seemed hesitant around most of the team. It would just take time, I guessed.

I turned to Fitz. Distance still lingered between us. I cleared my throat and tried for a bit of normalcy.

"If they'd asked me in my job interviews where I saw myself in ten years, my answer would not have been sitting in a conference room with witches and elves getting ready to discuss a powerful villain on a foreign planet," I whispered to Fitz.

Fitz's energy flurried from amused to uncertain and back, before he chuckled softly in response.

"I know what you mean. It wasn't in my career trajectory either," he agreed. His eyes cut to mine. He was feeling me out as much as I was him.

"It's nice not having to hide who we are. Now, if we can just get Charles to start including us, I'll be a lot happier."

Fitz reached toward me, hesitating a few seconds before taking my hand in his. And there it was—our energies calmed slightly.

"I wonder how Jordan's feeling today?" he asked.

We leaned forward, glancing down the table to find the human in question, who was seated by Henry. Henry had become more protective of Jordan since we'd crossed the portal. And if Henry wasn't close by, Isaac sure was. They were both trying to ensure she was comfortable as she acclimated to her new reality.

Charles crossed the threshold, a hush immediately falling over the group.

"Well, I hope you're prepared to hit the ground running today." He met my gaze. "We received some troubling information this morning."

"And this is regarding Lorenzo's forces?" Ian asked.

"I'm afraid so."

Charles's assistant, Brigitta, fixed her hazel eyes on the far wall and leaned forward in her chair. She tucked a few stray strands of her shoulder-length chestnut hair behind her ear before flicking her wrist in the direction of the wall, causing a large screen to descend from the ceiling. After another flick, this time toward the windows, thick covers drew closed and blocked the light. A map displayed on the screen.

Charles directed his attention toward our table of crusaders. "We are in Novam Terram. We're the most populous nation on Opimae and one of eight nations on the continent of Magna Terra."

Nods went around the table.

"Lorenzo is in the bordering nation of Arregaithel," Charles said, pointing on the map. Though I attempted to keep my energy even, Charles's reference to Lorenzo's fortress location made me bristle. He stole a glance at me.

Charles walked us through the main points of the map, reacquainting us with where we were in relation to Lorenzo's fortress, which was tucked into a small valley that sat high in the mountains looming above the small town of Terra Firma in Arregaithel. I resisted the urge to look toward Molly. Charles told us that many villagers had been murdered in Lorenzo's first attack, and unfathomably, countless others had enlisted as some of Lorenzo's first followers.

"These reports from Intelligence this morning show that his numbers are far greater than we imagined," Charles concluded. "We underestimated him at best."

"I don't understand," Isaac began. "How is he so successful at recruiting for a cause like this?"

"We've wondered that ourselves," Charles said. "But he is very charismatic, and I suppose these beings believe their lives would improve under his rule."

"Do you know exactly what he's promising beings who join him?" I asked.

Had he made the same pitch to the Opimaean beings as he'd given me?

"Well, for those from Earth, he promises to overthrow your government. He claims he will ask far less than the current government and promises unregulated power. One of our agents heard him speak last year in New York."

"Wait," James began. "In New York? He's crossed the portal again?"

"We sent word."

"Which we never received," Solomon said, turning to me and Fitz. Our silent look said it all—we'd discuss this after the meeting.

Charles's face was grave.

"What did your agents learn in New York?" James asked.

"He guaranteed that he would not only offer safety, but that humankind was no concern of his. We would not live in fear of witchkind government, nor remain in secret from the humans. He promised we would rule over them."

"It surprises me that so many beings want to have humankind ruled over, rather than coexisted with," James said.

"Power . . ." Charles began, "is a dangerous thing to offer. Even well-intentioned beings can be compromised by its lure."

"And what does he offer residents of this world?" Fitz asked.

"A bit of the same. He claims we've been brainwashed by Earth's governments and that we assist Earth's witchkind councils with holding the planet's witches in captivity."

"What a boldfaced lie!" James exclaimed.

"It's a fine strategy on Lorenzo's part," Henry said. "He knows exactly what he's doing."

"Agreed," Charles responded, rolling his sleeves absentmindedly. In doing so, he revealed tattoos the color of snow, showing starkly against his dark brown skin. The tattoos seemed to dance, slinking themselves around the width of his forearm.

"So, what are the implications of this, Charles? Where do we go from here?" Ian asked.

"We've called in our field agents, who will return to the city by late afternoon. They'll brief us once they arrive. Then we build our strategy. And we'll need to recruit additional warriors."

"Recruit?" Ian asked.

"The nations on other continents have avoided our efforts entirely, and even some of Magna Terra's leaders have not yet pledged full military support. We'll pitch them again at the chamber meeting later, especially considering this new information. And we'll try to recruit more soldiers for the militia regimens we already have. In this world, there is no draft. If we cannot garner enough support, then it does not happen."

"Would this current crisis with Lorenzo not warrant stronger action?" Isaac asked. "Not that I favor war, but Lorenzo is a real threat to us all."

"The nations won't favor it. We don't warmonger here, and the idea of a growing military has been a difficult one for the folk of Opimae to accept. We've only had a military presence to defend our world should something threatening come through that portal."

"You believed the only threat would come from Earth," Henry observed.

"Don't forget we are a planet of refugees," Charles said. "We certainly haven't."

I was buzzing with anxiety by the time we broke for recess, and I took a deep breath as Fitz and I found our seats at the old, wooden table with the rest of the team.

". . .and it seems like strange timing," Henry was saying.

"What's strange timing?" Fitz asked.

"That Opimae teams have just learned this information on Lorenzo right after we've arrived," Isaac answered.

"I don't think it's chance at all," Molly said, her eyes fixed on the food she was pushing around with her fork.

"What's your theory?" Jordan asked.

"I think Lorenzo knew when we were arriving, and he's been strategic in allowing Opimae's forces to discover information at certain times."

"You think—I'm sorry, what on earth is *that?*" Isaac asked, nodding in my direction.

I held up the food item in question. "Seafood, I think?"

"It looks like an octopus mated a seahorse," Henry said, his face scrunched in thought.

"I'd say it looks like an alien, but . . ." I said.

"We're the aliens in this scenario?" Jordan finished, laughing.

"Well, enough of that," I said. "I'll stick with the veggies today."

Isaac laughed. "Anyway, back to the point. So, you're saying Lorenzo's making a statement now that we're here?"

"Based on Hadley's report on her encounter with Lorenzo and the reports from previous agents, he seems like the type. I think he enjoys toying with others," Molly said.

Tanner let out a low whistle.

"Did you feel that way when you interacted with him, Hadley?" Solomon asked.

I nodded. "I think Molly's right."

"So, he's letting us believe we're making progress, and then releasing information that demonstrates how much we still don't know," Jordan said.

"Aye, but unless he's hiding more information, his numbers aren't strong enough that he's confident in victory," Henry added. "They're braw numbers, but they aren't enough for a decisive victory."

"I think he just means to rattle us and make us question if we're strong enough," Fitz said.

"And we're currently doing exactly what he meant for us to do," Jordan said.

"It feels like we're in a game of chess with Lorenzo," I said. "And I think it's time for us to finally make a move."

After lunch, we wound our way through headquarters to a larger meeting room, where our afternoon session with the chamber awaited. Though the full team wouldn't typically be in attendance, we wanted Magna Terra's rulers to meet all of us and give our team some insight into the chamber. Though I expected we'd have more barriers to break through with Charles, this was a start.

Molly and I fell to the back of the group, and I rejoiced at the opportunity to talk to her further. I hadn't realized we were missing Chloe until she passed us and caught up with Tanner.

I couldn't quite decide what was happening between Tanner and Chloe. They weren't together—they certainly weren't mated, yet the bond between them was more than friendship. The way they held each other's gaze was enough to arouse suspicion. They gravitated toward each other, trusted each other; their energy reacted excitedly to each other . . . I stopped. I was getting entirely too close to unintentional mind-reading territory. I tore my attention away from them.

"You've noticed it, too," Molly whispered.

"Noticed what?"

I was feigning ignorance, and Molly knew it.

"Really? I know you're watching them."

I lowered my voice. "You mean Tanner and Chloe?"

We both slowed our pace, and Molly cut her eyes toward me, one eyebrow raised—a signal to cut the crap.

"What do you think is going on?" I asked.

"*No idea, but something is off.*" Molly's voice echoed through my mind. "*You know Tanner better than I do, but I swear he's into Chloe. And it seems like she's drawn to him, or something.*"

I followed Molly's lead and switched to telepathy. "*But they aren't mated.*"

I thought of my connection to Fitz, recalling the way our worlds had shifted when it formed. Our energies had mingled together in a new way—it had been identifiable to even Henry and Tanner. I was certain that hadn't happened between Tanner and Chloe.

"*Maybe there's another connection we don't know about,*" Molly said. "*It's not right. They're more than friends.*"

"*I might just ask him about it. I'll at least know if he's lying. If there's something happening within the group, I'd like to know.*"

"*It's more than that—you need to know. We can't afford to have anything pull focus from the mission. Too much is at stake,*" Molly said. "*If I notice anything else, I'll tell you. But keep me posted, will you?*"

It was an interesting start to our alliance, but I jumped at her offer just the same. After all, part of Molly's purpose was to confer over strategy—to help maintain harmony within the group and offer an unbiased perspective.

I could only hope Molly and I were ready for whatever this was. Our team couldn't afford for this situation to evolve into an issue, though I already suspected it would.

We stepped into the chamber where the representatives of the nations of Opimae convened, and I turned my attention toward the magical beings filling the room. From witches and elves to druids and faeries, much of the magical species in Opimae were represented in the room. They took their seats in armchairs that lined the long rows of tables, which accounted for much of the room's floor space.

A familiar icy gaze rested on me. I met Mia's pale blue eyes.

"Good to see you, Mia," I said, hoping my attempt at pleasantry was more convincing than it felt. "How was your crossing?"

Mia's eyebrows rose. "Bumpy."

Her cross expression was humorous, and I stifled a laugh. I didn't think it would be welcome.

"Well, it's good you're here—we need to make some progress on these Parisian stalkers."

"I should've known you'd be the first one to find trouble."

"Nice, Mia."

She smirked. "You don't think they noticed you?"

"There weren't any signs, but . . ." I trailed off.

"What is it?" Mia asked.

"I just don't see how this could be coincidence."

She nodded. "It does seem unlikely, but we'll have to find the evidence to support that."

Charles called the meeting to order, so Fitz and I made our way to the front of the room.

"I thought only Earth's crusade leaders would be joining the chamber," a man toward the back of the room said. I wasn't familiar with the leaders yet, but his forest-colored robe looked like those of the druids.

"I thought it would be nice for Opimaean leaders to meet the team of crusaders. They'll join us just for today. Moving forward, Earth will be represented by five leaders in the chamber."

"Five?" the man challenged. "Why so many?"

"Our nations have one to two representatives each. But these leaders from Earth represent an entire planet. Five seems more than fair when you think about it."

The man muttered under his breath, but Charles signaled for Fitz and me to begin.

A total of eight nations were banding together in the fight against Lorenzo, and their representatives turned eager gazes toward us. Fitz and I gave a brief recap of our team, introducing each member to the chamber, along with our qualifications. While most of the chamber seemed interested, some of their attention felt positive, and some of it . . . not so much. The prime minister of Arregaithel, Evander, rose during the middle of our recap and rushed through the doors. Though it felt odd, we pressed on.

We were just finishing up when a tall, young elf opened the chamber doors. She quickly slipped a note into Charles's grasp before whispering to him and leaving the chamber. The look on Charles's face was grave, and he quickly shut his laptop to approach the podium.

"I apologize for the interruption, but we have an urgent matter to discuss," Charles said.

Fitz and I took our seats quickly.

"We have just received word that Adamo has fallen."

Gasps and murmurs filled the chamber. Fitz and I locked eyes. Adamo was a part of Arregaithel—we had been near it just a few days prior when we visited Róisín. Róisín. I had to find out if she and Laisrén were okay.

"How bad is it, Charles?" Bakari, the prime minister of Thalassa, asked. Thalassa was the kingdom of water witches, and they seemed to hold a lot of weight in Opimae's governing bodies. Prime Minister Bakari wore a silver tunic embroidered in navy appliqué. His soft green eyes were indicative of his water witch heritage and were set below a strong brow. His curly hair was cropped short, and his deep brown arms held white tattoos that encircled his wrists before dotting down the back of his hands and stretching to his fingertips.

"According to the agents, there's no hope of recovery. Lorenzo's army was swift."

"We need a full briefing," another voice called.

"Our field agents are almost here, and I've asked them to join us directly and share details," Charles said.

Charles called for a short recess so leaders could make calls and disseminate information. I found Lana in the crowd, typing furiously on her phone.

"Have you heard from Saoirse?" I asked.

Lana stopped typing, and her eyes turned soft. "She's okay." She released a deep sigh. "She was assigned to a mission near Adamo, so I messaged her right when Charles made the announcement."

"I'm so glad she's okay." I could only imagine how Lana had felt awaiting Saoirse's response. My chest tightened, and I instinctively looked for Fitz in the crowd. He was lost in conversation with Henry.

"I'm sure you're busy, but I need to know if Róisín is okay. How do I find out?"

"I'm happy to look into it for you."

Saoirse entered the room along with Sadie. Lana studied Saoirse, and her expression relaxed. Though Sadie carried herself with the same self-assuredness I'd seen in training, her green eyes were troubled. Charles greeted them, and the crowds settled as the two agents took command of the room.

"Today at fourteen hundred hours, a coordinated attack was launched on Adamo, a city in the northern terrain of Arregaithel," Saoirse began. "My and Sadie's teams were scheduled for a routine visit around the outskirts of Lorenzo's territory for an intelligence sweep. We called for backup and immediately moved toward the perimeter of the city. However, Lorenzo's troops were vast in number. We quickly realized that not only were we outnumbered, but that the attack had been a swift and decisive victory in Lorenzo's favor."

"The attack was ruthless," Sadie said. "Many are wounded or dead, but they are in Lorenzo's charge now."

My eyes swept the room, finding looks of horror, anguish, and disgust. Prime Minister Evander's chair remained empty. The druid in the green robe—the king of Bain, I thought—paced the room restlessly.

"How many troops from Lorenzo's side?" Prime Minister Bakari asked.

Saoirse and Sadie exchanged glances.

"Our best guess is around four thousand soldiers," Sadie said.

Everyone around the room looked as stunned as I felt. Those were big numbers to take on a small, unsuspecting city.

"*Four thousand?*" I followed the voice to its source—the king of Bain had stopped pacing. His mouth was agape above a long, gray beard, and his gray eyes widened. He reminded me of the wizards I'd seen depicted in film, which would have been humorous under different circumstances.

"Yes, your majesty," Sadie answered drily. "Even though many of the residents fought back, this is why Lorenzo's victory was quick."

"Do we have any reports on how many were killed?" Prime Minister Bakari asked.

"No, and I don't know that we'll be able to obtain that information now," Saoirse said.

A tall, domineering elf stood. His blond hair hung loosely beneath a gold crown, which sat atop a strong brow, and he wore a robe the color of the sea that was intricately woven with silver stitching. I recognized him from the Autumn Festival. King Copandir.

"Was Adamo the only area targeted or did others take fire?" he asked.

"It was a targeted attack. The surrounding areas are safe—for now," Saoirse said.

I met Lana's gaze, partially relieved. It was likely Laisrén and Róisín wouldn't have been in Adamo, but I wanted a definite answer. Lana wiggled her phone.

"They're safe," she mouthed.

Relief washed through me. Though my heart broke for my fire witch brethren, at least I knew two of them were safe.

"When can we expect a full intelligence report from your teams?" King Copandir asked.

"By this evening. We'll join the rest of our team to draft a report as soon as we're done here," Saoirse said.

The king looked to Charles, who nodded.

"We won't hold you up any longer with our discussions," Charles said to Saoirse and Sadie. "Thank you for your time."

The agents nodded and made their way to the door. Saoirse's fingers discreetly grazed Lana's arm as she passed by her, and as quickly as she and Sadie had entered, they were gone. The door closed with a thud.

Brigitta flicked her wrist to toss an orb of light toward the screen descending from the ceiling. A map spread across the screen, and we studied the area around Adamo.

"This is a great tragedy," Queen Min-Ji of Hurlee said, shaking her head of long raven hair, which was topped by a golden crown. It spilled across her pale gray tunic reaching halfway down her back, and her deep brown eyes were filled with anger. "And a major setback."

"This is a call for a shift in strategy," Charles said. "It shows us that something more must be done. As horrific as it is, the town was always at risk, and this should come as a surprise to no one."

"I'm tired of this chamber dodging responsibility, Charles," Queen Min-Ji said. "This is unacceptable. We should have fought harder from the moment Lorenzo's troops took Terra Firma."

"Many of us did vote for firmer tactics, but we were overruled," another voice called out. I leaned forward and found the source: the king of Kevardhu, the faerie kingdom. King Jowan was a petite man who looked no more than thirty. His blond strands were swept back and his pale skin was a stark contrast to his royal blue tunic.

"Yes, so let us learn from our past," Prime Minister Bakari said. "We cannot allow ourselves to repeat this mistake. Now, we must answer Lorenzo's action."

"We need better intelligence regarding today's tragedy before we make any decisions," King Copandir said.

They needed Jordan, I thought.

"And better intelligence is exactly what we've been working on," Charles said. He pointed to the screen as facts and figures about Lorenzo's army took shape. "And that information has shown us how great a threat we're truly dealing with now."

Gasps sounded from the chamber members.

"Yes," he said. "The size of his army has nearly doubled in the past six months."

"While you've been fraternizing with Earth, Lorenzo has been busy building an army!" King Jowan's face was set tight, his cheeks flushing with his anger.

"You believe these crusaders are those of the prophecy, but you have no evidence to support that. It's unlikely they'd come from *Earth* anyway. They'll protect themselves before they protect us!" the king of Bain exclaimed.

"That is unfair, Alden," Prime Minister Bakari said. "The prophecy clearly states they'll come from Earth. And you don't know these crusaders well enough to make that statement."

"Our alliance with Earth is important, and their support will be vital in our efforts. We are strengthening our numbers, as well," Charles said. "Our attention hasn't been divided from Lorenzo."

King Alden swept his eyes contemptuously across us. "You put too much faith in Earth. They'll turn their backs on us by the end. It's not their world that's in immediate danger."

"You have no basis for that opinion. That is prejudice, plain and simple," Prime Minister Bakari said. "We have no space for that in this chamber."

King Alden muttered under his breath, but he held his tongue.

"*Not the warmest welcome to the chamber, is it?*" I asked Fitz telepathically.

"*The team's energy is troubled,*" he returned.

Fitz was right. As the chamber continued on into the late afternoon, our group's energy was a muddled web of frustrated, offended, and surprised. I was relieved when the session adjourned for the evening.

After a security sweep of the apartment, Fitz and I sat across from James, Chloe, Solomon, Ian, and Mia.

"I don't like that information was withheld from us," I said, getting straight to the point.

"Yeah, it's concerning," Chloe agreed.

"Quite concerning," James conceded. He was slow to criticize the councils of either Earth or Opimae, but it had been made obvious today how little we still knew about Lorenzo.

"Has it been like this since you've arrived?" Mia asked.

"They've basically had us playing tourist," I said, "learning about the world, sightseeing. I can appreciate that they want us to understand the folk we're fighting alongside, but . . ."

"But now we discover that Lorenzo's power has extended significantly and that not all of Opimae is in agreement on our mission," Ian finished.

"I know some of the information on Lorenzo's forces is new, but not all of it," I said. "We should have been informed sooner. Plus, Charles said this information came from an investigation—an investigation we knew nothing about."

"Wait, someone catch me up here," Mia said.

We shared the information from the morning session. Mia shook her head.

"I can't stop asking myself if they withheld this because they distrust us, or . . . if there's something else," I said.

James nodded, his lips pulled tightly.

"What do you make of that bit about New York?" Fitz asked.

"Oh, aye. Another critical piece of the puzzle."

"This is no accidental mismanagement of information," I said, shaking my head. "And we all know it."

"But we have no proof," Solomon argued.

"Other than the fact that information *that* critical never reached us. Lorenzo crossed the portal again—*twice.*"

"We need to find out if this information was withheld from us on purpose," Mia said.

"Aye. Was it the work of a select few agents? Or is there something larger at play here?" Fitz speculated.

"We must send word back to the rest of the Cardinal Court," Solomon said. "Carefully."

"Should we run our own reconnaissance?" I asked. "See what we can come up with?"

"I think the court would be wholly divided on this issue," Chloe said.

"Which side of the aisle are you on?" I asked.

Chloe hesitated, but then said, "I don't think it would hurt."

"Chloe, are you serious?" Mia asked.

"I had a meeting with Charles during lunch today to discuss Jess's assignment to the team and our concerns over his behavior. Charles dismissed it."

With all that had happened, I hadn't received that update yet. Chloe eyed me sympathetically. Disappointment seeped straight into my bones, though I wouldn't give up just yet. I'd speak with Charles directly.

"And we both spoke to him about information sharing between teams, and that hasn't changed either—clearly," Solomon said.

Mia's face turned pensive. "Okay, I see your point."

"We have to consider this option," Fitz said.

"This will make the rest of the court nervous," Ian said.

"They should be nervous," I countered.

James stared through the window momentarily, weighing our choices.

"What are your thoughts, James?" I asked.

"Honestly, I'm no sure," he finally conceded.

My eyebrows raised.

"I ken." He smirked. "But as optimistic as I've been about Opimae, there is much as stake—we'll do what we must, I think."

"You think we should collect more data," Chloe guessed.

"I do."

"Fitz?" Chloe asked.

"We should collect our own data to verify the information being given to us and make decisions based on our own findings."

Ian released a low whistle. "That's a meaty objective."

"It is," Fitz said. "But we have the talent to do it. And I don't trust that Opimae is giving us a complete look at the situation."

"How would we begin such a mission?" James asked.

"Jordan would be a great start. She's supposedly gaining access to the system this week," Fitz said.

"She can dig around undetected. I'm sure of it." I nodded.

"This is more covert than I expected," James said.

"If we do this, it must be that way. The Opimaean teams can't discover what we're doing," Solomon said.

James's energy stirred restlessly.

"I know this makes you uneasy, James," I said. "We can leave you out of the loop if you'd prefer, but I agree with Fitz on this one. We need to know for sure who we can trust."

James nodded, lost in thought. "I'm no keen on it," he admitted. "But I ken you'll do this regardless."

"James—" I began.

"No, Hadley. I dinnae mean that despairingly. I only mean I ken you'll follow your convictions. But I want to be a part of this—especially if the court members condone it."

It was Fitz's turn to raise an eyebrow.

"I ken it surprises you. But there are no rules here. We must follow our instincts, and we need to ken the truth, as well. I cannae trust the fate of our world to half-truths from Opimae. Let us do what must be done."

I smiled, both surprised and encouraged by James's agreement.

"I wonder if it's worth Hadley spirit-travelling back to the fortress?" Ian asked.

"Dad . . . no," Fitz said.

"She's brought information back with her each time she's gone to Lorenzo's fortress," Ian argued.

"Aye, but the last time, things escalated. We learned there are consequences with Lorenzo, and I think it's a bad idea to send her alone."

I remained quiet. Truthfully, I wasn't certain of my opinion. I wanted to believe I could be useful again in that way, but now that I knew everything at stake, I needed to be smart about this decision.

"What if we run a stealth mission to the fortress—just a couple folks," Chloe said. "You could transport just outside and take a look around."

"We haven't seen anything of the exterior," I said. "It could be useful for future missions."

Fitz nodded. "Aye, that I agree with."

I offered Fitz a tight smile as I considered our first Opimaean mission coming together.

"A fine idea, Chloe," said James.

"I don't think you two should go together," Mia said, looking to me and Fitz.

"And why not?" I asked.

"Because Fitz's protective instincts are still too strong."

"I can manage," Fitz said.

"I disagree."

The room fell silent.

"They make a good team," Ian said. "And when they combine their powers, they're a force I've not seen before."

"I can imagine," Mia said. "But I still worry about Fitz's instincts. My concern is that he won't be able to curb them, and he'll leave himself vulnerable."

I wanted to argue, but I couldn't. I'd had the same worry since our encounter with Jess.

Chloe sighed. "I hear your concern, Mia. This should be pretty low impact though. It's a transport in and out."

"Molly could go with us," I proposed. "Then we'd have two time-walkers."

"As could I," Solomon said.

"Three time-walkers are good odds," James said.

I hadn't realized Solomon was a time-walker.

"It does increase the group size," Ian said. "Which concerns me for a stealth mission. But . . . I ken Solomon is quite experienced in this area."

"I've scouted more times than I can count," Solomon said. "My background is military—I served for several years after university before joining the council. The four of us would be fine, I believe."

His expertise put some of my nerves at ease. At least we'd have an experienced scout traveling with us on our first mission in Opimae.

In the end, we all agreed that the four of us would scout the area around Lorenzo's fortress in two days' time. The following day would be too busy, and Jordan could use the extra time to dig around in the system for more information.

"Let's keep this mission between us for now," I proposed. "I don't want the rest of the team distracted with this."

"A good call," Solomon said.

"And we should schedule a meeting with Charles to discuss our concerns," Ian added.

"Aye," James said. "Charles is reasonable. We should see where we get with him."

Chloe's mouth twisted at James's words.

"What is it, Chloe?" Mia asked.

"He didn't seem all that reasonable in our meeting."

"I can't believe he was against our request with Jess," I said.

"I got the feeling he wasn't necessarily against it. But more like his hands were tied."

"He'll likely need consent from the others in the chamber in order to increase our involvement," James said. "But he's influential with the others—I believe he does hold the power to sway them into being more direct with us."

Fitz nodded. "You're right. We should find a way to promote trust between us and Charles so he'll be willing to fight with us for what we need. Trust is the only way this is going to work."

A smile spread across James's lips.

"What is it?" I asked.

"We're already in deep. But you're thinking like leaders."

CHAPTER TWELVE

The following morning, I took a deep breath and knocked on Charles's office door. He beckoned me inside, and I took a seat.

"I'm just finishing up this report. Please, make yourself comfortable."

"No rush," I said, looking around absentmindedly.

Charles had done little in the way of decorating his space. The stone walls were covered haphazardly in maps. Burgundy rugs with swirling patterns of faded white, navy, and gold covered the wooden floors. It was quiet except for Charles's pen scratching across paper.

I studied Charles's maps. Most of them were Opimae-based, but he also displayed maps of Earth. The High Divide Trail, Olympic National Park, Washington State. I thought of the first time I'd seen similar maps in another witch's office—the maps Lorenzo had utilized to flee to Opimae with Fitz's family's ring.

"Do you miss home?" Charles asked, breaking my focus. He slid his note into an envelope.

"In some ways, sure. But despite the reason we're here, it's been nice to see your world."

Charles nodded. He sealed the envelope, snapped his fingers, and it disappeared.

"Brigitta said you wished to speak with me about Jess. Chloe raised your concerns to me yesterday."

"I thought it might be helpful to hear directly from me."

Charles nodded for me to proceed.

"I'm uncomfortable with Jess, and I'm formally requesting a different trainer."

"Chloe mentioned that Jess looked in on you."

"He stalked me," I said firmly.

Charles held my gaze for a moment and then nodded.

"Fitz and I were stalked by two other witches who are still unknown to us," I said. "After we lost them, Jess showed up. He watched me several times—it was unnerving, and Fitz and I wondered for months about his identity, only to have him show up in Opimae and be assigned as my trainer."

Charles nodded. "I did speak with Jess about the matter. He informed me he was doing some due diligence with you—observing you so he could formulate training plans."

"I hadn't even been approached about the crusade when this began, so I certainly hadn't accepted this mission," I said. Charles held my gaze but remained quiet. "And then there's the fact that he didn't watch anyone else."

"While I understand your concern about that, you are the only witch who came into her powers as an adult. That does set you apart."

I shook my head. "It still makes no sense. Why would he go through the trouble of crossing over to Earth just to observe a witch who hadn't even been assigned to his program yet?"

"You would have to ask Jess about that," Charles said.

"I don't want to ask him, Charles. I don't want to talk to him at all."

Charles sighed. "Hadley . . . I understand that you're unhappy with this decision. And I apologize that Jess alarmed you. But I'm going to be straight with you—he is the best fit for this role, and the chamber won't support a change."

"Why?"

"Because you're preparing for battle, and he's the best trainer we have."

"You're certain about that?" I asked skeptically.

"Just give him a chance," Charles said. "His intentions are in the right place, and even though I hate that you're uncomfortable, training with Jess is what's going to give you a fighting chance in the field. He has trained our very best agents. You deserve the same."

I was quiet, calculating my next move. I understood Jess was good at his job, but I still couldn't get past what he'd done. My heart sank.

"Jess is willing to forgive the incident from the other night. Perhaps we'll call it even and move on."

"You know about that?" I asked, my pulse quickening.

"Fitz wasn't easy on him. Jess's injuries were apparent the following morning, and when I asked him about it, he shrugged it off. I checked his medical records, and he hadn't logged anything that matched his injuries. When I questioned him the second time, he couldn't avoid the truth."

"Will there be any consequences for this?" I asked.

Charles dropped his gaze momentarily.

"There should be, but . . . you can thank the Adamo crisis for a shift in focus. No one is thinking of Fitz's violence right now."

Fitz's violence—I didn't much like the sound of that.

"I understand violence is frowned upon, but Jess found me alone and made me uncomfortable—again. I find it interesting that you overlook Jess's indiscretions while claiming there should be consequences for Fitz defending me."

Charles sighed. "It's not the same."

"Oh, I can agree with that."

Charles raised his eyebrows. "I understand your position, but if something like this happens again, I'm afraid it won't be overlooked. The nations of Opimae are still divided regarding your relation to the prophecy, and even if you two are the promised leaders, there are limits to what we are willing to overlook."

That wasn't what I had hoped to hear, but at least it had been said.

"There's no changing your mind about Jess being reassigned, is there?" I asked.

"I'm afraid not."

"So much for being the land of progress," I said.

"What do you mean?" Charles asked, though I was certain he already knew the answer to that.

"I tell you that a guy stalked me, made me uncomfortable, and you try to explain away the behavior. I tell you I'm uncomfortable working with him now, and you tell me to give him a chance? Give a chance to the guy who stalked me?"

And then you claim my mate should be punished for defending me against him.

I shook my head.

"No, Charles." My voice rose. "I guess I don't have much choice when it comes to training with him. But I won't give him a chance. He doesn't deserve that from me."

I stood and made my way to the door.

"I won't hold you up any longer, but just know this: you handled this poorly, and I won't forget what you've done here today. When you're ready to be an institution deserving of its title, let me know."

I shut the door a bit more forcefully than I meant to as I exited the room. Fitz was waiting in a chair nearby.

"Any lu—" Fitz hesitated, scanning my face. "He said no to the reassignment."

"Yep."

"Do you want me to give it a try?"

I shook my head. "Thank you—I know it comes from a place of concern, but it's not going to do us any good. Charles knows about your scuffle with Jess."

His face fell. "I'm sorry, love," he said, embracing me. "I'm sorry about all of it."

I pulled back, looking into his eyes. "I'm sorry too."

"You don't need to apologize," he said.

"Yeah, I do. I lost my temper. And I know when I went after Lorenzo, it scared you, and it was a reckless move, and . . ." I sighed. "Unfortunately, I know I'd do the same thing all over again if he walked down this hallway right now."

Fitz nodded slowly, his energy tight. "And unfortunately, I'll lose my temper with Jess again because I think the bastard still isn't done meddling with you."

My lips twisted as I sorted out my response. Finally, I said, "I thought I'd still be angry with you about that, but I'm not."

"Not to question my luck, but why is that?" he asked.

"Because we're going on this mission tomorrow. With all the factors we're dealing with and the danger to come, and I don't want to spend our time arguing." I thought of Henry and Molly. I thought of the time they hadn't had with their mates.

Fitz rested his hand on my shoulder, his finger rubbing along my jawline.

"I don't want to end up in this situation again with Jess, though," I said, pointing toward Charles's office.

"I wish Charles had listened to you."

"You and me both," I said. "But I have a plan."

Fitz's gaze was questioning.

"I'm going to focus on getting through training quickly," I said. "But if Jess pulls anything else with me, you don't need to intervene. I swear to the heavens I'll use my fire power and take care of this issue myself."

Fitz kissed the top of my head. "There's my wee firecracker. I hope I'm around to see it."

My anger was already dissolving into disappointment, but I managed a laugh.

"Let's go find Molly and finish prepping for this intelligence mission. I'll be damned if we're relying on Opimae for anything we don't have to."

CHAPTER THIRTEEN

The following morning, I stood in an obscure training room alongside Fitz, Solomon, and Molly. Chloe, Mia, and Ian sat at a nearby table. Should anyone come calling, they'd share that we were doing some additional training on transport.

We moved into place, and the time-walkers began a quick meditation to focus on our destination. Observing Fitz's transport prowess was fascinating. We operated so differently, not only because our powers drew from different sources, but also because of the way we accessed them. I was forever asking the elements to move and shift to help me complete my needs. Though Fitz also drew upon the elements, his power simply connected to them without request, constantly in communion. While the rest of us were taking those extra few seconds to connect, he was already influencing the elements, effectively remaining a step ahead.

Fitz extended his arm, signaling that he was ready for me. I tucked myself in front of him, and he wrapped his arms around me as I laid my head against his chest. We stood motionless. The hum of the heater was distracting, but it blocked the noise of the city well. The tile flooring was cold and lifeless, and I wished more than anything to be outside with my feet planted firmly in the earth.

"Focus," Fitz whispered. "It's time to go."

I pulled my mind back to our mission.

"Ready," I whispered back.

The air rippled around us, wavering until everything fell out of focus.

It all happened quite quickly—and differently from the last time we'd traveled through the in-between together. The darkness and then the stars came into focus, but gravity maintained a firmer hold on us, and I wondered if that was due to the change in planet.

Finally, the darkness cleared, and we stumbled on to a cliff's edge blanketed in snow.

"We did it," Fitz said, relief palpable in his voice.

"Of course you did." I smiled.

I peered over the cliffside, and the world swam. The drop-off was one of the least forgiving I'd ever seen—and I'd seen many over the years hiking the Olympic Mountains with my father. Fitz tightened his grip on my hand, and we waited for our companions.

"I'm surprised we arrived first. I thought I would slow you down," I said.

"Gravity meddled with me a bit, but the journey was easier than normal. I think your focus helped now that you've mastered your spirit-travel—it gave us an advantage."

Fitz's magic seemed to meld with mine when we worked as a team, making us a powerful unit. Just another way in which we felt seamless.

The air beside us rippled, and Molly stepped through the elements. She was quickly followed by Solomon. A satisfied grin spread across my lips.

Molly pulled a map from her coat pocket and opened it. A red dotted line snaked across the paper.

"If we've met our mark, we should be really close," she said.

"Let's find out." I looked ahead of us.

The snow was thick, though we'd already planned for that.

We each whispered to the elements, asking the snow to support us. Solomon took a confident step ahead, and though his shoes crunched against the snow, he didn't sink. Molly followed suit, and I turned to Fitz. He nodded. I took a deep breath, and then a timid step forward. Sure enough, the snow held firm.

A thick cluster of trees lay ahead, confirming we were headed in the right direction. The snow was heavy on the tree branches, and under their canopy, we found a reprieve from the blustering wind. We collectively sighed in relief. The path was dark, but we wouldn't risk a light—we were too close to the fortress. We pressed forward slowly, leaning heavily on our witches' eyes and minding our steps.

I stifled a gasp as we emerged from the tree line. A towering fortress reached toward the sky, a bulk of gray stonework that seemingly erupted from the snow-covered ground. Steep mountainsides stretched upward, surrounding the fortress on three sides, and snowflakes fell in a thick flurry all around us.

"Who would live here?" I muttered. But, of course, it made sense for this to serve as Lorenzo's headquarters. The elements were brutal enough to contribute to the area's isolation, even if a war-mongering witch hadn't made the stretch of wasteland above us his home.

We tucked ourselves back into the tree line and squatted under the cover of shadows. On the east side of the fortress lay a road that ran through the mountain pass, which was currently empty though clearly used, as the snow was kept clear. To the south of the fortress, a small ridge line ran from the western mountain to the tree line where we currently sought refuge. "The ridge line would offer the most coverage," I said.

"Aye," Fitz agreed. "We can transport just over there."

He pointed toward a section of eroded stone along the ridge line that would offer ample footing.

"That seems like a good position to see more," Molly said. "Solomon?"

"I don't see a better option," he said, scanning the area. "Let's go."

I held on to Fitz, and before I could even register the in-between, we were on the other side of the clearing.

From our new position, the backside of the fortress was clearly in view. The walls looked impenetrable, but I strained my eyes, searching for anything useful.

"I see a small opening," Solomon said. "I think I'll check it out quickly."

We nodded, and Solomon disappeared. When he materialized, he stood near the stone wall. He jumped and then hovered a few feet in the air. He brushed the snow around, attempting to hide his tracks.

"He's going to wear himself out with all this magic," Molly observed.

"This is a lot. How are you two feeling?" I asked.

"Just fine so far," Molly answered.

"Aye, I'm good," Fitz said. "But we should keep track of our vitals. You know how it can sneak up on you."

Molly nodded.

Solomon floated closer to the small opening he'd noticed and halted abruptly. He pushed himself against the wall but made no move to return to us. I closed my eyes and opened my witch's eye at full capacity. I found another witch's energy near Solomon. I wanted to use my spirit travel to investigate, but I couldn't leave my uninhabited body to be Fitz's burden until we had Solomon's report. I opened my eyes instead and waited. Finally, Solomon returned.

"There are guard stations along the walls. Hadley, can you spirit-travel to locate them all and report back?"

"Absolutely."

"Fitz, you said Hadley could speak to your mind in her spirit form?"

"Aye."

"Hadley, report your findings to Fitz, and Molly can document them on the map. We'll be here with your body, and Fitz will alert you if we need to depart quickly."

I tucked myself against the rock wall that shielded us from the snow, and Fitz slid an arm around me to support my body. A bit of apprehension flashed through his eyes, and I offered a soft smile.

"Be careful, Hads." His lips thinned with concern.

I nodded, cradling his face in my hands. "Don't worry about me. I'll be right back."

I closed my eyes and sank deep into my mind—and with a gentle push, my spirit separated from my body. I moved quickly toward the fortress, not wanting to waste any time. I wandered around the perimeter searching for openings and reported my findings to Fitz. I worked my way around until I came to the north side of the structure.

The snow still flurried all around me and stacked itself high against the fortress wall. But one small section, roughly the size of a garage door, was free of snow. As I moved closer, I focused on my connection to my body and waited for my senses to heighten. Sure enough, the air grew warmer. Though I saw no source of heat, the snow sizzled as it met the dark soil near the fortress wall.

I felt along the stones and recognized the threads of Lorenzo's energy—a protection spell to keep snooping witches from entering his lair. But something else nipped at my fingertips—there was a break in Lorenzo's spell, and the current of another witch's magic spanned the warm space until it connected with Lorenzo's energy at the other side. The spell wasn't for protection . . . it was some sort of break in Lorenzo's magic to allow entry . . .

Which meant that someone besides me had worked loophole magic.

Curious, I reached my hand through the wall.

"*Hadley.*" Fitz's voice passed through my mind, effectively halting my progress. "*Is everything all right?*"

"*Yes. I'm on to something. Give me just a moment.*"

I passed through the wall into Lorenzo's fortress. The space was dim, and I waited for my eyes to adjust. Slowly, the room came into focus. Rows of supplies spanned countless shelves, and I walked past every-thing from bandages to clothing racks before reaching a wooden door with an iron ring. I walked through it and into a long hallway.

The hallway seemed familiar, though I couldn't be sure if it was the same one from my previous spirit-travels. I'd meandered halfway down the hall when a wooden door caught my attention. I stepped through it into a familiar room. Unlike the day I'd found Gabriella and Camille warming themselves by the fireside, the space was empty. I stopped to consider where Lorenzo's office lay in relation when a face forever seared into my memory materialized only a few feet from me.

From his inky eyes to his dark hair and his chiseled athletic build, there was no mistaking Lorenzo Belmonte for anyone else.

His eyes lit in recognition.

"Lorenzo," I said softly. My breath hitched and I shifted my stance slightly, readying myself for whatever he had planned.

"You *are* a fighter, aren't you?" He grinned. "What are you doing here?"

"I saw you at the celebration, but you left before we could talk. So, I've come to speak with you."

"I see you're more forthcoming than you were in our last conversation. A wise choice," he said.

"Why did you leave so quickly?" I asked, deciding it was best to keep him talking.

"It was too crowded. There was no place to talk. But it was worth the journey to see you in your true form, instead of this." He waved in my direction. "It was just as I'd imagined it. Though I wish we'd had more time."

"What did you want to discuss?" I asked.

"Have you given any more thought to my proposal?"

"To join your side?" I asked. "No, I haven't."

Lorenzo shook his head. "I hate to see your potential wasted by the councils, Hadley."

"Why would I join you?"

"I told you—I want to create a world free from oppression. You know better than anyone what the witchkind governments are capable of. They've grown too powerful, and their power is unchecked."

I instinctively took a step back.

"I think they'd say the same of you," I challenged.

"Perhaps," he said dismissively. "But I only want to restore what they've broken."

"My, what an altruistic mission."

Lorenzo took a step closer, and I followed suit, stepping left, feigning leisurely movements in my attempt to distance myself from him.

"Your sarcasm stings, Hadley."

"Oh, I think you'll be just fine."

Lorenzo and I continued our silent dance. After my last encounter with him in this fortress, I couldn't allow him to get close to me this time. I took a deep breath, fighting to steady my racing heart.

"You are an interesting case. You want the same thing that I do, yet you fight against me. You truly are the most complex little creature."

I looked around the room, thinking through my options. My spirit was still connected with the air, so I might be able to transport out of the room without issue. The windowpanes would likely be cloaked in Lorenzo's protection spell, but if I needed to break through it to find my way out, I was confident I could. There was no other escape except for the door, but that would only lead me further into the fortress.

My eyes flickered back to Lorenzo. He was moving in the direction of the door. He thought that would be my plan.

Good.

"Surely, you're not thinking of leaving just yet. We've hardly had time to talk."

He was positioned just in front of a large painting near the doorway. I recalled the way the painting had nipped at my intuition the first time I'd been in the room. It depicted a scene around a fireside. A figure stood brightly against the scene in a red cloak. The figure seemed to be watching another, with . . .

With auburn hair in a navy cloak.

Oh god.

It couldn't be . . . except it was.

The two of us at the autumnal festival. I had to leave the fortress immediately.

Lorenzo drew nearer, and my head began to cloud at his thick scent, just as it had during my last spirit travel to his fortress. I couldn't risk him preventing me from leaving, so I called to the air and disappeared faster than I had even thought possible. When I woke back in my body, I sat up quickly, much to my team's alarm.

"What happened?" Fitz asked, his brows knit.

"Sorry," I said, my voice urgent, my mind spinning. Why did Lorenzo have a painting of us at the autumnal festival? "We have to go. Lorenzo . . . saw me."

"He what?" Molly said.

"Let's go—now," I ordered.

The sound of voices floated on the breeze. I tugged at Fitz's arm. "Fitz!"

He nodded and pulled me into his embrace.

Solomon closed his eyes for a mere second. "They're coming from above us. Quickly."

The voices grew closer.

Something crunched in the snow above us, and I gasped, looking up. The last thing I saw was a flurry of snowflakes before the world started spinning, and everything went black.

CHAPTER FOURTEEN

Mia wasn't pleased with my decision to enter Lorenzo's fortress, especially since he'd seen me, but Solomon pointed out that I was merely following a lead.

Truthfully, it was a gray area, but I had chosen to follow my instincts. In the end, we'd identified several entry points in Lorenzo's fortress, along with the strange opening that I thought might have escaped Lorenzo's notice. I'd also told Fitz of my revelation about the painting, though we'd decided not to share that information with Opimaean forces, at least not yet.

Jordan and I wandered through Magna Park the following afternoon on our lunch break. The prime minister of Arregaithel had returned home to deal with the aftermath of Adamo, but he was due back that afternoon to give a report. We took advantage of the delay to get some fresh air.

The grounds of the park were impressive, rivaling New York's

Central Park. We'd walked on its southern end near headquarters many times, but Jordan and I wanted to explore the northern area, as it adjoined a sizable lake that pooled from the city's snaking river.

We were joined by Keoni, who was a fast favorite of the team. He was telling us about an annual festival in Constantina, the southern elven kingdom, when he halted, touching his ear. The chatter from his earpiece wasn't discernible, but the tone of voice sounded urgent. His eyes narrowed.

"We must return to the offices immediately."

A black SUV pulled onto the sidewalk near us, and we ran across the distance and climbed into the backseat. The car quickly gained speed.

"What's going on?" I asked.

"Someone infiltrated the government system," Keoni said.

"Whoever it is knows where we all are," Jordan said gravely.

"Exactly. You've been requested back at headquarters. You'll be safe there."

"Hurry, please," I called to the driver. "Keoni, do they know anything yet?"

"I don't have details—just orders. They'll send more information shortly. We'll have you briefed as soon as possible."

The radio buzzed with feedback just before a shrill noise sounded through the comms system. Keoni pulled out his earpiece, his face scrunched in pain.

"What an awful noise," Jordan said. "Was that . . ."

"Yes," Keoni answered.

"Someone get me up to speed," I said.

"They're back in, and they've disconnected the system. We've gone dark, at least for now," Jordan offered calmly. It was difficult to rattle Jordan after a couple of years at the FBI.

"Shit." I stared through the windshield, whispering a prayer under my breath, when I realized something odd.

"Hey, where are we going?" I asked.

Jordan leaned forward. "You took the wrong freeway entrance."

There was nothing but silence from the front seats. And suddenly—it hit me. A wave of familiar energy radiated from the driver seat of the car.

"No, it can't be," I said.

"What is it?" Jordan asked.

The driver's eyes flickered to mine and I was sure.

"Parisian stalker," I said simply.

Jordan's eyes grew wide, horrified.

"Yes, you lost us in Paris, and we had to come all the way over here to find you again," he said in a thick German accent.

"Why come all this way just for me?" I asked.

His jaw set tight, and his eyes focused back on the road.

Keoni swore. "Stop the car right now!"

More silence.

Keoni reached for the gun on his belt when a being seemingly appeared from nowhere in the third row, striking Keoni with such a blow that he instantly lost consciousness.

"Leave him alone!" Jordan yelled.

I glanced at Keoni's belt, at the gun resting in the holster, but the man pulled my braid and reached for the gun. I connected with the air and sent the gun flying out of his reach. I shot forward, but he yanked my hair and pulled me back before I could grab it. The man leaned forward and snatched the weapon before I had the chance, but I channeled my power and blasted energy toward his hand. It was forceful enough to knock the gun from his grasp, shattering the car window. The man yelled and leaned back in his seat, his dark hair falling back to reveal his pointed ears.

Something struck my head with force, and the world went black.

I opened my eyes, startled. I looked around, and quickly realized something was wrong.

Shit.

The violent elf had knocked me unconscious, and my spirit had separated from my body. Jordan was holding my still form, her eyes filled with a burning rage. The elf held a knife in his hands as he studied her.

Think, Hadley.

I felt my connection back to my physical form. I was okay, I realized, but not quite ready to wake up.

Keoni's eyelids fluttered, and I thought there might be hope for us yet. We had to act fast, but I hardly knew what to do. I connected to the elements, thinking through our options.

"Keoni," I whispered to his mind. "*If you can hear me, stay still. Keep your eyes closed.*"

His eyelids squeezed tightly.

"*Wiggle your left thumb.*"

He did.

"*I think I have an idea, but I need you to stay still for a minute. Okay?*"

His thumb wiggled again. Still too disoriented to speak back into my mind, I guessed. I switched to a wavelength leading to Jordan.

"*Jordan, if you can hear me, look out the window. I have an idea.*"

Jordan's eyes widened, but she followed the instructions.

"*Just a minute, and I'll let you know what to do.*"

I studied the driver once more. This made no sense . . . an Earthside being traveling all this way. And where was he taking me?

I looked in the passenger seat. The being's energy was familiar in some way. And then it clicked—he was a druid. From his energy to his gray robe, he was every bit a Bain resident. He unknowingly caught my gaze and his eyes narrowed as his brows furrowed, clearly sensing that something was amiss. Yes, this was a druid all right.

I waited for the car to make the next turn, mentally thumbing through the maps we'd painstakingly committed to memory. We turned north toward Bain and Arregaithel.

My mind raced. I had the distinct feeling we were heading for Bain. Not only was King Alden against our involvement in the mission, but his hostility toward us was palpable. It was clear that even his staff was displeased with our presence in Opimae . . . but were they angry enough for this? Studying the druid in the front seat, I couldn't discredit the idea.

We needed to exit the car before we drove over the border into Bain. Even if I could wake up, if we attacked now, we'd fly off the bridge. We'd have time to float ourselves into the air, but Jordan's levitation was so new, and I wasn't sure if Keoni would be able to call on that power in his current state. But if we waited to return to solid ground, I thought we might find ourselves already in the mountain passes, which were just as dangerous—maybe more so.

I followed my path to Keoni.

"If I'm able to stop the car, can we take these guys?"

"Honestly . . . I don't think so," he said. It was a good sign that he could respond, though I shivered. It was always eerie having someone else in your head. *"I don't think we have the time or the numbers to take them on. Jordan is doing well with her combat training, but she's new to it, and she's human. I can rally through this head injury, but I don't know if you and I are enough. If we attack the driver, we'll likely just crash, and we can't anticipate their reactions. The car makes this delicate."*

Then it clicked. We would cross a lake just before the road forked to head into the mountain passes. That was our chance. I hovered as closely to my physical form as I could without connecting and felt around. I was ready—I could wake myself up.

"I could wreak havoc on the car's engine—make a real scene. We'd have the element of surprise, and I could do it once we're over the lake."

"I don't know . . ."

"I don't think we'll figure out a better plan."

Silence. And then, *"You're right. If we wait for the passes, I think we have little chance of coming back."*

"We'll crash, but I don't know how badly," I said.

"Protect your head as best you can."

"When we make impact, I need you to blow out every window this thing has, and I'll have the air pull the car straight to the water instead of rolling on the pavement. Can you do that?"

"Yeah. It'll be quite a few moving parts, but let's knock their heads against the dash, and then we'll only have the one guy behind us to deal with," Keoni answered.

I relayed the plan to Jordan, who nodded subtly and held tightly to the door handle.

It was going to be difficult to carry out the act and ground ourselves to our seats at the same time—especially since I needed to spot Jordan. But it was our only shot.

Our driver moved into the right lane, making the implementation of my plan easier. A little luck was on our side, at least. A sign flashed by indicating our exit-only lane would soon take us into Bain. The exit was already in view. We were almost out of time.

I focused my energy into reconnecting with my body, and suddenly, I was back. My chest felt heavy, and my head pounded so badly I thought it might explode. My neck ached, I guessed from the way the elf had made impact, and I resisted the urge to rub it, remaining incredibly still. I took a chance and allowed my eyelids to flutter open.

The elf was typing on his device, his knife still poised in one hand, ready to strike. I peered around Keoni, and the beautiful blue water of the alpine lake came into view.

My heart beat so wildly, I thought it would flee my chest. I closed my eyes, concentrating on the front of the car. I felt its vibrations. I listened to the hum of the engine. And then I wished it was no longer intact. And suddenly—it wasn't.

An explosion sounded through the quiet as flames leapt from the engine. We hit the bridge's barrier and flipped. I concentrated on keeping myself and Jordan safe, while Keoni blew the windows open. Glass flew across the space, and for a second, time slowed. Tiny fragments floated through the air, catching the light of the afternoon sun, before I saw past them. The world was a blur, and my mind couldn't make sense of what my eyes were seeing. It could have been seconds that passed—I hardly knew—before my side of the car made impact with the water, and aqua blue rushed into focus. My sinuses burned as the water rushed through my nose, and I beat back the panic rising in my body.

The car was filling with water faster than I imagined possible, and I pushed my head against the ceiling, gasping for air. Panic coursed through my veins as I dipped my head back underwater. Keoni's eyes were closed, and his limbs floated lazily beside him. I turned to Jordan, who also appeared unconscious. I shook her furiously, hoping for some sort of reaction, and miraculously, it worked. As she opened her eyes, a thud sounded through the water like an explosion, causing ripples. The world was growing fuzzy, but two orbs of amber light glowed distinctly beside me.

Someone grabbed my arm and pulled me from the window as the car attempted to drag us down with it. In a matter of seconds, I was on top of the water, and the two orbs stared back at me.

Jordan. The glowing orbs were her eyes.

I thought of her odd reaction to the water our second day in Opimae, what Saoirse had mentioned about glowing eyes, Jordan's unbelievable ability underwater . . . and it clicked.

Water witch.

"I'm going back for Keoni," Jordan said. "Can you levitate to the bridge?"

I stared wordlessly for a second too long.

"Hadley!" she yelled.

"Yes—go!"

Jordan shot underwater, and I focused my attention on the bridge above. Cars had stopped, and a crowd was forming along the railing. I locked my eyes on a woman with the most beautiful long, gray hair, and I asked the elements to guide me toward her. Soft energy nudged my body, and I realized the witches above were helping me navigate the elements.

Once my feet were on solid ground, I turned, looking for Jordan.

"How many others are there?" a man yelled.

"Two of my companions. We were taken hostage. Three of our captors are still down there, too."

"I'll help."

The witch's eyes emitted a strange blue light. It was captivating. He dove over the side, and shortly after, Jordan popped up with Keoni.

"Are you okay?" I shouted to Jordan.

"I'm fine. Just levitate Keoni up to the bridge for me."

In the end, Jordan and our new water witch companion, Gustavo, brought two of our captors to the surface. One had sustained a fatal injury during the crash and was pronounced dead on scene. Our driver— one of my Parisian stalkers—had sustained life-threatening injuries and was transported to the hospital by two time-walkers and a military medic. And the third, the elf who'd injured Keoni, had disappeared. He was either lost to the lake or had somehow escaped.

I turned to Jordan. "Holy shit, J."

She hugged me fiercely. "I don't know where it came from. When we hit the water, something in me changed."

"I think you just became the witch you were meant to be. And I was lucky enough to witness it."

CHAPTER FIFTEEN

The sight of headquarters was a welcome one. Fitz and Solomon came running from the front of the building. I leapt from the car and into Fitz's arms.

"Thank god you're here," Fitz said, his breathy voice betraying his fear.

"It's okay. I'm okay."

He pulled back, running his hands along my body. "Are you hurt?"

My shoulder was loud with pain, but I didn't want to worry him further.

"I'm a little banged up, but I'll be fine."

"Let's get you inside. Medical is waiting."

Solomon threw an arm supportively around Keoni and walked toward the entrance as Henry burst through the door. He hugged me fiercely before looking at Jordan, his face relaxing at the sight of her. She enveloped him in a hug, and he promptly carried her inside. Though she could walk, her ankle had taken a beating, and Henry wouldn't hear of it.

Shouting erupted from the far side of the room as we entered the medical triage area. Tanner was in Jess's face.

"You better tell us where he is right now!" Tanner bellowed.

"I already told you I don't know where he is," Jess shot back.

"What's going on?" I asked.

"It's James—he's been captured. A live feed was sent to our intelligence teams," Chloe said.

"Tanner, *stand down!*" Mia shouted.

"You had something to do with this. I can smell it on you!" Tanner yelled, ignoring Mia.

"Someone better calm him down right now, or I'll make him." I'd never seen Mia so angry. Her fingertips were tinged an icy hue.

"Hey!" I called to Mia. "You're entirely too worked up—you need to dial back your anger."

Her glare shifted to me. "Don't tell me what to do."

I dropped my gaze to her fingertips, which had turned fully blue.

"I'd never lose control," she said.

Normally, I would have agreed. But I'd never seen Mia like this. She huffed, and my fingertips blazed red. She dropped her gaze to my fingers and rolled her eyes.

Chloe shoved her way in between Tanner and Jess and stared at Tanner until he made eye contact. His jaw was set tight, but I already saw defeat in his eyes. I realized he didn't have it in him to ignore Chloe. Even in the chaos, my eyes met Molly's, and she arched an eyebrow.

"Let's get some fresh air, Tanner," Chloe said.

Tanner held Jess's gaze for a few seconds longer, his eyes shimmering in gold—his electrokinesis was at full capacity, ready to strike. He finally nodded and walked toward the door.

Chloe turned to face Jess. "You'd better be telling the truth, Jess. Because if you did have anything to do with this, I'll gut you myself."

Jess stared wordlessly; his face was impassible. Chloe followed Tanner's footsteps, and the room fell quiet.

"It wasn't Jess," I offered unceremoniously. Every set of eyes in the room fell on me.

"How do you know that?" Fitz asked.

"Because the male stalker from Paris just tried to abduct us. So my money's on Ms. Parisian Stalker."

"Did your captors say anything, Hadley?" Ian asked.

"Nothing about his intentions or where we were headed. But we were driving toward the mountain passes—toward Bain."

"Bain?" Charles said.

"We were in the exit lane. There was a druid in the front seat. And then I started thinking . . . King Alden would wish us gone if he could."

"Let's not get ahead of ourselves, Hadley," Charles said. "King Alden would not condone an act like this."

"At the very least, he's been vocal about his opposition to us. The Parisian stalker clearly has allies, so perhaps Bain helped him. Or perhaps that's where he's coincidentally set up shop . . . in the nation that's against us."

"That's unfair," Charles said.

"Is it?" I asked.

"There are enough hints to arouse suspicion," Jordan said. I could see her analyst mind ticking through the facts.

"We should consider this as a possibility and investigate it," Fitz said.
  Charles sighed.

"Do you have a more plausible theory, Charles?" Ian asked.

"I think we must consider Lorenzo. Perhaps they're working together."

"There's currently no evidence to support that claim, although if the druids are involved . . ."

"Hadley," Charles interjected, pinching the bridge of his nose.

I raised my hands in mock surrender, letting it go—for now.

"I don't know what would have prompted this, though," Charles said. "It doesn't make sense to me that this was Lorenzo's next move."

There was one reason I could think of.

A flurry of glances were exchanged between me, Fitz, Mia, Solomon, and Molly.

"What are you not saying?" Charles asked.

I started to answer but hesitated. Fitz released a low sigh.

"The longer you wait, the longer it'll take us to find James," Charles said.

"We conducted a quick scouting mission yesterday," Solomon said.

Charles tilted his head in Solomon's direction, his eyebrows arched.

"Hadley was in her spirit form, but Lorenzo recognized her," he continued.

"Why would you do this? Why wasn't I informed?" Charles demanded.

"If you're not going to be forthcoming with us, why do you demand that we be forthcoming with you?" I asked.

"What?" Charles asked, taken aback.

"You've kept us at arm's length," Fitz said. "We learned nothing from Intelligence until the day Adamo fell. And even then, it was only because we fought for it after information was shared in front of us by accident."

"We were allowing time for you to acclimate," Charles argued.

"I didn't buy that excuse the other day, and I don't buy it now," I said, trying to keep my tone even.

"We're doing what we can to help you adjust to Opimae, learn about this world, and keep you safe. But we can't do that if you're running around doing covert missions that we know nothing about." Charles voice was terse.

"Oh, here we go," Mia muttered.

"Keep us safe? Is that why you put a witch who stalked me in charge of my training? Is that your idea of safety?" I yelled.

"And is your idea of collaboration keeping information from us?" Charles asked.

"I don't know, Charles. You tell me. You seem to be good at that. You didn't even let us know Lorenzo had returned to *Earth*!"

"Enough!" Solomon said. "Both of you need to calm down."

"We need to focus on finding James," Mia interjected. "And Hadley, you need to sit down so the healers can evaluate your injuries."

I was fuming, and my heart raced wildly in my chest. I refused to release Charles's gaze.

"Come on, Hads," Fitz said, resting his hand gently on mine. "Take a seat, and let's make sure you're all right."

Finally, I nodded and answered his request. Jordan followed suit, and the healers set to work as conversations continued.

"Now, why does Tanner think Jess had something to do with

this?" Fitz asked.

"Because I was with James when he was abducted," Jess said.

Fitz's energy rustled at Jess's voice, but he remained civil.

"What happened?" I asked.

Charles crossed his arms and turned his attention to Jess.

"James asked to have our session today in the park. I had no issue with that. We were mid-session when two witches showed up and took him."

"Was there a fight? Was he injured?" Jordan asked, concern flooding her face.

"There was a skirmish, but we were surprised, and they were quick. He was a little scuffed up, but not bad."

I hadn't noticed the fresh cuts on Jess's skin or the sizable bruise along his strong cheekbone.

"Why would they leave you behind?" I asked.

It didn't make sense. Why wouldn't they capture them both?

"It's real work to transport with someone," Molly said. "But if that person is struggling . . . both abductors would have been needed to transport James."

Something nipped at the back of my mind, but Molly's theory made sense.

"Do we have any leads on who these witches are?" I asked.

"None," Charles said flatly.

"Intelligence is working hard to identify leads, I'm sure," Keoni said. He'd remained quiet through the heated exchange, but his complexion was returning to its warm, golden hue.

"Yes, of course. This is the hardest part," Charles said. "The waiting."

I tapped my foot anxiously, and Fitz reached for my hand. Gustavo was escorted into the room, and a healer signaled him over.

"Jordan, what happened out there?" Isaac asked. "Your eyes . . ."

"Apparently, they changed once we hit the water."

"Once we were submerged and she opened her eyes, this muffled explosion sounded through the water. And then her eyes began to glow, illuminating the whole area around us. And then . . ." I prompted.

"And then I just knew what to do. I could breathe. I could swim better than I ever thought possible. And I brought Hadley to the surface."

"Thank you," Fitz said. "Jordan, I don't know how to thank you."

"You know you don't need to thank me for that. Anyway, she saved my life first, so I returned the favor. We'd never let anything happen to each other." She squeezed my other hand. "Isaac, why did you ask about my eyes? Are they still glowing?"

"They aren't glowing now, don't worry," he answered, smiling. "But they are a different color. They're lighter, like amber."

"That's normal," Gustavo said, grimacing as the healer whispered words that closed a wound on his shoulder. Lacerations scattered across his muscular forearms. He'd obtained most of his injuries pulling a suspect from the vehicle, and after unwittingly walking straight into a major incident, he'd have to give an official statement.

"When kids come into their powers, their eyes lighten," Gustavo continued. "It's because your eyes are adapting to better see under water. It makes them more sensitive to sunlight—you'll never leave home without sunglasses again. But they'll adjust quickly underwater and to low light in general."

Jordan's sudden light sensitivity—it was all making sense.

Jordan swore under her breath. I cocked my head in her direction.

"No, it's nothing. It's just . . . a lot."

"I can only imagine, Jordan," Gustavo said. "If I can help you in any way, answer any questions . . . I'm here."

Jordan hesitated, holding Gustavo's gaze. "Thank you, Gustavo. I'd like that very much."

Gustavo smiled in return, pushing his dark, curly hair away from his face. He was attractive, but more than that, he was ethereal. A warm energy radiated around him, and there was something kind in his soft blue eyes. His cream-colored tunic was pulled over his shoulder where the healer was working, revealing a bronzed, sculpted torso.

He and Jordan studied each other. I wondered if she found something familiar in her fellow water witch's energy.

Once the healers were done with their work, Solomon ensured that Jordan would be allowed straight into Intelligence to assist with the efforts to find James. Jordan eagerly followed Keoni down the hallway to get started.

Charles sighed before turning to me. "We need to know what you learned at the fortress."

Fitz closed our bedroom door softly, his fingers lingering on the handle. I laid my hand on his shoulder, and he turned to me, tears staining the length of his face.

"Oh, Fitz."

His back slid along the door until he was a heap on the ground, and I fell to the floor in front of him. His hands cradled my face.

"I'm so sorry you were worried," I said.

"Don't apologize . . ." He closed his eyes. "I wasn't there. I couldn't find you."

"And that isn't your fault. None of us saw this coming."

"That's the problem," he said.

"You know Jordan will make sure that system gets locked in so tightly. Charles should have given her an expanded role the moment we arrived. It shouldn't have taken this."

Fitz nodded.

"It won't happen again," I said.

He pulled me to him, and I curled into his lap.

"What happened to James might be my fault," I said.

"Why do you think that?"

"I stirred Lorenzo up yesterday. If he's the one behind this, then it's my fault."

"We don't know if he's involved. But even if he is, you can't blame yourself for that, Hadley."

"Oh, but I can," I said. "I shouldn't have done it."

"That's debatable. There's no clear right or wrong."

"Isn't there?"

"No," he shook his head. "There isn't. We'll be faced with more of these quick decisions in the field, and they'll all have a heavy price attached."

We fell silent.

"Hadley, I could feel you today—your nerves, your heartbeat."

I took his face in my hands, but there were no words. I couldn't imagine the tables reversed.

"I knew you were in the water."

"How?"

"A few beads of moisture streaked down my face, I guess when you launched into the water."

My pulse quickened. Our bond was even stronger than I'd realized. Whatever the source of this connection between us truly was, wherever it came from, one thing was certain: it was undeniable.

"The horror on Henry's face will haunt me forever," Fitz continued. "He was afraid for us. The pain he carries from losing Emily . . . it filled my chest."

"But you didn't lose me. Fate favored us today. I'm here now."

Another tear rolled down his cheek, but his hands were firm as he pulled my face to his. I felt the fear leave his body as our lips met, and a surge of adrenaline drummed through mine. He tugged at the hem of my shirt before pausing, his eyes intensely on mine.

"Are you in pain?" he asked, his breath short.

"My shoulder hurts," I admitted. "But . . . don't stop."

He helped me shed my clothing carefully, holding my gaze as the layers between us were removed. Warm adrenaline pumped through my veins, and I closed my eyes to better navigate our connection. Fear and anger still lingered underneath the surface, but slowly, those emotions lessened, replaced with relief and desire that built with each tender touch. He kissed my shoulder gently, his eyes searching mine as his face rose to kiss me properly. My breath came short, but Fitz was only getting started.

I closed my eyes, feeling each subtle change of our energy, every shift in our bodies. The trials of the day and the fear of tomorrow faded away, and I leaned into the reckless joy that bubbled under the surface. I didn't know what the morning would bring, but for tonight, I'd allow myself to feel every single part of being alive and in that moment with Fitz.

CHAPTER SIXTEEN

The following evening finally brought information on James's whereabouts. After much debate, we fought for Jordan to lead a team to track James utilizing her own methods of information gathering. The Earth-side crusaders crowded around a table in a small conference room as Jordan led us through her process and assigned roles to each of us.

Fitz and I were combing through traffic footage when something strange caught my eye. A van rolled through an intersection without stopping, almost causing an accident. The driver looked familiar.

Her long blonde hair was braided to the side, and her brown eyes were lost in the shadows of the dimly lit street.

I paused my screen.

"Fitz. Does she look familiar to you?"

"Parisian stalker."

I nodded. The second half of the Parisian stalker duo was barreling through traffic lights yesterday afternoon shortly following

James's disappearance.

We called Jess into the room, who confirmed she was one of their attackers from the park.

"Great work!" Jordan said. She assigned a few team members to track the van through the city to start narrowing down our suspect's routes. Charles called for additional Opimaean team members to help trace information that would lead to identifying her.

Finally, sometime around ten in the evening, we found the witch's last known location.

Our team was dispatched to investigate. Keoni and Lana loaded everyone into the van, except for Jordan and Mia, who remained behind to run communications with our team. Our van was joined by two more full of agents to assist with our mission.

From the outside of the building, I hadn't expected a theater. The three stories that were visible from the street were covered in faded red brick, and it wasn't until we moved closer that I could read the various posters advertising the shows. We moved quickly into position and surrounded the building, uniting under one common goal: bring James home.

I tapped on the small radio connecting me to the rest of our team before moving casually toward a side door. Opimae City's magical beings were still wandering the streets, and discretion was imperative. We shielded Isaac as he picked the lock on the door, and we filtered into the dim light of the theater.

The building was eerily quiet, and I fought against the rising hysteria swelling in my chest. I couldn't shake the feeling that we were walking into a trap. A notification flashed on our comms system—we were marking off the areas that were clear. We happened upon a long row of doors and split off to investigate. I turned the doorknob nearest me and stepped into a dark office.

A small desk sat along the far wall just in front of a window, which had been left open. A gentle breeze rustled the papers on the desk, and a clock ticked from the wall beside me. I crossed the room to investigate a set of massive wooden cabinets. I threw open the doors and found no one. I scanned the space again, just as a hooded figure slipped into the room and shut the door softly. They turned and removed the hood.

A familiar witch with honey-colored hair and dark eyes stared back at me. Curls escaped from her braid, and her high cheekbones were tinged with a rosy hue.

"Where's James?" I asked.

"He's here. He's not who we're after." Her voice was raspy, her accent distinctly French.

"Then why did you take him?"

"We didn't intend to take him. Fitz wasn't where he was meant to be. Anyway, it worked out because here you both are."

"Hadley, where are you?" Fitz sounded through the comms system.

"What do you want? Why have you been following us?" I asked.

"We're after the same thing," she said.

"Which is?"

"Hadley, do you copy?" Henry's voice sounded in my earpiece.

"The ring," she said. "Isn't that why you're in Opimae?"

Her objective was especially troubling if she was working with Bain. I considered why King Alden might want the ring, and my heart thumped.

"Hadley? Who are you talking to?" Fitz asked, his voice tinged with fear.

"We're here to stop Lorenzo," I said.

The witch laughed softly. "I'm not as naive as the witchkind government."

The door handle turned, and the witch sighed.

She dropped her voice to a whisper. "I must go, but I hope we can finish our little chat."

Fitz, Lana, and Henry ran into the room as she disappeared.

"Are you all right?" Henry asked as Fitz rushed to my side.

"I'm fine."

"Was that . . . ?" Lana trailed off.

"The other stalker? Yes."

"What was she saying?" Lana asked.

"Nothing that's going to help us right now. I'll fill you in later. Have we found James?"

"Not yet, but we're closing in on the auditorium," Lana said.

He had to be there. We ran from the room past a small café and into the auditorium. I passed the seemingly endless rows of chairs, every second feeling like a lifetime in our search for James. Though the theater was dark, we made out James's figure on the front row at the right of the stage. He was struggling to speak, and I imagined he must be gagged by a spell, but he was conscious, and that was the most important thing.

Ian made it to James first and was loosening his bonds when a bright light flipped on. My eyes strained momentarily before opposing forces descended from a balcony overhead and burst through the red curtain on the stage. I ran toward James and assisted Ian in freeing him.

I scanned his injuries quickly—cuts and bruises were scattered across his skin, and blood was still trickling from a fresh gash on his cheek.

The last binding was a spell, and I fought against it until I found its edges and pulled it apart.

"Find a couple teammates and get him back to headquarters," Ian said.

It wasn't Ian's call, and he knew it. But it was a good one, so I nodded before taking James by the hand and rushing for the door. The team was locked in combat, though it was clear that our opposition was outnumbered. Numbers didn't always win battles, but I hoped it boded well for us. Molly and Chloe came to our aid as Fitz caught up to us and ran ahead to ensure a clear path. We exited the stage doors into a small parking area when a group of three descended on us.

"Keep going, Molly!" I yelled. "Get James back to headquarters!"

She took James by the hand, and they ran toward a nearby alleyway. Molly stopped at the entrance and turned on her heel wrapping her arms around James. They grew hazy and disappeared.

Fitz and Chloe were already locked in combat when I turned back around. Fitz had just taken down one warrior, and Chloe was holding off two more. Fitz turned to help her, and I hurled fire at his new opponent. The idea was to take down and capture opposing forces if possible, so I hoped my fire wasn't charged enough to kill. The fire flung the warrior into a nearby wall just as Chloe won her battle.

A witch with long blonde hair raced toward the alley where Molly and James had just slipped through the in-between. Fitz and I exchanged a quick glance and took off running in her direction, Chloe hard on our heels.

"I take it you've met?" Chloe huffed.

"She's the other Parisian stalker," I shot back. "We can't let her get away!"

I mustered my strength and threw a fireball down the alley, praying it would meet its mark. Sure enough, it landed right in front of her. She jumped back, which caused her to stumble before picking up her pace. I called another fireball and shot again. She swerved around it and kept going.

"Find a memory!" I yelled to Fitz.

Fitz nodded and set to work. When he stopped running, I knew she would follow suit.

"No!" the witch screamed, spinning around violently. Gusts of wind raced around Chloe through the small alley disturbing the calm air on its way to our target, and a funnel cloud engulfed her.

The cloud was nearly transparent, only slightly distorting our view of James's abductor. She sat on the ground, her mind clearly still captivated by her memory, and we hesitated.

"When I break through the funnel, have Fitz stop the vision," Chloe said.

I nodded.

Chloe swept her fingertips through the edge of the funnel, disturbing its perfect pattern. She reached toward the sky, and her fingertips grew bright with warm light.

"Now!" Chloe yelled.

"*Stop the vision*," I whispered to Fitz's mind.

The witch's eyes cleared, and she looked around, confused.

Chloe slid her hand through the funnel and ripped it apart. Fitz and I rushed in and grabbed the woman's arms, pulling them behind her back before she could even make sense of it. Her power felt weak, and I realized Chloe was crafting a spell that would suppress her power until removed.

A van pulled onto the sidewalk at the end of the alleyway. Henry rolled down the window.

"Need a lift?"

"Right on time, as usual," Fitz said.

We loaded the woman into the middle row of the van and scanned the street quickly, ensuring we hadn't left any traces behind.

"What did you show her?" I asked.

Fitz shook his head, a frown spreading across his features. "Don't ask me that, Hadley."

We were about to sound the all-clear when two figures ran toward the van. One was unfamiliar, but the other wasn't.

"That's one of my abductors—the one that hit Keoni!" I yelled. Fitz and I ran toward the van, but Chloe and Henry were already fighting against our latest combatants. Fitz entered the scuffle, and I jumped into the van with my stalker, who was inching her way toward the door while pulling at the ties around her wrist.

"I don't think so," I muttered, pulling her back to me. "You wanted to talk to me, remember?"

Henry took down the unfamiliar witch, but Chloe and Fitz were still struggling against the large elf. It was then, as I focused on his energy, that I realized he must be half witch. Witch magic lived inside him, and he was powerful. He spun out of Chloe's grasp and ran across the street. Fitz was hard on his heels as I called a fireball forward, but I was too late. Fitz's opponent slipped through time, and much to my horror, Fitz disappeared behind him.

CHAPTER SEVENTEEN

Charles was waiting for us at headquarters' front door when we arrived.

"Still no news?" I asked.

He shook his head. "Let's join Jordan in Intelligence."

Headquarters was overwhelming. Countless magical beings were rushing through the hallways, some talking into comms systems or on phones, others hurrying around with updates. Papers were flying from desk to desk.

Jordan materialized from a door at the far end of the hall.

"Hads! How you holding up?" she asked, moving toward me.

"We *have* to find Fitz."

"We're doing everything we possibly can. We have the best agents on this case. I think we—" Jordan trailed off.

Jordan was maybe ten feet away when the air between us rippled. The vibrations grew stronger, and Fitz came tumbling through the air and fell to the ground. Jordan gasped, and I rushed to his side.

"Fitz!"

Charles helped me assess him quickly while Jordan ran for medical assistance. We flipped him on to his back, and I knelt beside him, pushing his hair from his forehead. I followed a path of cuts and bruises along his face, which seemingly held the most trauma. Fitz was barely conscious, and my heart skipped a beat.

"His jaw," I whispered. The jagged gash on his jaw looked deep, and I swallowed hard.

Fitz's eyelids fluttered.

"Fitz. Hey, can you hear me?"

He opened his eyes weakly but nodded.

"What happened?" I asked.

"Isamu," he said.

"What are you talking about?"

"Isamu. The elf."

"He fought you?"

"Aye."

"What happened to your jaw?" I asked, eyeing the wound. Blood trickled on to my tunic, creating a dark pool. We needed to have it looked at quickly.

"His shoes—spikes on them."

I tried to keep my expression even. I nodded.

Fitz closed his eyes. I was no healer, but I knew he needed to stay awake.

"No, Fitz. Open your eyes. You have to stay with me, okay?"

Nothing.

I jumped as two witches materialized next to me.

Mia and Jordan turned the corner, running.

"Ma'am," one of the witches said. "We're going to take him to the healers now. We just need you to step away."

I hesitated, fear gripping my heart.

"It's okay, Hads. They've got him," Jordan said.

My eyes flickered to Mia.

She nodded. "He needs to be seen—quickly."

I carefully slid away and lowered Fitz's weight on to one of the transporters. The other held to his legs, and with a nod, they were gone.

"Don't you do this to me," I whispered to Fate. "Don't you bring him into my life just to rip him away from me."

We moved quickly toward the medical wing and rounded the corner into Lana and Isaac, who joined us. A splitting pain erupted through my head as we neared the healing rooms.

"What's happening to him?" I whispered, unable to use my full voice.

"He's being healed," Solomon said, catching me off guard. I hadn't noticed his arrival.

I staggered down the hallway, and Jordan looped her arm around me. Isaac scooped me up and followed Charles to a small, windowless room. He set me in a chair next to Fitz.

"We need space," one of the healers protested.

"Isaac, could you—"

"No," Solomon said. "She stays there, or we'll bring in a physician who can help him with her near."

The healer sneered at Solomon but fell back to work.

Stitches already ran from the bottom of Fitz's left cheek and snaked under his jawline to form a "u" shaped hook.

"This is from a shoe?" Jordan asked.

"He said there were spikes on the shoes." I gripped my head as a sharp pain seared through me. I squeezed my eyes shut, pushing away invasive thoughts. "He's unconscious?" I asked.

"Medically sedated—to keep him from feeling the pain," Solomon said.

I nodded wordlessly and reached for Fitz's hand. Pain shot through my head like lightning bolts, and I focused on our connection, checking for any sign that Fitz was okay. Nothing else mattered in that moment.

"What happened?" Tanner asked, walking into the room.

"We don't have many details just yet," Charles said.

"He'll be okay?" I asked the lead healer.

He held my gaze, still clearly annoyed by our presence but compassionate enough to answer a patient's mate.

"We were able to intervene quickly, which is a good thing. We'll know more soon."

"I'll bloody kill this elf," Henry seethed, passing through the door.

I clutched my head, doubling over in pain. The whole room went quiet.

Henry was quickly by my side. "What's the matter?"

"I think it's the connection," I whispered. Just as Fitz had experienced water rolling down his face, I was riddled with his pain. It was a fresh reminder of just how serious our bond was.

"I can help, if you'd like."

"How?"

"We can suppress the connection."

I shook my head, anxiety fluttering through me at the thought.

"You willnae lose anything. It's only temporary. You'll still feel the pain, but far less potently."

"I'd like to wait it out if I can, but I'll let you know if I change my mind."

The door swung open, and Ian burst into the room, his face falling as his eyes locked on to Fitz's motionless frame. Henry and Isaac were both quickly at his side. I extended my hand toward him in silent request, and he fell into my arms.

"This, this is too much," he whispered.

"I know. It's awful."

"He'll be all right?" he asked, his face expectant as he pulled away, searching my eyes for the truth.

"I think maybe it seems worse than it is, but we'll know more soon."

Ian shook his head softly, a humorless laugh escaping his lips.

"Lana, what are our current stats from this recovery?" Charles asked.

"We lost three Opimaean agents. Five are currently being treated," she said before turning toward Molly. "Molly surfaced with minor scrapes, but Isaac's were more extensive."

My head swiveled to Isaac. In my haste to get to Fitz, I'd barely even registered his appearance. His breastplate had protected his core, but his sleeves were torn and dotted with specks of blood.

"Are you okay?" I asked gently.

"Yes, love. Don't worry about me."

"Several of Isaac's left metacarpals were broken and his left humerus was bruised. They're healing now, but they'll be tender for about a week. All lacerations are healed," Lana continued.

And yet, Isaac had still picked me up. His strength was incredible.

"What happened?" Jordan asked.

"The corner of the stage." He started to shrug and winced.

Chloe rushed into the room, preventing further discussion, and the lead healer sighed loudly.

"No more," he said. "This is already far too much."

Chloe nodded, understanding. "I'll leave."

Jordan crossed the room and planted a kiss on my forehead. "I'll be just next door."

I nodded.

Isaac followed Chloe, Jordan, Molly, Tanner, and Mia from the room.

"Isaac," Henry called out.

"It's okay. I could really use a moment."

Henry hesitated but nodded solemnly.

"We'll all be just there," Solomon said to me, before following Charles and Lana through the exit.

I looked at Fitz. I'd think him asleep if not for the tubes and wires attached to his body. He looked at peace, though I knew that wasn't true. I focused again on our streams, hoping for more information. His energy seemed agitated, which I found odd considering he was sedated, and his pain still hit me in intense waves.

"He's fighting us," the lead healer mumbled almost to himself.

"What do you mean?"

The healer clearly wasn't interested in sharing, so I turned to June, the other healer working with him. Her expression was soft, kind.

"Even though he's sedated, his mind is still very active. My guess is he's reliving something unpleasant in his mind—most likely the scuffle. It's making our work tough."

I nodded, thinking through the possibilities.

"I see that look on your face, lass. And it's worth a try," Henry said.

"What are you talking about?" the lead healer asked gruffly.

"Hadley's connection to Fitz is one of the strongest I've seen,"

Henry said. "She's also a spirit-traveler and a mind reader."

"Absolutely not."

"I can do this—and not only that, I can do this very well," I countered.

"You want to enter his mind and do what?"

"Calm him. I'm the only one who can."

"I think it's a good idea," June announced.

"So do I," Ian added.

"You can't be serious," the lead countered.

"Perfectly serious. She can enter his mind and speak to him, calm him—and then we can finish our work quickly," June said.

"And what about the risks?" the lead asked. "Or do we not care about that?"

"What are the risks of not being able to complete Fitz's healing in a timely fashion?" I asked.

The lead healer met my gaze firmly, but I could see in his eyes we were winning.

"Well, it's not ideal," he admitted. "There could be some serious consequences if his head isn't healed soon."

"I don't want to risk that. And I know I can do this."

Silence. And then the lead said, "Very well. But if you experience anything unusual in there, you cut loose immediately."

Another wave of searing pain burned through my head.

"Breathe," Henry said calmly. "Hadley, you need to breathe deeply. Can you do that for me?"

I nodded, following his command, focusing my sight on his gaze and pulling air deep into my lungs. Henry's mouth moved quickly, but I couldn't register the words spilling out. Suddenly, the pain in my head lessened as Henry closed his eyes tightly.

"What was that?" I whispered.

"Just a bit of help. That should hold until you come back to yourself."

I embraced Henry tightly. "Thank you."

I turned to Fitz, and I focused on the connection, appreciating the tiny, glowing wires that carried information between the two of us. I anchored my consciousness to the river of light that traveled from me to Fitz, and I navigated until I found myself breaking into his consciousness. I wasn't sure what to expect, but the inner workings of his mind were very much alive—and agitated, just as June had suspected.

I was taken aback by the clarity of the scene that unfolded before me. The forest was filled with towering trees, and lavender-colored moss spread thickly across much of the ground. A small stone cottage was tucked into a clearing in the trees, smoke billowing thickly from the chimney.

My attention was torn from the scenery as two figures emerged from behind a large trunk. Battle raged as Fitz fought my former captor.

Fitz's hand connected to Isamu's face, but he recovered and tackled Fitz to the ground, rolling through the moss. I noticed a wrinkle in the air before me, and I touched my finger to the wavering ripple, attempting to understand it. I was able to separate the air, and I used all my strength to tug it into an opening, allowing me to view the altercation firsthand from Fitz's perspective. Though my intention had been to remain in Fitz's mind, my curiosity had further awakened my spirit-travel. I swore, focusing once more. It wasn't the time for aimless wandering in the past. I pulled at the opening, tearing it far enough to allow me back into Fitz's mind.

Observing the scuffle from Fitz's perspective was jarring, and I had to remind myself I was safe. Isamu couldn't hurt me. Fitz's mind had become a violent place, and I paused briefly, unsure of how to proceed. What would happen when I made my presence known? What if I made everything worse?

I'd followed the path he'd once placed for me and stepped inside his thoughts. He was my mate, and he needed me. I knew the answer to this. I took a deep breath and followed my instinct.

"Fitz!" I yelled. Isamu disappeared, and an image of my face replaced it. "Fitz," I called again.

"Hadley? Are you . . . inside my head?" he asked, clearly confused.

"Yes, I'm here."

"What happened? Why?"

"You're medically sedated so the physicians can heal you."

I granted him a chance to find his bearings.

"How did you make Isamu go away?" he asked.

"I didn't. You did that when you heard my voice."

"I've been trying to make the fighting stop. It's been on loop in my head."

"Oh, Fitz," I whispered. "That must have been awful."

"It's all right. You're here now."

"I'm here to help you relax. The fight was making you upset, which made the healer's work harder."

"I'm glad you're here. I need to explain things to you."

The same vivid scene that had unfolded came back to life before me. I was scanning the small stone cottage when a figure blurred in front of me, and the world tumbled out of focus.

"When I followed Isamu, we landed just outside a wee cottage," Fitz said. "Luckily, no one else was around, but Isamu picked up on my energy immediately. He turned and engaged me in a fight. It happened so quickly.

"I slammed into him one good time and took him down," Fitz continued. "But he rolled over and slipped away. That's when he kicked me in the jaw, the bastard. I got in a braw hit, and he fell back. He was barely conscious, and I was going to try transporting with him. But I didn't hear someone else approach, and I was tackled from behind. There were three agents, and I knew I was too weak to take them on. One of them threw a punch that was disorienting. I transported here not long after."

"I'm so glad you made it here. I can't believe this happened, but you're safe now. You're going to be okay."

Even though the healer hadn't confirmed Fitz's recovery, I had to tell myself he would be fine—it *had* to be true. We had moved mountains to be together and fought against all odds. I wasn't going to lose him like this. I thought again of Henry, of Molly. *That couldn't be me.*

"*You will not take him from me,*" I whispered to Fate.

"I almost forgot—one of the witches realized who I was. He instructed the other agents to be careful with me. He said I was one of the two crusaders from the prophecy—the ones there was a 'no kill' order on. He said they needed me for the ring."

Realization sparked inside of me. "The stalker said she needed us for the ring."

"You must be the other crusader protected under the 'no kill' order."

Why did she need me? My blood ran cold at the thought.

"Did anything indicate where the cottage was? Bain or Arregaithel?"

"Nae," Fitz said.

I felt the vague sensation of someone tugging at my hand. And though it was barely perceptible, intuition told me it was important. A distant whisper called me back to myself.

"I think it's time for me to go," I said.

"How do you know?"

"Someone is pulling at the edges of my consciousness."

"Aye, let's do this then," he answered, a slight edge in his voice.

"I'll see you soon. I love you."

"Hadley? Is everything all right, lass?" Henry's voice sounded distantly in my ear.

"Yes. Just a bit disoriented is all. I'll be fine in a minute."

"How's your head?" Ian asked anxiously.

"Pounding."

"Perhaps now we dampen the connection a bit?" Henry asked.

"Please," I whispered, rubbing my temples.

I felt the chain as Henry looped it around the glowing wires. The tension in my head released, and I took in a deep breath, focusing my energy. My sight was clearing, and the disorientation eased.

"We're done," the lead healer announced. "We'll wake him up now."

"Is he going to be in much pain?" Ian asked.

"No. He'll be groggy, but his headache should be bearable with the magic and medication we've administered."

"Is there anything you can do for Hadley?"

The lead still looked less than amused, but he beckoned me over to him. Henry helped me to my feet.

I crossed the space to the lead healer, and he laid his hands on either side of my face. He closed his eyes and muttered unintelligibly under his breath.

With his work completed, he stepped back to Fitz's side. "Leave the chain on for just a few moments while the spell takes effect, but your headache should be gone shortly."

I thanked him, and he began the process of waking Fitz.

"I'll be just next door with the others, then," Henry said softly, exiting the room.

"I'll come back," Ian offered.

"Ian . . . are you sure? Fitz will want to see you."

"You two need a moment before anyone else is added to the mix." Ian nodded in Fitz's direction. "He'd want it this way."

I smiled tightly.

"Send for me as soon as he's ready."

"Thank you," I whispered, nodding.

Ian squeezed my arm lightly and shuffled from the room. The lead healer again muttered under his breath, and with a snap of his fingers, Fitz opened his eyes.

"Hadley," he mouthed.

"I'm here, Fitz. I'm right here."

"Fitz, can you hear me?" The healer asked.

"Aye," he returned, his voice gravelly.

The lead healer ran through a few questions with Fitz. Both healers stepped away for a few minutes, letting us know they'd return shortly with a follow up list.

"I didn't mean to worry you," Fitz said, running his hand along my face.

His own face was littered with bruises that were already darkening to purples and blues as the healers' magic coursed through him. Though I knew it was a good sign, I fought back tears at the sight. His face was swollen from the trauma, and the stitches were unsettling—how were there so many?

"You've been to hell and back, and you're worried about me?" I asked.

"I cannae help it."

"How are you feeling?"

"Like someone kicked me in the head," he said.

My face fell.

"That was meant to be a joke."

"This is me laughing," I said, a tear falling down my face.

"I dinnae think I can sit up just yet. Come here."

I paused. I wanted nothing more than the reassurance his touch brought, but I wasn't sure it was a good idea for me to touch him in his current condition.

"Am I going to hurt you?"

"I dinnae care if you do." His brows knit before he shut his eyes and leaned back.

"You need to be still, Fitz." My heart ached seeing him in such a state, and my anxiety raged. I wanted to make things better for him, but I didn't know how to even begin.

"Then, come here."

"I don't want to make anything worse."

"Hadley, I need you closer. Our connection feels weak."

I nodded and climbed onto the bed, gently placing myself next to him, one leg looped around his. "Give me just a moment."

I closed my eyes, seeking the light of our connection. I loosened the tiny chain, and our streams roared back to full capacity.

Fitz's eyes widened. "What the hell was that?"

"My head was hurting—badly. Henry helped me suppress the flow of information, so the pain would ease."

Fitz nodded.

Henry had shown me more than he realized—he'd shown me that the connection between mates could be dampened. I added that to my mental file to consider later.

"Your dad is in the next room," I said. "Well, everyone is. They just wanted to give us a few minutes before you're bombarded."

He smiled weakly.

"What the hell were you thinking, Fitz?"

"I couldn't let him get away."

"You could have been killed. What if you couldn't transport back out?"

"But I did."

"Yeah, and you're a wreck." I scanned his face again, as if it would illustrate my point.

"You should see the other bloke." A smile tugged at his lips, but then he shut his eyes tightly in pain.

"Stop," I whispered. "Be still."

I didn't want to overload his body after the healer's magic, but I pushed a small amount of healing energy through the connection.

Fitz breathed deeply, closing his eyes for a moment. When he opened them, his gaze was tender.

"I know you're scared. I was, too, when you were nearly taken. But dinnae be angry."

"You just can't do things like that."

"I had a split second to make that decision, just like your decision at the fortress. That bastard tried to take you before. And he paid for it, too." His eyes clouded.

I shook my head.

"Can we talk about this later?" he asked.

I gave no answer.

"Please?"

I nodded.

Fitz tugged at my body until it molded to his, and we held each other tightly until the healers returned.

CHAPTER EIGHTEEN

"Are you sure you don't want me to call a car?" I asked Fitz.

"My legs are fine," he said.

"Suit yourself," I returned, my voice edgier than I intended. "Sorry, I don't mean to sound rude. I'm just . . ." I trailed off. What was I feeling?

"You're tired and sore. It's been a rough few days, and we have a full schedule today with a difficult meeting first on the agenda."

And my mind has been filled with questions about Fate.

Fitz kissed the top of my head. "Give yourself some grace, Hads."

We waved our hands overhead, asking the elements to shield us from the precipitation, and I winced at the pain that shot through my shoulder. Though it had been a few days since the crash, the pain was slow to fade. I had another healing appointment scheduled for the afternoon, and I hoped I'd see more progress.

It was a cool, rainy morning, and the comfort of the weather allowed me to relax as we walked from the coffee shop toward the council offices with James and Ian. Our first meeting of the day was to ask Charles to be more collaborative with us, and truthfully, I was anxious about the path it would take.

"Do we have a strategy with this meeting?" I asked.

Ian sighed. "I've learned over the years that it's difficult to extract the truth from leaders like Charles."

"What do you mean by that, Dad?"

"Charles holds an esteemed position. He's sitting on more information than we can possibly imagine."

"There are many beings he answers to in some capacity or the other," James said. "And that means he cannae be as forthcoming as perhaps he'd care to be."

I nodded, digesting this information.

I noticed James was having some difficulty keeping up with us, and I slowed my pace. His injuries were healing well, but we were all a little weathered after the events of the last few days.

"Maybe we just dive in headfirst and ask him why he isn't open with us."

"I dinnae ken, Hadley," James said. He cleared his throat before continuing. "I'm uncertain Charles will take well to that."

"I dinnae ken that he's the type to appreciate a slow dance though," Ian said. "Even if he has to be tightlipped, I think he'll appreciate candor from us."

"I know . . ." I trailed off momentarily. "I know you all believe in me, but I'll be honest with you . . . I don't know about this. I don't even know what to think about our current circumstances."

"I think we're all feeling a bit of that, Hads," Fitz said.

"Hadley, James and I have played at this game a long time, but we dinnae ken all the answers either. This is incredibly complex."

"Aye," James said. "Dinnae doubt yourself. You're meant to be here. You have a strong intuition and a way of promoting honesty and enthusiasm for the mission."

"You'll find your footing, lass," Ian said. "Give it time."

"Charles, I'm not going to tiptoe around this," I said. "You have to be more open with us." I was unsure if this direct strategy would work, but it was time to test the theory. James fidgeted in his seat. "We came here to help you, to strategize alongside you—but you aren't letting us help."

"That's not quite true. You and your team have been helpful since Adamo fell. It takes time to integrate teams, and it's been a busy few days with the abductions."

"You know what Hadley's getting at," Fitz said. "You're still withholding information instead of forming a true partnership with us."

"Charles, is there something we need to know here?" Ian asked.

Charles sighed. "There's been some discord in Opimae's upper ranks. Not everyone is on the same page about Earth's government."

"Like King Alden," I said.

Charles nodded.

"Oh, dear me," James said. "That's quite serious."

"It's old animosities. Nothing to worry yourselves with," Charles assured us.

"I'm afraid that's impossible." James was pacing the room, shaking his head. "This is discouraging news. We've given them no room to doubt us. What can we do to promote trust?"

"I think it will just take time," Charles said. "The longer we work together, the more we'll assuage the hesitation some of our leaders have about partnering with Earth."

Unless Bain *was* responsible for my abduction.

"We can appreciate the position you're in," Fitz said. "There are loads of opinions and even more information to consider. We're all trying to strike our balance."

Charles nodded.

"That said, we've learned honesty is the best policy," I added. "The truth stings sometimes, but the more information we have the better off we are."

"I apologize, but I'm walking a fine line."

"Is there a way around that?" I asked.

His mouth twisted in thought. "Perhaps the leaders don't need to know everything I share. It would avoid a fair amount of conflict with some of them."

"So, we can count on you to truly partner together moving forward?"

Silence.

"I'll work with you. But this is delicate."

"We'll keep everything confidential, Charles. We'd never violate your trust," I said.

All eyes turned to Charles, and he exhaled deeply, nodding.

It was an unexpected response, and I honestly didn't quite trust that things would improve, but the following weeks would tell us what we needed to know.

"I think we have much to learn from one another," Ian offered.

Keoni entered the room, and he nodded in greeting as he took a seat.

"Now, if you'll excuse the change in subject," Charles said, "we have another matter that requires our attention."

"By all means," James said.

"It's about Gustavo. I think he can be useful."

"He's obviously powerful, and brave, but what do we even know about him, Charles?" I asked.

"You mean other than the fact that he'll be Jordan's mate?"

I stood. "Excuse me?"

Charles nodded. "Trust me, I know."

"But Jordan . . ."

"Jordan is still acquiring her power, but her matching is imminent. When she matches, I can assure you it will happen. Try and keep those two apart and see what happens."

"She would never," Ian responded warmly.

"Do you think Gustavo knows?" I asked.

Charles pinched the bridge of his nose. "Why do you think I haven't been able to get rid of him?"

"I'll be damned," Fitz muttered, shaking his head. "Well, there's no keeping him away then."

My mind rolled to the afternoon of our abduction attempt. I'd felt a small shift in energy and noticed Jordan and Gustavo studying each other, but I'd thought it was due to Jordan coming into her power. I'd misinterpreted the signs.

"Technically, we can do that—if you wish. But I wouldn't advise it," Keoni said.

"Absolutely not," I said authoritatively. Every pair of eyes in the room settled on me. "That was attempted before—with me and Fitz. I'll wreak total havoc before anyone in this group is ever subjected to that."

Charles nodded. "It's been decided, then."

"That leaves us with the decision about how involved he can be," James said.

Ian finished flipping through a chart and tossed the folder to Fitz. "This is information on Gustavo. Everyone should read through that before we decide, but it seems his skills would be useful to this team."

"If he's interested—and he will be—we can run him through our tests as a first step and make further decisions based on our findings," Keoni suggested.

"If we're all in agreement, let's have the conversation with Gustavo and begin testing," I said.

"Consider it done," Charles responded.

"And Jordan begins her training with the team from Thalassa tomorrow, correct?"

"Correct," Charles said.

"I need approval from the court for this, but I'd also like to bring over one of our trainers from Earth."

"Maka?" Fitz guessed.

I nodded, then addressed Charles and Keoni. "I trained with her when I discovered I was a witch, and I think she'd be a great addition to Jordan's training team."

"If you think it would be helpful, by all means," Charles said. "Jordan will match in no time. She's well past ready for this."

"Good morning, team. Let's meet the Parisian stalkers." Jordan nodded to Brigitta, and her report materialized on the screen.

"Hans Schmidt and Allette Toussaint," Jordan said.

Two photos flashed on the screen. I was surprised by how unsettled I felt seeing the images of the infamous pair.

"Hans is a real exemplary citizen," Jordan continued. "He did some hard time in a French prison with Allette's brother."

"Nice," Mia muttered.

"Allette was believed to be involved, but authorities couldn't find any solid evidence, so she walked," Jordan continued. "When Hans was released, he moved in with Allette. The two seemingly were doing well, but it appears our two young lovers returned to a life of crime about a year ago. This is where it gets interesting. According to traffic cam footage we obtained, these two wandered into a Parisian bar one night, where they would have heard . . ."

"Lorenzo."

"Ten points for Solomon," Jordan said. "Our charismatic nemesis was speaking at the bar."

"So, there's the connection," Chloe said.

I felt Charles's gaze shift to me, but I kept my eyes on Jordan.

Jordan paused. "Not exactly—or at least, not if Allette's confessions are true."

Our expressions betrayed our confusion.

"Apparently, Allette and Hans don't care about Lorenzo or his mission. They wanted the MacGregor family ring for themselves. They have their own plans for overthrowing the witchkind government."

"Is there any evidence suggesting they're lying?" Charles asked.

"No. The only thing we have that ties them to Lorenzo is the night when they heard him speak."

"And Bain?" I asked.

Jordan shook her head. "We're early on in this investigation, but so far . . . there's nothing that proves Allette and Hans worked with either Lorenzo or with Bain."

"Damn it," Chloe muttered, pushing her chair back to cross the room. Everyone fell silent. She stared out the window before finally turning to face us all. "Is there no end to this?"

It was sobering to see this side of the usually composed and optimistic Chloe.

"I don't know if we should believe her or not," I said.

Fitz's hand found mine and gave it a squeeze in support.

"If they *are* working for Lorenzo, then he's been watching you this whole time," Tanner said. "And if they aren't working for him, then they're just another dead end."

"But if they are working alone or with Bain, then we have two separate entities to deal with," Isaac said.

"Unless Lorenzo and Bain are connected," Mia said.

Charles sighed. "That's unfounded."

"Charles, whether you like it or not, we need to lay all theories on the table," Mia said. "Intelligence will investigate them and rule them in or out. But it would be irresponsible of us not to follow every potential lead."

Charles hesitated, but finally, he nodded. "We still need to make sense of why they abducted James," he said.

"I was meant to be with him," Fitz said softly. His voice already sounded tired. His energy had not yet recovered from the events of the previous day.

"Aye, that's true. We were meant to spar a bit, but Fitz was pulled into a last-minute meeting."

"You think they were after you?" Keoni asked Fitz.

"Aye." Fitz explained what he overheard outside of the mystery cottage. "So, I think they meant to capture Hadley and me."

"But how did they know where you were supposed to be?" Isaac said.

"How did they know where Hadley and I were? How did they know where to find James?" Jordan asked. "They knew our locations."

"There's a mole," Henry said, leaning forward in his chair.

"Aye," Ian agreed. "They kenned the locations before the security breach. They couldnae have moved so quickly unless they already kenned where to find you."

"The security breach was just a part of the plan to get us in motion. It was a distraction," I realized.

"Well, this opens up another can of worms," Solomon chimed in. "I'm sure you're already investigating this?"

"Of course," Jordan answered. "We've launched a full investigation to find out as much as we possibly can about these spies' prior whereabouts and connections. We'll find out everything we can, but if I can make a suggestion . . ."

"Of course, you can," I said.

"They've just made everything more complicated, and we need additional resources. Besides that, the intelligence protocols need a complete overhaul, and we'll require expanded teams to address that need." She looked to Charles. "I'm proposing we recruit here, but we also bring over teams from Earth."

Charles hesitated, looking to Keoni before dropping his gaze to the table. They weren't fooling anyone—some sort of silent exchange was happening.

"This partnership won't be successful until we find a way to truly integrate," I said.

Charles tapped his thumb on the conference table. He shook his head lightly and finally responded. "I'll fight for the intelligence team expansion. We'll do a thorough sweep in the offices and try to identify all potential breaches—technologically and with personnel. Jordan, let's work on this together."

"You got it," she said.

"Let's not discuss anything outside of this core team unless we all agree on it," Charles suggested.

"Agreed. We need to identify the breach so we know who we can trust," I said. The mole could be high ranking, or they could even be in the room with us.

"I'm afraid this will cause discord in the chamber," Charles said. "If Lorenzo was watching you from the beginning, well . . . the chamber will have concerns."

"And if the mole is in the chamber . . ." I trailed off.

"Then it could be someone like King Alden," Chloe said.

I didn't want that to be true—the implications of that scenario would be catastrophic—but I couldn't shake my suspicions from my mind. I hoped Jordan's research would yield more information soon.

I looked to Fitz. What had started as two mates searching for a family heirloom had turned into a more complicated web than I could have ever thought.

"While we're researching the stalkers, I propose we do some research into King Alden," Solomon said, looking to Charles. "And to follow all of our leads, we should do some reconnaissance across time to keep pressing forward on Lorenzo. We need to think outside of the box. Let's go back and track Lucio. We know Lucio was the original mastermind of Lorenzo's plans. Hadley uncovered his note to Lorenzo—perhaps there's useful information to be found in the past."

"You'll have to be very careful not to disturb anything in the past," Charles said, his expression grave. "The last thing we need is Fate against us."

"For what it's worth, I think that's a great idea," Molly said.

We unanimously agreed.

"Fitz will need a bit of recovery time, but I think you two make a great team with your skill sets," Keoni said.

"Does the chamber need to vote on this?" Ian asked.

Charles mulled over his question.

"Let's keep this between us for now."

I met Jordan at our favorite coffee shop, the Opimae City Coffee Roasters, for lunch.

Etain, our favorite mixologist, was behind the counter.

Her tiny figure was draped in Opimae's signature Celtic inspired style, but her tunic was a pastel blue, which brought out her aqua eyes. Her gaze swept over us as her lips curled into a warm smile.

Jordan sought herbal tea with shots of calm and relaxation. She'd been working around the clock for days, and she was heading back to our house to sleep for a few hours. I needed black tea with an extra boost of energy to start my afternoon meetings.

We stood transfixed on Etain's process. Though we'd observed her at work many times, we were still fascinated. It was after she steeped the tea that things grew interesting. She waved her hands over the black tea, and a glowing orb materialized in the palm of her hand. She mouthed a few words I didn't understand—Latin, maybe—and tossed the orb into my drink. Etain added the steamed milk and stirred the drink by moving her hand in a circular motion. She waved a finger, and my drink slid across the counter. The mug emitted a warm glow, and I was captivated by the light swirling slowly in time with the drink.

The light faded, and I pulled the mug to my lips. I closed my eyes, sighing contentedly.

Etain finished Jordan's drink, and we found a table on the patio above the river.

"So, how are you feeling?" I asked Jordan. "Have you even processed that you're a witch yet?"

"Honestly . . . no. With James's abduction, I rolled from that discovery right into the last few days of investigation. Sitting here right now is the first moment I've had to really think about it."

I understood the turmoil that came with realizing you're a witch. Life was about to get a bit more complicated—and much more magical—for my dear friend. But if Charles was right about Gustavo, she'd also gain a partner to help her navigate her newfound power.

I thought of Fitz, and my energy stirred.

"Hopefully you'll get some time to yourself over the next couple days."

"I heard your trainer from Earth is being called over," Jordan said. "And Charles sent for Queen Marina, so her arrival will force me to focus on my magic, too."

Queen Marina was the monarch of Thalassa, the kingdom of water witches.

"Do you think this is typical—that the queen would travel all this way to meet with a new water witch?" I asked.

"Charles said the fact that I came from Earth and my power awakened here was a big deal." Jordan shrugged. "He also said they're going to reference portal crossings with Earth's records to see if my family might have come from Opimae."

"I wonder if there are more water witches on Earth whose powers are dormant," I said.

"I think that's possible. They'd be like me and have no idea whatsoever," Jordan said. "I just wish Grandma Estelle were here to see this."

"I think she is, J," I said softly. "I think somehow in our magical lineage, we carry the spirits of our ancestors with us. She's thrilled. I just know she is."

Jordan smiled. "You know, she never gave up on tracing her father's story."

"I have a feeling his story is going to hold some answers about your magic."

We grew quiet, and I twirled my finger, asking the air to stir my tea. Watching Jordan finding herself as a witch strengthened my belief that Fate had led her here. If I had won in my opposition to Jordan joining the crusade, I would have blocked my best friend from her destiny.

"I can't believe this is real life," Jordan said, her eyes glued to my mug.

I nodded. "Yeah, and you're basically a mermaid, J."

Her eyes widened playfully. "The first thing I asked Charles was if water witches grew tails."

"What did he say?"

"Well, after he stopped laughing, he said no. I think it's just folklore that humans came up with to explain something they can't understand."

I laughed. "I think I'm relieved by this news, honestly."

"Growing a damn tail was going to be the last straw."

"You're like the rest of us. My power comes from fire. Fitz's from the earth. Yours, from water. That's all."

Jordan nodded.

"You're one of us, Jordan. You always have been, and now you have the magic to prove it."

CHAPTER NINETEEN

I lay wrapped in Fitz's arms the following evening. We'd decided to retire early and skip dinner with the team, seeking solace after the chaos of the last few days. We'd ordered takeout from a pub down the street and eaten by the open window in our room.

"Your energy is distant," Fitz said. "It's been off for a while."

Truthfully, I needed a little quiet time to think through the series of events and ease my muddled mind. Between my abduction and Fitz's altercation with Isamu, I was rattled, even without the Opimaean politics and questioning of mates and Fate. I didn't meet his gaze.

I parsed through my thoughts before responding. "There's a lot going on lately."

"I'm sure the recent events haven't helped, but I noticed it before the stalkers showed up—before the festival, even."

I remained quiet.

"One minute things feel normal between us, and the next, they don't.

My head's mince, Hadley."

I sighed. How could I tell my mate, the man who loved me more than anything else in this world, that I was certain he loved me, but that perhaps Fate had made his choice for him?

"Fitz . . ." I began, still unsure of the words that would come tumbling out. "I don't want you worried about me."

He started to speak, but I was faster.

"Hold on," I said.

He nodded for me to continue.

"I don't want you worried about me because there's nothing to be concerned about. When we accepted this mission, a weight settled on my shoulders. And that weight has grown heavier as we've navigated this planet."

Fitz's eyes were hard on mine. He nodded, though his energy told a different story. He wasn't convinced.

"You've been distant, too. Is it the altercation, or is there more to it?" I asked.

"A great many things are on my mind," he admitted. "But right now, I'm worried our training won't be adequate. I want to be sure our team is prepared for the fight ahead. The stakes are high."

"I worry about that, too. But we'll fight for our team."

"Aye, you're right. We'll sort this. We have to."

I nodded, considering our partnership on this crusade.

"You know, we make each other better," I said.

That was something I knew without a shadow of a doubt to be true.

"We make each other stronger—braver. That's the way it should be," Fitz said.

"Fitz . . ." I paused. "Are you afraid of what's going to happen to us?"

"The only thing I fear is losing you. I could bear anything else."

"Have a little faith," I said.

"It's not that at all, and you know it. You're fierce. Your power is strong. And nothing will ever happen to you, not as long as I'm around. I'll always have your back."

"You have to learn to focus on yourself in battle, remember?"

Fitz smiled. We both knew better.

"And how do you think you'll fare at prioritizing yourself in battle?" he asked.

I grimaced.

"I thought so. But . . . we work best as a team anyway," he said.

"That's something we can agree on."

Fitz nodded. "The council has never been any good at sorting out what's best for us. Why would this be any different?"

"It isn't," I said.

"We'll sort this ourselves."

"You know, I believe in my best moments we can do this, but in my worst moments, I'm afraid of the outcome," I said.

"Are you afraid of your fate?"

"I'm not afraid of dying. I see it like this: we've already died in a way. We've chosen it, at the very least."

He looked at me, perplexed.

"Our former selves have died—the beings we might have been. We sacrificed our lives for this cause, and we make that sacrifice every morning when we wake up and choose to continue this mission. I've known from the beginning that death is the most likely end."

"And you still signed up."

"And I still signed up," I said. "So did you. And Henry, and Jordan, and all the others standing with us."

"We've had our first wee encounter with what's to come," Fitz said.

"And did it make you want to turn back?" I asked.

"I'm more determined than ever."

"Exactly. The day I decided to stand against Lorenzo, I knew there was no turning back. I think we all did." I paused. "No, I'm not afraid of death."

"You never cease to amaze me."

My mouth twisted into the awkward, lopsided grin that I always seemed to wear when I didn't know what to say.

"Don't you dare."

"Don't I dare, what?"

"You were just thinking about how to deflect my praise, and I won't stand for it," he responded mischievously.

I smiled, but I couldn't hide my troubled mind from Fitz.

"What is it, Hads?" he asked.

I couldn't seem to shake the fear that had gripped both my mind and body for days. The thought of losing Fitz had plagued me, and it had been especially present after recent events . . . and after talking with Henry and Molly.

Still, I hesitated.

"Out with it," he said.

"I've never known fear like I did the other day. Every minute that you were gone and I didn't know what was happening . . ." I trailed off. "It scares me to feel so deeply."

Fitz nodded slowly.

"Aye, I understand. We've both tasted that fear now."

I studied the stitches along his jaw.

"How are you feeling tonight?"

"The stitches come out tomorrow," he said. "I'm glad to be rid of them. They're itching, and it's making me mental."

"They look uncomfortable."

"How's your shoulder?" he asked, his fingers tracing the area in question.

"Better today. I was starting to get worried, so I'm relieved."

I reached for his hand. Warm, fuzzy energy pulsed through me. When I allowed my mind to quiet, there was great comfort in that simple act. "I'll never tire of this, you know? The peace you give me."

"Come on, Hadley. Don't make me greet."

I leaned over and planted a soft kiss just under his jawline, carefully avoiding his injuries.

"Now, *that* you may do any time."

"I'll keep that in mind."

Fitz leaned back in his chair and tugged at my arm. I moved onto his lap, and he wrapped me in a warm embrace. I tucked my leg around his and rested my head on his chest as he kissed the top of my head.

"I'm so thankful for you," he whispered.

CHAPTER TWENTY

The following day brought the promise of routine. Fitz and I arrived at headquarters just in time for his physical therapy session, and I wandered off to training. I groaned at the thought of working with Jess, but I focused on my resolution to work as hard as I possibly could to complete his training program quickly.

At least Tanner is in today's session with me, I thought.

I stepped into the training room, and the first face to greet me stopped me in my tracks.

"Oh my god. Maka!" I exclaimed. I crossed the space quickly and embraced my favorite trainer. Maka had moved around the world to work with Earth's witchkind council, but she hailed from the Cheyenne River Sioux Tribe of the American Dakotas. "I'm so glad you're here."

Maka's long raven hair was pulled into a loose braid that fell down her back. The coat she wore was brightly colored, and the modern shapes of her clothing felt out of place after I'd grown accustomed to the style of Opimae. My heart tightened at the sight of her Earth-side clothing.

"I'm excited to work with Jordan. I've never worked with a water witch before. And this," Maka said, gesturing broadly. I'd always found her husky, gravelly voice soothing. Her smile was bright and genuine—I'd missed her. "Being here is wild."

"Yeah, nothing like training crusaders on a foreign planet to add to your resume," I said.

She laughed deeply.

Chloe entered the room, pulling our focus to training, and Jess called me over to begin our sparring session.

Maka was adept at reading energy, and I whispered to her mind, sharing my history with Jess. *"I don't trust him. Let me know your opinion once you've had a chance to observe him—please."*

Maka nodded discreetly.

Sadie met me on the mat. She was Opimae's best fighter, and she was as smug as she was talented in the art of war. I reached out to shake her hand—the way we'd been taught to begin every training session. Sadie looked from my hand to my eyes before crossing her arms and looking away. I rolled my eyes but nodded to Jess. We'd get started regardless of her behavior.

Jess ran us through a series of moves.

I had been cleared for sparring with Opimae warriors just that morning. Continued training was mandated for all crusaders from both planets to keep our battle skills sharp. It sounded great in theory; however, my first session with Sadie was brutal. It became quickly obvious that Sadie had come to the session not to train me but to make me her punching bag. She made no effort to hide the fact that she wanted to be anywhere else, but I gritted my teeth and powered through the session.

We were in the middle of an intense fight training maneuver when the full weight of Sadie's blow connected with my chin, sending searing pain exploding through my jaw. I staggered backward, determined to stay upright, though it took everything in me. A menacing grin spread across her lips.

"Hey! That's enough," Chloe yelled from across the room. "She's supposed to be identifying our weaknesses, not exploiting them."

"Sadie, you heard Chloe. That's enough," Jess called across the space. He turned to Chloe. "I'm sorry. I don't know what's gotten into her lately."

"You mean, aside from us being here?" Tanner quipped.

Jess held Tanner's gaze before returning his focus to Sadie. He dismissed her for the day while he made a few notes in my chart.

Sadie rolled her eyes. "This shouldn't be my problem, you know."

"Do I even want to know what you're getting at, Sadie?" I asked, rubbing my aching chin.

"You should have already been trained before you got here. You make us weak."

"Why are you so against helping us?"

I thought it was only that she disliked us, but perhaps it was more than that. The mole could be anyone. Did Sadie's disdain run deeper than I suspected?

"Because this entire thing is Earth's fault, and then they send you and your team to us, like we're supposed to be grateful or something." She scoffed. "It's not right."

I crossed my arms, willing my fire magic to stay dormant. "How exactly is this Earth's fault?"

"This is an Earth-side being who's trying to destroy your world. Then he comes over here and starts wreaking havoc on *our* world. Now it's our problem, and the court sends us *you* when you haven't even been trained properly."

"That's not a fair assessment, and you know it."

"What's not fair is that Earth isn't going to send troops to help us."

"Our councils never said they weren't sending troops."

"I think that's enough for you two today," Jess interrupted, his glacial eyes wide under arched brows.

"Don't worry, Coach. I'm finished here."

Sadie stormed out, slamming the door behind her.

"I'm sorry about Sadie," Keoni said. I hadn't even noticed he'd slipped into the room.

I waved my arms, cutting his apology short. "Don't be. I know not everyone is happy to have us here."

"Well, I certainly am."

I thanked him for his kindness, and he left to escort Maka to meet Jordan. Jess and I began our sparring session.

I veered to the right, trying to escape an impending blow, but in my rush, I left my core unprotected. Jess's fist met its mark, and I tumbled to the floor. Pain shot through my abdomen, but not before my hand met Jess's jaw. The cold mat took my weight along with my breath. Jess rolled to the ground, his fall much more graceful than my own. As my breath returned, a wave of nausea rolled through my stomach, and I shifted to my side.

Jess extended his hand in my direction, but I slapped it away in protest.

"We're on the same team, Hadley."

"Could've fooled me," I muttered, pulling myself from the floor.

"You all right, Hads?" Tanner called from across the room.

"Yeah, I'm good." I turned to face Jess again.

"Okay, what went wrong there?"

"I lost focus. I left myself unprotected."

"I know it's a lot to remember, especially in the moment, but the more focused you are, the less I'll hurt you. And I really hate hurting you."

I scoffed.

"Hadley," Jess said sternly. "I do *not* like this part. But I'll rough you guys up as much as I need to right now. It'll save your life in the field."

I nodded curtly.

"Again, from the top."

I shifted my body into position.

"Not like that." He sighed. "Here, let me show you."

Jess's hands grazed my sides, gripping just above my hips as he shifted my body into position. A violent mix of emotions flurried through me. Embarrassment washed over me, inexplicable as it was. I had done nothing wrong, but Jess's behavior left me humiliated and anxious. I just wanted training to be over.

Tanner's heavy footsteps echoed through the open space, and Jess's hands dropped at his approach.

"I think she's got it, Jess."

"Her stance was off. I can handle my own training."

"Enough, you two." Chloe's authoritative voice silenced them both. Her eyes fell hard on Jess.

Tanner held Jess's gaze for a moment longer, but he eventually relented, stalking back to Chloe's side.

"Your friends don't like me," Jess said.

"You're not exactly a likable guy."

"Still irritated with me, I see."

"Just keep your hands off me, and stop antagonizing everyone who cares about me."

"I care about you."

I sneered.

"I do. I care that you're trained properly, so you have a better chance of survival in the field." He shot a glance at Tanner, clearly irritated at his interference.

"Tanner cares about me more than you do . . ." I paused. "And Fitz cares most of all."

The look on Jess's face was impassible, and I wanted to know more than ever what hid behind his cool demeanor. Though I wanted to be objective as I thought about who the mole could be, Jess pulled at my mind more than anyone.

"I don't get it. Why are you doing this?" I asked.

Another set of footsteps interrupted our conversation, but to my surprise, it wasn't Tanner.

"Surely we're not done for the day," Chloe bristled.

"Oh no, we were just about to pick up where we left off before the interruption."

"I don't know if you need to pick up exactly where you left off, but yeah, I agree that it's time to get back to work."

When the awkward session ended, Tanner was quickly by my side. He gripped my chin, pulling my face from side to side and swore.

"Come here," he said. Tanner pulled out a fresh butterfly bandage and replaced the current one above my eye.

"I know this part sucks. But you're making so many gains."

"It's okay. Honestly, I'd rather get a little beat up here than god knows what in the field."

"Getting knocked around in training is one thing. But getting knocked around by that guy . . ." Tanner shook his head. "You need to see a healer for this, by the way."

"I'll ask Maka to stop by after work."

Tanner eyed me suspiciously.

"I promise I'll have it looked at. I just . . . I need to get out of here, Tanner."

He offered to walk with me to the exit.

"Dude's an asshole," Tanner said. "Did he make you too uncomfortable?"

"No more than usual. Thanks for stepping in, though."

"He better not touch you like that again."

My witch's eye prickled. "What are you not telling me?"

Tanner's mouth twitched slightly. "I threatened to kick Jess's ass after your first session with him. Chloe smoothed things over—told me I'd land in a lot of trouble, and then I wouldn't be able to help at all."

"Tanner!" I laughed. "Oh my god. Well, thanks . . ."

"Yeah, at least Fitz got him good the one time."

My expression was dry, but I didn't comment.

"He's getting more blatant," I said instead.

"It's weird. I thought he would back off—you're a force to be reckoned with."

I laughed.

"Nah, Hads, don't do that."

"Do what?"

"Laugh off my compliment. You know you're a force. Maybe call up your fire magic again. That seemed to scare the hell out of him."

"I haven't exactly been a delicate flower."

"That's a fact."

"What do you think he's doing? We have so many theories floating around, but I honestly don't think he wants me . . . not like that."

"Damn, Hads. I don't even know at this point."

"Whatever his endgame is, he's definitely trying to piss us off."

"It's working," Tanner said.

"His actions don't make sense—my witch's eye can't seem to understand any of it. When he watched me before, it didn't feel romantic. And when he touches me, it doesn't feel sexual—he's almost always glancing away, like he's curious about who's watching. It's almost like . . . he's trying to stir up trouble, but it's not specifically with me and Fitz."

I paused at the building's exit, still considering Jess's intentions. Tanner held the door open for me.

"Thanks for everything today," I said.

"Don't mention it. See you at home, Weston."

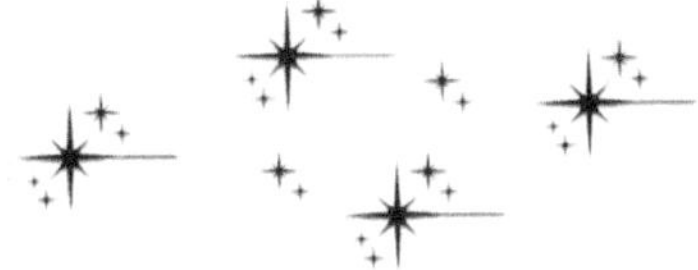

I walked into the great room of our home to find Fitz talking strategy with Henry and Isaac. His face fell as his eyes swept my injuries, and he rushed to my side.

"What happened?"

"The ground? Jess's fist? Hurricane Sadie? I'm not sure."

Fitz's eyes betrayed his anger.

"Just another day in training. It's nothing to worry about," I said.

Fitz pulled the bandage back. "Hads . . . you should've seen the healer before you left." He ran his thumb gingerly across my cheek just beneath my broken skin.

I waved him off. "I was tired, and . . ."

"And what?"

I sighed.

"Out with it."

"I didn't want to be there any longer than I had to be."

Fitz's eyes darkened.

"Jess is too rough with you."

"I asked Maka to take look at these cuts. She's going to catch a ride with Jordan."

Fitz nodded.

I walked over to a large window and gazed across the valley. One of the two suns had set, and the other hung low on the horizon. Its pale glow fell softly through the arched window.

"We were just talking about Jess when you walked in," Isaac said, pulling our attention to the large dining table.

Fitz took me by the hand, and we settled next to each other at the table. He pulled me close and slid his arm around me, cradling me protectively.

"I'm afraid I have more fuel for the fire," I said.

I shared my experience with Jess in the afternoon session. I didn't want to tell Fitz just yet, but we needed to compile all the information on Jess we possibly could. I felt Fitz's rage burning.

"I'm telling you, that bastard is up to something," Henry said.

"It'll be a miracle if I don't kill this bastard," Fitz said, seething.

"He'd deserve it, that one," Henry said. "But you'll no do that."

A sly expression crossed Isaac's face. "I don't think anyone can tell Fitz much of anything right now."

"Fitz," I said plainly.

It took a moment, but finally he met my gaze.

"I'm going to work extra hard over the next week or so and move on from Jess's training. I can do this."

He closed his eyes briefly and nodded. "What's your plan?"

"I want us to all train together when we get home. Let's just blow through this training and be done with him."

"Aye, that's a braw thought," Henry said. He gave me a soft smile and a wink.

"Count me in," Isaac said. "I know everyone will say yes to this."

Fitz opened his eyes and looked deeply into mine. "Aye. Let's do it."

I knew better than to think he'd let this go. But hopefully Henry, Isaac, and I could run interference between Fitz and Jess long enough to get through training.

"Jordan will have an update on Jess when she arrives," Isaac said. "She was digging into his files today."

I had been nervous since we'd made the decision to have Jordan investigate Jess. I worried about her getting caught, but Jordan was good—I knew she would be careful.

"Good. I know we're supposed to be learning from Jess, but I don't know if I even trust his teaching," I said.

"Do you think he was planted in the mission?" Henry asked. It was the question we'd all undoubtedly considered, but this was the first time it was being brought to the table.

Isaac let out a long, slow whistle.

"You're asking if he's the mole?" I clarified.

"Damn, mate. Do you understand how bad that would be?" Fitz asked.

"If the mole is the witch assigned to train us, then this would be deadly," Isaac added.

"It's a heavy accusation. He's suspicious, but him being the mole might be a stretch," Henry said. "We'll see what Jordan found."

Conversation paused as the door opened, and Jordan and Maka stepped into the great room.

"I'm sorry." I grimaced, looking at Maka.

"Don't be. I'm happy to take a look."

She sat next to me and removed the bandage.

"Yep. That's a bad one. And it *does* need medical attention, by the way." She eyed me pointedly.

I sighed. "Fine, but I don't want to hold you up. I'll see if the healer has left headquarters yet."

"Don't be silly. I can take care of this real quick. Do you guys have any of—oh, wait. I remember where mine is." Maka closed her eyes. She extended her hand, and a jar materialized. "Izzy has been teaching me about natural remedies that are local to Scotland. This healing salve she makes is legit."

My heart ached at the thought of Izzy. Fitz's face was distant, and I felt the same sadness pass through him.

"Okay, hold tight, Hadley. I'll be quick."

Fitz, Isaac, Henry, and Jordan moved closer, and I rolled my eyes. I could've done without an audience, but Maka didn't seem to mind.

Her fingers hovered just over my open wound. She whispered unintelligibly under her breath, and the air shifted. She was calling on the elements. My skin grew warm and tingly, and my pulse thumped through my wound as the air thrummed in my ears. Then, my skin itched, renewing itself under Maka's healing touch.

Maka swiped her fingertips through the salve and dabbed it over my injury. I felt no pain during the act, and I imagined the wound must be closed.

"Okay, that should do it. Go easy on it tomorrow—good thing you're not training with Jess—but get good rest tonight and drink plenty of water."

With my wounds tidied up, we asked for Jordan's update on Jess. I turned to Maka.

"We're investigating Jess. No mention whatsoever to anyone else about this."

Maka nodded. "Got it."

Jordan sighed. "Most of his records are sealed or have heavy redactions. Anything historical is sealed, so I'm curious about what happened in his past."

"I wonder if sealing records here falls under the same general protocols as Earth," I said.

"Aye. What type of information calls for the sealing of a record here—do we know?"

We turned to Jordan.

"I'll find out. Right now, I'm rolling up all sensitive information, and the director makes those types of decisions."

"Did we find anything useful at all?" Isaac asked.

"I have his address, so we could always run some surveillance there. And most of his previous addresses were redacted, but there was one I caught part of—Terra Firma."

"Wait, that's the first city Lorenzo took control of," I said.

The city where Molly had lost her mate. The fallen city we'd known nothing about.

"I'll follow up on that for sure." Jordan typed notes on to her tablet. "I'll send you all a full report tonight, and we'll go from there."

The group dispersed for the evening. Maka looked at my jaw again before leaving, and she added a bit more salve to the wound.

"You know, Hadley. You asked me to observe Jess earlier."

She paused.

"Even disregarding everything that was talked about or speculated on here tonight . . . something is off with that guy. So no, I don't trust him. And neither should you."

"I need to ask you a favor," I said.

"Anything."

"Teach me how to break a mind shield."

—— CHAPTER TWENTY-ONE ——

The hum of espresso machines paired with the chatter of conversation culminated in the distinct sound of a coffee house that apparently was universal. The rise and fall of elven music permeated the air as we approached the bar to order.

"Morning, Etain!" I called out.

"Well, if it isn't two of my favorite customers," she grinned. "The usual, folks?"

We both nodded enthusiastically.

Etain called a drink order, and the being who collected it was roughly my height and wore a long navy robe. A druid, I realized. When his eyes swept over me, I felt a slight pressure against my skin. His dark eyes held the faintest hint of burgundy and something else—contempt.

I smiled when he stood next to me to grab his drink, and his features grew even more severe. He stared at me a few seconds longer than necessary, procured his coffee, and stalked back to a table of beings dressed in robes of the same style.

I pushed back the question of what his mind held, and instead listened for their words on the air.

"We don't need them here. Look at them—what are they going to do to help us?" a druid in green said.

His neighbor, who was draped in maroon, spun his finger above his drink—stirring it, I guessed, before weighing into the conversation. "Earth allowed this to happen, and now they think they're helping us. We don't need anything else from them."

I turned back to Etain, who was studying me with a sympathetic look in her bright eyes.

"It makes sense that everyone isn't pleased to see us," I said.

Etain shook her head. "The druids are especially negative about this whole deal. No one can please them, so don't take it personally."

I turned to study them once more and caught the glare of the druid in green. I held his gaze for longer than I was comfortable, though something in me refused to back down. When I faced Etain, I gave her a grateful smile. Regardless of whether the druids were involved with Allette and Hans, their disapproval of us was clear. I wasn't sure how to change a nation's opinion of us, but that wouldn't stop me from trying.

"So, you guys are meeting the Queen today?" Etain asked, tucking a stray strand of pink hair behind her ear.

"Yes," Jordan replied. "I'm so nervous."

Queen Marina of Thalassa had arrived the previous evening, and Jordan and I were scheduled to meet her later in the afternoon.

"Don't be!" Etain called over the noise of the espresso machine. "Everyone adores Queen Marina—kind of like how you guys all follow the British royal family."

"I'm surprised you know about them!" Jordan said.

"Not all of us keep up with Earth, but I do. I think humans are fascinating."

I chuckled. "You could say that."

Etain slid my London Fog across the counter. "I know you asked for the usual, but I also added a shot of wellness today. Your system is a little cloudy. This should help."

Jordan and I took a seat and waited for Molly. She'd had an early morning training session and had messaged Jordan and me to meet about Tanner and Chloe. Though I'd spoken with both Jordan and Molly about our speculations, this was our first discussion as a team.

I scanned the space, searching for any sign that something was amiss.

"What's wrong, Hadley?" Jordan asked.

I shook my head. "I'm just feeling a little paranoid, I think."

"We've been through a lot lately. That makes sense. But if some-one's watching, we'll know."

Molly slid into the chair next to me and sighed. A sizable bruise was forming underneath one of her dark eyes.

"Rough morning?" I asked.

"I've had better, that's for sure. I would've been here sooner, but I stopped to see the healer. Sorry about that," Molly said.

"So, what prompted your text this morning?" I asked.

"Chloe joined our session, and I heard her say something to Tanner."

"What did she say?" Jordan asked.

"She told Tanner she thinks she's under an enchantment. It's funny because I couldn't hear anything else during their entire conversation. Then I heard that clearly—it was almost like the elements were throwing those words in my direction."

"That's so odd."

"Do you think he's trying to help her figure out if she's enchanted?" Jordan questioned.

Molly took a deep breath, her gaze shifting downward.

I placed my hand over hers briefly. "Molly. You're not going to be judged over anything you say here today, even if it's bizarre or if you think you'll upset us. Just spit it out."

Molly tilted her head back slowly, eyes turned toward the ceiling. She nodded before continuing. "I think he's the one who placed her under an enchantment."

The table went silent, and I turned my gaze to Jordan. Disbelief clouded her features.

"Don't be angry," Molly said.

"Hold on, no . . . I'm not," I said. "I'm just processing. What makes you think that?"

"A couple of things." She paused, looking from me to Jordan, gauging our expressions. "Okay, so they're close. Weirdly close for two witches who aren't mated. Their body language is all wrong. Then she said she's under an enchantment. And I know you understand this, Hadley—I just have this feeling he enchanted her. My gut tells me that."

"Okay, yeah. I understand that. All of it, honestly," I acknowledged.

Jordan nodded. "I'm with you so far."

"So, get this. Recently, someone was telling me about a friend of hers. She fell in love with a human, and . . ." she glanced around. She paused briefly, and the air shifted.

"She's creating a privacy shield," I whispered to Jordan.

"Okay, sorry," Molly said. "So, she fell in love with a human, and then her local council found out. Someone reported it."

"Jerk," I muttered under my breath.

Jordan and Molly nodded.

"The council gave her an ultimatum. Break things off or they'd do something about it."

"Like what?"

"I don't know," Molly said, shaking her head. "But the rumor has always been that the council will wipe the human's memory and place a spell on them. Then they relocate them."

It was no rumor, but I didn't want to open that conversation with Molly today. My heart ached as I recalled what the councils had put me through. Jordan rested her hand on mine. I smiled weakly in return.

"That makes me sick," Jordan finally said.

Molly nodded. "Anyway, she gave them her word that he didn't know anything about her being a witch, and that she'd take care of it. She placed an enchantment on him so he wouldn't recognize her the same way."

"What do you mean by that—the same way?" Jordan asked.

"Basically, it's a mind trick. It's altering the way someone perceives you to form a detachment."

My stomach twisted.

"So, they could still be around each other technically. But he wouldn't feel anything for her?" Jordan asked.

"Exactly. I mean, I think he would still feel *something*, but not as intensely—not love. She shallowed out his feelings."

"Is that . . . allowed?"

"God, no. Usually, you'd be in some deep shit if anyone found out. But in this case . . . the council looked the other way."

"Of course they did. It suited their interests." I shook my head but returned my focus to her real point. "So, you think Tanner is trying to create some distance between himself and Chloe?"

"Yeah. I think they're mates."

"Oh god," I whispered.

"Look, I might be wrong. I just don't think I am."

"It would explain the connection," I said, thinking of mine with Fitz. It was impossible to deny the similarities in the way they conducted themselves when they were together.

Molly nodded. "The pull of mates is strong. It's nearly impossible to break." Molly paused. Something flickered across her eyes . . . sadness, maybe. "No enchantment could cut off those feelings completely."

The ache in my heart returned, thinking of Molly's loss. Even if I was Fated into love, I found comfort in what coursed between Fitz and me.

"Poor Chloe," I said, my voice strained.

"You okay, Hads?" Jordan asked.

"Yeah, I'm good." I cleared my throat, realizing that I wasn't. And it wasn't only because of Fate. We'd been moving so quickly to get to Opimae, I had stuffed down my feelings about the councils. But Molly's story was reminding me that my wounds hadn't quite healed.

"I can't quite wrap my head around this," Jordan said. "This shit sounds scary to me."

A nerve shot through my stomach. If Charles was right about Gustavo, I would be having an in-depth conversation with Jordan on this very topic soon.

"Yeah, it might feel odd at first, but then . . . I don't know. It feels natural," I said, my mind growing distant.

"You sound unsure," Jordan said.

"It's an odd concept," I admitted. "Everything is heightened between mates. You're left open and vulnerable to your partner. But there is this sense inside of you that it's meant to be this way."

"I think I'm having trouble with this because it just doesn't sound like Tanner," Jordan said. "What would make him do something like that?"

"That's what we need to find out. I think he's guarding her heart, and there could be a few different reasons for that," Molly said.

"This must be painful for him too. He wouldn't do something like this lightly," I said.

"I'm wondering—will Fate see this as Tanner tampering with the natural progression of events? Will he suffer consequences for this?" Molly asked.

"Shit. I didn't even think about that," I said. "I have a feeling the answer to that question is yes."

Jordan rested her elbows on the table and dropped her chin to her hands, sighing.

"But we need to figure out if that's even what's happening," Molly said.

"It would explain what we're seeing right now. The attraction, the suppression of feelings, the confusion . . ."

"Right. There would still be a connection. Complicated feelings. The whole thing . . . they just wouldn't feel that final click."

If Molly's theory was correct, then Tanner was actively choosing not to be Chloe's mate. I didn't know if he could implement the solution long term, but his actions led me to think that maybe—just maybe— Fitz had made a choice when he formed his stream long ago. Maybe he hadn't just given into Fate. Maybe our destiny hadn't been solely up to her. Maybe Fitz had chosen to love me.

"What is it, Hads?" Jordan asked.

"It's nothing, really. I've just been thinking about Fate a lot."

"What do you mean?" Molly asked.

I wasn't ready to discuss the depth of my personal questioning, not even with Jordan. I focused on its relation to Tanner and Chloe instead.

"I'm wondering how much control Fate allows us in our own destinies.

She brings us to our mates, and there's this incredibly strong bond that forms. But the draw is strong even before your streams are created. With that being said . . . I can only imagine how difficult this would be for Tanner to fight if Fate has led him to Chloe."

Jordan nodded, parsing through my information.

"And ultimately, how long can you fight Fate anyway?" Molly asked.

"Exactly," I said. "Is he just fighting time? Or can this distance hold?"

"So, if that's what Tanner's doing, then he's fighting against his nature and against Fate," Jordan said.

I recalled how difficult it was when the council had forced Fitz and me apart. They'd forced us to fight our nature, and it had been hell on me, even though I was still human. If Molly's theory was correct, I couldn't imagine how difficult this would be for Tanner, nor how confusing it would be for Chloe. My chest tightened again at the thought.

"Damn," Jordan said, forcefully. "This is screwed up."

"You know what's even more screwed up?"

"What?"

"I think Molly's right."

Jordan and I settled on to plush velvet chairs in a small meeting room at headquarters. The space was like the training room we'd been in our first afternoon there, but the windows were smaller, forcing us to rely mostly on the flickering magical lamps around the space. The room was eerily quiet, and I was glad to see Charles, Keoni, and Brigitta cross the threshold.

Charles settled into the chair beside me.

Our conversation ended abruptly when the queen's arrival was announced. We stood to greet her. Jordan's energy shifted wildly, and I closed my eyes briefly, sending her as much calming energy as I could muster. When I opened my eyes, Brigitta's were closed—and she was facing Jordan in much the same way. I smiled, grateful for her support.

Queen Marina glided effortlessly into the room, flanked by guards on each side of her, which I imagined was a new safety precaution in the age of Lorenzo. She was stunning, the living embodiment of sailor's tales of ethereal beings from the sea, and I couldn't help but study her. Hair as dark as a midnight sky was swept back toward the crown of her head, though curls escaped around her face. Her skin was dark brown, and her hazel eyes bordered on a true green, amplified by her extravagant lavender robes.

The queen halted before Charles. We could've heard a pin drop.

"Queen Marina," Charles finally said. "Lovely to see you, as always." He bowed, and we all followed suit.

"Likewise, Charles. I'm pleased to be here on such business."

"As are we."

"I know there are many formalities to be followed, but I'm anxious to see the young woman. Could I please be introduced straight away?"

"As you wish, of course. Jordan?" Charles called, turning to face my best friend.

Jordan moved timidly toward the queen. She paused and curtsied, and the queen's eyes widened. Queen Marina placed her hand beneath Jordan's jaw and guided her to stand. She studied Jordan carefully, and I realized I was holding my breath.

"You're a water witch, without any doubt. Welcome to our kingdom, my child."

"Thank you, your majesty."

"There is much to learn. And we haven't much time now, do we?"

"I'm sure your representatives have you up to speed on the latest from the crusade. Thank you for your full support in bringing over the Earth-side teams—and of our latest efforts," Charles said.

"We all wish these circumstances were different, but they aren't. The discord from Bain and Athdara are unnecessary distractions. We must strike an accord and move forward collaboratively if we're to dampen Lorenzo's rebellion."

Though I knew Bain wasn't pleased with Earth's involvement, the information about Athdara surprised me. Another chamber meeting was only days away, and I resolved to pay further attention to King Copandir.

"And speaking of collaboration," Charles said, "we're grateful you've sent trainers from Thalassa to work with Jordan. Since she's working diligently with intelligence teams and her travel to Thalassa must wait, this is inordinately helpful."

"I thought it would be so. I've brought a few more of my best trainers with me. However, I'd like to arrange at least a brief trip for her to see the land of our folk whenever she might be spared for a couple of days."

"I'm sure that can be done."

"If you'd like that, that is?" Queen Marina asked Jordan.

"I'd like nothing more," Jordan answered.

"Wonderful. I'd also like to meet Hadley and Fitz."

Charles turned to me, and I followed Jordan's example.

"We'll arrange for you to meet Fitz soon, but Hadley joined us today."

She shifted her gaze to me. "After all this time . . . here you are, the promised crusader of the prophecy. Oh, how we've waited for you. The fate of our world rests on your shoulders. Know that you have my full support."

"I'm afraid I'm at a loss for words—I can't thank you enough for your support. Not only for the crusade, but also with Jordan."

"You two have a bond that is tightly woven—I sense it. Try not to worry while you're focused on the mission, Hadley. Jordan will be learning and growing into the witch she's destined to become."

I bowed my head in gratitude.

"Now then. I've brought gifts. Come, you two. Charles has been kind enough to lend us a magnificently large room for us to become better acquainted."

Jordan and I spent the afternoon with Queen Marina. I hadn't expected her to involve me in the rest of the day's conversations, but she seemed to sense that Jordan was most comfortable with that arrangement.

We learned that Thalassa was one of the oldest reigning kingdoms in Opimae. Since so many water witches had come over at once from Earth during the Great Passage, the entire nation had been born in the blink of an eye.

Queen Marina had brought an astonishing number of records with her. Volumes of lineages were stacked neatly upon tables, and witches arrived to assist us through our research. Encyclopedias and various books on the history of their kingdom were being organized by the kingdom's brightest scholars for Jordan's review. Various garments hung on racks near the window, the traditional clothing of the water witches, right down to their preferred garments for spending extended periods of time in the ocean.

"I'm in awe. I honestly . . . I have no idea what to even say except thank you."

"You're welcome. I know this must be an overwhelming amount of information, but we'll guide you through it bit by bit. You'll have the best teachers walking you through it all. And Hadley—you're welcome here with Jordan any time you'd like."

"Thank you, Queen Marina. This is . . . well, it's magnificent."

"We're just getting started. Jordan, over the next few months, you'll experience an awakening you can't even imagine. We rarely have the honor of welcoming one of our own back into the fold, and we are so pleased the tides of Fate have called you home."

After decompressing from the day, I updated Fitz on the Tanner and Chloe situation as we got ready for bed.

"Molly thinks I should talk to him."

"What do you think?"

"I think I need to wait a while. I want to be sure about this."

"Aye," Fitz's voice sounded through the open door. "You don't want to waltz into training and ask Tanner if he enchanted Chloe to prevent the two of them from mating. That's a heavy charge to have gotten wrong."

"Oh yes, that definitely would have been my strategy." I rolled my eyes, laughing. "You're such a dork."

"Aye, but a lovable one."

"You bet."

I bounded into the bedroom, having killed the lights in our bathroom. I climbed onto Fitz's lap, and he pulled the covers around us. "No, I'd wait to get him alone *after* training, and then attack."

Fitz wore his most horrified expression, and we both laughed.

"Focus!" I said playfully, my hands resting on either side of his beautiful face. I stared into his eyes, my mind echoing questions that my conversation with Molly and Jordan had produced. Had our course been irrevocably charted by Fate? Or had we truly made our own decisions in loving each other?

Our eyes locked for a second too long, and energy burst wildly in the space between us. I closed my eyes, shaking off the intensity of the connection. Fitz pulled me close, tucking his head under my chin. I released a long, slow breath and focused my mind back to Tanner.

"Maybe he'll be fine if I just casually mention I've noticed something odd between him and Chloe. I'll decide my next course of action based on how he reacts."

"I hope you know there won't be anything *casual* about this conversation."

"Aye," I said, emulating Fitz.

"And if he's angry?" he asked. I heard the humor in his voice.

"Then he can be angry, which will probably be the case, and it'll turn into a fight. But you can't go around placing Cardinal Court members under enchantment."

"Now, *that* is true."

"What would happen if a council member found out?"

"He'd be in loads of trouble—immediately suspended from his job and likely from the crusade entirely, therefore ending his career."

"Great."

"Talk to him when you're ready, and we'll sort it from there. He trusts you more than anyone else on the team. You'll get it right."

"You know what's interesting about all this?"

"What's that?" he asked.

"The councils will force someone away from their mate and make harmful decisions for them, but they'd punish Tanner for this," I said, before sharing Molly's story from dinner. "Fitz, that could have been us."

Fitz raised his head to face me. "Not unless you told me that's what you wanted."

My eyes searched his. "Even if I hadn't matched to my power? You still would've fought to be with me?"

"Aye. I'd have fought the councils until the very end, even with my dying breath."

I thought about his plans, how he had been prepared to give up everything to disappear with me if that's what it had come to, if the councils had given us the same ultimatum.

"I would have, too. Even before I matched to my power, our connection was too strong. I can't imagine a scenario where we gave up," I said.

And I couldn't. Regardless of the questions in my mind, I knew I would have fought until the bitter end for him. I still would. I thought of Tanner and shivered. What could have happened to prompt him to fight against himself like this?

"There isn't one."

"I feel sorry for that witch . . . sacrificing her happiness to keep the person she loves safe."

He cradled my head with his hand. "Aye. She's better than I was."

"No," I said firmly. "Maybe she didn't know how to build a network like you did, or maybe she was just too scared to find a way around the councils. But *you* didn't give up on us. You're a fighter . . . we both are. And I'd go through that hell all over again to be where we are now."

Fitz's eyes grew distant.

"What is it?"

"Imagine enchanting your mate . . ." He shook his head.

"Would you ever have done that to me?"

"Enchant you? Not under any circumstance."

"Good, but I'm a little surprised."

"Why?"

"You've been so protective of me."

"Before you matched to your power, I protected you so you *wouldn't* be enchanted. I'd never enchant you. I wouldn't take this away from you for anything, and I would be pissed if you did that to me. If anyone stole the knowledge of my mate, for any reason . . ." He trailed off.

"No, Hadley. I'd never make this decision for you. It's your decision, and yours alone."

My heart swelled as I considered how Fitz had fought for me to make my own decision. It was comforting to know that he believed it was mine.

"I can't imagine not knowing you . . . or waking up one day and not knowing you the way I do now," I said softly.

"For years, I wondered about you—where you were, what your laugh sounded like, what your opinion would be about this and that." He rubbed his thumb across my cheek. His lips followed. "What we have . . . I'd pay any price for it."

— CHAPTER TWENTY-TWO —

The following morning was a tense scene. Though it had only been a few days since the accident, and even though he wasn't anywhere near healed, the trainers insisted Fitz attempt a quick time-walk with me to test his recovery.

"This is absurd," I argued, stalking across the training room.

"Yeah, this is a really bad idea," Molly said.

"We have Molly here so she can trace you if you run into trouble. She can follow your threads and bring you back," the trainer argued.

Though Molly was a time-walker, there was no guarantee that she'd be able to trace us. These trainers had to know that, and my pulse quickened as I questioned their true motivation for this test.

"I've spoken with the trainers at length, and they've assured me they can mitigate all risks," Keoni said.

"I appreciate what you're saying," I said diplomatically, despite my true feelings. "But there's no way to mitigate all the risks with this situation. This is *dangerous*."

"There's truly nothing to be concerned about," the trainer said. His tone was dismissive, and I didn't miss the annoyed look he gave the other trainer in the room.

"I won't take Hadley with me," Fitz said.

Fitz took a seat at a small wooden table near the window. He looked a little pale, and his speech betrayed his fatigue. It was difficult for me to maintain my composure seeing the trainers push Fitz in this condition, and my fingers tingled as anger built within me.

"Yes, you will," I argued. "I'm not letting you time-walk alone right now."

"Aye, because you know how dangerous this is, which is exactly why you should stay behind," he said.

"What if Molly goes with him?" Keoni asked.

"No," one of the trainers said sternly. "She will unintentionally help him, even if she tries not to. Her magic will assist him. We need to know what he can do on his own."

My magic would also assist him to some extent, but the trainers didn't need to know that.

"He's not going alone. Final answer." My eyes flashed to Fitz, daring him to contradict me.

He exhaled angrily.

Our argument continued, but we eventually agreed on a brief walk into the recent past.

"I'll take just a moment to meditate," he told the trainers, his voice terse enough to make it clear they'd follow his timeline.

I nodded approvingly, and the rest of us wandered to the far side of the room to grant him some space. I stood near the doorway with Molly, my gaze lingering on Fitz.

"I still don't understand the point of this. Why does it have to be today?" Molly whispered.

"Apparently, they think it's vital to get a read on how he's healing."

"You buy that?"

"Of course not. And neither does he."

"What do you think is going on?" she asked.

"Honestly? I don't think these trainers are fans of Earth. I think they're pushing us out of spite."

"You could take this to Charles."

"I could."

But it wouldn't change anything. Even though we'd started turning a corner with Charles, his dismissal of Jess's behavior led me to believe he'd support these trainers.

Molly smirked.

"What?"

"I'm surprised you aren't making a bigger stink about this."

"Was that fight not loud enough for you?"

"Plenty. But you let it go."

"It's Fitz's call."

"And you're more protective of him than this."

I sighed. "I'm trusting his judgement."

Molly let out a whistle.

"Now what?"

"Oh, nothing. I'm just anticipating the repressed anger that's going to show up in my session with you later today."

"I mean, you're not wrong."

Once Fitz's meditation was over, Molly and I joined him. I wrapped my arms around his torso, holding him tightly.

"You sure you're good?" I asked, feeling his nerves. "We have the power to walk away."

He paused. "I feel like I need to try. This injury put me behind schedule, and we don't have the luxury of time."

I shook my head. "I don't know why you put so much pressure on yourself."

"Of course, you do."

"Let's just get this over with so you can rest a bit."

"I'll track Fitz's energy," Molly said. "I'll do everything I can to find you if anything goes wrong."

"Thank you, Molly," I said softly.

Fitz nodded his head. "Here goes nothing."

The in-between welcomed us, the elements of time and space

swirling dreamily. I'd grown accustomed to floating through the night sky, though I was constantly suppressing the urge to reach out and touch the dancing constellations. They were mesmerizing. I was attempting to pull back toward our destination when a nagging sensation crept into the back of my mind.

"Hadley . . ." Fitz's voice sounded through the haze. It was muffled, and a twinge of anxiety hit the pit of my stomach.

"What's wrong?" I asked.

"I don't know. Something just isn't right."

I felt his heart rate increase through our connection.

"Fitz. It's okay. Just take a second."

"The threads are jumbled. They're usually easier to navigate than this."

"Do you know where we came from?" I asked.

"Aye. Or at least, I think so. I've been trying not to lose that path, just in case. But it's hard to focus on both the present and the past."

He paused, looking around.

"Take your time. I have all the faith in the world in you," I responded with every ounce of sincerity in me. This was delicate, but I knew he could do it.

Fitz kissed my forehead, the act ripe with concern, before he returned to the task at hand.

"So, where did we come from, exactly?" I asked, hoping to be useful.

"This way." He pointed. "There are two possible threads. It's just . . ."

"It's just what?"

"My head is pounding, and my senses aren't heightened like they should be."

"You're going to be okay, right?" My voice held a hint of panic, and I swallowed hard. I didn't want to add to his own fear. "I mean, should I be worried?"

"The healers said the pain would be bad for a bit longer. It feels like someone is splitting my head in two. But if I can ease this pain, my vision should clear, and I'll be able to reconnect properly to the elements to navigate us out."

"We'll figure this out. I guess we can sit here until your head clears."

"Aye, but I do have to maintain focus, so we don't go drifting off into the constellations."

"Yeah, let's not get lost in time, please." I shuddered, recalling Fitz's words from our first time travel escapade. The thought of getting trapped in time was more than unsettling.

"I know you can't close your eyes, but at least it's dim where we are. Maybe keep sight of the threads while we do some deep breathing together? Try to relax your body a bit?"

We ran through various exercises, and Fitz was able to maintain focus on the potential paths home. I wanted nothing more than to be helpful, but there was precious little I could do in this situation, and that only added to my growing nerves. The fear of being trapped in time settled in my bones, but I did my best to calm myself, knowing that panic would only make our situation worse.

The only solution was to calm Fitz's body so he could lead us back out.

Fitz sat cross legged on what looked like a smooth mass of clouds that glowed with warm light. He pulled my near-weightless body onto his lap. I channeled as much peace and calm as I could, pushing healing energy to Fitz's body while thinking about the training room. In that moment, I was especially grateful for our energy streams. His hand landed on mine, his thumb running across the back of my hand, and I felt our connection intensifying. Finally, Fitz broke the silence.

"I know the way home," he said simply.

Fitz stood, pulling me up with him, and my feet settled on to the glowing cloud.

"What are we standing on?"

"There are thousands of threads underneath us, all different colors. Some are vibrant, some are dull. They link all of time and space together. We glide just above them."

"It looks like a hazy cloud to me."

"Wait, you can see them? How strange."

"I shouldn't be able to see anything, should I?"

"No . . . But I'll bet it's another bit of your loophole magic," he said. "We should head back."

"Let's go, captain."

I jumped back into his arms, and he picked up the thread that would lead us home. I tucked my head under his chin, and before I knew it, the bright lights of the training room welcomed us back to our time.

"Fitz! Hadley! Can you hear us?" Molly's voice broke through my groggy consciousness.

"Loud and clear," I answered grumpily.

"Are you all right?" Keoni whispered urgently.

"I think so. Fitz?"

"Aye, I'm good. My head is killing me, though. More than it should."

"We should get you checked out immediately."

I registered the medical staff nearby.

"How long were we gone?" I asked.

"Three hours."

"Longest fifteen-minute time travel journey I've ever been on," I said.

"The trainers knew something was off almost instantly. We've had Molly and other trackers looking for you and medical staff on standby for hours."

"Yeah, that's what happens when you push someone to do something before they're ready—before they're healed."

Fire burned through my veins, and my fingertips tingled with the threat of my anger overflowing.

"Hadley," Fitz warned.

"Not this time, Fitz," I said. "We could have gotten lost in time today. You'd better not push anyone else like you pushed Fitz. These are real lives on the line."

The venom in my voice was impossible to miss.

"We're very sorry," the lead trainer said. "Truly. It won't happen again."

"We'll have plenty of time to discuss this," Keoni interjected. "But let's get you both somewhere comfortable right now so you can be assessed by the medical staff."

I tore my eyes from the trainers. Something wasn't right, and I knew immediately I wouldn't allow these trainers the opportunity to make the same "mistake" twice.

"Come on, Hadley," Molly said. "We'll deal with this later, but right now, Fitz needs you."

My eyes flashed to Fitz, who was holding the back of a chair in a death grip. I was by his side quickly, and we held each other tightly as we crossed the training room. Seeing him in this state was enough to boil my blood.

"Keoni, will you let Charles know I'll stop by his office this afternoon?"

"Of course."

I hoped Charles was ready for some changes to the training department.

CHAPTER TWENTY-THREE

The chamber was unusually quiet as we entered the meeting space. The rows of leaders seemed to be focused on information packets on the long tables in front of them. We knew Jordan was due to provide an update today, and based on the atmosphere, it would be serious. Fitz and I found our seats close to the front row.

I stole a quick glance at Fitz. His bruises had faded to soft shades of yellow, his cuts were fading, and the deep gash on his jaw was scabbed over. The healers had been able to ease the pain that stemmed from the transport misfire, and they confirmed what we suspected—the trainers shouldn't have asked him to attempt time travel during that stage of the healing process. They were reprimanded and placed on probation while we investigated whether the trainers had been under any influence of Lorenzo. With the severity of recent events, we were more desperate than ever to identify our security breaches—technological and otherwise.

I picked up the information packet just as Jordan entered the room, flanked by Charles, Keoni, and Brigitta. Jordan and Charles took to the platform.

Discovering there was at least one informant in our ranks was unsettling, and though Jess was our main suspect, I still found myself watching each Opimaean agent carefully.

"Good morning, everyone. As I'm sure you've seen, we'll start today by reviewing an intelligence update." Charles turned to Jordan. "For those of you who haven't had the pleasure, this is Jordan Moore. She is an analyst with our Earth crusaders. As she made these discoveries, we'll hear directly from her today."

"Thank you, Charles," Jordan said, stepping forward. Jordan had always been unapologetically herself, but today she carried herself with even more confidence.

My witch's eye picked up on a warm magical glow around her, much like the amber light of her eyes. It seemed my dear friend had come into her magic.

I smiled as she began her report.

"After the abduction attempts on the Earth-side teams and the system break-in, I've been working on identifying weaknesses in the databases here and with Opimaean teams to secure them. In doing so, I've discovered some troubling information." She turned to Brigitta, who pulled Jordan's presentation on to the screen.

"One of our largest issues right now is a communication breakdown. Simply put, there are far too many instances of miscommunication. Information is being lost between teams."

Bakari, the prime minister of Thalassa, stood. "What type of information is being lost?"

"The first break in communication I noticed was between Opimae and Earth. Information was being sent to agents to then be transmitted by couriers across the portal. But the information never made it to Earth. Earth's teams didn't even know that Lorenzo had crossed the portal again."

"Likely a breakdown on Earth's side," King Alden of Bain said, running his fingers along his beard.

I almost stood, but Jordan was quick with her response.

"The breakdown was on the Opimaean side. The information never reached the couriers; I checked the system. There was a deliberate attempt to prevent the information from being shared."

The king and his advisors looked less than convinced. Their contempt for us held strong.

"Are there any leads on who did this?" King Brennus of Constantina, the southern elven kingdom, asked.

"Not yet. The teams are currently sweeping the database to find all instances of these communication failures, and we're working on identifying patterns within the information. We'll have a full report to you as soon as possible."

"Thank you, Jordan."

Jordan nodded and took a seat beside me as Charles returned to the platform.

"We cannot ignore the perpetrators of the recent abduction attempts. They've clearly infiltrated our systems. We are currently unsure which issues are the work of the abductors and which to attribute to Lorenzo, but Intelligence is working diligently to find out," Charles said. "But of course, Lorenzo is our main concern. And for now, the chamber must address the fall of Adamo. I propose we take action against Lorenzo quickly."

Queen Min-Ji of Hurlee stood. I studied her closely, wondering if she was with us or against us. Her dark eyes were troubled, but she carried herself with grace, holding her head high. "I'm just going to say what I know many are thinking. We should move to take Adamo back."

The room fell to disorder. Murmurs, agreements and objections, and chatter between chamber members roared through the space. Charles called the chamber back to order.

I looked to Fitz and then to Chloe, Solomon, and Mia. Though I knew we'd need to discuss our stance, I didn't suspect we'd be opposed to the idea. Though it meant battle for the team, something had to be done.

"Queen Min-Ji, you still have the floor," Charles said.

"Lorenzo is growing in power, and if we do not check it soon, he will grow beyond our reach. Our intelligence is compromised. We're going to spend how much in resources to find the informants, and I ask each of you here today to think about these questions: will it make a difference, or will we be too late?"

King Alden stood. "While I agree with Queen Min-Ji, I think we take this one step further. We should commission a team to enter Lorenzo's fortress and capture him."

The queen seconded his motion.

I looked to Fitz, and he nodded. We needed to volunteer the team for this mission. It was the perfect opportunity for us to obtain Fitz's family ring. Whether or not we could capture Lorenzo, we could obtain the ring. I looked to the Cardinal Court members. Through quick nods, we settled on an answer—I would volunteer us for the mission.

King Copandir of Athdara stood. "I don't know that I like the thought." He paused. "Though I understand the sentiment—and the appeal—our forces are not ready for that."

"Respectfully, I disagree." It was Evander, the prime minister of Arregaithel who spoke. "It is easy to have this opinion when the carnage isn't happening to your folk. Ask yourself how you would feel if Lorenzo were killing citizens in your nations and taking their homes from them. Their peace, their security.

"The Northern Realm of the elves has always been an ally to us. We ask for your continued partnership. Do not abandon us when we need you most."

The king remained quiet.

Prime Minister Evander's appeal heightened my fire magic, which only fueled my connection to the witches of Adamo. Warm adrenaline pulsed through my veins as I stood. Every set of eyes in the room turned to me.

"Earth will stand with you, Prime Minister. The witches of the fire nation have our support."

Prime Minister Evander nodded gratefully. "We appreciate your partnership."

I looked to my team. Fitz nodded, encouraging me further. "I know the thought of sending your warriors into Adamo is a heavy burden to carry, but we all understand what we've signed up for. Many more lives will be lost if Lorenzo continues to grow in power. We can't afford to stand by and watch." I turned to King Copandir. "And with all due respect, your majesty, many lives in your kingdom will be lost if we do not stop Lorenzo. You'll sacrifice many more later."

The king held my gaze. When he spoke again, his eyes were lost in reflection. "You have given me much to consider," he said. I smiled at his diplomacy.

Prime Minister Bakari stood. "The folk of Thalassa do not favor the side of war. However, if we do not stand as one now and fight, together we will fall later. Today, it is Adamo. Tomorrow, it is Pluvia Silva. And the next? The border nations of Athdara, Bain, Novam Terram. He will come for us all."

A somber quiet spread across the room.

Charles was the first to break it. "Bakari is right about Pluvia Silva."

"Aye," Fitz agreed. "Lorenzo is working his way down the mountain. It will not be long before he finds his way to Opimae City and beyond."

"How large is Pluvia Silva?" Solomon asked.

"A hundred thousand beings," Prime Minister Evander said.

"Gaining control of Pluvia Silva would be a wise move for Lorenzo, strategically speaking," Charles responded. "The town is of great military significance for us. It's the proper spot in the mountainside to launch an attack on Lorenzo's fortress."

"And a great place for Lorenzo to further his cause. The strategic position works both ways," Prime Minister Evander said.

King Brennus stood. "Constantina will support Arregaithel. You have been a steadfast ally to many of us during difficult times. And if Lorenzo takes Arregaithel, it will not only be a great loss to its folk, but for all of us."

King Alden stood. "We should discuss what the attack to regain Adamo would require from each nation, along with the resources for the fortress mission."

We had to be a part of that mission. I stood again.

"The fortress team should be small. I'd like to propose my team, along with a solid set of transporters from Opimae."

"We don't need Earth taking over this mission," King Alden said, condescension clear in his tone.

"That's not what we're trying to do," I argued. "But I've entered Lorenzo's fortress several times now. I have the necessary experience—and so does the rest of this team."

The king huffed.

Prime Minister Bakari stood. "Like it or not, Hadley has a point. The Earth-side team has collected our best intelligence regarding Lorenzo's fortress."

"Opimaean troops can handle this," the king said.

"You can't just barge into Lorenzo's fortress. That won't work," I said.

"I wasn't suggesting that," King Alden said, sneering. "I just don't trust this team."

"You have no basis for that," Mia said, standing. "How many of your warriors or agents have the power to find loopholes in other witch's spells?"

The room was silent.

"Please," Mia continued. "If there's anyone here today who can answer this question, please do. How many of your folk work loophole magic?"

Silence.

Finally, Mia said, "That's what I thought. Then, no one else can lead a team into the fortress with stealth."

I stifled a smile, both stunned and gratified.

Mia returned to her seat, smug. She paused before turning to me, her eyes flickering quickly to mine as the chamber's conversation resumed.

CHAPTER TWENTY-FOUR

The arguments in the chamber continued well into the afternoon, but they couldn't reach a decision. The chamber would meet again over the next week and try to reach an accord regarding Adamo. In the meantime, we were to continue our training, attend meetings, and study the intelligence briefings Jordan sent to us.

The following afternoon, post-practice, I happily left Jess and my suspicions behind to update Jordan on some intelligence of our own.

Molly and I took Jordan to a local wine bar. A private room awaited us, and we settled in for an evening of conversation.

Gustavo had been called away on business, wrapping up his responsibilities to join our crusade. He'd aced his tests with surprisingly high scores. He was due back the following morning, and we needed to have a conversation with Jordan about what this meant.

We were led down an iron spiral staircase and seated at a rustic wooden table. We lost ourselves momentarily to the beauty of the space.

Torches were mounted on the beige stone walls, casting the warm glow of magical light. A fire crackled at one corner of the room, while a small waterfall trickled down the opposite wall—from a natural spring, the waiter shared.

Even wine was different on Opimae. Though it held many of the same characteristics of Earth's wine, the colors seemed more vibrant, and the taste was bolder. My wine selection was a deep ruby, and it trickled slowly down the sides of the glass once it was swirled.

"J, I know you've talked to Gustavo since he left—a few times?"

"Yeah, actually he's called me every day to check in." She paused. "Do y'all think that's normal?"

"You know it isn't, Jordan. That's why you asked the question," Molly said.

Jordan chuckled. "Straight to the point, as always."

"Here's the thing," I began. "We have a theory . . ."

"Don't do that tiptoe thing."

"What tiptoe thing?"

"Spit it out, Hads."

"Fine," I said, though I paused nervously for just a second. "Gustavo is your mate."

"What?" she exclaimed, nearly choking on her wine.

"You two are magnetic," Molly said. "You had a pull to each other even before you came into your powers. Now that you've matched, the connection between the two of you will want to solidify."

Jordan looked at me, bewildered.

"I know. I almost said something sooner, but you were acclimating to so much—you still are—and then everything with Adamo. But Gustavo is back tomorrow, and you've matched to your magic, so it really couldn't wait any longer."

"What does this mean? Like—oh god—am I just going to want to jump his bones tomorrow, or what?"

It was my turn to choke on my wine. Molly laughed so hard she snorted, which was something I'd never seen from her before.

"Okay, but seriously. A little help here," Jordan pleaded.

"Well, your connection won't solidify instantly," I said, recalling that my own experience would be different from Jordan's. I'd already grown to love Fitz as a human well before I'd come into my magic. "That is, unless you've already fallen for this man."

Jordan's expression turned pensive. "There's something there, for sure, but it's not love . . ."

"Do you think it will be love?" I asked.

"There's this sense that I already know him. That I've known him forever. Which is odd, considering we've mostly just talked on the phone," she said, her brows furrowing. "It's not quite love at first sight; it's knowledge at first sight."

That was exactly how it had felt for me and Fitz.

"And that's normal," Molly said.

"What happens if this connection forms?" Jordan asked.

I thought of my first reaction to Fitz after matching to my power and smiled.

"What? What is it?" Jordan asked.

"It wasn't the physical connection that surprised me," I said, thinking of Jordan's earlier question. "I mean, don't get me wrong, the physical attraction is intense. But I was suddenly so completely aware of him in a new way. His power, his scent, his feelings . . . everything was amplified. I had this need to explore our connection. And that first contact . . ." I shook my head. "It's intense."

"Explain," Jordan demanded.

I thought of the feelings that had swirled through me when we matched, of the peace that accompanied our streams, how the painful shocking between us had ceased.

"Everything fell into place. It sounds so damn corny, but it did. Our world was turned upside down, and none of it still made much sense, but suddenly I knew the two of us belonged together. We made sense, and that mattered more than anything. I knew that no matter what happened, it would be okay in the end if we were together."

Jordan dropped her head on to Molly's shoulder.

"What else?"

"The first time I saw Fitz after matching to my power . . . it was clarity. Oh, and we had these little energy streams form. I don't know if they always form the same, but ours are these bright wires that look like filament in old-timey light bulbs. It's the manifestation of our connection, and it carries information between the two of us. It's how Fitz knew we were in trouble the day we met Gustavo."

"Fitz said water dripped down his face?"

I nodded. "That should tell you what you need to know about the connection. I know when he's in pain. He knows when I'm frightened. If I close my eyes right now and concentrate, I can feel his heartbeat. It's . . . reassuring."

"And this might happen to me tomorrow," Jordan said, her eyes narrowing.

"Yeah, it's a real possibility," I said. "Even if you're not quite ready to form your streams, things will intensify between you two."

"Which is why we wanted to talk to you about it," Molly said.

"I know you understand some of it from hearing about me and Fitz, and with... whatever is happening between Tanner and Chloe. But to take on all these new things in this foreign world, and then to find your mate . . . it feels scary as hell when you don't understand what's happening."

"We weren't sure at first if we should warn you," Molly said. "I mean, a part of me still thinks you should have the whole experience without our commentary, but we didn't want you feeling freaked out."

"You did the right thing. I feel like running away, even now." Jordan chewed at her bottom lip as her gaze fell to the table.

I grasped her hand, and it shook violently in my own. Jordan wasn't easily rattled, and it took me off guard. She was one of the steadiest, calmest beings I knew.

"Oh, Jordan."

Jordan's gaze was fixed on her drink. But finally, she looked at me.

"What if I don't want this?" she whispered.

"Honestly?" I paused searching for an answer. "I have no idea."

"Gustavo is a good guy," Molly said. "I can feel that, so I know you can, too. I don't think you'll have to worry about not wanting this."

"That's not the issue. The issue is that this feels like something that isn't my choice but is going to change my entire life. What if I don't want to fall in love? What if I don't want to rearrange my entire life over all this stuff that's happened lately?"

Jordan questioned the one element of the mate connection that I had been wondering about myself.

Did we truly have a choice?

"Jordan."

"No. Hadley, I'm serious. I came to this foreign planet, and then it turns out I'm a witch? And immediately after discovering that, this man shows up who I'm destined to fall in love with?" Her voice rose. "This is too much."

"I know," I said simply.

Jordan searched my eyes. "What aren't you saying, Hads?"

I hesitated, breaking eye contact.

"Just say it," she said. "You know you can say it here, whatever it is."

I knew I could.

"Honestly, Jordan's question is my question, too. Do we make this choice, or is it decided for us? And if so, doesn't that change the way we look at our relationships?"

"You're worried Fate has predestined our love," Molly said.

"Yeah."

"Do you have doubts with Fitz?" Jordan asked.

"Here's the thing: I have no doubt that Fitz and I love each other. I have no doubt that our connection is strong. The feel of his energy, his heartbeat, all of it—it's comforting."

"But . . ." Jordan prompted after I hesitated.

"But I've been questioning Fate and her involvement in our lives lately."

"You mentioned something about that the other day," Molly said.

I nodded. "It's been nipping at me. I mean, I'm confident I love Fitz, but did I have a choice? Did he choose to love me, or did Fate decide that for him?" I asked. "It's just bothering me that I don't know the answer to that question, I guess."

Molly's eyes softened, and so did Jordan's features. The fear I'd pushed down inside of me must have finally shown on my face.

"Why is this bothering you so much?" Molly asked.

"I guess I just want to know that we've chosen our lives. And if Fate does decide this path for us, then who's to say she won't decide to break our bond one day?"

Molly exhaled deeply.

"You hadn't thought about that before," I said.

Molly shook her head. "I guess you don't always question things when you've grown up in them."

"Does your bond feel . . . I don't know . . . wrong?" Jordan asked.

I hesitated before answering. She was worried about me, but my answers could shape her own perspective before she had the experience firsthand. I didn't want that for her—I wanted her to form her own opinions solely based on her personal experience. When I voiced my concern, she shook her head.

"That's for me to decide. It'll be fine. We have to talk about this, Hadley."

Finally, I proceeded. "Our connection doesn't feel wrong at all. It's felt a bit overwhelming at times while adjusting to it, but that feeling isn't a constant. For the most part, it feels natural."

"So, really it's just that you want to know it wasn't decided for you— that this is real because the two of you chose it," Jordan said.

"Exactly."

"That's what I'm wondering, too. And it really does scare me," Jordan said.

"I know this feels scary, but I've seen this process happen with friends of mine, and you're lucky you've found Gustavo. Having some-one you can count on like this . . . well, it's a gift," Molly offered, skirting the truth about Finn.

"But if I can't control my feelings, then is it really a gift? Or is it a life sentence? Just another assignment?"

"It's not going to feel like an assignment, Jordan. You'll want this," Molly said. "Even though Hadley's wondering about the origin of this feeling, she doesn't want to give it up. Or at least, I don't think she does."

Molly looked to me.

"No. I don't want that at all."

Jordan sighed.

"What?" Molly asked, her eyebrows raised.

"This meant-to-be bullshit is too much, especially with Hadley's question mark over Fate."

Molly eyed me, a hint of amusement hiding in her demeanor.

"Bullshit?" I asked.

"This sounds crazy, and you know it. Like a cult or something."

"Jordan, it's not a cult," I said.

Jordan eyed me dubiously.

"I know how it must sound."

"But?"

"I don't know," I answered, exasperated. "It's just how we're made. You can resist it if you want, but I don't think you'll be very happy."

We sat wordlessly for a moment before Jordan broke the silence.

"So after questioning all this . . . do you have any idea what's true? Do you feel like maybe you had a choice?"

I paused only long enough to organize my thoughts.

"I'm still wavering back and forth. Everyone I've talked with thinks we have a choice, and I've seen some things that strengthen that argument."

"Like what?" she asked.

"Like Tanner. I think we're right about him, and if so, that means he's resisting his mate. And we know others have done that when forced by the council. So it seems it's possible."

"Honestly, I think you're asking a question that's relevant for all species," Molly said.

"How so?" I asked.

"You two are focusing on this Fate issue so heavily because this is a new concept to you, and being a witch feels different than being a human, right?"

We nodded.

"But really, how much different is it for witches to fall in love than it is for humans?" Molly asked. "Yes, the connection is *stronger*, but humans fall in love every day. It isn't like they have much control over who they fall in love with. They might make the choice to distance themselves from the one they love, just as we might. I guess what I'm saying is . . . this isn't all that weird. The choice is the same."

Molly had a point. Though it didn't clear up my question, it did make me wonder . . . perhaps we were all destined to be this way, witch, human, or otherwise.

"I think what I'm struggling with is that this seems so permanent," Jordan said.

I nodded. "It can be."

"If you and your mate continue to share the same core values, then it's damn near unbreakable. If you don't . . . from what I understand, you could decide to break your connection and move forward without them. It's just rare," Molly added.

"This isn't something you thought you'd ever deal with, and I understand that more than most," I said. "You thought you were human. And now you know this is coming . . ."

Jordan nodded, encouraging me forward.

"The only thing I want to ask of you is this: just wait until tomorrow to decide how you feel about it all. Forget Fate. Forget all of this, and just see Gustavo again. Feel what you feel, and then decide what you want. Because right now, I think you're letting your feelings sweep you away over something you don't have all the information on yet."

"Not really in character for someone who analyzes the facts every day, is it?"

"You're allowed a variance now and then."

Jordan smiled. It was a welcome sight.

"You're one of the most intelligent, capable, badass witches I know," Molly said. "Don't doubt yourself. Your instincts will guide you tomorrow. You're going to be just fine."

"Thanks, Molly. I think I'm going to be fixated on this all night."

"Perfectly normal."

"I'm sorry if we messed this up, J," I said.

"Oh, Hadley. There was no right way to do this."

A humorless smile crossed my lips.

Jordan set her hands on to the table with a gentle thud.

"I am not letting this guy unsettle me all night, though. I'll tell you that," Jordan said.

"You trying to convince us or yourself?" Molly asked.

"Damn it, Molly," Jordan said, though she laughed.

"Wine and potions can help take your mind off things—at least for a little while," I teased.

"Hey, maybe she decided she wants to daydream about Gustavo all night after all. Ever think of that?" Molly said.

"Different day, same sweet Molly."

"Okay." Jordan cleared her throat. "Whatever happens, I'm going to be just fine. I can handle this. I'm not wasting the rest of the evening bathing in anxiety."

I smiled. "No, that wouldn't be very you."

Jordan reached for my hand. "And you'll figure out your answer too, Hadley. I've been around you and Fitz long enough to know you love each other. Wherever that originated, I see the way you two show up for each other. You're good for each other. Nothing can take away from that—not even Fate herself."

I smiled.

"Perfect. A toast, then!" Molly called out, raising her glass, and we followed suit.

"Here's to the next phase of Jordan's life. Jordan, so much has been tossed at you in the last couple weeks, but you've taken every curveball in stride. I know we're all excited to watch you grow into the powerful witch you are meant to be."

Jordan met my gaze. She smiled, and a bit of tension released. I found great comfort in the fact that no matter what lay ahead of us, we had one another. I had found the women who made me feel more myself when I was with them than apart. I'd found my sisters—the ones the world forgot were mine all along.

"This crusade has its challenges, but it's given us a new family," I said.

"To sisterhood!" Jordan exclaimed.

"To sisterhood!" our voices rose in unison.

I rolled over, my eyes aching as they met the green numbers of the alarm clock, which shone brightly against the darkness of the room: *5:30 a.m.* I groaned. Almost an hour earlier than my alarm. I had stayed up far too late with Jordan and Molly, which wouldn't help my growing fatigue. The past few weeks had been relentless, and I hardly knew if my memories were real or dreams.

I rolled back over to Fitz, resolving to push everything from my mind, at least for another hour. I slid my hand on to his firm chest, and even in sleep, he responded, his hand finding mine. I watched the low-hanging fog's slow movement through the valley, occasionally catching a warm flicker of Opimae City's lights, until I drifted back to sleep.

Bright morning light poured through an open window along with a slight breeze. The sun cast golden rays across everything it found, warming the worn floor and the top of a curly-headed beauty seated at the breakfast table. I floated across the room, seeking a better view of the paper in front of Chloe and found a list of baby names scribbled across it. Was this a dream or another time? Though I wasn't a seer— the future wasn't mine to ponder—I wondered if my magic had found a loophole after expending so much energy on the puzzle of Tanner and Chloe.

Heavy footsteps sounded in the hallway, and Tanner emerged shirtless, wearing a faded pair of jeans. He peered over Chloe's head, resting his hands gently on her shoulders.

"Now I know what they mean by glowing," he whispered sweetly, leaning over to plant a quick kiss on her parted lips.

The vision dissipated as the alarm clock sounded violently in my ear.

What on earth had I just seen?

CHAPTER TWENTY-FIVE

The offices were buzzing when we arrived the following morning. Fitz and I walked down the hallway heading toward a small training room to test Fitz's recovery—responsibly.

Fitz and I were always reaching for each other, but we'd barely made contact all morning, nor had we really talked. I had been lost in my conversation with Jordan and Molly from the night before, and the strange dream had only muddled my mind further. My energy was off, and he surprisingly hadn't brought it up.

Fitz glanced at me from the corner of his eye, and I was about to break the ice when Keoni interrupted my thoughts.

"Fitz, Hadley!" Keoni called. "This way, please."

Fitz and I locked eyes before following him to Charles's office. It couldn't be good news.

"Morning, you two. Take a seat, please."

"What's going on?" Fitz asked.

"I've just received news that I want to share with Hadley before the rest of the team."

"Let's have it."

"It's about your abductor—the one who's been in the hospital."

"Did he wake up?"

"I'm afraid not. The lead healer phoned first thing this morning. He said there's zero brain function as of last night."

"They're taking him off life support?" I guessed.

"That's what they're recommending. They need my approval, though."

"What are you going to do?"

"Whatever you and Jordan would like me to do."

"Thank you . . . but why are you leaving that decision up to us?"

"You asked for more agency when it comes to important matters."

I nodded.

"And I know this was personal for you. This witch stalked you, even on Earth. It seemed right to pull you into this decision." He paused, considering. "But if this feels more like a burden rather than closure, I am happy to make the decision for you."

"Thank you." I hesitated. "I think we'll make the decision ourselves. But can it wait until later today?"

"I hear Gustavo is due back this morning," Charles said.

"Right. I'd like to give Jordan a little time before we discuss. I know what we'll have to do. But it's a life we're talking about, so I feel like we should discuss it before any orders are given."

"A wise call, Hadley."

"Thank you for this, Charles," Fitz said. "Sincerely."

"My pleasure, Fitz. Now, I'll let you two get to work."

"Today's the day Jordan is supposed to find love," I said as we walked out of Charles's office, "not make a decision on whether or not to end another witch's life."

"I know, Hads."

"Every joy has its cost in this crusade." My heart felt heavy.

"It's the price we pay as leaders. We'll feel their joy and their pain in equal strides," he said.

"I'll talk to Jordan tonight."

Fitz nodded.

"Everything okay?" I asked, feeling his strained energy.

He pursed his lips. "You've been a bit distant since you came home last night."

His words made me feel worse. The last thing I wanted was to make him feel like something was wrong, especially when I wasn't ready to talk about it with him.

"I'm tired. Last night took it out of me. There's a lot going on and a lot to think about, you know?"

He nodded, but his energy didn't match. This wasn't my first deflection, but he wouldn't press me in the hallway at the office.

"I know you have to discuss the stalker with Jordan tonight, but perhaps we can find some time to relax after."

I reached for Fitz's jaw, resting my hand against it lightly. A bit of tension eased.

"But for now," Fitz said, "I supposed we'd better get to training."

"Actually, I have one quick task first," I said.

Fitz followed my gaze and waved to Gustavo. His lips brushed my forehead. "I'll see you in there."

"Gustavo."

"Hadley—greetings."

"Welcome back. I hope your return home went well."

"It went very well, thank you. You probably already know this, but Queen Marina helped me find a quick replacement at work, and I'm ready to focus on the mission ahead."

"Glad to hear it. Have you been briefed on your day yet?"

"I haven't. I'm meeting Keoni now."

I nodded. "Your task for today is going to be a bit unconventional."

"Unconventional? I don't understand."

"Your assignment is to simply spend the day with Jordan."

A spark of recognition flitted across his face.

"You know, don't you?" I asked.

He smiled shyly. "From the second I saw her rise from the water that day on the bridge."

"But you didn't say anything."

"She hadn't matched yet. I thought it best to let things run their course."

"You're aware she's matched now?"

"She mentioned that on the phone a couple nights ago."

"Then you know what today holds. I'm happy for you two."

And I was. I prayed Jordan and Gustavo would know the same love Fitz and I did, though I hoped the concept of Fate didn't continue to trouble her as it did me.

"She knows?"

"Yes," I said simply. "She understands it about as well as she can right now. Be easy with her, Gustavo. This is all so new."

Gustavo nodded. I felt his nerves stirring. "I know you and Jordan are close—like sisters."

I nodded.

"You don't need to worry about her. I'll ease her into all this. I'll be good to her—you have my word."

He placed his hand on my shoulder, and mine fell on his.

"One last thing before you go."

His gaze shifted worriedly.

"I'll need to talk with Jordan tonight, so don't stray too far this evening."

"Is it serious?"

"Yes. I won't share details with anyone before I brief Jordan, but she and I have a big decision ahead of us. Fitz and I bought some time, but I'm afraid it can't wait until tomorrow."

"I understand. We'll see you at dinner."

I smiled. "I won't keep you from your destiny any longer. Welcome to the family, Gustavo."

Gustavo was true to his word. He and Jordan were seated on the couch when I returned. Fitz and I had gone on a successful, uneventful time-jump a few years into the past, which was encouraging after the last time-travel debacle. Jordan's glow was evident, and I felt a weight settle on my chest at the heavy task I had to lay before her.

"I'm sorry to bring this to you today."

"Hey—none of that. None of us can help the timing of anything on this mission."

"Speaking of which—how are you?" I asked.

"I'm okay."

I gave her a questioning glance.

"I think it's going to take me a long time to understand this—if I can ever truly understand it. But you were right about this feeling natural . . . I'm going to be fine."

"Did you form your streams?" I asked.

She shook her head. "I told him I wasn't ready to do that. He's withholding his stream too until we're ready."

They were making a choice.

"Hadley . . ." Jordan trailed off, lost in thought.

"What is it?" I asked.

"Fate leads us where we should be, but it's up to us to decide to jump. I know I'm still teetering on the edge of love, but . . . I think there's a choice. I don't know with certainty just yet, but even if I've got it all wrong . . . I don't know that I care." Jordan clasped her hand over her mouth playfully.

I had to laugh.

She pulled her hands away. "Isn't that an awful thing to admit, though? I mean, you've been so worried about Fate."

"Not at all, J. I completely understand the sentiment. It's okay to be happy, you know."

She nodded. "It just feels like it's going to be right."

It pained me to change the subject to our abductor on such a happy day for her, but I poured a couple glasses of whisky and switched the conversation to fill her in on the details of my conversation with Charles.

"I almost feel like I'm a conspiracy theorist, but honestly—we shouldn't trust anyone or anything right now. Not absolutely," Jordan said.

"I've been teetering back and forth on it all day," I admitted. "Maybe it's the mystery around the mole tugging at me, but I can't seem to trust anyone outside of our core team right now."

"I feel the same. Between the informant and Lorenzo and these stalkers, there's too many questions that still aren't answered," Jordan said. "I wonder if you and I could bring in an independent healer before we make the decision?"

"So we can confirm there's no brain function?"

"Exactly."

"Okay. Let's find someone first—a healer who won't have any idea what this is all about—and then present the idea to Charles."

"We'll have to work fast."

I nodded. "Okay, let's throw all the conspiracy theories on the table."

"Hold on." Jordan grabbed a notepad lying on the nearby counter.

"So, back to Hans. Maybe he shouldn't be brain dead right now . . . not naturally."

"That could've been—what does Bob Ross call it? A happy accident."

I nearly choked on my whisky.

"Sorry, too soon? I've been spending too much time with Molly lately, I think."

"You have to warn me before you say things like that," I said, laughing.

Jordan giggled.

"If someone wanted to silence him for good, they've likely already had their chance," I said. "Maybe someone made sure this witch wouldn't remember anything later—even if it meant an accidental brain bleed."

"Right, because we don't know for sure where that bleed came from. Accident, or surgery?"

"Exactly. The other possibility is that he might still have brain function."

"So, we'd pull the plug and do someone a favor." Jordan sighed, scribbling the theory across the page. "That would be horrible."

"It's too convenient that the witch we capture ends up with a brain injury."

"But okay, if someone was concerned about him sharing information . . . why not finish him off?"

"Maybe our new security measures have them worried," I said.

"Yeah, or maybe they don't want to flat out kill him—they want us to do it because it makes us believe that they weren't involved and that we were in control."

"You're on to something there. I wish my gut didn't agree with yours."

"What if this is the work of the mole?" Jordan asked.

I paused, considering the possibilities. "What if this is Jess?"

"You still suspect him?"

"He makes the most sense right now. He's suspicious, he's already caused plenty of problems, and he's hiding something."

She nodded hesitantly.

"You're not convinced," I said.

"I operate on facts. It's the analyst in me." Jordan was right. We didn't have solid evidence yet. "But we have good reason to be suspicious of him."

Jordan reached for my hand.

"I wish we didn't have to make a decision about ending a life."

"We'll figure this out."

"I know," she whispered.

And in the end, we decided it was only fair to bring Keoni into the mix. He was one of the few witches we trusted in Opimae, and after all, he was a part of the whole affair. It made sense that the three of us should end this horrible situation together. And it just so happened that Keoni's childhood best friend was a healer in a neighboring town. Keoni had him on the phone in no time, and he agreed to help us with our project. He would meet us the following morning at the hospital, where we'd brief Charles—and Charles alone.

The morning air was heavy. The pale suns and the thin air were something I'd finally grown accustomed to, and the newly thick, humid air—though cool—was unusual. It reminded me of the Pacific Northwest, and my heart ached at the reminder. Opimae City was beautiful, and I'd been thankful many times over that the air didn't harbor oppressive heat from an overbearing sun. But even in its ethereal beauty, I found myself longing for the autumn days of Edinburgh.

I found myself longing for home.

Keoni's friend, Healer Krause, was a tall, domineering witch who might have been attractive if he'd had any personality. It seemed he had little in common with Keoni, but he was apparently brilliant and willing to help, so we welcomed his presence.

Charles was close behind us, a frown seeping on to his features.

"Are you sure this is absolutely necessary?" he asked in a low voice.

"I know you think this is too much, but I need to know all the facts with certainty."

Charles motioned for me to lead the way.

Healer Krause reached his conclusion quickly. "His charts don't make sense."

"What do you mean?" Charles asked.

"You said he lost brain function two nights ago?"

"Yes," Charles said. "The lead healer said they ran more tests that night at twenty-two hundred hours, and that's when they were able to confirm loss of brain function."

"This test is dated from yesterday morning—zero five hundred hours, to be precise. See that? That indicates brain function."

"So the healer was wrong about the time, at best," Charles surmised.

"And lied to you, at worst," I said.

"There's more," Keoni said, tucking a loose strand of his dark hair behind his ear.

"He does, indeed, have no brain function now," Healer Krause confirmed.

"So, at this point, we still need to make a decision," Keoni said.

"What's your recommendation, Healer Krause?" Jordan asked.

"My recommendation is to pull him from life support. No matter what happened the other night—and I think you should find out—he's gone now. And he won't come back."

I looked to Charles. "I demand we investigate this. I want to know what happened."

Charles nodded. "Of course, Hadley."

Jordan put her head in her hands. "We were right, Hadley."

"What do you mean by that?" Charles asked.

"We believe there's been foul play."

"Jordan," Charles said. "Let's not jump to any conclusions before the investigation is underway."

"Based on these charts, I support her claim."

"Please elaborate, Healer Krause," I said.

"If you read his charts over the past week, I believe the patient was gaining strength—physically and mentally. His charts indicate improvement. That sharply declines yesterday morning at zero six hundred hours, and yet there is no documentation to actively support the idea that anything was done about it."

I looked pointedly at Charles.

"I'm taking this seriously," he said.

"I would make an emergency call to your office to gain custody of these records now, and create digital and hard copies," Healer Krause continued. "If you don't—and we're correct about this being foul play— these will disappear or be altered the moment the word 'investigation' is whispered through these hallways."

In the end, Jordan, Keoni, and I decided to remove Hans Schmidt from life support. There was nothing left to be done, no hope of recovery. Our stipulations were that Healer Krause perform the duties, and that the three of us remain in the room.

With the recent questions filling my mind regarding Fate and mates, the thought of Hans's death brought with it a certain gravity. It didn't matter what force had brought them together, nor what control they had: Allette was losing a mate. Despite Hans and Allette's wrongdoings, this would crush her—and I carried that weight with me.

I studied the lifeless body of my former stalker lying in the hospital bed. Blond strands were pulled away from his face into a ponytail, and I thought hard, attempting to recall the color of his eyes, knowing I had seen them during our brief time together.

The color of his eyes suddenly seemed important. My memory failed me, and I realized there was no reason not to infiltrate his mind to see what I could discover. I closed my eyes as the healing staff continued their end-of-life preparations and pushed my way toward Hans's mind.

I immediately wished my attempt hadn't been successful. My chest tightened at the overwhelming feeling of emptiness. There was absolutely nothing there—no thoughts, no activity. There was only utter darkness. This witch was truly gone, and the loss of activity within his mind caused a heaviness in the pit of my stomach.

The soft beep of the machines brought me back to myself. Jordan's gaze grew questioning. I shook my head and focused on slowing both my breath and my heart rate. I looked again to my former captor.

He had entered my life to do nothing but harm, and he had paid the ultimate price for it. There was a small part of me that worried I wanted him dead—I didn't want to harbor hate like that in my heart. But ultimately, I knew that things were much more complicated than that. I knew that, despite his unfortunate entrance into my life, his life shouldn't have ended this way. He shouldn't have been murdered in our custody. And as Healer Krause declared the time of death, I joined hands with Jordan and Keoni, and I vowed to deliver justice.

I vowed to find the truth.

CHAPTER TWENTY-SIX

Fitz and I called a team meeting the following morning, and we all crowded around our large makeshift table to get started. Henry and Jordan emerged from the kitchen with the last of the fruit and jam to accompany our robust breakfast spread and completed our party.

"Thanks for joining us this morning, everyone. We'd like to touch base about a few different matters," I said. "First off, the chamber is far from reaching a decision on Adamo, but the mission to Lorenzo's fortress looks like it'll move forward."

"We need to be a part of that team," Solomon said.

"Aye," Fitz said. "And though Hadley and I will continue to advocate for that in and out of the chamber, we need more."

"The information gathering mission to the fortress impressed some of the leaders, you said?" Ian asked.

"Yes, and Jordan's efforts are paying off as well. But if there are other advances we can make as a team, it wouldn't hurt," I said.

"The Parisian stalker capture was a win for Intelligence," Jordan said. "We're working hard to make the most of that. Let's make sure the chamber sees how capable we are as a team."

"And you fended off abduction attempts. That was a great win, despite the challenges it caused," Chloe said.

Tanner's gaze lingered on Chloe, capturing my attention. Even with everything going on, I couldn't help but notice their interactions.

"Reports show that training is going well, even with Opimae's indiscretion with Fitz's transport test," Mia said.

"We'll do what we can with this," I said.

"There's one other matter before Charles joins us," Fitz said. "We need to reach a decision on our next move with Jess."

"I'd like to propose we track Jess for a couple days and see if we catch anything suspicious," I said. "Solomon said with my loophole power, we can work out a way to follow Jess without him feeling our presence."

"It'll be tricky, but Hadley's capable," Solomon said.

"Molly and I would go with Hadley," Fitz said. "We can transport out quickly if necessary, and our observance will remain on Hadley so we don't accidentally throw our energy on to Jess."

"Maka is helping me with using my loophole power for mind reading, so I can hopefully break through Jess's shield soon."

"I thought you'd mastered that," Isaac said. "Didn't you read Lorenzo's mind when you were in the fortress once?"

"Yeah, but I couldn't break through Jess's."

"Why is that?" Henry asked.

"Breaking a shield is tough, and sometimes, we just can't break through," Maka said. "Each witch's energy is different. Hadley's loophole power seems to understand Lorenzo's energy very well, but not Jess's. So, it's taking some time to strategize."

"So, what's the timeframe we're looking at?" Tanner asked.

I looked to Maka.

"Hadley's almost ready. We're just working on the subtle nuances right now. I think we'll be done with her training by the end of today. But if it still doesn't work, then we're in trouble."

Charles entered the room, so we shifted to the next topic.

"Charles is joining us to discuss the Parisian stalkers here, rather than at headquarters," Fitz explained. "While we conduct this investigation regarding the informants, we'll silo some information. Perhaps it'll even help us track the mole."

I didn't miss that Charles was alone—Lana and Keoni must have been asked to wait outside our home.

"Hans was a loss yesterday," I said. "Allette remains in Opimaean confinement. She was slow to reveal information, but agents continue to question her as Jordan's team produces more information about her and Hans."

"Do we believe they were connected to Lorenzo or not?" Isaac asked.

"I have a report prepared on her confessions." Jordan passed around a briefing. "We currently have no information to indicate they were connected to Lorenzo. And Allette is holding firm to her statement that she and Hans wanted the ring for themselves."

"Something just doesn't add up here," I said.

"I agree," Jordan said. "There's more to her story, but if we only focus on a possible connection to Lorenzo, we might miss a greater truth."

"Aye, a good call," Ian said. "She could be hiding any number of things."

"I'm sure she isn't the only witch besides Lorenzo who wants the ring for herself," James said. "But she might be the only one who's had the resources to attempt something like this."

"Aye, that's true. She must have an expanded network to pull off what she has."

I turned to Charles. "You have an update from Hans's case, correct?"

"After our meeting with Healer Krause yesterday morning, I consulted five independent physicians on the case," he said. "After reviewing the information, they've all confirmed the same opinion: foul play."

"Good instinct," Mia said, looking to Jordan and then to me. I was surprised to discover that her acknowledgement mattered to me.

"Jordan and I just knew something wasn't right."

"Good work, indeed. We'd have missed this if not for you," Charles admitted.

"What do you propose happens next?" I asked.

"I'd like to launch a full investigation into the matter. Perhaps this will lead us somewhere with this larger case."

"I think I can speak for the team when I say that we support that decision. Though, I'd like to propose that this be a joint investigation."

Charles agreed.

"Did you already have someone in mind to run point for us?" Solomon asked me.

I decided there was no time like the present to take a leap of faith. The words almost caught in my throat, but I took a deep breath and made my proposal.

"I was thinking Mia would be a good fit."

Mia's eyes flickered quickly to mine, and I found the faintest hint of surprise in them. She nodded once and turned to the rest of the room.

Solomon smiled. "I agree. Make your case, and we'll vote."

"Mia will be the least biased in the group for this investigation. She has a great skill set and the discretion necessary to lead an internal investigation. And since she was working their case originally, this is a natural progression."

"Mia, do you accept this nomination?" Solomon asked.

"I do."

"All those in favor, raise your hand."

"It's unanimous," Fitz said.

"You'll do a fine job, Mia," said James.

CHAPTER TWENTY-SEVEN

Our first day of following Jess yielded absolutely nothing. He went straight to work and returned home directly afterward. Jordan tracked his devices, and he made no calls and did nothing out of the ordinary. It was discouraging for our first day, so our second day began with a little less hope. After a normal morning, I attended my training session with Jess, which was filled with the usual discomfort, before we traced him from headquarters. Instead of going home, he turned in the opposite direction, and Fitz, Molly, and I exchanged eager glances before following his path.

Jess meandered down the rain-soaked streets of Opimae, seemingly in no hurry. He nodded to passersby and whistled as he strolled along the cobblestones. An elven band performed at the center of a court-yard, drawing a small crowd despite the rain. Jess stopped and clapped through the duration of the song they were performing. He smiled and sang along.

It wasn't only Jess's behavior that was completely different from the Jess we knew from training—his energy was light and free.

I took the opportunity to probe Jess's mind, hoping his distraction would increase the chances of my success. I moved all along the edges of his mind, seeking immersion, but at every turn, I was met by an invisible barrier. I circled his mind several times, searching for an opening, a wisp of energy, anything that might useful, but to no avail. I whispered to the elements. I tried it all—and yet, nothing would open his thoughts. What secrets did he hold to be expending so much magic to protect them constantly?

I sighed. I looked to Fitz and then to Molly and nodded for them to casually observe Jess's behavior. Fitz grew wary, and Molly shrugged, her face pensive. I returned my focus to him just as he began walking through the crowds. I snaked my way through the magical beings, remaining focused on Jess's energy.

As we neared the opposite side of the courtyard I fell back, considering the waning crowd. Jess hadn't noticed my presence yet, and I hoped that pattern would hold. The sidewalk split into two paths, and Jess steered himself to the right. The path led along the river, with faded brick buildings rising to our right. Trees provided a canopy from much of the rain, though a few large drops fell from the leaves and splashed against my raincoat. I glanced over my shoulder to ensure Fitz and Molly were keeping pace, and upon seeing them round a corner, I powered forward.

Jess paused in front of a stone building that was flanked on each side by red brick facades, and I tucked myself behind a tree as I awaited his move. He looked around, but the path was quiet. Only the rush of the river and the falling raindrops disturbed the peaceful scene. Jess slowly opened the door and disappeared.

Fitz and Molly were quickly beside me.

"I think I should spirit travel to follow him," I said.

Fitz's mouth tugged downward as he thought through my suggestion. He surprised me by nodding his head.

"Really? No opposition from you?" I asked.

"If you can handle Lorenzo, I reckon you can handle that bloke," he said.

Molly laughed. "We passed a bench not far back."

We ran back to the bench and took a seat quickly. I positioned myself in Fitz's arms, feigning sleep, with Molly seated casually beside us. I closed my eyes and focused on separating my spirit from my body. The first moment of success was always a tad jarring, and I shook my limbs, dispelling the excess energy. I ran down the sidewalk and through the wooden door.

The door opened to a dark foyer with two torches illuminating the space, their magical light flickering across beige stone walls. The passageway immediately dropped down a set of steps, and it struck me that this building felt old, even for Opimae City. I followed the last traces of Jess's energy down the drafty stairwell until the next source of light illuminated the steps more brightly. With another few steps, I found myself at a wooden door. I passed through and found a room roughly the same size as the great room at our house. Jess stood near the far wall, flipping through a book.

I stepped closer to examine the antique volume. His eyes were transfixed on the pages, and I made a mental note of the book, *Elven Magic Systems*, before examining the rest of the room. A fireplace held the remnants of a forgotten fire. The coals still emitted a faint glow, and the stonework was warm to the touch.

I moved on to the bookshelves lining either side of the fireplace. They were filled with aged volumes, focused on everything from witches and elves to faeries and druids.

I halted as the door opened and an elf entered the room. Jess closed the book with a pop and returned it to the shelf before greeting the new addition.

"Hello, old friend," Jess said, bowing slightly.

The elf nodded, and Jess straightened as the elf moved closer.

"You are most welcome here," the elf said. "Much time has passed since our last visit."

"I'm afraid it's been difficult to get away. The Earth crusaders are here, and we've been busy with our preparations."

"A noble cause, as always." The elf smiled. His teeth were as white as freshly fallen snow, a stark contrast to his long raven hair. "But do not grow too distracted and forget your true purpose."

True purpose. A prickle nipped at the nape of my neck.

"I do not forget my duties, I can assure you."

The elf moved closer and placed a hand on Jess's shoulder.

"You worry too much, my friend."

"There is too much at stake," Jess said.

"And much will be restored in the end."

I couldn't make sense of their conversation. Did they speak vaguely out of caution? Were they hoping the Opimaean government would bring restoration . . . or Lorenzo? My blood ran cold as I considered the implications.

The door opened a second time, and a young girl, no more than five, ran across the room and into Jess's arms.

"Uncle!" she said excitedly.

Her enthusiasm was jarring. I'd thought of Jess as many things: stalker, trainer, agent, possible mole. But for the first time, I thought about the other titles he held: uncle, son, brother . . . perhaps even mate?

Jess twirled the girl around and set her back on her feet. He wore a bright smile, but his energy raged as violently as a storm.

"There's my Luna girl," he said warmly. "Did you have a pleasant trip?"

Luna nodded enthusiastically.

"Well, I have some fresh caora bread with me. Perhaps you'd like some?"

"Yes!" Luna shouted. "My favorite."

Jess laughed. He waved his hand against a bare stone wall, and a door materialized.

"All right, into the kitchen you go. We'll be right there."

Luna bounced through the door, and Jess turned. In the commotion I'd missed another witch entering the room. She looked so much like Jess: her icy blue eyes somehow seemed less severe than his, but they held the same hue and sat in an angular face. Her skin was the same warm brown as Jess's, and her curly raven hair was swept into a loose braid.

Simply put, she was beautiful. I wondered if they were twins.

But she was also frail. She moved softly, light of foot, and fell into

Jess's arms. He hugged her tightly, his face scrunched in conflict.

"You should not have come here," he said.

"It's nice to see you too, brother."

"You know better," he said sternly. "It is still too dangerous."

"We've had no news of you for weeks," she said, her eyes challenging Jess's. "And Luna was worried."

Jess sighed. "It does not change the fact that this is quite dangerous. Do you know what they'll do if they discover you lived?" His voice rose ever so slightly. "Do you not understand? They will use you against me! And then where will we be?"

His sister dropped her head.

"I am doing what I must to protect you both. If you cannot find it in your heart to protect yourself, at least think of Luna."

"I am tired, Jess."

I didn't doubt that. She was a shell of a woman. I wondered what ailed her, and soon enough, the answer crossed my mind.

War.

She had been gravely injured in the fall of Terra Firma, and by the looks of it, she'd never recovered.

"And I'm not?" His eyebrows rose. "I have not slept well since Terra Firma."

The elf took a seat in the corner, clearly avoiding the family spat.

"Surely, they wouldn't harm us."

"You have no idea what we're up against," he said.

Luna reemerged from the kitchen holding the remnants of what must have once been caora bread. Crumbs littered her gray tunic. She smiled brightly at her uncle and raised her arms to him. He answered her request and picked her up, and she rested her head on his chest.

Jess gazed at his sister over the top of his niece's curls.

She opened her mouth to speak, but stopped, looking at Jess with wide eyes.

"Someone is among us," she whispered.

"What do you mean?"

"A spirit-traveler."

"Here?" the elf asked. "In this room?"

She nodded.

I took a deep breath and asked the elements to return me to my body before Jess had a chance to follow my energy—to sit with it long enough to recognize me.

I startled awake next to Fitz.

"We should go—transport back to the courtyard."

Fitz nodded, and we were soon standing among the bustling streets. I ran my hands through my hair, pulling it into a ponytail. I moved my hands along my ears to pull any hair free that might have entangled with my favorite earrings—Gram's earrings—when I realized one was missing.

I halted.

"What is it?" Fitz asked.

"My earring," I said, horrified.

"You could have lost it anywhere, "Molly said. "We've covered so much ground today."

I nodded, but the thought of losing such a special tie to my grandmother made me feel sick.

I attempted a tracking spell, but the elements wouldn't lead me to the earring. Fitz tried too, and then Molly, but nothing worked.

We retraced our steps from the courtyard back to headquarters, but we found nothing. We decided to return to the area around the building where Jess had met his family, but we'd have to wait until we knew he had left.

We meandered back to the lively courtyard, combing the streets one last time before sitting on a bench. I filled Fitz and Molly in on the details I'd learned, and sat with them in silence for a moment before Molly spoke.

"I don't understand this at all."

"He's in some kind of trouble," I said. "But they kept things vague enough that I don't know what."

"Aye," Fitz said. "He could've been speaking of our government, or of Lorenzo, or of the stalkers, or something else entirely."

"We don't know what's wrong, but we do know something's wrong," Molly said.

"Aye. It confirms that Jess is up to something."

"I think we should get this information to Jordan, but I honestly think we should keep the team really tight on this one."

"Why?" Fitz asked.

"I have a few reasons," I said. "But the biggest and most compelling reason is Luna. There's a child tangled up in this . . . and Jess's sister is clearly ill. We need to protect them while we investigate Jess."

"Perhaps we loop Jordan in for intelligence, but we ask the rest of the team to remain focused on their other duties while we investigate further?" Fitz suggested.

The three of us agreed and rose to return home for the day. And as we wandered the streets of Opimae City, I couldn't shake Luna from my mind. I had a feeling there was much more to Jess's story than I'd realized.

CHAPTER TWENTY-EIGHT

Jordan's tablet sounded with several notifications the following morning, just as we entered headquarters. She pulled the device from her bag and started reading.

"Oh my god," she whispered.

I turned to face her. "What's wrong?"

Her eyes were troubled as they met mine. "There's been an attack on Pluvia Silva."

Lana rushed around the corner, nearly slamming into Isaac.

"Sorry," she muttered. "Have you heard the news?"

"Aye. Jordan was just filling us in," Ian said.

When we made it to the main room, Charles led us through a quick recap.

Lorenzo had just attacked the mountain town, and the Earth-side team was joining a convoy being sent in to help.

We left headquarters as soon as we were briefed.

Cars and aid vehicles dotted the cobblestone streets of Opimae City for as far as I could see, all joining our effort. A few choppers had already landed in the town, but due to the mountainous terrain, it was tricky. We climbed rapidly and were high above the city before I'd even wrapped my mind around our situation. Gray rock and verdant grass blurred in my peripheral vision as we turned.

For the first time, it really sunk in: if we didn't figure things out quickly, we might lose to Lorenzo—and a lot of magical beings were going to suffer.

Fitz and I were seated across from Lana and Charles, listening as she recounted the events over an intercom system connected to each of the special teams' vehicles. Lorenzo had devised dynamite spells and carefully laid them around the town. At exactly zero seven hundred hours, they'd detonated in sync, blowing buildings apart and sending the town into complete chaos.

"It's not good," she said gravely. "Reports from our first responders indicate there are many dead, and we can't begin to guess at how many beings could be trapped under the rubble. When we arrive on scene, your job is to work where your strengths lie. You'll each receive your assignments as you exit the vehicles. Please keep your eyes open—our tactical units are completing their sweep of the town now, but remember, Lorenzo's carnage might not be over. I'll be back in communication shortly."

She set down her radio and swiped across her small tablet, checking for the latest updates.

"Prime Minister Bakari and Fitz were right the other day in the chamber. Lorenzo is working his way down the mountain," I said.

Charles had been thumbing across intelligence updates on his tablet and taking phone calls, but he paused at my statement.

"Charles, we're only seeing the things Lorenzo's allowing us to see," I said. "I don't think Fate favors him, but we're not doing everything we should be."

He exhaled forcefully and cut his eyes to mine. "I'm afraid you're right," he conceded.

"I know our teams are strong—the best there are. But we have to figure out what we're missing," I said.

"You agreed to work with additional teams from Earth. It's time to bring them over," Fitz said.

"I haven't been able to garner full support yet. It's been complicated," Charles said.

"Then uncomplicate it. Lives are on the line," I snapped.

Charles hesitated, but finally said, "You're right. I'll find a way around the opposition."

The cars slowed in front of us, and as we turned the last switchback, a grave scene unfolded before us. Smoke billowed from the buildings sprawling through the mountainsides, and a thick sheet of ash covered everything in sight. A being flanked in lightweight armor walked to the first car and signaled us down a street that was being cleared.

Lana took to the radio. "We're headed directly into the center of Pluvia Silva, where central command and medical are being established. Once these cars come to a halt, I need everyone out and focused immediately. The things you will be exposed to today will be difficult to understand. I'm not telling you this to frighten you, but to prepare you. We have much to do and very little time. May Fate be with us all."

The radio buzzed with feedback as it fell into her lap, and central command came into view. The cars slammed to a halt, and we all poured from the vehicles into the mayhem of the streets, seeking our assignments.

Mia was to spend the day with Lana, working to keep all parts moving.

Fitz and Henry were tasked with finding the deceased and tagging them with red ribbons, so rescuers knew to keep moving. The most important task was to find the wounded and save as many as possible.

Molly and Maka quickly ran into the medical tent to help in triage. Though Maka was here to train Jordan, she'd offered her services as a healer immediately. Tanner, Gustavo, and Isaac were to work as a team to bring the wounded back to the healers.

James and Chloe were assigned to the tents where beings who weren't gravely injured gathered, seeking information on their family members or friends, or to simply seeking solace away from their leveled homes. It was one of the more grueling tasks, but they both had the right temperament and stamina for it.

Ian and Solomon were assigned to the rescue teams. They were to help them with coordination and be lead communicators with dispatch.

And finally, Jordan and I were assigned to help in central command. We were tasked with coordinating between all teams and ensuring smooth communication. We worked in tandem to keep tabs on where various teams were located and what their task loads were. We had line of sight through cameras that were being placed by teams in all areas of the city, and we had direct radio contact with the leads of every team. It was almost overwhelming to see how much information lay at our fingertips.

Jordan and I scanned the system, learning our new job as quickly as we could. Opimaean troops had pushed Lorenzo's forces toward the edge of the city, and for the time being, the lines held.

At one point, I noticed Fitz and Henry on camera. They were moving rubble away from the side of a building. They finally pulled a body from the debris, and they knelt beside her. Henry checked for a pulse, but I saw him mouth the words to Fitz. He pulled her eyelids down and slapped the ground beside him. Fitz turned and threw up in the nearby bushes. His anguish poured through me, along with a wave of nausea. I took a deep breath, steadying myself, and pushed a bit of calm through our connection.

I bit my lip and turned back to Jordan, who had watched along with me. I nodded to her, and we returned to work, knowing that even mere seconds could save additional lives.

After hours of coordination, I paused briefly, shutting my eyes for a few seconds. They burned in protest after staring at the screens for so long. Jordan checked the combat lines for an update. Lorenzo's troops had been pushed out of the city, and the fighting seemed to be at a stalemate.

Suddenly, the ground beneath us rumbled.

"Jordan, Hadley, what's happening?" Isaac's voice sounded over the loudspeaker in our room.

Jordan and I were flipping through every camera feed we had.

"Isaac, we don't see anything unusual. We're looking."

"It feels so strange . . . like an earthquake," Jordan whispered.

"There's something odd in the sky," Fitz said. "Flip over to us, Hadley."

Sure enough, a dark cloud was moving fast on the horizon. But something was off. The cloud moved fluidly, almost as though it was alive.

"Hadley, are you seeing this?" Jordan murmured.

"What the hell is that?" I asked, enlarging the feed.

"Oh, shit."

"What? Jordan, what is it?" Henry asked.

"Lana, come to central command. Now," I said, ignoring Henry's question.

"Hadley!" Fitz called.

"Fitz, you and Henry take cover now. Find somewhere to seek shelter."

"Hadley." His voice grew stern. "What is it?"

"I don't know, Fitz. It looks like . . . a swarm of giant . . . bats."

"Excuse me?" Isaac demanded.

"It looks like bats," Jordan confirmed. "But like . . . mutant bats. They're huge."

"How many?" Lana asked.

"I couldn't tell you," Jordan said. "They're thick—like dark clouds snaking across the horizon."

"Oh, that's not good at all. Teams should seek shelter," Lana said, keeping her voice level. "I'm almost at command. Announce it over the loudspeaker—tell all teams that woodland vampire bats are flying over and to take cover immediately."

"Vampire bats?" Chloe asked. "Like the ones on Earth that drink blood?"

"Yes, they drink blood," Lana said, out of breath.

"But bigger, Chloe," I added. They were nearing the camera feed. "Their wingspan is probably six feet."

Lana burst through the door as Jordan made the announcement over the speaker. We heard screams and watched helplessly as everyone scrambled to seek shelter. I didn't yet understand the damage the woodland vampire bats could cause, but clearly, it was bad.

"Fitz, are you and Henry somewhere safe?"

"Yes, love. Don't worry about us. We found a building stable enough to hide in."

We scanned the cameras, ensuring everyone had taken shelter to the best of their ability. And suddenly, the bats were upon us.

They were horrid looking creatures, with squished faces and fangs that protruded from their mouths as if they were always ready for blood. They scoured the area for any living creature, and I exhaled once they'd passed over Fitz and Henry's hiding spot. Finally, they found their way to our makeshift hospitals. The creatures bit and tore at the canvas, their flapping wings beating violently against the shelters. Though the tents had been magically constructed and secured, that didn't make them infallible. But we had little time to fret as the military assembled nearby, trained to take on their assault. They released fire on the creatures, killing a few instantly.

We heard scratches against the canvas of our own tent, and my breath hitched. One of the nightmarish creatures broke through the flap, sticking its smashed face through the opening.

"Your fire!" Lana yelled. "They hate fire."

My fire magic answered my call swiftly, and the creature released an ear-shattering screech as flames shot from my palms, though it made no attempt to back away. I shaped my fire into a bow and released an arrow in the bat's direction. The flaming arrow met its mark, and the bat again screeched before pulling away from the tent wildly.

The structure swayed in protest amidst the bat's departure, and Lana and Jordan held the nearest stakes to stabilize the tent. I closed my eyes, whispering to the elements, and they answered my request. The ropes pulled tightly. The swaying ceased and the rips in the fabric disappeared, returning the tent to its former stability.

The three of us joined together at the center of the tent, awaiting a second attack, but the military moved swiftly and the bats soon left, seeking their next victims. I released a deep sigh, but my relief was short lived.

The ground rumbled again, but this time the reverberations were far more intense. An explosion pounded through the air. Violent shaking forced us to our knees. Jordan and I reached for each other, bracing ourselves.

"Lana!" Jordan yelled.

Lana covered her head as she inched closer to us. The ground shook angrily for another few minutes before we were able to find our balance, taking stock of ourselves and our surroundings.

"Fitz," I whispered, feeling for our connection. It was strained, and I raced to the camera feed. Though several cameras survived the blast, the one near Fitz and Henry was out, and the intercom system had been interrupted. I looked to Jordan and Lana, panicked.

"Hadley, you need to stay here," Lana said.

"Out of the question," I shot back.

"We have no idea what just happened. It's entirely too dangerous for you to run out there right now."

"I don't care how dangerous it is. Fitz is out there, and I need to find him. What if he's hurt?" I asked, panicked.

"You'd feel it. How does the connection feel?"

"Strained."

"But not like he's hurt, right?" Lana said.

I felt his heart racing, but not much else, not like normal. Something was off. I had to find him.

"Lana, what if that was Saoirse out there?" I asked, ignoring her question.

Lana looked hard, her eyes searching mine. I'd found the soft spot in her armor.

"If you were in my shoes, what would you do? Tell me what you would do if your mate was out there."

She sighed. "I'd go find her."

"Exactly."

I threw open the tent flap and ran into the panicked streets of Pluvia Silva, staggering as my feet hit the ruptured cobblestones. I paused, scanning the area to gain my bearings. Ash fell from the smoke-filled sky as beings scurried through the debris. I made eye contact with Molly, who was doing her best to push a stake back into the ground. I ran over and used my weight to help her pull it into place.

"Why aren't you in central command?" she asked.

"I'm going to find Fitz."

"No, you aren't," a harsh voice called out over my shoulder. Sadie. "Do you not grasp the situation, Hadley? This is reckless."

"Let me be loud and clear," I said, closing the gap between me and Sadie. "I'm going to find Fitz whether you like it or not. Now, get out of my way."

Sadie's face showed the slightest hint of surprise before she regained her carefully placed cynicism. "I'm coming with you."

"Fantastic," I said sarcastically. "Just don't slow me down."

Molly pulled me into a quick embrace. "Be careful. It's bad out there."

"I will. Promise." And with that, Sadie and I ran through the havoc toward Fitz's last known location.

As we passed the last of the medical tents, we ran by the stations where residents waited desperately to hear news of their loved ones. James was just emerging from an entrance when he noticed us running toward the edge of the park. We didn't stop, but I registered his face long enough to see it fall.

"Hadley, no! It's too dangerous! Sadie!"

"Sorry, James," I muttered under my breath.

CHAPTER TWENTY-NINE

The streets were already roaring back to life as rescue teams emerged from where they'd taken shelter during the attack. I could barely distinguish them through all the ash obstructing my vision as they raced back into the field. Sadie and I pushed onward, navigating the commotion as best we could. We ran three blocks before either of us said a word. It was Sadie who first broke the silence.

"Where was Fitz last seen?"

"A few blocks north of here. He and Henry were by this quirky tea shop with strange creatures all over it."

"Carved in stone?"

"Yes, you know it?"

She nodded. "The Goblin's Goblet."

Sadie and I reached toward each other as a huge chunk of stone fell several stories and landed half a block from where we stood. Debris flew everywhere from the collision. We hit the ground, protecting ourselves as best we could.

"You okay?" I asked as soon as the initial impact was over.

Sadie looked at me, her eyes unreadable as small pieces of dust, ash, and random debris floated lazily around us. She nodded, pulling a chunk of concrete from her hair.

"You can turn back any time, Sadie."

"This is what we've trained for. I'm not turning back now."

I nodded once and rose from the carnage. My arm hurt, and when I touched my dark tunic, I realized it was soaked in blood. Sadie stood and reached for my arm.

"That's a bad gash, Hadley. I can patch it up," she said, her eyes flickering to mine in question.

I wanted to keep moving, but the wound seemed severe enough to require attention. I nodded.

"Quickly, if you can," I said.

She closed her eyes, still holding my arm while hovering her free hand just above my wound. My skin grew warm—uncomfortably so— before a searing pain shot through me. Something scratched against my arm—Sadie's magic, I supposed—before I felt my skin pulling back together. The wound still ached, but the flow of blood ceased. She opened her eyes and nodded once.

"This will work—at least for now," she said.

"Thank you," I said before closing my eyes to focus on my connection to Fitz, hoping it would guide me closer to his location.

"What are you doing?" Sadie asked. A few seconds passed. "Hadley!"

I raised my hand, one finger extended. "Just a second."

I expected pushback, but it seemed Sadie was going to let this one go. And finally, Fitz's energy grew stronger.

"He's close. This way," I whispered.

With our intended route obstructed, we retraced our path and ran around the block. The streets grew quieter the further we ran, casting an eerie atmosphere over our mission. I wasn't even sure what I was truly feeling. If fear or anxiety lingered in my mind or body, it escaped me in my all-consuming need to drive myself forward and find my other half.

We had almost reached the bridge to cross the river when the sounds of conflict arose. We halted and looked to each other.

"Should we go around?" I asked.

"The next bridge is several blocks down the river. Let's investigate first."

We moved swiftly, and as we reached the end of the block, we peered around the edge of the building. The windows had been blown out, and the cold breeze sweeping across the river ripped through the holes in the building.

A skirmish had begun between our forces and Lorenzo's.

"I thought his soldiers had been pushed further back than this," I whispered.

Sadie nodded. "I think we press through. It looks like it's almost over, and everyone is well paired off."

I took a deep breath, thinking. I needed to get to Fitz. "Let's go, then."

Sadie and I ran for the bridge. She was right—the soldiers were paired off. We were navigating through the conflict when something odd caught my eye. At the far end of the bridge, Keoni was in heated debate with a witch who appeared to be one of Lorenzo's soldiers. Keoni looked up and caught sight of us, his eyes widening in surprise. I was distracted just long enough to miss the soldier running toward me. Before I could react, someone blurred in my periphery and took the brunt of a fireball that had been intended for me.

"Oh my god, Jess!"

I turned and threw a fireball back at the witch who'd attacked me.

Sadie transported from my side to the opposing soldier faster than I could blink and took him down swiftly. I dropped to Jess's side.

"Jess! Are you okay?"

He had taken a nasty hit on his abdomen. Keoni was by my side in an instant, radioing for backup.

"What are you doing here?" Keoni asked me as he assessed Jess's injuries.

"Recovery—we're looking for Fitz and Henry."

Keoni nodded as he continued his assessment.

"What happened here?" I asked.

Our eyes locked for a few seconds too long. Something wasn't right, and I knew it.

"Stragglers. We're trying to capture as many as possible for questioning," Keoni finally said. "Do you and Sadie need backup?"

"I don't think so, but truthfully, I don't know. I can report back once we've found them," I answered, though my mind was still caught up in what I'd seen. "Who was that soldier you were speaking with?"

He sighed. Just when I thought he wouldn't answer, he began.

"I grew up with him. We were close all through school. I hadn't seen him in a few years, and now I know why."

"He joined Lorenzo."

Keoni nodded. "He had the chance to kill me, Hadley. But he didn't."

"You let him go," I guessed.

"Yes." His brows knitted tightly.

"He showed you mercy, and you showed him the same. That's okay, Keoni."

He closed his eyes briefly, then nodded.

"I've got Jess. You can press forward," he said.

I looked at Jess, whose eyes were shut tight. I hesitated for a moment longer, thinking of Jess's sister . . . thinking of Luna. I couldn't shake that from my bones. I whispered a calming spell his way, something to ease his pain.

Keoni rested his hand on mine. "Go find Fitz."

I nodded and rose, searching for Sadie. She'd jumped in to help finish off the skirmish but was walking my way.

"Ready?"

"Let's go," she said.

As we raced across the bridge, I focused on mine and Fitz's connection, letting it guide me closer to him. We were rounding the corner of a clothing store where the windows had been blown out when I almost slammed into Fitz. We both stumbled backward, and his face lit with recognition—then relief. I threw myself into his arms before I could even think to make sure he wasn't injured, and he closed his arms around me, succumbing to instinct.

"Thank god you're all right," he mumbled before pulling back, his eyes scanning my body. "You are all right, aren't you?"

"Yeah, I'm just fine. Are you okay?"

"Aye, nothing major, anyway. But if you're both all right," he said, his eyes widening at the realization that it was Sadie who'd accompanied me, "I need your help. It's Henry."

A muted voice called from the other side of a pile of rubble that lay next to the remains of some type of office building.

"I think I'm mostly all right, but get me the hell out of here!"

It was Henry all right.

"We're working on it, mate. Just hang in there," Fitz called back.

"How in the hell did he survive that?" Sadie asked in quiet disbelief.

"I—I have no idea. He cannae see much in there, but something must be shielding him from most of the debris," Fitz said.

I walked around the pile, doing my best to assess the situation.

"Fitz, can you transport back to central command and get us some help?" I asked.

"I wish I could. I'm all right, but . . . I took a bit of a beating myself. It'll take some time before I'm able to transport."

In our haste, I hadn't really stopped to register the scrapes on Fitz or consider how taxing the situation must have been when he wasn't fully recovered yet. It pulled at my heartstrings to see him like this.

"It is your most draining power. That makes sense." I nodded, a taut smile on my face. I knew he'd be beating himself up for that one and moved quickly to my next plan before he had time to dwell on it. "We have to levitate the debris, then."

Sadie whistled. "We can try, but those stones are heavy."

"We have to try."

With my power at full strength alongside Sadie's and a boost from Fitz, who luckily had enough energy for levitation, the top piece of debris flew from the pile. The crumbling building's outdoor patio was on the second floor, and it had survived the blast. Henry had tucked himself in the corner of the stairwell by the wall, and it seemed that when a large iron beam had fallen, the patio was elevated enough to bear the impact, preventing it from crushing Henry.

"Henry!" I called down. "Can you levitate yourself out?"

"Nae," he grunted. "Something has my right leg."

"We'll need to levitate it, then. How are you two feeling?" Fitz asked.

"I'm still good," Sadie said.

"Me, too. Are you still okay to give us a boost?"

"Aye, I can manage that."

"Are you sure?"

"Positive." Fitz nodded reassuringly.

We pooled our strength yet again, and the iron beam slid carefully out of place, allowing us in. We rushed to Henry's side and found the problem. Fitz's face fell.

"What is it, mate?" Henry asked. "The truth."

I knelt, taking Henry's hand in mine. He was coated in dust, and cuts and bruises scattered across his skin.

"It's your leg. It's stuck under some rubble."

"I see. Can you move it?"

"Aye," Fitz answered. "But there's blood, so I dinnae know what we'll find."

"Sadie is trained as a paramedic," I said. "We'll figure this out."

Henry smiled weakly and squeezed my hand. "Of course you will, lass."

Reserving our power as much as possible, Fitz and Sadie tried moving the debris from Henry's leg, while I held Henry, his head propped in my lap. As the debris was cleared, the pool of blood expanded.

"Shite," Fitz muttered under his breath. "What do we do?"

Sadie's eyes were scanning over the wound rapidly, and she extended her hands, whispering something unintelligible under her breath. She ripped the leg of his trousers to better assess the wound. His lower leg had taken a beating, but it was his thigh that made my gut twist. A deep gash ran the length of his femur. Blood spilled out of the open wound. I had never seen an injury like this before, and I steeled myself.

"We need to stop the bleeding."

Sadie had been trained well enough to keep her voice level, but the desperate undertone in the statement was clear. Sadie pulled a strap off her pack and tied it tight around Henry's leg, buying us time.

Blood still flowed from the wound. "Why isn't it working?" I asked, my tone desperate.

When Sadie looked at me, her torn expression took my breath away.

"It's bad," she whispered. "He needs healing, but Hadley, this requires a lot of power. And I . . . don't have the power for it right now."

We stared wordlessly as seconds ticked by.

"Would—would cauterization work?" Fitz asked.

Sadie nodded.

"Hadley," Henry muttered. "I think you're up, lass."

My blood ran cold. He meant my fire magic.

"Henry, do you understand how unbelievably controlled I'd have to be to do something like this?"

"Good thing you've had all that practice," he mumbled, barely coherent as he weakened.

"It's bleeding too much for me to assess it well," Sadie said. "And we have all this ash and dirt falling everywhere. I'm worried it's already been compromised, and that's assuming . . ." she dropped her voice. "That's assuming he makes it out of here. We have minutes, Hadley."

"He could lose his leg, or . . ." Fitz eyed me meaningfully.

Or he could die.

My gaze then shifted to Sadie. She nodded.

My hands were shaking, but I knew what I had to do.

"Fitz, come trade places with me. Quick."

As I settled down by Henry's leg, Sadie whispered urgently in my ear, telling me exactly what was needed while carefully remaining out of Henry's earshot.

I glanced at Henry's face one last time.

"Fitz. Take his mind somewhere else . . . if you still have the power for it."

Fitz nodded, closing his eyes tightly. "Aye, I can do it."

"While you work on the bleeding, I'm going to follow your path and heal what I can," Sadie said.

"Is there anything you can do to reduce the feeling before I . . ." I trailed off. Before I seared his wound—but the words stuck in my throat.

Sadie nodded and set to work.

I bent near the wound and swallowed hard before connecting to the elements. Everything moved in slow motion, though from shock or the focus of that moment, I wasn't sure. I sensed where the punctures were and breathed deeply. My finger blazed hot with fire, and I concentrated until the flame was bursting from one tiny sliver of my skin. When it was as hot as I could channel, I nodded to Sadie, and I touched fire to the wound. I was barely aware of anything outside of my task, though I registered Fitz talking to Henry, attempting to keep him alert. As my fire met the last of the wound, the flow of blood ceased. I wasn't sure if that was it—would this work? But we had bought ourselves time and stopped the bleeding, and that was a hell of a victory.

Sadie ran through a series of motions, though I was hardly aware of what she was doing, but she soon laid her hand on my shoulder and announced she was going to find help. I offered to join her, but she shook her head.

"Henry can't move yet. Stay here in case anything happens."

"Thank you," I returned, my voice shaking. And with that, she was gone.

Sadie was quick, and Henry was readied for transport to Opimae City without delay. The team urged me to join Fitz back at the hospital with Henry, but I refused. They needed me at central command. I could still help, and I needed to do that.

"Here you were all this time worried I'd risk it all for you, but look at what you did today." Fitz shook his head. "You risked everything to find me."

"I couldn't help it," I admitted.

I would have risked anything at all, gone through the depths of hell, to make sure he was safe. And I'd do it all over again without question.

"I love you."

"I love you. Now, go take care of Henry, and I'll see you when I'm done here."

He brushed his lips against mine and jumped into the chopper just as they finished loading Henry inside. I waited until the helicopter cleared the nearby mountaintop before returning to work.

Jordan wrapped her arms around me as I entered the tent.

The cameras were all nearly restored, and I flipped through them quickly to take stock and reorient myself after my adventure. Brigitta appeared by our side with steaming mugs of tea. I wondered when she had arrived onsite, though there was no time for chatter.

"They're laced with several spells—energy, comfort, and focus. It should help." I was beyond grateful for her at that moment. She squeezed my hand and disappeared back through the door.

I video conferenced into the triage room to let Molly know Tanner's teams were bringing in a slew of badly wounded beings. She nodded quickly before turning back to a patient, closing her eyes and laying her fingers across the man's abdomen. I heard cries for help wailing in the distance, and I wondered how difficult it must be to remain focused on healing with so many voices filling the air. Behind her, Tanner, Isaac, and Gustavo rushed through the door, placing their most critical patients on the newly opened beds.

The night brought a fresh wave of responders, along with additional Opimaean council members. As they took over our positions, all the first wave responders gathered. Ian appeared in the crowd and embraced me tightly, his eyes damp.

"What you did today was unspeakably dangerous," he said. "Thank you. Thank you for loving my son enough to do that."

"You know you don't have to thank me for that."

Ian nodded, his lips quivering.

"I cannae keep doing this," he whispered.

"I know, Ian."

"If anything had happened to Fitz . . ." He trailed off. "Well, you understand, of course. But I couldnae lose you either, Hadley. You're a daughter to me now."

I tucked my head against Ian's chest, finally forced to acknowledge all that had happened.

"I was so scared, Ian. Henry . . ."

"I ken, lass."

Ian and I released each other, and he laid his hand comfortingly on my shoulder. I knew the fear of losing a mate. That fear had propelled me straight into the eye of the storm that afternoon. But the fear of losing a child—I could only guess at the mix of emotions swirling through Ian, especially without Ann there to share his burden.

"You did good today, kiddo. I'm proud of you."

"That means a lot, Ian. Thank you," I said softly.

The rest of the team found us, and we embraced warmly, happy to lay our eyes on each other again. Jordan slipped an arm around me, and we held on to each other.

There were so many other unspoken words in the air, so many things I couldn't even voice aloud—not yet. I breathed deeply, willing my mind back from the brink of release. I couldn't allow myself to feel the full force of the day's events—not yet, and not amid the growing crowd.

Charles joined us, looking tired and bloodied. Most of his day had been spent in command with us, but he'd also worked in the healing stations, encouraging staff and helping with patients as he could. The pale sunlight cast a soft glow behind him, and despite his fatigue, he carried himself with strength as he addressed the crowd.

"What is there to say in the face of such evil? Today, these beings were robbed of all security. Their safety, homes, family, and friends were taken from them. But even on a day like today, I see hope. I see courage. I see goodness. Because today, I see each one of you."

His eyes swept the crowd.

"I watched you offer everything you had to these beings. I watched you help. Heal. Comfort. And though we are still operating in the carnage evil has left behind, we have banded together to demonstrate that goodness will always prevail.

"From the bottom of my heart, I thank you all. And let me say this loud and clear: the perpetrator of this attack will suffer the consequences of his actions. Justice will have the last word."

The crowd erupted in cheers and shouts, and I looked across the sea of my magical brethren. We were exhausted, soaked in ash, dirt, and the blood of our brothers and sisters. We were sore and shaking and ridden with anger.

But we were also full of love and concern for those affected.

We were full of hope that Lorenzo would not have the last word.

And we were itching for the fight that lay ahead.

CHAPTER THIRTY

Fitz was waiting for me when the team made it home. I rushed into his arms.

"How's Henry?" I asked.

"He's doing fine. They're about to release him. He sent me home, but Keoni is with him."

"How is that possible?"

"It's incredible what medicine and magic can do together."

"So, his leg will be fine?"

"He'll take antibiotics because of the infection risk, but aye—he'll make a full recovery."

Relief washed over me, though it was short lived. I hesitated before asking my next question. "What about Jess? Is he okay?"

Fitz's energy shifted, and he eyed me before answering. "He's still in surgery last I checked. I'm waiting for a report."

I nodded. Fitz understood why I wanted to know, why I *needed* to know. He was one of the few beings who knew what Jess's loss would mean to a young woman and her daughter.

The team expressed their relief over Henry.

"I'm going to rinse off this . . . grime. Then I'll be here in the great room if anyone needs to talk about what happened today," I said.

Fitz closed our door gently before enveloping me again in his arms. I hadn't noticed before that I was trembling.

"How are you feeling?" he asked.

"I have no idea, honestly."

"Me neither," he admitted. "No matter how much training you go through, nothing prepares you for that."

I nodded in agreement, tears threatening to spill from my lashes. "I thought I'd lost you, Fitz."

"Hey," he whispered. "But you found me, my brave witch."

My grip tightened.

"How do we process this?" he asked, almost to himself.

I cleared my throat. "We talk about it. We don't keep it in. And then we find a way to channel this pain into power. We make Lorenzo pay for what he's done."

I wanted that ring out of his grasp more than ever.

Fitz tightened his hold on me, and the pressure felt safe. I leaned deeper into our connection.

"Are you sure you're ready to talk the others through what happened?"

"No, of course not." I released my grip slightly, looking into his eyes. "Are you?"

"Not really."

"But it's our job as leaders," I said. "So, we'll do it."

"Aye," he agreed. "Let's get cleaned up. The warm water will help with the shaking, I think."

Fitz and I helped each other rid ourselves of the physical markings from the day. I'd spent the last few weeks questioning witches' bonds with their mates, discussing with Jordan and Molly, scrutinizing Tanner. But whether Fitz and I had been destined to love each other or not didn't matter on a day like today. What mattered was that we had returned home together, and we would be okay. What mattered was that I had a mate like Fitz to walk through life with me. I'd sort out the rest later.

Henry returned while we were cleaning up, and once I emerged from the bedroom, I found him moving around the great room on crutches. We met each other in a tight embrace.

"You saved me," he murmured.

Tears ran hot down my face.

"You scared the hell out of me today, Henry."

"If it's any consolation, I was pretty scared myself."

"I love you. You know that, right?"

"Aye, I love you too. And I'm damn grateful for you."

Fitz and I took our place on the couch, hand in hand, and Jordan sat next to me, one arm linked through mine as she leaned against Gustavo. Molly curled into a ball and tucked herself under Isaac's arm, and he hugged her tightly to him. Henry tended to a laceration on Tanner's forearm, courtesy of a piece of jagged metal in the field. We wanted Henry to rest, but he said he needed to feel useful.

Chloe sat next to Tanner while she worked over a laptop with Solomon and Mia, pushing themselves to dispatch an early report to Earth. James and Ian shared a quick embrace before settling down.

James flicked his wrist, and the fireplace rid itself of our last fire's charred remains. He muttered under his breath, and fresh kindling and logs stacked themselves. James turned expectantly to me.

I nodded, and the fire roared to life. The soft crackle of wood was familiar, comforting.

"No quite the same as sitting around the fireplace at Henry's," Ian said, breaking the silence.

"I miss the sitting room more than I can put into words," Isaac said.

Nods and faint smiles were offered before the room became somber. Henry was first to break the silence, a Gaelic song escaping his lips. His voice was strained, but it was a welcome sound. I'd heard the tune once before on a much different night around Henry's fireplace—a Celtic prayer for peace sung in Scots Gaelic. Soon, other voices followed— Fitz, Ian, and then James—as they offered their prayer to the countless souls in need of comfort on that dark night.

gum beannaich
an tighearn' thu
gun deàlraich a ghnùis ort 's gum bi e gràsmhor dhut
gun togadh
e ghnùis riut
agus sìth thoirt dhut

biodh a gràs ort is grach beannachd
mile cinneach a chuid fhàbhar
's air do theaghlach 's do chuid chloinne
's an cuid chloinne, 's an cuid chloinne

May the road rise to meet you
May the wind be always at your back
May the sun shine warm upon your face
the rain fall soft upon your fields

And until we meet again
may God hold you in the palm of His hand
And until we meet again
may God hold you in the palm of His hand

PART THREE

CHAPTER THIRTY-ONE

Opimae's leaders were called into session the day after Lorenzo's attack, and Fitz and I joined them to give a report on the carnage. Charles asked us to present our experiences and observations to the room—his way of garnering support for new military strategies and financial support. From the looks of what Lorenzo had already accomplished, we needed it.

After hearing our report on the attack, already referred to as Red Monday, there was outrage across the chamber.

"What more do you need to hear?" King Alden asked. "How many more lives must we sacrifice before we act? We must regain control of Adamo!"

"I'm not yet convinced this is the right course of action," King Copandir said. "Do we not have another choice?"

"What about the mission to the fortress?" King Brennus suggested. "Could we not start there and make a decision about Adamo based on the outcome?"

"If the fortress mission fails, we'll lose the element of surprise with Adamo," Prime Minister Bakari said. "I understand your hesitation, but this is the best course of action."

"Our teams handled Pluvia Silva exceptionally well," Prime Minister Evander said. "The Opimaean forces and the Earth forces worked well together to neutralize a threat that took us by surprise."

"We should have done something before now. We could have prevented the tragedy in Pluvia Silva," Queen Min-Ji said. "Our inaction directly resulted in the loss of innocent lives. This chamber has blood on its hands!"

Silence fell as she made eye contact with her fellow leaders.

Finally, Prime Minister Bakari broke the silence. "Pluvia Silva should have never occurred—but it did. What can we learn from it? We must act against Lorenzo—that's clear. But we also learned that our forces are prepared for a fight against him. If we could take back Pluvia Silva under those circumstances, I believe we can regain Adamo."

"I agree," Charles said. "And I think our top teams from Opimae and Earth should lead the attack. They have proved themselves worthy of the responsibility."

The corner of Fitz's mouth curved slightly as he met my gaze. After fighting for more agency and breaking through Charles's walls, his belief in us felt good. For the first time, I felt like Charles truly trusted us.

"These crusade leaders are considered by many to be the ones from the prophecy," Queen Min-Ji said. "In the beginning, I was unsure if that was true, but my doubts have been assuaged. Their tie to the prophecy is something I ask each of you to consider."

"That is a bold statement, Min-Ji," King Brennus said flatly. I found nothing in his air to determine if he disagreed, and I wondered what his opinion of us truly was.

"We are not all convinced they are the crusaders promised by the prophecy," a woman said. I didn't recognize the voice, and I strained to see the source. A tall elf with long dark hair stood next to King Copandir. Queen Emlyn. I hadn't seen her since the autumnal celebration, as she split her time between the chamber and her duties in Athdara, but there was no forgetting this ethereal elf.

"Respectfully, you do not have the firsthand knowledge the rest of us have," Queen Min-Ji said.

Queen Emlyn bristled at her statement. Her blue eyes burned defiantly. "No, I've been taking care of my folk, but the king has kept me apprised of these proceedings."

"I do not mean to imply you are not educated on these issues. I only mean to state that you have not yet had the opportunity to know Earth's crusaders."

Queen Emlyn's eyes swept across me and Fitz, but she was quiet.

King Alden stood. "I don't think it's any secret that I've opposed Earth's help, but . . . I'm thinking about things differently after the events of Red Monday." He hesitated, clearly struggling to find the right words. "This team has proven themselves capable."

My breath hitched. Fitz and I met each other's gaze. This was the turning point we'd been waiting for.

Conversation carried on for a while longer, but we were talking in circles. Charles ended the morning session, and we adjourned for a quick break before he called the afternoon session to order.

Jordan walked to the platform. I smiled proudly as my best friend called the meeting to order.

"Thank you for making time for me today. I know you're busy, so I'll keep this brief. We uncovered information on the MacGregor ring this morning."

Whispers sounded through the crowd. Fitz's energy stirred within me. I reached for his hand and took in a deep breath, steadying myself. Despite all the reasons we'd come to Opimae, this was where it had all begun for Fitz and me.

"It appears that Lucio Belmonte, Lorenzo's father, time-walked to 1662 and extracted the ring from the past."

Gasps and exclamations echoed through the chamber. Fitz's energy grew tight, and Chloe leaned back in her seat, shaking her head.

Jordan waited for the chatter to die down before continuing.

"We located several sealed records earlier this week—an alarming pattern in Opimaean archives, I'm afraid. This morning, we received approval to open them. Much of the information had been redacted, but our specialized teams are working on countering the spells."

Though the information was concerning, Jordan had just given us a new lead to follow. We'd investigate Lucio immediately.

"Progress is slow," she continued. "The redaction spells are powerful, so it's taking a while to sort them out. But we've discovered that the guards were incapacitated outside the room where the ring was being kept. That's as far as we've gotten.

"This is a forbidden act, and the team is already discussing the repercussions that might come from Fate. But we are in the early phase of our investigation, so there's still a lot to be learned."

Solomon raised his hand. Jordan nodded for him to speak.

"Our main worry, at this point, is the threads of Fate?" he asked.

Jordan nodded. "We don't know what Lucio might have jumbled up as he left the past, and we don't know what this means for the future. Whether Lorenzo accesses its power or we neutralize the threat of the ring, there could be consequences from Fate for altering the ring's natural course. We must proceed with caution."

Jordan signaled through question after question. She was a natural, in total command of the room. Her time in the FBI had truly prepared her for this role.

Eventually, the final hand raised.

"Fitz," Jordan said.

"So, what's the plan of action? Where do we go from here?"

"Intelligence will remain focused on our research through the archives. If we need assistance, I'll be in touch as necessary." Jordan scanned the crowd before nodding to Charles.

Charles took to the floor. "I know we'll need time to deliberate with our nations and with each other. But now, more than ever, we must consider the consequences of our inaction. I propose a vote on Adamo and on Lorenzo's fortress at the end of the week—that gives us four days to deliberate."

Charles swept his eyes across the crowd.

"Meeting adjourned."

We filed into the dining hall after our meeting, intent on joining our team for lunch. We were surrounded by now familiar stone walls, though this space boasted large windows that allowed more natural light than most of the other rooms. Circular iron chandeliers held magical flames, and rows of wooden tables were spread across the stone floors. I found Molly in a back corner, waiting for the line to grow shorter, and stood next to her.

I scanned the tables. Jess sat at the far end of the room. He'd been in rough shape in Pluvia Silva, but he was recovering well. Sadie gestured intensely as she debated something with a colleague. I smiled. Tanner and Chloe were at the back of the line, lost in discussion.

Molly sighed loudly.

"What?"

"Enough of this already. Talk to Tanner."

"Molly . . ."

"You're stalling. And I get it. But you can't stall forever."

I wanted to argue with her. Truthfully, I wanted to do anything other than have this conversation with Tanner. But Molly was right—I needed to talk to him. Tanner left the line and headed for the wooden double doors that led to an outdoor patio, and I followed him, taking my chance.

I met Fitz's gaze before leaving the room and felt the uncertainty on my face. He nodded once, his support palpable.

Why would Tanner fight this?

I took a deep breath and stepped through the doors.

"Hey," I said. Tanner turned. "I need to ask you something."

"Okay, shoot."

I looked around and found a corner space on the patio that was unoccupied. I led us over and pulled a quick privacy shield into place.

"I've noticed something going on with you and Chloe."

"I have no idea what you mean." His face was blank, but his eyes darted away from me. I didn't need his break in eye contact to tell me something was off—it was enough to rouse a small thread in the air that told me he wasn't being truthful.

"I wouldn't mention it, except it's become obvious. I can see you aren't mated, but this isn't friendship."

"There's nothing going on with us. I mean, we're working closely to make sure we're ready for what's coming. That's all."

"That's not what your body language says."

"You said it yourself: we aren't mated. I know things are uncertain right now with all the speculation around Jess and all that, but you're letting your imagination run wild."

"Don't do that, Tanner."

"What?"

"Don't act like I'm an idiot. I know what I see."

Tanner scoffed.

"I'm not the only one who sees what's happening."

"So, what? You're all spying and forming stupid opinions about us?"

"Why the hell are you being so defensive?"

"What the hell are you trying to imply?"

"Did you enchant Chloe?"

Tanner stepped back, staring at me like I had grown another head.

"Are you kidding me? This is bullshit, Hadley." His voice was barely more than a whisper, but I winced at the venom in his tone. He turned to leave.

"Don't talk to me that way, and don't you dare walk away from me."

"Do you realize what you just asked me?" he asked, pausing.

"Yes, and I want the truth."

His body was rigid. I held his gaze, refusing to look away from the lightning storm in his eyes.

Finally, he shook his head and stalked away from me, disappearing through the doorway without so much as a look back.

CHAPTER THIRTY-TWO

The following morning, the team voted for Fitz and me to return to Opimae's past.

Jordan had identified a period when Lucio was confirmed to be in Opimae. The idea was that we'd return to that time and collect any information on Lucio we could find. Fitz's injuries had healed enough for the journey, and we all decided it was worth the effort. The mission was to remain secret—though we did inform Charles of our plans, maintaining our new pact with him.

Fitz and I stood in a small training room at headquarters, donning Opimaean fashion circa 1940. The fashion trends in Opimae weren't on the same course as the Old World. That decade had apparently seen heavy influence from elven royalty of old.

"This is too much." I threw my hands up, laughing at Fitz's attire. His outfit was some combination of a Celtic ruler's garb crossed with parachute pants.

"Aye. These designers were ahead of their time. But you know, yours isn't bad."

"I thought their dress had always been traditional. What happened here in the forties? This is like a Halloween costume," I argued, glancing down at my long gown. It was sage green with gold embroidery around the hemline, and the sleeves were fitted to the elbow before flaring out.

"Mine, aye. You look like you stepped off the set of a film."

"If we end up in a different time, we are going to look ridiculous," I said.

"I don't know what you're talking about," Fitz countered. "Now come here. Your tiara is crooked."

Then he wrapped his arms around me, and the world faded away. Headquarters swirled back into focus just as a young woman ran breathlessly down the hallway in front of us, her burgundy dress billowing in her wake. It appeared very little about headquarters had changed in the last eighty years. The beige stone walls and magically lit torches were just the same.

"Do you feel that?" Fitz asked.

"Yeah," I said roughly, distracted by the elements. "The air is wild."

Fitz nodded. "I think we chose an interesting day to visit."

We took in each of the subtle clues buzzing in the elements. Vibrations rang through the air. We followed their path, moving quickly to the floor above us. It didn't take long to identify the source. Magical beings ran toward a door at the far end of the hallway, and we followed suit, rushing down the stone corridor. The room was huge, and I couldn't recall having ever seen it at the present-day headquarters. It was well lit with floor-to-ceiling windows on two of the walls. Bright lights hung above countless wooden desks, and lamps sat atop each of the surfaces in the room.

An elf brushed my shoulder as he rushed past, uttering a distracted apology as he moved toward two men fighting at the center of the large room. One of the witches looked familiar, and it took my brain only a few seconds to register who he was. I had seen his likeness in Jordan's last intelligence update——and again just before our time-travel journey.

"Fitz!" I whispered urgently to his mind. *"It's Lucio. Right there!"*

Fitz's gaze zeroed in on Lucio just as a young woman ran up to us and pulled us aside.

"Stop! You must go. Both of you." Her accent was familiar—like Queen Marina's and Gustavo's. Her hazel eyes were wide, horrified. "Out! Now!"

"Why?" I asked.

"Don't let Lucio see you. Follow me."

Fitz and I met each other's gaze, but we followed the young woman quickly from the room.

Suddenly, I placed her. She was the dark-haired witch I'd seen during my spirit travels to Lorenzo's fortress.

Gabriella.

We followed her lead to the stairwell and stepped inside.

"I recognize you from the fortress. You spoke to me when I traveled there."

"I thought that was you," she said, her eyes flickering in hope. "Lucio knows who you are, but he can't see you—not today."

"And why is that?" Fitz asked.

"Because unlike Lorenzo, Lucio will kill you immediately."

"There's two of us and one of him."

"Correction," Gabriella said. "There are two of you, and roughly fifty of him. His agents are scattered everywhere in the building."

"Why?" I asked.

"He's stealing files from the archives. I'm surprised you transported to this day."

"This isn't in the records. We checked this date before coming back."

Gabriella furrowed her brow. "Then your records are flawed."

"They've been altered," Fitz whispered with realization.

"I came to warn you," Gabriella said. "An ally of mine saw that you were coming here today. I arrived as quickly as I could."

"Why are you helping us?" I asked.

"That's not important at this moment. We'll meet later, and I'll tell you everything. But for now, you must return to your time."

I nodded, and Fitz put his arms around me.

"I'll see you soon," she promised, and the world went black.

I opened my eyes to the future—or present, as it were—and rushed alongside Fitz to find Charles. He was in a meeting with Keoni when we entered his office, though he ushered us in.

"We have news from today's mission," Fitz said, eyeing Keoni.

Charles hesitated before prompting us to proceed.

"Unbelievable," Charles muttered once we'd relayed the details to him.

"I didn't realize you were conducting a time-travel mission today," Keoni said. "It wasn't on my briefing."

Keoni's tone betrayed his frustration. I met Charles's gaze, and he looked to Keoni, considering his response.

"It was a highly classified mission," Charles finally said. "We kept it quiet."

Keoni pursed his lips, then nodded.

"It's no accident we landed on that day, at that time, in the midst of Lucio's mission," I said.

"You believe Fate charted your course," Charles guessed.

"Don't you? The facts led us there, but what are the odds?"

"Aye, I think she's shown us favor," Fitz agreed.

Charles nodded.

"We should get this information over to Jordan so she can factor it into her teams' research," I said.

"Agreed. And Keoni, can you get us a list of everyone who's had access to the archives for the last—what—eighty years?"

Keoni arched his eyebrow.

"I know," Charles said, his head resting in his hands.

"I'm sure you're already thinking this, but if someone wiped this incident, they might have also wiped the record of their access," I said.

Keoni nodded distractedly. "A good thought."

"Nothing can be covered up, at least not completely." Our questioning glances pulled an explanation from Charles. "We can trace a cover up.

Jordan is doing a bit of that already."

Keoni's gaze narrowed. "Is that possible?"

"That protection was built into the system since its inception."

"I've never heard of that before. That's certainly not common knowledge," Keoni said stiffly.

"Of course not. And it doesn't leave this room. Understood?"

A chorus of agreement echoed through the office.

"Don't mention Gabriella to anyone—not even to Charles," I whispered into Fitz's mind.

I returned my focus to Charles and Keoni, studying them intently. I trusted Charles, and Keoni, too. But I couldn't ignore the nagging in my gut that something wasn't right. Perhaps I was simply suspicious of everyone after news of a mole in our ranks. Perhaps not. But Keoni's agitated energy certainly wasn't helping.

"Don't worry," Charles said. "If there's something to be found, we'll find it."

"Charles, I—" I paused. "I don't know who we can trust with this. I don't know who we can trust with anything, really."

Charles sighed, staring through the window. I looked to Keoni, who offered me a tight smile as he nodded toward Charles. I understood his silent request.

Give him a moment.

"Truthfully, I don't either," Charles finally admitted.

—— CHAPTER THIRTY-THREE ——

The birds sang a bittersweet song as I ran through the park, and a heavy chill lingered in the afternoon air. Winter had finally set in. The second sun seemed to fade into the distance—smaller than it had been before—and cast a dimmer light across the city.

I passed Henry, who was out for a walk. His recovery was going well, and I was glad to see him returning to normal. I passed Ian next, who seemed to be wandering aimlessly, lost in his own thoughts. I waved but remained focused on my path until I saw him—the elf who'd abducted me. And more importantly, the being who'd harmed my fiancé. I circled back quickly, but he was already waiting for me, propped against a towering oak tree.

"What do you want?" I asked crisply, foregoing formalities.

"Lovely to see you again, Hadley."

"I can't say the same. Now, what do you want, Isamu?"

"I want you to come talk with me."

"I'm not going anywhere with you."

"We have a lot to discuss. So, you'll come back with me, and that's exactly what we'll do."

I rolled my eyes. "Planning to abduct me again?"

"Is that what you call it? Huh."

"I think that's what everyone would call it."

"Well, regardless, I don't think that's necessary, because you'll make the right decision this time."

"What makes you think I'd go anywhere with you?"

"I'd imagine you want to keep that mate of yours alive."

My blood boiled. "You say that one more time, and you won't live to threaten anyone ever again."

His lips pulled tightly against his teeth. "And what makes Fitz so special to you? I understand he lied to you."

"Stop talking."

"Well, he did. To protect you?" Isamu laughed. "From the very government that's meant to help you? To keep you safe?"

How does he know about that?

I didn't want to lose control, but Isamu was thoroughly testing my patience.

"I know what you're trying to do, but your mind games don't work on me."

"What mind games? I only speak the truth. You would have never experienced something like that in the world we're fighting to build."

"And to do that, you need to capture and harm other beings? Stalk people? If you're 'fighting to build' anything, you're going about garnering support the wrong way. Your logic doesn't hold up."

"We didn't want it to happen like that, but your governments are so narrow minded. They've complicated everything."

"Don't you dare stand there and try to justify your actions to me. You can't place that on anyone but yourselves. You made these choices, and now you're telling me it's someone else's fault? You're pathetic."

"Okay, that's enough," he said, dropping his foot from against the tree. "You're leaving with me right now."

"Like hell I am."

The corner of his mouth turned upward into a smile, clearly amused at my protest—and ignorant of my abilities. I had trained hard for this very moment.

"I know you mean to put up a fight. I wouldn't expect any less of you, crusader."

"Don't test me."

Isamu laughed, picking at my temper. He seemed confident, but my magic identified the many holes in his energetic armor. Even outnumbered, Fitz must have thoroughly roughed him up.

"Oh, don't be angry, Hadley," he said, his hands raised in mock surrender. "I love how feisty you are. The last time we met, we had all kinds of fun, didn't we? You blew up a car engine."

I attempted to access his mind, but it was carefully protected, and I didn't have time to break in—I'd navigate this skirmish relying entirely on instinct. Fire prickled all through my body, threatening to spill out, and I knew my eyes must have been blazing. Isamu tilted his head, watching me warily, before stepping toward me. He was quick, but not quick enough to match the fire that tingled at my fingertips.

I took my shot.

Flames leapt from my fingers across the short distance, slamming into Isamu's shoulder. He jumped back and slapped his shoulder furiously in hopes of extinguishing the flames.

I took advantage of those few seconds and anchored myself against a nearby tree, whispering through the elements.

"Ian. Henry. If you can hear me, I'm by the center grove of trees in the park. I need backup, ASAP."

I wasn't positive I needed backup, but it sure wouldn't hurt.

Isamu moved toward me assuredly, though I registered how the burst of flames had weakened him. I breathed deeply, reassessing my connection to the elements, and concentrated my fire into a bow and arrow. I pulled back, minding my form, and released the arrow.

Isamu was better able to anticipate this attack and attempted to jump out of the way but didn't have enough time to fully remove himself from the line of fire. My arrow met the same shoulder again, knocking him back. When he rose from the ground, he staggered, gripping his arm tightly. The force seemed to have dislocated his shoulder. His tunic hadn't withstood the flames, and his flesh was burnt. I steeled myself for what would happen next and formed another arrow, but before I could launch it, a force settled around me and the arrow fizzled out. Another figure materialized next to Isamu.

I recalled my training around flame suppression. Isamu formed a cloud that settled all around me, dampening my fire magic. But luckily, I'd learned to fight back and focused myself to combat his counterattack. Isamu approached quicker than I'd anticipated, especially in his condition, and I was just disintegrating his cloud when he reached me. We tumbled on to the ground, and I asked the air to pull me from his grasp. I slid from underneath him, and he turned toward me. He thought I'd be easier to wrangle than this. A slow smile spread across his face. I called my fire back to the surface, just as he launched himself at me again. But before I could fire, a figure blurred in between us, tackling Isamu to the ground.

Henry. I turned. Ian was locked in battle with Isamu's companion, rolling across the grass. Isamu jumped from the ground, running toward a nearby grove of trees, when a translucent rope projected from Henry's hand and wrapped itself around Isamu's feet. Henry pulled him back, utilizing the air against him, but Isamu waved his hands, cutting himself loose from Henry's grasp.

Isamu launched himself back toward us, but I'd had enough. As Henry sent Isamu flying, I asked the air to pull Isamu's companion away from Ian and whispered instructions to Henry. I raised my hands to the sky and brought them down with such force that my fire exploded. Henry blanketed us in protection, but Isamu and his friend weren't quite so lucky. The blast sent them sailing through the air, and when we emerged from Henry's protection, Isamu and our second attacker were passed out on the ground before us.

I met Henry's gaze. "How's your leg holding up?"

"Fine, lass."

Relief ran through me. "Ian's arm looks bad. I'll check on him while you get these guys tied up."

Henry nodded.

I pulled Ian's arm carefully into my grasp. "How bad is it?"

"Nothing to concern yourself with, lass. Just scuffed up a bit."

"Still, you need to get checked out," I said protectively. Ian had become a second father to me, and I wasn't taking any chances.

I stepped aside to call Fitz, pausing briefly to survey Henry's work.

"Henry, don't take your eyes off Isamu for even a second—he's a slippery one."

I stood next to Henry in the medical wing of headquarters, waiting on the healers to triage Ian. Isaac and Molly entered the room, looking for us.

"We have to stop meeting like this," Isaac joked.

I laughed and embraced him. "I know. It's getting old, isn't it?"

"I swear to god, I'm going to kill this creature myself," Fitz said, his eyes narrowing as he barged through the door.

"You'll do no such thing," I replied.

"Oh, is that so?"

"He's a resource now, and you know it."

"He knows it, but feel that energy." Isaac whistled. "My man is pissed."

"And he has good reason," I said. "But once he's out of healing, Isamu could really fill in some blanks for us."

Fitz scanned me for injuries.

"Only minor scrapes and a burn from my own carelessness. The healers have already cleared me." I nodded in Ian's direction. "He has a nasty gash on his arm, but he wouldn't hear of being seen until the healers had attended to me."

"Dad." Fitz followed my hint, and he softened as he pulled his dad's arm into view.

"It's not bad," Ian said, though he winced at Fitz's contact.

"Let's have you checked out just the same," Fitz said, throwing his arm around his dad as they shuffled to a nearby chair.

"I don't know how tough this guy will be to crack open," Molly said, pulling me into an embrace. "But one thing I do know is he underestimated our little firecracker."

"Aye, aye!" Isaac said.

"Damn straight he did," Henry added.

"Yes, well that might be so, but Henry and Ian showed up just in time to pull me out of a bind."

"You'd have sorted it yourself soon enough, lass," Henry said. "But I was happy to lend another pair of hands just the same."

Jordan and Mia entered the room, quickly followed by Tanner. He and I locked eyes. His face was tense, his energy worried. His eyes swept my body, searching for injuries, I guessed, and when he realized I was okay, his features softened. He nodded at me and then quickly went to check on Ian.

"This is a damn good team. That's what this shows us," Jordan added, pulling me from Molly to hug me tightly. "Thank God and Fate and everything else."

Mia was right behind her. "Not to break up a good time, but I need to check in with Hadley and Henry. Ian, I'll come back for you in a bit."

"Of course, Mia. Lead the way," Henry said.

Mia ran us through a full list of questions that would appease the Earth and Opimaean councils alike, though she concluded her interrogation with a smile.

"You're smiling. That seems suspicious."

"Oh, come now, Hadley. Mia can be quite pleasant," Henry said.

"That seems like a backhanded compliment," Mia said, before clearing her throat. "Actually, I just wanted to say that I'm impressed. You handled this situation well."

"That's high praise," Henry said.

"The councils have done their best to prepare us, and we've done our best to learn," I said. "The only thing I ever worry about is losing my temper."

"How so?"

"My fire magic is a life force of its own. I'm able to control it most times, but occasionally, it slips out too strongly."

"And what? You can't reel it back in?" Mia asked.

"I can. But the damage is done by then."

Mia looked around cautiously, registering that we were alone.

"I don't know that I'm terribly concerned about that," she whispered.

Henry chuckled softly.

"What?" she asked sharply.

"Oh, nothing."

"Henry," I prompted, sensing Mia's humor falling into questionable territory.

"I didnae expect that from you, that's all."

"Why not?" Mia looked affronted.

"You're a rule follower. And you preach control to us constantly."

Mia paused, choosing her words carefully, I guessed.

"Yes, we preach control ad nauseum, and that's because you do need to exercise caution and discernment. But if you weren't passionate about this mission, then you wouldn't be here. Sometimes passion leads us down a slippery slope. I don't love that, but it's reality."

I was pretty sure my jaw dropped.

"I know. I gave you hell for breaking the rules, but that was when I distrusted you. I distrusted your judgment. But . . ." she paused, seemingly unsure of what she wanted to say. "Well . . . I've learned some things in Opimae, and your judgement isn't as questionable as I thought. If Isamu hadn't come through today's skirmish, it would have been a loss to Intelligence, but it's battle. It's life and death sometimes, and I understand that."

I nodded, still in shock.

"Isamu has done nothing but hurt you and harass you, and he has consistently put this mission in jeopardy. But we'll work on furthering your control anyway, Hadley," Mia added, standing. "And with that, I'm off to check on Ian."

CHAPTER THIRTY-FOUR

The following morning found me sparring with Sadie. We'd decided to continue our sessions together to challenge ourselves and grow further in combat, and there was always something more to learn.

Sadie swung at me, the full weight of her body flying mere inches from my face, but I pulled back just in time. I lunged forward, pushing her on to the mat, and swung around until I had her locked in a chokehold, my magic helping keep her in check. She tapped the floor beside me, and I released her.

"Finally." She smirked. "You're proficient."

We pulled each other up from the mat. Something had shifted between us that day in the field; there was a newfound respect between us. She'd still give me hell until the bitter end—I was sure of that—but I was fine with being colleagues who could respect each other, even if we'd never be friends.

Sadie wiped the sweat from her face and tossed my water bottle to me.

"Question," she said.

"Shoot."

"What's going on with the chamber? The energy in this building is about to blow the windows out, and there's chatter like you wouldn't believe all through the lower ranks."

I couldn't argue that the energy in the building was off, but I felt like Sadie was skirting around the real issue at hand. "You're usually more direct than this. What are you really asking?"

"Is the chamber sending us to fight?"

I dropped to the mat, mulling over what I should share with her. I looked at Sadie, considering her. I had to wonder if she could be the mole, but truthfully, I had no reason to suspect her. As rough as our start had been, Sadie had changed my opinion of her in Pluvia Silva. She had been willing to risk her own life to run into danger with me to find Fitz. She'd healed my arm and she had been a major factor in saving Henry's life.

"I'll never hear the end of it if I tell you," I said, still hesitant.

"No one will ever know. You have my word."

I searched for the threads around her that would tell me she was lying. The air remained undisturbed, and I nodded, knowing I could trust her statement.

"That's what we're fighting about in that chamber every day."

"Since that last big update meeting a couple of days ago?"

"Yep. I've sat in every meeting since the attack, and we just can't seem to reach a consensus. We vote in two days."

"What do you think will happen?"

"I think we'll be sent to regain Adamo."

Sadie's eyes widened.

I continued. "Everyone is still upset—angry—over the attack. Which I understand, because I am, too."

"I heard your team proposed the attack."

"That's not true. But we do support it."

She nodded, seemingly lost in thought.

"We need to start taking ground back from Lorenzo. Preventing him from moving further down the mountain is important, but we need to do more than that. We need to push him back."

"When I first heard about it, I was against it," she admitted.

"And now?"

"Now, I understand what we have to do if we want to win this."

"I hate that there isn't a better solution than engaging in another battle against him, but this is what we have to do. I think the chamber will see that in the end."

"And we were successful in Pluvia Silva."

"Exactly. We were able to pull out a win, even when Lorenzo held the upper hand by surprising us."

Sadie nodded.

"Thank you for telling me," she finally said.

"I'm glad I felt like I could."

There were no greetings this morning from Charles. We filed wordlessly into the chamber, preparing ourselves for the outcome of a life-altering decision for countless magical beings—ourselves included.

My nerves were high, despite my attempts to calm them, though I couldn't blame that solely on the vote. Fitz was unusually quiet. Though he didn't seem angry, his energy was off, and he had been distant since yesterday. We took a seat, and Fitz finally looked at me— really looked at me—for the first time that morning. He took my hand, offering a bit of comfort, though his energy and his blank expression remained the same.

Charles walked to the platform, the echo of his shoes permeating the otherwise still air. I breathed deeply, suddenly realizing I was holding my breath.

"Today, this chamber convenes to decide the fate of two missions," he began. "The first will decide whether to mobilize our teams and take back Adamo. The second will decide on sending in a group of special forces to claim Lorenzo's fortress."

My heart skipped a beat at his mention of the latter. That was us—our team. The crusaders of the prophecy. I thought of Esther MacGregor's ring and the chain of events it had set into motion.

"Let us begin," he said.

He loked at Brigitta, who nodded, and then turned back to the chamber. "Earth Crusaders."

I dropped Fitz's hand and stood, my own hands trembling.

"Your votc on the Adamo attack," he said.

Roísín flashed through my mind.

"Aye," I answered.

"Your vote on the mission to Lorenzo's fortress," he continued.

"Aye."

"Thank you," he offered.

I took my seat. Fitz nodded reassuringly.

"Arregaithel," he called.

This pattern continued through Bain, Novam Terram, Hurlee, and each nation pledged their support of both missions. When the time came for King Copandir of Athdara to vote, the room grew still.

The king stood, tall and domineering. I took Fitz's hand as Charles asked for Athdara's decision. The nerves that fluttered through our connection matched the energy that whipped around the room.

King Copandir hesitated for only a moment before answering. "Aye," he said.

His decision on Lorenzo followed—affirmative.

Nods and faint whispers echoed through the chamber. I caught Charles's gaze, and relief was apparent in his eyes. Fitz's energy eased.

The southern elven kingdom followed Athdara, as did Kevandhu, the kingdom of the faeries.

The vote was a resounding yes.

Even as I scanned the room, I could hardly believe it. In over-whelming numbers, it was decided that our team would partner with Opimae's most specialized forces to take back Adamo—and capture Lorenzo.

And it would happen quickly.

"We have an update on the attack," I said, entering the great room.

The temperature dropped and every gaze settled on me and Fitz.

"When?" Isaac asked, already guessing at the council's decision.

"One week from today," Fitz said, his eyes flickering quickly to mine and away again.

"Both Adamo and Lorenzo's fortress," I said.

Murmurs sounded across the table.

"We're ready for this," I said, "and we'll fight as a team and return from this together."

"Are Gustavo and I to fight, as well?" Jordan asked.

"Yes," I answered softly. "The councils signed off on your training."

"I don't feel ready."

"None of us do," Fitz assured her.

"None of us could," Henry said. "We haven't seen real battle yet. I think that confidence only comes from experience . . . unfortunately." He looked to Solomon, who nodded.

"Yes, but we are ready, and we just have to keep reminding ourselves of that. We're going to be okay," Isaac said, speaking far more confidently than his energy felt.

I smiled. Encouraging one another was one of the most important things we could do.

"What does the next week look like?" Ian asked his son.

"Loads of last-minute training and reviewing of strategy. If there's any area where we're feeling deficient, we'll address it."

"And if there are any skills we identify in each other as lacking, we'll work on those, so keep an eye out for your teammates," I added.

"We're meant to have a thorough assessment of our battle skills, but as lightly as possible so we don't sustain any injuries this close to battle," Fitz explained.

"I can't believe we're doing this," Molly said.

"Me neither." I offered her a small smile. "But we fought hard for this decision, and now we must face what that means."

"Yeah. We spent all this time training and planning, but it just felt like some abstract future. It still doesn't seem real," Jordan added.

"And after seeing Pluvia Silva, we know exactly what we're up against," Molly said.

"It's a lot to wrap our minds around," I said simply. "But we'll have time to process and prepare."

The room fell silent.

"We will win this," Fitz said quietly. "We'll come back together."

CHAPTER THIRTY-FIVE

Fitz remained distant as the evening wore on. I had assumed it was the result of his father and me both being injured, or the weight of the impending mission, but I knew it was more than that. Even at the team dinner, he was unusually quiet, garnering a few curious looks from our teammates. I'd shrugged it off then, but as we returned to our room, I pulled the elements into a privacy shield and turned to Fitz.

"Okay, enough," I said. "I can't take this any longer."

"What?"

"I said, enough."

"Oh, I heard you," he said, eyebrows raised. "But I don't know what you're pissed about."

"I'm not pissed. I'm tired of you walking around not saying whatever it is you need to say."

"I don't have anything to say."

"Bullshit," I said firmly.

"Aye, it is. You're accusing me of the very thing you've been doing for weeks."

Everything suddenly seemed to be too much, and I felt my patience break. I walked toward him, halting only when we were mere inches apart. We were standing so closely together I felt the tension rolling off him. His energy cut through the still air like a bolt of lightning.

"Why don't you tell me what's got you so worked up," he said slowly.

"Why won't you talk to me?" I hissed.

"I am talking to you. I have been talking to you."

"Don't be coy with me. You know exactly what I'm talking about. You've been weird for two days, and I know the team notices. We're supposed to be leaders."

"We are leaders."

"You're holding something back that's eating at you. Don't you realize that your anxious energy is consuming me?"

"Stop," his voice rang out. He turned toward the windows. I walked across the space to pour a dram from our supply of whisky and sank into the nearby chair.

"I'm worried," he finally began.

"About what?"

"About your safety."

"Why?"

"The vote. I know we're for the recovery of Adamo, but the reality is that we'll head straight into battle. I need to make sure you come out of this all right. I felt that stronger than ever after Pluvia Silva, and then Isamu came calling again."

"Well, you need to be concerned with your own safety. I don't want to live without you."

"Dinnae say things like that, Hadley," he warned.

"What are you pissed about now?"

"You know I cannae have that thought cross my mind."

"Oh, that I don't want to live?"

I knew what I'd done. Anything that made us reflect on a world without each other was excruciating.

I continued. "Well, you're not doing me any favors either."

"Listen . . . I know we might die. But it's more than that. The thought of what we might do to survive haunts me."

"I know exactly how you feel," I admitted. "It haunts me, too."

We paused, silent for a moment.

Finally, I said, "We need to focus on our strategy. Worrying about dying and leaving me unprotected is only distracting you from doing your best."

"Well, that's pretty fresh, coming from you."

"What?" I asked, stunned.

"You've no been yourself either. You've had me second-guessing myself ever since we landed in Opimae. I've been patient, thinking you've just been sorting out your thoughts with everything going on, but I know there's more to it."

I dropped my gaze.

"One minute you feel normal, happy even. And the next . . ." He shook his head. "The next, you feel so distant."

I took a deep breath. "So, where does that leave us, then?"

"I'll talk to you if you'll talk to me," he replied.

He walked across the room, and we shook hands. The gesture was playful, though the anger hadn't yet cleared the room.

"Let's start with what else you aren't telling me," I said. "Something else is bothering you."

"It's nothing, really."

A small, wavering thread took shape next to Fitz. A lie.

"Fitz, you can't get away with this with me. In case you forgot, I'm a witch now, and a damn powerful one. You can't lie to me."

"It's no a lie."

"It's not the truth, either."

Fitz walked back to the window and stood motionless, collecting his thoughts. I stewed quietly from my side of the room. I wasn't in any hurry, but the anxiety gripping my chest was growing with each tick of the clock. After what seemed an eternity, Fitz turned toward me, his hands in his pockets, his face downcast. Slowly, he raised his gaze.

"Truthfully, it took me a minute to sort out my head—to even work out what's truly bothering me."

"Take your time."

A hoarse laugh escaped his lips. "I feel your anxiety, and I'm going to put you out of your misery quickly, I promise."

I nodded.

"This whole mission is bothering me, of course. But I'm realizing how much of a toll these altercations took on me."

He paused.

"I've struggled more with this recovery than I wanted to admit— even to myself. I wasn't healed before Pluvia Silva, so it just sort of built on top of one another."

"It's normal for you to have struggled with all that."

"Aye, but it's more than that. I feel like I've held us back, and now I'm wondering if I'm as prepared as I should be after the setbacks."

"You've done exactly what you should've been doing: healing," I half whispered. "Even with the hits you took, you still pushed through sparring sessions and chamber meetings. I honestly don't know how you did it."

Fitz shook his head.

"You're never fair to yourself. But what you've done is amazing. I've watched you recover over the last couple weeks, and you are ready for this."

I crossed the room and took his hands in mine, my eyes searching his.

"I know what you're struggling with now, and it has nothing to do with your physical strength. But please find a way to believe in yourself, because you've not held anyone back, not even yourself."

His energy roared through the space, disrupting the quiet night air. I reached for his face, hesitating briefly before brushing my fingertips along the length of the fresh scar that ran from under his jawline to his cheek.

It occurred to me this wasn't the only part of Fitz that had been irrevocably altered from our experience in Opimae—we all bore our scars from this journey, physical and otherwise— but it was one that would always boil my blood. It was a constant reminder that someone had harmed him. My breath hitched at the thought of what I would do to Isamu if I could. I took a deep, ragged breath before pressing my lips to the scar, and when I pulled back, his eyes were softer than before—although I found something new in his energy.

"What is it?" I asked.

"You'll find it silly, but I hate this scar."

"I don't find that silly at all. I understand the sentiment, but I love it."

He rolled his eyes. "Come on, Hadley."

"No, I'm serious. It makes me beyond angry to think about why it's there, but that scar reminds me how resilient you are. How much of a fighter you are. Whether or not you want it, it's a part of you now. And I love every part of you. I want you—all of you. Wasn't that what you said back in London when I matched to my power?"

Fitz smiled, pulling me closer.

"This isn't a flaw. It's character."

"Aye, whatever you say." He paused. "You know, battle is imminent. You say I'm resilient . . . but I'm no completely healed. I might no be back to normal in a few days."

It hit me then: he felt he wasn't ready for battle, and he wanted to be sure I'd be all right if he didn't make it. The realization blew through me like a gust of wind.

"What are you always telling me I need to practice? Oh right, patience."

Fitz smirked.

"I think you're healing normally. Keep taking care of yourself, and you'll get there."

Fitz nodded.

"You need to talk to me when you're feeling like this," I said. "You trying to hide it is more distracting than the truth ever could be."

"I know. But lately I hardly know my own thoughts."

"So, it takes you a while to work out what's even wrong."

"I think I compartmentalize my life sometimes. It's . . ."

"It's a coping mechanism," I finished for him.

He nodded.

"Fitz. There's no shame in that. We all have our own coping mechanisms."

"What's yours?" he asked.

"Sometimes my mind wanders to what our life would be like if we hadn't joined this crusade."

"What do you see?" he asked.

"You, teaching that new course you were developing before we left. Me, running the donor event at the castle. Decorating our new home."

I longed for cozy mornings by the fireside, set to the tune of gentle rainfall against our flat's windowpanes. I dreamed of simple afternoons, Fitz grading papers while I sipped Earl Grey tea and devoured a good book. Evenings spent cooking dinner, just like our first night together at our flat.

I longed for the beings we had been before this crusade began.

Fitz traced circles up and down my forearm.

"We're all trying our best to manage this shite," Fitz said, pulling my attention back from Edinburgh. "Truthfully, I've been worried about myself, and I didnae want to say it out loud. It made it more real somehow."

"But it's good that you've said it out loud," I said. "You've spoken your fear—and now that we can name it, we can defeat it. We can face anything together."

He rested his forehead against mine.

"Come with me to my follow up appointment tomorrow?"

"Of course," I whispered. "I wouldn't miss it."

"Now, tell me what's been troubling you."

I looked away, caught, but he took my chin between his fingers and pulled my gaze back to him. My nerves rang through our streams.

"Fitz . . . did you fall in love with me on purpose? I mean, did you fall in love with me willingly, I guess? Or do you think you even had a choice in the first place?"

Fitz grazed my face with his fingertips, and his gaze turned tender.

"What's brought that question to mind, my love?" he asked.

"Everything. The council forcing us apart. Molly and Henry's losses. Molly's story about the woman who'd enchanted her mate. Jordan and Gustavo finding love. Tanner."

"You *have* been thinking on this."

"Yeah. I'm grateful for what we have, and I believe Fate led us to each other. I think I made a conscious choice with you." My head dipped, unable to hold his gaze. "But do you feel the same?"

"Hadley, look at me," he said.

I did as he asked. He stared deeply into my eyes, and I saw something flicker in his expression. He pulled me to the nearby bench, and we sat quietly, turning to face each other.

"The truth is . . . I loved you before my eyes even knew you, before my mind could catch up with my heart. I saw you standing in that clearing with Izzy, and I knew I'd been bested. Your energy mingled with mine, and I ran headfirst into a world full of trouble."

He paused.

"Did I have a choice in the matter? I'll tell you this: every day that I was apart from you, I loved you. And every day since I've known you, I've chosen you. Even if my soul cares little for my mind's opinion on the matter, and even if my soul already loves you beyond all reason, I still wake up every single day and choose to love you."

My breath quickened at the intensity of his words.

"So, even if I was meant to love you, I love you on purpose."

Tension released from somewhere deep within me. I nodded, tears threatening to spill down my cheeks.

"Oh, Hadley," he said.

"I choose you, Fitz. Every single day, I choose *you.*"

Fitz tugged at my arm.

"Come here," he whispered gently. "I need to feel you."

I climbed onto Fitz's lap and wrapped my legs around his waist, facing him. I stared into his emerald eyes as I traced his jawline with my fingers, stopping again at his scar, and smiled softly. I'd remind him that I loved every part of him, even the scars, until he believed it.

He reached for my hand and kissed my fingers gently. I closed my eyes, savoring the feel of his touch, longing to stay in the magic of this moment forever. Warm desire filled my veins, and Fitz's longing pulsed through our connection. I kissed him as his hands explored my body, from my chest to my waist to my thighs. He found his grip on my thighs and stood, cradling me to him as he tugged off my chemise. I slid until my feet met the ground, and I pulled his shirt over his head.

I brushed my fingers lightly over Fitz's forearm, tracing a sizable bruise. He pulled my hand away and brushed his lips across my fingers. I closed my eyes, sparks racing through me.

"Don't trouble yourself with those," he whispered.

I shook my head, meeting his gaze. "Do you not understand why I can't help myself?"

His eyebrows rose. "You think I dinnae understand? How do you think I feel when I see this?" He pointed to my forearm where a large, purplish bruise had formed around my slow-healing gash from Pluvia Silva.

His eyes grew stormy as he flipped my arm over and pointed to another large bruise. "Or this?"

He knelt before me and reached for the button on my pants. I placed my hand over his, halting his progress. There was a wound on my hip from my scuffle with Isamu, and I'd carefully hidden it so Fitz wouldn't worry. His eyes shot to mine, and I knew it was too late.

"You think you can hide your wounds from me? That willnae work, Hadley."

I hesitated, but I was only delaying the inevitable. I leaned over to inspect the bruise as he slid the soft fabric below it. It was worse than I thought it would be. My hip and the front of my thigh were both covered in red and purple, and a cut ran halfway down my leg. An intake of air betrayed Fitz's surprise, and I grimaced. His face softened as he rose, his hands cradling my face.

"What happened? Who did this to you?"

"Isamu. It's kind of a blur, but I think it happened when we tumbled to the ground."

"He'll no have another chance to harm you—I'll see to that."

"Fitz. No."

His eyes searched mine, and I knew it was a lost cause. "I know how badly that must hurt, because even I can feel it."

"It's the worst I've had," I admitted.

"Did the healers look at it?"

"They said this one would take another day or two to heal."

Disapproval registered on his face. "I can help with the pain."

I nodded.

He knelt again, and his hands hovered inches from my hip. A cooling energy radiated across the wound, and slowly, the pain numbed as he worked slowly down to my thigh.

Fitz carefully kissed the wound, making his way up my hip. I pulled him toward me and kissed him deeply, this man who'd chosen to love me. We shed the remaining layers between us, our clothes soon littering the bedroom floor. I kissed him, and we dissolved into a tangled mess of limbs and whispered promises. Tiny bursts of energy exploded as we moved together, coursing through me like an awakening.

My body fell into rhythm with his, creating a symphony only we could hear.

CHAPTER THIRTY-SIX

Even though Fitz and I agreed with the decision to take back Adamo and invade Lorenzo's fortress, we still carried the weight of what this meant for our team. We felt the need to seek peace in the wake of the decision reached and decided to have a tranquil night with the team. There was something to be said for celebrating the wins we'd had the last couple weeks.

At least we still had each other.

I longed to sit around a fireside away from the city and feel the comfort of ancient things. Lana and Saoirse owned a property by the ocean overlooking a cliff outside of town, and they offered the old stone structure to us as a retreat. As we entered through the wooden door at twilight, we were greeted by worn stone floors, thick rugs, and a roaring fire. Huge leather chairs were strewn around the living room along with bottles of whisky.

I cast a glance toward Lana, smirking.

"I know my audience," she joked.

"You sure do."

I noticed a guitar near one of the chairs and pointed to the instrument. "Ian, look."

"Oh, aye, I see it!"

"We'll have some music, then," said James, clapping excitedly.

Isaac grinned. "Gustavo, you're in for a treat."

"Based on the excitement, I can see that. What type of songs will we have?"

"Scottish tales, to be sure," Henry said, clasping a hand on Gustavo's back. "Do you know much of the Scottish culture of Earth?"

Fitz and I found each other's gaze and smiled.

"Not much more than what I've observed being around the lot of you." He grinned. "But I've heard of your stories. This is truly an honor."

"Dinnae get too excited, lad," Ian said. "This willnae be all that grand—but it'll be merry, just the same."

"That's all we need tonight," Lana said.

"Perhaps we can hear some elven music, as well?" I asked.

"I'd love that."

"And Gustavo—what of the water folk? Do you have your own music to share?" Fitz asked.

"Indeed, we do. I could share a song or two if you'd like."

Jordan beamed. "That would be wonderful."

We gathered around the fire and passed cups of whisky around. The air on Opimae was always cool, but the temperature had dropped that afternoon, and the mix of the cold, salty breeze, the warmth of the fire, and the burn of the whisky was pure magic.

Wind gusted through the room, disturbing the fire, and we turned to find Keoni rushing through the door.

"Okay, now it's cold."

Laughter resounded.

"Join us by the fire," Henry offered, extending a cup in his direction.

Keoni accepted and settled on the floor near my feet. He'd seemed distant and unhappy lately; Pluvia Silva had been tough on us all, and the pressure on his shoulders must have been substantial. I understood why he was detached, stressed . . . but I still hated to see it.

"You know, Keoni, I've never asked how you landed in your role," I said.

"Well, I served in my nation's military for about fifty years, and after reaching the top rank, I needed a fresh challenge. I knew I was as far as I'd ever get, and I was feeling restless. I met Charles on an assignment, and the pieces fell into place."

Even though witches aged slowly, I was surprised by Keoni's age—he looked like he couldn't have been older than his late twenties.

"Where are you from, if you don't mind my asking?"

"I hail from Hurlee originally. You haven't had the chance to learn much of my folk, but we're a quiet nation of witches southeast of here. I grew up on the coast and always dreamed of seeing the world—and of seeing yours, too."

"Have you made it to Earth yet?"

"No, but I'm keen to go. I've been all over this planet through my service. Earth is the final frontier."

"You can say that again," Henry quipped.

Keoni smiled before continuing. "One day, I hope to cross into the Wild West with you."

His reference brought a smile to my face. "I hope that too, Keoni."

Saoirse dropped on to the couch next to me, and Ian began his musical efforts.

"The Bonnie Lass o Fyvie" was his opening number, and Henry joined him. I took the song as an opportunity to gaze across the fire and study Gustavo closely.

The water folk were truly ethereal. His eyes glowed a mesmerizing aqua in the dim firelight, set brightly against his golden-brown skin. Sitting next to Jordan, whose amber eyes glowed alongside his, they were a pair to be seen. He swayed along to the rhythm, gazing at Jordan often. I smiled, thinking of the love that had found my best friend, and leaned into Fitz.

Lana sang a captivating elven tune that sounded Nordic to my ears, and Saoirse joined her at the chorus. She was followed by Gustavo, who strummed the guitar and sang of his folks' passage from Earth to

Opimae and how they formed their nation. It left me longing for more, and I hoped to have time to dig further into the books Queen Marina brought for Jordan.

The music paused for dinner, and the team scattered across the space to enjoy a spread of elven fare along with specialties from Opimae City.

"Here you go." Molly set another pastry on my plate. They were flaky and sweetened with dates—and delicious.

"Hey, has Tanner talked to you tonight?" Molly continued.

"No."

"Have you given him an opportunity?"

I grimaced.

"You need to give him a chance to talk to you."

"He doesn't want to."

"You're wrong," Molly said decidedly.

"You don't mince words, do you?"

She grinned. "Maybe not, but I'm right about this."

"Explain it to me, then."

"You're missing the subtle clues in his energy. Yes, it's agitated—all muddled up. I feel doubt, fear, confusion, but not anger. He was worried about you after Pluvia Silva. When we hold secrets like Tanner's, we really want to get them off our chests to someone who cares about us."

I paused momentarily, trying to pick out what Molly had found in Tanner's emotions. The woman read feelings like a wine connoisseur smelled all the complexities in a glass of Malbec. I found her gift astonishing.

"You think he's ready for that?"

"The shock has worn off. He needs to share his burden."

I nodded.

"You know, no one is in the kitchen right now, and I'd love some more mead," she said.

"You're devious," I said.

"You should probably ask Fitz if he needs anything."

I followed Molly's eyes to a burgundy leather couch, where Fitz, Solomon, and Tanner sat.

"Fitz, you need anything from the kitchen?" I offered, hoping I didn't sound too rehearsed.

"I'm good, love. Thanks."

I caught Tanner's glance from the corner of my eye and strolled into the kitchen. Trying to grant him enough time, I found no shortage of tasks to be completed. I moved stacks of plates into the sink while floating trash into the nearby receptacle. I grabbed two bottles of mead from the fridge and turned to find Tanner across the kitchen island.

"Oh, hey."

"Hey."

I stood awkwardly, holding our bottles.

"Double fisting it, huh?"

I laughed, feeling better instantly.

"I'm sorry about the other day," Tanner said.

"It's okay. I'm sorry, too. I could've been more tactful."

"Nah, don't apologize." He paused, tapping his finger on the worn wooden surface. "Especially since you're right."

I set the mead on the counter and opened mine quickly. Tanner's eyebrows rose.

"Sorry. I think I'm going to need this to get through the conversation we're about to have."

"Me too, honestly."

I slid Molly's mead into Tanner's grasp and waited for him to begin.

"A friend of mine from school is a seer," he finally said. "No one you've met, but I've known her since we were kids. We don't talk much anymore, but she asked to meet up right before I left the States for Edinburgh. I thought it was strange, but I met her in Seattle." He paused, draining a good portion of the bottle. "She said she'd seen something about my future and had debated about whether or not to tell me, but ultimately thought it would save my life."

He took another sip, his nerves radiating through the space. "She said she foresaw my mate and I joining a dangerous mission. She couldn't figure out what we were doing, but she said that while on the mission, I would be killed."

My blood ran cold.

"Oh my god, Tanner."

"Let me finish."

It took a minute, but I nodded for him to proceed.

"I knew this was the right thing to do. I might die. I might not. Any number of things could change, but I knew I was supposed to be a part of this."

"For God's sake, Tanner. You don't need to do this."

"Yeah, I do. I'm destined as much as anyone else on this team. We both know there will be more than one casualty by the time this is all over." He paused, shutting his eyes tightly. "And that's okay. This is important, and a lot more innocent beings are going to die if we don't get the job done."

I chewed my lip, my mind racing. I knew Tanner well enough to understand how he operated. He'd made up his mind, and I'd never convince him to opt out. Instead, I focused my effort on an area where I might make some headway.

"Your belief that you might not make it back to Earth . . . that's what's going on with Chloe?"

"Yeah. My friend saw enough for us to identify that it was Chloe. I wrestled with it a long time, but once I was scheduled to meet her in person, I kind of panicked."

"You enchanted her."

"Yeah."

"Why?"

"Because I might not make it to the end of this mission, and I want to protect Chloe from that. She'll spend these few months with me, and then what? She lives with the fact that we'll never get married, never have a life together? It's not fair to her."

"Do you understand what will happen if the court figures out you've enchanted her?"

"I'll probably be dead before they figure it out."

"What the hell, Tanner? Don't say things like that. You just said something can still change."

"I'm just operating right now like it won't. We both know it isn't likely."

"You're all over the place. You think you'll die, then you think you won't. You say you joined us because things might change, and then you say they likely won't . . ."

"Honestly, my opinion changes by the hour."

"I think you should tell Chloe," I said plainly.

"That's not the plan."

"This isn't fair to her, Tanner."

"You don't know that. You don't know her as well as you think you do."

"I know more than you think. Are you forgetting what I went through?" I said angrily, thinking of all that had been concealed from me while Fitz and I were apart: the confusion and fear I'd felt while Fitz had tried to protect me from the government. The hurt and anger I'd felt when everything finally came to light, when I realized just how many beings had banded together to hide the truth from me.

I still hadn't quite healed from it.

"What, with the council? That was different."

"You're right. It was different." I paused. "There were serious consequences attached to our situation. Fitz didn't just up and decide to hide something this important from me."

Tanner's jaw was set tightly.

"You know what that did to me. You saw it," I said, my voice breaking. "This will do the same to Chloe."

"No," he said firmly, though his eyes flickered with uncertainty.

"You think you know her . . ."

"Yeah, I know her pretty damn well," he said, cutting me off. "Don't you realize I'm carrying the grief for both of us right now?"

I leaned across the counter, taking Tanner's hand in mine. He flinched, but he didn't pull away. "You know I care about you. I'm angry right now, but that's because I care. I want you to live, and I want you to have a good life as long as you're with us."

He hesitated, but finally he nodded. "I know."

"You can do what you want, and I know you will. But please, just think about telling her. Yes, it'll be a disaster if it comes out, but I've been in her position. I might not know her as well as you do, but I know she'd want this time with you. Chloe would want the chance to love you and be loved."

Tanner's gaze dropped.

"Shit, Hads. How did things get so complicated? Remember when we were just living on mountains with no cell reception?"

He sighed, releasing some of his anger. That was a good sign, at least.

"I don't want her to go through what you did."

"That's exactly what's happening to her right now," I said. "The confusion, the conflicted feelings, the uncertainty . . . it's horrible. Release her from that, Tanner."

Tanner chewed at his lip, his eyes lost in thought.

"We leave for Adamo in a few days," I said. "Battle is imminent. You're out of time. Tell her before it's too late."

Tanner hesitated, but finally, he nodded. "Okay."

Everything else fell away the moment we walked into the living room and Tanner leaned over, whispering into Chloe's ear. She nodded, and they disappeared into a dim hallway, leaving the rest of us for a lengthy stretch of time.

I didn't realize until that moment how much of a toll Tanner and Chloe's situation had taken on me. Not only had I been worried, but Tanner's enchantment had ripped the bandage off my own wounds, which had only just begun to heal. Fitz crossed the room and took a seat on the couch, slipping his arm around me.

"I know this was hard on you," he said softly. "But you had the courage to stand up to Tanner and encourage him to make the right choice."

"It'll take time for Chloe to heal from this."

"Aye. But the two of you will help each other—that much I know. And . . ." Fitz trailed off. "And I think it's good that Chloe will understand what you went through now. It's not the same, but it's enough."

Fitz was right about that, and it sparked something inside me. "She'll understand what it feels like when the councils force witches to do this to their human mates."

"She's nearing the end of her investigation on how our case was handled. It's braw timing."

When footsteps sounded again in the hallway and the two witches in question reemerged, I squeezed Fitz's hand as we waited in suspense.

Chloe met my gaze and made a beeline for my arms. I glanced over her shoulder at Tanner, who nodded.

"Thank you," Chloe whispered, releasing me.

"For what?"

"For helping Tanner realize he needed to tell me the truth."

"You deserved to know. I would want that if I were in your shoes."

Chloe rejoined Tanner, gripping his hand in both of hers, and they called for everyone's attention. Fitz pulled me close. As Tanner announced they were officially together, Molly caught my eye, winking. Isaac shouted enthusiastically, thoroughly startling me.

He boomed with laughter. "Sorry, Hads. I *love* love."

It wasn't only my joy that permeated the air. The team was happy, relieved of our burdens for a few hours.

Stay in the magic, I thought.

The night wore on happily, and when it grew late, the songs turned Gaelic. Finally, Ian began one of my favorites: "The Bonnie Banks of Loch Lomond."

Though the lyrics could slightly differ, the message was always the same. Somewhere in its history, the lament of Jacobite widows had become an anthem for a nation. Wrapped securely in a blanket with Fitz, we sang for the heartache of lost love, and my own heart ached for home. I longed for Scotland.

> *Oh, ye'll tak' the high road, and I'll tak' the low road*
> *And I'll be in Scotland afore ye*
> *Where me and my true love will never meet again,*
> *On the bonnie, bonnie banks of Loch Lomond*

"Solomon, would you sing us an Ethiopian song to close us out?"

"I'd be honored, Chloe," Solomon began. "This is a lullaby my mother would always sing before bed, from my childhood right up until we lost her. It wards off bad dreams. The perfect song to end the night with."

Eshururu ruru
Eshururu ruru

Yemamuye enate tolo neyilete
Wetetun beguya dabowun bahiya yizechilete

Eshururu ruru
Eshururu ruru

Yemamuye enate tolo neyilete
Wetetun beguya dabowun bahiya yizechilete

Eshururu ruru
Eshururu ruru

"Go with God. Go in peace. And may Fate grant you favor always." Solomon bowed, and the room was silent, lost in the magic of the moment.

Ferns lined the walkway of the park just across from headquarters. Sunlight fell softly through the gaps of the plants, leaving patterns along the red brick walkway. Something about the light was reminiscent of early spring, which would be approaching in Edinburgh. The very thought pulled at my heart. The songs of the prior evening had pushed my almost-home to the front of my mind, and I lingered in that nostalgia, allowing myself to daydream.

My life would look so different if we hadn't agreed to this mission.

A nearby bench was unoccupied, and I slid on to the seat, dropping my head in my hands. I needed a moment to mourn the loss of that life, a moment to remind myself it could still lie in our future. A moment to trust that we'd all live to see the other side of Adamo.

The bench shook from the weight of another being dropping beside me. It scared me for a second before I recognized the energy.

"Too much today?" Tanner asked.

"Too much lately." I sighed, raising my head to meet his gaze.

"Yeah, I feel that."

"How are things going with you and Chloe?"

"Good. I removed the enchantment last night at Lana's before we told you all, and we talked most of last night. I thought she'd be angrier than she is, but I also think she's scared, since we leave for Adamo this week. We're working everything out."

"My arguments with Fitz blow over quickly, too. We forgive and move on. You never know when your mate might be ripped away from you."

"That's so real. I'm going to worry about her more than ever. If I don't make it, you know?"

I nodded.

"And then, I think . . . what if we hadn't done this?" Tanner continued. "What if I hadn't signed up? What if Fate had just allowed me to have a normal life?"

"I never would have blamed you for not coming with us, even before I knew this."

"Yeah, but I knew that wasn't in the cards for me. I'm meant to be here," he said.

I mulled over his words. Finally, I found my thoughts. "I've questioned Fate quite a bit over the last few months. With this mission, with mates . . . with everything, honestly."

"What answers did you find?"

"That we have a choice. She led us to one another. She led us to this mission. But ultimately, we had to accept her call to love and her call to arms."

"She led us to a prophecy," Tanner said. "I still can't wrap my mind around that one."

I sighed. "If it's even true."

"You think it isn't?"

"I can't say. Maybe it is. Maybe we're destined to save our worlds from Lorenzo. But I don't know, Tanner. It's difficult to think of myself as a powerful witch destined to save the world."

Tanner nodded in understanding. Silence fell over us.

"Chloe is good for you," I said after a long, contemplative moment. "I already sense that. I'm happy for you, Tanner."

"Thank you. I wouldn't have gotten here without you. I feel like I'm finally whole, and you helped make it happen."

"I know how risky it feels to pursue love under these circumstances, but it's worth it."

"I know that now," he said.

I thought of my dream—of Tanner's other potential future.

"I don't know if this helps, but I believe you're going to return home from Opimae. Not long before I first spoke with you about Chloe, I had a dream, but now I don't think it was a dream."

"What do you mean? You think it was some sort of vision?"

"I know it's not one of my gifts, but I think Fate showed me a piece of your future."

"What did you see?"

"You and Chloe. I saw you together in what I think is your future apartment. And Tanner . . . she was pregnant."

He exhaled deeply, taking a moment to find his response. "I hope to god you're right."

"And if I am, do you know what that means?"

He smiled. "Yeah. That I come home."

Tanner slid his arm around me and squeezed gently. I rested my head on his shoulder for just a moment.

We couldn't change what we couldn't change, and we had a mission to fulfill. But for a few minutes, we were just two friends sharing the quiet of a sunlit morning, finding comfort in a common dream.

CHAPTER THIRTY-SEVEN

The following morning, Chloe, Solomon, Mia, and James asked to meet with Fitz and me. We settled into a small office at our house, and Solomon pulled a privacy shield against the door. Fitz and I eyed each other.

"James, would you like to start?" Chloe prompted.

"I had an idea," James began. "But I wasn't sure if the council would support it, so I spoke with Solomon, Chloe, and Mia before pitching it to you two. I ken there will be opposition to it, but it's worth discussing."

Solomon nodded, though his expression was severe. Mia crossed her arms and leaned back in her seat. I had a feeling this was about to get interesting.

"We approved of him moving forward with the discussion," Chloe added pragmatically, though her energy stirred nervously. "But not before ample discussion. It's something that would normally be rejected by the court, and fast."

"But this is a dire situation we've found ourselves in, and we need a solution outside of the box. Something Lorenzo willnae see coming."

"James . . . what on Earth is this idea?" I asked.

"I'd like to propose that you and Fitz travel to Scotland—specifically to 1662—and return with Esther's ring," he said.

"What?" Fitz's voice rose. He leaned forward in his chair, dropping my hand under the table.

I studied Fitz, feeling his surprise course through my body. I couldn't name what I felt, though I wondered how many more trials we would be pushed into.

"I know that sounds shocking," Chloe said, "but I promise you, we've considered all options."

"I dinnae see how this could be a viable option," Fitz said. "I know we've broken the rules before, but this . . . this is *forbidden*."

"I understand that. And we wouldn't have approved such a request had we seen another way forward," Solomon said.

"This is ludicrous," Fitz said.

"Aye. It's forbidden for a reason. It's risky, and sure to be met with forceful opposition," James agreed.

"But?"

"We've discussed how to get ahead of Lorenzo, and we have to consider another option in case the mission to his fortress fails," James said. He paused, allowing his statement to sink in. "We should consider solutions Lorenzo willnae anticipate—and that includes options that he believes we'd never consider."

"It's not ideal. But it's worth considering," Solomon said.

Mia was unusually silent.

"What are your thoughts on this, Mia?" I asked.

She and Chloe looked at each other before she spoke.

"I'm against it. Not only is it forbidden, I don't think we have cause to consider this right now."

"You'd consider it if our circumstances worsened?" Fitz asked. His expression was cloaked in surprise, much like my own energy.

"Yes. If the Adamo mission fails. Or if the mission to the fortress reveals matters are a lot worse than we thought. Then I would consider this proposal. That doesn't mean I'd agree—but I'd consider it."

I nodded. "Look, we don't have any reason to suspect that Adamo will end badly. Don't get me wrong—I understand the risks, and I know they're serious. But it's hard for me to reason that we should tempt Fate just yet."

"Aye," Fitz said. "I agree with Hadley. It's too risky, and I willnae anger Fate."

"I ken the risks are quite serious," James said. "But Lorenzo's forces are greater than anticipated, and he willnae underestimate us after Pluvia Silva."

"We have the element of surprise, but will that be enough?" Solomon asked.

"Regardless of the outcome of Adamo, if this mission to the fortress should fail, then we have to take this proposal seriously," Chloe said. "Once we go on these missions, there's no turning back."

"Aye," James agreed. "We'll have struck at the beast, and it'll be war after this."

We sat in silence.

"We'll see how things turn out in Adamo and with the fortress mission," Fitz finally said. "This is a massive risk, and I dinnae think we should even look at it seriously unless we've run out of all other options."

"Nor do I," I said. "I know this comes from a good place, and I appreciate that, but I agree with Fitz, and with Mia—there's too much at stake. Let's just stay focused on Adamo and on the fortress, and we'll see where Fate leads."

— CHAPTER THIRTY-EIGHT —

I stopped by my locker on my way out of headquarters. I pulled a team photo from the door and studied it, smiling. Keoni had taken it one morning shortly after we'd arrived. So much had happened since we'd crossed into Opimae, and I knew in that moment, studying the faces smiling back at me, I wasn't the same witch who'd come through the portal.

I had just secured the locker when Jess rounded the corner. He was walking faster than I'd seen him move since Pluvia Silva, and his gashes were fading into faint scars, just like mine.

"You're leaving now?" he questioned, his words slow and soft.

"Skipping the formalities today, I see."

Jess smiled slightly, a humorless act as far as I could tell.

"Early tomorrow morning," I said.

"I . . . truthfully, I don't understand this mission."

"Well . . ." I paused, unsure of how much to disclose.

"No, that's okay. Don't tell me." He shifted his weight, clearly uncomfortable. "I mean . . . I know it's classified, so I understand you can't give me much. None of the lower ranks really know what you're doing."

"I'm sure there are plenty of wild theories floating around."

"Tons," he muttered distractedly.

My mind was racing. Jess's energy was wild . . . untamed. He had worked tirelessly during our entire acquaintance to check his emotions, to check his energy. As far as I was aware, he was always in control, and it was unnerving to see him like this.

"Jess, I haven't had a chance to talk to you since Pluvia Silva. Thank you," I said awkwardly. I wasn't sure how to properly thank someone who was literally willing to die for me, especially considering what I knew about his family. Sacrifice felt different when you understood what someone had to lose.

He waved his hand in protest. "Don't mention it."

"I have to. What you did was brave. And selfless. I just want you to know how grateful I am."

He nodded.

"How are you healing up?" I asked.

"I'm getting there. The recovery is much easier than last time."

"I'm sorry, have you . . . have you had that happen before?"

"Once, years ago. But that's a story for another time." He smiled sadly. "I have something for your mission," he continued, holding out a small crystal dangling from a silver chain. As my fingers met the rough surface of the black tourmaline, I gasped softly, feeling the intense energy radiating from it.

"It'll settle in once you've had it on for a while—that is, if you'll accept it."

I nodded, and Jess released the necklace into my waiting palm. I had studied black tourmaline when I learned about crystals and their properties. This type of crystal was used for protection. It was meant to both ground a space and to clear negativity, but this particular stone buzzed with an extra boost of energy—Jess's energy. He'd placed a spell over it, granting extra protection to its wearer. The energy would settle into my own, sure enough, but it would take time to find its rhythm. I was stunned. Even with everything I thought I knew about Jess, I was beginning to realize I didn't know anything at all.

"This is for protection..."

"Yes," he answered softly.

Jess paused, carefully registering my expression. "I know you've been skeptical of me, and you have every right to be. But you have a strong intuition. You know you can trust me when I say this will protect you."

"You've already protected me once. Doesn't seem like such a stretch," I said. I gazed down at the crystal, feeling its energy washing through my hand.

If Jess was the mole, then why was he helping me? None of this made sense.

"Why do you conceal your thoughts, Jess?"

I hadn't intended to ask him, but the words came tumbling out before I could stop them.

Jess laughed lightly. "I was wondering how long it would take you to ask me."

"You knew I would pry into your thoughts?"

"I don't mean to offend you . . . or to imply that you do that to others unprovoked. But I know you and the team haven't trusted me. It's a natural course of action."

"So . . ." I prompted.

"Hadley . . ." he paused, dropping his gaze for a moment before returning his icy eyes to mine. "I can't tell you. The time has not come for that."

I tried to steady my heart rate. I knew he was hiding something, and it was overwhelming to hear him confirm my suspicions.

"There are things that have happened to me . . . things in my past that I'm not ready to discuss. Things I don't want anyone to know. I will make you a promise, though. I will tell you everything one day, but you have to come back from this mission in order for me to keep that promise, okay?"

I narrowed my eyes. "You know I'm not patient."

He laughed—a real, genuine laugh. "I'm aware. And I know I've tested your patience many times over."

"Well, I'm glad you're aware."

"I won't ask you to trust me on this, because even though your gut tells you that you can, I know you won't—not completely. And that's okay. But . . . know that my intentions are good, and that what I conceal now will benefit us all in the end."

"Jess . . . are you in trouble?"

His eyebrows rose, surprise flickering in his eyes. "No."

I knew that wasn't true, even before the faint thread formed near his head.

"Just go on your mission. Focus on that and forget the rest for now." Jess shifted uncomfortably before his eyes flickered back to mine, more intense than I'd ever seen. "Take care of yourself. And Hadley . . . come back."

Not awaiting my response, he turned and left the room.

I held the crystal in my line of sight, examining it closely. I slipped the necklace over my head before I froze.

I swore, removing the crystal from my neck. Before I could wear the charm, I needed to have one very difficult conversation with the being I loved most.

The being who would understand this gift the least.

I found Fitz cooking dinner alongside Henry and Jordan when I returned to our flat, the sounds of their banter and laughter echoing down the hallway. Fitz moved to my side when I entered the kitchen, the promise of a kiss resting on his lips, but he halted inches from my face, his body going rigid. All movement, all noise in the space ceased, as our tension radiated through the air, undoubtedly hitting Henry and Jordan in waves.

Fitz breathed deeply before breaking the silence.

"Why do I feel Jess's energy on you?" he whispered slowly.

"I was just speaking with him. Let's go to our room and talk about it."

I reached for Fitz's hand, but he refused the offer. His jaw clenched.

"Fitz. Our room. Now."

He sighed before starting down the hallway.

"Sorry," I mouthed to Henry and Jordan.

"*Good luck*," Jordan's voice sounded through my thoughts.

I shut the door behind us and pulled a privacy shield into place.

Fitz turned quickly to rest his hands against the door on either side of my shoulders, his face inches from mine. He breathed in deeply, deliberately, allowing my scent to permeate his senses. He was searching for other signs of Jess.

"You feel of Jess. You smell of Jess. Do you also—"

"Don't you dare finish that question," I spit out through clinched teeth. He had a right to ask questions, but not that one. "Open your eyes."

I waited. Nothing.

"I said open your eyes. Look at me."

His eyes flew open. Rage burned behind them.

"You feel of him, Hadley." A deep rumble escaped from his chest. A growl, almost. But it was more energy than voice, a release of his anger. It was a bad sign.

I was dealing with a primal Fitz.

I took a long, deep breath and released it. I needed to tread lightly. Anger burned in my chest, but I knew that if the roles were reversed, I'd behave the same way. It was our nature. But it was also in our nature to exercise control.

"Yes. And I will explain that. But before I say anything, I want to make one thing very clear. I have something from Jess, something I'm going to share with you. That's why you feel him. But that's the extent of it, Fitz."

Fitz's lips quivered in rage, and I rested my hands on either side of his face. He shook his head in protest, but I refused to release him, forcing him to look into my eyes.

"His energy doesn't pulse through me. My body has never ached from his absence. That intimacy only belongs to you."

Fitz's breath caught in his throat as he inched closer, though he withheld his lips. He'd make me wait longer still.

"His scent and his energy aren't intertwined with mine. But yours are. You are *on* me, *in* me, *around* me."

Fitz's hand slapped the door, struggling for control.

"Hadley," he growled.

I cradled his face in my hands, and his eyes burned into my own. "Look deeply. Feel deeply. You'll only find me . . . and you."

His breath grew calmer, deeper, as he searched my energy.

"I hate this," he admitted. "I hate feeling this way."

"I know. But it's normal," I said. "For us, anyway."

"You'd feel the same way."

"There's no denying that. But we can control how deeply we fall into this emotion."

"I'll try," he said, grimacing.

"Talk to me about it."

"Hadley. I dinnae know . . ."

"Talk to me. Please," I coaxed.

"I'm focusing on you. Feeling our connection."

"What else?"

"You know what else."

"Say it."

"I want to . . . harm him."

"I know you do."

"It's a horrible thing to admit," he continued, gritting his teeth. "Especially considering he took fire for you."

"We have a complicated history with Jess," I said. "And his heroics on the battlefield probably didn't help this situation."

"Aye, it mixed me up worse, I think."

"Of course, it did. But you're strong enough that you won't attack him again."

"I'll long for it." His eyes were shut tightly—in shame, I guessed.

"Look at me."

Fitz shook his head.

"My love. Open your eyes."

Fitz sighed, but his eyes opened. It was progress.

"Now, look at me."

It took a moment, but his eyes flickered to mine.

"I am yours."

He nodded. "I know. I still feel him."

"So, fix it."

His breath hitched. "Your eyes . . ." he whispered.

I cocked my head in question.

"Your fire magic."

I smiled. "I'm learning anger isn't the only emotion that brings my fire to the surface."

"That'll be fun to get under control Earth-side."

I groaned.

"But I love it," he continued. "All the fiery colors blazing in your eyes. You're mesmerizing."

My fingers grazed his lips before resting on his firm chest. "Remove the traces of him."

Fitz's lips lingered along my neck before pulling the woolen tunic over my head and ripping the chemise underneath. He traced his way along my collarbone and then lower before returning to my neck, my lips. I gasped, and his hands made short work of the remains of my chemise. He drew back, allowing his eyes to linger just as his lips had done only moments before.

He lifted me from the ground, his muscles tensed, and the air carried the two of us to the chaise near the windows. No one would see us, but it seemed like the whole world stretched below us as far as the eye could see, though the scene was barely real in my hazy mind. Fitz gripped me firmly as he traced the length of my shoulder down my back, and suddenly, the world didn't exist at all.

He took his time studying my body, working diligently until there was nothing left but the two of us.

The delicate chemise was ruined, but it was nothing a little magic couldn't fix. I pulled the torn heap from the floor and watched it float lazily in the air while the tears disappeared.

"You're worried about mending your shirt at a time like this?" Fitz asked, eyebrows raised.

"Hey, I really like this one. Lana gave it to me."

Fitz chuckled softly.

"I'm glad your humor is returning. We're going to need it," I said, allowing the mended shirt to fall on to a nearby chair.

He reached for me, pulling me onto his lap. I wrapped my legs tightly around his waist.

"Do you feel me?" I asked.

He slid his hands the length of my thighs, grasping my hips.

"Aye," he whispered.

"Not just physically. Here, too," I said softly. I placed my hand on his chest, feeling for his reassuring heartbeat.

"Aye. I feel your energy in my veins."

I closed my eyes. An extra rush of energy channeled through our connection, and Fitz gasped as it entered his body. I kissed his parted lips before meeting his gaze.

"You are the only being who will ever feel that. Do you hear me?"

He nodded.

"Tell me what you feel."

"I feel . . . light. I feel *you*."

"Who else do you feel?"

"No one. Only us."

"And for all of eternity, who else will be able to feel this?"

"No one," he whispered.

"Good boy," I breathed into his ear, allowing my lips to trace its outline lightly. He quivered under my touch, and my legs tightened their grip around his waist, provoking a sigh from him.

"Now that we've established that bit, are you ready to discuss that necklace?"

Fitz met my lips hungrily but pulled away before he lost himself again. "Aye. I'm ready."

I told him everything about my conversation with Jess as we held each other close, reminding his instincts—his nature—that there was nothing amiss between us. He wasn't easily convinced of Jess's intentions, but he had learned to trust my instincts well enough to let it pass. Though it was clear he wasn't thrilled with the prospect of me wearing a piece of jewelry from Jess, much less jewelry that reeked of his energy.

"I dinnae understand why you need this from him," Fitz said.

"It's just an extra layer of protection. Don't you want me to have as much protection as possible? I mean honestly, Fitz, isn't that what you're always worried about?"

"Aye, and you dinnae need to take that tone about it. You know I want you to be safe more than anything. It's just . . . are you sure about this?"

"Positive. I told you there was more under the surface there. We've known things didn't quite add up. I think there's a very good reason why." I paused. "What is it, my love? What is it really?"

He hesitated.

"Spit it out."

"I dinnae know how I'll stand that energy on you. It'll pain me."

I mulled over the options in my head. "You could amplify your energy in my moonstone ring. Honestly, Fitz, if you think about that in addition to your energy that already radiates from me . . ." I stopped, kissing him softly. "I don't think you'll mind Jess's protection charm."

He nodded. "A braw thought. We'll try it."

"I know this isn't easy . . . but I do know it's right to do."

"Have you changed your mind about him being the mole?" Fitz asked.

I paused, considering the question. "I'm confident there's something odd going on, but I don't know if it's that he's the mole, or what."

Fitz nodded, his eyes distant.

"All I know for sure is that you can feel the energy on this stone. You can feel its positive power."

Fitz rolled the stone through his fingers a second time. "There's no denying that."

Jess's recent actions made me question everything. But if he wasn't the mole, then who was?

CHAPTER THIRTY-NINE

It must have been my imagination, but the world looked darker than ever in the early morning hours. The suns had not yet risen, and the planet's moon was nowhere to be seen.

I pulled my hair tightly into a French braid that plaited down my back as Fitz slid his chainmail into place. I removed my engagement ring, which sparkled even in the dim light, and pulled it onto the silver chain next to Jess's gift. I then removed my moonstone ring, and my heart tightened as my energy slightly dulled. It had grown accustomed to Fitz's energy boost over the last couple of years, and it moved around slowly, seeking the missing energy.

I quickly added the ring to the chain and clasped it around my neck. My energy readjusted with the feel of the ring against my chest before zipping around at the addition of Jess's protection charm. I took a deep breath and caught Fitz's gaze. He was studying me, his face impossible to read.

Fitz crossed the room and stepped into my view in the mirror, his features turning grave, as he placed an arm supportively around my shoulder. "Ready?"

I turned to face him. "As I'll ever be."

The team gathered in the driveway, ready to be whisked away to the mountain pass where Adamo lay. Jordan was talking quietly with Gustavo, and a pang in my chest caught me off guard. She had been asked to stay at headquarters last minute and run intelligence during the battle. We needed that skill set of hers most. She wandered over, and Tanner put his arms around us both.

"Three musketeers," Jordan mused.

"Always. No matter what," Tanner said.

"How are you both holding up?" I asked.

"You know, just wondering which battle might be my last."

"Tanner!" Jordan and I chastised in unison.

"Don't ask if you don't want to know." He shrugged.

Jordan rolled her eyes. "Well, it sure as hell isn't going to be this one. Right?"

"Right," he answered studiously.

"I'm really upset I won't be there with y'all," Jordan said. "It's going to be impossible not to worry."

"Nah, J. You have to push that aside."

"Tanner's right. The best way to keep us safe—to keep Gustavo safe—is to focus on absolutely nothing but doing your best work."

She nodded. "I can do that."

"Bring it in, musketeers," I said.

A tear trickled down Jordan's cheek. "Love you guys."

"Always," Tanner said.

"Forever," I said.

The silence in the car was oppressive as we wound our way up the mountainside.

The front lines would already be in position by now, awaiting orders. They were instructed to attack and distract, taking down anything in their path. The second wave was tactical units meant to clear a path for our team. We had been assigned to enter the deepest parts of the city that had the heaviest protection from Lorenzo's forces and commandeer their newly established command station. We couldn't know how many of Lorenzo's troops were stationed in the city, but we were certain we'd see battle, and I prayed fervently that we all came back alive.

The cars pulled down a gravel road about a mile from the city gates. We jumped from the vehicles and paired off quickly for transport. I tucked myself into Fitz's embrace, and the world spun away. The transport was seamless, and we emerged from the tree line bordering the roadway and noted our short distance from the edge of the city.

At the city gates, we paused and awaited the break of dawn. The quiet was so intense, I swore our breath alone would wake the entirety of the city. It would have been peaceful under different circumstances. The morning was cold, and Fitz slipped his arms around me as we waited for the first wave of the attack. Our armor was lightweight and even the wool underneath was hardly sufficient as we lay in the dew of a cold, winter morning.

Finally, the first sun rose, revealing the foggy valley below us. I strained to make out the fuzzy shapes in the distance, but the haze was just thick enough to obscure my vision. The sun reflected across the top of the fog bank, casting a bright glow around the city. Our military escort signaled us forward, and we crawled silently over the last few feet that separated us from the picturesque city of Adamo.

Ancient stone structures towered overhead, sprawling just beyond the crumbling stone walls of the city's entrance. How much life had existed within these very walls before Lorenzo had ripped away the city's heart and soul? Fog crept over the wall, puffing along the cobblestone streets and casting an eerie atmosphere over our battleground. There were far too many dark alleyways and coved doors for my liking, and my heart raced as I imagined the troops that might be hiding.

I breathed deeply, dragging the cold air into my lungs before releasing it slowly. I glanced toward Fitz, who seemed to be scanning the area for danger, and then to the team, who were doing the same.

I reached for Jess's protection charm. The energy was a bit distracting, but I was grateful for the added boost.

Soon enough, we heard the distant sound of metal breaking through the atmosphere, and I followed the noise to our military planes dropping countless beings from the sky straight into the city. The troops were on the ground.

And then, chaos ensued.

The sounds of battle broke through the still morning air. This was it. Our time was now. I released Fitz's hand, and we readied ourselves for attack. Fitz met my gaze, his features troubled, but he nodded softly at me.

"For the fire folk!" I yelled as we broke into a run.

We propelled ourselves through the city gates. Beige stonework and battling bodies blurred in my periphery. Equal parts fight and flight warred inside of me, but we had to keep moving.

City Center materialized in the distance, a beacon of hope amongst streets that were already stained with the blood of beings from both sides of the conflict. Opposition was minimal until we grew closer.

A soldier jumped at Henry, who spun quickly on his heel and channeled a powerful burst of energy, sending the witch flying across the courtyard and into a stone wall. Henry's instincts were good—he hadn't even hesitated.

Fitz nodded. "Nice work, mate."

Our tactical units could no longer hold back Lorenzo's forces, and troops ran toward us, ready for battle. Mia swept her arm in front of her and ice crackled across the courtyard, creating a line that slowed the attack of our opposing forces. I anchored into my fire magic and felt Fitz's power shift as he prepared himself for the onslaught. Tanner's fingertips were charged with electricity, and he released lightning bolts toward a soldier who had just cleared Mia's ice. Molly vanished and then reappeared near a large patch of ice, quickly taking down an enemy soldier.

An agent I recognized from headquarters was struggling against a rival soldier. He looked weak as he dropped to his knees, clutching his head. I gasped, but before I could pivot, the opposing soldier detonated a blast that sent our ally flying. When he landed, there was no movement. The soldier's gaze turned to meet mine, and we ran toward each other.

I closed my eyes for a second, exploring my connection with the air. She was steady, and I picked up my pace. My opponent called forward some sort of energy bomb, which glowed brightly against the morning light. The power within it would be charged enough to kill, and it swirled ceaselessly, flickering as it hovered just above his open palm. He hurled the threat in my direction, and I raised my hands, recalling my training with Jess. I reflected the energy and flung it back faster than I'd thought possible. Apparently, it caught him off guard as well, though he managed to duck out of the way. I called to the air and asked it to pull the energy back in my direction.

I made contact with my opponent, looking into his youthful face and bright green eyes. As our bodies connected, I allowed him to overpower me and throw me to the ground, but in doing so, he created a clear path for his own energy to return to him. His eyes widened as the burst of energy slammed into his chest, and a bright light flashed across the courtyard. I felt the first real horror of battle as I rolled to my left, allowing him to fall lifelessly to the ground next to me.

I hesitated, understanding now what my survival meant for the soldiers I battled. My throat clenched as a familiar energy washed over me.

Fitz.

"Hadley!" he shouted over the noise surrounding us. Desperation lingered in his voice—he was scared for me. "My love, we have to keep moving."

I nodded, but my body wouldn't budge. Fitz looked around, gauging how much time we had, and I noticed a scratch on his jawline. I put my hand to his face, registering his blood on my fingertips.

"Hadley, it's nothing. Let's go."

I nodded, and he looped his hand through mine, pulling me into a jog.

Shock, I realized. Shock had slowed my mind. I shook my head and prayed for clarity, forcing myself to reconnect to the elements as we ran through another courtyard.

"This way!" Tanner yelled ahead of us, and we followed him down a narrow alleyway, the world momentarily looking as dark as I felt.

Troops ran toward us as we emerged from the shadows.

Fitz and I positioned our backs against each other as soldiers neared us. I was hardly aware of anyone else around me in that moment, focused as I was on the large man running toward me. I waited until he was close before blasting my fire magic at him. He fell backward, revealing a horror I was sure none of us had anticipated.

"Oh god, no."

"Hadley, what?" Fitz called as he turned to stand beside me. "Oh, shite."

The woman that stood before me wore armor around her chest and core but couldn't hide her bulging belly. I was horrified.

"Fitz, we can't—"

"*I know.*" His voice sounded in my head.

"*Let's try to take her down softly and capture her?*"

"*Aye. Let her make the first move. Let's see what kind of power we're dealing with.*"

The woman walked slowly toward us, a slight smile on her face. She knew she'd taken us off guard. I wondered if the pregnancy was a decoy, and I had time to enter her unprotected mind. It was real—and her first move would be to blast us with fire magic. I whispered to Fitz's mind, and he nodded. He'd let me deflect while he slipped away to take her by surprise.

She was quick, tossing fireball after fireball, but I threw my arms up, sending each one flying to the ground. I could have quenched her fire. I could have fired back even faster, but I wasn't taking her down. I was keeping her occupied. Fitz left my side, making his way toward a far wall. Her eyes followed, and she fired at him. He disappeared, and I extinguished her flame before it was even halfway to where he had stood.

I couldn't help but smirk. Her gaze flew to me, and the flames in her eyes grew wilder. She wasn't used to having her power matched.

Somewhere in my periphery, I registered Sadie's presence and heard her gasp when she registered the situation.

"Fitz," I whispered to her mind.

She nodded and ran out of sight.

After another few deflections, the woman grew angry and reckless. Fitz materialized behind her, his arms extended toward the sky. He nodded, and I suppressed her flames. She looked around wildly, flinging her arms in all directions trying to throw out her fire.

I walked closer, and suddenly Sadie was standing next to Fitz. Fitz dropped his arms, and the young woman fell gently toward the ground, her knees hovering inches above the stone. Sadie looped her wrists, and the woman's arms pulled unwillingly behind her back, where Fitz twirled a hand around hers, and a magical thread appeared, binding her wrists.

Sadie hoisted her from the ground. "Walk."

"I'll do no such thing."

"You're coming with us. You don't have a say in the matter."

"I'm not going anywhere with you," the woman returned through gritted teeth.

"You don't have a choice. Now, you can walk, or I'll carry you. Don't try me," Sadie said.

"Armana," I called gently.

"How the hell do you know my name?"

"We don't want to harm you. We just need you to cooperate with us."

Realization lit in her eyes. "You're a mind reader."

"Only when necessary."

"Well, how about you stay the hell out of my head?" she spat.

"That can be arranged. Walk with us, and I'll stay out of your mind."

Armana stared at me, but she didn't resist when we started forward.

We turned toward the rest of the group, doing my best to ignore the bodies that lay on the ground. Some were merely unconscious it seemed, but others . . . I couldn't think about it.

"Who's this?" Henry asked as we approached.

Armana sneered, pulling a smirk from Henry.

"You look like shite," Fitz said, pulling a proper laugh from Henry.

He pulled Fitz into a quick embrace. "Aye, and you've looked better yourself."

Chloe ran in from a nearby alleyway. "Okay, we have our window.

Troops are holding steady."

"Up these steps. Follow me." Lana ran ahead of us, bow pulled back and ready to strike. We wound up the old stone stairs, and Lana halted outside a wooden door. "The soldiers in here are trained to kill anything that comes through that door. We eliminate without question. Understood?"

We all nodded, and a nearby soldier blasted open the door. The world moved in slow motion as the occupants of the command center rose, ready to fight. Half of us deflected their assaults, and the other half fired.

In the end, we took the room and rushed into place in front of the equipment. My head was pounding, but I took a deep breath and focused on my task at hand. I stationed myself in front of a large monitor system and swept my eyes across the keypads when I noticed drops of blood. Confused, I looked above me but found nothing there. I looked again to the keyboard and noticed blood dripping again—and then my foggy mind caught up.

I was bleeding.

"What's wrong?" Fitz demanded, suddenly by my side. His eyes grew wide when he saw my head. "Sadie!"

"What happened, Hadley?" she asked, kneeling in front of me.

"I'm not sure," I said, thinking hard. "Is it bad?"

"The swelling isn't good, but I've got it. Just hold still a minute."

Sadie muttered unintelligibly under her breath. My skin grew itchy and the pressure in my head eased. A good sign.

"It's not healed, but this will hold for now."

I nodded, returning my focus to the keyboard. Mia took a seat to my right and Molly to my left. Mia directed us through inputting all the necessary codes she and Jordan had devised to break into the system. When we were done, I turned the last dial as instructed, and Jordan's smiling face popped onto the screen.

"Oh, thank god! You're alive."

I smiled. "Hi, J."

"Is everyone okay?"

"Yeah, the core team is good. Gustavo is guarding the door."

Jordan breathed a sigh of relief. "Okay, I'm going to get started downloading everything I can. Lorenzo's agents already know we're in. They're trying to shut down the system, but we'll fight them and get as much data as we can."

"Rad," Chloe said.

"This is such a waste of your resources," Armana said from her chair in the corner.

"And why is that?" Isaac asked, humoring her. He'd taken on the task of keeping watch over her while we waited.

"Because this will change nothing. You took us by surprise this one time, but Lorenzo is so many steps ahead of you."

"He has been," Henry agreed. "But that's changing."

"You're wasting your breath trying to reason with her," Mia said distractedly as she typed another code into the computer.

Armana scoffed. "You're wasting lives. Time. Money. In the end, we'll just take it all back."

"You can believe that if it gives you comfort," Isaac said softly.

Armana rolled her eyes.

Tanner radioed from the bottom of the stairs that the teams continued to hold off opposing troops. Time ticked on slowly, and my nerves rose with every passing minute before Jordan finally spoke.

"And that's it. We've been kicked out. But we got a whole lot of data."

"Great work, J."

"Y'all get out of there, and once the city's secure, we have Intelligence coming in to work on the system."

"Any reports on how we're doing out there?" Molly asked.

Jordan flicked through her screens. "Y'all almost have it. We're doing the damn thing."

Sighs of relief sounded through the room, though our work wasn't quite over.

"Let's get moving, then," Fitz commanded. "See you in a few hours, Jordan."

"Go get 'em, y'all."

CHAPTER FORTY

We filed out of the room, and Chloe hugged Tanner tightly upon reaching his post. We moved along as a unit, protecting all sides as we slinked through the city. The sudden quiet unnerved me, and I gripped Fitz's hand. He squeezed it in response, his nerves flitting through my body.

Finally, near the opposite side of the city from where we entered, we found the last remaining battle and jumped in while Ian stood guard over Armana. The troops were growing tired on either side, but I pushed through my exhaustion to tousle with a powerful witch who'd had her offensive magic stunted. Her ability to still defend herself was impressive, her skills impeccable.

I rolled from the ground, finding my balance as I turned to face the witch, pulling my fire bow and arrow before me. A cloud settled around me, fizzling my flames before the woman tossed a light ring in my direction. The light ring grew as it neared me, just as I had seen

Jess's expand to engulf Tanner in training. I recalled Jess's instructions on deflection, but the witch had surprised me, and I hesitated a second too long.

The edge of the light ring made impact with the left side of my body. I gasped at the surge of energy that blew through me, capping my magic.

My thoughts ticked quickly through the consequences. Jess had said the effects would last roughly ten minutes—more than enough time for this witch to take me down. I needed to be smart. The witch began hurling energy in my direction, and though I could deflect it, my power waned with each block. If she continued to fire, I couldn't hold her off for much longer. I needed a few seconds to think—to breathe—but the blows kept coming.

Then, it hit me.

There was a chance I could hurl her energy back at her. It would require gathering all my energy into one decisive blow, but it could work. I took a deep breath and channeled every ounce of magic into my hands as I ran around my opponent. Confusion flashed across her features, surely wondering what I was doing. When my magic was fully charged, I jumped away from the energy blast coming my way, rather than shielding it. The woman cocked her head, and I saw indecision flicker across her features.

She hesitated before calling another swirling orb of energy to the surface. She was expending an absurd amount of energy; she had to be tiring herself. She flung the glowing orb at me, and just before it connected with my outstretched arms, I pulled back and used my magic to bat the energy orb like a baseball. The witch jumped out of the orb's trajectory, but I hadn't released control of the energy and tapped it to follow her path. The orb connected, and she flew backward as the energy traveled through her core.

My relief was short lived; I was in danger. My head ached, and the loss of power left me feeling drained. I turned away from the witch, intent on finding a hiding spot to allow my magic to recharge, when Tanner caught my eye. He was locked into battle, hurling electricity at an opponent. He took the man down, but as he turned, another witch fired from across the courtyard. Their energy slammed into Tanner, and he fell to the ground.

My heart was heavy with fear as I raced toward him. I looked in the direction the energy had come from and found Fitz transporting in front of the witch to blast energy in a surprise attack. The witch fell as I dropped to Tanner's side.

I rolled him on to his back in horror.

"Tanner!" I yelled.

I shook him, trying to wake him from what I hoped was unconsciousness, fear gripping my body.

"Tanner!" I screamed once more.

Finally, his eyes opened.

"Hadley." He smiled weakly. "Just give me a minute."

He sat up slowly, gripping his shoulder, but he swayed off balance. He fell back, and I caught his head in my hands, steering him gently to the ground. I tried not to panic, but his energy was waning. He was far too weak—he needed medical attention quickly. The rest of the team was finishing up their work, and Fitz ran over to me. Sadie was right behind him. She knelt next to us.

Chloe's scream pierced my soul.

"Chloe," Tanner mumbled weakly.

She rushed to his side.

"What happened?" Chloe asked, her eyes filled with fear.

"Tanner took a nasty hit. Careful, he's hurt . . . badly, I think."

Sadie swore. "It's one of those radiating energy orbs." She looked at me. "We have to get the excess energy out immediately."

"Tell us what to do."

"Get behind him and hold him up," Sadie ordered Chloe, clearly understanding that Chloe needed to do something to help him. "Timing is everything right now."

Chloe followed her instructions and held Tanner upright.

"Hold him tightly. His body is going to fight you as soon as this thing comes to the surface."

Chloe nodded, and Isaac came in to reinforce her.

"Fitz, create an energy barrier around his body," Sadie said. "These can be pretty volatile, and we don't want it to fly out and impair anyone else."

"Aye, I'm on it."

"Hadley, I need you to locate the orb. Feel around. You'll know it as soon as you run across it. Then, call it slowly to the surface."

I assessed my power quickly, which was slowly returning as the effects of the light ring wore off. Even with the progress, I was nervous. I swallowed hard but nodded.

"As soon as you pull it out, I'm going to catch it and toss it against that far wall. Henry, make sure no one comes near that area. Make a shield."

"Aye, I've got it."

"Hadley—you're up."

My nerves were on edge, but I took a deep breath and focused on Tanner.

"Tanner, I'm going to start feeling around. If you want this thing out, try not to fight me."

Tanner looked at me, his brows creased in pain. He nodded.

I closed my eyes, moving my energy slowly toward Tanner. I connected to him and pushed my way around until I met the currents of his energy. They were charged with the other witch's energy, threatening to kill him from the inside. I understood the urgency in that very moment and pushed forward until a surge of energy made me gasp.

"Hadley!" I heard Fitz's panic, but I had to stay focused.

"She's okay. She found it," Sadie said, her voice echoing distantly.

The energy was fighting me, and I worried I was still too weak to tame it. I paused to take stock of it—to understand it. I felt around the edges and found where it connected to Tanner, slowly unwinding the ties before bringing the energy toward the surface. It wanted to attach to me, and I found the only solution was to push the wisps away as I slowly called the orb forward. When it reached the surface, I had to tug harder, and I understood why Sadie had asked for the shield around Tanner. With a pop, he was free of the energy, but it bounced toward Sadie. She was ready. She expertly bound the wisps back to the bulk of energy and tossed it against a wall, where it exploded into tiny fragments and faded from existence.

"Get him to medical," Solomon barked at nearby soldiers.

They picked Tanner up and ran out of sight, Chloe hard on their heels. The rest of the team pressed on, but I remained on the ground for a few seconds and focused on my breathing. Fitz laid a hand on my face.

"You good?" he asked.

I nodded.

"We have to keep moving."

He pulled me from the ground, and we jogged over to the last of the action. I scanned the scene and realized we really weren't needed. This was it—this was the end.

As we entered the last skirmish, I spotted Keoni, who tumbled on to the ground a few yards ahead of us. Before I understood what was happening, an energy bullet connected with his chest. Surprise crossed his face, and I yelled.

I ran toward Keoni, quickly followed by Molly and Sadie, but he fell before we reached him. Fitz, Isaac, and Solomon ran toward the source of the energy.

I dropped to Keoni's side.

His eyes were distant. The energy bullet must have sent searing pain through his body, but he was silent. A bad sign, I thought.

"Keoni, can you hear me?" I asked.

Silence.

"Keoni!"

His eyes flickered to mine.

"Stay with us, okay? Sadie can help."

"I'm sorry," Keoni mouthed.

"For what?" I asked.

But it was too late. His stared into nothingness, and his body relaxed.

"No," I whispered, willing the tears to stay inside. I turned to Sadie, who looked shellshocked. Molly's eyes watered, but she wouldn't allow her tears to spill over. I turned back to Keoni, offering a blessing for peace, and closed his eyelids.

A familiar energy radiated from Keoni—not just his own, but that of another witch I recognized. I couldn't place it. Was this familiar energy radiating from the bullet that had been fired at Keoni?

Tanner's injuries had terrified me, and Keoni . . . my mind was muddled by grief.

"This isn't happening," I said.

Molly wrapped her arms around me and held me. Finally, Sadie broke the moment.

"We have to keep moving forward," she said, though I didn't miss the crack in her voice. "We need to make sure the others are okay."

I heard the subtext in her words. We didn't want to lose anyone else today.

I nodded, and we ran toward the direction I'd last seen Fitz.

Mia had caught up with the guys, and the four of them were doing their best to take these last soldiers alive, as best I could tell, but it was Isaac that caught my attention. He was locked into an intense battle with a face I recognized all too well.

Isamu.

"Impossible," I muttered.

And then everything connected. The energy I had felt on Keoni was from Isamu—the energy bullet had come from him.

"How?" Molly asked, exasperation in her voice.

I didn't hesitate. I pulled back on my fire bow, directing my arrow carefully around Isaac. I met my mark and readied my fire again when Molly stopped me. I pulled away from her and ran to Isamu, gripping his shirt tightly, shaking him.

Molly's arms were around me in a second, pulling me away from him. "Hadley, stop!"

The fire raged in my eyes, tingled all through my body, pulsed from my fingertips. And I knew it—I was out of control. Molly knew it too.

She knew I'd kill him.

"I don't care!" I yelled. "He doesn't deserve to live!"

Anguish filled my voice, and it matched the look on Molly's face. She tried to calm me as Sadie and Isaac tied Isamu's hands, preparing him for transport. Fitz was by my side in an instant, and I fell into his arms.

"Fitz, I . . ."

"I know. It's all right," he coaxed.

"He almost killed you. He hurt Ian, and he killed Keoni. I know he did."

"And he'll pay for that," Fitz said.

I looked in Isamu's direction. He was unconscious. Good.

"We need to find out how in the hell he got out of headquarters," Gustavo barked.

"Can you radio back?" Molly asked Sadie. "Make sure everything's okay there?"

Lana ran from around the corner. She was battered, but she wore a smile. "It's done. We've taken the city."

Cheers erupted from those around us, despite the losses we'd suffered.

No more soldiers had to die today.

Just then, an enemy soldier rounded the corner with one of our agents right behind her. She turned and smiled as she caught my gaze before her figure grew hazy.

"Allette!" I called. But it was too late. She was gone.

"How did she . . ." Isaac trailed off.

"She was with Isamu," I said.

"We don't know that yet," Fitz said.

"If she was with Isamu, and they were both here today fighting," Molly said.

"Then she works for Lorenzo. They both do," Henry finished.

Fitz slipped an arm protectively around me.

"Fitz is right," I said. "We don't know anything yet."

"Let's radio this information back to Jordan," Fitz said.

"A good call," Lana said.

"We're down Tanner, Chloe, and Keoni," Fitz said. "Do we push forward with the fortress?"

The team was silent.

"Everyone had assignments, so we'd need to add three more members back to the team," Mia said.

"Aye, and we have soldiers we can recruit here," Henry said. "We'll just brief them before transport."

"I know it feels impossible to push Tanner and Keoni from our minds now, but once we're on the ground, our adrenaline will kick in and we'll be mission-focused," Lana said.

I considered everyone's words as I assessed my power. I certainly wasn't at full strength, but it was enough to move forward.

"I'm going to make a case that we proceed," I said, clearing my throat. "I know Adamo just took a lot out of us—physically and emotionally. But we still have the element of surprise—Lorenzo won't expect us."

Several team members nodded.

"We came to Opimae to take Fitz's family ring away from this monster. We came here to stop him. And we have the opportunity today to do that. If we are successful, we accomplish both of those goals. Today is our best chance. We can do this—Fate has favored us."

CHAPTER FORTY-ONE

The stars of the in-between faded as we stepped on to fresh snow outside of Lorenzo's fortress.

We'd met our mark. We stood just where I'd discovered the crack in Lorenzo's otherwise impenetrable shield only a few weeks ago. I moved closer to the wall and felt for the threads of Lorenzo's protection spells. Sure enough, the differing energy remained intact. It was satisfying that Lorenzo hadn't figured out how I'd broken in.

I turned to the team. "This way."

We lined up in pairs for the transporters to set to work. Molly stood next to Fitz and me. We nodded at each other and materialized on the other side of the wall.

Nothing had changed since my last spirit travel. The rows of shelving that lined the space were still covered in supplies, and I motioned toward the far side door that was our path to the magical ring.

Molly studied our surroundings before looking to me. "Why do I feel like this is a trap?"

I took a deep breath, calming my rising nerves. "Even if it is, there's no turning back now."

I signaled forward, and the team followed me to the door. We stepped into the stone hallway that had grown familiar to me. It was almost unnerving to be back in a space I'd visited outside of my body on several occasions. The hallways were eerily quiet, and I had to give Molly's fear some credit. Did Lorenzo already know we were within his walls?

The Opimaean soldiers wore masks of determination, though I felt their energy radiating through the space. Despite their best efforts, they were nervous.

We pressed on.

Finally, we reached Lorenzo's office door. I moved closer to it, listening intently, hearing nothing but the buzz of Lorenzo's energy—his protection spell. I focused on the wisps of his energy—now familiar to me—and tugged at the edges. The protection fell away, and I met the eyes of my mate.

Fitz was poised beside me, ready to strike. For a fleeting second, everything fell away. He was ready to die for me, and I was prepared to do the same for him. Though our silent exchange was quick, it was powerful.

It was too risky for me to leave my body to scout out the other side of the door, so we'd walk in sight unseen. I gave the signal and opened the door.

Fitz and I split up, looking for any sign of the ring. The team joined us.

"What are you doing?" one of the Opimaean soldiers asked.

Though the Opimaean government believed the mission was only about Lorenzo's capture, we refused to miss an opportunity to bring the ring home with us.

"We're looking for the magical ring," I said. "Help us? It looks exactly like this one," I said, pulling the chain from underneath my armor and holding the magical ring closer to the light.

"That's not why we're here," another soldier said. "We're supposed to capture Lorenzo."

I paused, turning back to the Opimaean forces. They all wore similar expressions of concern and doubt.

"It's one of the reasons. Yes, we're supposed to capture Lorenzo. But this ring is deadly in the wrong hands. We need to remove it from this fortress, so it doesn't remain with the enemy."

The soldiers exchanged glances. Finally, one of them decided. "They're our commanders. We should follow orders."

"I'll help," another said.

"We must work quickly," Fitz said.

The soldiers nodded and set to work.

The surface of Lorenzo's desk had been cleared. I rummaged through the drawers, which were empty, showing no signs of the former protection spell. I moved on. One of the leather armchairs was indented from use, but the small table—the one where I'd first seen Esther MacGregor's magical ring—held only classic volumes of literature: *The Count of Monte Cristo, The Hound of the Baskervilles, Frankenstein.*

We opened drawers, moved books, looked for hiding spots. I carefully felt for other protections spells, but to no avail—the ring wasn't there.

The disappointment on Fitz's face was clear, but the ring had to be in the fortress—we wouldn't give up that easily.

I walked past Lorenzo's desk, and a glimmer of gold on the floor caught my attention. I stooped to take a closer look. It wasn't the MacGregor ring, but rather a simple gold band. I picked it up, and the vision that materialized took my breath away.

A young woman with long, golden hair sat at a piano. I was unfamiliar with the tune, but the notes that bled from the instrument were a deep, beautiful sort of melancholy. An ache gripped my chest, inexplicable as it was. Her eyes flickered to mine, pale as a winter's sky, and her expression filled with anguish. I was overcome with the strange urge to comfort this sad girl.

She was Lorenzo's mate. I knew it with the same certainty that always accompanied my "knowing."

And Lorenzo was leaving her.

"Goodbye, Anya," Lorenzo said. "I wish you well."

The vision dissipated, leaving me disoriented.

"You good, Hads?" Fitz asked.

"Yeah, let's move on," I said, tucking the ring in my pocket.

Door after door, we found the rooms unprotected and devoid of Lorenzo. Finally, we came to a wooden set of double doors, and I felt it—a familiar energy that brought a sense of dread along with it.

Lorenzo was on the other side. It was now or never.

"Ready?" I asked the team.

They nodded unanimously, and I threw open the door.

The room was empty. The team swept the space. We cast unsure glances at one another. Something was wrong.

"We should go—now," Solomon said.

Fitz wrapped his arms around me and stepped toward the in-between. We were met by an invisible force, and we stumbled backward, clutching our heads. The others were in a similar state.

"What the hell was that?" Lana muttered.

"Oh god," Molly said. "I've felt this once before."

"What?" I asked.

"Aye, in training," Fitz said. "We're being blocked."

"What do you mean, we're being blocked?" I asked.

"Lorenzo is preventing our exit, and the only person who can find the loophole in Lorenzo's powers isn't a time-walker," Solomon said, looking to me. "We'll have to find our way out of here on foot."

"There's nothing I can do?" I asked, desperate.

"Nothing," Fitz said.

My heart pounded in my chest, and I was certain the whole room could hear it. Fitz took my hand in his.

"We can do this," Fitz said. "Let's retrace our steps and leave."

"Can you transport to the room where we entered?" I asked.

"Let's try it," he said.

Miraculously, it worked. We stepped through the in-between and into the large supply room. We ran to the wall where we'd entered and paused. I realized something I hadn't before: the energy was familiar to me. I couldn't place it. Something was odd, and as I registered that the energy was weaker than before, a prickle worked down my spine.

I shook it off and focused on making it out of Lorenzo's fortress. The transporters closed their eyes and whispered prayers, hoping against all odds, the elements would grant us favor and carry us to the other side of the wall.

We stepped forward and were again met by the invisible barrier. My breath hitched.

"He found the opening," I said flatly, staring at the wall like it might suddenly allow us through. Had Lorenzo found it earlier and left it open on purpose?

"Do we know where the exit is?" Molly asked.

"We can't just walk out the front door," Mia said.

"Thanks for clarifying, Mia. That's exactly what I was suggesting."

"Hads, if another witch created a loophole, so can you," Fitz said.

I could do it, but my full power still hadn't returned. I paused, considering the idea. "I can try."

"We might as well search for anything we've missed while Hadley's sorting the exit," Henry said.

"Aye, but don't stray too far," Fitz instructed.

I studied Lorenzo's protection spell, feeling for weak spots along the wall. His magic held strong, so I realized I'd just have to choose a spot and begin my work. I closed my eyes, heightening my focus on his energy, and felt for a wisp. When I'd identified the thread, I pulled at it. This spell was too intricate to unravel quickly, and it would also be risky. I'd learned on one of my early spirit travels from Earth that Lorenzo's spells would attach themselves to whoever broke them. No—I'd have to tie my own magic into it.

I'd just attached my first thread to the edge of Lorenzo's when a loud noise disturbed me.

I turned to find the door opening, and Lorenzo Belmonte stepped through.

He was flanked by a tall witch with cropped blond hair, and both men were dressed in battle regalia. He moved closer, and several figures wearing dark armor materialized behind Lorenzo. Though they were clearly his backup, none were positioned to fight. One of them caught my attention with her long, blonde hair.

Allette.

And to her left was Gabriella. This was about to get interesting.

Lana moved her hand to her side, signaling that everyone should hold fire. Lorenzo approached Fitz and me, cocking his head ever so slightly.

"What are you doing here?" he asked. There was no venom in his voice today, but I suspected that wouldn't last.

"We've come for the ring," I said. There was no point in lying.

Lorenzo shook his head. "You're not leaving with that ring, Hadley."

"It's no yours to keep," Fitz said. "It belongs to my family."

Lorenzo shifted his gaze to Fitz, and I used the opportunity to scan the room. We had hoped to catch Lorenzo off guard, which was clearly out of the question now. But there were only a few guards in the room—leaving with Lorenzo was still a possibility.

"Your family was careless with it, so it belongs to me now. But come join me, and we'll use the ring for good."

"*Excuse me?*" I spat. I knew I should control my temper, but I was tired, grieving, and angry—angry, especially, with the witch standing across from me.

Lorenzo's eyes narrowed, his expression hardening.

"For *good?*" I continued.

"Hadley, you know my intentions."

"Well, I don't," Mia said. "Why don't you explain it to the rest of us?"

"*He doesn't have many guards with him. Should we still attack?*" Mia asked telepathically.

"You are part of the problem, court member." His voice was dry, and the disdain on his face was impossible to miss.

"*Yes,*" I answered Mia. "*I'll give the order. Keep him talking for a moment.*"

"Hadley and Fitz aren't going to help you," Lana said.

"Quiet, *elf.* This does not concern you," Lorenzo said, the venom in his voice taking me by surprise.

Lana shifted her grip on her bow. Mia laid a hand on Lana's and shook her head ever so slightly.

"A wise decision," Lorenzo said.

It wasn't only Lana who bristled at the comment, but Mia was entirely too controlled to allow herself to make a bad decision. I felt the shift in her energy—she was strategizing. I met her gaze.

"I know what you want from Fitz, but why me?" I asked, turning to Lorenzo.

"You know my reasons," he said. "Don't play dumb with me, Hadley."

Fitz's energy tightened.

"None of your team needs to be further harmed today. Not if you come with me."

"It's too late for negotiations," I said. "I've already lost someone dear to me."

"And that wouldn't have happened if you'd just listened to me from the beginning. You believe Fate to be on your side. You believe our situation is that of the prophecy." Lorenzo shook his head. "No. Fate has favored me and my forces, and she will continue to do so."

Fitz signaled me to commence our attack. I caught Lorenzo's gaze and smiled before throwing flames, creating a line of fire between us.

Lorenzo jumped out of the way as Fitz's voice rang loudly through the room.

"Now!"

Fitz and I ran toward Lorenzo as the rest of the crusaders raced toward the guards, each of us meeting our opponents in battle.

I hurled fire at Lorenzo, but he expertly batted it away. Fitz grounded himself to the soil beneath the fortress, and the stones below Lorenzo rippled and cracked with Fitz's controlled earthquake. I threw another fireball as Lorenzo lost his balance, but he swept his arm, creating an energy shield. He deflected the fireball and rolled back to his feet. As Fitz and I reached Lorenzo, the witch he had entered with materialized in front of us. A time-walker.

"Careful, Alexander," Lorenzo said. "Try not to harm them."

Alexander set his sights on Fitz, and the two of them locked into battle. I reached Lorenzo, and our fight turned physical. He tried to overpower me, but I fueled my magic into strength, leveling the playing field. My fist connected with Lorenzo's jaw, but he swept his feet under mine, throwing me on to the ground. He dropped on top of me, and we wrestled for control. He tried pulling my hands together in a binding spell, but I pushed fire from my fingers, burning him. Lorenzo pulled back, and Isaac seemingly came out of nowhere, tackling him.

Gabriella sneaked along the edge of the skirmish, and I ran to meet her. She pushed me toward the fortress wall, and we struggled in a mock battle as she spoke telepathically.

"You should leave."

"Not without Lorenzo."

"If he overpowers you, you won't leave this fortress."

I considered her words.

"We could draw him outside and continue fighting there. If we capture him, we'll have to get out of this fortress anyway to transport back."

"Your power wanes," Gabriella said. *"What happened?"*

"Adamo took a lot of it."

She shoved me behind a tall shelf. *"I'll channel some power your way."*

My breath hitched as Gabriella's magical energy entered my body. She was powerful herself, and she filled my veins with the same warmth as Maka's healing energy. It was a small comfort in the midst of hell.

When she had finished, she nodded. *"Okay, work your loophole and get the team on the other side of the wall. Then, do what you must. But Hadley . . . if you see you will lose, leave. Do not allow him to take you captive."*

I ran back to the wall, scanning the battle scene. Fitz was still fighting against Alexander, and Mia had joined Isaac in the fight against Lorenzo.

I quickly located a wisp of Lorenzo's energy and tugged. I called my magic forward to tie it to the edge of his protection spell, which crackled and popped through the air. I tied my thread to it, and the spell opening held. I repeated the process and tied both ends of my magic together.

"Crusaders, fall back!" I yelled, pointing to the opening.

The scene fell into chaos as the team fought their way to the wall. I prayed we had enough transporters to get everyone through. Fitz escaped Alexander's grasp and raced to my side.

He wrapped his arms around me, and we stepped into the freshly fallen powder outside.

Two by two, our forces materialized around us.

"We'll draw him out, take him down, and transport back to headquarters," I relayed to the team.

They nodded.

A moment passed, and then Lorenzo and Alexander stepped through the wall, followed by the guards who hadn't fallen.

Lorenzo advanced toward me, and I tossed fire in his path, contemplating the best way to take him down without killing him. He stopped, his hands rising to protect his face. I took advantage of his delay and raced toward him. He was anticipating my attack by the time I reached him, though he made no attempt to stop me. I threw fire, but he deflected it and allowed me to make contact. I knocked him off balance, and we tumbled to the ground, once again locked in combat.

"Stop fighting me, Hadley," Lorenzo said.

"No. You're coming back to headquarters with me," I panted.

A gust of wind pulled me away from Lorenzo, sending me flying across the snowbank. I wrestled with it, trying to break free so I could consult with the elements, but I couldn't seem to do so. I found Fitz below and he reached a hand toward the sky. The air suddenly cradled me and deposited me into his arms.

I located Lorenzo. He was arguing with Alexander. This was our chance to catch them off guard. Fitz and I ran toward them as I spoke to Lana's mind.

"Call for the dragons."

Lorenzo must have perceived our progress, and he turned his gaze to us before registering the sparring across the open space. Another set of guards arrived, but Lana had called for backup of our own. I couldn't decide which side was winning.

Seeing my lifeless comrades filled me with rage, a tingling sensation that hummed through my body. I felt flushed. I paused several yards short of Lorenzo.

Lorenzo's eyes widened, though the emotion they held wasn't fear.

"*Bellissima*," he marveled.

I raised my hand, turning it over in a quick study. Flames spread across my whole body. Quite literally . . . I was on fire.

"I've got this," I whispered to Fitz before sprinting toward Lorenzo.

"Sir! You must stop her. She'll kill you if she makes contact!"

I was pleased by the fear in Alexander's voice. Lorenzo stared, transfixed. For a second, I thought he wasn't going to react. But before I made contact, he moved away, faster than I thought possible—the work of some sort of magic.

"No!" I yelled, before turning my gaze to Alexander.

I hurled a fireball in his direction. It connected with his left shoulder, and his face contorted in pain just before he disappeared. Fitz was by my side in an instant.

"Where is Lorenzo?" Fitz muttered. He looked around warily, awaiting an assault. I followed his gaze around the waning crowd of warriors.

My heart sank. We couldn't return to Opimae City without Lorenzo.

Finally, I spotted Molly fighting against Lorenzo. I recalled her words to me when she'd told me of Finn—and of her rage toward Lorenzo. *I'll gut him*, she'd said. I tapped Fitz's shoulder and ran toward them as a high-pitched shriek filled the air. I recognized the sound instantly, and my heart swelled as my energy roared.

Róisín.

A thunder of dragons flew overhead, their wings slicing through the air, their cries disturbing the sounds of battle.

Exclamations of "dragons!" echoed through the space.

Róisín flew second in command to a solid black dragon who contrasted beautifully with the fiery hair of its rider. Laisrén led the thunder atop the magnificently large dragon, and dressed in armor, he looked every bit a warrior. The witch who had led Róisín to meet me was positioned to his left, and her chariot was a beautiful silver dragon. Each of the dragons held a rider . . . except for Róisín.

"Looks like the air force has arrived," I said.

The new wave of attackers worked swiftly alongside us, and with this new element of surprise, the battle turned in our favor. My faith resurfaced—we had a real chance of leaving with Lorenzo.

Lorenzo's head tilted to the sky, granting Molly the upper hand. She launched energy that connected with Lorenzo's shoulder, but Lorenzo countered her attack and pulled the air back. It rippled around him before he released, sending Molly flying back several feet. Fitz reached

Lorenzo first, knocking him to the ground.

My heart faltered. I couldn't stand there and do nothing, but they were too tangled for me to get in a clean shot. Molly tried to jump back in, but another guard rushed at her and they wrestled with each other. I returned my focus to Fitz, who had gotten his arms around Lorenzo and was attempting to transport out with him. Their bodies wavered in and out of focus in their silent battle. I fell to the ground and called my energy to my hands. If I could get a clean hit, I'd zap Lorenzo's power enough for Fitz to be successful, but I quickly realized their power was too enmeshed. It wouldn't work.

Lorenzo finally grabbed Fitz's arms and hit him with energy—not enough to gravely injure him, but enough to push him back. When Lorenzo separated from Fitz, I threw an energy orb at him, which connected with his torso. He doubled over in pain, then looked around at his few guards left and took a step like he meant to leave.

I called to the elements, creating ripples through the air. Lorenzo moved toward the fortress, but the elements wouldn't allow him access. He glanced around and found my gaze, shaking his head lightly.

"Stop this game you're playing," he called.

"I will," I returned. "As soon as you hand over the ring."

I wondered how far away his reinforcements could be, trying to recall the distance from his fortress to Terra Firma. But the last threads of this battle were tying themselves up: Róisín dropped to the ground next to me, snow scattering in her wake.

It was over, and Lorenzo knew it. His eyes were desperate when they met mine. Flames burst from my fingertips, and they flowed like a river from Róisín's mouth. Fitz reached my side first, as connected to the elements as he was, ripples of air visible at his fingertips. Lana reached the other side of Róisín, her bow poised, and Molly materialized next to Fitz, the air sparking around her. I'd never seen the team so fully engaged in the elements, or so enraged, and they were a sight to behold.

Lorenzo swept his eyes across us, and when he looked back to me, he was calm.

"Alexander," he called. The witch in question materialized beside him. This was our only chance to catch him before he disappeared.

I took a step closer. "You know, you're always inviting me to your fortress, but you know where I've been. Why don't you come with me?"

Lorenzo laughed. "Why? So they can lock me behind bars? Spellbind me? That doesn't sound like such a good idea."

"Wouldn't you do the same to me?"

Before he could answer, Fitz launched toward him. Alexander threw up a shield of energy, and Fitz slammed against the crackling force before falling to the ground. Lorenzo turned to Fitz and took a step forward.

"Fitz!" Ian yelled.

Ian threw energy that knocked Lorenzo backward. I ran to Fitz.

"I'm all right," Fitz said. "But damn, that hurt."

"Your dad is fighting Lorenzo."

"What? No," he exclaimed.

Fitz stood, but he wavered.

"You need to take a beat," I said.

Without awaiting a response, I ran toward Lorenzo and Ian, hoping to intervene quickly. Ian was powerful, but Lorenzo's magic was stronger. I felt like I couldn't move fast enough, and my heart pounded quicker with every passing second. Ian and Lorenzo were exchanging fire while the rest of the crusaders were attempting to take down the few remaining guards. Lorenzo sent an energy orb flying toward Ian.

My scream pierced the valley as Ian fell to the ground.

Alexander reached Lorenzo. Their shouting was indiscernible, but heated. Lorenzo looked around the battlefield and then his eyes met mine. Alexander grasped for Lorenzo, and they disappeared.

I reached Ian at the same time as Fitz, and we knelt in the snow to assess his injuries. He was unconscious, but he was alive.

"We have to get him back," Fitz said.

"Take him."

"I dinnae think I can, Hadley."

I paused, my muddled mind slowly registering what he meant.

"I'll take him," Molly said, out of breath as she dropped to her knees beside us.

"Where's your partner?" I asked, scanning the small group of crusaders locked into battle.

"Dead," Molly said.

I swallowed hard.

"Can you make it to headquarters?" Fitz asked.

Molly hesitated briefly. "Yeah. I can do it."

"Are you sure?" he pressed.

"Yes. You and Hadley finish up here, and I'll get him to medical."

"Thank you," Fitz said, touching her shoulder.

Molly nodded. She wiggled into the snow behind Ian and wrapped her arms around him. She closed her eyes, and with that, they were gone.

"We might have won out here," I said, "but we won't be successful if we go after him again."

"Aye, he'll have backup coming from Terra Firma by now," Fitz said.

"You can't transport us?" I asked Fitz, wondering if my boost would make a difference this time.

"That shield was a nasty hit," he said. "I think I have it in me, but . . ." He trailed off.

I turned to Roísín. "I have a better idea."

CHAPTER FORTY-TWO

Magna Valley stretched below us, basked in the soft light of sunset. Fitz and I sat in silence as Roísín steered us toward headquarters, following Laisrén's capable lead atop the large dragon he'd ridden into battle. We'd never seen the valley from this perspective, and it took some of the edge off my nerves, at least for now. I both longed for and feared information on Tanner's and Ian's conditions. They were both in surgery, and that was all we could expect as an update for a while.

Roísín turned north directly into the sunset. The cold air made me shiver, even with Roísín's warmth, but it kept me alert, which was inordinately helpful, as drained as I was. Fitz's arms were around me, and he leaned forward, resting his head against the crook of my neck. His energy was exhausted, and I knew we'd both require rest to return to our normal levels. I laced my fingers through his and fought against the urge to close my eyes.

Instead, I scanned the scene below us. We had just soared over the last of the foothills and were following the river through Opimae City. Its citizens were walking along the riverside, meandering through court-yards, driving along the cobblestone streets . . . living their lives. We had fought today for their rights to a peaceful life. A few of them caught sight of us: some pointed in surprise, others smiled and waved. It wasn't every day they'd see a dragon gracing the city skies.

Laisrén navigated to the sidewalk outside of headquarters, and Róisín landed gently near the door. A young woman emerged through the doorway, looking over her shoulder distractedly at our team who was assembled just inside. When she looked in our direction, her eyes widened as they swept over Róisín.

Róisín nudged my shoulder.

"You're such a brave girl," I whispered.

"She wouldn't let anyone ride with her into battle," Laisrén said. "She hasn't bonded with anyone yet—I think she's been waiting for you."

My throat ached. "I might have to leave for a while," I said, recalling the consequences of our failed mission to Lorenzo's fortress.

"She'll wait," Laisrén said, matter-of-factly.

"You think I have it in me to be a fire warrior?" I asked sheepishly.

"Maybe even more than we do," he returned.

"Now, that is something I know to be false."

Laisrén chuckled. "You're made for it. This won't be the last of your battles, but it's the last you'll meet without your dragon."

I wrapped my arms around Róisín once more. She rested her head on top of mine, and we stood quietly locked in our goodbye.

"I'll see you as soon as I can. I promise."

Róisín nodded her head. She released a sigh, along with sparks that floated in the space around us. I said my goodbyes to Laisrén before taking Fitz's hand and walking into headquarters.

Our group was solemn. The hallways buzzed annoyingly with chatter. There'd been victory and defeat in equal measure, and part of me under-stood the excitement, but I needed quiet. I needed to know Ian and Tanner would be okay. I needed respect for the dead. Anything above a whisper felt intrusive after what we'd witnessed.

The hallways fell silent at our approach. Eyes followed us, and countless beings offered timid smiles, bows, and soft-spoken appreciation. I looked at the team, realizing we reflected the hell we'd been through. We were battered, bruised, and exhausted. We were covered in sweat, dirt, and blood. But I did my best to smile, and to nod in acknowledgment of their words, kind as they were.

"Thank you," a gray-haired witch said, stepping forward with tears in his eyes. "My son was killed in the initial attack, and today I feel like his death has been avenged in some way."

I smiled softly, taking his hand briefly before moving on.

As we neared Charles's office, Jordan burst through the door to greet us. Her face fell for only a fraction of a second, but it was enough to confirm our appearance was rough. She rushed to Gustavo and paused.

"Are you . . . hurt?"

Gustavo pulled her close, assuaging her fears. His shoulder was beaten up, but other than that, his injuries were merely minor scrapes and bruises.

She gasped when she turned to me. "What happened to your head?" she asked.

"I'm not really sure. Does it look bad?"

"There's a lot of dried blood." She chewed at her lip, her energy betraying her concern.

I reached absentmindedly toward my head, and winced as I touched the blood caked into my hair.

"Time to get that looked at, Hads," Fitz said.

After hugging me tightly, Jordan pulled us into Charles's office. Healers, including Maka, were waiting inside, and they tended to our wounds as we debriefed. My head gave them a bit of trouble, but it only took a few moments of me grimacing in pain before I was healed.

"Sadie might have just saved your life," Maka whispered softly for only me to hear.

"It was that bad?" I asked.

"Swelling near your brain is always a bad thing. If you had continued fighting in that condition . . . well, it would have been bad, to say the very least."

I nodded. "Thank you for telling me."

I heard a soft intake of air from Jordan.

Isaac had lifted his shirt to show Healer June a wound on his torso, a deep gash that was a bloody mess. Burn marks stretched across his skin, angry and weeping.

"When did that happen?" I demanded.

"Isaac, you said it wasn't bad." Henry shook his head.

"It looks worse than it is," he protested.

"You should have told us, mate." Fitz's voice was soft.

Chloe walked in, and the room fell silent. I stood quickly and crossed the room. She embraced me tightly, and I held her quietly until she was ready to talk.

"How is he?" I finally asked.

She chewed on her bottom lip and blinked back tears.

"He's still in surgery. They said the energy orb was one of the most powerful they've seen. It caused a lot of internal damage, so it's taking them a long time to work through the injuries."

"Is he going to be okay?" I asked, suddenly growing anxious and lightheaded.

Her eyes flickered to mine. "I don't know, Hadley. The healers don't know."

I shook my head. This couldn't be the end for Tanner. He had too much fight ahead of him. A mate who was only just coming to know his love. A family who wouldn't let him go.

"No," I whispered to Fate.

Fight, Tanner.

Chloe tightened her grip on my hand.

"After that vision, he should've stayed away from all this," I said.

"What?" Chloe asked.

Her brows scrunched with confusion, and I knew immediately what I'd done. Tanner hadn't shared the vision with her.

"It's nothing," I said quickly.

"Hadley, what are you talking about?"

Chloe held my gaze, and I shifted uncomfortably. I couldn't share the information with her after he'd chosen to conceal it, could I?

"You need to tell me right now." Chloe's tone held both panic and anger.

"Chloe . . ." I said, realizing this was the worst possible timing. "Tanner didn't enchant you just because he was worried about the mission. A friend of Tanner's had a vision. She foresaw Tanner's death—and she said it would happen on this mission."

Chloe shook her head, tears spilling from her sea-colored eyes. "No. No, that can't be true."

"He was trying to protect you because he believes he won't make it through this crusade."

Chloe's eyes were desperate when they landed on mine.

"But he's not going to die today," I said. "And I believe he has the power to change his future. It isn't certain, remember?"

She remained silent. The rest of the room was quiet, frozen as my conversation with Chloe continued.

"No one else is dying today," I said firmly.

"I just found him," Chloe said. "I can't lose him already, Hadley."

I moved closer and pulled her into an embrace, holding her as she fell apart. I found Fitz over her shoulder, and he eyed me sympathetically. Chloe's situation was a worst-case scenario for us all. I could only imagine how Henry and Molly felt in that moment.

Charles entered the room and paused briefly, taking in the sight of us. He recovered and advanced toward us, shaking hands and offering thanks as he made his way around the room.

When he made it to Chloe and me, he smiled sadly.

"I just heard they've made progress with Tanner."

Chloe's head snapped up.

"They've almost made it through his core—his internal organs are mostly repaired. He's still critical, but that's a good sign, at least."

"I'm going back to the wait station," Chloe said urgently.

"Do you want someone to come with you?" I asked.

"No. You all debrief. I could use a few moments anyway. But thank you."

Chloe left the room, and I turned my focus to Charles.

"We don't know how Ian's surgery will turn out, but so far, it is going well," Charles said.

"Thank you, Charles," Fitz said, his eyes filled with pain.

Ian would be okay. He had to be.

"I'm sorry, Charles. I'm so sorry about Keoni," I said.

"Thank you. It's worse than you know."

"What do you mean?"

"We're waiting for more information," James said. "Jordan's teams are already digging furiously through all of Keoni's devices, his home, everything we have access to . . . but it appears Keoni betrayed us."

Murmurs sounded all through the room.

"Jordan?" I asked.

"We've pulled camera footage. Keoni sent Isamu's guard on an errand this afternoon. The guard didn't even question it—which was wrong, but I mean, it was Keoni. Keoni released Isamu from his cell. Then they freed Allette, and they all left together."

My mind was spinning.

"Hadley, what is it?" James nudged.

"I'm trying to make sense of all this. It's . . . when Keoni was killed, I'm positive it was Isamu who did it. If they were working together, why would he kill Keoni?"

"You're positive?"

"When I bent down to tend to Keoni . . ." I swallowed hard, collecting myself. "It was too late, but I recognized the energy from the wound. It was Isamu. I'm certain."

"So, Keoni releases Isamu and Allette and travels with them to Adamo. But then Isamu kills him. Why?" James asked.

"I mean, it could've even been an accident," Molly said.

"Keoni could have been a captive by the time they left the building. Perhaps he was blackmailed into helping Isamu and Allette, so Isamu eliminated Keoni on the battlefield," Henry said.

"I could see Lorenzo making some sort of threat that prompted Keoni to act as he did," I added.

"This raises another question, though," Solomon mused. "How long has this gone on? How much information could Lorenzo have extracted through Keoni?"

"All of it," Charles said, his head in his hands. "Keoni could have leaked everything."

"If the mole was so high ranking, it would explain how Lorenzo stayed ahead of us," I said.

Isaac let out a low whistle.

"Let's not get ahead of ourselves," Fitz said. "Let's see what Jordan's teams come up with and go from there."

"There's something else," I said.

The energy in the room turned curious. I shared the information I'd learned from the ring still resting in my pocket. Perhaps I should have handed it over to Intelligence, but for some reason I couldn't name, I held on to it.

"So, you think this was Lorenzo's mate?" Mia asked.

"No," I shook my head. "I *know* she was Lorenzo's mate."

"You said her name was Anya?" Jordan confirmed, reaching for her tablet.

I gave a physical description to Jordan.

"We'll work on identifying her," Jordan said.

"I think . . . I think one of them broke their connection, but I don't know why."

I looked at Fitz. He took my hand in his.

"If Lorenzo has a mate out there, we have to find her," Molly said. "This could be huge."

"Definitely. I'll go brief the teams," Jordan said.

"And as much as I hate to tell you this," Charles said, turning to Fitz and me, "the chamber has been called to session this evening."

Fitz sighed. "How long do we have?"

Charles checked his watch. "Oh, about fifteen minutes."

CHAPTER FORTY-THREE

We returned to our home different witches than the ones who'd left it early that morning. I wanted nothing more than to curl up alone in a ball in a dark room and forget everything that had happened today. My body wouldn't stop shaking, my head was aching, and I was growing nauseous. I realized Fitz and I hadn't eaten all day. But most of the team was assembled in the great room.

"You're all here," I said.

"Of course, we are," Mia said. I crossed the room and took her hand briefly. Mia was as tough as God ever made anyone. Despite all our differences, I was beginning to respect her.

"You two should clean up," Isaac said. "It helps to rinse everything away—I promise."

Molly emerged from the kitchen. "We have food for you," she said. "I know you're probably not hungry, but you've got to choke something down." She narrowed her eyes at me, clearly anticipating protest.

"Maybe I'll try a little bread first," I said, after considering what my body would keep down.

"Aye, me too," Fitz said. "Let's ease in with just a bit of scran."

"Coming right up," she said, and disappeared into the kitchen.

Chloe padded down the hallway wearing Tanner's lucky Mariners hat, her blonde curls spilling from it.

I smiled. I hadn't seen that hat since we crossed over.

"I know," Chloe said, like she was the one who read minds. "They wouldn't let me leave it with him, but I thought maybe one of us should wear it."

"A good idea," I said. "What's the latest?"

"Surgery was successful. They think he's going to be okay," she said, her eyes misting.

I embraced her with relief. When we pulled away, I realized just how troubled her blue eyes were.

"He'll be weak for a couple of days—his energy really took a hit—but the healers said he just needs a lot of rest to help him heal now."

"Thank god he's going to be okay," I said. "I—we can't lose Tanner."

Chloe squeezed my hand.

Molly returned with caora bread and water, which Fitz and I accepted gratefully. Once we'd finished eating, we showered. It didn't wash away the emptiness in the pit of my stomach, but Isaac was right—it helped.

We dressed slowly, using gentle movements with our aching bodies, before returning to the great room and taking a seat on the couch nearest the fire. I snugged up against Fitz.

"What's the latest on Ian?" Henry asked.

"He's out of surgery and resting in an induced coma. They won't wake him until tomorrow," I said, relieving Fitz from having to answer. He slipped his hand in mine.

"I sent for Mum and Izzy," Fitz said softly. "I'm trying to be positive, but it doesn't look good."

"He'll turn a corner," Henry said. "He has to."

"Aye," Fitz said. "I'm sure you're right."

The rest of the team soon spread themselves across the living area.

"I'm exhausted, but how are we supposed to sleep tonight?" Chloe said.

"I don't know if I can shut my eyes just yet," Molly said. "I'm . . . well, I'm a little scared of what'll surface."

Isaac held out his hand, and Molly took it willingly. He pulled her close, and she curled into a ball under the weight of his protective bulk. I was surprised by Molly's admission, but pleasantly so. The last thing any of us needed was to clam up.

"Aye, me too," Henry said. "We saw some real shite today."

"I keep seeing this one image in my head," Molly said, a quick glance at me betraying her thoughts.

"Keoni?" I guessed.

She nodded. "I just see Hadley dropping beside him. I see her closing his eyelids. And . . ." She trailed off, her eyes distant as she found what she wanted to say. "And then I think about his betrayal. I just wonder what his last moments were like."

"And wonder if we should be angry at his choices," Solomon added.

She nodded.

"I am angry," I admitted. "I'm angry at his decisions. I'm angry that I had to feel his lifeless body because of them. I'm angry that he did this to us, and . . . I'm just confused."

I tumbled through memories with Keoni, from lighthearted moments spent in companionship right down to his perturbed looks when Lana had mentioned Lorenzo.

Lorenzo.

"I can't stop thinking about the way Lorenzo engaged with us in the fortress either," I said.

"The entire fortress mission felt weird from the moment we stepped through that wall," Molly said.

"He seems to think he has some sort of right to Hadley and Fitz," Gustavo said. "It was odd."

"A god complex, I think," Solomon said. "He thinks he's the best candidate to restructure all of witchkind, and I think he believes Hadley and Fitz will help him do that."

"It's so odd that he focuses on us," I said.

"He wants your power," Fitz said. "He's intoxicated by it."

"And he wants yours, too. You're the most powerful living MacGregor, and I'll wager he's decided you'll release the power of the ring to him," Henry said.

"He probably thinks that once you join him, the rest of us will follow," Jordan added.

I nodded. "And he believes Fate is on his side."

"Did you face opposition at the chamber meeting today?" Henry asked.

"Today was solely a briefing. But the next chamber meeting should be interesting," I said.

The group fell silent. And then finally—

"I can't believe I took a life today. *Lives* . . ."

Everyone looked to Gustavo.

"We all knew it was coming, but damn. The reality of it was awful," Isaac said.

"I don't think we'll ever be over it," Molly said. "We'll find a way to live with what we had to do. What we'll have to do again. But I don't think any of us will ever be the same."

Solomon nodded. "I was involved in conflicts in my youth back in Ethiopia. I promise, this pit in your stomach will ease. But Molly's right. It changes you."

"You're such a positive being," Mia said. "How?"

"With lots of practice. When you see the worst of our worlds, the path back to happiness is a choice. I *choose* happiness."

"How?" Gustavo echoed.

"I think of each of you." He smiled. "I think of the many beings we are protecting. Yes, we must do some horrible things to reach our goal, but we're preventing an evil being from destroying countless innocent lives. I have the privilege of protecting the innocent—and I do that alongside each of you."

"When we experienced the attack at Pluvia Silva, I thought I'd never feel okay again," I said. "But we've fought through that as a group."

"We made our mental health a priority, and we haven't allowed each other to slip into darkness. This will be the same," Fitz said.

The conversation continued into the evening. We shared our

burdens with one another. We shared our guilt. We discussed therapy and battle and even my loss of control, harming Isamu when I knew we needed a live capture for intelligence. Nothing was off-topic; nothing was taboo. And we agreed that we'd hold each other's hands and walk through the darkness together until the last of us emerged into the light.

No one wanted to be alone at the end of the evening, so we dragged pillows and blankets into the great room until everyone had a comfortable place to sleep. I'd thought I wanted some time alone, but as it turned out, I wasn't quite ready for that either. I needed my team more than ever, and I guessed they felt the same.

The subtle noises of the medical equipment and a soft patter of rain were the only perceptible noises in an otherwise quiet afternoon. The stormy skies of Opimae City cast an appropriate gloom through the windows, and consequentially, across the seven witches scattered through the healing room. Fitz and Izzy were seated on either side of Ann, who was holding Ian's hand. I sat on the edge of the couch next to Fitz, my arm draped supportively around his shoulders. Henry and Isaac were seated near the window. They'd offered to give us some privacy, but they were an integral part of the family—and they now would help offer a blessing of peace for Ian's departure from our world and into the next.

The healers had fought hard to save Ian over the course of the last two days, but in the end, his earthly body just couldn't do it. We learned that he had internal damage from Isamu's attack that hadn't healed properly, and his body wasn't strong enough to recover from his altercation with Lorenzo. His organs were failing, so the healers had administered medication to grant Ian enough time for Ann and Izzy to arrive in Opimae.

Magic was a powerful force, but as Henry had once told me, there were some wounds even magic couldn't heal.

Ann wept as Ian weakly relayed his brief goodbyes to his family. It was taxing on him, but one by one he left us with the love that only Ian could give. There had always been something about Ian: warm and inviting; powerful, yet kind.

Ian believed in our ability to persevere, but we couldn't believe the same. Not without him.

He spent his last moments of consciousness speaking with us all. He told Fitz and Izzy how proud he was of them, how incredibly brave and kind they'd both grown to be. He told Fitz he was a fierce leader and a beautiful partner, and how he wished he could've stayed with us long enough to see our wedding one day. He shared that had Fate allowed, he'd have followed Fitz's lead anywhere. His gaze settled on Izzy as he told her the world of Opimae was about to discover the most talented healer he'd ever known and how her gentle spirit gave him hope for our worlds.

There were countless tender moments between him and Ann, and we were privileged to witness the whispers of love between two witches who'd stood by each other's side for ninety years. Their love was steadfast, encouraging despite the earth-shattering ending. My heart broke into a thousand pieces at the thought of Ann's loss.

And then Ian asked to speak to me. I dropped to my knees next to the bed as he placed his hand into mine.

"Hadley, my child."

"I didn't think I'd ever have to do this again, Ian," I said, my voice breaking. "I can't lose another father."

"I ken it seems that way, lass. But you'll be all right—you all will."

I shook my head.

"I want you to ken how precious you are to me. You have become a daughter to me, and I thank God for the time we had together. Thank you. . . for being you, for having the courage to do what's right, and for loving my son so fiercely."

"It's my honor."

"The love and power you and Fitz share is simply extraordinary."

I nodded.

"Take care of each other."

In the end, we all gathered as Ian took his last breath, each of us clinging to one another for comfort. The raindrops rolling down the windowpane kept time with our tears. The sky darkened. Ian's soul was free, but a part of my own left with him.

His death marked a new chapter in our lives, and with it would come my vengeance.

CHAPTER FORTY-FOUR

Fitz and I were granted a few days' leave to mourn the loss of his father. It seemed far too short a time for us to grieve such a being. Losing Ian awakened trauma I thought I had dealt with; the wounds from my father's death had still been healing when this crusade began.

A crusade that had led to Keoni's death, and then to Ian's.

A crusade that had shown me death on the battlefield and even beyond.

A crusade that had forced me to kill or be killed.

I wanted to say I was fine—that we all were—but that couldn't be further from the truth, and it seemed that would remain the case for the foreseeable future.

Fitz wasn't ready to talk about his loss, preferring to bury himself in caring for his mother and preparing for what lay ahead.

On our first day back from leave, we entered the chamber, and a sea of faces turned expectantly toward us. My stomach tightened at the sight. Fitz reached for my hand, and we followed Charles to the front row to take our seats.

A small envelope was sitting on my chair, and I picked it up curiously, tugging it open. I reached inside and pulled out an earring.

I gasped.

There, in my hand, was my missing earring from the afternoon I'd tracked Jess. As thrilled as I was to have it back in my possession, the implications were unsettling.

Fitz eyed me suspiciously, and I passed the earring off to him. His eyes widened as he met my gaze.

"Is this . . ." He trailed off.

I nodded.

"Then he knows," Fitz said.

"That I was tracking him that day? Maybe. Someone does, anyway."

Charles began the meeting, and I slid the envelope into my bag. The rest of our conversation would have to wait.

"Jordan will run us through her report on Keoni, which was just finalized this morning."

Jordan took the stage.

"Morning, everyone. Our teams have been combing through records and cross-referencing Keoni's devices and whereabouts. In doing so, we've discovered quite a bit of information that he leaked to Lorenzo's forces."

The chamber filled with gasps and heated exclamations.

"There is more detailed information in the reports that were just sent your way, but it's currently bringing about more questions than answers.

"We have learned a few things with certainty—we confirmed Keoni worked with Lorenzo's forces in some capacity in Pluvia Silva."

I stood. "I have some information on that."

Jordan signaled for me to proceed.

I told the chamber of my experience with Keoni when I'd seen him speaking with his friend from Hurlee.

"An old friend? I can't imagine he'd betray us over that," a voice called out from the back of the chamber. King Jowan of Kevardhu.

"He lied to you."

"He wasn't lying about the connection," I said. "I'm gifted in that area, and I would know if he lied. So, there's something to it. Perhaps, that information can be helpful."

"Of course, it's helpful. It's a good lead, Hadley. Thank you," Jordan said.

I nodded and sat down.

"We also know that Keoni leaked information regarding Hadley and Fitz's time-jump where they encountered Lucio, Hadley's location when Isamu found her at the park, and information regarding some of our military plans. We're currently working through the records to determine what other issues were caused by his intelligence leaks."

Chatter rumbled through the chamber, and Jordan quickly called us back to order. "I'd like to point out that Keoni also provided false information. He gave Lorenzo's forces the wrong date for the Adamo attack."

I gasped, realization settling in. Jordan met my gaze.

"And he was killed for it," Fitz said.

"We believe so," Jordan said. "It seems he may have given other false information as well."

"Do we have any idea why?" King Copandir asked.

"We have some early theories, but I'd like to withhold those until they gain credibility," Jordan said.

My mind was racing. Why had Keoni played double agent? It didn't make sense. There was certainly more to this story, but if anyone could sort it out, it was Jordan.

"We've also confirmed Hans and Allette's involvement with Lorenzo. After sending new information back to Earth's teams, they were able to cross reference dates and facial recognition software. They've been spotted with Lorenzo on several occasions. Again, there's more about that in my report."

Jordan nodded to Charles, and he stood.

"We'll discuss this further in the afternoon session, but we'll hear from King Alden now—he'd like to raise a concern with the chamber."

The king stood but hesitated before he began, sweeping his gaze across the chamber. When his eyes settled on mine, I had anticipated animosity, but I found something else instead: regret.

Finally, he began. "I know we need to review the full report from Intelligence, but in light of the news regarding Lorenzo's connection to these stalkers, we must discuss the repercussions of Hadley and Fitz's place in this mission."

I stood. "Our place?"

King Alden pursed his lips. "I know I've had objections to the Earth crusaders in the past, but I assure you all this does not stem from those former objections."

He looked to me and then to Fitz before continuing.

"If Lorenzo has been watching these two crusaders since before they traveled to Opimae, we must ask ourselves this question: why did he allow them to cross over? Why didn't he prevent them from ever doing so in the first place?"

Queen Min-Ji spoke. "Because he wanted them to cross over. He wanted them here."

"We know he wants Fitz and me for his own purposes," I said, "but it doesn't matter what he wants. We're not going to help him."

"I understand the sentiment," King Alden said. "But you have to understand the risk we're taking by keeping you here. It is a risk to your safety, and it is also a risk to the safety of our world. What if he captures you? What if he forces you to do his bidding?"

"It's too risky," Queen Min-Ji said. "It would be irresponsible of us to allow you to continue on."

King Copandir stood. "What of the prophecy? Do we not consider that in this chamber?"

"The prophecy is still in question," King Alden said.

"It clearly states that a team of crusaders will be led by Fate to Opimae from Earth. It also states two of these crusaders will be strongly connected to each other," King Copandir said.

"Are you saying you don't believe Earth has sent us the proper team, Alden? Is that your concern?" King Brennus asked.

"I am concerned over all of it," King Alden said.

"The prophecy is long-revered," Prime Minister Bakari said. "We do not discredit it now. There is no question in my mind that these two are those who were foretold."

"Nor in mine," King Copandir said.

"Nor mine," King Brennus agreed.

"I'm not discrediting the prophecy, nor these crusaders," Queen Min-Ji said. "I've made that clear in previous sessions. But I am questioning if it is responsible of this chamber to play right into Lorenzo's hands. We must consider whether it is wise to continue with our current trajectory. We have a responsibility to our folk."

I looked at Fitz, my heart racing. We couldn't be removed from this mission. We'd come too far to slip further away from the ring.

I pushed my shoulders back, standing tall, as Fitz rose next to me.

"I'd like to say something about this," I began. "You say our safety is of concern. I'd like to ask you to remove that from your considerations."

"Though we appreciate your concern, this mission has been risky from its inception," Fitz said. "We understand the risks perfectly."

"Our entire team has known since the beginning that we might not survive this crusade. We signed up anyway. This confirmation, though disturbing, does not increase our risk of death."

"I've heard rumor of a no-kill order," King Brennus said.

"Aye," Fitz said. "We previously believed that order to have come from our stalkers. When we realized their involvement with Lorenzo, coupled with Lorenzo's behavior toward us, everything clicked."

"Though your deaths would be a great loss, this news is almost more troubling. Lorenzo is clearly set on your capture," Queen Emlyn said.

"And if he captures you, he will force you to help him. This witch is ruthless," King Alden said. "You've seen that firsthand. Don't you understand who you're up against?"

"What if Lorenzo tries time travel? What if he goes back in time to have Fitz release the power of the ring?" King Brennus asked.

"A good question," Charles said. "But I don't think even Lorenzo would risk those consequences."

"His father time traveled to the past and stole the ring," King Brennus argued.

"But Lorenzo isn't his father," King Copandir said. "I'll admit that

I've had the same concern, but Lorenzo already had his chance to force Fitz to access the ring's power. For whatever reason, he didn't. He's waited for Hadley and Fitz to arrive in Opimae."

"Which is incredibly concerning," Queen Min-Ji said. "We're missing something."

The room fell silent.

I shifted my footing. "I know there is a lot of uncertainty, but Queen Min-Ji mentioned your responsibility to your folk. What of our responsibility? Fitz and I have proven ourselves. We have already stood against Lorenzo on multiple occasions."

"That is true," Queen Min-Ji said. "But you are two of the most powerful witches this world has seen—and we have seen many marvels. If Lorenzo were to capture you, it would be catastrophic. The risk might outweigh the reward on this one."

Charles stood. "If I may assert my stance, I stand with Hadley and Fitz. But I propose we put this to a vote. Consider the consequences of our actions here. Weigh your choices tonight. We'll reconvene tomorrow."

The chamber filled with the chatter of voices and the footsteps of the leaders exiting the room.

Fitz and I sat in our chairs, shellshocked, unable to move.

CHAPTER FORTY-FIVE

The following morning, our team gathered in the great room awaiting the decision of the chamber. Fitz and I had been asked not to attend the session, and I paced the room relentlessly to expel my nervous energy. And I wasn't the only one—the entire team was on edge. Finally, Fitz's phone rang, and the two of us stepped on to the patio.

Fitz answered and placed the phone on speaker.

"I wish I had better news," Charles said.

"They've voted us off the mission," Fitz said.

Charles hesitated. "Yes. I can't tell you how disappointed I am by this decision."

The world tilted off its axis, and I sank into a nearby chair.

"No," I said, shaking my head. "This can't be happening."

Fitz knelt near the chair and held my hand. My agony was beyond words.

"I'm sorry, Hadley," Charles said. "I'm sorry to you both."

"You have nothing to apologize for," Fitz said. "You've done your best, and we appreciate your support far more than you know."

Charles told us how he and several other members had fought against the decision, but I hardly heard Charles's explanations. I felt like someone had knocked all the wind out of me. My mind couldn't seem to accept reality, and everything was distant. Tears fell down my face, a mix of countless emotions swirling through me. I was just as frustrated as I was upset, and I didn't know how to remedy it.

"I haven't given up, and I hope you won't either," Charles finally said.

"What do you mean?" I asked, sniffling.

"If I know you and your team at all, you're not going to accept this. I can't turn the tides in the chamber right now, so it'll have to be something outside of the box."

My mind started ticking through possibilities.

"I'm on my way to your home now. Let's talk further when I arrive."

The call disconnected, and I stared wordlessly at Fitz.

The morning air nipped at my neck, but I couldn't move just yet. I didn't know how to face the team after Charles's news.

"They'll all be waiting on us," Fitz said. "But take your time. We dinnae have to rush this."

"How are you feeling?" I asked.

"Like shite," he said.

We both did. Ian's death . . . and Keoni's. Tanner's brush with death. And now this.

"There's a part of me that wants to pack my bags and not look back."

"Aye, but I know you better than that."

He was right.

"We can't just leave our team. We can't leave without that ring either," I said.

"Aye, I agree. We didnae come this far to stop now. I just wish—"

Fitz's energy stirred sadly.

"What is it?" I asked.

"I wish Dad was here. He'd know just what to do right now."

"We'll make him proud, Fitz."

Fitz wiped the tears from my face before kissing my forehead tenderly.

I gave the bravest smile I had in me.

"Let's go in," I said. "We can't put this off forever."

The room was silent as we entered, but they knew instantly. Fitz was attempting to hide it, but his face had fallen. I was certain I didn't look any better.

"They've voted to remove you," Chloe guessed.

"Aye. Hadley and I are no longer your crusade leaders," Fitz said.

The room fell into exclamations and chatter.

I swept my eyes across my little family. Many of them had joined because of Fitz and me.

Finally, Solomon broke through the noise of our team. "All right, everyone. Let's settle down. We need to discuss this rationally."

He motioned toward the large breakfast table. The team gathered round, and we sat for a moment.

"Did Charles give the chamber's reasoning?" Henry asked.

"In the end, Charles said they were unwilling to take the risk. They fear our capture. So, they're sending us back to Earth."

"What? No," Jordan said. "They can't send you back."

"They feel we'll be out of Lorenzo's grasp on Earth."

"That's no quite true though, is it?" Henry said. "Lorenzo has crossed the portal several times. If he means to use you to access the ring, he'll find his way back to Earth."

"I keep asking myself why he didn't do that from the beginning," I said.

"Aye, me too," Fitz said. "But Queen Min-Ji was right about one thing: for whatever reason, he wanted us to come here."

"We can't just accept this," Isaac said. "We have to fight."

"Charles made it clear that the chamber wouldn't be swayed," I said.

"And they'll shut us down if we go rogue over here," Tanner said. Even amid this horror, it was good to see Tanner up and moving around again. His progress was slow, but he was healing.

"I'm here because of Hadley and Fitz," Jordan said. "And I know many of you feel the same way."

"Aye, most of us," Henry agreed.

"So, stay for us," I said. "Fitz and I aren't going to accept this decision."

"You're right, Hadley. We shouldn't accept this. So, let's fight back,"

Solomon said.

"But what is there to be done, Solomon?" James asked.

I pushed my seat away from the table and stood. "I have a proposal."

"By all means, let's hear it," Solomon said.

"I think we revisit James's idea of time travel."

"His what?" Jordan asked.

"You're serious?" Fitz asked.

"I am." I met his gaze. I had opposed it adamantly, but everything had looked different then. "We're out of options, and we're not going to sway the chamber. But we can run our own mission—on Earth."

"I dinnae know that I like it, Hads," Fitz said. "But... let's discuss."

"James," I said, turning to him. "If you're still invested in the proposal, I'd like to have you pitch it to the team."

When James explained his idea, the team erupted into chaos.

"Let's listen to what they have to say," Jordan called above the sea of voices.

"The floor is yours," Isaac said, though his tone was terse.

"We understand the apprehension completely," James said. "This is risky, and we ken that well. This willnae even work if Fate decides to hold history true to its current course. But we are in a delicate situation, and Lorenzo must be prevented from using the ring against us. He's much too powerful already, and we ken the ring could amplify his power greatly."

"What if we forge our own ring to fight against Lorenzo?" Henry asked.

Chloe and James cut him a disapproving look.

"I'm no suggesting we do it," he defended, leaning back in his chair. "But I am proposing another idea so we can say that we have truly thought of everything else."

"It is forbidden, but forbidden acts don't seem to be of much concern right now," Isaac said.

"We can't ask that of others—to sacrifice their powers while they're still living," Solomon said.

"But there are witches dying every day," Molly said.

"Yes, that's true," Chloe nodded thoughtfully. "But the real issue with that option is that it, once again, gives someone entirely too much power. I don't care who wields it, that amount of power takes on its own personality, its own desires. It speaks to you, haunts your thoughts . . . your dreams, even."

"It takes on a dark personality in time, and the problem with that is there is no way to evaluate the power within each witch," James said thoughtfully. "Many witches have darkness inside of them, even if you cannae see it. So, how do you assess that?"

"Right, the ring's power could summon its bearer to evil."

"So, it could be perfectly fine and helpful, or it could be dark and destroy us. What you get is a total gamble?" I asked.

"Yes," Chloe confirmed.

"All right, that one's out," Henry said. "What's next?"

"Well, our only option here is war. More battles like Adamo," Tanner added. "Things will escalate, and we'll lose a lot of good folk."

"*Shit.* I hate to acknowledge this, but I don't think we have a better option," Isaac said.

"We don't," Chloe admitted. "We have honestly gone over everything we could think of so many times. We've spent hours arguing over this, posing every idea we could think of and every kink we could throw into the plans. This one is the most viable option. I understand we might fail, but I think we have to try."

"Molly," I said, turning to face her. "What do you think?"

Molly was an observer, rational, very rarely succumbing to emotion.

"I think it's a good idea," she stated plainly. "I understand the concerns completely; I have the same concerns. However, I agree that we're out of viable options. It's our best chance to get the upper hand right now because Lorenzo will never see it coming. He'd never expect the council to break the rules. But it's not up to me, because I'm not the one that'll time travel to an incredibly dangerous time and place. So, you two have to decide."

I looked to Mia.

"I'm not for it," she said simply.

"I have to say, I don't like the thought of it either," Tanner said. "I mean, I get it. I just . . . I think the risk of altering Fate is too high."

"Aye, that's my main concern as well," Henry said. "Fitz and Hadley can handle this mission, but I think there could be serious consequences."

"If Fate wanted us tampering with the past, I think she would have led us down another path—not to Opimae," Mia said.

"Exactly. Fate has laid out the path, and yeah, we have to decide what's right and wrong, but this is a big departure from our course," Tanner said.

"More than that, it feels misaligned with the prophecy," Mia said.

"But the prophecy *is* vague," Chloe countered. "We know of the outcome, but it tells us nothing regarding the events that will bring it to fruition."

"I think the leaders of Magna Terra voted against the prophecy today," Solomon said. "I think they've already altered the course of Fate. Lucio did as well. This is our solution to set the path right."

Mia nodded, considering. "I do see your point."

James looked at Fitz and me, sympathy written on his face.

"If we come to an agreement here . . . you still believe Fitz and I are the best candidates for this mission," I said.

"Yes. For a couple of reasons," Chloe began. "But the most important of them all is that whoever goes back in time will be working with Fitz's ancestors. We believe that crusader should be Fitz—he'll need you, Hadley."

"And we promised to never separate you again," Solomon added.

"No more than two witches can do this. You'll already create a disturbance, but anyone else would be too much," James said.

Fitz nodded thoughtfully and turned to me, reaching again for my hand. "You really want to do this?"

"I have no idea what I want," I answered truthfully. "But we've been backed into a corner, and I think we should try."

"I hate to say this, but there's risk associated with this mission—including something happening to you two," Molly said, her brows knit tightly. "Are we willing to take that risk?"

"I think we all know I'm not keen on Hadley being in danger," Fitz said, "but there's no helping it here. There are risks no matter our path forward. What are we to do on Earth if not accept this mission? Wait for Lorenzo to find us?"

Fitz met my gaze, and we lingered, feeling each other's energy.

"I feel the same way," I agreed. "There's no guarantee we'll make it, but we have to try. I can't sit around and do nothing."

"Well, we know the chamber will never go for this," Isaac said.

"We're not asking for the chamber's approval," Solomon said. "This is an Earth matter. They have no say there."

The room fell silent.

"But we haven't reached a consensus, even amongst our team," Mia said.

"Does Solomon's point about Fate sway your mind at all?" I asked.

She paused, and the entire room seemed to wait in suspense. "If I'm being honest, I'm struggling between how I feel and how I think I should feel about all this."

"How so?" Jordan asked.

"Earth has put far too much effort into this mission for them to rip our crusade leaders off this case. It's not right. But the bureaucrat in me still thinks it's irresponsible to green light this plan," Mia said, looking to Solomon and then Chloe. "However, Solomon could be right about Fate. There's no clear right and wrong anymore."

"I also believe the ring is still the key to all this," I said. "We won't be able to get closer to the ring here in Opimae, but we do have the power to reach it in the past."

"A fine point, Hadley," James said.

"This mission began with the ring for us, and I think it'll also end with the ring. I know we're feeling uncertain and divided. I know there are a lot of factors to parse through and the risks are high, but so are the stakes. They're higher than ever."

"And what of Fate's potential consequences?" Henry asked.

"We're already facing consequences from Lucio's disturbance of the past, and the chamber's decision to deviate from the prophecy," Chloe said.

"Aye. Realistically, we're stepping into a mess no matter which course of action we decide on," Fitz said.

"And Fate could see Hadley and Fitz's inaction as contempt," Solomon said.

"I hadn't even considered that," I admitted.

"There is no certain track at this point, but I think we must try this," James said. "We cannae sit idle and allow this current course to be charted."

"Isaac?" I asked, recalling his former opposition. "What do you think?"

"I'm for it. It's no more dangerous than what we've been doing here, and I agree with Mia. The chamber made the wrong decision today. Let's do what we do best: fight the man."

I smiled, despite the circumstances. This wouldn't be the first time I'd gone rogue.

"Henry?" Fitz asked.

"Aye, I'm for it."

One by one, our companions pledged their support for the mission.

A door closed at the far end of the hallway, and footsteps echoed loudly through the space. Soon, Charles, Prime Minister Bakari, and Queen Marina stepped into the great room. The energy that blustered in held a bit of anger and a soft nudge of curiosity.

We rose from our seats, offering a half bow to the queen.

"Please, take your seats," she said, waving us off.

"It's always a pleasure to see you, but I feel something odd in your energy," I said. "Apologies for my directness, but—why have you come?"

Prime Minister Bakari smiled.

"We've all come to help," Charles said.

"Help?" Fitz asked.

The queen stepped forward. "Yes. We will stand with the prophecy's promised crusaders. So, please—tell us your plans."

CHAPTER FORTY-SIX

As much as Chloe and Solomon had fought for our time to grieve, Fitz and I were ordered to depart expeditiously because the chamber was concerned Lorenzo would abduct us before we had the chance to leave Opimae. As such, they had assigned additional guards to travel back to Earth with us.

Their presence at the house was unnerving. I felt more like a prisoner than someone under protection.

I worried at Fitz's ability to even begin to process his father's death under these circumstances. He was as close to his father as I had been with mine. I'd tried to talk with him, but he clearly wasn't ready, still burying himself in our work.

The night before our departure to Earth, Fitz and I were packing when a soft rap at the door halted our progress.

"Come in!" Fitz called.

Jordan stepped inside, a bittersweet smile forming on her lips.

"Queen Marina would like a word with you, Hadley."

"Lead the way."

The queen stood in the great room of our home. The lights were low, and the firelight flickered across her lavender robes.

"Hadley, my child, come and sit," she beckoned, her hand outstretched.

I grasped her hand, taking a seat next to her.

"You and Fitz are leaders now more than ever. You are a symbol of hope. We've placed our trust in you."

A symbol of hope?

"I'm honored," I said. Her words took my breath away. I was more determined than ever to fight for both of our worlds . . . for our folk.

"How are you feeling tonight?"

"It feels surreal. I'll be back on Earth tomorrow at this time."

"Home won't feel the same as it once did."

"Because I've changed?"

"Yes. And because your team is here. Home will feel familiar, but different. Comforting, and yet not."

"It sounds like you speak from experience."

The queen smiled, her eyes distant.

"I, too, once left on a mission. When I returned home, everything was the same except for me. It is a strange feeling."

I nodded expectantly.

"Lucio caused quite a stir in our kingdom," she continued. "You see, Lorenzo's father was a very powerful water witch. His parents relocated to Italy, causing Lucio's powers to wane over the years. He returned here to regain his power, but then he began pushing his agenda about ruling the humans of Earth."

"And he brought his mate back with him, right? Lorenzo's mother."

"Yes, and when they returned together, they caused an uprising in my kingdom. Ultimately, their rebellion was stifled. Lucio and Adelina returned to Earth, and you know the rest."

"I'm surprised they didn't include the rebellion in our training."

"It's rarely spoken of now—a piece of history we've tried to forget. My older brother ruled at the time, but he was killed in the uprising . . . by Lucio."

"Oh, that's awful. I am so incredibly sorry."

"Thank you." Her gaze was transfixed on the flames in the fireplace. "His wife left with their children and found a new life elsewhere."

"And you became queen."

"I was never meant to rule. But I've done my best."

"You've found your way. Everyone adores you."

The queen smiled.

"Do you think they'd ever want to return home?"

"I couldn't say. They haven't contacted me since their departure. I thought it would be selfish of me to reach out to them. Hopefully, they've made peace with it all. If they wanted to come home, they would have by now," the queen said. "Well, let's get to it, shall we?"

Jordan called for the queen's guards. They stepped forward, accompanying a water witch I knew well.

"Hi, Gustavo."

"Hadley." He smiled warmly.

Gustavo extended a box in Queen Marina's direction, and she opened it carefully before removing its contents.

"Hadley, this gift is meant to protect you," she explained, dangling a beautiful necklace that shimmered as it caught the light. "It won't glimmer on Earth, so it won't be so conspicuous."

It was a simple gold chain that held a glass amulet. Water moved inside of it like tides pulled by the moon, and I noticed an inscription around the glass. Though I couldn't read it, I recognized the language from Queen Marina's records she'd brought for Jordan. The letters were beautifully rounded script that was reminiscent of calligraphy from Earth.

I gasped. "Oh, it's stunning!"

"The inscription is a powerful protection spell crafted by my mother long ago. And this is enchanted water from our homeland. The glass is under magical protection, so it will not break, even in a skirmish."

"Incredible," I murmured, mesmerized by the movement of the water. "I'm honored."

Queen Marina bowed her head slightly in my direction—another sign of her allegiance to us during this mission.

"May I?" she asked, gesturing to the amulet.

"Of course."

She slipped the necklace over my head, and a flutter went through me as it settled on my chest.

"Your energy will adjust."

"Oddly enough, it doesn't feel strange at all. It feels good."

"Perhaps there's a bit of water witch somewhere inside you," the queen returned, smiling.

"Only if I'm lucky."

"I think you have a great deal more than luck."

I tucked the amulet underneath my sweater and grasped Jordan's hand.

"There's another amulet for Fitz. I only wanted to speak with you first."

She nodded to Gustavo, who walked in the direction of our room.

"We appreciate this very much," I said.

"We couldn't let you two run off without sending a bit of ourselves with you. Hadley, if anything were to happen to you . . ." Jordan's eyes glazed over, tears threatening to spill out.

"Hey, now. None of that." I pulled Jordan close. "I'll be back."

"Promise?"

"Promise. We still have to kick Lorenzo's ass. I can't do that if I'm dead."

Jordan laughed softly. "A solid point, Hads."

I rested my head gently against hers, taking in the last of the time we had together. Friends, sisters, and teammates, resolute in our shared goal. I couldn't guarantee anything at this point, but I knew one thing: we had a hell of a lot of soul on this side of the fight, and that was something Lorenzo could never match.

It was nearing dusk as we approached the portal. It would be midday when we stepped on to Earth's soil. Fitz, Chloe, Solomon, Ann, Izzy, and I stood gazing at the strange passageway to our home planet with guards flanked on each side, ready to protect us from harm . . . and to prevent us from fleeing, I was sure. Chloe's energy was sad, and I could only imagine how difficult it must have been for her to leave Tanner. She was meant to come back in a couple weeks, but that must have felt like years away with him staying behind in Opimae, especially considering his recent injury. I gave her a weak smile as we stepped near the portal.

It almost shocked me to feel the portal's pull. Something about it was magnetic, and I had to focus all my energy into not running straight for its opening. I thought of the trouble we encountered on our outbound journey, recalling I'd need to push myself toward Earth.

Fitz slipped his hand in mine and squeezed gently. My energy warmed at his touch.

How different we were on this journey back.

I succumbed to the urge to step into the portal, Fitz right beside me. A flash of light accompanied the roar of our passage through space and time. I shut my eyes tightly against the dazzling rays, and just like that . . .

We were home.

EPILOGUE

Forfar, Scotland
September 1662
Esther

It was hot for late September, but I stopped by the garden gate, allowing the sun's warmth to envelop me. I'd been cold all the way through since my recent vision, and Katherine's troubled energy when she had called on me this afternoon hadn't helped matters. I sighed, reaching for the latch. The midges were still thick from summer, and I struck the air as I continued toward the house, endeavoring to move the wee beasties away from my face.

Hamish was walking down the old path beside our home, and I dawdled until he reached me. He smiled weakly—I hadn't seen a real smile on his face in months—and he kissed me.

"Did ye have a braw visit with Katherine?" he asked.

"Aye, agreeable enough," I said, hoping he wouldnae push the matter.

Since the death of her husband, Katherine had become a wisp of a woman, and her sorrow clung to her. Most women in the burgh—both witch and human—avoided her as though they'd catch her grief like the plague. I'd asked her to tea no long after his death, and she'd called on me every sennight since.

"I nearly believe ye," Hamish said.

I rested my hands on my hips and narrowed my gaze. Hamish's amusement was plain on his lips.

"Her sorrow is taxing," I finally said. "It seems she's sinking further into it rather than rising above it."

"Hmph." Hamish's face crumpled. I dearly loved how his face turned pensive as he weighed his thoughts.

"I found it especially vexing this day . . . I reckon it was due to the vision . . ."

Hamish's face turned to stone. "Nae, Esther. That vision willnae come to pass."

I smiled without humor. Fate had given her say. Hamish's denial concerned me. In truth, Katherine's grief left me hollow because I feared Hamish would share in her fate—that he wouldnae recover after the witch hunters had come for me.

I slapped once more at the midges. "Shall we walk inside? I cannae take the beasties any longer," I said.

Hamish nodded and reached for my hand. We walked in silence until the wind shifted, bringing a chill to the afternoon air. I halted, the breath leaving my body as a scene took hold of me. Two figures passed through the in-between, weightless in the strange expanse. *Fitz and Hadley.* The light brightened as they stepped on to rocky ground.

"Esther, can ye hear me?" Hamish's voice was distant, echoing through my mind.

I nodded as my sight cleared.

"A vision?" he asked.

"Aye. It's Fitz and Hadley," I said.

"Has anything happened?"

"They've returned to Earth," I said, quite breathlessly.

"It's been set into motion, then."

"So it seems," I said, meeting his gaze.

"I dinnae ken if I should be pleased or no."

I considered his words.

"I cannae say," I said. "But they mean us nae harm, I'm certain of it. Though they are in trouble, Hamish. That much I ken."

He nodded.

"We will welcome them into our home," I said.

Hamish held my gaze. Finally, "Aye. As ye wish."

I gathered my skirts, ready to move forward, and Hamish supported my weight as we progressed slowly. The vision had left me disoriented—they'd grown worrisomely vivid over the last fortnight.

We'd neared the house when Annabel rushed around the corner, her mouth set into a hard line and her eyes determined. Once she distinguished us, she halted and swallowed hard before she pressed on.

"Are ye well, child?" she asked, reaching for me.

"Aye. Dinnae fash, Aunt. It is only the work of a vision."

She nodded. She attempted to hide her troubled energy, but it was like a wild horse refusing to be tamed. Her eyes swept across my garden table. Murdina had no yet cleared the dishes. "Did ye host Katherine again?"

I met her gaze, wordlessly—defiantly.

"Esther, what have I told ye? Ye must leave her be."

"She is alone, Aunt. She is troubled, and the women of this burgh treat her like a sickness."

"With good reason. Rumors are running wild among the servants, Esther."

"I willnae abandon her when she most needs an ally."

"Yer stubborn nature will be yer own downfall. Do ye no see that, child?"

My anger bubbled inside of me like water in a kettle.

"That is enough, Annabel," Hamish said sternly.

"Ye cannae look away from the truth any longer. The new minister will see to it that we all burn if he has his way," she continued.

"I cannae hear any more of this." I meant to press on, but Annabel laid a hand on my arm.

"Esther . . ." She paused. The tears in her eyes sent a chill through me.

"Oh, Aunt," I said. "What are ye no telling me?"

She looked down, and I met Hamish's stare. His eyes betrayed his fear. It would be bad news.

"Annabel, out with it," I said, though my tone softened.

"I've just come from the market. It is all the burgh is speaking of. It's Helen, Esther," she said. "She's been taken to the tollbooth. She's been accused of witchcraft."

I looked to Hamish, fear gripping my body. His grasp tightened—an anchor holding me steady as my sight blurred.

I closed my eyes. "Then it's begun."

PRONUNCIATION GUIDE

Beings
Copandir – co-pan-deer
Emlyn – em-lin
Etain – ee-tane
Jowan –joh-ahn
Laisrén – les-ren

Places
Adamo – ah-dah-mo
Arregaithel – air-eh-gay-thahl
Athdara – aeth-dah-rah
Bain – bane
Constantina – con-stan-teen-a
Hurlee – hur-lee
Iter – ih-tair
Kevardhu – keh-var-doo
Opimae – oh-peh-may
Pluvia Silva – ploo-vee-ah sil-vah
Thalassa – thah-lah-suh

Other
Caora – coo-rah
Roísín – roh-sheen
Samhain – sah-win

GLOSSARY

Aye – yes

Bairn – kid

Bonnie – handsome, pretty, beautiful.

Braw – good looking, beautiful, really nice.

Cannae – can't

Couldnae – couldn't

Didnae – didn't

Dinnae – don't

Gonnae – will you

Greet – to cry

Ken – to know

Nae – no

No – (in certain contexts) used in place of not

Och Aye – (Old Scots) oh yes

Scran – food

Shouldnae – shouldn't

Tartan – a plaid textile design of Scottish origin, usually patterned to designate a distinctive clan

Wee – little

Willnae – won't

Wouldnae – wouldn't

ACKNOWLEDGEMENTS

Wow, a bindup! This means I've written two books, y'all. Over the course of the last couple years, there are many wonderful people to whom I owe a hearty thank you for their support.

My first thank you is for evermore to my husband, Trent, for sharing a home with an author who is always taking on more than she should. Thank you for putting up with my shenanigans. From all-night editing sessions to hangry episodes to the amount of money we spend on coffee (seriously, we need to buy stock), you take it all in stride and remind me every day that I can do this (and to not complain because I chose this path). Thank you. For all of it.

A massive thank you to my editor, Jamie Ryu for seeing the potential in Summoned and walking this path with me hand in hand. Thank you for believing in my world, and even more miraculously, thank you for believing in me. You have pushed me to learn and grow in ways I couldn't have imagined. Thank you for elevating this story and maintaining your professionalism even when this process grew overwhelming… and let's be real here; that was for most of it. But look—we did it! There never was, and never will be, a more powerful duo. You are the real magic, Jamie.

Thank you to my family and friends for your support and patience through this process. I know I was far too absent, and I'm grateful y'all understand me. To my parents, my sister, and my Aunt Elaine, I'd like to say an especially strong thank you—for all of it.

Thank you to the Miller Tree Inn family: Bella, Julia, Marissa, Triana, and Jalisa. You give Trent and I purpose. Thank you for everything—every bit of it.

Thank you to Samantha Rose Baldwin for lending your many skill-sets to this process and for your vision with the Summoned-verse. I couldn't ask for a better business partner or friend. You've made so many projects possible, and you've been a constant from the very beginning—I'll never be able to thank you enough for that. Summoned and I will always be better for it. Hadley and I are both beyond grateful for you.

Thank you to Monique Messman and Cherish Danae for being the best Summoned Patreon team to ever grace this planet—or the next. And another thank you to Cherish Danae for creating incredible original Summoned music.

Thank you to Vee Elle, Kathryn Gaddy, Britt Byrd, Anna McGuinness, Ash Harvey, and Charlotte Gilgallon for reading my work with keen eyes and care. You've left your mark on these pages, and they are the better for it.

Thank you to Jon Stubbington for continuing to bring my book cover dreams into reality. This special edition cover literally took my breath away.

Thank you to the ARA PR team for your incredibly hard work and for moving mountains. You amaze me every day. Grateful for you.

And to the Summoned Patrons… you are everything. Thank you for your love, support, and encouragement. Y'all bring so much magic to my life and to this series.

M.B. Thurman traded her career as an executive assistant to fulfill her lifelong dream of becoming an author. She spends her time writing and operating her bed and breakfast, the notable Miller Tree Inn. Though her Southern roots run deep, Thurman has embraced the lifestyle of the magical Pacific Northwest with her husband and feisty feline, Midnight.

Thurman's book settings echo her love of travel—especially areas of the world that brim with magic and echo ancient marvels. Her company, Firecracker Entertainment, is dedicated to bringing Thurman's novels to life through immersive storytelling in mediums ranging from screen to audio and beyond. Visit her at mbthurman.com, @mbt_writes on Instagram and Threads, or @mbtwrites on TikTok.

Into the Flames is a bind-up of the first two books in the Summoned Series. Learn more at thesummonedseries.com or @thesummonedseries

www.ingramcontent.com/pod-product-compliance
Lightning Source LLC
Chambersburg PA
CBHW030324010826
48973CB00004B/851